Don Quixote
Vol - I

MAVEN BOOKS

Don Quixote
Vol - I

Miguel de Cervantes Saavedra

Chennai　　　Trichy　　　Tirunelveli　　　NewDelhi

MAVEN BOOKS

An Imprint of **MJP Publishers**

ISBN 978-93-87488-73-1 **Maven Books**

All rights reserved No. 44, Nallathambi Street,
Printed and bound in India Triplicane, Chennai 600 005

MJP 494 © Publishers, 2018

Publisher : C. Janarthanan

To the Duke of Bejar, Marquis of Gibraleon,
Count of Benalcazar
and
Banares, Vicecount of the Puebla De Alcocer,
Master of the Towns of Capilla,
Curiel and Burguillos

In belief of the good reception and honours that Your Excellency bestows on all sort of books, as prince so inclined to favor good arts, chiefly those who by their nobleness do not submit to the service and bribery of the vulgar, I have determined bringing to light The Ingenious Gentleman Don Quixote of la Mancha, in shelter of Your Excellency's glamorous name, to whom, with the obeisance I owe to such grandeur, I pray to receive it agreeably under his protection, so that in this shadow, though deprived of that precious ornament of elegance and erudition that clothe the works composed in the houses of those who know, it dares appear with assurance in the judgment of some who, trespassing the bounds of their own ignorance, use to condemn with more rigour and less justice the writings of others. It is my earnest hope that Your Excellency's good counsel in regard to my honourable purpose, will not disdain the littleness of so humble a service.

                  Miguel de Cervantes

Publisher's Note

The legacy of a country is in its varied cultural heritage, historical literature, developments in the field of economy and science. The top nations in the world are competing in the field of science, economy and literature. This vast legacy has to be conserved and documented so that it can be bestowed to the future generation. The knowledge of this legacy is slowly getting perished in the present generation due to lack of documentation.

Keeping this in mind, the concern with retrospective acquiring of rare books has been accented recently by the burgeoning reprint industry. Maven Books is gratified to retrieve the rare collections with a view to bring back those books that were landmarks in their time.

In this effort, a series of rare books would be republished under the banner, "Maven Books". The books in the reprint series have been carefully selected for their contemporary usefulness as well as their historical importance within the intellectual. We reconstruct the book with slight enhancements made for better presentation, without affecting the contents of the original edition.

Most of the works selected for republishing covers a huge range of subjects, from history to anthropology. We believe this reprint edition will be a service to the numerous researchers and practitioners active in this fascinating field. We allow readers to experience the wonder of peering into a scholarly work of the highest order and seminal significance.

Maven Books

Translator's Preface

I ABOUT THIS TRANSLATION

It was with considerable reluctance that I abandoned in favour of the present undertaking what had long been a favourite project: that of a new edition of Shelton's "Don Quixote," which has now become a somewhat scarce book. There are some—and I confess myself to be one—for whom Shelton's racy old version, with all its defects, has a charm that no modern translation, however skilful or correct, could possess. Shelton had the inestimable advantage of belonging to the same generation as Cervantes; "Don Quixote" had to him a vitality that only a contemporary could feel; it cost him no dramatic effort to see things as Cervantes saw them; there is no anachronism in his language; he put the Spanish of Cervantes into the English of Shakespeare. Shakespeare himself most likely knew the book; he may have carried it home with him in his saddle-bags to Stratford on one of his last journeys, and under the mulberry tree at New Place joined hands with a kindred genius in its pages.

But it was soon made plain to me that to hope for even a moderate popularity for Shelton was vain. His fine old crusted English would, no doubt, be relished by a minority, but it would be only by a minority. His warmest admirers must admit that he is not a satisfactory representative of Cervantes. His translation of the First Part was very hastily made and was never revised by him. It has all the freshness and vigour, but also a full measure of the faults, of a hasty production. It is often very literal—barbarously literal frequently—but just as often very loose. He had evidently a good colloquial knowledge of Spanish, but apparently not much more. It never seems to occur to him that the same translation of a word will not suit in every case.

It is often said that we have no satisfactory translation of "Don Quixote." To those who are familiar with the original, it savours of truism or platitude to say so, for in truth there can be no thoroughly satisfactory translation of "Don Quixote" into English or any other language. It is not that the Spanish idioms are so utterly unmanageable, or that the untranslatable words, numerous enough no doubt, are so superabundant, but rather that the sententious terseness to which the humour of the book owes its flavour is peculiar to Spanish, and can at best be only distantly imitated in any other tongue.

The history of our English translations of "Don Quixote" is instructive. Shelton's, the first in any language, was made, apparently, about 1608, but not published till 1612. This of course was only the First Part. It has been asserted that the Second, published in 1620, is not the work of Shelton, but there is nothing to support the assertion save the fact that it has less spirit, less of what we generally understand by "go," about it than the first, which would be only natural if the first were the work of a young man writing currente calamo, and the second that of a middle-aged man writing for a bookseller. On the other hand, it is closer and more literal, the style is the same, the very same translations, or mistranslations, occur in it, and it is extremely unlikely that a new translator would, by suppressing his name, have allowed Shelton to carry off the credit.

In 1687 John Phillips, Milton's nephew, produced a "Don Quixote" "made English," he says, "according to the humour of our modern language." His "Quixote" is not so much a translation as a travesty, and a travesty that for coarseness, vulgarity, and buffoonery is almost unexampled even in the literature of that day.

Ned Ward's "Life and Notable Adventures of Don Quixote, merrily translated into Hudibrastic Verse" (1700), can scarcely be reckoned a translation, but it serves to show the light in which "Don Quixote" was regarded at the time.

A further illustration may be found in the version published in 1712 by Peter Motteux, who had then recently combined tea-dealing with literature. It is described as "translated from the original by several hands," but if so all Spanish flavour has entirely evaporated under the manipulation of the several hands. The flavour that it has, on the other hand, is distinctly Franco-cockney. Anyone who compares it carefully with the original will have little doubt that it is a concoction from Shelton and the French of Filleau de Saint Martin, eked out by borrowings from Phillips, whose mode of treatment it adopts. It is, to be sure, more decent and decorous, but it treats "Don Quixote" in the same fashion as a comic book that cannot be made too comic.

To attempt to improve the humour of "Don Quixote" by an infusion of cockney flippancy and facetiousness, as Motteux's operators did, is not merely an impertinence like larding a sirloin of prize beef, but an absolute falsification of the spirit of the book, and it is a proof of the uncritical way in which "Don Quixote" is generally read that this worse than worthless translation—worthless as failing to represent, worse than worthless as misrepresenting—should have been favoured as it has been.

It had the effect, however, of bringing out a translation undertaken and executed in a very different spirit, that of Charles Jervas, the portrait painter, and friend of Pope, Swift, Arbuthnot, and Gay. Jervas has been allowed little credit for his work, indeed it may be said none, for it is known to the world in general as Jarvis's. It was not published until after his death, and the printers gave the name according to the current pronunciation of the day. It has been the most freely used and the most freely abused of all the translations. It has seen far more editions than any other, it is admitted on all hands to be by far the most faithful, and yet nobody seems to have a good word to say for it or for its author. Jervas no doubt prejudiced readers against himself in his preface, where among many true words about Shelton, Stevens, and Motteux, he rashly and unjustly charges Shelton with having translated not from the Spanish, but from the Italian version of Franciosini, which did not appear until ten years after Shelton's first volume. A suspicion of incompetence, too, seems to have attached to him because he was by profession a painter and a mediocre one (though he has given us the best portrait we have of Swift), and this may have been strengthened by Pope's remark that he "translated 'Don Quixote' without understanding Spanish." He has been also charged with borrowing from Shelton, whom he disparaged. It is true that in a few difficult or obscure passages he has followed Shelton, and gone astray with him; but for one case of this sort, there are fifty where he is right and Shelton wrong. As for Pope's dictum, anyone who examines Jervas's version carefully, side by side with the original, will see that he was a sound Spanish scholar, incomparably a better one than Shelton, except perhaps in mere colloquial Spanish. He was, in fact, an honest, faithful, and painstaking translator, and he has left a version which, whatever its shortcomings may be, is singularly free from errors and mistranslations.

The charge against it is that it is stiff, dry—"wooden" in a word,-and no one can deny that there is a foundation for it. But it may be pleaded for Jervas that a good deal of this rigidity is due to his abhorrence of the light, flippant, jocose style of his predecessors. He was one of the few, very few, translators that have shown any apprehension of the unsmiling gravity which is the essence of Quixotic humour; it seemed to him a crime to bring Cervantes forward smirking and grinning at his own good things, and to this may be attributed in a great measure the ascetic abstinence from everything savouring of liveliness which is the characteristic of his translation. In most modern editions, it should be observed, his style has been smoothed and smartened, but without any reference to the original Spanish, so that if he has been made to read more agreeably he has also been robbed of his chief merit of fidelity.

Smollett's version, published in 1755, may be almost counted as one of these. At any rate it is plain that in its construction Jervas's translation was very freely drawn upon, and very little or probably no heed given to the original Spanish.

The later translations may be dismissed in a few words. George Kelly's, which appeared in 1769, "printed for the Translator," was an impudent imposture, being nothing more than Motteux's version with a few of the words, here and there, artfully transposed; Charles Wilmot's (1774) was only an abridgment like Florian's, but not so skilfully executed; and the version published by Miss Smirke in 1818, to accompany her brother's plates, was merely a patchwork production made out of former translations. On the latest, Mr. A. J. Duffield's, it would be in every sense of the word impertinent in me to offer an opinion here. I had not even seen it when the present undertaking was proposed to me, and since then I may say vidi tantum, having for obvious reasons resisted the temptation which Mr. Duffield's reputation and comely volumes hold out to every lover of Cervantes.

From the foregoing history of our translations of "Don Quixote," it will be seen that there are a good many people who, provided they get the mere narrative with its full complement of facts, incidents, and adventures served up to them in a form that amuses them, care very little whether that form is the one in which Cervantes originally shaped his ideas. On the other hand, it is clear that there are many who desire to have not merely the story he tells, but the story as he tells it, so far at least as differences of idiom and circumstances permit, and who will give a preference to the conscientious translator, even though he may have acquitted himself somewhat awkwardly.

But after all there is no real antagonism between the two classes; there is no reason why what pleases the one should not please the other, or why a translator who makes it his aim to treat "Don Quixote" with the respect due to a great classic, should not be as acceptable even to the careless reader as the one who treats it as a famous old jest-book. It is not a question of caviare to the general, or, if it is, the fault rests with him who makes so. The method by which Cervantes won the ear of the Spanish people ought, mutatis mutandis, to be equally effective with the great majority of English readers. At any rate, even if there are readers to whom it is a matter of indifference, fidelity to the method is as much a part of the translator's duty as fidelity to the matter. If he can please all parties, so much the better; but his first duty is to those who look to him for as faithful a representation of his author as it is in his power to give them, faithful to the letter so long as fidelity is practicable, faithful to the spirit so far as he can make it.

My purpose here is not to dogmatise on the rules of translation, but to indicate those I have followed, or at least tried to the best of my ability to follow, in the present instance. One which, it seems to me, cannot be too rigidly followed in translating "Don Quixote," is to avoid everything that savours of affectation. The book itself is, indeed, in one sense a protest against it, and no man abhorred it more than Cervantes. For this reason, I think, any temptation to use antiquated or obsolete language should be resisted. It is after all an affectation, and one for which there is no warrant or excuse. Spanish has probably undergone less change since the seventeenth century than any language in Europe, and by far the greater and certainly the best part of "Don Quixote" differs but little in language from the colloquial Spanish of the present day. Except in the tales and Don Quixote's speeches, the translator who uses the simplest and plainest everyday language will almost always be the one who approaches nearest to the original.

Seeing that the story of "Don Quixote" and all its characters and incidents have now been for more than two centuries and a half familiar as household words in English mouths, it seems to me that the old familiar names and phrases should not be changed without good reason. Of course a translator who holds that "Don Quixote" should receive the treatment a great classic deserves, will feel himself bound by the injunction laid upon the Morisco in Chap. IX not to omit or add anything.

II ABOUT CERVANTES AND DON QUIXOTE

Four generations had laughed over "Don Quixote" before it occurred to anyone to ask, who and what manner of man was this Miguel de Cervantes Saavedra whose name is on the title-page; and it was too late for a satisfactory answer to the question when it was proposed to add a life of the author to the London edition published at Lord Carteret's instance in 1738. All traces of the personality of Cervantes had by that time disappeared. Any floating traditions that may once have existed, transmitted from men who had known him, had long since died out, and of other record there was none; for the sixteenth and seventeenth centuries were incurious as to "the men of the time," a reproach against which the nineteenth has, at any rate, secured itself, if it has produced no Shakespeare or Cervantes. All that Mayans y Siscar, to whom the task was entrusted, or any of those who followed him, Rios, Pellicer, or Navarrete, could do was to eke out the few allusions Cervantes makes to himself in his various prefaces with such pieces of documentary evidence bearing upon his life as they could find.

This, however, has been done by the last-named biographer to such good purpose that he has superseded all predecessors. Thoroughness is the chief characteristic of Navarrete's work. Besides sifting, testing, and methodising with rare patience and judgment what had been previously brought to light, he left, as the saying is, no stone unturned under which anything to illustrate his subject might possibly be found. Navarrete has done all that industry and acumen could do, and it is no fault of his if he has not given us what we want. What Hallam says of Shakespeare may be applied to the almost parallel case of Cervantes: "It is not the register of his baptism, or the draft of his will, or the orthography of his name that we seek; no letter of his writing, no record of his conversation, no character of him drawn ... by a contemporary has been produced."

It is only natural, therefore, that the biographers of Cervantes, forced to make brick without straw, should have recourse largely to conjecture, and that conjecture should in some instances come by degrees to take the place of established fact. All that I propose to do here is to separate what is matter of fact from what is matter of conjecture, and leave it to the reader's judgment to decide whether the data justify the inference or not.

The men whose names by common consent stand in the front rank of Spanish literature, Cervantes, Lope de Vega, Quevedo, Calderon, Garcilaso de la Vega, the Mendozas, Gongora, were all men of ancient families, and, curiously, all, except the last, of families that traced their origin to the same mountain district in the North of Spain. The family of Cervantes is commonly said to have been of Galician origin, and unquestionably it was in possession of lands in Galicia at a very early date; but I think the balance of the evidence tends to show that the "solar," the original site of the family, was at Cervatos in the north-west corner of Old Castile, close to the junction of Castile, Leon, and the Asturias. As it happens, there is a complete history of the Cervantes family from the tenth century down to the seventeenth extant under the title of "Illustrious Ancestry, Glorious Deeds, and Noble Posterity of the Famous Nuno Alfonso, Alcaide of Toledo," written in 1648 by the industrious genealogist Rodrigo Mendez Silva, who availed himself of a manuscript genealogy by Juan de Mena, the poet laureate and historiographer of John II.

The origin of the name Cervantes is curious. Nuno Alfonso was almost as distinguished in the struggle against the Moors in the reign of Alfonso VII as the Cid had been half a century before in that of Alfonso VI, and was rewarded by divers grants of land in the neighbourhood of Toledo. On one of his acquisitions, about two leagues from the city, he built himself a castle which he called Cervatos, because "he was lord of the solar of Cervatos in the Montana," as the mountain region extending from the Basque Provinces to Leon was always called. At his death in battle in 1143, the castle passed by his will to his son Alfonso Munio, who, as territorial or local surnames were then coming into vogue in place of the simple patronymic, took the additional name of Cervatos. His eldest son Pedro succeeded him in the possession of the castle, and followed his example in adopting the name, an assumption at which the younger son, Gonzalo, seems to have taken umbrage.

Everyone who has paid even a flying visit to Toledo will remember the ruined castle that crowns the hill above the spot where the bridge of Alcantara spans the gorge of the Tagus, and with its broken outline and crumbling walls makes such an admirable pendant to the square solid Alcazar towering over the city roofs on the opposite side. It was built, or as some say restored, by Alfonso VI shortly after his occupation of Toledo in 1085, and called by him San Servando after a Spanish martyr, a name subsequently modified into San Servan (in which form it appears in the "Poem of the Cid"), San Servantes, and San Cervantes: with regard to which last the "Handbook for Spain" warns its readers against the supposition that it has anything to do with the author of "Don Quixote." Ford, as all know who have taken him for a companion and counsellor on the roads of Spain, is seldom wrong in matters of literature or history. In this instance, however, he is in error. It has everything to do with the author of "Don Quixote," for it is in fact these old walls that have given to Spain the name she is proudest of to-day. Gonzalo, above mentioned, it may be readily conceived, did not relish the appropriation by his brother of a name to which he himself had an equal right, for though nominally taken from the castle, it was in reality derived from the ancient territorial possession of the family, and as a set-off, and to distinguish himself (diferenciarse) from his brother, he took as a surname the name of the castle on the bank of the Tagus, in the building of which, according to a family tradition, his great-grandfather had a share.

Both brothers founded families. The Cervantes branch had more tenacity; it sent offshoots in various directions, Andalusia, Estremadura, Galicia, and Portugal, and produced a goodly line of men distinguished in the service of Church and State. Gonzalo himself, and apparently a son of his, followed Ferdinand III in the great campaign of 1236-48 that gave Cordova and Seville to Christian Spain and penned up the Moors in the kingdom of Granada, and his descendants intermarried with some of the noblest families of the Peninsula and numbered among them soldiers, magistrates, and Church dignitaries, including at least two cardinal-archbishops.

Of the line that settled in Andalusia, Deigo de Cervantes, Commander of the Order of Santiago, married Juana Avellaneda, daughter of Juan Arias de Saavedra, and had several sons, of whom one was Gonzalo Gomez, Corregidor of Jerez and ancestor of the Mexican and Columbian branches of the family; and another, Juan, whose son Rodrigo married Dona Leonor de Cortinas, and by her had four children, Rodrigo, Andrea, Luisa, and Miguel, our author.

The pedigree of Cervantes is not without its bearing on "Don Quixote." A man who could look back upon an ancestry of genuine knights-errant extending from well-nigh the time of Pelayo to the siege of Granada was likely to have a strong feeling on the subject of the sham chivalry of the romances. It gives a point, too, to what he says in more than one place about families that have once been great and have tapered away until they have come to nothing, like a pyramid. It was the case of his own.

He was born at Alcala de Henares and baptised in the church of Santa Maria Mayor on the 9th of October, 1547. Of his boyhood and youth we know nothing, unless it be from the glimpse he gives us in the preface to his "Comedies" of himself as a boy looking on with delight while Lope de Rueda and his company set up their rude plank stage in the plaza and acted the rustic farces which he himself afterwards took as the model of his interludes. This first glimpse, however, is a significant one, for it shows the early development of that love of the drama which exercised such an influence on his life and seems to have grown stronger as he grew older, and of which this very preface, written only a few months before his death, is such a striking proof. He gives us to understand, too, that he was a great reader in his youth; but of this no assurance was needed, for the First Part of "Don Quixote" alone proves a vast amount of miscellaneous reading, romances of chivalry, ballads, popular poetry, chronicles, for which he had no time or opportunity except in the first twenty years of his life; and his misquotations and mistakes in matters of detail are always, it may be noticed, those of a man recalling the reading of his boyhood.

Other things besides the drama were in their infancy when Cervantes was a boy. The period of his boyhood was in every way a transition period for Spain. The old chivalrous Spain had passed away. The new Spain was the mightiest power the world had seen since the Roman Empire and it had not yet been called upon to pay the price of its greatness. By the policy of Ferdinand and Ximenez the sovereign had been made absolute, and the Church and Inquisition adroitly adjusted to keep him so. The nobles, who had always resisted absolutism as strenuously as they had fought the Moors, had been divested of all political power, a like fate had befallen the cities, the free constitutions of Castile and Aragon had been swept away, and the only function that remained to the Cortes was that of granting money at the King's dictation.

The transition extended to literature. Men who, like Garcilaso de la Vega and Diego Hurtado de Mendoza, followed the Italian wars, had brought back from Italy the products of the post-Renaissance literature, which took root and flourished and even threatened to extinguish the native growths. Damon and Thyrsis, Phyllis and Chloe had been fairly naturalised in Spain, together with all the devices of pastoral poetry for investing with an air of novelty the idea of a dispairing shepherd and inflexible shepherdess. As a set-off against this, the old historical and traditional ballads, and the true pastorals, the songs and ballads of peasant life, were being collected assiduously and printed in the cancioneros that succeeded one another with increasing rapidity. But the most notable consequence, perhaps, of the spread of printing was the flood of romances of chivalry that had continued to pour from the press ever since Garci Ordonez de Montalvo had resuscitated "Amadis of Gaul" at the beginning of the century.

For a youth fond of reading, solid or light, there could have been no better spot in Spain than Alcala de Henares in the middle of the sixteenth century. It was then a busy, populous university town, something more than the enterprising rival of Salamanca, and altogether a very different place from the melancholy, silent, deserted Alcala the traveller sees now as he goes from Madrid to Saragossa. Theology and medicine may have been the strong points of the university, but the town itself seems to have inclined rather to the humanities and light literature, and as a producer of books Alcala was already beginning to compete with the older presses of Toledo, Burgos, Salamanca and Seville.

A pendant to the picture Cervantes has given us of his first playgoings might, no doubt, have been often seen in the streets of Alcala at that time; a bright, eager, tawny-haired boy peering into a book-shop where the latest volumes lay open to tempt the public, wondering, it may be, what that little book with the woodcut of the blind beggar and his boy, that called itself "Vida de Lazarillo de Tormes, segunda impresion," could be about; or with eyes brimming over with merriment gazing at one of those preposterous portraits of a knight-errant in outrageous panoply and plumes with which the publishers of chivalry romances loved to embellish the title-pages of their folios. If the boy was the father of the man, the sense of the incongruous that was strong at fifty was lively at ten, and some such reflections as these may have been the true genesis of "Don Quixote."

For his more solid education, we are told, he went to Salamanca. But why Rodrigo de Cervantes, who was very poor, should have sent his son to a university a hundred and fifty miles away when he had one at his own door, would be a puzzle, if we had any reason for supposing that he did so. The only evidence is a vague statement by Professor Tomas Gonzalez, that he once saw an old entry of the matriculation of a Miguel de Cervantes. This does not appear to have been ever seen again; but even if it had, and if the date corresponded, it would prove nothing, as there were at least two other Miguels born about the middle of the century; one of them, moreover, a Cervantes Saavedra, a cousin, no doubt, who was a source of great embarrassment to the biographers.

That he was a student neither at Salamanca nor at Alcala is best proved by his own works. No man drew more largely upon experience than he did, and he has nowhere left a single reminiscence of student life-for the "Tia Fingida," if it be his, is not one—nothing, not even "a college joke," to show that he remembered days that most men remember best. All that we know positively about his education is that Juan Lopez de Hoyos, a professor of humanities and belles-lettres of some eminence, calls him his "dear and beloved pupil." This was in a little collection of verses by different hands on the death of Isabel de Valois, second queen of Philip II, published by the professor in 1569, to which Cervantes contributed four pieces, including an elegy, and an epitaph in the form of a sonnet. It is only by a rare chance that a "Lycidas" finds its way into a volume of this sort, and Cervantes was no Milton. His verses are no worse than such things usually are; so much, at least, may be said for them.

By the time the book appeared he had left Spain, and, as fate ordered it, for twelve years, the most eventful ones of his life. Giulio, afterwards Cardinal, Acquaviva had been sent at the end of 1568 to Philip II by the Pope on a mission, partly of condolence, partly political, and on his return to Rome, which was somewhat brusquely expedited by the King, he took Cervantes with him as his camarero (chamberlain), the office he himself held in the Pope's household. The post would no doubt have led to advancement at the Papal Court had Cervantes retained it, but in the summer of 1570 he resigned it and enlisted as a private soldier in Captain Diego Urbina's company, belonging to Don Miguel de Moncada's regiment, but at that time forming a part of the command of Marc Antony Colonna. What impelled him to this step we know not, whether it was distaste for the career before him, or purely military enthusiasm. It may well have been the latter, for it was a stirring time; the events, however, which led to the alliance between Spain, Venice, and the Pope, against the common enemy, the Porte, and to the victory of the combined fleets at Lepanto, belong rather to the history of Europe than to the life of Cervantes. He was one of those that sailed from Messina, in September 1571, under the command of Don John of Austria; but on the morning of the 7th of October, when the Turkish fleet was sighted, he was lying below ill with fever. At the news that the enemy was in sight he rose, and, in spite of the remonstrances of his comrades and superiors, insisted on taking his post, saying he preferred death in the service of God and the King to health. His galley, the Marquesa, was in the thick of the fight, and before it was over he had received three gunshot wounds, two in the breast and one in the left hand or arm. On the morning after the battle, according to Navarrete, he had an interview with the commander-in-chief, Don John, who was making a personal inspection of the wounded, one result of which was an addition of three crowns to his pay, and another, apparently, the friendship of his general.

How severely Cervantes was wounded may be inferred from the fact, that with youth, a vigorous frame, and as cheerful and buoyant a temperament as ever invalid had, he was seven months in hospital at Messina before he was discharged. He came out with his left hand permanently disabled; he had lost the use of it, as Mercury told him in the "Viaje del Parnaso" for the greater glory of the right. This, however, did not absolutely unfit him for service, and in April 1572 he joined Manuel Ponce de Leon's company of Lope de Figueroa's regiment, in which, it seems probable, his brother Rodrigo was serving, and shared in the operations of the next three years, including the capture of the Goletta and Tunis. Taking advantage of the lull which followed the recapture of these places by the Turks, he obtained leave to return to Spain, and sailed from Naples in September 1575 on board the Sun galley, in company with his brother Rodrigo, Pedro Carrillo de Quesada, late Governor of the Goletta, and some others, and furnished with letters from Don John of Austria and the Duke of Sesa, the Viceroy of Sicily, recommending him to the King for the command of a company, on account of his services; a dono infelice as events proved. On the 26th they fell in with a squadron of Algerine galleys, and after a stout resistance were overpowered and carried into Algiers.

By means of a ransomed fellow-captive the brothers contrived to inform their family of their condition, and the poor people at Alcala at once strove to raise the ransom money, the father disposing of all he possessed, and the two sisters giving up their marriage portions. But Dali Mami had found on Cervantes the letters addressed to the King by Don John and the Duke of Sesa, and, concluding that his prize must be a person of great consequence, when the money came he refused it scornfully as being altogether insufficient. The owner of Rodrigo, however, was more easily satisfied; ransom was accepted in his case, and it was arranged between the brothers that he should return to Spain and procure a vessel in which he was to come back to Algiers and take off Miguel and as many of their comrades as possible. This was not the first attempt to escape that Cervantes had made. Soon after the commencement of his captivity he induced several of his companions to join him in trying to reach Oran, then a Spanish post, on foot; but after the first day's journey, the Moor who had agreed to act as their guide deserted them, and they had no choice but to return. The second attempt was more disastrous. In a garden outside the city on the sea-shore, he constructed, with the help of the gardener, a Spaniard, a hiding-place, to which he brought, one by one, fourteen of his fellow-captives, keeping them there in secrecy for several months, and supplying them with food through a renegade known as El Dorador, "the Gilder." How he, a captive himself, contrived to do all this, is one of the mysteries of the story. Wild as the project may appear, it was very nearly successful. The vessel procured by Rodrigo made its appearance off the coast, and under cover of night was proceeding to take off the refugees, when the crew were alarmed by a passing fishing boat, and beat a hasty retreat. On renewing the attempt shortly afterwards, they, or a portion of them at least, were taken prisoners, and just as the poor fellows in the garden were exulting in the thought that in a few moments more freedom would be within their grasp, they found themselves surrounded by Turkish troops, horse and foot. The Dorador had revealed the whole scheme to the Dey Hassan.

When Cervantes saw what had befallen them, he charged his companions to lay all the blame upon him, and as they were being bound he declared aloud that the whole plot was of his contriving, and that nobody else had any share in it. Brought before the Dey, he said the same. He was threatened with impalement and with torture; and as cutting off ears and noses were playful freaks with the Algerines, it may be conceived what their tortures were like; but nothing could make him swerve from his original statement that he and he alone was responsible. The upshot was that the unhappy gardener was hanged by his master, and the prisoners taken possession of by the Dey, who, however, afterwards restored most of them to their masters, but kept Cervantes, paying Dali Mami 500 crowns for him. He felt, no doubt, that a man of such resource, energy, and daring, was too dangerous a piece of property to be left in private hands; and he had him heavily ironed and lodged in his own prison. If he thought that by these means he could break the spirit or shake the resolution of his prisoner, he was soon undeceived, for Cervantes contrived before long to despatch a letter to the Governor of Oran, entreating him to send him some one that could be trusted, to enable him and three other gentlemen, fellow-captives of his, to make their escape; intending evidently to renew his first attempt with a more trustworthy guide. Unfortunately the Moor who carried the letter was stopped just outside Oran, and the letter being found upon him, he was sent back to Algiers, where by the order of the Dey he was promptly impaled as a warning to others, while Cervantes was condemned to receive two thousand blows of the stick, a number which most likely would have deprived the world of "Don Quixote," had not some persons, who they were we know not, interceded on his behalf.

After this he seems to have been kept in still closer confinement than before, for nearly two years passed before he made another attempt. This time his plan was to purchase, by the aid of a Spanish renegade and two Valencian merchants resident in Algiers, an armed vessel in which he and about sixty of the leading captives were to make their escape; but just as they were about to put it into execution one Doctor Juan Blanco de Paz, an ecclesiastic and a compatriot, informed the Dey of the plot. Cervantes by force of character, by his self-devotion, by his untiring energy and his exertions to lighten the lot of his companions in misery, had endeared himself to all, and become the leading spirit in the captive colony, and, incredible as it may seem, jealousy of his influence and the esteem in which he was held, moved this man to compass his destruction by a cruel death. The merchants finding that the Dey knew all, and fearing that Cervantes under torture might make disclosures that would imperil their own lives, tried to persuade him to slip away on board a vessel that was on the point of sailing for Spain; but he told them they had nothing to fear, for no tortures would make him compromise anybody, and he went at once and gave himself up to the Dey.

As before, the Dey tried to force him to name his accomplices. Everything was made ready for his immediate execution; the halter was put round his neck and his hands tied behind him, but all that could be got from him was that he himself, with the help of four gentlemen who had since left Algiers, had arranged the whole, and that the sixty who were to accompany him were not to know anything of it until the last moment. Finding he could make nothing of him, the Dey sent him back to prison more heavily ironed than before.

The poverty-stricken Cervantes family had been all this time trying once more to raise the ransom money, and at last a sum of three hundred ducats was got together and entrusted to the Redemptorist Father Juan Gil, who was about to sail for Algiers. The Dey, however, demanded more than double the sum offered, and as his term of office had expired and he was about to sail for Constantinople, taking all his slaves with him, the case of Cervantes was critical. He was already on board heavily ironed, when the Dey at length agreed to reduce his demand by one-half, and Father Gil by borrowing was able to make up the amount, and on September 19, 1580, after a captivity of five years all but a week, Cervantes was at last set free. Before long he discovered that Blanco de Paz, who claimed to be an officer of the Inquisition, was now concocting on false evidence a charge of misconduct to be brought against him on his return to Spain. To checkmate him Cervantes drew up a series of twenty-five questions, covering the whole period of his captivity, upon which he requested Father Gil to take the depositions of credible witnesses before a notary. Eleven witnesses taken from among the principal captives in Algiers deposed to all the facts above stated and to a great deal more besides. There is something touching in the admiration, love, and gratitude we see struggling to find expression in the formal language of the notary, as they testify one after another to the good deeds of Cervantes, how he comforted and helped the weak-hearted, how he kept up their drooping courage, how he shared his poor purse with this deponent, and how "in him this deponent found father and mother."

On his return to Spain he found his old regiment about to march for Portugal to support Philip's claim to the crown, and utterly penniless now, had no choice but to rejoin it. He was in the expeditions to the Azores in 1582 and the following year, and on the conclusion of the war returned to Spain in the autumn of 1583, bringing with him the manuscript of his pastoral romance, the "Galatea," and probably also, to judge by internal evidence, that of the first portion of "Persiles and Sigismunda." He also brought back with him, his biographers assert, an infant daughter, the offspring of an amour, as some of them with great circumstantiality inform us, with a Lisbon lady of noble birth, whose name, however, as well as that of the street she lived in, they omit to mention. The sole foundation for all this is that in 1605 there certainly was living in the family of Cervantes a Dona Isabel de Saavedra, who is described in an official document as his natural daughter, and then twenty years of age.

With his crippled left hand promotion in the army was hopeless, now that Don John was dead and he had no one to press his claims and services, and for a man drawing on to forty life in the ranks was a dismal prospect; he had already a certain reputation as a poet; he made up his mind, therefore, to cast his lot with literature, and for a first venture committed his "Galatea" to the press. It was published, as Salva y Mallen shows conclusively, at Alcala, his own birth-place, in 1585 and no doubt helped to make his name more widely known, but certainly did not do him much good in any other way.

While it was going through the press, he married Dona Catalina de Palacios Salazar y Vozmediano, a lady of Esquivias near Madrid, and apparently a friend of the family, who brought him a fortune which may possibly have served to keep the wolf from the door, but if so, that was all. The drama had by this time outgrown market-place stages and strolling companies, and with his old love for it he naturally turned to it for a congenial employment. In about three years he wrote twenty or thirty plays, which he tells us were performed without any throwing of cucumbers or other missiles, and ran their course without any hisses, outcries, or disturbance. In other words, his plays were not bad enough to be hissed off the stage, but not good enough to hold their own upon it. Only two of them have been preserved, but as they happen to be two of the seven or eight he mentions with complacency, we may assume they are favourable specimens, and no one who reads the "Numancia" and the "Trato de Argel" will feel any surprise that they failed as acting dramas. Whatever merits they may have, whatever occasional they may show, they are, as regards construction, incurably clumsy. How completely they failed is manifest from the fact that with all his sanguine temperament and indomitable perseverance he was unable to maintain the struggle to gain a livelihood as a dramatist for more than three years; nor was the rising popularity of Lope the cause, as is often said, notwithstanding his own words to the contrary. When Lope began to write for the stage is uncertain, but it was certainly after Cervantes went to Seville.

Among the "Nuevos Documentos" printed by Senor Asensio y Toledo is one dated 1592, and curiously characteristic of Cervantes. It is an agreement with one Rodrigo Osorio, a manager, who was to accept six comedies at fifty ducats (about 6l.) apiece, not to be paid in any case unless it appeared on representation that the said comedy was one of the best that had ever been represented in Spain. The test does not seem to have been ever applied; perhaps it was sufficiently apparent to Rodrigo Osorio that the comedies were not among the best that had ever been represented. Among the correspondence of Cervantes there might have been found, no doubt, more than one letter like that we see in the "Rake's Progress," "Sir, I have read your play, and it will not doo."

He was more successful in a literary contest at Saragossa in 1595 in honour of the canonisation of St. Jacinto, when his composition won the first prize, three silver spoons. The year before this he had been appointed a collector of revenues for the kingdom of Granada. In order to remit the money he had collected more conveniently to the treasury, he entrusted it to a merchant, who failed and absconded; and as the bankrupt's assets were insufficient to cover the whole, he was sent to prison at Seville in September 1597. The balance against him, however, was a small one, about 26l., and on giving security for it he was released at the end of the year.

It was as he journeyed from town to town collecting the king's taxes, that he noted down those bits of inn and wayside life and character that abound in the pages of "Don Quixote:" the Benedictine monks with spectacles and sunshades, mounted on their tall mules; the strollers in costume bound for the next village; the barber with his basin on his head, on his way to bleed a patient; the recruit with his breeches in his bundle, tramping along the road singing; the reapers gathered in the venta gateway listening to "Felixmarte of Hircania" read out to them; and those little Hogarthian touches that he so well knew how to bring in, the ox-tail hanging up with the landlord's comb stuck in it, the wine-skins at the bed-head, and those notable examples of hostelry art, Helen going off in high spirits on Paris's arm, and Dido on the tower dropping tears as big as walnuts. Nay, it may well be that on those journeys into remote regions he came across now and then a specimen of the pauper gentleman, with his lean hack and his greyhound and his books of chivalry, dreaming away his life in happy ignorance that the world had changed since his great-grandfather's old helmet was new. But it was in Seville that he found out his true vocation, though he himself would not by any means have admitted it to be so. It was there, in Triana, that he was first tempted to try his hand at drawing from life, and first brought his humour into play in the exquisite little sketch of "Rinconete y Cortadillo," the germ, in more ways than one, of "Don Quixote."

Where and when that was written, we cannot tell. After his imprisonment all trace of Cervantes in his official capacity disappears, from which it may be inferred that he was not reinstated. That he was still in Seville in November 1598 appears from a satirical sonnet of his on the elaborate catafalque erected to testify the grief of the city at the death of Philip II, but from this up to 1603 we have no clue to his movements. The words in the preface to the First Part of "Don Quixote" are generally held to be conclusive that he conceived the idea of the book, and wrote the beginning of it at least, in a prison, and that he may have done so is extremely likely.

There is a tradition that Cervantes read some portions of his work to a select audience at the Duke of Bejar's, which may have helped to make the book known; but the obvious conclusion is that the First Part of "Don Quixote" lay on his hands some time before he could find a publisher bold enough to undertake a venture of so novel a character; and so little faith in it had Francisco Robles of Madrid, to whom at last he sold it, that he did not care to incur the expense of securing the copyright for Aragon or Portugal, contenting himself with that for Castile. The printing was finished in December, and the book came out with the new year, 1605. It is often said that "Don Quixote" was at first received coldly. The facts show just the contrary. No sooner was it in the hands of the public than preparations were made to issue pirated editions at Lisbon and Valencia, and to bring out a second edition with the additional copyrights for Aragon and Portugal, which he secured in February.

No doubt it was received with something more than coldness by certain sections of the community. Men of wit, taste, and discrimination among the aristocracy gave it a hearty welcome, but the aristocracy in general were not likely to relish a book that turned their favourite reading into ridicule and laughed at so many of their favourite ideas. The dramatists who gathered round Lope as their leader regarded Cervantes as their common enemy, and it is plain that he was equally obnoxious to the other clique, the culto poets who had Gongora for their chief. Navarrete, who knew nothing of the letter above mentioned, tries hard to show that the relations between Cervantes and Lope were of a very friendly sort, as indeed they were until "Don Quixote" was written. Cervantes, indeed, to the last generously and manfully declared his admiration of Lope's powers, his unfailing invention, and his marvellous fertility; but in the preface of the First Part of "Don Quixote" and in the verses of "Urganda the Unknown," and one or two other places, there are, if we read between the lines, sly hits at Lope's vanities and affectations that argue no personal good-will; and Lope openly sneers at "Don Quixote" and Cervantes, and fourteen years after his death gives him only a few lines of cold commonplace in the "Laurel de Apolo," that seem all the colder for the eulogies of a host of nonentities whose names are found nowhere else.

In 1601 Valladolid was made the seat of the Court, and at the beginning of 1603 Cervantes had been summoned thither in connection with the balance due by him to the Treasury, which was still outstanding. He remained at Valladolid, apparently supporting himself by agencies and scrivener's work of some sort; probably drafting petitions and drawing up statements of claims to be presented to the Council, and the like. So, at least, we gather from the depositions taken on the occasion of the death of a gentleman, the victim of a street brawl, who had been carried into the house in which he lived. In these he himself is described as a man who wrote and transacted business, and it appears that his household then consisted of his wife, the natural daughter Isabel de Saavedra already mentioned, his sister Andrea, now a widow, her daughter Constanza, a mysterious Magdalena de Sotomayor calling herself his sister, for whom his biographers cannot account, and a servant-maid.

Meanwhile "Don Quixote" had been growing in favour, and its author's name was now known beyond the Pyrenees. In 1607 an edition was printed at Brussels. Robles, the Madrid publisher, found it necessary to meet the demand by a third edition, the seventh in all, in 1608. The popularity of the book in Italy was such that a Milan bookseller was led to bring out an edition in 1610; and another was called for in Brussels in 1611. It might naturally have been expected that, with such proofs before him that he had hit the taste of the public, Cervantes would have at once set about redeeming his rather vague promise of a second volume.

But, to all appearance, nothing was farther from his thoughts. He had still by him one or two short tales of the same vintage as those he had inserted in "Don Quixote" and instead of continuing the adventures of Don Quixote, he set to work to write more of these "Novelas Exemplares" as he afterwards called them, with a view to making a book of them.

The novels were published in the summer of 1613, with a dedication to the Conde de Lemos, the Maecenas of the day, and with one of those chatty confidential prefaces Cervantes was so fond of. In this, eight years and a half after the First Part of "Don Quixote" had appeared, we get the first hint of a forthcoming Second Part. "You shall see shortly," he says, "the further exploits of Don Quixote and humours of Sancho Panza." His idea of "shortly" was a somewhat elastic one, for, as we know by the date to Sancho's letter, he had barely one-half of the book completed that time twelvemonth.

But more than poems, or pastorals, or novels, it was his dramatic ambition that engrossed his thoughts. The same indomitable spirit that kept him from despair in the bagnios of Algiers, and prompted him to attempt the escape of himself and his comrades again and again, made him persevere in spite of failure and discouragement in his efforts to win the ear of the public as a dramatist. The temperament of Cervantes was essentially sanguine. The portrait he draws in the preface to the novels, with the aquiline features, chestnut hair, smooth untroubled forehead, and bright cheerful eyes, is the very portrait of a sanguine man. Nothing that the managers might say could persuade him that the merits of his plays would not be recognised at last if they were only given a fair chance. The old soldier of the Spanish Salamis was bent on being the Aeschylus of Spain. He was to found a great national drama, based on the true principles of art, that was to be the envy of all nations; he was to drive from the stage the silly, childish plays, the "mirrors of nonsense and models of folly" that were in vogue through the cupidity of the managers and shortsightedness of the authors; he was to correct and educate the public taste until it was ripe for tragedies on the model of the Greek drama—like the "Numancia" for instance—and comedies that would not only amuse but improve and instruct. All this he was to do, could he once get a hearing: there was the initial difficulty.

He shows plainly enough, too, that "Don Quixote" and the demolition of the chivalry romances was not the work that lay next his heart. He was, indeed, as he says himself in his preface, more a stepfather than a father to "Don Quixote." Never was great work so neglected by its author. That it was written carelessly, hastily, and by fits and starts, was not always his fault, but it seems clear he never read what he sent to the press. He knew how the printers had blundered, but he never took the trouble to correct them when the third edition was in progress, as a man who really cared for the child of his brain would have done. He appears to have regarded the book as little more than a mere libro de entretenimiento, an amusing book, a thing, as he says in the "Viaje," "to divert the melancholy moody heart at any time or season." No doubt he had an affection for his hero, and was very proud of Sancho Panza. It would have been strange indeed if he had not been proud of the most humorous creation in all fiction. He was proud, too, of the popularity and success of the book, and beyond measure delightful is the naivete with which he shows his pride in a dozen passages in the Second Part. But it was not the success he coveted. In all probability he would have given all the success of "Don Quixote," nay, would have seen every copy of "Don Quixote" burned in the Plaza Mayor, for one such success as Lope de Vega was enjoying on an average once a week.

And so he went on, dawdling over "Don Quixote," adding a chapter now and again, and putting it aside to turn to "Persiles and Sigismunda"—which, as we know, was to be the most entertaining book in the language, and the rival of "Theagenes and Chariclea"— or finishing off one of his darling comedies; and if Robles asked when "Don Quixote" would be ready, the answer no doubt was: En breve-shortly, there was time enough for that. At sixty-eight he was as full of life and hope and plans for the future as a boy of eighteen.

Nemesis was coming, however. He had got as far as Chapter LIX, which at his leisurely pace he could hardly have reached before October or November 1614, when there was put into his hand a small octave lately printed at Tarragona, and calling itself "Second Volume of the Ingenious Gentleman Don Quixote of La Mancha: by the Licentiate Alonso Fernandez de Avellaneda of Tordesillas." The last half of Chapter LIX and most of the following chapters of the Second Part give us some idea of the effect produced upon him, and his irritation was not likely to be lessened by the reflection that he had no one to blame but himself. Had Avellaneda, in fact, been content with merely bringing out a continuation to "Don Quixote," Cervantes would have had no reasonable grievance. His own intentions were expressed in the very vaguest language at the end of the book; nay, in his last words, "forse altro cantera con miglior plettro," he seems actually to invite some one else to continue the work, and he made no sign until eight years and a half had gone by; by which time Avellaneda's volume was no doubt written.

In fact Cervantes had no case, or a very bad one, as far as the mere continuation was concerned. But Avellaneda chose to write a preface to it, full of such coarse personal abuse as only an ill-conditioned man could pour out. He taunts Cervantes with being old, with having lost his hand, with having been in prison, with being poor, with being friendless, accuses him of envy of Lope's success, of petulance and querulousness, and so on; and it was in this that the sting lay. Avellaneda's reason for this personal attack is obvious enough. Whoever he may have been, it is clear that he was one of the dramatists of Lope's school, for he has the impudence to charge Cervantes with attacking him as well as Lope in his criticism on the drama. His identification has exercised the best critics and baffled all the ingenuity and research that has been brought to bear on it. Navarrete and Ticknor both incline to the belief that Cervantes knew who he was; but I must say I think the anger he shows suggests an invisible assailant; it is like the irritation of a man stung by a mosquito in the dark. Cervantes from certain solecisms of language pronounces him to be an Aragonese, and Pellicer, an Aragonese himself, supports this view and believes him, moreover, to have been an ecclesiastic, a Dominican probably.

Any merit Avellaneda has is reflected from Cervantes, and he is too dull to reflect much. "Dull and dirty" will always be, I imagine, the verdict of the vast majority of unprejudiced readers. He is, at best, a poor plagiarist; all he can do is to follow slavishly the lead given him by Cervantes; his only humour lies in making Don Quixote take inns for castles and fancy himself some legendary or historical personage, and Sancho mistake words, invert proverbs, and display his gluttony; all through he shows a proclivity to coarseness and dirt, and he has contrived to introduce two tales filthier than anything by the sixteenth century novellieri and without their sprightliness.

But whatever Avellaneda and his book may be, we must not forget the debt we owe them. But for them, there can be no doubt, "Don Quixote" would have come to us a mere torso instead of a complete work. Even if Cervantes had finished the volume he had in hand, most assuredly he would have left off with a promise of a Third Part, giving the further adventures of Don Quixote and humours of Sancho Panza as shepherds. It is plain that he had at one time an intention of dealing with the pastoral romances as he had dealt with the books of chivalry, and but for Avellaneda he would have tried to carry it out. But it is more likely that, with his plans, and projects, and hopefulness, the volume would have remained unfinished till his death, and that we should have never made the acquaintance of the Duke and Duchess, or gone with Sancho to Barataria.

From the moment the book came into his hands he seems to have been haunted by the fear that there might be more Avellanedas in the field, and putting everything else aside, he set himself to finish off his task and protect Don Quixote in the only way he could, by killing him. The conclusion is no doubt a hasty and in some places clumsy piece of work and the frequent repetition of the scolding administered to Avellaneda becomes in the end rather wearisome; but it is, at any rate, a conclusion and for that we must thank Avellaneda.

The new volume was ready for the press in February, but was not printed till the very end of 1615, and during the interval Cervantes put together the comedies and interludes he had written within the last few years, and, as he adds plaintively, found no demand for among the managers, and published them with a preface, worth the book it introduces tenfold, in which he gives an account of the early Spanish stage, and of his own attempts as a dramatist. It is needless to say they were put forward by Cervantes in all good faith and full confidence in their merits. The reader, however, was not to suppose they were his last word or final effort in the drama, for he had in hand a comedy called "Engano a los ojos," about which, if he mistook not, there would be no question.

Of this dramatic masterpiece the world has no opportunity of judging; his health had been failing for some time, and he died, apparently of dropsy, on the 23rd of April, 1616, the day on which England lost Shakespeare, nominally at least, for the English calendar had not yet been reformed. He died as he had lived, accepting his lot bravely and cheerfully.

Was it an unhappy life, that of Cervantes? His biographers all tell us that it was; but I must say I doubt it. It was a hard life, a life of poverty, of incessant struggle, of toil ill paid, of disappointment, but Cervantes carried within himself the antidote to all these evils. His was not one of those light natures that rise above adversity merely by virtue of their own buoyancy; it was in the fortitude of a high spirit that he was proof against it. It is impossible to conceive Cervantes giving way to despondency or prostrated by dejection. As for poverty, it was with him a thing to be laughed over, and the only sigh he ever allows to escape him is when he says, "Happy he to whom Heaven has given a piece of bread for which he is not bound to give thanks to any but Heaven itself." Add to all this his vital energy and mental activity, his restless invention and his sanguine temperament, and there will be reason enough to doubt whether his could have been a very unhappy life. He who could take Cervantes' distresses together with his apparatus for enduring them would not make so bad a bargain, perhaps, as far as happiness in life is concerned.

Of his burial-place nothing is known except that he was buried, in accordance with his will, in the neighbouring convent of Trinitarian nuns, of which it is supposed his daughter, Isabel de Saavedra, was an inmate, and that a few years afterwards the nuns removed to another convent, carrying their dead with them. But whether the remains of Cervantes were included in the removal or not no one knows, and the clue to their resting-place is now lost beyond all hope. This furnishes perhaps the least defensible of the items in the charge of neglect brought against his contemporaries. In some of the others there is a good deal of exaggeration. To listen to most of his biographers one would suppose that all Spain was in league not only against the man but against his memory, or at least that it was insensible to his merits, and left him to live in misery and die of want. To talk of his hard life and unworthy employments in Andalusia is absurd. What had he done to distinguish him from thousands of other struggling men earning a precarious livelihood? True, he was a gallant soldier, who had been wounded and had undergone captivity and suffering in his country's cause, but there were hundreds of others in the same case. He had written a mediocre specimen of an insipid class of romance, and some plays which manifestly did not comply with the primary condition of pleasing: were the playgoers to patronise plays that did not amuse them, because the author was to produce "Don Quixote" twenty years afterwards?

The scramble for copies which, as we have seen, followed immediately on the appearance of the book, does not look like general insensibility to its merits. No doubt it was received coldly by some, but if a man writes a book in ridicule of periwigs he must make his account with being coldly received by the periwig wearers and hated by the whole tribe of wigmakers. If Cervantes had the chivalry-romance readers, the sentimentalists, the dramatists, and the poets of the period all against him, it was because "Don Quixote" was what it was; and if the general public did not come forward to make him comfortable for the rest of his days, it is no more to be charged with neglect and ingratitude than the English-speaking public that did not pay off Scott's liabilities. It did the best it could; it read his book and liked it and bought it, and encouraged the bookseller to pay him well for others.

It has been also made a reproach to Spain that she has erected no monument to the man she is proudest of; no monument, that is to say, of him; for the bronze statue in the little garden of the Plaza de las Cortes, a fair work of art no doubt, and unexceptionable had it been set up to the local poet in the market-place of some provincial town, is not worthy of Cervantes or of Madrid. But what need has Cervantes of "such weak witness of his name;" or what could a monument do in his case except testify to the self-glorification of those who had put it up? Si monumentum quoeris, circumspice. The nearest bookseller's shop will show what bathos there would be in a monument to the author of "Don Quixote."

Nine editions of the First Part of "Don Quixote" had already appeared before Cervantes died, thirty thousand copies in all, according to his own estimate, and a tenth was printed at Barcelona the year after his death. So large a number naturally supplied the demand for some time, but by 1634 it appears to have been exhausted; and from that time down to the present day the stream of editions has continued to flow rapidly and regularly. The translations show still more clearly in what request the book has been from the very outset. In seven years from the completion of the work it had been translated into the four leading languages of Europe. Except the Bible, in fact, no book has been so widely diffused as "Don Quixote." The "Imitatio Christi" may have been translated into as many different languages, and perhaps "Robinson Crusoe" and the "Vicar of Wakefield" into nearly as many, but in multiplicity of translations and editions "Don Quixote" leaves them all far behind.

Still more remarkable is the character of this wide diffusion. "Don Quixote" has been thoroughly naturalised among people whose ideas about knight-errantry, if they had any at all, were of the vaguest, who had never seen or heard of a book of chivalry, who could not possibly feel the humour of the burlesque or sympathise with the author's purpose. Another curious fact is that this, the most cosmopolitan book in the world, is one of the most intensely national. "Manon Lescaut" is not more thoroughly French, "Tom Jones" not more English, "Rob Roy" not more Scotch, than "Don Quixote" is Spanish, in character, in ideas, in sentiment, in local colour, in everything. What, then, is the secret of this unparalleled popularity, increasing year by year for well-nigh three centuries? One explanation, no doubt, is that of all the books in the world, "Don Quixote" is the most catholic. There is something in it for every sort of reader, young or old, sage or simple, high or low. As Cervantes himself says with a touch of pride, "It is thumbed and read and got by heart by people of all sorts; the children turn its leaves, the young people read it, the grown men understand it, the old folk praise it."

But it would be idle to deny that the ingredient which, more than its humour, or its wisdom, or the fertility of invention or knowledge of human nature it displays, has insured its success with the multitude, is the vein of farce that runs through it. It was the attack upon the sheep, the battle with the wine-skins, Mambrino's helmet, the balsam of Fierabras, Don Quixote knocked over by the sails of the windmill, Sancho tossed in the blanket, the mishaps and misadventures of master and man, that were originally the great attraction, and perhaps are so still to some extent with the majority of readers. It is plain that "Don Quixote" was generally regarded at first, and indeed in Spain for a long time, as little more than a queer droll book, full of laughable incidents and absurd situations, very amusing, but not entitled to much consideration or care. All the editions printed in Spain from 1637 to 1771, when the famous printer Ibarra took it up, were mere trade editions, badly and carelessly printed on vile paper and got up in the style of chap-books intended only for popular use, with, in most instances, uncouth illustrations and clap-trap additions by the publisher.

To England belongs the credit of having been the first country to recognise the right of "Don Quixote" to better treatment than this. The London edition of 1738, commonly called Lord Carteret's from having been suggested by him, was not a mere edition de luxe. It produced "Don Quixote" in becoming form as regards paper and type, and embellished with plates which, if not particularly happy as illustrations, were at least well intentioned and well executed, but it also aimed at correctness of text, a matter to which nobody except the editors of the Valencia and Brussels editions had given even a passing thought; and for a first attempt it was fairly successful, for though some of its emendations are inadmissible, a good many of them have been adopted by all subsequent editors.

The zeal of publishers, editors, and annotators brought about a remarkable change of sentiment with regard to "Don Quixote." A vast number of its admirers began to grow ashamed of laughing over it. It became almost a crime to treat it as a humorous book. The humour was not entirely denied, but, according to the new view, it was rated as an altogether secondary quality, a mere accessory, nothing more than the stalking-horse under the presentation of which Cervantes shot his philosophy or his satire, or whatever it was he meant to shoot; for on this point opinions varied. All were agreed, however, that the object he aimed at was not the books of chivalry. He said emphatically in the preface to the First Part and in the last sentence of the Second, that he had no other object in view than to discredit these books, and this, to advanced criticism, made it clear that his object must have been something else.

One theory was that the book was a kind of allegory, setting forth the eternal struggle between the ideal and the real, between the spirit of poetry and the spirit of prose; and perhaps German philosophy never evolved a more ungainly or unlikely camel out of the depths of its inner consciousness. Something of the antagonism, no doubt, is to be found in "Don Quixote," because it is to be found everywhere in life, and Cervantes drew from life. It is difficult to imagine a community in which the never-ceasing game of cross-purposes between Sancho Panza and Don Quixote would not be recognized as true to nature. In the stone age, among the lake dwellers, among the cave men, there were Don Quixotes and Sancho Panzas; there must have been the troglodyte who never could see the facts before his eyes, and the troglodyte who could see nothing else. But to suppose Cervantes deliberately setting himself to expound any such idea in two stout quarto volumes is to suppose something not only very unlike the age in which he lived, but altogether unlike Cervantes himself, who would have been the first to laugh at an attempt of the sort made by anyone else.

The extraordinary influence of the romances of chivalry in his day is quite enough to account for the genesis of the book. Some idea of the prodigious development of this branch of literature in the sixteenth century may be obtained from the scrutiny of Chapter VII, if the reader bears in mind that only a portion of the romances belonging to by far the largest group are enumerated. As to its effect upon the nation, there is abundant evidence. From the time when the Amadises and Palmerins began to grow popular down to the very end of the century, there is a steady stream of invective, from men whose character and position lend weight to their words, against the romances of chivalry and the infatuation of their readers. Ridicule was the only besom to sweep away that dust.

That this was the task Cervantes set himself, and that he had ample provocation to urge him to it, will be sufficiently clear to those who look into the evidence; as it will be also that it was not chivalry itself that he attacked and swept away. Of all the absurdities that, thanks to poetry, will be repeated to the end of time, there is no greater one than saying that "Cervantes smiled Spain's chivalry away." In the first place there was no chivalry for him to smile away. Spain's chivalry had been dead for more than a century. Its work was done when Granada fell, and as chivalry was essentially republican in its nature, it could not live under the rule that Ferdinand substituted for the free institutions of mediaeval Spain. What he did smile away was not chivalry but a degrading mockery of it.

The true nature of the "right arm" and the "bright array," before which, according to the poet, "the world gave ground," and which Cervantes' single laugh demolished, may be gathered from the words of one of his own countrymen, Don Felix Pacheco, as reported by Captain George Carleton, in his "Military Memoirs from 1672 to 1713." "Before the appearance in the world of that labour of Cervantes," he said, "it was next to an impossibility for a man to walk the streets with any delight or without danger. There were seen so many cavaliers prancing and curvetting before the windows of their mistresses, that a stranger would have imagined the whole nation to have been nothing less than a race of knight-errants. But after the world became a little acquainted with that notable history, the man that was seen in that once celebrated drapery was pointed at as a Don Quixote, and found himself the jest of high and low. And I verily believe that to this, and this only, we owe that dampness and poverty of spirit which has run through all our councils for a century past, so little agreeable to those nobler actions of our famous ancestors."

To call "Don Quixote" a sad book, preaching a pessimist view of life, argues a total misconception of its drift. It would be so if its moral were that, in this world, true enthusiasm naturally leads to ridicule and discomfiture. But it preaches nothing of the sort; its moral, so far as it can be said to have one, is that the spurious enthusiasm that is born of vanity and self-conceit, that is made an end in itself, not a means to an end, that acts on mere impulse, regardless of circumstances and consequences, is mischievous to its owner, and a very considerable nuisance to the community at large. To those who cannot distinguish between the one kind and the other, no doubt "Don Quixote" is a sad book; no doubt to some minds it is very sad that a man who had just uttered so beautiful a sentiment as that "it is a hard case to make slaves of those whom God and Nature made free," should be ungratefully pelted by the scoundrels his crazy philanthropy had let loose on society; but to others of a more judicial cast it will be a matter of regret that reckless self-sufficient enthusiasm is not oftener requited in some such way for all the mischief it does in the world.

A very slight examination of the structure of "Don Quixote" will suffice to show that Cervantes had no deep design or elaborate plan in his mind when he began the book. When he wrote those lines in which "with a few strokes of a great master he sets before us the pauper gentleman," he had no idea of the goal to which his imagination was leading him. There can be little doubt that all he contemplated was a short tale to range with those he had already written, a tale setting forth the ludicrous results that might be expected to follow the attempt of a crazy gentleman to act the part of a knight-errant in modern life.

It is plain, for one thing, that Sancho Panza did not enter into the original scheme, for had Cervantes thought of him he certainly would not have omitted him in his hero's outfit, which he obviously meant to be complete. Him we owe to the landlord's chance remark in Chapter III that knights seldom travelled without squires. To try to think of a Don Quixote without Sancho Panza is like trying to think of a one-bladed pair of scissors.

The story was written at first, like the others, without any division and without the intervention of Cide Hamete Benengeli; and it seems not unlikely that Cervantes had some intention of bringing Dulcinea, or Aldonza Lorenzo, on the scene in person. It was probably the ransacking of the Don's library and the discussion on the books of chivalry that first suggested it to him that his idea was capable of development. What, if instead of a mere string of farcical misadventures, he were to make his tale a burlesque of one of these books, caricaturing their style, incidents, and spirit?

In pursuance of this change of plan, he hastily and somewhat clumsily divided what he had written into chapters on the model of "Amadis," invented the fable of a mysterious Arabic manuscript, and set up Cide Hamete Benengeli in imitation of the almost invariable practice of the chivalry-romance authors, who were fond of tracing their books to some recondite source. In working out the new ideas, he soon found the value of Sancho Panza. Indeed, the keynote, not only to Sancho's part, but to the whole book, is struck in the first words Sancho utters when he announces his intention of taking his ass with him. "About the ass," we are told, "Don Quixote hesitated a little, trying whether he could call to mind any knight-errant taking with him an esquire mounted on ass-back; but no instance occurred to his memory." We can see the whole scene at a glance, the stolid unconsciousness of Sancho and the perplexity of his master, upon whose perception the incongruity has just forced itself. This is Sancho's mission throughout the book; he is an unconscious Mephistopheles, always unwittingly making mockery of his master's aspirations, always exposing the fallacy of his ideas by some unintentional ad absurdum, always bringing him back to the world of fact and commonplace by force of sheer stolidity.

By the time Cervantes had got his volume of novels off his hands, and summoned up resolution enough to set about the Second Part in earnest, the case was very much altered. Don Quixote and Sancho Panza had not merely found favour, but had already become, what they have never since ceased to be, veritable entities to the popular imagination. There was no occasion for him now to interpolate extraneous matter; nay, his readers told him plainly that what they wanted of him was more Don Quixote and more Sancho Panza, and not novels, tales, or digressions. To himself, too, his creations had become realities, and he had become proud of them, especially of Sancho. He began the Second Part, therefore, under very different conditions, and the difference makes itself manifest at once. Even in translation the style will be seen to be far easier, more flowing, more natural, and more like that of a man sure of himself and of his audience. Don Quixote and Sancho undergo a change also. In the First Part, Don Quixote has no character or individuality whatever. He is nothing more than a crazy representative of the sentiments of the chivalry romances. In all that he says and does he is simply repeating the lesson he has learned from his books; and therefore, it is absurd to speak of him in the gushing strain of the sentimental critics when they dilate upon his nobleness, disinterestedness, dauntless courage, and so forth. It was the business of a knight-errant to right wrongs, redress injuries, and succour the distressed, and this, as a matter of course, he makes his business when he takes up the part; a knight-errant was bound to be intrepid, and so he feels bound to cast fear aside. Of all Byron's melodious nonsense about Don Quixote, the most nonsensical statement is that "'t is his virtue makes him mad!" The exact opposite is the truth; it is his madness makes him virtuous.

In the Second Part, Cervantes repeatedly reminds the reader, as if it was a point upon which he was anxious there should be no mistake, that his hero's madness is strictly confined to delusions on the subject of chivalry, and that on every other subject he is discreto, one, in fact, whose faculty of discernment is in perfect order. The advantage of this is that he is enabled to make use of Don Quixote as a mouthpiece for his own reflections, and so, without seeming to digress, allow himself the relief of digression when he requires it, as freely as in a commonplace book.

It is true the amount of individuality bestowed upon Don Quixote is not very great. There are some natural touches of character about him, such as his mixture of irascibility and placability, and his curious affection for Sancho together with his impatience of the squire's loquacity and impertinence; but in the main, apart from his craze, he is little more than a thoughtful, cultured gentleman, with instinctive good taste and a great deal of shrewdness and originality of mind.

As to Sancho, it is plain, from the concluding words of the preface to the First Part, that he was a favourite with his creator even before he had been taken into favour by the public. An inferior genius, taking him in hand a second time, would very likely have tried to improve him by making him more comical, clever, amiable, or virtuous. But Cervantes was too true an artist to spoil his work in this way. Sancho, when he reappears, is the old Sancho with the old familiar features; but with a difference; they have been brought out more distinctly, but at the same time with a careful avoidance of anything like caricature; the outline has been filled in where filling in was necessary, and, vivified by a few touches of a master's hand, Sancho stands before us as he might in a character portrait by Velazquez. He is a much more important and prominent figure in the Second Part than in the First; indeed, it is his matchless mendacity about Dulcinea that to a great extent supplies the action of the story.

His development in this respect is as remarkable as in any other. In the First Part he displays a great natural gift of lying. His lies are not of the highly imaginative sort that liars in fiction commonly indulge in; like Falstaff's, they resemble the father that begets them; they are simple, homely, plump lies; plain working lies, in short. But in the service of such a master as Don Quixote he develops rapidly, as we see when he comes to palm off the three country wenches as Dulcinea and her ladies in waiting. It is worth noticing how, flushed by his success in this instance, he is tempted afterwards to try a flight beyond his powers in his account of the journey on Clavileno.

In the Second Part it is the spirit rather than the incidents of the chivalry romances that is the subject of the burlesque. Enchantments of the sort travestied in those of Dulcinea and the Trifaldi and the cave of Montesinos play a leading part in the later and inferior romances, and another distinguishing feature is caricatured in Don Quixote's blind adoration of Dulcinea. In the romances of chivalry love is either a mere animalism or a fantastic idolatry. Only a coarse-minded man would care to make merry with the former, but to one of Cervantes' humour the latter was naturally an attractive subject for ridicule. Like everything else in these romances, it is a gross exaggeration of the real sentiment of chivalry, but its peculiar extravagance is probably due to the influence of those masters of hyperbole, the Provencal poets. When a troubadour professed his readiness to obey his lady in all things, he made it incumbent upon the next comer, if he wished to avoid the imputation of tameness and commonplace, to declare himself the slave of her will, which the next was compelled to cap by some still stronger declaration; and so expressions of devotion went on rising one above the other like biddings at an auction, and a conventional language of gallantry and theory of love came into being that in time permeated the literature of Southern Europe, and bore fruit, in one direction in the transcendental worship of Beatrice and Laura, and in another in the grotesque idolatry which found exponents in writers like Feliciano de Silva. This is what Cervantes deals with in Don Quixote's passion for Dulcinea, and in no instance has he carried out the burlesque more happily. By keeping Dulcinea in the background, and making her a vague shadowy being of whose very existence we are left in doubt, he invests Don Quixote's worship of her virtues and charms with an additional extravagance, and gives still more point to the caricature of the sentiment and language of the romances.

One of the great merits of "Don Quixote," and one of the qualities that have secured its acceptance by all classes of readers and made it the most cosmopolitan of books, is its simplicity. There are, of course, points obvious enough to a Spanish seventeenth century audience which do not immediately strike a reader now-a-days, and Cervantes often takes it for granted that an allusion will be generally understood which is only intelligible to a few. For example, on many of his readers in Spain, and most of his readers out of it, the significance of his choice of a country for his hero is completely lost. It would be going too far to say that no one can thoroughly comprehend "Don Quixote" without having seen La Mancha, but undoubtedly even a glimpse of La Mancha will give an insight into the meaning of Cervantes such as no commentator can give. Of all the regions of Spain it is the last that would suggest the idea of romance. Of all the dull central plateau of the Peninsula it is the dullest tract. There is something impressive about the grim solitudes of Estremadura; and if the plains of Leon and Old Castile are bald and dreary, they are studded with old cities renowned in history and rich in relics of the past. But there is no redeeming feature in the Manchegan landscape; it has all the sameness of the desert without its dignity; the few towns and villages that break its monotony are mean and commonplace, there is nothing venerable about them, they have not even the picturesqueness of poverty; indeed, Don Quixote's own village, Argamasilla, has a sort of oppressive respectability in the prim regularity of its streets and houses; everything is ignoble; the very windmills are the ugliest and shabbiest of the windmill kind.

Translator's Preface xxxix

To anyone who knew the country well, the mere style and title of "Don Quixote of La Mancha" gave the key to the author's meaning at once. La Mancha as the knight's country and scene of his chivalries is of a piece with the pasteboard helmet, the farm-labourer on ass-back for a squire, knighthood conferred by a rascally ventero, convicts taken for victims of oppression, and the rest of the incongruities between Don Quixote's world and the world he lived in, between things as he saw them and things as they were.

It is strange that this element of incongruity, underlying the whole humour and purpose of the book, should have been so little heeded by the majority of those who have undertaken to interpret "Don Quixote." It has been completely overlooked, for example, by the illustrators. To be sure, the great majority of the artists who illustrated "Don Quixote" knew nothing whatever of Spain. To them a venta conveyed no idea but the abstract one of a roadside inn, and they could not therefore do full justice to the humour of Don Quixote's misconception in taking it for a castle, or perceive the remoteness of all its realities from his ideal. But even when better informed they seem to have no apprehension of the full force of the discrepancy. Take, for instance, Gustave Doré's drawing of Don Quixote watching his armour in the inn-yard. Whether or not the Venta de Quesada on the Seville road is, as tradition maintains, the inn described in "Don Quixote," beyond all question it was just such an inn-yard as the one behind it that Cervantes had in his mind's eye, and it was on just such a rude stone trough as that beside the primitive draw-well in the corner that he meant Don Quixote to deposit his armour. Gustave Doré makes it an elaborate fountain such as no arriero ever watered his mules at in the corral of any venta in Spain, and thereby entirely misses the point aimed at by Cervantes. It is the mean, prosaic, commonplace character of all the surroundings and circumstances that gives a significance to Don Quixote's vigil and the ceremony that follows.

Cervantes' humour is for the most part of that broader and simpler sort, the strength of which lies in the perception of the incongruous. It is the incongruity of Sancho in all his ways, words, and works, with the ideas and aims of his master, quite as much as the wonderful vitality and truth to nature of the character, that makes him the most humorous creation in the whole range of fiction. That unsmiling gravity of which Cervantes was the first great master, "Cervantes' serious air," which sits naturally on Swift alone, perhaps, of later humourists, is essential to this kind of humour, and here again Cervantes has suffered at the hands of his interpreters. Nothing, unless indeed the coarse buffoonery of Phillips, could be more out of place in an attempt to represent Cervantes, than a flippant, would-be facetious style, like that of Motteux's version for example, or the sprightly, jaunty air, French translators sometimes adopt. It is the grave matter-of-factness of the narrative, and the apparent unconsciousness of the author that he is saying anything ludicrous, anything but the merest commonplace, that give its peculiar flavour to the humour of Cervantes. His, in fact, is the exact opposite of the humour of Sterne and the self-conscious humourists. Even when Uncle Toby is at his best, you are always aware of "the man Sterne" behind him, watching you over his shoulder to see what effect he is producing. Cervantes always leaves you alone with Don Quixote and Sancho. He and Swift and the great humourists always keep themselves out of sight, or, more properly speaking, never think about themselves at all, unlike our latter-day school of humourists, who seem to have revived the old horse-collar method, and try to raise a laugh by some grotesque assumption of ignorance, imbecility, or bad taste.

It is true that to do full justice to Spanish humour in any other language is well-nigh an impossibility. There is a natural gravity and a sonorous stateliness about Spanish, be it ever so colloquial, that make an absurdity doubly absurd, and give plausibility to the most preposterous statement. This is what makes Sancho Panza's drollery the despair of the conscientious translator. Sancho's curt comments can never fall flat, but they lose half their flavour when transferred from their native Castilian into any other medium. But if foreigners have failed to do justice to the humour of Cervantes, they are no worse than his own countrymen. Indeed, were it not for the Spanish peasant's relish of "Don Quixote," one might be tempted to think that the great humourist was not looked upon as a humourist at all in his own country.

The craze of Don Quixote seems, in some instances, to have communicated itself to his critics, making them see things that are not in the book and run full tilt at phantoms that have no existence save in their own imaginations. Like a good many critics now-a-days, they forget that screams are not criticism, and that it is only vulgar tastes that are influenced by strings of superlatives, three-piled hyperboles, and pompous epithets. But what strikes one as particularly strange is that while they deal in extravagant eulogies, and ascribe all manner of imaginary ideas and qualities to Cervantes, they show no perception of the quality that ninety-nine out of a hundred of his readers would rate highest in him, and hold to be the one that raises him above all rivalry.

To speak of "Don Quixote" as if it were merely a humorous book would be a manifest misdescription. Cervantes at times makes it a kind of commonplace book for occasional essays and criticisms, or for the observations and reflections and gathered wisdom of a long and stirring life. It is a mine of shrewd observation on mankind and human nature. Among modern novels there may be, here and there, more elaborate studies of character, but there is no book richer in individualised character. What Coleridge said of Shakespeare in minimis is true of Cervantes; he never, even for the most temporary purpose, puts forward a lay figure. There is life and individuality in all his characters, however little they may have to do, or however short a time they may be before the reader. Samson Carrasco, the curate, Teresa Panza, Altisidora, even the two students met on the road to the cave of Montesinos, all live and move and have their being; and it is characteristic of the broad humanity of Cervantes that there is not a hateful one among them all. Even poor Maritornes, with her deplorable morals, has a kind heart of her own and "some faint and distant resemblance to a Christian about her;" and as for Sancho, though on dissection we fail to find a lovable trait in him, unless it be a sort of dog-like affection for his master, who is there that in his heart does not love him?

But it is, after all, the humour of "Don Quixote" that distinguishes it from all other books of the romance kind. It is this that makes it, as one of the most judicial-minded of modern critics calls it, "the best novel in the world beyond all comparison." It is its varied humour, ranging from broad farce to comedy as subtle as Shakespeare's or Moliere's that has naturalised it in every country where there are readers, and made it a classic in every language that has a literature.

SOME COMMENDATORY VERSES URGANDA THE UNKNOWN

To the book of Don Quixote of la Mancha

If to be welcomed by the good,
O Book! thou make thy steady aim,
No empty chatterer will dare
To question or dispute thy claim.
But if perchance thou hast a mind
To win of idiots approbation,
Lost labour will be thy reward,
Though they'll pretend appreciation.

They say a goodly shade he finds
Who shelters 'neath a goodly tree;
And such a one thy kindly star
In Bejar bath provided thee:
A royal tree whose spreading boughs
A show of princely fruit display;
A tree that bears a noble Duke,
The Alexander of his day.

Of a Manchegan gentleman
Thy purpose is to tell the story,
Relating how he lost his wits
O'er idle tales of love and glory,
Of "ladies, arms, and cavaliers:"
A new Orlando Furioso-
Innamorato, rather—who
Won Dulcinea del Toboso.

Put no vain emblems on thy shield;
All figures—that is bragging play.
A modest dedication make,
And give no scoffer room to say,
"What! Alvaro de Luna here?
Or is it Hannibal again?
Or does King Francis at Madrid
Once more of destiny complain?"

Since Heaven it hath not pleased on thee
Deep erudition to bestow,
Or black Latino's gift of tongues,
No Latin let thy pages show.
Ape not philosophy or wit,
Lest one who cannot comprehend,
Make a wry face at thee and ask,
"Why offer flowers to me, my friend?"

Be not a meddler; no affair
Of thine the life thy neighbours lead:
Be prudent; oft the random jest
Recoils upon the jester's head.
Thy constant labour let it be
To earn thyself an honest name,
For fooleries preserved in print
Are perpetuity of shame.

A further counsel bear in mind:
If that thy roof be made of glass,
It shows small wit to pick up stones
To pelt the people as they pass.
Win the attention of the wise,
And give the thinker food for thought;
Whoso indites frivolities,
Will but by simpletons be sought.

AMADIS OF GAUL
To Don Quixote of la Mancha

SONNET

Thou that didst imitate that life of mine
When I in lonely sadness on the great
Rock Pena Pobre sat disconsolate,
In self-imposed penance there to pine;
Thou, whose sole beverage was the bitter brine
Of thine own tears, and who withouten plate
Of silver, copper, tin, in lowly state
Off the bare earth and on earth's fruits didst dine;
Live thou, of thine eternal glory sure.
So long as on the round of the fourth sphere
The bright Apollo shall his coursers steer,
In thy renown thou shalt remain secure,
Thy country's name in story shall endure,
And thy sage author stand without a peer.

DON BELIANIS OF GREECE
To Don Quixote of la Mancha

SONNET

In slashing, hewing, cleaving, word and deed,
I was the foremost knight of chivalry,
Stout, bold, expert, as e'er the world did see;
Thousands from the oppressor's wrong I freed;
Great were my feats, eternal fame their meed;
In love I proved my truth and loyalty;
The hugest giant was a dwarf for me;
Ever to knighthood's laws gave I good heed.

My mastery the Fickle Goddess owned,
And even Chance, submitting to control,
Grasped by the forelock, yielded to my will.
Yet—though above yon horned moon enthroned
My fortune seems to sit—great Quixote, still
Envy of thy achievements fills my soul.

THE LADY OF ORIANA
To Dulcinea del Toboso

SONNET

Oh, fairest Dulcinea, could it be!
It were a pleasant fancy to suppose so—
Could Miraflores change to El Toboso,
And London's town to that which shelters thee!
Oh, could mine but acquire that livery
Of countless charms thy mind and body show so!
Or him, now famous grown—thou mad'st him grow so—
Thy knight, in some dread combat could I see!
Oh, could I be released from Amadis
By exercise of such coy chastity
As led thee gentle Quixote to dismiss!
Then would my heavy sorrow turn to joy;
None would I envy, all would envy me,
And happiness be mine without alloy.

GANDALIN, SQUIRE OF AMADIS OF GAUL,
To Sancho Panza, squire of Don Quixote

SONNET

All hail, illustrious man! Fortune, when she
Bound thee apprentice to the esquire trade,
Her care and tenderness of thee displayed,
Shaping thy course from misadventure free.
No longer now doth proud knight-errantry
Regard with scorn the sickle and the spade;
Of towering arrogance less count is made
Than of plain esquire-like simplicity.
I envy thee thy Dapple, and thy name,
And those alforjas thou wast wont to stuff
With comforts that thy providence proclaim.
Excellent Sancho! hail to thee again!

To thee alone the Ovid of our Spain
Does homage with the rustic kiss and cuff.

FROM EL DONOSO, THE MOTLEY POET,
On Sancho Panza and Rocinante

ON SANCHO

I am the esquire Sancho Pan—
Who served Don Quixote of La Man—;
But from his service I retreat-,
Resolved to pass my life discreet-;
For Villadiego, called the Si—,
Maintained that only in reti—
Was found the secret of well-be—,
According to the "Celesti—:"
A book divine, except for sin—
By speech too plain, in my opin—

ON ROCINANTE

I am that Rocinante fa—,
Great-grandson of great Babie—,
Who, all for being lean and bon—,
Had one Don Quixote for an own—;
But if I matched him well in weak—,
I never took short commons meek—,
But kept myself in corn by steal—,
A trick I learned from Lazaril—,
When with a piece of straw so neat—
The blind man of his wine he cheat—.

ORLANDO FURIOSO
To Don Quixote of La Mancha

SONNET

If thou art not a Peer, peer thou hast none;
Among a thousand Peers thou art a peer;
Nor is there room for one when thou art near,
Unvanquished victor, great unconquered one!
Orlando, by Angelica undone,
Am I; o'er distant seas condemned to steer,
And to Fame's altars as an offering bear
Valour respected by Oblivion.
I cannot be thy rival, for thy fame

And prowess rise above all rivalry,
Albeit both bereft of wits we go.
But, though the Scythian or the Moor to tame
Was not thy lot, still thou dost rival me:
Love binds us in a fellowship of woe.

THE KNIGHT OF PHOEBUS
To Don Quixote of La Mancha

My sword was not to be compared with thine
Phoebus of Spain, marvel of courtesy,
Nor with thy famous arm this hand of mine
That smote from east to west as lightnings fly.
I scorned all empire, and that monarchy
The rosy east held out did I resign
For one glance of Claridiana's eye,
The bright Aurora for whose love I pine.
A miracle of constancy my love;
And banished by her ruthless cruelty,
This arm had might the rage of Hell to tame.
But, Gothic Quixote, happier thou dost prove,
For thou dost live in Dulcinea's name,
And famous, honoured, wise, she lives in thee.

FROM SOLISDAN
To Don Quixote of La Mancha

SONNET

Your fantasies, Sir Quixote, it is true,
That crazy brain of yours have quite upset,
But aught of base or mean hath never yet
Been charged by any in reproach to you.
Your deeds are open proof in all men's view;
For you went forth injustice to abate,
And for your pains sore drubbings did you get
From many a rascally and ruffian crew.
If the fair Dulcinea, your heart's queen,
Be unrelenting in her cruelty,
If still your woe be powerless to move her,
In such hard case your comfort let it be
That Sancho was a sorry go-between:
A booby he, hard-hearted she, and you no lover.

DIALOGUE
Between Babieca and Rocinante

SONNET

B: "How comes it, Rocinante, you're so lean?"
R: "I'm underfed, with overwork I'm worn."
B: "But what becomes of all the hay and corn?"
R: "My master gives me none; he's much too mean."
B: "Come, come, you show ill-breeding, sir, I ween;
   'T is like an ass your master thus to scorn."
R: He is an ass, will die an ass, an ass was born;
   Why, he's in love; what's what's plainer to be seen?"
B: "To be in love is folly?"—R. "No great sense."
B: "You're metaphysical."—R. "From want of food."
B: "Rail at the squire, then."—R. "Why, what's the good?
   I might indeed complain of him, I grant ye,
   But, squire or master, where's the difference?
   They're both as sorry hacks as Rocinante."

The Author's Preface

Idle reader: thou mayest believe me without any oath that I would this book, as it is the child of my brain, were the fairest, gayest, and cleverest that could be imagined. But I could not counteract Nature's law that everything shall beget its like; and what, then, could this sterile, illtilled wit of mine beget but the story of a dry, shrivelled, whimsical offspring, full of thoughts of all sorts and such as never came into any other imagination—just what might be begotten in a prison, where every misery is lodged and every doleful sound makes its dwelling? Tranquillity, a cheerful retreat, pleasant fields, bright skies, murmuring brooks, peace of mind, these are the things that go far to make even the most barren muses fertile, and bring into the world births that fill it with wonder and delight. Sometimes when a father has an ugly, loutish son, the love he bears him so blindfolds his eyes that he does not see his defects, or, rather, takes them for gifts and charms of mind and body, and talks of them to his friends as wit and grace. I, however—for though I pass for the father, I am but the stepfather to "Don Quixote"—have no desire to go with the current of custom, or to implore thee, dearest reader, almost with tears in my eyes, as others do, to pardon or excuse the defects thou wilt perceive in this child of mine. Thou art neither its kinsman nor its friend, thy soul is thine own and thy will as free as any man's, whate'er he be, thou art in thine own house and master of it as much as the king of his taxes and thou knowest the common saying, "Under my cloak I kill the king;" all which exempts and frees thee from every consideration and obligation, and thou canst say what thou wilt of the story without fear of being abused for any ill or rewarded for any good thou mayest say of it.

My wish would be simply to present it to thee plain and unadorned, without any embellishment of preface or uncountable muster of customary sonnets, epigrams, and eulogies, such as are commonly put at the beginning of books. For I can tell thee, though composing it cost me some labour, I found none greater than the making of this Preface thou art now reading. Many times did I take up my pen to write it, and many did I lay it down again, not knowing what to write. One of these times, as I was pondering with the paper before me, a pen in my ear, my elbow on the desk, and my cheek in my hand, thinking of what I should say, there came in unexpectedly a certain lively, clever friend of mine, who, seeing me so deep in thought, asked the reason; to which I, making no mystery of it, answered that I was thinking of the Preface I had to make for the story of "Don Quixote," which so troubled me that I had a mind not to make any at all, nor even publish the achievements of so noble a knight.

"For, how could you expect me not to feel uneasy about what that ancient lawgiver they call the Public will say when it sees me, after slumbering so many years in the silence of oblivion, coming out now with all my years upon my back, and with a book as dry as a rush, devoid of invention, meagre in style, poor in thoughts, wholly wanting in learning and wisdom, without quotations in the margin or annotations at the end, after the fashion of other books I see, which, though all fables and profanity, are so full of maxims from Aristotle, and Plato, and the whole herd of philosophers, that they fill the readers with amazement and convince them that the authors are men of learning, erudition, and eloquence. And then, when they quote the Holy Scriptures!—anyone would say they are St. Thomases or other doctors of the Church, observing as they do a decorum so ingenious that in one sentence they describe a distracted lover and in the next deliver a devout little sermon that it is a pleasure and a treat to hear and read. Of all this there will be nothing in my book, for I have nothing to quote in the margin or to note at the end, and still less do I know what authors I follow in it, to place them at the beginning, as all do, under the letters A, B, C, beginning with Aristotle and ending with Xenophon, or Zoilus, or Zeuxis, though one was a slanderer and the other a painter. Also my book must do without sonnets at the beginning, at least sonnets whose authors are dukes, marquises, counts, bishops, ladies, or famous poets. Though if I were to ask two or three obliging friends, I know they would give me them, and such as the productions of those that have the highest reputation in our Spain could not equal.

"In short, my friend," I continued, "I am determined that Senor Don Quixote shall remain buried in the archives of his own La Mancha until Heaven provide some one to garnish him with all those things he stands in need of; because I find myself, through my shallowness and want of learning, unequal to supplying them, and because I am by nature shy and careless about hunting for authors to say what I myself can say without them. Hence the cogitation and abstraction you found me in, and reason enough, what you have heard from me."

Hearing this, my friend, giving himself a slap on the forehead and breaking into a hearty laugh, exclaimed, "Before God, Brother, now am I disabused of an error in which I have been living all this

1   *Author's Preface*

long time I have known you, all through which I have taken you to be shrewd and sensible in all you do; but now I see you are as far from that as the heaven is from the earth. It is possible that things of so little moment and so easy to set right can occupy and perplex a ripe wit like yours, fit to break through and crush far greater obstacles? By my faith, this comes, not of any want of ability, but of too much indolence and too little knowledge of life. Do you want to know if I am telling the truth? Well, then, attend to me, and you will see how, in the opening and shutting of an eye, I sweep away all your difficulties, and supply all those deficiencies which you say check and discourage you from bringing before the world the story of your famous Don Quixote, the light and mirror of all knight-errantry."

"Say on," said I, listening to his talk; "how do you propose to make up for my diffidence, and reduce to order this chaos of perplexity I am in?"

To which he made answer, "Your first difficulty about the sonnets, epigrams, or complimentary verses which you want for the beginning, and which ought to be by persons of importance and rank, can be removed if you yourself take a little trouble to make them; you can afterwards baptise them, and put any name you like to them, fathering them on Prester John of the Indies or the Emperor of Trebizond, who, to my knowledge, were said to have been famous poets: and even if they were not, and any pedants or bachelors should attack you and question the fact, never care two maravedis for that, for even if they prove a lie against you they cannot cut off the hand you wrote it with.

"As to references in the margin to the books and authors from whom you take the aphorisms and sayings you put into your story, it is only contriving to fit in nicely any sentences or scraps of Latin you may happen to have by heart, or at any rate that will not give you much trouble to look up; so as, when you speak of freedom and captivity, to insert

Non bene pro toto libertas venditur auro;

and then refer in the margin to Horace, or whoever said it; or, if you allude to the power of death, to come in with—

Pallida mors Aequo pulsat pede pauperum tabernas, Regumque turres.

"If it be friendship and the love God bids us bear to our enemy, go at once to the Holy Scriptures, which you can do with a very small amount of research, and quote no less than the words of God himself: Ego autem dico vobis: diligite inimicos vestros. If you speak of evil thoughts, turn to the Gospel: De corde exeunt cogitationes malae. If of the fickleness of friends, there is Cato, who will give you his distich:

Donec eris felix multos numerabis amicos, Tempora si fuerint nubila, solus eris.

"With these and such like bits of Latin they will take you for a grammarian at all events, and that now-a-days is no small honour and profit.

"With regard to adding annotations at the end of the book, you may safely do it in this way. If you mention any giant in your book contrive that it shall be the giant Goliath, and with this alone, which will cost you almost nothing, you have a grand note, for you can put—The giant Golias or Goliath was a Philistine whom the shepherd David slew by a mighty stone-cast in the Terebinth valley, as is related in the Book of Kings—in the chapter where you find it written.

"Next, to prove yourself a man of erudition in polite literature and cosmography, manage that the river Tagus shall be named in your story, and there you are at once with another famous annotation, setting forth—The river Tagus was so called after a King of Spain: it has its source in such and such a place and falls into the ocean, kissing the walls of the famous city of Lisbon, and it is a common belief that it has golden sands, etc. If you should have anything to do with robbers, I will give you the story of Cacus, for I have it by heart; if with loose women, there is the Bishop of Mondonedo, who will give you the loan of Lamia, Laida, and Flora, any reference to whom will bring you great credit; if with hard-hearted ones, Ovid will furnish you with Medea; if with witches or enchantresses, Homer has Calypso, and Virgil Circe; if with valiant captains, Julius Caesar himself will lend you himself in his own 'Commentaries,' and Plutarch will give you a thousand Alexanders. If you should deal with love, with two ounces you may know of Tuscan you can go to Leon the Hebrew, who will supply you to your heart's content; or if you should not care to go to foreign countries you have at home Fonseca's 'Of the Love of God,' in which is condensed all that you or the most imaginative mind can want on the subject. In short, all you have to do is to manage to quote these names, or refer to these stories I have mentioned, and leave it to me to insert the annotations and quotations, and I swear by all that's good to fill your margins and use up four sheets at the end of the book.

"Now let us come to those references to authors which other books have, and you want for yours. The remedy for this is very simple: You have only to look out for some book that quotes them all, from A to Z as you say yourself, and then insert the very same alphabet in your book, and though the imposition may be plain to see, because you have so little need to borrow from them, that is no matter; there will probably be some simple enough to believe that you have made use of them all in this plain, artless story of yours. At any rate, if it answers no other purpose, this long catalogue of authors will serve to give a surprising look of authority to your book. Besides, no one will trouble himself to verify whether you have followed them or whether you have not, being no way concerned in it; especially as, if I mistake not, this book of yours has no need of any one of those things you say it wants, for it is, from beginning to end, an attack upon the books of chivalry, of which Aristotle never dreamt, nor St. Basil said a word, nor Cicero had any knowledge; nor do the niceties of truth nor the observations of astrology come within the range of its fanciful vagaries; nor have geometrical measurements or refutations of the arguments used in rhetoric anything to do with it; nor does it mean to preach to anybody, mixing up things human and divine, a sort of motley in which no Christian understanding should dress itself. It has only to avail itself of truth to nature in its composition, and the more perfect the imitation the better the work will be. And as this piece of yours aims at nothing more than to destroy the authority and influence which books of chivalry have in the world and with the public, there is no need for you to go a-begging for aphorisms from philosophers, precepts from Holy Scripture, fables from poets, speeches from orators, or miracles from saints; but merely to take care that your style and diction run musically, pleasantly, and plainly, with clear, proper, and well-placed words, setting forth your purpose to the best of your power, and putting your ideas intelligibly, without confusion or obscurity. Strive, too, that in reading your story the melancholy may be moved to laughter, and the merry made merrier still; that the simple shall not be wearied, that the judicious shall admire the invention, that the grave shall not despise it, nor the wise fail to praise it. Finally, keep your aim fixed on the destruction of that ill-founded edifice of the books of chivalry, hated by some and praised by many more; for if you succeed in this you will have achieved no small success."

In profound silence I listened to what my friend said, and his observations made such an impression on me that, without attempting to question them, I admitted their soundness, and out of them I determined to make this Preface; wherein, gentle reader, thou wilt perceive my friend's good sense, my good fortune in finding such an adviser in such a time of need, and what thou hast gained in receiving, without addition or alteration, the story of the famous Don Quixote of La Mancha, who is held by all the inhabitants of the district of the Campo de Montiel to have been the chastest lover and the bravest knight that has for many years been seen in that neighbourhood. I have no desire to magnify the service I render thee in making thee acquainted with so renowned and honoured a knight, but I do desire thy thanks for the acquaintance thou wilt make with the famous Sancho Panza, his squire, in whom, to my thinking, I have given thee condensed all the squirely drolleries that are scattered through the swarm of the vain books of chivalry. And so—may God give thee health, and not forget me. Vale.

Contents

I	Which Treats of the Character and Pursuits of the Famous Gentleman Don Quixote of La Mancha	1
II	Chapter IIWhich Treats of the First Sally the Ingenious Don Quixote made from Home	6
III	Wherein is Related the Droll Way in Which Don Quixote had himself Dubbed a Knight	11
IV	Of What Happened to Our Knight When he Left the Inn	16
V	In Which the Narrative of our Knight's Mishap is Continued	22
VI	Of the Diverting and Important Scrutiny which the Curate and the Barber made in the Library of our Ingenious Gentleman	26
VII	Of the Second Sally of Our Worthy Knight Don Quixote of La Mancha	33
VIII	Of the Good Fortune which the Valiant Don Quixote had in the Terrible and Undreamt of Adventure of the Windmills, with other Occurrences Worthy to be Fitly Recorded	38
IX	In Which is Concluded and Finished the Terrific Battle between the Gallant Biscayan and the Valiant Manchegan	45
X	Of the Pleasant Discourse that passed between Don Quixote and his Squire Sancho Panza	50
XI	What Befell Don Quixote with Certain Goatherds	55
XII	Of What a Goatherd Related to those with Don Quixote	61
XIII	In Which is ended the Story of the Shepherdess Marcela, with Other Incidents	66
XIV	Wherein are inserted the Despairing Verses of the Dead Shepherd, Together with other Incidents not Looked for	74
XV	In Which is Related the Unfortunate Adventure that Don Quixote fell in with when he fell out with Certain Heartless Yanguesans	82

XVI	Of What Happened to the Ingenious Gentleman in the Inn which he took to be a Castle	89
XVII	In Which are Contained the Innumerable Troubles which the Brave Don Quixote and his Good Squire Sancho Panza Endured in the Inn, which to his Misfortune he took to be a Castle	96
XVIII	In Which is Related the Discourse Sancho Panza held with his Master, Don Quixote, and Other Adventures Worth Relating	104
XIX	Of the Shrewd Discourse which Sancho held with his Master, and of the Adventure that Befell him with a Dead Body, together with other Notable Occurrences	113
XX	Of the Unexampled and Unheard of Adventure which was Achieved by the Valiant Don Quixote of La Mancha with less Peril than any ever Achieved by any Famous Knight in the World	120
XXI	Which Treats of the Exalted Adventure and Rich Prize of Mambrino's Helmet, Together with Other Things that happened to our Invincible Knight	131
XXII	Of the Freedom Don Quixote Conferred on Several Unfortunates who Against their will were being carried Where they had no wish to go	141
XXIII	Of What Befell Don Quixote in the Sierra Morena, which was One of the Rarest Adventures related in this Veracious History	151
XXIV	In Which ss Continued the Adventure of the Sierra Morena	161
XXV	Which Treats of the Strange things that Happened to the Stout Knight of La Mancha in the Sierra Morena, and of his Imitation of the Penance of Beltenebros	169
XXVI	In Which are Continued the Refinements Where with Don Quixote Played the Part of a Lover in the Sierra Morena	183
XXVII	Of how the Curate and the Barber Proceeded with their Scheme; together with Other Matters Worthy of Record in this Great History	190
XXVIII	Which Treats of the Strange and Delightful Adventure that Befell the Curate and the Barber in the Same Sierra	204

XXIX	Which Treats of the Droll Device and Method adopted to Extricate our Love-Stricken Knight from the Severe Penance he had imposed upon himself	216
XXX	Which Treats of Address Displayed by the Fair Dorothea, with Other Matters Pleasant and Amusing	226
XXXI	Chapter Of the Delectable Discussion between Don Quixote and Sancho Panza, his Squire, Together with Other Incidents	235
XXXII	Which Treats of what Befell Don Quixote's Party at the Inn	243
XXXIII	In Which is related the Novel of "The Ill-Advised Curiosity"	249
XXXIV	In Which is Continued the Novel of "The Ill-Advised Curiosity"	265
XXXV	Which Treats of the Heroic and Prodigious Battle Don Quixote had with Certain Skins of Red Wine, and brings the Novel of "The Ill-Advised Curiosity" to a Close	281
XXXVI	Which Treats of more Curious incidents that Occurred at the Inn	289
XXXVII	In Which is continued the Story of the Famous Princess Micomicona, with Other Droll Adventures	297
XXXVIII	Which Treats of the Curious Discourse Don Quixote Delivered on Arms and Letters	306
XXXIX	Wherein the Captive Relates his Life and Adventures	310
XL	In Which the Story of the Captive is Continued	317
XLI	In Which the Captive Still Continues his Adventures	327
XLII	Which Treats of what further took place in the Inn, and of Several Other Things Worth Knowing	343
XLIII	Wherein is related the Pleasant Story of the Muleteer, together with other Strange Things that came to pass in the Inn	349
XLIV	In Which are Continued the Unheard of Adventures of the Inn	358
XLV	In Which the Doubtful Question of Mambrino's Helmet and the Pack-Saddle is Finally Settled, with Other Adventures that Occurred in Truth and Earnest	366
XLVI	Of the End of the Notable Adventure of the officers of the Holy Brotherhood; and of the Great Ferocity of our Worthy Knight, Don Quixote	373

XLVII	Of the Strange Manner in Which Don Quixote of La Mancha was Carried Away Enchanted, Together with other Remarkable Incidents	380
XLVIII	In Which the Canon Pursues the Subject of the Books of Chivalry, with other Matters Worthy of his Wit	388
XLIX	Which Treats of the Shrewd Conversation which Sancho Panza held with his Master Don Quixote	395
L	Of the Shrewd Controversy which Don Quixote and the Canon held, Together with Other Incidents	401
LI	Which Deals with what the Goatherd told those who were Carrying off Don Quixote	407
LII	Of the Quarrel that Don Quixote had with the Goatherd, together with the rare Adventure of the Penitents, which with an Expenditure of Sweat he brought to a Happy Conclusion	412

CHAPTER I

WHICH TREATS OF THE CHARACTER AND PURSUITS OF THE FAMOUS GENTLEMAN DON QUIXOTE OF LA MANCHA

In a village of La Mancha, the name of which I have no desire to call to mind, there lived not long since one of those gentlemen that keep a lance in the lance-rack, an old buckler, a lean hack, and a greyhound for coursing. An olla of rather more beef than mutton, a salad on most nights, scraps on Saturdays, lentils on Fridays, and a pigeon or so extra on Sundays, made away with three-quarters of his income. The rest of it went in a doublet of fine cloth and velvet breeches and shoes to match for holidays, while on week-days he made a brave figure in his best homespun. He had in his house a housekeeper past forty, a niece under twenty, and a lad for the field and market-place, who used to saddle the hack as well as handle the bill-hook. The age of this gentleman of ours was bordering on fifty; he was of a hardy habit, spare, gaunt-featured, a very early riser and a great sportsman. They will have it his surname was Quixada or Quesada (for here there is some difference of opinion among the authors who write on the subject), although from reasonable conjectures it seems plain that he was called Quexana. This, however, is of but little importance to our tale; it will be enough not to stray a hair's breadth from the truth in the telling of it.

You must know, then, that the above-named gentleman whenever he was at leisure (which was mostly all the year round) gave himself up to reading books of chivalry with such ardour and avidity that he almost entirely neglected the pursuit of his field-sports, and even the management of his property; and to such a pitch did his eagerness and infatuation go that he sold many an acre of tillageland to buy books of chivalry to read, and brought home as many of them as he could get. But of all there were none he liked so well as those of the famous Feliciano de Silva's composition, for their lucidity of style and complicated conceits were as pearls in his sight, particularly when in his reading he came upon courtships and cartels, where he often found passages like "the reason of the unreason with which my reason is afflicted so weakens my reason that with reason I murmur at your beauty;" or again, "the high heavens, that of your divinity divinely fortify you with the stars, render you deserving of the desert your greatness deserves." Over conceits of this sort the poor gentleman lost his wits, and used to lie awake striving to understand them and worm the meaning out of them; what Aristotle himself could not have made out or extracted had he come to life again for that special purpose. He was not at all easy about the wounds which Don Belianis gave and took, because it seemed to him that, great as were the surgeons who had cured him, he must have had his face and body covered all over with seams and scars. He commended, however, the author's way of ending his book with the promise of that interminable adventure, and many a time was he tempted to take up his pen and finish it properly as is there proposed, which no doubt he would have done, and made a successful piece of work of it too, had not greater and more absorbing thoughts prevented him.

Many an argument did he have with the curate of his village (a learned man, and a graduate of Siguenza) as to which had been the better knight, Palmerin of England or Amadis of Gaul. Master Nicholas, the village barber, however, used to say that neither of them came up to the Knight of Phoebus, and that if there was any that could compare with him it was Don Galaor, the brother of Amadis of Gaul, because he had a spirit that was equal to every occasion, and was no finikin knight, nor lachrymose like his brother, while in the matter of valour he was not a whit behind him. In short, he became so absorbed in his books that he spent his nights from sunset to sunrise, and his days from dawn to dark, poring over them; and what with little sleep and much reading his brains got so dry that he lost his wits. His fancy grew full of what he used to read about in his books, enchantments, quarrels, battles, challenges, wounds, wooings, loves, agonies, and all sorts of impossible nonsense; and it so possessed his mind that the whole fabric of invention and fancy he read of was true, that to him no history in the world had more reality in it. He used to say the Cid Ruy Diaz was a very good knight, but that he was not to be compared with the Knight of the Burning Sword who with one back-stroke cut in half two fierce and monstrous giants. He thought more of Bernardo del Carpio because at Roncesvalles he slew Roland in spite of enchantments, availing himself of the artifice of Hercules when he strangled Antaeus the son of Terra in his arms. He approved highly of the giant Morgante, because, although of the giant breed which is always arrogant and ill-conditioned, he alone was affable and well-bred. But above all he admired Reinaldos of Montalban, especially when he saw him sallying forth from his castle and robbing everyone he met, and when beyond the seas he stole that image of

Mahomet which, as his history says, was entirely of gold. To have a bout of kicking at that traitor of a Ganelon he would have given his housekeeper, and his niece into the bargain.

In short, his wits being quite gone, he hit upon the strangest notion that ever madman in this world hit upon, and that was that he fancied it was right and requisite, as well for the support of his own honour as for the service of his country, that he should make a knight-errant of himself, roaming the world over in full armour and on horseback in quest of adventures, and putting in practice himself all that he had read of as being the usual practices of knights-errant; righting every kind of wrong, and exposing himself to peril and danger from which, in the issue, he was to reap eternal renown and fame. Already the poor man saw himself crowned by the might of his arm Emperor of Trebizond at least; and so, led away by the intense enjoyment he found in these pleasant fancies, he set himself forthwith to put his scheme into execution.

The first thing he did was to clean up some armour that had belonged to his great-grandfather, and had been for ages lying forgotten in a corner eaten with rust and covered with mildew. He scoured and polished it as best he could, but he perceived one great defect in it, that it had no closed helmet, nothing but a simple morion. This deficiency, however, his ingenuity supplied, for he contrived a kind of half-helmet of pasteboard which, fitted on to the morion, looked like a whole one. It is true that, in order to see if it was strong and fit to stand a cut, he drew his sword and gave it a couple of slashes, the first of which undid in an instant what had taken him a week to do. The ease with which he had knocked it to pieces disconcerted him somewhat, and to guard against that danger he set to work again, fixing bars of iron on the inside until he was satisfied with its strength; and then, not caring to try any more experiments with it, he passed it and adopted it as a helmet of the most perfect construction.

He next proceeded to inspect his hack, which, with more quartos than a real and more blemishes than the steed of Gonela, that "tantum pellis et ossa fuit," surpassed in his eyes the Bucephalus of Alexander or the Babieca of the Cid. Four days were spent in thinking what name to give him, because (as he said to himself) it was not right that a horse belonging to a knight so famous, and one with such merits of his own, should be without some distinctive name, and he strove to adapt it so as to indicate what he had been before belonging to a knight-errant, and what he then was; for it was only reasonable that, his master taking a new character, he should take a new name, and that it should be a distinguished and full-sounding one, befitting the new order and calling he was about to follow. And so, after having composed, struck out, rejected, added to, unmade, and remade a multitude of names out of his memory and fancy, he decided upon calling him Rocinante, a name, to his thinking, lofty, sonorous, and significant of his condition as a hack before he became what he now was, the first and foremost of all the hacks in the world.

Having got a name for his horse so much to his taste, he was anxious to get one for himself, and he was eight days more pondering over this point, till at last he made up his mind to call himself "Don Quixote," whence, as has been already said, the authors of this veracious history have inferred that his name must have been beyond a doubt Quixada, and not Quesada as others would have it. Recollecting, however, that the valiant Amadis was not content to call himself curtly Amadis and nothing more, but added the name of his kingdom and country to make it famous, and called himself Amadis of Gaul, he, like a good knight, resolved to add on the name of his, and to style himself Don Quixote of La Mancha, whereby, he considered, he described accurately his origin and country, and did honour to it in taking his surname from it.

So then, his armour being furbished, his morion turned into a helmet, his hack christened, and he himself confirmed, he came to the conclusion that nothing more was needed now but to look out for a lady to be in love with; for a knight-errant without love was like a tree without leaves or fruit, or a body without a soul. As he said to himself, "If, for my sins, or by my good fortune, I come across some giant hereabouts, a common occurrence with knights-errant, and overthrow him in one onslaught, or cleave him asunder to the waist, or, in short, vanquish and subdue him, will it not be well to have some one I may send him to as a present, that he may come in and fall on his knees before my sweet lady, and in a humble, submissive voice say, 'I am the giant Caraculiambro, lord of the island of Malindrania, vanquished in single combat by the never sufficiently extolled knight Don Quixote of La Mancha, who has commanded me to present myself before your Grace, that your Highness dispose of me at your pleasure'?" Oh, how our good gentleman enjoyed the delivery of this speech, especially when he had thought of some one to call his Lady! There was, so the story goes, in a village near his own a very good-looking farm-girl with whom he had been at one time in love, though, so far as is known, she never knew it nor gave a thought to the matter. Her name was Aldonza Lorenzo, and upon her he thought fit to confer the title of Lady of his Thoughts; and after some search for a name which should not be out of harmony with her own, and should suggest and indicate that of a princess and great lady, he decided upon calling her Dulcinea del Toboso—she being of El Toboso—a name, to his mind, musical, uncommon, and significant, like all those he had already bestowed upon himself and the things belonging to him.

CHAPTER II

WHICH TREATS OF THE FIRST SALLY THE INGENIOUS DON QUIXOTE MADE FROM HOME

These preliminaries settled, he did not care to put off any longer the execution of his design, urged on to it by the thought of all the world was losing by his delay, seeing what wrongs he intended to right, grievances to redress, injustices to repair, abuses to remove, and duties to discharge. So, without giving notice of his intention to anyone, and without anybody seeing him, one morning before the dawning of the day (which was one of the hottest of the month of July) he donned his suit of armour, mounted Rocinante with his patched-up helmet on, braced his buckler, took his lance, and by the back door of the yard sallied forth upon the plain in the highest contentment and satisfaction at seeing with what ease he had made a beginning with his grand purpose. But scarcely did he find himself upon the open plain, when a terrible thought struck him, one all but enough to make him abandon the enterprise at the very outset. It occurred to him that he had not been dubbed a knight, and that according to the law of chivalry he neither could nor ought to bear arms against any knight; and that even if he had been, still he ought, as a novice knight, to wear white armour, without a device upon the shield until by his prowess he had earned one. These reflections made him waver in his purpose, but his craze being stronger than any reasoning, he made up his mind to have himself dubbed a knight by the first one he came across, following the example of others in the same case, as he had read in the books that brought him to this pass. As for white armour, he resolved, on the first opportunity, to scour his until it was whiter than an ermine; and so comforting himself he pursued his way, taking that which his horse chose, for in this he believed lay the essence of adventures.

Thus setting out, our new-fledged adventurer paced along, talking to himself and saying, "Who knows but that in time to come, when the veracious history of my famous deeds is made known, the sage who writes it, when he has to set forth my first sally in the early morning, will do it after this fashion? 'Scarce had the rubicund Apollo spread o'er the face of the broad spacious earth the golden threads of his bright hair, scarce had the little birds of painted plumage attuned their notes to hail with dulcet and mellifluous harmony the coming of the rosy Dawn, that, deserting the soft couch of her jealous spouse, was appearing to mortals at the gates and balconies of the Manchegan horizon, when the renowned knight Don Quixote of La Mancha, quitting the lazy down, mounted his celebrated steed Rocinante and began to traverse the ancient and famous Campo de Montiel;'" which in fact he was actually traversing. "Happy the age, happy the time," he continued, "in which shall be made known my deeds of fame, worthy to be moulded in brass, carved in marble, limned in pictures, for a memorial for ever. And thou, O sage magician, whoever thou art, to whom it shall fall to be the chronicler of this wondrous history, forget not, I entreat thee, my good Rocinante, the constant companion of my ways and wanderings." Presently he broke out again, as if he were love-stricken in earnest, "O Princess Dulcinea, lady of this captive heart, a grievous wrong hast thou done me to drive me forth with scorn, and with inexorable obduracy banish me from the presence of thy beauty. O lady, deign to hold in remembrance this heart, thy vassal, that thus in anguish pines for love of thee."

So he went on stringing together these and other absurdities, all in the style of those his books had taught him, imitating their language as well as he could; and all the while he rode so slowly and the sun mounted so rapidly and with such fervour that it was enough to melt his brains if he had any. Nearly all day he travelled without anything remarkable happening to him, at which he was in despair, for he was anxious to encounter some one at once upon whom to try the might of his strong arm.

Writers there are who say the first adventure he met with was that of Puerto Lapice; others say it was that of the windmills; but what I have ascertained on this point, and what I have found written in the annals of La Mancha, is that he was on the road all day, and towards nightfall his hack and he found themselves dead tired and hungry, when, looking all around to see if he could discover any castle or shepherd's shanty where he might refresh himself and relieve his sore wants, he perceived not far out of his road an inn, which was as welcome as a star guiding him to the portals, if not the palaces, of his redemption; and quickening his pace he reached it just as night was setting in. At the door were standing two young women, girls of the district as they call them, on their way to Seville with some carriers who had chanced to halt that night at the inn; and as, happen what might to our adventurer, everything he saw or imaged seemed to him to be and to happen after the fashion of what he read of, the moment he saw the inn he pictured it to himself as a castle with its four turrets and pinnacles of shining silver, not forgetting the drawbridge and moat and all the belongings usually ascribed to castles of the sort. To this inn, which to him seemed a castle, he advanced, and at a short distance from it he checked Rocinante, hoping that some dwarf would show himself upon the battlements, and by sound of trumpet give notice that a knight was approaching the castle. But seeing that they were slow about it, and that Rocinante was in a hurry to reach the stable, he made for the inn door, and perceived the two gay damsels who were standing there, and who seemed to him to be two fair maidens or lovely ladies taking their ease at the castle gate.

At this moment it so happened that a swineherd who was going through the stubbles collecting a drove of pigs (for, without any apology, that is what they are called) gave a blast of his horn to bring them together, and forthwith it seemed to Don Quixote to be what he was expecting, the signal of some dwarf announcing his arrival; and so with prodigious satisfaction he rode up to the inn and to the ladies, who, seeing a man of this sort approaching in full armour and with lance and buckler, were turning in dismay into the inn, when Don Quixote, guessing their fear by their flight, raising his pasteboard visor, disclosed his dry dusty visage, and with courteous bearing and gentle voice addressed them, "Your ladyships need not fly or fear any rudeness, for that it belongs not to the order of knighthood which I profess to offer to anyone, much less to highborn maidens as your appearance proclaims you to be." The girls were looking at him and straining their eyes to make out the features which the clumsy visor obscured, but when they heard themselves called maidens, a thing so much out of their line, they could not restrain their laughter, which made Don Quixote wax indignant, and say, "Modesty becomes the fair, and moreover laughter that has little cause is great silliness; this, however, I say not to pain or anger you, for my desire is none other than to serve you."

The incomprehensible language and the unpromising looks of our cavalier only increased the ladies' laughter, and that increased his irritation, and matters might have gone farther if at that moment the landlord had not come out, who, being a very fat man, was a very peaceful one. He, seeing this grotesque figure clad in armour that did not match any more than his saddle, bridle, lance, buckler, or corselet, was not at all indisposed to join the damsels in their manifestations of amusement; but, in truth, standing in awe of such a complicated armament, he thought it best to speak him fairly, so he said, "Senor Caballero, if your worship wants lodging, bating the bed (for there is not one in the inn) there is plenty of everything else here." Don Quixote, observing the respectful bearing of the Alcaide of the fortress (for so innkeeper and inn seemed in his eyes), made answer, "Sir Castellan, for me anything will suffice, for

> 'My armour is my only wear,
> My only rest the fray.'"

The host fancied he called him Castellan because he took him for a "worthy of Castile," though he was in fact an Andalusian, and one from the strand of San Lucar, as crafty a thief as Cacus and as full of tricks as a student or a page. "In that case," said he,

> "'Your bed is on the flinty rock,
> Your sleep to watch alway;'

and if so, you may dismount and safely reckon upon any quantity of sleeplessness under this roof for a twelvemonth, not to say for a single night." So saying, he advanced to hold the stirrup for Don Quixote, who got down with great difficulty and exertion (for he had not broken his fast all day), and then charged the host to take great care of his horse, as he was the best bit of flesh that ever ate bread in this world. The landlord eyed him over but did not find him as good as Don Quixote said, nor even half as good; and putting him up in the stable, he returned to see what might be wanted by his guest, whom the damsels, who had by this time made their peace with him, were now relieving of his armour. They had taken off his breastplate and backpiece, but they neither knew nor saw how to open his gorget or remove his make-shift helmet, for he had fastened it with green ribbons, which, as there was no untying the knots, required to be cut. This, however, he would not by any means consent to, so he remained all the evening with his helmet on, the drollest and oddest figure that can be imagined; and while they were removing his armour, taking the baggages who were about it for ladies of high degree belonging to the castle, he said to them with great sprightliness:

> "Oh, never, surely, was there knight
> So served by hand of dame,
> As served was he, Don Quixote hight,
> When from his town he came;
> With maidens waiting on himself,
> Princesses on his hack—

or Rocinante, for that, ladies mine, is my horse's name, and Don Quixote of La Mancha is my own; for though I had no intention of declaring myself until my achievements in your service and honour had made me known, the necessity of adapting that old ballad of Lancelot to the present occasion has given you the knowledge of my name altogether prematurely. A time, however, will come for your ladyships to command and me to obey, and then the might of my arm will show my desire to serve you."

The girls, who were not used to hearing rhetoric of this sort, had nothing to say in reply; they only asked him if he wanted anything to eat. "I would gladly eat a bit of something," said Don Quixote, "for I feel it would come very seasonably." The day happened to be a Friday, and in the whole inn there was nothing but some pieces of the fish they call in Castile "abadejo," in Andalusia "bacallao," and in some places "curadillo," and in others "troutlet;" so they asked him if he thought he could eat troutlet, for there was no other fish to give him. "If there be troutlets enough," said Don Quixote, "they will be the same thing as a trout; for it is all one to me whether I am given eight reals in small change or a piece of eight; moreover, it may be that these troutlets are like veal, which is better than beef, or kid, which is better than goat. But whatever it be let it come quickly, for the burden and pressure of arms cannot be borne without support to the inside." They laid a table for him at the door of the inn for the sake of the air, and the host brought him a portion of ill-soaked and worse cooked stockfish, and a piece of bread as black and mouldy as his own armour; but a laughable sight it was to see him eating, for having his helmet on and the beaver up, he could not with his own hands put anything into his mouth unless some one else placed it there, and this service one of the ladies rendered him. But to give him anything to drink was impossible, or would have been so had not the landlord bored a reed, and putting one end in his mouth poured the wine into him through the other; all which he bore with patience rather than sever the ribbons of his helmet.

While this was going on there came up to the inn a sowgelder, who, as he approached, sounded his reed pipe four or five times, and thereby completely convinced Don Quixote that he was in some famous castle, and that they were regaling him with music, and that the stockfish was trout, the bread the whitest, the wenches ladies, and the landlord the castellan of the castle; and consequently he held that his enterprise and sally had been to some purpose. But still it distressed him to think he had not been dubbed a knight, for it was plain to him he could not lawfully engage in any adventure without receiving the order of knighthood.

CHAPTER III

WHEREIN IS RELATED THE DROLL WAY IN WHICH DON QUIXOTE HAD HIMSELF DUBBED A KNIGHT

Harassed by this reflection, he made haste with his scanty pothouse supper, and having finished it called the landlord, and shutting himself into the stable with him, fell on his knees before him, saying, "From this spot I rise not, valiant knight, until your courtesy grants me the boon I seek, one that will redound to your praise and the benefit of the human race." The landlord, seeing his guest at his feet and hearing a speech of this kind, stood staring at him in bewilderment, not knowing what to do or say, and entreating him to rise, but all to no purpose until he had agreed to grant the boon demanded of him. "I looked for no less, my lord, from your High Magnificence," replied Don Quixote, "and I have to tell you that the boon I have asked and your liberality has granted is that you shall dub me knight to-morrow morning, and that to-night I shall watch my arms in the chapel of this your castle; thus tomorrow, as I have said, will be accomplished what I so much desire, enabling me lawfully to roam through all the four quarters of the world seeking adventures on behalf of those in distress, as is the duty of chivalry and of knights-errant like myself, whose ambition is directed to such deeds."

The landlord, who, as has been mentioned, was something of a wag, and had already some suspicion of his guest's want of wits, was quite convinced of it on hearing talk of this kind from him, and to make sport for the night he determined to fall in with his humour. So he told him he was quite right in pursuing the object he had in view, and that such a motive was natural and becoming in cavaliers as distinguished as he seemed and his gallant bearing showed him to be; and that he himself in his younger days had followed the same honourable calling, roaming in quest of adventures in various parts of the world, among others the Curing-grounds of Malaga, the Isles of Riaran, the Precinct of Seville, the Little Market of Segovia, the Olivera of Valencia, the Rondilla of Granada, the Strand of San Lucar, the Colt of Cordova, the Taverns of Toledo, and divers other quarters, where he had proved the nimbleness of his feet and the lightness of his fingers, doing many wrongs, cheating many widows, ruining maids and swindling minors, and, in short, bringing himself under the notice of almost every tribunal and court of justice in Spain; until at last he had retired to this castle of his, where he was living upon his property and upon that of others; and where he received all knights-errant of whatever rank or condition they might be, all for the great love he bore them and that they might share their substance with him in return for his benevolence. He told him, moreover, that in this castle of his there was no chapel in which he could watch his armour, as it had been pulled down in order to be rebuilt, but that in a case of necessity it might, he knew, be watched anywhere, and he might watch it that night in a courtyard of the castle, and in the morning, God willing, the requisite ceremonies might be performed so as to have him dubbed a knight, and so thoroughly dubbed that nobody could be more so. He asked if he had any money with him, to which Don Quixote replied that he had not a farthing, as in the histories of knights-errant he had never read of any of them carrying any. On this point the landlord told him he was mistaken; for, though not recorded in the histories, because in the author's opinion there was no need to mention anything so obvious and necessary as money and clean shirts, it was not to be supposed therefore that they did not carry them, and he might regard it as certain and established that all knights-errant (about whom there were so many full and unimpeachable books) carried well-furnished purses in case of emergency, and likewise carried shirts and a little box of ointment to cure the wounds they received. For in those plains and deserts where they engaged in combat and came out wounded, it was not always that there was some one to cure them, unless indeed they had for a friend some sage magician to succour them at once by fetching through the air upon a cloud some damsel or dwarf with a vial of water of such virtue that by tasting one drop of it they were cured of their hurts and wounds in an instant and left as sound as if they had not received any damage whatever. But in case this should not occur, the knights of old took care to see that their squires were provided with money and other requisites, such as lint and ointments for healing purposes; and when it happened that knights had no squires (which was rarely and seldom the case) they themselves carried everything in cunning saddle-bags that were hardly seen on the horse's croup, as if it were something else of more importance, because, unless for some such reason, carrying saddle-bags was not very favourably regarded among knights-errant. He therefore advised him (and, as his godson so soon to be, he might even command him) never from that time forth to travel without money and the usual requirements, and he would find the advantage of them when he least expected it.

Don Quixote promised to follow his advice scrupulously, and it was arranged forthwith that he should watch his armour in a large yard at one side of the inn; so, collecting it all together, Don Quixote placed it on a trough that stood by the side of a well, and bracing his buckler on his arm he grasped his lance and began with a stately air to march up and down in front of the trough, and as he began his march night began to fall.

The landlord told all the people who were in the inn about the craze of his guest, the watching of the armour, and the dubbing ceremony he contemplated. Full of wonder at so strange a form of madness, they flocked to see it from a distance, and observed with what composure he sometimes paced up and down, or sometimes, leaning on his lance, gazed on his armour without taking his eyes off it for ever so long; and as the night closed in with a light from the moon so brilliant that it might vie with his that lent it, everything the novice knight did was plainly seen by all.

Meanwhile one of the carriers who were in the inn thought fit to water his team, and it was necessary to remove Don Quixote's armour as it lay on the trough; but he seeing the other approach hailed him in a loud voice, "O thou, whoever thou art, rash knight that comest to lay hands on the armour of the most valorous errant that ever girt on sword, have a care what thou dost; touch it not unless thou wouldst lay down thy life as the penalty of thy rashness." The carrier gave no heed to these words (and he would have done better to heed them if he had been heedful of his health), but seizing it by the straps flung the armour some distance from him. Seeing this, Don Quixote raised his eyes to heaven, and fixing his thoughts, apparently, upon his lady Dulcinea, exclaimed, "Aid me, lady mine, in this the first encounter that presents itself to this breast which thou holdest in subjection; let not thy favour and protection fail me in this first jeopardy;" and, with these words and others to the same purpose, dropping his buckler he lifted his lance with both hands and with it smote such a blow on the carrier's head that he stretched him on the ground, so stunned that had he followed it up with a second there would have been no need of a surgeon to cure him. This done, he picked up his armour and returned to his beat with the same serenity as before.

Shortly after this, another, not knowing what had happened (for the carrier still lay senseless), came with the same object of giving water to his mules, and was proceeding to remove the armour in order to clear the trough, when Don Quixote, without uttering a word or imploring aid from anyone, once more dropped his buckler and once more lifted his lance, and without actually breaking the second carrier's head into pieces, made more than three of it, for he laid it open in four. At the noise all the people of the inn ran to the spot, and among them the landlord. Seeing this, Don Quixote braced his buckler on his arm, and with his hand on his sword exclaimed, "O Lady of Beauty, strength and support of my faint heart, it is time for thee to turn the eyes of thy greatness on this thy captive knight on the brink of so mighty an adventure." By this he felt himself so inspired that he would not have flinched if all the carriers in the world had assailed him. The comrades of the wounded perceiving the plight they were in began from a distance to shower stones on Don Quixote, who screened himself as best he could with his buckler, not daring to quit the trough and leave his armour unprotected. The landlord shouted to them to leave him alone, for he had already told them that he was mad, and as a madman he would not be accountable even if he killed them all. Still louder shouted Don Quixote, calling them knaves and traitors, and the lord of the castle, who allowed knights-errant to be treated in this fashion, a villain and a low-born knight whom, had he received the order of knighthood, he would call to account for his treachery. "But of you," he cried, "base and vile rabble, I make no account; fling, strike, come on, do all ye can against me, ye shall see what the reward of your folly and insolence will be." This he uttered with so much spirit and boldness that he filled his assailants with a terrible fear, and as much for this reason as at the persuasion of the landlord they left off stoning him, and he allowed them to carry off the wounded, and with the same calmness and composure as before resumed the watch over his armour.

But these freaks of his guest were not much to the liking of the landlord, so he determined to cut matters short and confer upon him at once the unlucky order of knighthood before any further misadventure could occur; so, going up to him, he apologised for the rudeness which, without his knowledge, had been offered to him by these low people, who, however, had been well punished for their audacity. As he had already told him, he said, there was no chapel in the castle, nor was it needed for what remained to be done, for, as he understood the ceremonial of the order, the whole point of being dubbed a knight lay in the accolade and in the slap on the shoulder, and that could be administered in the middle of a field; and that he had now done all that was needful as to watching the armour, for all requirements were satisfied by a watch of two hours only, while he had been more than four about it. Don Quixote believed it all, and told him he stood there ready to obey him, and to make an end of it with as much despatch as possible; for, if he were again attacked, and felt himself to be dubbed knight, he would not, he thought, leave a soul alive in the castle, except such as out of respect he might spare at his bidding.

Thus warned and menaced, the castellan forthwith brought out a book in which he used to enter the straw and barley he served out to the carriers, and, with a lad carrying a candle-end, and the two damsels already mentioned, he returned to where Don Quixote stood, and bade him kneel down. Then, reading from his account-book as if he were repeating some devout prayer, in the middle of his delivery he raised his hand and gave him a sturdy blow on the neck, and then, with his own sword, a smart slap on the shoulder, all the while muttering between his teeth as if he was saying his prayers. Having done this, he directed one of the ladies to gird on his sword, which she did with great self-possession and gravity, and not a little was required to prevent a burst of laughter at each stage of the ceremony; but what they had already seen of the novice knight's prowess kept their laughter within bounds. On girding him with the sword the worthy lady said to him, "May God make your worship a very fortunate knight, and grant you success in battle." Don Quixote asked her name in order that he might from that time forward know to whom he was beholden for the favour he had received, as he meant to confer upon her some portion of the honour he acquired by the might of his arm. She answered with great humility that she was called La Tolosa, and that she was the daughter of a cobbler of Toledo who lived in the stalls of Sanchobienaya, and that wherever she might be she would serve and esteem him as her lord. Don Quixote said in reply that she would do him a favour if thenceforward she assumed the "Don" and called herself Dona Tolosa. She promised she would, and then the other buckled on his spur, and with her followed almost the same conversation as with the lady of the sword. He asked her name, and she said it was La Molinera, and that she was the daughter of a respectable miller of Antequera; and of her likewise Don Quixote requested that she would adopt the "Don" and call herself Dona Molinera, making offers to her further services and favours.

Having thus, with hot haste and speed, brought to a conclusion these never-till-now-seen ceremonies, Don Quixote was on thorns until he saw himself on horseback sallying forth in quest of adventures; and saddling Rocinante at once he mounted, and embracing his host, as he returned thanks for his kindness in knighting him, he addressed him in language so extraordinary that it is impossible to convey an idea of it or report it. The landlord, to get him out of the inn, replied with no less rhetoric though with shorter words, and without calling upon him to pay the reckoning let him go with a Godspeed.

CHAPTER IV

OF WHAT HAPPENED TO OUR KNIGHT WHEN HE LEFT THE INN

Day was dawning when Don Quixote quitted the inn, so happy, so gay, so exhilarated at finding himself now dubbed a knight, that his joy was like to burst his horse-girths. However, recalling the advice of his host as to the requisites he ought to carry with him, especially that referring to money and shirts, he determined to go home and provide himself with all, and also with a squire, for he reckoned upon securing a farm-labourer, a neighbour of his, a poor man with a family, but very well qualified for the office of squire to a knight. With this object he turned his horse's head towards his village, and Rocinante, thus reminded of his old quarters, stepped out so briskly that he hardly seemed to tread the earth.

He had not gone far, when out of a thicket on his right there seemed to come feeble cries as of some one in distress, and the instant he heard them he exclaimed, "Thanks be to heaven for the favour it accords me, that it so soon offers me an opportunity of fulfilling the obligation I have undertaken, and gathering the fruit of my ambition. These cries, no doubt, come from some man or woman in want of help, and needing my aid and protection;" and wheeling, he turned Rocinante in the direction whence the cries seemed to proceed. He had gone but a few paces into the wood, when he saw a mare tied to an oak, and tied to another, and stripped from the waist upwards, a youth of about fifteen years of age, from whom the cries came. Nor were they without cause, for a lusty farmer was flogging him with a belt and following up every blow with scoldings and commands, repeating, "Your mouth shut and your eyes open!" while the youth made answer, "I won't do it again, master mine; by God's passion I won't do it again, and I'll take more care of the flock another time."

Seeing what was going on, Don Quixote said in an angry voice, "Discourteous knight, it ill becomes you to assail one who cannot defend himself; mount your steed and take your lance" (for there was a lance leaning against the oak to which the mare was tied), "and I will make you know that you are behaving as a coward." The farmer, seeing before him this figure in full armour brandishing a lance over his head, gave himself up for dead, and made answer meekly, "Sir Knight, this youth that I am chastising is my servant, employed by me to watch a flock of sheep that I have hard by, and he is so careless that I lose one every day, and when I punish him for his carelessness and knavery he says I do it out of niggardliness, to escape paying him the wages I owe him, and before God, and on my soul, he lies."

"Lies before me, base clown!" said Don Quixote. "By the sun that shines on us I have a mind to run you through with this lance. Pay him at once without another word; if not, by the God that rules us I will make an end of you, and annihilate you on the spot; release him instantly."

The farmer hung his head, and without a word untied his servant, of whom

Don Quixote asked how much his master owed him.

He replied, nine months at seven reals a month. Don Quixote added it up, found that it came to sixty-three reals, and told the farmer to pay it down immediately, if he did not want to die for it.

The trembling clown replied that as he lived and by the oath he had sworn (though he had not sworn any) it was not so much; for there were to be taken into account and deducted three pairs of shoes he had given him, and a real for two blood-lettings when he was sick.

"All that is very well," said Don Quixote; "but let the shoes and the blood-lettings stand as a setoff against the blows you have given him without any cause; for if he spoiled the leather of the shoes you paid for, you have damaged that of his body, and if the barber took blood from him when he was sick, you have drawn it when he was sound; so on that score he owes you nothing."

"The difficulty is, Sir Knight, that I have no money here; let Andres come home with me, and I will pay him all, real by real."

"I go with him!" said the youth. "Nay, God forbid! No, senor, not for the world; for once alone with me, he would ray me like a Saint Bartholomew."

"He will do nothing of the kind," said Don Quixote; "I have only to command, and he will obey me; and as he has sworn to me by the order of knighthood which he has received, I leave him free, and I guarantee the payment."

"Consider what you are saying, senor," said the youth; "this master of mine is not a knight, nor has he received any order of knighthood; for he is Juan Haldudo the Rich, of Quintanar."

"That matters little," replied Don Quixote; "there may be Haldudos knights; moreover, everyone is the son of his works."

"That is true," said Andres; "but this master of mine—of what works is he the son, when he refuses me the wages of my sweat and labour?"

"I do not refuse, brother Andres," said the farmer, "be good enough to come along with me, and I swear by all the orders of knighthood there are in the world to pay you as I have agreed, real by real, and perfumed."

"For the perfumery I excuse you," said Don Quixote; "give it to him in reals, and I shall be satisfied; and see that you do as you have sworn; if not, by the same oath I swear to come back and hunt you out and punish you; and I shall find you though you should lie closer than a lizard. And if you desire to know who it is lays this command upon you, that you be more firmly bound to obey it, know that I am the valorous Don Quixote of La Mancha, the undoer of wrongs and injustices; and so, God be with you, and keep in mind what you have promised and sworn under those penalties that have been already declared to you."

So saying, he gave Rocinante the spur and was soon out of reach. The farmer followed him with his eyes, and when he saw that he had cleared the wood and was no longer in sight, he turned to his boy Andres, and said, "Come here, my son, I want to pay you what I owe you, as that undoer of wrongs has commanded me."

"My oath on it," said Andres, "your worship will be well advised to obey the command of that good knight—may he live a thousand years—for, as he is a valiant and just judge, by Roque, if you do not pay me, he will come back and do as he said."

"My oath on it, too," said the farmer; "but as I have a strong affection for you, I want to add to the debt in order to add to the payment;" and seizing him by the arm, he tied him up again, and gave him such a flogging that he left him for dead.

"Now, Master Andres," said the farmer, "call on the undoer of wrongs; you will find he won't undo that, though I am not sure that I have quite done with you, for I have a good mind to flay you alive." But at last he untied him, and gave him leave to go look for his judge in order to put the sentence pronounced into execution.

Andres went off rather down in the mouth, swearing he would go to look for the valiant Don Quixote of La Mancha and tell him exactly what had happened, and that all would have to be repaid him sevenfold; but for all that, he went off weeping, while his master stood laughing.

Thus did the valiant Don Quixote right that wrong, and, thoroughly satisfied with what had taken place, as he considered he had made a very happy and noble beginning with his knighthood, he took the road towards his village in perfect self-content, saying in a low voice, "Well mayest thou this day call thyself fortunate above all on earth, O Dulcinea del Toboso, fairest of the fair! since it has fallen to thy lot to hold subject and submissive to thy full will and pleasure a knight so renowned as is and will be Don Quixote of La Mancha, who, as all the world knows, yesterday received the order of knighthood, and hath to-day righted the greatest wrong and grievance that ever injustice conceived and cruelty perpetrated: who hath to-day plucked the rod from the hand of yonder ruthless oppressor so wantonly lashing that tender child."

He now came to a road branching in four directions, and immediately he was reminded of those cross-roads where knights-errant used to stop to consider which road they should take. In imitation of them he halted for a while, and after having deeply considered it, he gave Rocinante his head, submitting his own will to that of his hack, who followed out his first intention, which was to make straight for his own stable. After he had gone about two miles Don Quixote perceived a large party of people, who, as afterwards appeared, were some Toledo traders, on their way to buy silk at Murcia. There were six of them coming along under their sunshades, with four servants mounted, and three muleteers on foot. Scarcely had Don Quixote descried them when the fancy possessed him that this must be some new adventure; and to help him to imitate as far as he could those passages he had read of in his books, here seemed to come one made on purpose, which he resolved to attempt. So with a lofty bearing and determination he fixed himself firmly in his stirrups, got his lance ready, brought his buckler before his breast, and planting himself in the middle of the road, stood waiting the approach of these knights-errant, for such he now considered and held them to be; and when they had come near enough to see and hear, he exclaimed with a haughty gesture, "All the world stand, unless all the world confess that in all the world there is no maiden fairer than the Empress of La Mancha, the peerless Dulcinea del Toboso."

The traders halted at the sound of this language and the sight of the strange figure that uttered it, and from both figure and language at once guessed the craze of their owner; they wished, however, to learn quietly what was the object of this confession that was demanded of them, and one of them, who was rather fond of a joke and was very sharp-witted, said to him, "Sir Knight, we do not know who this good lady is that you speak of; show her to us, for, if she be of such beauty as you suggest, with all our hearts and without any pressure we will confess the truth that is on your part required of us."

"If I were to show her to you," replied Don Quixote, "what merit would you have in confessing a truth so manifest? The essential point is that without seeing her you must believe, confess, affirm, swear, and defend it; else ye have to do with me in battle, ill-conditioned, arrogant rabble that ye are; and come ye on, one by one as the order of knighthood requires, or all together as is the custom and vile usage of your breed, here do I bide and await you relying on the justice of the cause I maintain."

"Sir Knight," replied the trader, "I entreat your worship in the name of this present company of princes, that, to save us from charging our consciences with the confession of a thing we have never seen or heard of, and one moreover so much to the prejudice of the Empresses and Queens of the Alcarria and Estremadura, your worship will be pleased to show us some portrait of this lady, though it be no bigger than a grain of wheat; for by the thread one gets at the ball, and in this way we shall be satisfied and easy, and you will be content and pleased; nay, I believe we are already so far agreed with you that even though her portrait should show her blind of one eye, and distilling vermilion and sulphur from the other, we would nevertheless, to gratify your worship, say all in her favour that you desire."

"She distils nothing of the kind, vile rabble," said Don Quixote, burning with rage, "nothing of the kind, I say, only ambergris and civet in cotton; nor is she one-eyed or humpbacked, but straighter than a Guadarrama spindle: but ye must pay for the blasphemy ye have uttered against beauty like that of my lady."

And so saying, he charged with levelled lance against the one who had spoken, with such fury and fierceness that, if luck had not contrived that Rocinante should stumble midway and come down, it would have gone hard with the rash trader. Down went Rocinante, and over went his master, rolling along the ground for some distance; and when he tried to rise he was unable, so encumbered was he with lance, buckler, spurs, helmet, and the weight of his old armour; and all the while he was struggling to get up he kept saying, "Fly not, cowards and caitiffs! stay, for not by my fault, but my horse's, am I stretched here."

One of the muleteers in attendance, who could not have had much good nature in him, hearing the poor prostrate man blustering in this style, was unable to refrain from giving him an answer on his ribs; and coming up to him he seized his lance, and having broken it in pieces, with one of them he began so to belabour our Don Quixote that, notwithstanding and in spite of his armour, he milled him like a measure of wheat. His masters called out not to lay on so hard and to leave him alone, but the muleteers blood was up, and he did not care to drop the game until he had vented the rest of his wrath, and gathering up the remaining fragments of the lance he finished with a discharge upon the unhappy victim, who all through the storm of sticks that rained on him never ceased threatening heaven, and earth, and the brigands, for such they seemed to him. At last the muleteer was tired, and the traders continued their journey, taking with them matter for talk about the poor fellow who had been cudgelled. He when he found himself alone made another effort to rise; but if he was unable when whole and sound, how was he to rise after having been thrashed and well-nigh knocked to pieces? And yet he esteemed himself fortunate, as it seemed to him that this was a regular knight-errant's mishap, and entirely, he considered, the fault of his horse. However, battered in body as he was, to rise was beyond his power.

CHAPTER V

IN WHICH THE NARRATIVE OF OUR KNIGHT'S MISHAP IS CONTINUED

Finding, then, that, in fact he could not move, he thought himself of having recourse to his usual remedy, which was to think of some passage in his books, and his craze brought to his mind that about Baldwin and the Marquis of Mantua, when Carloto left him wounded on the mountain side, a story known by heart by the children, not forgotten by the young men, and lauded and even believed by the old folk; and for all that not a whit truer than the miracles of Mahomet. This seemed to him to fit exactly the case in which he found himself, so, making a show of severe suffering, he began to roll on the ground and with feeble breath repeat the very words which the wounded knight of the wood is said to have uttered:

> Where art thou, lady mine, that thou
> My sorrow dost not rue?
> Thou canst not know it, lady mine,
> Or else thou art untrue.

And so he went on with the ballad as far as the lines:

> O noble Marquis of Mantua,
> My Uncle and liege lord!

As chance would have it, when he had got to this line there happened to come by a peasant from his own village, a neighbour of his, who had been with a load of wheat to the mill, and he, seeing the man stretched there, came up to him and asked him who he was and what was the matter with him that he complained so dolefully.

Don Quixote was firmly persuaded that this was the Marquis of Mantua, his uncle, so the only answer he made was to go on with his ballad, in which he told the tale of his misfortune, and of the loves of the Emperor's son and his wife all exactly as the ballad sings it.

The peasant stood amazed at hearing such nonsense, and relieving him of the visor, already battered to pieces by blows, he wiped his face, which was covered with dust, and as soon as he had done so he recognised him and said, "Senor Quixada" (for so he appears to have been called when he was in his senses and had not yet changed from a quiet country gentleman into a knight-errant), "who has brought your worship to this pass?" But to all questions the other only went on with his ballad.

Seeing this, the good man removed as well as he could his breastplate and backpiece to see if he had any wound, but he could perceive no blood nor any mark whatever. He then contrived to raise him from the ground, and with no little difficulty hoisted him upon his ass, which seemed to him to be the easiest mount for him; and collecting the arms, even to the splinters of the lance, he tied them on Rocinante, and leading him by the bridle and the ass by the halter he took the road for the village, very sad to hear what absurd stuff Don Quixote was talking.

Nor was Don Quixote less so, for what with blows and bruises he could not sit upright on the ass, and from time to time he sent up sighs to heaven, so that once more he drove the peasant to ask what ailed him. And it could have been only the devil himself that put into his head tales to match his own adventures, for now, forgetting Baldwin, he bethought himself of the Moor Abindarraez, when the Alcaide of Antequera, Rodrigo de Narvaez, took him prisoner and carried him away to his castle; so that when the peasant again asked him how he was and what ailed him, he gave him for reply the same words and phrases that the captive Abindarraez gave to Rodrigo de Narvaez, just as he had read the story in the "Diana" of Jorge de Montemayor where it is written, applying it to his own case so aptly that the peasant went along cursing his fate that he had to listen to such a lot of nonsense; from which, however, he came to the conclusion that his neighbour was mad, and so made all haste to reach the village to escape the wearisomeness of this harangue of Don Quixote's; who, at the end of it, said, "Senor Don Rodrigo de Narvaez, your worship must know that this fair Xarifa I have mentioned is now the lovely Dulcinea del Toboso, for whom I have done, am doing, and will do the most famous deeds of chivalry that in this world have been seen, are to be seen, or ever shall be seen."

To this the peasant answered, "Senor—sinner that I am!—cannot your

worship see that I am not Don Rodrigo de Narvaez nor the Marquis of

Mantua, but Pedro Alonso your neighbour, and that your worship is neither

Baldwin nor Abindarraez, but the worthy gentleman Senor Quixada?"

"I know who I am," replied Don Quixote, "and I know that I may be not only those I have named, but all the Twelve Peers of France and even all the Nine Worthies, since my achievements surpass all that they have done all together and each of them on his own account."

With this talk and more of the same kind they reached the village just as night was beginning to fall, but the peasant waited until it was a little later that the belaboured gentleman might not be seen riding in such a miserable trim. When it was what seemed to him the proper time he entered the village and went to Don Quixote's house, which he found all in confusion, and there were the curate and the village barber, who were great friends of Don Quixote, and his housekeeper was saying to them in a loud voice, "What does your worship think can have befallen my master, Senor Licentiate Pero Perez?" for so the curate was called; "it is three days now since anything has been seen of him, or the hack, or the buckler, lance, or armour. Miserable me! I am certain of it, and it is as true as that I was born to die, that these accursed books of chivalry he has, and has got into the way of reading so constantly, have upset his reason; for now I remember having often heard him saying to himself that he would turn knight-errant and go all over the world in quest of adventures. To the devil and Barabbas with such books, that have brought to ruin in this way the finest understanding there was in all La Mancha!"

The niece said the same, and, more: "You must know, Master Nicholas"—for that was the name of the barber—"it was often my uncle's way to stay two days and nights together poring over these unholy books of misventures, after which he would fling the book away and snatch up his sword and fall to slashing the walls; and when he was tired out he would say he had killed four giants like four towers; and the sweat that flowed from him when he was weary he said was the blood of the wounds he had received in battle; and then he would drink a great jug of cold water and become calm and quiet, saying that this water was a most precious potion which the sage Esquife, a great magician and friend of his, had brought him. But I take all the blame upon myself for never having told your worships of my uncle's vagaries, that you might put a stop to them before things had come to this pass, and burn all these accursed books—for he has a great number—that richly deserve to be burned like heretics."

"So say I too," said the curate, "and by my faith to-morrow shall not pass without public judgment upon them, and may they be condemned to the flames lest they lead those that read to behave as my good friend seems to have behaved."

All this the peasant heard, and from it he understood at last what was the matter with his neighbour, so he began calling aloud, "Open, your worships, to Senor Baldwin and to Senor the Marquis of Mantua, who comes badly wounded, and to Senor Abindarraez, the Moor, whom the valiant Rodrigo de Narvaez, the Alcaide of Antequera, brings captive."

At these words they all hurried out, and when they recognised their friend, master, and uncle, who had not yet dismounted from the ass because he could not, they ran to embrace him.

"Hold!" said he, "for I am badly wounded through my horse's fault; carry me to bed, and if possible send for the wise Urganda to cure and see to my wounds."

"See there! plague on it!" cried the housekeeper at this: "did not my heart tell the truth as to which foot my master went lame of? To bed with your worship at once, and we will contrive to cure you here without fetching that Hurgada. A curse I say once more, and a hundred times more, on those books of chivalry that have brought your worship to such a pass."

They carried him to bed at once, and after searching for his wounds could find none, but he said they were all bruises from having had a severe fall with his horse Rocinante when in combat with ten giants, the biggest and the boldest to be found on earth.

"So, so!" said the curate, "are there giants in the dance? By the sign of the Cross I will burn them to-morrow before the day over."

They put a host of questions to Don Quixote, but his only answer to all was—give him something to eat, and leave him to sleep, for that was what he needed most. They did so, and the curate questioned the peasant at great length as to how he had found Don Quixote. He told him, and the nonsense he had talked when found and on the way home, all which made the licentiate the more eager to do what he did the next day, which was to summon his friend the barber, Master Nicholas, and go with him to Don Quixote's house.

CHAPTER VI

OF THE DIVERTING AND IMPORTANT SCRUTINY WHICH THE CURATE AND THE BARBER MADE IN THE LIBRARY OF OUR INGENIOUS GENTLEMAN

He was still sleeping; so the curate asked the niece for the keys of the room where the books, the authors of all the mischief, were, and right willingly she gave them. They all went in, the housekeeper with them, and found more than a hundred volumes of big books very well bound, and some other small ones. The moment the housekeeper saw them she turned about and ran out of the room, and came back immediately with a saucer of holy water and a sprinkler, saying, "Here, your worship, senor licentiate, sprinkle this room; don't leave any magician of the many there are in these books to bewitch us in revenge for our design of banishing them from the world."

The simplicity of the housekeeper made the licentiate laugh, and he directed the barber to give him the books one by one to see what they were about, as there might be some to be found among them that did not deserve the penalty of fire.

"No," said the niece, "there is no reason for showing mercy to any of them; they have every one of them done mischief; better fling them out of the window into the court and make a pile of them and set fire to them; or else carry them into the yard, and there a bonfire can be made without the smoke giving any annoyance." The housekeeper said the same, so eager were they both for the slaughter of those innocents, but the curate would not agree to it without first reading at any rate the titles.

The first that Master Nicholas put into his hand was "The four books of Amadis of Gaul." "This seems a mysterious thing," said the curate, "for, as I have heard say, this was the first book of chivalry printed in Spain, and from this all the others derive their birth and origin; so it seems to me that we ought inexorably to condemn it to the flames as the founder of so vile a sect."

"Nay, sir," said the barber, "I too, have heard say that this is the best of all the books of this kind that have been written, and so, as something singular in its line, it ought to be pardoned."

"True," said the curate; "and for that reason let its life be spared for the present. Let us see that other which is next to it."

"It is," said the barber, "the 'Sergas de Esplandian,' the lawful son of Amadis of Gaul."

"Then verily," said the curate, "the merit of the father must not be put down to the account of the son. Take it, mistress housekeeper; open the window and fling it into the yard and lay the foundation of the pile for the bonfire we are to make."

The housekeeper obeyed with great satisfaction, and the worthy "Esplandian" went flying into the yard to await with all patience the fire that was in store for him.

"Proceed," said the curate.

"This that comes next," said the barber, "is 'Amadis of Greece,' and, indeed, I believe all those on this side are of the same Amadis lineage."

"Then to the yard with the whole of them," said the curate; "for to have the burning of Queen Pintiquiniestra, and the shepherd Darinel and his eclogues, and the bedevilled and involved discourses of his author, I would burn with them the father who begot me if he were going about in the guise of a knight-errant."

"I am of the same mind," said the barber.

"And so am I," added the niece.

"In that case," said the housekeeper, "here, into the yard with them!"

They were handed to her, and as there were many of them, she spared herself the staircase, and flung them down out of the window.

"Who is that tub there?" said the curate.

"This," said the barber, "is 'Don Olivante de Laura.'"

"The author of that book," said the curate, "was the same that wrote 'The Garden of Flowers,' and truly there is no deciding which of the two books is the more truthful, or, to put it better, the less lying; all I can say is, send this one into the yard for a swaggering fool."

"This that follows is 'Florismarte of Hircania,'" said the barber.

"Senor Florismarte here?" said the curate; "then by my faith he must take up his quarters in the yard, in spite of his marvellous birth and visionary adventures, for the stiffness and dryness of his style deserve nothing else; into the yard with him and the other, mistress housekeeper."

"With all my heart, senor," said she, and executed the order with great delight.

"This," said the barber, "is The Knight Platir.'"

"An old book that," said the curate, "but I find no reason for clemency in it; send it after the others without appeal;" which was done.

Another book was opened, and they saw it was entitled, "The Knight of the Cross."

"For the sake of the holy name this book has," said the curate, "its ignorance might be excused; but then, they say, 'behind the cross there's the devil; to the fire with it."

Taking down another book, the barber said, "This is 'The Mirror of Chivalry.'"

"I know his worship," said the curate; "that is where Senor Reinaldos of Montalvan figures with his friends and comrades, greater thieves than Cacus, and the Twelve Peers of France with the veracious historian Turpin; however, I am not for condemning them to more than perpetual banishment, because, at any rate, they have some share in the invention of the famous Matteo Boiardo, whence too the Christian poet Ludovico Ariosto wove his web, to whom, if I find him here, and speaking any language but his own, I shall show no respect whatever; but if he speaks his own tongue I will put him upon my head."

"Well, I have him in Italian," said the barber, "but I do not understand him."

"Nor would it be well that you should understand him," said the curate, "and on that score we might have excused the Captain if he had not brought him into Spain and turned him into Castilian. He robbed him of a great deal of his natural force, and so do all those who try to turn books written in verse into another language, for, with all the pains they take and all the cleverness they show, they never can reach the level of the originals as they were first produced. In short, I say that this book, and all that may be found treating of those French affairs, should be thrown into or deposited in some dry well, until after more consideration it is settled what is to be done with them; excepting always one 'Bernardo del Carpio' that is going about, and another called 'Roncesvalles;' for these, if they come into my hands, shall pass at once into those of the housekeeper, and from hers into the fire without any reprieve."

To all this the barber gave his assent, and looked upon it as right and proper, being persuaded that the curate was so staunch to the Faith and loyal to the Truth that he would not for the world say anything opposed to them. Opening another book he saw it was "Palmerin de Oliva," and beside it was another called "Palmerin of England," seeing which the licentiate said, "Let the Olive be made firewood of at once and burned until no ashes even are left; and let that Palm of England be kept and preserved as a thing that stands alone, and let such another case be made for it as that which Alexander found among the spoils of Darius and set aside for the safe keeping of the works of the poet Homer. This book, gossip, is of authority for two reasons, first because it is very good, and secondly because it is said to have been written by a wise and witty king of Portugal. All the adventures at the Castle of Miraguarda are excellent and of admirable contrivance, and the language is polished and clear, studying and observing the style befitting the speaker with propriety and judgment. So then, provided it seems good to you, Master Nicholas, I say let this and 'Amadis of Gaul' be remitted the penalty of fire, and as for all the rest, let them perish without further question or query."

"Nay, gossip," said the barber, "for this that I have here is the famous 'Don Belianis.'"

"Well," said the curate, "that and the second, third, and fourth parts all stand in need of a little rhubarb to purge their excess of bile, and they must be cleared of all that stuff about the Castle of Fame and other greater affectations, to which end let them be allowed the over-seas term, and, according as they mend, so shall mercy or justice be meted out to them; and in the mean time, gossip, do you keep them in your house and let no one read them."

"With all my heart," said the barber; and not caring to tire himself with reading more books of chivalry, he told the housekeeper to take all the big ones and throw them into the yard. It was not said to one dull or deaf, but to one who enjoyed burning them more than weaving the broadest and finest web that could be; and seizing about eight at a time, she flung them out of the window.

In carrying so many together she let one fall at the feet of the barber, who took it up, curious to know whose it was, and found it said, "History of the Famous Knight, Tirante el Blanco."

"God bless me!" said the curate with a shout, "'Tirante el Blanco' here! Hand it over, gossip, for in it I reckon I have found a treasury of enjoyment and a mine of recreation. Here is Don Kyrieleison of Montalvan, a valiant knight, and his brother Thomas of Montalvan, and the knight Fonseca, with the battle the bold Tirante fought with the mastiff, and the witticisms of the damsel Placerdemivida, and the loves and wiles of the widow Reposada, and the empress in love with the squire Hipolito—in truth, gossip, by right of its style it is the best book in the world. Here knights eat and sleep, and die in their beds, and make their wills before dying, and a great deal more of which there is nothing in all the other books. Nevertheless, I say he who wrote it, for deliberately composing such fooleries, deserves to be sent to the galleys for life. Take it home with you and read it, and you will see that what I have said is true."

"As you will," said the barber; "but what are we to do with these little books that are left?"

"These must be, not chivalry, but poetry," said the curate; and opening one he saw it was the "Diana" of Jorge de Montemayor, and, supposing all the others to be of the same sort, "these," he said, "do not deserve to be burned like the others, for they neither do nor can do the mischief the books of chivalry have done, being books of entertainment that can hurt no one."

"Ah, senor!" said the niece, "your worship had better order these to be burned as well as the others; for it would be no wonder if, after being cured of his chivalry disorder, my uncle, by reading these, took a fancy to turn shepherd and range the woods and fields singing and piping; or, what would be still worse, to turn poet, which they say is an incurable and infectious malady."

"The damsel is right," said the curate, "and it will be well to put this stumbling-block and temptation out of our friend's way. To begin, then, with the 'Diana' of Montemayor. I am of opinion it should not be burned, but that it should be cleared of all that about the sage Felicia and the magic water, and of almost all the longer pieces of verse: let it keep, and welcome, its prose and the honour of being the first of books of the kind."

"This that comes next," said the barber, "is the 'Diana,' entitled the 'Second Part, by the Salamancan,' and this other has the same title, and its author is Gil Polo."

"As for that of the Salamancan," replied the curate, "let it go to swell the number of the condemned in the yard, and let Gil Polo's be preserved as if it came from Apollo himself: but get on, gossip, and make haste, for it is growing late."

"This book," said the barber, opening another, "is the ten books of the

'Fortune of Love,' written by Antonio de Lofraso, a Sardinian poet."

"By the orders I have received," said the curate, "since Apollo has been Apollo, and the Muses have been Muses, and poets have been poets, so droll and absurd a book as this has never been written, and in its way it is the best and the most singular of all of this species that have as yet appeared, and he who has not read it may be sure he has never read what is delightful. Give it here, gossip, for I make more account of having found it than if they had given me a cassock of Florence stuff."

He put it aside with extreme satisfaction, and the barber went on, "These that come next are 'The Shepherd of Iberia,' 'Nymphs of Henares,' and 'The Enlightenment of Jealousy.'"

"Then all we have to do," said the curate, "is to hand them over to the secular arm of the housekeeper, and ask me not why, or we shall never have done."

"This next is the 'Pastor de Filida.'"

"No Pastor that," said the curate, "but a highly polished courtier; let it be preserved as a precious jewel."

"This large one here," said the barber, "is called 'The Treasury of various Poems.'"

"If there were not so many of them," said the curate, "they would be more relished: this book must be weeded and cleansed of certain vulgarities which it has with its excellences; let it be preserved because the author is a friend of mine, and out of respect for other more heroic and loftier works that he has written."

"This," continued the barber, "is the 'Cancionero' of Lopez de Maldonado."

"The author of that book, too," said the curate, "is a great friend of mine, and his verses from his own mouth are the admiration of all who hear them, for such is the sweetness of his voice that he enchants when he chants them: it gives rather too much of its eclogues, but what is good was never yet plentiful: let it be kept with those that have been set apart. But what book is that next it?"

"The 'Galatea' of Miguel de Cervantes," said the barber.

"That Cervantes has been for many years a great friend of mine, and to my knowledge he has had more experience in reverses than in verses. His book has some good invention in it, it presents us with something but brings nothing to a conclusion: we must wait for the Second Part it promises: perhaps with amendment it may succeed in winning the full measure of grace that is now denied it; and in the mean time do you, senor gossip, keep it shut up in your own quarters."

"Very good," said the barber; "and here come three together, the 'Araucana' of Don Alonso de Ercilla, the 'Austriada' of Juan Rufo, Justice of Cordova, and the 'Montserrate' of Christobal de Virues, the Valencian poet."

"These three books," said the curate, "are the best that have been written in Castilian in heroic verse, and they may compare with the most famous of Italy; let them be preserved as the richest treasures of poetry that Spain possesses."

The curate was tired and would not look into any more books, and so he decided that, "contents uncertified," all the rest should be burned; but just then the barber held open one, called "The Tears of Angelica."

"I should have shed tears myself," said the curate when he heard the title, "had I ordered that book to be burned, for its author was one of the famous poets of the world, not to say of Spain, and was very happy in the translation of some of Ovid's fables."

CHAPTER VII

OF THE SECOND SALLY OF OUR WORTHY KNIGHT DON QUIXOTE OF LA MANCHA

At this instant Don Quixote began shouting out, "Here, here, valiant knights! here is need for you to put forth the might of your strong arms, for they of the Court are gaining the mastery in the tourney!" Called away by this noise and outcry, they proceeded no farther with the scrutiny of the remaining books, and so it is thought that "The Carolea," "The Lion of Spain," and "The Deeds of the Emperor," written by Don Luis de Avila, went to the fire unseen and unheard; for no doubt they were among those that remained, and perhaps if the curate had seen them they would not have undergone so severe a sentence.

When they reached Don Quixote he was already out of bed, and was still shouting and raving, and slashing and cutting all round, as wide awake as if he had never slept.

They closed with him and by force got him back to bed, and when he had become a little calm, addressing the curate, he said to him, "Of a truth, Senor Archbishop Turpin, it is a great disgrace for us who call ourselves the Twelve Peers, so carelessly to allow the knights of the Court to gain the victory in this tourney, we the adventurers having carried off the honour on the three former days."

"Hush, gossip," said the curate; "please God, the luck may turn, and what is lost to-day may be won to-morrow; for the present let your worship have a care of your health, for it seems to me that you are over-fatigued, if not badly wounded."

"Wounded no," said Don Quixote, "but bruised and battered no doubt, for that bastard Don Roland has cudgelled me with the trunk of an oak tree, and all for envy, because he sees that I alone rival him in his achievements. But I should not call myself Reinaldos of Montalvan did he not pay me for it in spite of all his enchantments as soon as I rise from this bed. For the present let them bring me something to eat, for that, I feel, is what will be more to my purpose, and leave it to me to avenge myself."

They did as he wished; they gave him something to eat, and once more he fell asleep, leaving them marvelling at his madness.

That night the housekeeper burned to ashes all the books that were in the yard and in the whole house; and some must have been consumed that deserved preservation in everlasting archives, but their fate and the laziness of the examiner did not permit it, and so in them was verified the proverb that the innocent suffer for the guilty.

One of the remedies which the curate and the barber immediately applied to their friend's disorder was to wall up and plaster the room where the books were, so that when he got up he should not find them (possibly the cause being removed the effect might cease), and they might say that a magician had carried them off, room and all; and this was done with all despatch. Two days later Don Quixote got up, and the first thing he did was to go and look at his books, and not finding the room where he had left it, he wandered from side to side looking for it. He came to the place where the door used to be, and tried it with his hands, and turned and twisted his eyes in every direction without saying a word; but after a good while he asked his housekeeper whereabouts was the room that held his books.

The housekeeper, who had been already well instructed in what she was to answer, said, "What room or what nothing is it that your worship is looking for? There are neither room nor books in this house now, for the devil himself has carried all away."

"It was not the devil," said the niece, "but a magician who came on a cloud one night after the day your worship left this, and dismounting from a serpent that he rode he entered the room, and what he did there I know not, but after a little while he made off, flying through the roof, and left the house full of smoke; and when we went to see what he had done we saw neither book nor room: but we remember very well, the housekeeper and I, that on leaving, the old villain said in a loud voice that, for a private grudge he owed the owner of the books and the room, he had done mischief in that house that would be discovered by-and-by: he said too that his name was the Sage Munaton."

"He must have said Friston," said Don Quixote.

"I don't know whether he called himself Friston or Friton," said the housekeeper, "I only know that his name ended with 'ton.'"

"So it does," said Don Quixote, "and he is a sage magician, a great enemy of mine, who has a spite against me because he knows by his arts and lore that in process of time I am to engage in single combat with a knight whom he befriends and that I am to conquer, and he will be unable to prevent it; and for this reason he endeavours to do me all the ill turns that he can; but I promise him it will be hard for him to oppose or avoid what is decreed by Heaven."

"Who doubts that?" said the niece; "but, uncle, who mixes you up in these quarrels? Would it not be better to remain at peace in your own house instead of roaming the world looking for better bread than ever came of wheat, never reflecting that many go for wool and come back shorn?"

"Oh, niece of mine," replied Don Quixote, "how much astray art thou in thy reckoning: ere they shear me I shall have plucked away and stripped off the beards of all who dare to touch only the tip of a hair of mine."

The two were unwilling to make any further answer, as they saw that his anger was kindling.

In short, then, he remained at home fifteen days very quietly without showing any signs of a desire to take up with his former delusions, and during this time he held lively discussions with his two gossips, the curate and the barber, on the point he maintained, that knights-errant were what the world stood most in need of, and that in him was to be accomplished the revival of knight-errantry. The curate sometimes contradicted him, sometimes agreed with him, for if he had not observed this precaution he would have been unable to bring him to reason.

Meanwhile Don Quixote worked upon a farm labourer, a neighbour of his, an honest man (if indeed that title can be given to him who is poor), but with very little wit in his pate. In a word, he so talked him over, and with such persuasions and promises, that the poor clown made up his mind to sally forth with him and serve him as esquire. Don Quixote, among other things, told him he ought to be ready to go with him gladly, because any moment an adventure might occur that might win an island in the twinkling of an eye and leave him governor of it. On these and the like promises Sancho Panza (for so the labourer was called) left wife and children, and engaged himself as esquire to his neighbour.

Don Quixote next set about getting some money; and selling one thing and pawning another, and making a bad bargain in every case, he got together a fair sum. He provided himself with a buckler, which he begged as a loan from a friend, and, restoring his battered helmet as best he could, he warned his squire Sancho of the day and hour he meant to set out, that he might provide himself with what he thought most needful. Above all, he charged him to take alforjas with him. The other said he would, and that he meant to take also a very good ass he had, as he was not much given to going on foot. About the ass, Don Quixote hesitated a little, trying whether he could call to mind any knight-errant taking with him an esquire mounted on ass-back, but no instance occurred to his memory. For all that, however, he determined to take him, intending to furnish him with a more honourable mount when a chance of it presented itself, by appropriating the horse of the first discourteous knight he encountered. Himself he provided with shirts and such other things as he could, according to the advice the host had given him; all which being done, without taking leave, Sancho Panza of his wife and children, or Don Quixote of his housekeeper and niece, they sallied forth unseen by anybody from the village one night, and made such good way in the course of it that by daylight they held themselves safe from discovery, even should search be made for them.

Sancho rode on his ass like a patriarch, with his alforjas and bota, and longing to see himself soon governor of the island his master had promised him. Don Quixote decided upon taking the same route and road he had taken on his first journey, that over the Campo de Montiel, which he travelled with less discomfort than on the last occasion, for, as it was early morning and the rays of the sun fell on them obliquely, the heat did not distress them.

And now said Sancho Panza to his master, "Your worship will take care, Senor Knight-errant, not to forget about the island you have promised me, for be it ever so big I'll be equal to governing it."

To which Don Quixote replied, "Thou must know, friend Sancho Panza, that it was a practice very much in vogue with the knights-errant of old to make their squires governors of the islands or kingdoms they won, and I am determined that there shall be no failure on my part in so liberal a custom; on the contrary, I mean to improve upon it, for they sometimes, and perhaps most frequently, waited until their squires were old, and then when they had had enough of service and hard days and worse nights, they gave them some title or other, of count, or at the most marquis, of some valley or province more or less; but if thou livest and I live, it may well be that before six days are over, I may have won some kingdom that has others dependent upon it, which will be just the thing to enable thee to be crowned king of one of them. Nor needst thou count this wonderful, for things and chances fall to the lot of such knights in ways so unexampled and unexpected that I might easily give thee even more than I promise thee."

"In that case," said Sancho Panza, "if I should become a king by one of those miracles your worship speaks of, even Juana Gutierrez, my old woman, would come to be queen and my children infantes."

"Well, who doubts it?" said Don Quixote.

"I doubt it," replied Sancho Panza, "because for my part I am persuaded that though God should shower down kingdoms upon earth, not one of them would fit the head of Mari Gutierrez. Let me tell you, senor, she is not worth two maravedis for a queen; countess will fit her better, and that only with God's help."

"Leave it to God, Sancho," returned Don Quixote, "for he will give her what suits her best; but do not undervalue thyself so much as to come to be content with anything less than being governor of a province."

"I will not, senor," answered Sancho, "specially as I have a man of such quality for a master in your worship, who will know how to give me all that will be suitable for me and that I can bear."

CHAPTER VIII

OF THE GOOD FORTUNE WHICH THE VALIANT DON QUIXOTE HAD IN THE TERRIBLE AND UNDREAMT-OF ADVENTURE OF THE WINDMILLS, WITH OTHER OCCURRENCES WORTHY TO BE FITLY RECORDED

At this point they came in sight of thirty forty windmills that there are on plain, and as soon as Don Quixote saw them he said to his squire, "Fortune is arranging matters for us better than we could have shaped our desires ourselves, for look there, friend Sancho Panza, where thirty or more monstrous giants present themselves, all of whom I mean to engage in battle and slay, and with whose spoils we shall begin to make our fortunes; for this is righteous warfare, and it is God's good service to sweep so evil a breed from off the face of the earth."

"What giants?" said Sancho Panza.

"Those thou seest there," answered his master, "with the long arms, and some have them nearly two leagues long."

"Look, your worship," said Sancho; "what we see there are not giants but windmills, and what seem to be their arms are the sails that turned by the wind make the millstone go."

"It is easy to see," replied Don Quixote, "that thou art not used to this business of adventures; those are giants; and if thou art afraid, away with thee out of this and betake thyself to prayer while I engage them in fierce and unequal combat."

So saying, he gave the spur to his steed Rocinante, heedless of the cries his squire Sancho sent after him, warning him that most certainly they were windmills and not giants he was going to attack. He, however, was so positive they were giants that he neither heard the cries of Sancho, nor perceived, near as he was, what they were, but made at them shouting, "Fly not, cowards and vile beings, for a single knight attacks you."

A slight breeze at this moment sprang up, and the great sails began to move, seeing which Don Quixote exclaimed, "Though ye flourish more arms than the giant Briareus, ye have to reckon with me."

So saying, and commending himself with all his heart to his lady Dulcinea, imploring her to support him in such a peril, with lance in rest and covered by his buckler, he charged at Rocinante's fullest gallop and fell upon the first mill that stood in front of him; but as he drove his lance-point into the sail the wind whirled it round with such force that it shivered the lance to pieces, sweeping with it horse and rider, who went rolling over on the plain, in a sorry condition. Sancho hastened to his assistance as fast as his ass could go, and when he came up found him unable to move, with such a shock had Rocinante fallen with him.

"God bless me!" said Sancho, "did I not tell your worship to mind what you were about, for they were only windmills? and no one could have made any mistake about it but one who had something of the same kind in his head."

"Hush, friend Sancho," replied Don Quixote, "the fortunes of war more than any other are liable to frequent fluctuations; and moreover I think, and it is the truth, that that same sage Friston who carried off my study and books, has turned these giants into mills in order to rob me of the glory of vanquishing them, such is the enmity he bears me; but in the end his wicked arts will avail but little against my good sword."

"God order it as he may," said Sancho Panza, and helping him to rise got him up again on Rocinante, whose shoulder was half out; and then, discussing the late adventure, they followed the road to Puerto Lapice, for there, said Don Quixote, they could not fail to find adventures in abundance and variety, as it was a great thoroughfare. For all that, he was much grieved at the loss of his lance, and saying so to his squire, he added, "I remember having read how a Spanish knight, Diego Perez de Vargas by name, having broken his sword in battle, tore from an oak a ponderous bough or branch, and with it did such things that day, and pounded so many Moors, that he got the surname of Machuca, and he and his descendants from that day forth were called Vargas y Machuca. I mention this because from the first oak I see I mean to rend such another branch, large and stout like that, with which I am determined and resolved to do such deeds that thou mayest deem thyself very fortunate in being found worthy to come and see them, and be an eyewitness of things that will with difficulty be believed."

"Be that as God will," said Sancho, "I believe it all as your worship says it; but straighten yourself a little, for you seem all on one side, may be from the shaking of the fall."

"That is the truth," said Don Quixote, "and if I make no complaint of the pain it is because knights-errant are not permitted to complain of any wound, even though their bowels be coming out through it."

"If so," said Sancho, "I have nothing to say; but God knows I would rather your worship complained when anything ailed you. For my part, I confess I must complain however small the ache may be; unless this rule about not complaining extends to the squires of knights-errant also."

Don Quixote could not help laughing at his squire's simplicity, and he assured him he might complain whenever and however he chose, just as he liked, for, so far, he had never read of anything to the contrary in the order of knighthood.

Sancho bade him remember it was dinner-time, to which his master answered that he wanted nothing himself just then, but that he might eat when he had a mind. With this permission Sancho settled himself as comfortably as he could on his beast, and taking out of the alforjas what he had stowed away in them, he jogged along behind his master munching deliberately, and from time to time taking a pull at the bota with a relish that the thirstiest tapster in Malaga might have envied; and while he went on in this way, gulping down draught after draught, he never gave a thought to any of the promises his master had made him, nor did he rate it as hardship but rather as recreation going in quest of adventures, however dangerous they might be. Finally they passed the night among some trees, from one of which Don Quixote plucked a dry branch to serve him after a fashion as a lance, and fixed on it the head he had removed from the broken one. All that night Don Quixote lay awake thinking of his lady Dulcinea, in order to conform to what he had read in his books, how many a night in the forests and deserts knights used to lie sleepless supported by the memory of their mistresses. Not so did Sancho Panza spend it, for having his stomach full of something stronger than chicory water he made but one sleep of it, and, if his master had not called him, neither the rays of the sun beating on his face nor all the cheery notes of the birds welcoming the approach of day would have had power to waken him. On getting up he tried the bota and found it somewhat less full than the night before, which grieved his heart because they did not seem to be on the way to remedy the deficiency readily. Don Quixote did not care to break his fast, for, as has been already said, he confined himself to savoury recollections for nourishment.

They returned to the road they had set out with, leading to Puerto Lapice, and at three in the afternoon they came in sight of it. "Here, brother Sancho Panza," said Don Quixote when he saw it, "we may plunge our hands up to the elbows in what they call adventures; but observe, even shouldst thou see me in the greatest danger in the world, thou must not put a hand to thy sword in my defence, unless indeed thou perceivest that those who assail me are rabble or base folk; for in that case thou mayest very properly aid me; but if they be knights it is on no account permitted or allowed thee by the laws of knighthood to help me until thou hast been dubbed a knight."

"Most certainly, senor," replied Sancho, "your worship shall be fully obeyed in this matter; all the more as of myself I am peaceful and no friend to mixing in strife and quarrels: it is true that as regards the defence of my own person I shall not give much heed to those laws, for laws human and divine allow each one to defend himself against any assailant whatever."

"That I grant," said Don Quixote, "but in this matter of aiding me against knights thou must put a restraint upon thy natural impetuosity."

"I will do so, I promise you," answered Sancho, "and will keep this precept as carefully as Sunday."

While they were thus talking there appeared on the road two friars of the order of St. Benedict, mounted on two dromedaries, for not less tall were the two mules they rode on. They wore travelling spectacles and carried sunshades; and behind them came a coach attended by four or five persons on horseback and two muleteers on foot. In the coach there was, as afterwards appeared, a Biscay lady on her way to Seville, where her husband was about to take passage for the Indies with an appointment of high honour. The friars, though going the same road, were not in her company; but the moment Don Quixote perceived them he said to his squire, "Either I am mistaken, or this is going to be the most famous adventure that has ever been seen, for those black bodies we see there must be, and doubtless are, magicians who are carrying off some stolen princess in that coach, and with all my might I must undo this wrong."

"This will be worse than the windmills," said Sancho. "Look, senor; those are friars of St. Benedict, and the coach plainly belongs to some travellers: I tell you to mind well what you are about and don't let the devil mislead you."

"I have told thee already, Sancho," replied Don Quixote, "that on the subject of adventures thou knowest little. What I say is the truth, as thou shalt see presently."

So saying, he advanced and posted himself in the middle of the road along which the friars were coming, and as soon as he thought they had come near enough to hear what he said, he cried aloud, "Devilish and unnatural beings, release instantly the highborn princesses whom you are carrying off by force in this coach, else prepare to meet a speedy death as the just punishment of your evil deeds."

The friars drew rein and stood wondering at the appearance of Don Quixote as well as at his words, to which they replied, "Senor Caballero, we are not devilish or unnatural, but two brothers of St. Benedict following our road, nor do we know whether or not there are any captive princesses coming in this coach."

"No soft words with me, for I know you, lying rabble," said Don Quixote, and without waiting for a reply he spurred Rocinante and with levelled lance charged the first friar with such fury and determination, that, if the friar had not flung himself off the mule, he would have brought him to the ground against his will, and sore wounded, if not killed outright. The second brother, seeing how his comrade was treated, drove his heels into his castle of a mule and made off across the country faster than the wind.

Sancho Panza, when he saw the friar on the ground, dismounting briskly from his ass, rushed towards him and began to strip off his gown. At that instant the friars muleteers came up and asked what he was stripping him for. Sancho answered them that this fell to him lawfully as spoil of the battle which his lord Don Quixote had won. The muleteers, who had no idea of a joke and did not understand all this about battles and spoils, seeing that Don Quixote was some distance off talking to the travellers in the coach, fell upon Sancho, knocked him down, and leaving hardly a hair in his beard, belaboured him with kicks and left him stretched breathless and senseless on the ground; and without any more delay helped the friar to mount, who, trembling, terrified, and pale, as soon as he found himself in the saddle, spurred after his companion, who was standing at a distance looking on, watching the result of the onslaught; then, not caring to wait for the end of the affair just begun, they pursued their journey making more crosses than if they had the devil after them.

Don Quixote was, as has been said, speaking to the lady in the coach: "Your beauty, lady mine," said he, "may now dispose of your person as may be most in accordance with your pleasure, for the pride of your ravishers lies prostrate on the ground through this strong arm of mine; and lest you should be pining to know the name of your deliverer, know that I am called Don Quixote of La Mancha, knight-errant and adventurer, and captive to the peerless and beautiful lady Dulcinea del Toboso: and in return for the service you have received of me I ask no more than that you should return to El Toboso, and on my behalf present yourself before that lady and tell her what I have done to set you free."

One of the squires in attendance upon the coach, a Biscayan, was listening to all Don Quixote was saying, and, perceiving that he would not allow the coach to go on, but was saying it must return at once to El Toboso, he made at him, and seizing his lance addressed him in bad Castilian and worse Biscayan after his fashion, "Begone, caballero, and ill go with thee; by the God that made me, unless thou quittest coach, slayest thee as art here a Biscayan."

Don Quixote understood him quite well, and answered him very quietly, "If thou wert a knight, as thou art none, I should have already chastised thy folly and rashness, miserable creature." To which the Biscayan returned, "I no gentleman!—I swear to God thou liest as I am Christian: if thou droppest lance and drawest sword, soon shalt thou see thou art carrying water to the cat: Biscayan on land, hidalgo at sea, hidalgo at the devil, and look, if thou sayest otherwise thou liest."

""You will see presently," said Agrajes,'" replied Don Quixote; and throwing his lance on the ground he drew his sword, braced his buckler on his arm, and attacked the Biscayan, bent upon taking his life.

The Biscayan, when he saw him coming on, though he wished to dismount from his mule, in which, being one of those sorry ones let out for hire, he had no confidence, had no choice but to draw his sword; it was lucky for him, however, that he was near the coach, from which he was able to snatch a cushion that served him for a shield; and they went at one another as if they had been two mortal enemies. The others strove to make peace between them, but could not, for the Biscayan declared in his disjointed phrase that if they did not let him finish his battle he would kill his mistress and everyone that strove to prevent him. The lady in the coach, amazed and terrified at what she saw, ordered the coachman to draw aside a little, and set herself to watch this severe struggle, in the course of which the Biscayan smote Don Quixote a mighty stroke on the shoulder over the top of his buckler, which, given to one without armour, would have cleft him to the waist. Don Quixote, feeling the weight of this prodigious blow, cried aloud, saying, "O lady of my soul, Dulcinea, flower of beauty, come to the aid of this your knight, who, in fulfilling his obligations to your beauty, finds himself in this extreme peril." To say this, to lift his sword, to shelter himself well behind his buckler, and to assail the Biscayan was the work of an instant, determined as he was to venture all upon a single blow. The Biscayan, seeing him come on in this way, was convinced of his courage by his spirited bearing, and resolved to follow his example, so he waited for him keeping well under cover of his cushion, being unable to execute any sort of manoeuvre with his mule, which, dead tired and never meant for this kind of game, could not stir a step.

On, then, as aforesaid, came Don Quixote against the wary Biscayan, with uplifted sword and a firm intention of splitting him in half, while on his side the Biscayan waited for him sword in hand, and under the protection of his cushion; and all present stood trembling, waiting in suspense the result of blows such as threatened to fall, and the lady in the coach and the rest of her following were making a thousand vows and offerings to all the images and shrines of Spain, that God might deliver her squire and all of them from this great peril in which they found themselves. But it spoils all, that at this point and crisis the author of the history leaves this battle impending, giving as excuse that he could find nothing more written about these achievements of Don Quixote than what has been already set forth. It is true the second author of this work was unwilling to believe that a history so curious could have been allowed to fall under the sentence of oblivion, or that the wits of La Mancha could have been so undiscerning as not to preserve in their archives or registries some documents referring to this famous knight; and this being his persuasion, he did not despair of finding the conclusion of this pleasant history, which, heaven favouring him, he did find in a way that shall be related in the Second Part.

CHAPTER IX

IN WHICH IS CONCLUDED AND FINISHED THE TERRIFIC BATTLE BETWEEN THE GALLANT BISCAYAN AND THE VALIANT MANCHEGAN

In the First Part of this history we left the valiant Biscayan and the renowned Don Quixote with drawn swords uplifted, ready to deliver two such furious slashing blows that if they had fallen full and fair they would at least have split and cleft them asunder from top to toe and laid them open like a pomegranate; and at this so critical point the delightful history came to a stop and stood cut short without any intimation from the author where what was missing was to be found.

This distressed me greatly, because the pleasure derived from having read such a small portion turned to vexation at the thought of the poor chance that presented itself of finding the large part that, so it seemed to me, was missing of such an interesting tale. It appeared to me to be a thing impossible and contrary to all precedent that so good a knight should have been without some sage to undertake the task of writing his marvellous achievements; a thing that was never wanting to any of those knights-errant who, they say, went after adventures; for every one of them had one or two sages as if made on purpose, who not only recorded their deeds but described their most trifling thoughts and follies, however secret they might be; and such a good knight could not have been so unfortunate as not to have what Platir and others like him had in abundance. And so I could not bring myself to believe that such a gallant tale had been left maimed and mutilated, and I laid the blame on Time, the devourer and destroyer of all things, that had either concealed or consumed it.

On the other hand, it struck me that, inasmuch as among his books there had been found such modern ones as "The Enlightenment of Jealousy" and the "Nymphs and Shepherds of Henares," his story must likewise be modern, and that though it might not be written, it might exist in the memory of the people of his village and of those in the neighbourhood. This reflection kept me perplexed and longing to know really and truly the whole life and wondrous deeds of our famous Spaniard, Don Quixote of La Mancha, light and mirror of Manchegan chivalry, and the first that in our age and in these so evil days devoted himself to the labour and exercise of the arms of knight-errantry, righting wrongs, succouring widows, and protecting damsels of that sort that used to ride about, whip in hand, on their palfreys, with all their virginity about them, from mountain to mountain and valley to valley—for, if it were not for some ruffian, or boor with a hood and hatchet, or monstrous giant, that forced them, there were in days of yore damsels that at the end of eighty years, in all which time they had never slept a day under a roof, went to their graves as much maids as the mothers that bore them. I say, then, that in these and other respects our gallant Don Quixote is worthy of everlasting and notable praise, nor should it be withheld even from me for the labour and pains spent in searching for the conclusion of this delightful history; though I know well that if Heaven, chance and good fortune had not helped me, the world would have remained deprived of an entertainment and pleasure that for a couple of hours or so may well occupy him who shall read it attentively. The discovery of it occurred in this way.

One day, as I was in the Alcana of Toledo, a boy came up to sell some pamphlets and old papers to a silk mercer, and, as I am fond of reading even the very scraps of paper in the streets, led by this natural bent of mine I took up one of the pamphlets the boy had for sale, and saw that it was in characters which I recognised as Arabic, and as I was unable to read them though I could recognise them, I looked about to see if there were any Spanish-speaking Morisco at hand to read them for me; nor was there any great difficulty in finding such an interpreter, for even had I sought one for an older and better language I should have found him. In short, chance provided me with one, who when I told him what I wanted and put the book into his hands, opened it in the middle and after reading a little in it began to laugh. I asked him what he was laughing at, and he replied that it was at something the book had written in the margin by way of a note. I bade him tell it to me; and he still laughing said, "In the margin, as I told you, this is written: 'This Dulcinea del Toboso so often mentioned in this history, had, they say, the best hand of any woman in all La Mancha for salting pigs.'"

When I heard Dulcinea del Toboso named, I was struck with surprise and amazement, for it occurred to me at once that these pamphlets contained the history of Don Quixote. With this idea I pressed him to read the beginning, and doing so, turning the Arabic offhand into Castilian, he told me it meant, "History of Don Quixote of La Mancha, written by Cide Hamete Benengeli, an Arab historian." It required great caution to hide the joy I felt when the title of the book reached my ears, and snatching it from the silk mercer, I bought all the papers and pamphlets from the boy for half a real; and if he had had his wits about him and had known how eager I was for them, he might have safely calculated on making more than six reals by the bargain. I withdrew at once with the Morisco into the cloister of the cathedral, and begged him to turn all these pamphlets that related to Don Quixote into the Castilian tongue, without omitting or adding anything to them, offering him whatever payment he pleased. He was satisfied with two arrobas of raisins and two bushels of wheat, and promised to translate them faithfully and with all despatch; but to make the matter easier, and not to let such a precious find out of my hands, I took him to my house, where in little more than a month and a half he translated the whole just as it is set down here.

In the first pamphlet the battle between Don Quixote and the Biscayan was drawn to the very life, they planted in the same attitude as the history describes, their swords raised, and the one protected by his buckler, the other by his cushion, and the Biscayan's mule so true to nature that it could be seen to be a hired one a bowshot off. The Biscayan had an inscription under his feet which said, "Don Sancho de Azpeitia," which no doubt must have been his name; and at the feet of Rocinante was another that said, "Don Quixote." Rocinante was marvellously portrayed, so long and thin, so lank and lean, with so much backbone and so far gone in consumption, that he showed plainly with what judgment and propriety the name of Rocinante had been bestowed upon him. Near him was Sancho Panza holding the halter of his ass, at whose feet was another label that said, "Sancho Zancas," and according to the picture, he must have had a big belly, a short body, and long shanks, for which reason, no doubt, the names of Panza and Zancas were given him, for by these two surnames the history several times calls him. Some other trifling particulars might be mentioned, but they are all of slight importance and have nothing to do with the true relation of the history; and no history can be bad so long as it is true.

If against the present one any objection be raised on the score of its truth, it can only be that its author was an Arab, as lying is a very common propensity with those of that nation; though, as they are such enemies of ours, it is conceivable that there were omissions rather than additions made in the course of it. And this is my own opinion; for, where he could and should give freedom to his pen in praise of so worthy a knight, he seems to me deliberately to pass it over in silence; which is ill done and worse contrived, for it is the business and duty of historians to be exact, truthful, and wholly free from passion, and neither interest nor fear, hatred nor love, should make them swerve from the path of truth, whose mother is history, rival of time, storehouse of deeds, witness for the past, example and counsel for the present, and warning for the future. In this I know will be found all that can be desired in the pleasantest, and if it be wanting in any good quality, I maintain it is the fault of its hound of an author and not the fault of the subject. To be brief, its Second Part, according to the translation, began in this way:

With trenchant swords upraised and poised on high, it seemed as though the two valiant and wrathful combatants stood threatening heaven, and earth, and hell, with such resolution and determination did they bear themselves. The fiery Biscayan was the first to strike a blow, which was delivered with such force and fury that had not the sword turned in its course, that single stroke would have sufficed to put an end to the bitter struggle and to all the adventures of our knight; but that good fortune which reserved him for greater things, turned aside the sword of his adversary, so that although it smote him upon the left shoulder, it did him no more harm than to strip all that side of its armour, carrying away a great part of his helmet with half of his ear, all which with fearful ruin fell to the ground, leaving him in a sorry plight.

Good God! Who is there that could properly describe the rage that filled the heart of our Manchegan when he saw himself dealt with in this fashion? All that can be said is, it was such that he again raised himself in his stirrups, and, grasping his sword more firmly with both hands, he came down on the Biscayan with such fury, smiting him full over the cushion and over the head, that—even so good a shield proving useless—as if a mountain had fallen on him, he began to bleed from nose, mouth, and ears, reeling as if about to fall backwards from his mule, as no doubt he would have done had he not flung his arms about its neck; at the same time, however, he slipped his feet out of the stirrups and then unclasped his arms, and the mule, taking fright at the terrible blow, made off across the plain, and with a few plunges flung its master to the ground. Don Quixote stood looking on very calmly, and, when he saw him fall, leaped from his horse and with great briskness ran to him, and, presenting the point of his sword to his eyes, bade him surrender, or he would cut his head off. The Biscayan was so bewildered that he was unable to answer a word, and it would have gone hard with him, so blind was Don Quixote, had not the ladies in the coach, who had hitherto been watching the combat in great terror, hastened to where he stood and implored him with earnest entreaties to grant them the great grace and favour of sparing their squire's life; to which Don Quixote replied with much gravity and dignity, "In truth, fair ladies, I am well content to do what ye ask of me; but it must be on one condition and understanding, which is that this knight promise me to go to the village of El Toboso, and on my behalf present himself before the peerless lady Dulcinea, that she deal with him as shall be most pleasing to her."

The terrified and disconsolate ladies, without discussing Don Quixote's demand or asking who Dulcinea might be, promised that their squire should do all that had been commanded.

"Then, on the faith of that promise," said Don Quixote, "I shall do him no further harm, though he well deserves it of me."

CHAPTER X

OF THE PLEASANT DISCOURSE THAT PASSED BETWEEN DON QUIXOTE AND HIS SQUIRE SANCHO PANZA

Now by this time Sancho had risen, rather the worse for the handling of the friars' muleteers, and stood watching the battle of his master, Don Quixote, and praying to God in his heart that it might be his will to grant him the victory, and that he might thereby win some island to make him governor of, as he had promised. Seeing, therefore, that the struggle was now over, and that his master was returning to mount Rocinante, he approached to hold the stirrup for him, and, before he could mount, he went on his knees before him, and taking his hand, kissed it saying, "May it please your worship, Senor Don Quixote, to give me the government of that island which has been won in this hard fight, for be it ever so big I feel myself in sufficient force to be able to govern it as much and as well as anyone in the world who has ever governed islands."

To which Don Quixote replied, "Thou must take notice, brother Sancho, that this adventure and those like it are not adventures of islands, but of cross-roads, in which nothing is got except a broken head or an ear the less: have patience, for adventures will present themselves from which I may make you, not only a governor, but something more."

Sancho gave him many thanks, and again kissing his hand and the skirt of his hauberk, helped him to mount Rocinante, and mounting his ass himself, proceeded to follow his master, who at a brisk pace, without taking leave, or saying anything further to the ladies belonging to the coach, turned into a wood that was hard by. Sancho followed him at his ass's best trot, but Rocinante stepped out so that, seeing himself left behind, he was forced to call to his master to wait for him. Don Quixote did so, reining in Rocinante until his weary squire came up, who on reaching him said, "It seems to me, senor, it would be prudent in us to go and take refuge in some church, for, seeing how mauled he with whom you fought has been left, it will be no wonder if they give information of the affair to the Holy Brotherhood and arrest us, and, faith, if they do, before we come out of gaol we shall have to sweat for it."

"Peace," said Don Quixote; "where hast thou ever seen or heard that a knight-errant has been arraigned before a court of justice, however many homicides he may have committed?"

"I know nothing about omecils," answered Sancho, "nor in my life have had anything to do with one; I only know that the Holy Brotherhood looks after those who fight in the fields, and in that other matter I do not meddle."

"Then thou needst have no uneasiness, my friend," said Don Quixote, "for I will deliver thee out of the hands of the Chaldeans, much more out of those of the Brotherhood. But tell me, as thou livest, hast thou seen a more valiant knight than I in all the known world; hast thou read in history of any who has or had higher mettle in attack, more spirit in maintaining it, more dexterity in wounding or skill in overthrowing?"

"The truth is," answered Sancho, "that I have never read any history, for I can neither read nor write, but what I will venture to bet is that a more daring master than your worship I have never served in all the days of my life, and God grant that this daring be not paid for where I have said; what I beg of your worship is to dress your wound, for a great deal of blood flows from that ear, and I have here some lint and a little white ointment in the alforjas."

"All that might be well dispensed with," said Don Quixote, "if I had remembered to make a vial of the balsam of Fierabras, for time and medicine are saved by one single drop."

"What vial and what balsam is that?" said Sancho Panza.

"It is a balsam," answered Don Quixote, "the receipt of which I have in my memory, with which one need have no fear of death, or dread dying of any wound; and so when I make it and give it to thee thou hast nothing to do when in some battle thou seest they have cut me in half through the middle of the body—as is wont to happen frequently,—but neatly and with great nicety, ere the blood congeal, to place that portion of the body which shall have fallen to the ground upon the other half which remains in the saddle, taking care to fit it on evenly and exactly. Then thou shalt give me to drink but two drops of the balsam I have mentioned, and thou shalt see me become sounder than an apple."

"If that be so," said Panza, "I renounce henceforth the government of the promised island, and desire nothing more in payment of my many and faithful services than that your worship give me the receipt of this supreme liquor, for I am persuaded it will be worth more than two reals an ounce anywhere, and I want no more to pass the rest of my life in ease and honour; but it remains to be told if it costs much to make it."

"With less than three reals, six quarts of it may be made," said Don Quixote.

"Sinner that I am!" said Sancho, "then why does your worship put off making it and teaching it to me?"

"Peace, friend," answered Don Quixote; "greater secrets I mean to teach thee and greater favours to bestow upon thee; and for the present let us see to the dressing, for my ear pains me more than I could wish."

Sancho took out some lint and ointment from the alforjas; but when Don Quixote came to see his helmet shattered, he was like to lose his senses, and clapping his hand upon his sword and raising his eyes to heaven, be said, "I swear by the Creator of all things and the four Gospels in their fullest extent, to do as the great Marquis of Mantua did when he swore to avenge the death of his nephew Baldwin (and that was not to eat bread from a table-cloth, nor embrace his wife, and other points which, though I cannot now call them to mind, I here grant as expressed) until I take complete vengeance upon him who has committed such an offence against me."

Hearing this, Sancho said to him, "Your worship should bear in mind, Senor Don Quixote, that if the knight has done what was commanded him in going to present himself before my lady Dulcinea del Toboso, he will have done all that he was bound to do, and does not deserve further punishment unless he commits some new offence."

"Thou hast said well and hit the point," answered Don Quixote; and so I recall the oath in so far as relates to taking fresh vengeance on him, but I make and confirm it anew to lead the life I have said until such time as I take by force from some knight another helmet such as this and as good; and think not, Sancho, that I am raising smoke with straw in doing so, for I have one to imitate in the matter, since the very same thing to a hair happened in the case of Mambrino's helmet, which cost Sacripante so dear."

"Senor," replied Sancho, "let your worship send all such oaths to the devil, for they are very pernicious to salvation and prejudicial to the conscience; just tell me now, if for several days to come we fall in with no man armed with a helmet, what are we to do? Is the oath to be observed in spite of all the inconvenience and discomfort it will be to sleep in your clothes, and not to sleep in a house, and a thousand other mortifications contained in the oath of that old fool the Marquis of Mantua, which your worship is now wanting to revive? Let your worship observe that there are no men in armour travelling on any of these roads, nothing but carriers and carters, who not only do not wear helmets, but perhaps never heard tell of them all their lives."

"Thou art wrong there," said Don Quixote, "for we shall not have been above two hours among these cross-roads before we see more men in armour than came to Albraca to win the fair Angelica."

"Enough," said Sancho; "so be it then, and God grant us success, and that the time for winning that island which is costing me so dear may soon come, and then let me die."

"I have already told thee, Sancho," said Don Quixote, "not to give thyself any uneasiness on that score; for if an island should fail, there is the kingdom of Denmark, or of Sobradisa, which will fit thee as a ring fits the finger, and all the more that, being on terra firma, thou wilt all the better enjoy thyself. But let us leave that to its own time; see if thou hast anything for us to eat in those alforjas, because we must presently go in quest of some castle where we may lodge to-night and make the balsam I told thee of, for I swear to thee by God, this ear is giving me great pain."

"I have here an onion and a little cheese and a few scraps of bread," said Sancho, "but they are not victuals fit for a valiant knight like your worship."

"How little thou knowest about it," answered Don Quixote; "I would have thee to know, Sancho, that it is the glory of knights-errant to go without eating for a month, and even when they do eat, that it should be of what comes first to hand; and this would have been clear to thee hadst thou read as many histories as I have, for, though they are very many, among them all I have found no mention made of knights-errant eating, unless by accident or at some sumptuous banquets prepared for them, and the rest of the time they passed in dalliance. And though it is plain they could not do without eating and performing all the other natural functions, because, in fact, they were men like ourselves, it is plain too that, wandering as they did the most part of their lives through woods and wilds and without a cook, their most usual fare would be rustic viands such as those thou now offer me; so that, friend Sancho, let not that distress thee which pleases me, and do not seek to make a new world or pervert knight-errantry."

"Pardon me, your worship," said Sancho, "for, as I cannot read or write, as I said just now, I neither know nor comprehend the rules of the profession of chivalry: henceforward I will stock the alforjas with every kind of dry fruit for your worship, as you are a knight; and for myself, as I am not one, I will furnish them with poultry and other things more substantial."

"I do not say, Sancho," replied Don Quixote, "that it is imperative on knights-errant not to eat anything else but the fruits thou speakest of; only that their more usual diet must be those, and certain herbs they found in the fields which they knew and I know too."

"A good thing it is," answered Sancho, "to know those herbs, for to my thinking it will be needful some day to put that knowledge into practice."

And here taking out what he said he had brought, the pair made their repast peaceably and sociably. But anxious to find quarters for the night, they with all despatch made an end of their poor dry fare, mounted at once, and made haste to reach some habitation before night set in; but daylight and the hope of succeeding in their object failed them close by the huts of some goatherds, so they determined to pass the night there, and it was as much to Sancho's discontent not to have reached a house, as it was to his master's satisfaction to sleep under the open heaven, for he fancied that each time this happened to him he performed an act of ownership that helped to prove his chivalry.

CHAPTER XI

WHAT BEFELL DON QUIXOTE WITH CERTAIN GOAT-HERDS

He was cordially welcomed by the goatherds, and Sancho, having as best he could put up Rocinante and the ass, drew towards the fragrance that came from some pieces of salted goat simmering in a pot on the fire; and though he would have liked at once to try if they were ready to be transferred from the pot to the stomach, he refrained from doing so as the goatherds removed them from the fire, and laying sheepskins on the ground, quickly spread their rude table, and with signs of hearty good-will invited them both to share what they had. Round the skins six of the men belonging to the fold seated themselves, having first with rough politeness pressed Don Quixote to take a seat upon a trough which they placed for him upside down. Don Quixote seated himself, and Sancho remained standing to serve the cup, which was made of horn. Seeing him standing, his master said to him:

"That thou mayest see, Sancho, the good that knight-errantry contains in itself, and how those who fill any office in it are on the high road to be speedily honoured and esteemed by the world, I desire that thou seat thyself here at my side and in the company of these worthy people, and that thou be one with me who am thy master and natural lord, and that thou eat from my plate and drink from whatever I drink from; for the same may be said of knight-errantry as of love, that it levels all."

"Great thanks," said Sancho, "but I may tell your worship that provided I have enough to eat, I can eat it as well, or better, standing, and by myself, than seated alongside of an emperor. And indeed, if the truth is to be told, what I eat in my corner without form or fuss has much more relish for me, even though it be bread and onions, than the turkeys of those other tables where I am forced to chew slowly, drink little, wipe my mouth every minute, and cannot sneeze or cough if I want or do other things that are the privileges of liberty and solitude. So, senor, as for these honours which your worship would put upon me as a servant and follower of knight-errantry, exchange them for other things which may be of more use and advantage to me; for these, though I fully acknowledge them as received, I renounce from this moment to the end of the world."

"For all that," said Don Quixote, "thou must seat thyself, because him who humbleth himself God exalteth;" and seizing him by the arm he forced him to sit down beside himself.

The goatherds did not understand this jargon about squires and knights-errant, and all they did was to eat in silence and stare at their guests, who with great elegance and appetite were stowing away pieces as big as one's fist. The course of meat finished, they spread upon the sheepskins a great heap of parched acorns, and with them they put down a half cheese harder than if it had been made of mortar. All this while the horn was not idle, for it went round so constantly, now full, now empty, like the bucket of a water-wheel, that it soon drained one of the two wine-skins that were in sight. When Don Quixote had quite appeased his appetite he took up a handful of the acorns, and contemplating them attentively delivered himself somewhat in this fashion:

"Happy the age, happy the time, to which the ancients gave the name of golden, not because in that fortunate age the gold so coveted in this our iron one was gained without toil, but because they that lived in it knew not the two words "mine" and "thine"! In that blessed age all things were in common; to win the daily food no labour was required of any save to stretch forth his hand and gather it from the sturdy oaks that stood generously inviting him with their sweet ripe fruit. The clear streams and running brooks yielded their savoury limpid waters in noble abundance. The busy and sagacious bees fixed their republic in the clefts of the rocks and hollows of the trees, offering without usance the plenteous produce of their fragrant toil to every hand. The mighty cork trees, unenforced save of their own courtesy, shed the broad light bark that served at first to roof the houses supported by rude stakes, a protection against the inclemency of heaven alone. Then all was peace, all friendship, all concord; as yet the dull share of the crooked plough had not dared to rend and pierce the tender bowels of our first mother that without compulsion yielded from every portion of her broad fertile bosom all that could satisfy, sustain, and delight the children that then possessed her. Then was it that the innocent and fair young shepherdess roamed from vale to vale and hill to hill, with flowing locks, and no more garments than were needful modestly to cover what modesty seeks and ever sought to hide. Nor were their ornaments like those in use to-day, set off by Tyrian purple, and silk tortured in endless fashions, but the wreathed leaves of the green dock and ivy, wherewith they went as bravely and becomingly decked as our Court dames with all the rare and far-fetched artifices that idle curiosity has taught them. Then the love-thoughts of the heart clothed themselves simply and naturally as the heart conceived them, nor sought to commend themselves by forced and rambling verbiage. Fraud, deceit, or malice had then not yet mingled with truth and sincerity. Justice held her ground, undisturbed and unassailed by the efforts of favour and of interest, that now so much impair, pervert, and beset her. Arbitrary law had not yet established itself in the mind of the judge, for then there was no cause to judge and no one to be judged. Maidens and modesty, as I have said, wandered at will alone and unattended, without fear of insult from lawlessness or libertine assault, and if they were undone it was of their own will and pleasure. But now in this hateful age of ours not one is safe, not though some new labyrinth like that of Crete conceal and surround her; even there the pestilence of gallantry will make its way to them through chinks or on the air by the zeal of its accursed importunity, and, despite of all seclusion, lead them to ruin. In defence of these, as time advanced and wickedness increased, the order of knights-errant was instituted, to defend maidens, to protect widows and to succour the orphans and the needy. To this order I belong, brother goatherds, to whom I return thanks for the hospitality and kindly welcome ye offer me and my squire; for though by natural law all living are bound to show favour to knights-errant, yet, seeing that without knowing this obligation ye have welcomed and feasted me, it is right that with all the good-will in my power I should thank you for yours."

All this long harangue (which might very well have been spared) our knight delivered because the acorns they gave him reminded him of the golden age; and the whim seized him to address all this unnecessary argument to the goatherds, who listened to him gaping in amazement without saying a word in reply. Sancho likewise held his peace and ate acorns, and paid repeated visits to the second wineskin, which they had hung up on a cork tree to keep the wine cool.

Don Quixote was longer in talking than the supper in finishing, at the end of which one of the goatherds said, "That your worship, senor knight-errant, may say with more truth that we show you hospitality with ready good-will, we will give you amusement and pleasure by making one of our comrades sing: he will be here before long, and he is a very intelligent youth and deep in love, and what is more he can read and write and play on the rebeck to perfection."

The goatherd had hardly done speaking, when the notes of the rebeck reached their ears; and shortly after, the player came up, a very good-looking young man of about two-and-twenty. His comrades asked him if he had supped, and on his replying that he had, he who had already made the offer said to him:

"In that case, Antonio, thou mayest as well do us the pleasure of singing a little, that the gentleman, our guest, may see that even in the mountains and woods there are musicians: we have told him of thy accomplishments, and we want thee to show them and prove that we say true; so, as thou livest, pray sit down and sing that ballad about thy love that thy uncle the prebendary made thee, and that was so much liked in the town."

"With all my heart," said the young man, and without waiting for more pressing he seated himself on the trunk of a felled oak, and tuning his rebeck, presently began to sing to these words.

ANTONIO'S BALLAD

Thou dost love me well, Olalla;
   Well I know it, even though
Love's mute tongues, thine eyes, have never
   By their glances told me so.

For I know my love thou knowest,
   Therefore thine to claim I dare:
Once it ceases to be secret,
   Love need never feel despair.

True it is, Olalla, sometimes
   Thou hast all too plainly shown
That thy heart is brass in hardness,
   And thy snowy bosom stone.

Yet for all that, in thy coyness,
   And thy fickle fits between,
Hope is there—at least the border
   Of her garment may be seen.

Lures to faith are they, those glimpses,
   And to faith in thee I hold;
Kindness cannot make it stronger,
   Coldness cannot make it cold.

If it be that love is gentle,
   In thy gentleness I see
Something holding out assurance
   To the hope of winning thee.

If it be that in devotion
   Lies a power hearts to move,

That which every day I show thee,
  Helpful to my suit should prove.

Many a time thou must have noticed—
  If to notice thou dost care—
How I go about on Monday
  Dressed in all my Sunday wear.

Love's eyes love to look on brightness;
  Love loves what is gaily drest;
Sunday, Monday, all I care is
  Thou shouldst see me in my best.

No account I make of dances,
  Or of strains that pleased thee so,
Keeping thee awake from midnight
  Till the cocks began to crow;

Or of how I roundly swore it
  That there's none so fair as thou;
True it is, but as I said it,
  By the girls I'm hated now.

For Teresa of the hillside
  At my praise of thee was sore;
Said, "You think you love an angel;
  It's a monkey you adore;

"Caught by all her glittering trinkets,
  And her borrowed braids of hair,
And a host of made-up beauties
  That would Love himself ensnare."

'T was a lie, and so I told her,
  And her cousin at the word
Gave me his defiance for it;
  And what followed thou hast heard.

Mine is no high-flown affection,
  Mine no passion par amours—
As they call it—what I offer
  Is an honest love, and pure.

Cunning cords the holy Church has,
  Cords of softest silk they be;

> Put thy neck beneath the yoke, dear;
> Mine will follow, thou wilt see.
>
> Else—and once for all I swear it
> By the saint of most renown—
> If I ever quit the mountains,
> 'T will be in a friar's gown.

Here the goatherd brought his song to an end, and though Don Quixote entreated him to sing more, Sancho had no mind that way, being more inclined for sleep than for listening to songs; so said he to his master, "Your worship will do well to settle at once where you mean to pass the night, for the labour these good men are at all day does not allow them to spend the night in singing."

"I understand thee, Sancho," replied Don Quixote; "I perceive clearly that those visits to the wine-skin demand compensation in sleep rather than in music."

"It's sweet to us all, blessed be God," said Sancho.

"I do not deny it," replied Don Quixote; "but settle thyself where thou wilt; those of my calling are more becomingly employed in watching than in sleeping; still it would be as well if thou wert to dress this ear for me again, for it is giving me more pain than it need."

Sancho did as he bade him, but one of the goatherds, seeing the wound, told him not to be uneasy, as he would apply a remedy with which it would be soon healed; and gathering some leaves of rosemary, of which there was a great quantity there, he chewed them and mixed them with a little salt, and applying them to the ear he secured them firmly with a bandage, assuring him that no other treatment would be required, and so it proved.

CHAPTER XII

OF WHAT A GOATHERD RELATED TO THOSE WITH DON QUIXOTE

Just then another young man, one of those who fetched their provisions from the village, came up and said, "Do you know what is going on in the village, comrades?"

"How could we know it?" replied one of them.

"Well, then, you must know," continued the young man, "this morning that famous student-shepherd called Chrysostom died, and it is rumoured that he died of love for that devil of a village girl the daughter of Guillermo the Rich, she that wanders about the wolds here in the dress of a shepherdess."

"You mean Marcela?" said one.

"Her I mean," answered the goatherd; "and the best of it is, he has directed in his will that he is to be buried in the fields like a Moor, and at the foot of the rock where the Cork-tree spring is, because, as the story goes (and they say he himself said so), that was the place where he first saw her. And he has also left other directions which the clergy of the village say should not and must not be obeyed because they savour of paganism. To all which his great friend Ambrosio the student, he who, like him, also went dressed as a shepherd, replies that everything must be done without any omission according to the directions left by Chrysostom, and about this the village is all in commotion; however, report says that, after all, what Ambrosio and all the shepherds his friends desire will be done, and to-morrow they are coming to bury him with great ceremony where I said. I am sure it will be something worth seeing; at least I will not fail to go and see it even if I knew I should not return to the village tomorrow."

"We will do the same," answered the goatherds, "and cast lots to see who must stay to mind the goats of all."

"Thou sayest well, Pedro," said one, "though there will be no need of taking that trouble, for I will stay behind for all; and don't suppose it is virtue or want of curiosity in me; it is that the splinter that ran into my foot the other day will not let me walk."

"For all that, we thank thee," answered Pedro.

Don Quixote asked Pedro to tell him who the dead man was and who the shepherdess, to which Pedro replied that all he knew was that the dead man was a wealthy gentleman belonging to a village in those mountains, who had been a student at Salamanca for many years, at the end of which he returned to his village with the reputation of being very learned and deeply read. "Above all, they said, he was learned in the science of the stars and of what went on yonder in the heavens and the sun and the moon, for he told us of the cris of the sun and moon to exact time."

"Eclipse it is called, friend, not cris, the darkening of those two luminaries," said Don Quixote; but Pedro, not troubling himself with trifles, went on with his story, saying, "Also he foretold when the year was going to be one of abundance or estility."

"Sterility, you mean," said Don Quixote.

"Sterility or estility," answered Pedro, "it is all the same in the end. And I can tell you that by this his father and friends who believed him grew very rich because they did as he advised them, bidding them 'sow barley this year, not wheat; this year you may sow pulse and not barley; the next there will be a full oil crop, and the three following not a drop will be got.'"

"That science is called astrology," said Don Quixote.

"I do not know what it is called," replied Pedro, "but I know that he knew all this and more besides. But, to make an end, not many months had passed after he returned from Salamanca, when one day he appeared dressed as a shepherd with his crook and sheepskin, having put off the long gown he wore as a scholar; and at the same time his great friend, Ambrosio by name, who had been his companion in his studies, took to the shepherd's dress with him. I forgot to say that Chrysostom, who is dead, was a great man for writing verses, so much so that he made carols for Christmas Eve, and plays for Corpus Christi, which the young men of our village acted, and all said they were excellent. When the villagers saw the two scholars so unexpectedly appearing in shepherd's dress, they were lost in wonder, and could not guess what had led them to make so extraordinary a change. About this time the father of our Chrysostom died, and he was left heir to a large amount of property in chattels as well as in land, no small number of cattle and sheep, and a large sum of money, of all of which the young man was left dissolute owner, and indeed he was deserving of it all, for he was a very good comrade, and kind-hearted, and a friend of worthy folk, and had a countenance like a benediction. Presently it came to be known that he had changed his dress with no other object than to wander about these wastes after that shepherdess

Marcela our lad mentioned a while ago, with whom the deceased Chrysostom had fallen in love. And I must tell you now, for it is well you should know it, who this girl is; perhaps, and even without any perhaps, you will not have heard anything like it all the days of your life, though you should live more years than sarna."

"Say Sarra," said Don Quixote, unable to endure the goatherd's confusion of words.

"The sarna lives long enough," answered Pedro; "and if, senor, you must go finding fault with words at every step, we shall not make an end of it this twelvemonth."

"Pardon me, friend," said Don Quixote; "but, as there is such a difference between sarna and Sarra, I told you of it; however, you have answered very rightly, for sarna lives longer than Sarra: so continue your story, and I will not object any more to anything."

"I say then, my dear sir," said the goatherd, "that in our village there was a farmer even richer than the father of Chrysostom, who was named Guillermo, and upon whom God bestowed, over and above great wealth, a daughter at whose birth her mother died, the most respected woman there was in this neighbourhood; I fancy I can see her now with that countenance which had the sun on one side and the moon on the other; and moreover active, and kind to the poor, for which I trust that at the present moment her soul is in bliss with God in the other world. Her husband Guillermo died of grief at the death of so good a wife, leaving his daughter Marcela, a child and rich, to the care of an uncle of hers, a priest and prebendary in our village. The girl grew up with such beauty that it reminded us of her mother's, which was very great, and yet it was thought that the daughter's would exceed it; and so when she reached the age of fourteen to fifteen years nobody beheld her but blessed God that had made her so beautiful, and the greater number were in love with her past redemption. Her uncle kept her in great seclusion and retirement, but for all that the fame of her great beauty spread so that, as well for it as for her great wealth, her uncle was asked, solicited, and importuned, to give her in marriage not only by those of our town but of those many leagues round, and by the persons of highest quality in them. But he, being a good Christian man, though he desired to give her in marriage at once, seeing her to be old enough, was unwilling to do so without her consent, not that he had any eye to the gain and profit which the custody of the girl's property brought him while he put off her marriage; and, faith, this was said in praise of the good priest in more than one set in the town. For I would have you know, Sir

Errant, that in these little villages everything is talked about and everything is carped at, and rest assured, as I am, that the priest must be over and above good who forces his parishioners to speak well of him, especially in villages."

"That is the truth," said Don Quixote; "but go on, for the story is very good, and you, good Pedro, tell it with very good grace."

"May that of the Lord not be wanting to me," said Pedro; "that is the one to have. To proceed; you must know that though the uncle put before his niece and described to her the qualities of each one in particular of the many who had asked her in marriage, begging her to marry and make a choice according to her own taste, she never gave any other answer than that she had no desire to marry just yet, and that being so young she did not think herself fit to bear the burden of matrimony. At these, to all appearance, reasonable excuses that she made, her uncle ceased to urge her, and waited till she was somewhat more advanced in age and could mate herself to her own liking. For, said he—and he said quite right—parents are not to settle children in life against their will. But when one least looked for it, lo and behold! one day the demure Marcela makes her appearance turned shepherdess; and, in spite of her uncle and all those of the town that strove to dissuade her, took to going a-field with the other shepherd-lasses of the village, and tending her own flock. And so, since she appeared in public, and her beauty came to be seen openly, I could not well tell you how many rich youths, gentlemen and peasants, have adopted the costume of Chrysostom, and go about these fields making love to her. One of these, as has been already said, was our deceased friend, of whom they say that he did not love but adore her. But you must not suppose, because Marcela chose a life of such liberty and independence, and of so little or rather no retirement, that she has given any occasion, or even the semblance of one, for disparagement of her purity and modesty; on the contrary, such and so great is the vigilance with which she watches over her honour, that of all those that court and woo her not one has boasted, or can with truth boast, that she has given him any hope however small of obtaining his desire. For although she does not avoid or shun the society and conversation of the shepherds, and treats them courteously and kindly, should any one of them come to declare his intention to her, though it be one as proper and holy as that of matrimony, she flings him from her like a catapult. And with this kind of disposition she does more harm in this country than if the plague had got into it, for her affability and her beauty draw on the hearts of those that associate with her to love her and to court her, but her scorn and her frankness bring them to the brink of despair; and so they know not what to say save to proclaim her aloud cruel and hard-hearted, and other names of the same sort which well describe the nature of her character; and if you should remain here any time, senor, you would hear these hills and valleys resounding with the laments of the rejected ones who pursue her. Not far from this there is a spot where there are a couple of dozen of tall beeches, and there is not one of them but has carved and written on its smooth bark the name of Marcela, and above some a crown carved on the same tree as though her lover would say more plainly that Marcela wore and deserved that of all human beauty. Here one shepherd is sighing, there another is lamenting; there love songs are heard, here despairing elegies. One will pass all the hours of the night seated at the foot of some oak or rock, and there, without having closed his weeping eyes, the sun finds him in the morning bemused and bereft of sense; and another without relief or respite to his sighs, stretched on the burning sand in the full heat of the sultry summer noontide, makes his appeal to the compassionate heavens, and over one and the other, over these and all, the beautiful Marcela triumphs free and careless. And all of us that know her are waiting to see what her pride will come to, and who is to be the happy man that will succeed in taming a nature so formidable and gaining possession of a beauty so supreme. All that I have told you being such well-established truth, I am persuaded that what they say of the cause of Chrysostom's death, as our lad told us, is the same. And so I advise you, senor, fail not to be present to-morrow at his burial, which will be well worth seeing, for Chrysostom had many friends, and it is not half a league from this place to where he directed he should be buried."

"I will make a point of it," said Don Quixote, "and I thank you for the pleasure you have given me by relating so interesting a tale."

"Oh," said the goatherd, "I do not know even the half of what has happened to the lovers of Marcela, but perhaps to-morrow we may fall in with some shepherd on the road who can tell us; and now it will be well for you to go and sleep under cover, for the night air may hurt your wound, though with the remedy I have applied to you there is no fear of an untoward result."

Sancho Panza, who was wishing the goatherd's loquacity at the devil, on his part begged his master to go into Pedro's hut to sleep. He did so, and passed all the rest of the night in thinking of his lady Dulcinea, in imitation of the lovers of Marcela. Sancho Panza settled himself between Rocinante and his ass, and slept, not like a lover who had been discarded, but like a man who had been soundly kicked.

CHAPTER XIII

IN WHICH IS ENDED THE STORY OF THE SHEPHERD-ESS MARCELA, WITH OTHER INCIDENTS

Bit hardly had day begun to show itself through the balconies of the east, when five of the six goatherds came to rouse Don Quixote and tell him that if he was still of a mind to go and see the famous burial of Chrysostom they would bear him company. Don Quixote, who desired nothing better, rose and ordered Sancho to saddle and pannel at once, which he did with all despatch, and with the same they all set out forthwith. They had not gone a quarter of a league when at the meeting of two paths they saw coming towards them some six shepherds dressed in black sheepskins and with their heads crowned with garlands of cypress and bitter oleander. Each of them carried a stout holly staff in his hand, and along with them there came two men of quality on horseback in handsome travelling dress, with three servants on foot accompanying them. Courteous salutations were exchanged on meeting, and inquiring one of the other which way each party was going, they learned that all were bound for the scene of the burial, so they went on all together.

One of those on horseback addressing his companion said to him, "It seems to me, Senor Vivaldo, that we may reckon as well spent the delay we shall incur in seeing this remarkable funeral, for remarkable it cannot but be judging by the strange things these shepherds have told us, of both the dead shepherd and homicide shepherdess."

"So I think too," replied Vivaldo, "and I would delay not to say a day, but four, for the sake of seeing it."

Don Quixote asked them what it was they had heard of Marcela and Chrysostom. The traveller answered that the same morning they had met these shepherds, and seeing them dressed in this mournful fashion they had asked them the reason of their appearing in such a guise; which one of them gave, describing the strange behaviour and beauty of a shepherdess called Marcela, and the loves of many who courted her, together with the death of that Chrysostom to whose burial they were going. In short, he repeated all that Pedro had related to Don Quixote.

This conversation dropped, and another was commenced by him who was called Vivaldo asking Don Quixote what was the reason that led him to go armed in that fashion in a country so peaceful.

To which Don Quixote replied, "The pursuit of my calling does not allow or permit me to go in any other fashion; easy life, enjoyment, and repose were invented for soft courtiers, but toil, unrest, and arms were invented and made for those alone whom the world calls knights-errant, of whom I, though unworthy, am the least of all."

The instant they heard this all set him down as mad, and the better to settle the point and discover what kind of madness his was, Vivaldo proceeded to ask him what knights-errant meant.

"Have not your worships," replied Don Quixote, "read the annals and histories of England, in which are recorded the famous deeds of King Arthur, whom we in our popular Castilian invariably call King Artus, with regard to whom it is an ancient tradition, and commonly received all over that kingdom of Great Britain, that this king did not die, but was changed by magic art into a raven, and that in process of time he is to return to reign and recover his kingdom and sceptre; for which reason it cannot be proved that from that time to this any Englishman ever killed a raven? Well, then, in the time of this good king that famous order of chivalry of the Knights of the Round Table was instituted, and the amour of Don Lancelot of the Lake with the Queen Guinevere occurred, precisely as is there related, the go-between and confidante therein being the highly honourable dame Quintanona, whence came that ballad so well known and widely spread in our Spain—

> O never surely was there knight
> So served by hand of dame,
> As served was he Sir Lancelot hight
> When he from Britain came—

with all the sweet and delectable course of his achievements in love and war. Handed down from that time, then, this order of chivalry went on extending and spreading itself over many and various parts of the world; and in it, famous and renowned for their deeds, were the mighty Amadis of Gaul with all his sons and descendants to the fifth generation, and the valiant Felixmarte of Hircania, and the never sufficiently praised Tirante el Blanco, and in our own days almost we have seen and heard and talked with the invincible knight Don Belianis of Greece. This, then, sirs, is to be a knight-errant, and what I have spoken of is the order of his chivalry, of which, as I have already said, I, though a sinner, have made profession, and what the aforesaid knights professed that same do I profess, and so I go through these solitudes and wilds seeking adventures, resolved in soul to oppose my arm and person to the most perilous that fortune may offer me in aid of the weak and needy."

By these words of his the travellers were able to satisfy themselves of Don Quixote's being out of his senses and of the form of madness that overmastered him, at which they felt the same astonishment that all felt on first becoming acquainted with it; and Vivaldo, who was a person of great shrewdness and of a lively temperament, in order to beguile the short journey which they said was required to reach the mountain, the scene of the burial, sought to give him an opportunity of going on with his absurdities. So he said to him, "It seems to me, Senor Knight-errant, that your worship has made choice of one of the most austere professions in the world, and I imagine even that of the Carthusian monks is not so austere."

"As austere it may perhaps be," replied our Don Quixote, "but so necessary for the world I am very much inclined to doubt. For, if the truth is to be told, the soldier who executes what his captain orders does no less than the captain himself who gives the order. My meaning, is, that churchmen in peace and quiet pray to Heaven for the welfare of the world, but we soldiers and knights carry into effect what they pray for, defending it with the might of our arms and the edge of our swords, not under shelter but in the open air, a target for the intolerable rays of the sun in summer and the piercing frosts of winter. Thus are we God's ministers on earth and the arms by which his justice is done therein. And as the business of war and all that relates and belongs to it cannot be conducted without exceeding great sweat, toil, and exertion, it follows that those who make it their profession have undoubtedly more labour than those who in tranquil peace and quiet are engaged in praying to God to help the weak. I do not mean to say, nor does it enter into my thoughts, that the knight-errant's calling is as good as that of the monk in his cell; I would merely infer from what I endure myself that it is beyond a doubt a more laborious and a more belaboured one, a hungrier and thirstier, a wretcheder, raggeder, and lousier; for there is no reason to doubt that the knights-errant of yore endured much hardship in the course of their lives. And if some of them by the might of their arms did rise to be emperors, in faith it cost them dear in the matter of blood and sweat; and if those who attained to that rank had not had magicians and sages to help them they would have been completely baulked in their ambition and disappointed in their hopes."

"That is my own opinion," replied the traveller; "but one thing among many others seems to me very wrong in knights-errant, and that is that when they find themselves about to engage in some mighty and perilous adventure in which there is manifest danger of losing their lives, they never at the moment of engaging in it think of commending themselves to God, as is the duty of every good Christian in like peril; instead of which they commend themselves to their ladies with as much devotion as if these were their gods, a thing which seems to me to savour somewhat of heathenism."

"Sir," answered Don Quixote, "that cannot be on any account omitted, and the knight-errant would be disgraced who acted otherwise: for it is usual and customary in knight-errantry that the knight-errant, who on engaging in any great feat of arms has his lady before him, should turn his eyes towards her softly and lovingly, as though with them entreating her to favour and protect him in the hazardous venture he is about to undertake, and even though no one hear him, he is bound to say certain words between his teeth, commending himself to her with all his heart, and of this we have innumerable instances in the histories. Nor is it to be supposed from this that they are to omit commending themselves to God, for there will be time and opportunity for doing so while they are engaged in their task."

"For all that," answered the traveller, "I feel some doubt still, because often I have read how words will arise between two knights-errant, and from one thing to another it comes about that their anger kindles and they wheel their horses round and take a good stretch of field, and then without any more ado at the top of their speed they come to the charge, and in mid-career they are wont to commend themselves to their ladies; and what commonly comes of the encounter is that one falls over the haunches of his horse pierced through and through by his antagonist's lance, and as for the other, it is only by holding on to the mane of his horse that he can help falling to the ground; but I know not how the dead man had time to commend himself to God in the course of such rapid work as this; it would have been better if those words which he spent in commending himself to his lady in the midst of his career had been devoted to his duty and obligation as a Christian. Moreover, it is my belief that all knights-errant have not ladies to commend themselves to, for they are not all in love."

"That is impossible," said Don Quixote: "I say it is impossible that there could be a knight-errant without a lady, because to such it is as natural and proper to be in love as to the heavens to have stars: most certainly no history has been seen in which there is to be found a knight-errant without an amour, and for the simple reason that without one he would be held no legitimate knight but a bastard, and one who had gained entrance into the stronghold of the said knighthood, not by the door, but over the wall like a thief and a robber."

"Nevertheless," said the traveller, "if I remember rightly, I think I have read that Don Galaor, the brother of the valiant Amadis of Gaul, never had any special lady to whom he might commend himself, and yet he was not the less esteemed, and was a very stout and famous knight."

To which our Don Quixote made answer, "Sir, one solitary swallow does not make summer; moreover, I know that knight was in secret very deeply in love; besides which, that way of falling in love with all that took his fancy was a natural propensity which he could not control. But, in short, it is very manifest that he had one alone whom he made mistress of his will, to whom he commended himself very frequently and very secretly, for he prided himself on being a reticent knight."

"Then if it be essential that every knight-errant should be in love," said the traveller, "it may be fairly supposed that your worship is so, as you are of the order; and if you do not pride yourself on being as reticent as Don Galaor, I entreat you as earnestly as I can, in the name of all this company and in my own, to inform us of the name, country, rank, and beauty of your lady, for she will esteem herself fortunate if all the world knows that she is loved and served by such a knight as your worship seems to be."

At this Don Quixote heaved a deep sigh and said, "I cannot say positively whether my sweet enemy is pleased or not that the world should know I serve her; I can only say in answer to what has been so courteously asked of me, that her name is Dulcinea, her country El Toboso, a village of La Mancha, her rank must be at least that of a princess, since she is my queen and lady, and her beauty superhuman, since all the impossible and fanciful attributes of beauty which the poets apply to their ladies are verified in her; for her hairs are gold, her forehead Elysian fields, her eyebrows rainbows, her eyes suns, her cheeks roses, her lips coral, her teeth pearls, her neck alabaster, her bosom marble, her hands ivory, her fairness snow, and what modesty conceals from sight such, I think and imagine, as rational reflection can only extol, not compare."

"We should like to know her lineage, race, and ancestry," said Vivaldo.

To which Don Quixote replied, "She is not of the ancient Roman Curtii, Caii, or Scipios, nor of the modern Colonnas or Orsini, nor of the Moncadas or Requesenes of Catalonia, nor yet of the Rebellas or Villanovas of Valencia; Palafoxes, Nuzas, Rocabertis, Corellas, Lunas, Alagones, Urreas, Foces, or Gurreas of Aragon; Cerdas, Manriques, Mendozas, or Guzmans of Castile; Alencastros, Pallas, or Meneses of Portugal; but she is of those of El Toboso of La Mancha, a lineage that though modern, may furnish a source of gentle blood for the most illustrious families of the ages that are to come, and this let none dispute with me save on the condition that Zerbino placed at the foot of the trophy of Orlando's arms, saying,

'These let none move Who dareth not his might with Roland prove.'"

"Although mine is of the Cachopins of Laredo," said the traveller, "I will not venture to compare it with that of El Toboso of La Mancha, though, to tell the truth, no such surname has until now ever reached my ears."

"What!" said Don Quixote, "has that never reached them?"

The rest of the party went along listening with great attention to the conversation of the pair, and even the very goatherds and shepherds perceived how exceedingly out of his wits our Don Quixote was. Sancho Panza alone thought that what his master said was the truth, knowing who he was and having known him from his birth; and all that he felt any difficulty in believing was that about the fair Dulcinea del Toboso, because neither any such name nor any such princess had ever come to his knowledge though he lived so close to El Toboso. They were going along conversing in this way, when they saw descending a gap between two high mountains some twenty shepherds, all clad in sheepskins of black wool, and crowned with garlands which, as afterwards appeared, were, some of them of yew, some of cypress. Six of the number were carrying a bier covered with a great variety of flowers and branches, on seeing which one of the goatherds said, "Those who come there are the bearers of Chrysostom's body, and the foot of that mountain is the place where he ordered them to bury him." They therefore made haste to reach the spot, and did so by the time those who came had laid the bier upon the ground, and four of them with sharp pickaxes were digging a grave by the side of a hard rock. They greeted each other courteously, and then Don Quixote and those who accompanied him turned to examine the bier, and on it, covered with flowers, they saw a dead body in the dress of a shepherd, to all appearance of one thirty years of age, and showing even in death that in life he had been of comely features and gallant bearing. Around him on the bier itself were laid some books, and several papers open and folded; and those who were looking on as well as those who were opening the grave and all the others who were there preserved a strange silence, until one of those who had borne the body said to another, "Observe carefully, Ambrosia if this is the place Chrysostom spoke of, since you are anxious that what he directed in his will should be so strictly complied with."

"This is the place," answered Ambrosia "for in it many a time did my poor friend tell me the story of his hard fortune. Here it was, he told me, that he saw for the first time that mortal enemy of the human race, and here, too, for the first time he declared to her his passion, as honourable as it was devoted, and here it was that at last Marcela ended by scorning and rejecting him so as to bring the tragedy of his wretched life to a close; here, in memory of misfortunes so great, he desired to be laid in the bowels of eternal oblivion." Then turning to Don Quixote and the travellers he went on to say, "That body, sirs, on which you are looking with compassionate eyes, was the abode of a soul on which Heaven bestowed a vast share of its riches. That is the body of Chrysostom, who was unrivalled in wit, unequalled in courtesy, unapproached in gentle bearing, a phoenix in friendship, generous without limit, grave without arrogance, gay without vulgarity, and, in short, first in all that constitutes goodness and second to none in all that makes up misfortune. He loved deeply, he was hated; he adored, he was scorned; he wooed a wild beast, he pleaded with marble, he pursued the wind, he cried to the wilderness, he served ingratitude, and for reward was made the prey of death in the mid-course of life, cut short by a shepherdess whom he sought to immortalise in the memory of man, as these papers which you see could fully prove, had he not commanded me to consign them to the fire after having consigned his body to the earth."

"You would deal with them more harshly and cruelly than their owner himself," said Vivaldo, "for it is neither right nor proper to do the will of one who enjoins what is wholly unreasonable; it would not have been reasonable in Augustus Caesar had he permitted the directions left by the divine Mantuan in his will to be carried into effect. So that, Senor Ambrosia while you consign your friend's body to the earth, you should not consign his writings to oblivion, for if he gave the order in bitterness of heart, it is not right that you should irrationally obey it. On the contrary, by granting life to those papers, let the cruelty of Marcela live for ever, to serve as a warning in ages to come to all men to shun and avoid falling into like danger; or I and all of us who have come here know already the story of this your love-stricken and heart-broken friend, and we know, too, your friendship, and the cause of his death, and the directions he gave at the close of his life; from which sad story may be gathered how great was the cruelty of Marcela, the love of Chrysostom, and the loyalty of your friendship, together with the end awaiting those who pursue rashly the path that insane passion opens to their eyes. Last night we learned the death of Chrysostom and that he was to be buried here, and out of curiosity and pity we left our direct road and resolved to come and see with our eyes that which when heard of had so moved our compassion, and in consideration of that compassion and our desire to prove it if we might by condolence, we beg of you, excellent Ambrosia, or at least I on my own account entreat you, that instead of burning those papers you allow me to carry away some of them."

And without waiting for the shepherd's answer, he stretched out his hand and took up some of those that were nearest to him; seeing which Ambrosio said, "Out of courtesy, senor, I will grant your request as to those you have taken, but it is idle to expect me to abstain from burning the remainder."

Vivaldo, who was eager to see what the papers contained, opened one of them at once, and saw that its title was "Lay of Despair."

Ambrosio hearing it said, "That is the last paper the unhappy man wrote; and that you may see, senor, to what an end his misfortunes brought him, read it so that you may be heard, for you will have time enough for that while we are waiting for the grave to be dug."

"I will do so very willingly," said Vivaldo; and as all the by-standers were equally eager they gathered round him, and he, reading in a loud voice, found that it ran as follows.

CHAPTER XIV

WHEREIN ARE INSERTED THE DESPAIRING VERSES OF THE DEAD SHEPHERD, TOGETHER WITH OTHER INCIDENTS NOT LOOKED FOR

THE LAY OF CHRYSOSTOM

    Since thou dost in thy cruelty desire
The ruthless rigour of thy tyranny
From tongue to tongue, from land to land proclaimed,
The very Hell will I constrain to lend
This stricken breast of mine deep notes of woe
To serve my need of fitting utterance.
And as I strive to body forth the tale
Of all I suffer, all that thou hast done,
Forth shall the dread voice roll, and bear along
Shreds from my vitals torn for greater pain.
Then listen, not to dulcet harmony,
But to a discord wrung by mad despair
Out of this bosom's depths of bitterness,
To ease my heart and plant a sting in thine.

    The lion›s roar, the fierce wolf›s savage howl,
The horrid hissing of the scaly snake,
The awesome cries of monsters yet unnamed,
The crow's ill-boding croak, the hollow moan
Of wild winds wrestling with the restless sea,
The wrathful bellow of the vanquished bull,
The plaintive sobbing of the widowed dove,
The envied owl's sad note, the wail of woe
That rises from the dreary choir of Hell,
Commingled in one sound, confusing sense,
Let all these come to aid my soul's complaint,
For pain like mine demands new modes of song.

    No echoes of that discord shall be heard
Where Father Tagus rolls, or on the banks
Of olive-bordered Betis; to the rocks
Or in deep caverns shall my plaint be told,
And by a lifeless tongue in living words;
Or in dark valleys or on lonely shores,
Where neither foot of man nor sunbeam falls;

Or in among the poison-breathing swarms
Of monsters nourished by the sluggish Nile.
For, though it be to solitudes remote
The hoarse vague echoes of my sorrows sound
Thy matchless cruelty, my dismal fate
Shall carry them to all the spacious world.

   Disdain hath power to kill, and patience dies
Slain by suspicion, be it false or true;
And deadly is the force of jealousy;
Long absence makes of life a dreary void;
No hope of happiness can give repose
To him that ever fears to be forgot;
And death, inevitable, waits in hall.
But I, by some strange miracle, live on
A prey to absence, jealousy, disdain;
Racked by suspicion as by certainty;
Forgotten, left to feed my flame alone.
And while I suffer thus, there comes no ray
Of hope to gladden me athwart the gloom;
Nor do I look for it in my despair;
But rather clinging to a cureless woe,
All hope do I abjure for evermore.

   Can there be hope where fear is? Were it well,
When far more certain are the grounds of fear?
Ought I to shut mine eyes to jealousy,
If through a thousand heart-wounds it appears?
Who would not give free access to distrust,
Seeing disdain unveiled, and—bitter change!—
All his suspicions turned to certainties,
And the fair truth transformed into a lie?
Oh, thou fierce tyrant of the realms of love,
Oh, Jealousy! put chains upon these hands,
And bind me with thy strongest cord, Disdain.
But, woe is me! triumphant over all,
My sufferings drown the memory of you.

   And now I die, and since there is no hope
Of happiness for me in life or death,
Still to my fantasy I'll fondly cling.
I'll say that he is wise who loveth well,
And that the soul most free is that most bound
In thraldom to the ancient tyrant Love.
I'll say that she who is mine enemy

In that fair body hath as fair a mind,
And that her coldness is but my desert,
And that by virtue of the pain he sends
Love rules his kingdom with a gentle sway.
Thus, self-deluding, and in bondage sore,
And wearing out the wretched shred of life
To which I am reduced by her disdain,
I'll give this soul and body to the winds,
All hopeless of a crown of bliss in store.

Thou whose injustice hath supplied the cause
That makes me quit the weary life I loathe,
As by this wounded bosom thou canst see
How willingly thy victim I become,
Let not my death, if haply worth a tear,
Cloud the clear heaven that dwells in thy bright eyes;
I would not have thee expiate in aught
The crime of having made my heart thy prey;
But rather let thy laughter gaily ring
And prove my death to be thy festival.
Fool that I am to bid thee! well I know
Thy glory gains by my untimely end.

And now it is the time; from Hell›s abyss
Come thirsting Tantalus, come Sisyphus
Heaving the cruel stone, come Tityus
With vulture, and with wheel Ixion come,
And come the sisters of the ceaseless toil;
And all into this breast transfer their pains,
And (if such tribute to despair be due)
Chant in their deepest tones a doleful dirge
Over a corse unworthy of a shroud.
Let the three-headed guardian of the gate,
And all the monstrous progeny of hell,
The doleful concert join: a lover dead
Methinks can have no fitter obsequies.

Lay of despair, grieve not when thou art gone
Forth from this sorrowing heart: my misery
Brings fortune to the cause that gave thee birth;
Then banish sadness even in the tomb.

The "Lay of Chrysostom" met with the approbation of the listeners, though the reader said it did not seem to him to agree with what he had heard of Marcela's reserve and propriety, for Chrysostom complained in it of jealousy, suspicion, and absence, all to the prejudice of the good name and fame of Marcela; to which Ambrosio replied as one who knew well his friend's most secret thoughts, "Senor, to remove that doubt I should tell you that when the unhappy man wrote this lay he was away from Marcela, from whom he had voluntarily separated himself, to try if absence would act with him as it is wont; and as everything distresses and every fear haunts the banished lover, so imaginary jealousies and suspicions, dreaded as if they were true, tormented Chrysostom; and thus the truth of what report declares of the virtue of Marcela remains unshaken, and with her envy itself should not and cannot find any fault save that of being cruel, somewhat haughty, and very scornful."

"That is true," said Vivaldo; and as he was about to read another paper of those he had preserved from the fire, he was stopped by a marvellous vision (for such it seemed) that unexpectedly presented itself to their eyes; for on the summit of the rock where they were digging the grave there appeared the shepherdess Marcela, so beautiful that her beauty exceeded its reputation. Those who had never till then beheld her gazed upon her in wonder and silence, and those who were accustomed to see her were not less amazed than those who had never seen her before. But the instant Ambrosio saw her he addressed her, with manifest indignation:

"Art thou come, by chance, cruel basilisk of these mountains, to see if in thy presence blood will flow from the wounds of this wretched being thy cruelty has robbed of life; or is it to exult over the cruel work of thy humours that thou art come; or like another pitiless Nero to look down from that height upon the ruin of his Rome in embers; or in thy arrogance to trample on this ill-fated corpse, as the ungrateful daughter trampled on her father Tarquin's? Tell us quickly for what thou art come, or what it is thou wouldst have, for, as I know the thoughts of Chrysostom never failed to obey thee in life, I will make all these who call themselves his friends obey thee, though he be dead."

"I come not, Ambrosia for any of the purposes thou hast named," replied Marcela, "but to defend myself and to prove how unreasonable are all those who blame me for their sorrow and for Chrysostom's death; and therefore I ask all of you that are here to give me your attention, for will not take much time or many words to bring the truth home to persons of sense. Heaven has made me, so you say, beautiful, and so much so that in spite of yourselves my beauty leads you to love me; and for the love you show me you say, and even urge, that I am bound to love you. By that natural understanding which God has given me I know that everything beautiful attracts love, but I cannot see how, by reason of being loved, that which is loved for its beauty is bound to love that which loves it; besides, it may happen that the lover of that which is beautiful may be ugly, and ugliness being detestable, it is very absurd to say, "I love thee because thou art beautiful, thou must love me though I be ugly." But supposing the beauty equal on both sides, it does not follow that the inclinations must be therefore alike, for it is not every beauty that excites love, some but pleasing the eye without winning the affection; and if every sort of beauty excited love and won the heart, the will would wander vaguely to and fro unable to make choice of any; for as there is an infinity of beautiful objects there must be an infinity of inclinations, and true love, I have heard it said, is indivisible, and must be voluntary and not compelled. If this be so, as I believe it to be, why do you desire me to bend my will by force, for no other reason but that you say you love me? Nay—tell me—had Heaven made me ugly, as it has made me beautiful, could I with justice complain of you for not loving me? Moreover, you must remember that the beauty I possess was no choice of mine, for, be it what it may, Heaven of its bounty gave it me without my asking or choosing it; and as the viper, though it kills with it, does not deserve to be blamed for the poison it carries, as it is a gift of nature, neither do I deserve reproach for being beautiful; for beauty in a modest woman is like fire at a distance or a sharp sword; the one does not burn, the other does not cut, those who do not come too near. Honour and virtue are the ornaments of the mind, without which the body, though it be so, has no right to pass for beautiful; but if modesty is one of the virtues that specially lend a grace and charm to mind and body, why should she who is loved for her beauty part with it to gratify one who for his pleasure alone strives with all his might and energy to rob her of it? I was born free, and that I might live in freedom I chose the solitude of the fields; in the trees of the mountains I find society, the clear waters of the brooks are my mirrors, and to the trees and waters I make known my thoughts and charms. I am a fire afar off, a sword laid aside. Those whom I have inspired with love by letting them see me, I have by words undeceived, and if their longings live on hope—and I have given none to Chrysostom or to any other—it cannot justly be said that the death of any is my doing, for it was rather his own obstinacy than my cruelty that killed him; and if it be made a charge against me that his wishes were honourable, and that therefore I was bound to yield to them, I answer that when on this very spot where now his grave is made he declared to me his purity of purpose, I told him that mine was to live in perpetual solitude, and that the earth alone should enjoy the fruits of my retirement and the spoils of my beauty; and if, after this open avowal, he chose to persist against hope and steer against the wind, what wonder is it that he should sink in the depths of his infatuation? If I had encouraged him, I should be false; if I had gratified him, I should have acted against my own better resolution and purpose. He was persistent in spite of warning, he despaired without being hated. Bethink you now if it be reasonable that his suffering should be laid to my charge. Let him who has been deceived complain, let him give way to despair whose encouraged hopes have proved vain, let him flatter himself whom I shall entice, let him boast whom I shall receive; but let not him call me cruel or homicide to whom I make no promise, upon whom I practise no deception, whom I neither entice nor receive. It has not been so far the will of Heaven that I should love by fate, and to expect me to love by choice is idle. Let this general declaration serve for each of my suitors on his own account, and let it be understood from this time forth that if anyone dies for me it is not of jealousy or misery he dies, for she who loves no one can give no cause for jealousy to any, and candour is not to be confounded with scorn. Let him who calls me wild beast and basilisk, leave me alone as something noxious and evil; let him who calls me ungrateful, withhold his service; who calls me wayward, seek not my acquaintance; who calls me cruel, pursue me not; for this wild beast, this basilisk, this ungrateful, cruel, wayward being has no kind of desire to seek, serve, know, or follow them. If Chrysostom's impatience and violent passion killed him, why should my modest behaviour and circumspection be blamed? If I preserve my purity in the society of the trees, why should he who would have me preserve it among men, seek to rob me of it? I have, as you know, wealth of my own, and I covet not that of others; my taste is for freedom, and I have no relish for constraint; I neither love nor hate anyone; I do not deceive this one or court that, or trifle with one or play with another. The modest converse of the shepherd girls of these hamlets and the care of my goats are my recreations; my desires are bounded by these mountains, and if they ever wander hence it is to contemplate the beauty of the heavens, steps by which the soul travels to its primeval abode."

With these words, and not waiting to hear a reply, she turned and passed into the thickest part of a wood that was hard by, leaving all who were there lost in admiration as much of her good sense as of her beauty. Some—those wounded by the irresistible shafts launched by her bright eyes—made as though they would follow her, heedless of the frank declaration they had heard; seeing which, and deeming this a fitting occasion for the exercise of his chivalry in aid of distressed damsels, Don Quixote, laying his hand on the hilt of his sword, exclaimed in a loud and distinct voice:

"Let no one, whatever his rank or condition, dare to follow the beautiful Marcela, under pain of incurring my fierce indignation. She has shown by clear and satisfactory arguments that little or no fault is to be found with her for the death of Chrysostom, and also how far she is from yielding to the wishes of any of her lovers, for which reason, instead of being followed and persecuted, she should in justice be honoured and esteemed by all the good people of the world, for she shows that she is the only woman in it that holds to such a virtuous resolution."

Whether it was because of the threats of Don Quixote, or because Ambrosio told them to fulfil their duty to their good friend, none of the shepherds moved or stirred from the spot until, having finished the grave and burned Chrysostom's papers, they laid his body in it, not without many tears from those who stood by. They closed the grave with a heavy stone until a slab was ready which Ambrosio said he meant to have prepared, with an epitaph which was to be to this effect:

> Beneath the stone before your eyes
> The body of a lover lies;
> In life he was a shepherd swain,
> In death a victim to disdain.
> Ungrateful, cruel, coy, and fair,
> Was she that drove him to despair,
> And Love hath made her his ally
> For spreading wide his tyranny.

They then strewed upon the grave a profusion of flowers and branches, and all expressing their condolence with his friend ambrosio, took their Vivaldo and his companion did the same; and Don Quixote bade farewell to his hosts and to the travellers, who pressed him to come with them to Seville, as being such a convenient place for finding adventures, for they presented themselves in every street and round every corner oftener than anywhere else. Don Quixote thanked them for their advice and for the disposition they showed to do him a favour, and said that for the present he would not, and must not go to Seville until he had cleared all these mountains of highwaymen and robbers, of whom report said they were full. Seeing his good intention, the travellers were unwilling to press him further, and once more bidding him farewell, they left him and pursued their journey, in the course of which they did not fail to discuss the story of Marcela and Chrysostom as well as the madness of Don Quixote. He, on his part, resolved to go in quest of the shepherdess Marcela, and make offer to her of all the service he could render her; but things did not fall out with him as he expected, according to what is related in the course of this veracious history, of which the Second Part ends here.

CHAPTER XV

IN WHICH IS RELATED THE UNFORTUNATE ADVENTURE THAT DON QUIXOTE FELL IN WITH WHEN HE FELL OUT WITH CERTAIN HEARTLESS YANGUESANS

The sage Cide Hamete Benengeli relates that as soon as Don Quixote took leave of his hosts and all who had been present at the burial of Chrysostom, he and his squire passed into the same wood which they had seen the shepherdess Marcela enter, and after having wandered for more than two hours in all directions in search of her without finding her, they came to a halt in a glade covered with tender grass, beside which ran a pleasant cool stream that invited and compelled them to pass there the hours of the noontide heat, which by this time was beginning to come on oppressively. Don Quixote and Sancho dismounted, and turning Rocinante and the ass loose to feed on the grass that was there in abundance, they ransacked the alforjas, and without any ceremony very peacefully and sociably master and man made their repast on what they found in them.

Sancho had not thought it worth while to hobble Rocinante, feeling sure, from what he knew of his staidness and freedom from incontinence, that all the mares in the Cordova pastures would not lead him into an impropriety. Chance, however, and the devil, who is not always asleep, so ordained it that feeding in this valley there was a drove of Galician ponies belonging to certain Yanguesan carriers, whose way it is to take their midday rest with their teams in places and spots where grass and water abound; and that where Don Quixote chanced to be suited the Yanguesans' purpose very well. It so happened, then, that Rocinante took a fancy to disport himself with their ladyships the ponies, and abandoning his usual gait and demeanour as he scented them, he, without asking leave of his master, got up a briskish little trot and hastened to make known his wishes to them; they, however, it seemed, preferred their pasture to him, and received him with their heels and teeth to such effect that they soon broke his girths and left him naked without a saddle to cover him; but what must have been worse to him was that the carriers, seeing the violence he was offering to their mares, came running up armed with stakes, and so belaboured him that they brought him sorely battered to the ground.

By this time Don Quixote and Sancho, who had witnessed the drubbing of Rocinante, came up panting, and said Don Quixote to Sancho:

"So far as I can see, friend Sancho, these are not knights but base folk of low birth: I mention it because thou canst lawfully aid me in taking due vengeance for the insult offered to Rocinante before our eyes."

"What the devil vengeance can we take," answered Sancho, "if they are more than twenty, and we no more than two, or, indeed, perhaps not more than one and a half?"

"I count for a hundred," replied Don Quixote, and without more words he drew his sword and attacked the Yanguesans and excited and impelled by the example of his master, Sancho did the same; and to begin with, Don Quixote delivered a slash at one of them that laid open the leather jerkin he wore, together with a great portion of his shoulder. The Yanguesans, seeing themselves assaulted by only two men while they were so many, betook themselves to their stakes, and driving the two into the middle they began to lay on with great zeal and energy; in fact, at the second blow they brought Sancho to the ground, and Don Quixote fared the same way, all his skill and high mettle availing him nothing, and fate willed it that he should fall at the feet of Rocinante, who had not yet risen; whereby it may be seen how furiously stakes can pound in angry boorish hands.

Then, seeing the mischief they had done, the Yanguesans with all the haste they could loaded their team and pursued their journey, leaving the two adventurers a sorry sight and in sorrier mood.

Sancho was the first to come to, and finding himself close to his master he called to him in a weak and doleful voice, "Senor Don Quixote, ah, Senor Don Quixote!"

"What wouldst thou, brother Sancho?" answered Don Quixote in the same feeble suffering tone as Sancho.

"I would like, if it were possible," answered Sancho Panza, "your worship to give me a couple of sups of that potion of the fiery Blas, if it be that you have any to hand there; perhaps it will serve for broken bones as well as for wounds."

"If I only had it here, wretch that I am, what more should we want?" said Don Quixote; "but I swear to thee, Sancho Panza, on the faith of a knight-errant, ere two days are over, unless fortune orders otherwise, I mean to have it in my possession, or my hand will have lost its cunning."

"But in how many does your worship think we shall have the use of our feet?" answered Sancho Panza.

"For myself I must say I cannot guess how many," said the battered knight Don Quixote; "but I take all the blame upon myself, for I had no business to put hand to sword against men who where not dubbed knights like myself, and so I believe that in punishment for having transgressed the laws of chivalry the God of battles has permitted this chastisement to be administered to me; for which reason, brother Sancho, it is well thou shouldst receive a hint on the matter which I am now about to mention to thee, for it is of much importance to the welfare of both of us. It is at when thou shalt see rabble of this sort offering us insult thou art not to wait till I draw sword against them, for I shall not do so at all; but do thou draw sword and chastise them to thy heart's content, and if any knights come to their aid and defence I will take care to defend thee and assail them with all my might; and thou hast already seen by a thousand signs and proofs what the might of this strong arm of mine is equal to"—so uplifted had the poor gentleman become through the victory over the stout Biscayan.

But Sancho did not so fully approve of his master's admonition as to let it pass without saying in reply, "Senor, I am a man of peace, meek and quiet, and I can put up with any affront because I have a wife and children to support and bring up; so let it be likewise a hint to your worship, as it cannot be a mandate, that on no account will I draw sword either against clown or against knight, and that here before God I forgive the insults that have been offered me, whether they have been, are, or shall be offered me by high or low, rich or poor, noble or commoner, not excepting any rank or condition whatsoever."

To all which his master said in reply, "I wish I had breath enough to speak somewhat easily, and that the pain I feel on this side would abate so as to let me explain to thee, Panza, the mistake thou makest. Come now, sinner, suppose the wind of fortune, hitherto so adverse, should turn in our favour, filling the sails of our desires so that safely and without impediment we put into port in some one of those islands I have promised thee, how would it be with thee if on winning it I made thee lord of it? Why, thou wilt make it well-nigh impossible through not being a knight nor having any desire to be one, nor possessing the courage nor the will to avenge insults or defend thy lordship; for thou must know that in newly conquered kingdoms and provinces the minds of the inhabitants are never so quiet nor so well disposed to the new lord that there is no fear of their making some move to change matters once more, and try, as they say, what chance may do for them; so it is essential that the new possessor should have good sense to enable him to govern, and valour to attack and defend himself, whatever may befall him."

"In what has now befallen us," answered Sancho, "I'd have been well pleased to have that good sense and that valour your worship speaks of, but I swear on the faith of a poor man I am more fit for plasters than for arguments. See if your worship can get up, and let us help Rocinante, though he does not deserve it, for he was the main cause of all this thrashing. I never thought it of Rocinante, for I took him to be a virtuous person and as quiet as myself. After all, they say right that it takes a long time to come to know people, and that there is nothing sure in this life. Who would have said that, after such mighty slashes as your worship gave that unlucky knight-errant, there was coming, travelling post and at the very heels of them, such a great storm of sticks as has fallen upon our shoulders?"

"And yet thine, Sancho," replied Don Quixote, "ought to be used to such squalls; but mine, reared in soft cloth and fine linen, it is plain they must feel more keenly the pain of this mishap, and if it were not that I imagine—why do I say imagine?—know of a certainty that all these annoyances are very necessary accompaniments of the calling of arms, I would lay me down here to die of pure vexation."

To this the squire replied, "Senor, as these mishaps are what one reaps of chivalry, tell me if they happen very often, or if they have their own fixed times for coming to pass; because it seems to me that after two harvests we shall be no good for the third, unless God in his infinite mercy helps us."

"Know, friend Sancho," answered Don Quixote, "that the life of knights-errant is subject to a thousand dangers and reverses, and neither more nor less is it within immediate possibility for knights-errant to become kings and emperors, as experience has shown in the case of many different knights with whose histories I am thoroughly acquainted; and I could tell thee now, if the pain would let me, of some who simply by might of arm have risen to the high stations I have mentioned; and those same, both before and after, experienced divers misfortunes and miseries; for the valiant Amadis of Gaul found himself in the power of his mortal enemy Arcalaus the magician, who, it is positively asserted, holding him captive, gave him more than two hundred lashes with the reins of his horse while tied to one of the pillars of a court; and moreover there is a certain recondite author of no small authority who says that the Knight of Phoebus, being caught in a certain pitfall, which opened under his feet in a certain castle, on falling found himself bound hand and foot in a deep pit underground, where they administered to him one of those things they call clysters, of sand and snow-water, that well-nigh finished him; and if he had not been succoured in that sore extremity by a sage, a great friend of his, it would have gone very hard with the poor knight; so I may well suffer in company with such worthy folk, for greater were the indignities which they had to suffer than those which we suffer. For I would have thee know, Sancho, that wounds caused by any instruments which happen by chance to be in hand inflict no indignity, and this is laid down in the law of the duel in express words: if, for instance, the cobbler strikes another with the last which he has in his hand, though it be in fact a piece of wood, it cannot be said for that reason that he whom he struck with it has been cudgelled. I say this lest thou shouldst imagine that because we have been drubbed in this affray we have therefore suffered any indignity; for the arms those men carried, with which they pounded us, were nothing more than their stakes, and not one of them, so far as I remember, carried rapier, sword, or dagger."

"They gave me no time to see that much," answered Sancho, "for hardly had I laid hand on my tizona when they signed the cross on my shoulders with their sticks in such style that they took the sight out of my eyes and the strength out of my feet, stretching me where I now lie, and where thinking of whether all those stake-strokes were an indignity or not gives me no uneasiness, which the pain of the blows does, for they will remain as deeply impressed on my memory as on my shoulders."

"For all that let me tell thee, brother Panza," said Don Quixote, "that there is no recollection which time does not put an end to, and no pain which death does not remove."

"And what greater misfortune can there be," replied Panza, "than the one that waits for time to put an end to it and death to remove it? If our mishap were one of those that are cured with a couple of plasters, it would not be so bad; but I am beginning to think that all the plasters in a hospital almost won't be enough to put us right."

"No more of that: pluck strength out of weakness, Sancho, as I mean to do," returned Don Quixote, "and let us see how Rocinante is, for it seems to me that not the least share of this mishap has fallen to the lot of the poor beast."

"There is nothing wonderful in that," replied Sancho, "since he is a knight-errant too; what I wonder at is that my beast should have come off scot-free where we come out scotched."

"Fortune always leaves a door open in adversity in order to bring relief to it," said Don Quixote; "I say so because this little beast may now supply the want of Rocinante, carrying me hence to some castle where I may be cured of my wounds. And moreover I shall not hold it any dishonour to be so mounted, for I remember having read how the good old Silenus, the tutor and instructor of the gay god of laughter, when he entered the city of the hundred gates, went very contentedly mounted on a handsome ass."

"It may be true that he went mounted as your worship says," answered Sancho, "but there is a great difference between going mounted and going slung like a sack of manure."

To which Don Quixote replied, "Wounds received in battle confer honour instead of taking it away; and so, friend Panza, say no more, but, as I told thee before, get up as well as thou canst and put me on top of thy beast in whatever fashion pleases thee best, and let us go hence ere night come on and surprise us in these wilds."

"And yet I have heard your worship say," observed Panza, "that it is very meet for knights-errant to sleep in wastes and deserts, and that they esteem it very good fortune."

"That is," said Don Quixote, "when they cannot help it, or when they are in love; and so true is this that there have been knights who have remained two years on rocks, in sunshine and shade and all the inclemencies of heaven, without their ladies knowing anything of it; and one of these was Amadis, when, under the name of Beltenebros, he took up his abode on the Pena Pobre for—I know not if it was eight years or eight months, for I am not very sure of the reckoning; at any rate he stayed there doing penance for I know not what pique the Princess Oriana had against him; but no more of this now, Sancho, and make haste before a mishap like Rocinante's befalls the ass."

"The very devil would be in it in that case," said Sancho; and letting off thirty "ohs," and sixty sighs, and a hundred and twenty maledictions and execrations on whomsoever it was that had brought him there, he raised himself, stopping half-way bent like a Turkish bow without power to bring himself upright, but with all his pains he saddled his ass, who too had gone astray somewhat, yielding to the excessive licence of the day; he next raised up Rocinante, and as for him, had he possessed a tongue to complain with, most assuredly neither Sancho nor his master would have been behind him.

To be brief, Sancho fixed Don Quixote on the ass and secured Rocinante with a leading rein, and taking the ass by the halter, he proceeded more or less in the direction in which it seemed to him the high road might be; and, as chance was conducting their affairs for them from good to better, he had not gone a short league when the road came in sight, and on it he perceived an inn, which to his annoyance and to the delight of Don Quixote must needs be a castle. Sancho insisted that it was an inn, and his master that it was not one, but a castle, and the dispute lasted so long that before the point was settled they had time to reach it, and into it Sancho entered with all his team without any further controversy.

CHAPTER XVI

OF WHAT HAPPENED TO THE INGENIOUS GENTLEMAN IN THE INN WHICH HE TOOK TO BE A CASTLE

The innkeeper, seeing Don Quixote slung across the ass, asked Sancho what was amiss with him. Sancho answered that it was nothing, only that he had fallen down from a rock and had his ribs a little bruised. The innkeeper had a wife whose disposition was not such as those of her calling commonly have, for she was by nature kind-hearted and felt for the sufferings of her neighbours, so she at once set about tending Don Quixote, and made her young daughter, a very comely girl, help her in taking care of her guest. There was besides in the inn, as servant, an Asturian lass with a broad face, flat poll, and snub nose, blind of one eye and not very sound in the other. The elegance of her shape, to be sure, made up for all her defects; she did not measure seven palms from head to foot, and her shoulders, which overweighted her somewhat, made her contemplate the ground more than she liked. This graceful lass, then, helped the young girl, and the two made up a very bad bed for Don Quixote in a garret that showed evident signs of having formerly served for many years as a straw-loft, in which there was also quartered a carrier whose bed was placed a little beyond our Don Quixote's, and, though only made of the pack-saddles and cloths of his mules, had much the advantage of it, as Don Quixote's consisted simply of four rough boards on two not very even trestles, a mattress, that for thinness might have passed for a quilt, full of pellets which, were they not seen through the rents to be wool, would to the touch have seemed pebbles in hardness, two sheets made of buckler leather, and a coverlet the threads of which anyone that chose might have counted without missing one in the reckoning.

On this accursed bed Don Quixote stretched himself, and the hostess and her daughter soon covered him with plasters from top to toe, while Maritornes—for that was the name of the Asturian—held the light for them, and while plastering him, the hostess, observing how full of wheals Don Quixote was in some places, remarked that this had more the look of blows than of a fall.

It was not blows, Sancho said, but that the rock had many points and projections, and that each of them had left its mark. "Pray, senora," he added, "manage to save some tow, as there will be no want of some one to use it, for my loins too are rather sore."

"Then you must have fallen too," said the hostess.

"I did not fall," said Sancho Panza, "but from the shock I got at seeing my master fall, my body aches so that I feel as if I had had a thousand thwacks."

"That may well be," said the young girl, "for it has many a time happened to me to dream that I was falling down from a tower and never coming to the ground, and when I awoke from the dream to find myself as weak and shaken as if I had really fallen."

"There is the point, senora," replied Sancho Panza, "that I without dreaming at all, but being more awake than I am now, find myself with scarcely less wheals than my master, Don Quixote."

"How is the gentleman called?" asked Maritornes the Asturian.

"Don Quixote of La Mancha," answered Sancho Panza, "and he is a knight-adventurer, and one of the best and stoutest that have been seen in the world this long time past."

"What is a knight-adventurer?" said the lass.

"Are you so new in the world as not to know?" answered Sancho Panza. "Well, then, you must know, sister, that a knight-adventurer is a thing that in two words is seen drubbed and emperor, that is to-day the most miserable and needy being in the world, and to-morrow will have two or three crowns of kingdoms to give his squire."

"Then how is it," said the hostess, "that belonging to so good a master as this, you have not, to judge by appearances, even so much as a county?"

"It is too soon yet," answered Sancho, "for we have only been a month going in quest of adventures, and so far we have met with nothing that can be called one, for it will happen that when one thing is looked for another thing is found; however, if my master Don Quixote gets well of this wound, or fall, and I am left none the worse of it, I would not change my hopes for the best title in Spain."

To all this conversation Don Quixote was listening very attentively, and sitting up in bed as well as he could, and taking the hostess by the hand he said to her, "Believe me, fair lady, you may call yourself fortunate in having in this castle of yours sheltered my person, which is such that if I do not myself praise it, it is because of what is commonly said, that self-praise debaseth; but my squire will inform you who I am. I only tell you that I shall preserve for ever inscribed on my memory the service you have rendered me in order to tender you my gratitude while life shall last me; and would to Heaven love held me not so enthralled and subject to its laws and to the eyes of that fair ingrate whom I name between my teeth, but that those of this lovely damsel might be the masters of my liberty."

The hostess, her daughter, and the worthy Maritornes listened in bewilderment to the words of the knight-errant; for they understood about as much of them as if he had been talking Greek, though they could perceive they were all meant for expressions of good-will and blandishments; and not being accustomed to this kind of language, they stared at him and wondered to themselves, for he seemed to them a man of a different sort from those they were used to, and thanking him in pothouse phrase for his civility they left him, while the Asturian gave her attention to Sancho, who needed it no less than his master.

The carrier had made an arrangement with her for recreation that night, and she had given him her word that when the guests were quiet and the family asleep she would come in search of him and meet his wishes unreservedly. And it is said of this good lass that she never made promises of the kind without fulfilling them, even though she made them in a forest and without any witness present, for she plumed herself greatly on being a lady and held it no disgrace to be in such an employment as servant in an inn, because, she said, misfortunes and ill-luck had brought her to that position. The hard, narrow, wretched, rickety bed of Don Quixote stood first in the middle of this star-lit stable, and close beside it Sancho made his, which merely consisted of a rush mat and a blanket that looked as if it was of threadbare canvas rather than of wool. Next to these two beds was that of the carrier, made up, as has been said, of the pack-saddles and all the trappings of the two best mules he had, though there were twelve of them, sleek, plump, and in prime condition, for he was one of the rich carriers of Arevalo, according to the author of this history, who particularly mentions this carrier because he knew him very well, and they even say was in some degree a relation of his; besides which Cide Hamete Benengeli was a historian of great research and accuracy in all things, as is very evident since he would not pass over in silence those that have been already mentioned, however trifling and insignificant they might be, an example that might be followed by those grave historians who relate transactions so curtly and briefly that we hardly get a taste of them, all the substance of the work being left in the inkstand from carelessness, perverseness, or ignorance. A thousand blessings on the author of "Tablante de Ricamonte" and that of the other book in which the deeds of the Conde Tomillas are recounted; with what minuteness they describe everything!

To proceed, then: after having paid a visit to his team and given them their second feed, the carrier stretched himself on his pack-saddles and lay waiting for his conscientious Maritornes. Sancho was by this time plastered and had lain down, and though he strove to sleep the pain of his ribs would not let him, while Don Quixote with the pain of his had his eyes as wide open as a hare's.

The inn was all in silence, and in the whole of it there was no light except that given by a lantern that hung burning in the middle of the gateway. This strange stillness, and the thoughts, always present to our knight's mind, of the incidents described at every turn in the books that were the cause of his misfortune, conjured up to his imagination as extraordinary a delusion as can well be conceived, which was that he fancied himself to have reached a famous castle (for, as has been said, all the inns he lodged in were castles to his eyes), and that the daughter of the innkeeper was daughter of the lord of the castle, and that she, won by his highbred bearing, had fallen in love with him, and had promised to come to his bed for a while that night without the knowledge of her parents; and holding all this fantasy that he had constructed as solid fact, he began to feel uneasy and to consider the perilous risk which his virtue was about to encounter, and he resolved in his heart to commit no treason to his lady Dulcinea del Toboso, even though the queen Guinevere herself and the dame Quintanona should present themselves before him.

While he was taken up with these vagaries, then, the time and the hour—an unlucky one for him—arrived for the Asturian to come, who in her smock, with bare feet and her hair gathered into a fustian coif, with noiseless and cautious steps entered the chamber where the three were quartered, in quest of the carrier; but scarcely had she gained the door when Don Quixote perceived her, and sitting up in his bed in spite of his plasters and the pain of his ribs, he stretched out his arms to receive his beauteous damsel. The Asturian, who went all doubled up and in silence with her hands before her feeling for her lover, encountered the arms of Don Quixote, who grasped her tightly by the wrist, and drawing her towards him, while she dared not utter a word, made her sit down on the bed. He then felt her smock, and although it was of sackcloth it appeared to him to be of the finest and softest silk: on her wrists she wore some glass beads, but to him they had the sheen of precious Orient pearls: her hair, which in some measure resembled a horse's mane, he rated as threads of the brightest gold of Araby, whose refulgence dimmed the sun himself: her breath, which no doubt smelt of yesterday's stale salad, seemed to him to diffuse a sweet aromatic fragrance from her mouth; and, in short, he drew her portrait in his imagination with the same features and in the same style as that which he had seen in his books of the other princesses who, smitten by love, came with all the adornments that are here set down, to see the sorely wounded knight; and so great was the poor gentleman's blindness that neither touch, nor smell, nor anything else about the good lass that would have made any but a carrier vomit, were enough to undeceive him; on the contrary, he was persuaded he had the goddess of beauty in his arms, and holding her firmly in his grasp he went on to say in low, tender voice:

"Would that found myself, lovely and exalted lady, in a position to repay such a favour as that which you, by the sight of your great beauty, have granted me; but fortune, which is never weary of persecuting the good, has chosen to place me upon this bed, where I lie so bruised and broken that though my inclination would gladly comply with yours it is impossible; besides, to this impossibility another yet greater is to be added, which is the faith that I have pledged to the peerless Dulcinea del Toboso, sole lady of my most secret thoughts; and were it not that this stood in the way I should not be so insensible a knight as to miss the happy opportunity which your great goodness has offered me."

Maritornes was fretting and sweating at finding herself held so fast by Don Quixote, and not understanding or heeding the words he addressed to her, she strove without speaking to free herself. The worthy carrier, whose unholy thoughts kept him awake, was aware of his doxy the moment she entered the door, and was listening attentively to all Don Quixote said; and jealous that the Asturian should have broken her word with him for another, drew nearer to Don Quixote's bed and stood still to see what would come of this talk which he could not understand; but when he perceived the wench struggling to get free and Don Quixote striving to hold her, not relishing the joke he raised his arm and delivered such a terrible cuff on the lank jaws of the amorous knight that he bathed all his mouth in blood, and not content with this he mounted on his ribs and with his feet tramped all over them at a pace rather smarter than a trot. The bed which was somewhat crazy and not very firm on its feet, unable to support the additional weight of the carrier, came to the ground, and at the mighty crash of this the innkeeper awoke and at once concluded that it must be some brawl of Maritornes', because after calling loudly to her he got no answer. With this suspicion he got up, and lighting a lamp hastened to the quarter where he had heard the disturbance. The wench, seeing that her master was coming and knowing that his temper was terrible, frightened and panic-stricken made for the bed of Sancho Panza, who still slept, and crouching upon it made a ball of herself.

The innkeeper came in exclaiming, "Where art thou, strumpet? Of course this is some of thy work." At this Sancho awoke, and feeling this mass almost on top of him fancied he had the nightmare and began to distribute fisticuffs all round, of which a certain share fell upon Maritornes, who, irritated by the pain and flinging modesty aside, paid back so many in return to Sancho that she woke him up in spite of himself. He then, finding himself so handled, by whom he knew not, raising himself up as well as he could, grappled with Maritornes, and he and she between them began the bitterest and drollest scrimmage in the world. The carrier, however, perceiving by the light of the innkeeper candle how it fared with his ladylove, quitting Don Quixote, ran to bring her the help she needed; and the innkeeper did the same but with a different intention, for his was to chastise the lass, as he believed that beyond a doubt she alone was the cause of all the harmony. And so, as the saying is, cat to rat, rat to rope, rope to stick, the carrier pounded Sancho, Sancho the lass, she him, and the innkeeper her, and all worked away so briskly that they did not give themselves a moment's rest; and the best of it was that the innkeeper's lamp went out, and as they were left in the dark they all laid on one upon the other in a mass so unmercifully that there was not a sound spot left where a hand could light.

It so happened that there was lodging that night in the inn a caudrillero of what they call the Old Holy Brotherhood of Toledo, who, also hearing the extraordinary noise of the conflict, seized his staff and the tin case with his warrants, and made his way in the dark into the room crying: "Hold! in the name of the Jurisdiction! Hold! in the name of the Holy Brotherhood!"

The first that he came upon was the pummelled Don Quixote, who lay stretched senseless on his back upon his broken-down bed, and, his hand falling on the beard as he felt about, he continued to cry, "Help for the Jurisdiction!" but perceiving that he whom he had laid hold of did not move or stir, he concluded that he was dead and that those in the room were his murderers, and with this suspicion he raised his voice still higher, calling out, "Shut the inn gate; see that no one goes out; they have killed a man here!" This cry startled them all, and each dropped the contest at the point at which the voice reached him. The innkeeper retreated to his room, the carrier to his pack-saddles, the lass to her crib; the unlucky Don Quixote and Sancho alone were unable to move from where they were. The cuadrillero on this let go Don Quixote's beard, and went out to look for a light to search for and apprehend the culprits; but not finding one, as the innkeeper had purposely extinguished the lantern on retreating to his room, he was compelled to have recourse to the hearth, where after much time and trouble he lit another lamp.

CHAPTER XVII

IN WHICH ARE CONTAINED THE INNUMERABLE TROUBLES WHICH THE BRAVE DON QUIXOTE AND HIS GOOD SQUIRE SANCHO PANZA ENDURED IN THE INN, WHICH TO HIS MISFORTUNE HE TOOK TO BE A CASTLE

By this time Don Quixote had recovered from his swoon; and in the same tone of voice in which he had called to his squire the day before when he lay stretched "in the vale of the stakes," he began calling to him now, "Sancho, my friend, art thou asleep? sleepest thou, friend Sancho?"

"How can I sleep, curses on it!" returned Sancho discontentedly and bitterly, "when it is plain that all the devils have been at me this night?"

"Thou mayest well believe that," answered Don Quixote, "because, either I know little, or this castle is enchanted, for thou must know-but this that I am now about to tell thee thou must swear to keep secret until after my death."

"I swear it," answered Sancho.

"I say so," continued Don Quixote, "because I hate taking away anyone's good name."

"I say," replied Sancho, "that I swear to hold my tongue about it till the end of your worship's days, and God grant I may be able to let it out tomorrow."

"Do I do thee such injuries, Sancho," said Don Quixote, "that thou wouldst see me dead so soon?"

"It is not for that," replied Sancho, "but because I hate keeping things long, and I don't want them to grow rotten with me from over-keeping."

"At any rate," said Don Quixote, "I have more confidence in thy affection and good nature; and so I would have thee know that this night there befell me one of the strangest adventures that I could describe, and to relate it to thee briefly thou must know that a little while ago the daughter of the lord of this castle came to me, and that she is the most elegant and beautiful damsel that could be found in the wide world. What I could tell thee of the charms of her person!

of her lively wit! of other secret matters which, to preserve the fealty I owe to my lady Dulcinea del Toboso, I shall pass over unnoticed and in silence! I will only tell thee that, either fate being envious of so great a boon placed in my hands by good fortune, or perhaps (and this is more probable) this castle being, as I have already said, enchanted, at the time when I was engaged in the sweetest and most amorous discourse with her, there came, without my seeing or knowing whence it came, a hand attached to some arm of some huge giant, that planted such a cuff on my jaws that I have them all bathed in blood, and then pummelled me in such a way that I am in a worse plight than yesterday when the carriers, on account of Rocinante's misbehaviour, inflicted on us the injury thou knowest of; whence conjecture that there must be some enchanted Moor guarding the treasure of this damsel's beauty, and that it is not for me."

"Not for me either," said Sancho, "for more than four hundred Moors have so thrashed me that the drubbing of the stakes was cakes and fancy-bread to it. But tell me, senor, what do you call this excellent and rare adventure that has left us as we are left now? Though your worship was not so badly off, having in your arms that incomparable beauty you spoke of; but I, what did I have, except the heaviest whacks I think I had in all my life? Unlucky me and the mother that bore me! for I am not a knight-errant and never expect to be one, and of all the mishaps, the greater part falls to my share."

"Then thou hast been thrashed too?" said Don Quixote.

"Didn't I say so? worse luck to my line!" said Sancho.

"Be not distressed, friend," said Don Quixote, "for I will now make the precious balsam with which we shall cure ourselves in the twinkling of an eye."

By this time the cuadrillero had succeeded in lighting the lamp, and came in to see the man that he thought had been killed; and as Sancho caught sight of him at the door, seeing him coming in his shirt, with a cloth on his head, and a lamp in his hand, and a very forbidding countenance, he said to his master, "Senor, can it be that this is the enchanted Moor coming back to give us more castigation if there be anything still left in the ink-bottle?"

"It cannot be the Moor," answered Don Quixote, "for those under enchantment do not let themselves be seen by anyone."

"If they don't let themselves be seen, they let themselves be felt," said

Sancho; "if not, let my shoulders speak to the point."

"Mine could speak too," said Don Quixote, "but that is not a sufficient reason for believing that what we see is the enchanted Moor."

The officer came up, and finding them engaged in such a peaceful conversation, stood amazed; though Don Quixote, to be sure, still lay on his back unable to move from pure pummelling and plasters. The officer turned to him and said, "Well, how goes it, good man?"

"I would speak more politely if I were you," replied Don Quixote; "is it the way of this country to address knights-errant in that style, you booby?"

The cuadrillero finding himself so disrespectfully treated by such a sorry-looking individual, lost his temper, and raising the lamp full of oil, smote Don Quixote such a blow with it on the head that he gave him a badly broken pate; then, all being in darkness, he went out, and Sancho Panza said, "That is certainly the enchanted Moor, Senor, and he keeps the treasure for others, and for us only the cuffs and lamp-whacks."

"That is the truth," answered Don Quixote, "and there is no use in troubling oneself about these matters of enchantment or being angry or vexed at them, for as they are invisible and visionary we shall find no one on whom to avenge ourselves, do what we may; rise, Sancho, if thou canst, and call the alcaide of this fortress, and get him to give me a little oil, wine, salt, and rosemary to make the salutiferous balsam, for indeed I believe I have great need of it now, because I am losing much blood from the wound that phantom gave me."

Sancho got up with pain enough in his bones, and went after the innkeeper in the dark, and meeting the officer, who was looking to see what had become of his enemy, he said to him, "Senor, whoever you are, do us the favour and kindness to give us a little rosemary, oil, salt, and wine, for it is wanted to cure one of the best knights-errant on earth, who lies on yonder bed wounded by the hands of the enchanted Moor that is in this inn."

When the officer heard him talk in this way, he took him for a man out of his senses, and as day was now beginning to break, he opened the inn gate, and calling the host, he told him what this good man wanted. The host furnished him with what he required, and Sancho brought it to Don Quixote, who, with his hand to his head, was bewailing the pain of the blow of the lamp, which had done him no more harm than raising a couple of rather large lumps, and what he fancied blood was only the sweat that flowed from him in his sufferings during the late storm. To be brief, he took the materials, of which he made a compound, mixing them all and boiling them a good while until it seemed to him they had come to perfection. He then asked for some vial to pour it into, and as there was not one in the inn, he decided on putting it into a tin oil-bottle or flask of which the host made him a free gift; and over the flask he repeated more than eighty paternosters and as many more ave-marias, salves, and credos, accompanying each word with a cross by way of benediction, at all which there were present Sancho, the innkeeper, and the cuadrillero; for the carrier was now peacefully engaged in attending to the comfort of his mules.

This being accomplished, he felt anxious to make trial himself, on the spot, of the virtue of this precious balsam, as he considered it, and so he drank near a quart of what could not be put into the flask and remained in the pigskin in which it had been boiled; but scarcely had he done drinking when he began to vomit in such a way that nothing was left in his stomach, and with the pangs and spasms of vomiting he broke into a profuse sweat, on account of which he bade them cover him up and leave him alone. They did so, and he lay sleeping more than three hours, at the end of which he awoke and felt very great bodily relief and so much ease from his bruises that he thought himself quite cured, and verily believed he had hit upon the balsam of Fierabras; and that with this remedy he might thenceforward, without any fear, face any kind of destruction, battle, or combat, however perilous it might be.

Sancho Panza, who also regarded the amendment of his master as miraculous, begged him to give him what was left in the pigskin, which was no small quantity. Don Quixote consented, and he, taking it with both hands, in good faith and with a better will, gulped down and drained off very little less than his master. But the fact is, that the stomach of poor Sancho was of necessity not so delicate as that of his master, and so, before vomiting, he was seized with such gripings and retchings, and such sweats and faintness, that verily and truly he believed his last hour had come, and finding himself so racked and tormented he cursed the balsam and the thief that had given it to him.

Don Quixote seeing him in this state said, "It is my belief, Sancho, that this mischief comes of thy not being dubbed a knight, for I am persuaded this liquor cannot be good for those who are not so."

"If your worship knew that," returned Sancho—"woe betide me and all my kindred!—why did you let me taste it?"

At this moment the draught took effect, and the poor squire began to discharge both ways at such a rate that the rush mat on which he had thrown himself and the canvas blanket he had covering him were fit for nothing afterwards. He sweated and perspired with such paroxysms and convulsions that not only he himself but all present thought his end had come. This tempest and tribulation lasted about two hours, at the end of which he was left, not like his master, but so weak and exhausted that he could not stand. Don Quixote, however, who, as has been said, felt himself relieved and well, was eager to take his departure at once in quest of adventures, as it seemed to him that all the time he loitered there was a fraud upon the world and those in it who stood in need of his help and protection, all the more when he had the security and confidence his balsam afforded him; and so, urged by this impulse, he saddled Rocinante himself and put the pack-saddle on his squire's beast, whom likewise he helped to dress and mount the ass; after which he mounted his horse and turning to a corner of the inn he laid hold of a pike that stood there, to serve him by way of a lance. All that were in the inn, who were more than twenty persons, stood watching him; the innkeeper's daughter was likewise observing him, and he too never took his eyes off her, and from time to time fetched a sigh that he seemed to pluck up from the depths of his bowels; but they all thought it must be from the pain he felt in his ribs; at any rate they who had seen him plastered the night before thought so.

As soon as they were both mounted, at the gate of the inn, he called to the host and said in a very grave and measured voice, "Many and great are the favours, Senor Alcaide, that I have received in this castle of yours, and I remain under the deepest obligation to be grateful to you for them all the days of my life; if I can repay them in avenging you of any arrogant foe who may have wronged you, know that my calling is no other than to aid the weak, to avenge those who suffer wrong, and to chastise perfidy. Search your memory, and if you find anything of this kind you need only tell me of it, and I promise you by the order of knighthood which I have received to procure you satisfaction and reparation to the utmost of your desire."

The innkeeper replied to him with equal calmness, "Sir Knight, I do not want your worship to avenge me of any wrong, because when any is done me I can take what vengeance seems good to me; the only thing I want is that you pay me the score that you have run up in the inn last night, as well for the straw and barley for your two beasts, as for supper and beds."

"Then this is an inn?" said Don Quixote.

"And a very respectable one," said the innkeeper.

"I have been under a mistake all this time," answered Don Quixote, "for in truth I thought it was a castle, and not a bad one; but since it appears that it is not a castle but an inn, all that can be done now is that you should excuse the payment, for I cannot contravene the rule of knights-errant, of whom I know as a fact (and up to the present I have read nothing to the contrary) that they never paid for lodging or anything else in the inn where they might be; for any hospitality that might be offered them is their due by law and right in return for the insufferable toil they endure in seeking adventures by night and by day, in summer and in winter, on foot and on horseback, in hunger and thirst, cold and heat, exposed to all the inclemencies of heaven and all the hardships of earth."

"I have little to do with that," replied the innkeeper; "pay me what you owe me, and let us have no more talk of chivalry, for all I care about is to get my money."

"You are a stupid, scurvy innkeeper," said Don Quixote, and putting spurs to Rocinante and bringing his pike to the slope he rode out of the inn before anyone could stop him, and pushed on some distance without looking to see if his squire was following him.

The innkeeper when he saw him go without paying him ran to get payment of Sancho, who said that as his master would not pay neither would he, because, being as he was squire to a knight-errant, the same rule and reason held good for him as for his master with regard to not paying anything in inns and hostelries. At this the innkeeper waxed very wroth, and threatened if he did not pay to compel him in a way that he would not like. To which Sancho made answer that by the law of chivalry his master had received he would not pay a rap, though it cost him his life; for the excellent and ancient usage of knights-errant was not going to be violated by him, nor should the squires of such as were yet to come into the world ever complain of him or reproach him with breaking so just a privilege.

The ill-luck of the unfortunate Sancho so ordered it that among the company in the inn there were four woolcarders from Segovia, three needle-makers from the Colt of Cordova, and two lodgers from the Fair of Seville, lively fellows, tender-hearted, fond of a joke, and playful, who, almost as if instigated and moved by a common impulse, made up to Sancho and dismounted him from his ass, while one of them went in for the blanket of the host's bed; but on flinging him into it they looked up, and seeing that the ceiling was somewhat lower than what they required for their work, they decided upon going out into the yard, which was bounded by the sky, and there, putting Sancho in the middle of the blanket, they began to raise him high, making sport with him as they would with a dog at Shrovetide.

The cries of the poor blanketed wretch were so loud that they reached the ears of his master, who, halting to listen attentively, was persuaded that some new adventure was coming, until he clearly perceived that it was his squire who uttered them. Wheeling about he came up to the inn with a laborious gallop, and finding it shut went round it to see if he could find some way of getting in; but as soon as he came to the wall of the yard, which was not very high, he discovered the game that was being played with his squire. He saw him rising and falling in the air with such grace and nimbleness that, had his rage allowed him, it is my belief he would have laughed. He tried to climb from his horse on to the top of the wall, but he was so bruised and battered that he could not even dismount; and so from the back of his horse he began to utter such maledictions and objurgations against those who were blanketing Sancho as it would be impossible to write down accurately: they, however, did not stay their laughter or their work for this, nor did the flying Sancho cease his lamentations, mingled now with threats, now with entreaties but all to little purpose, or none at all, until from pure weariness they left off. They then brought him his ass, and mounting him on top of it they put his jacket round him; and the compassionate Maritornes, seeing him so exhausted, thought fit to refresh him with a jug of water, and that it might be all the cooler she fetched it from the well. Sancho took it, and as he was raising it to his mouth he was stopped by the cries of his master exclaiming, "Sancho, my son, drink not water; drink it not, my son, for it will kill thee; see, here I have the blessed balsam (and he held up the flask of liquor), and with drinking two drops of it thou wilt certainly be restored."

At these words Sancho turned his eyes asquint, and in a still louder voice said, "Can it be your worship has forgotten that I am not a knight, or do you want me to end by vomiting up what bowels I have left after last night? Keep your liquor in the name of all the devils, and leave me to myself!" and at one and the same instant he left off talking and began drinking; but as at the first sup he perceived it was water he did not care to go on with it, and begged Maritornes to fetch him some wine, which she did with right good will, and paid for it with her own money; for indeed they say of her that, though she was in that line of life, there was some faint and distant resemblance to a Christian about her. When Sancho had done drinking he dug his heels into his ass, and the gate of the inn being thrown open he passed out very well pleased at having paid nothing and carried his point, though it had been at the expense of his usual sureties, his shoulders. It is true that the innkeeper detained his alforjas in payment of what was owing to him, but Sancho took his departure in such a flurry that he never missed them. The innkeeper, as soon as he saw him off, wanted to bar the gate close, but the blanketers would not agree to it, for they were fellows who would not have cared two farthings for Don Quixote, even had he been really one of the knights-errant of the Round Table.

CHAPTER XVIII

IN WHICH IS RELATED THE DISCOURSE SANCHO PANZA HELD WITH HIS MASTER, DON QUIXOTE, AND OTHER ADVENTURES WORTH RELATING

Sancho reached his master so limp and faint that he could not urge on his beast. When Don Quixote saw the state he was in he said, "I have now come to the conclusion, good Sancho, that this castle or inn is beyond a doubt enchanted, because those who have so atrociously diverted themselves with thee, what can they be but phantoms or beings of another world? and I hold this confirmed by having noticed that when I was by the wall of the yard witnessing the acts of thy sad tragedy, it was out of my power to mount upon it, nor could I even dismount from Rocinante, because they no doubt had me enchanted; for I swear to thee by the faith of what I am that if I had been able to climb up or dismount, I would have avenged thee in such a way that those braggart thieves would have remembered their freak for ever, even though in so doing I knew that I contravened the laws of chivalry, which, as I have often told thee, do not permit a knight to lay hands on him who is not one, save in case of urgent and great necessity in defence of his own life and person."

"I would have avenged myself too if I could," said Sancho, "whether I had been dubbed knight or not, but I could not; though for my part I am persuaded those who amused themselves with me were not phantoms or enchanted men, as your worship says, but men of flesh and bone like ourselves; and they all had their names, for I heard them name them when they were tossing me, and one was called Pedro Martinez, and another Tenorio Hernandez, and the innkeeper, I heard, was called Juan Palomeque the Left-handed; so that, senor, your not being able to leap over the wall of the yard or dismount from your horse came of something else besides enchantments; and what I make out clearly from all this is, that these adventures we go seeking will in the end lead us into such misadventures that we shall not know which is our right foot; and that the best and wisest thing, according to my small wits, would be for us to return home, now that it is harvest-time, and attend to our business, and give over wandering from Zeca to Mecca and from pail to bucket, as the saying is."

"How little thou knowest about chivalry, Sancho," replied Don Quixote; "hold thy peace and have patience; the day will come when thou shalt see with thine own eyes what an honourable thing it is to wander in the pursuit of this calling; nay, tell me, what greater pleasure can there be in the world, or what delight can equal that of winning a battle, and triumphing over one's enemy? None, beyond all doubt."

"Very likely," answered Sancho, "though I do not know it; all I know is that since we have been knights-errant, or since your worship has been one (for I have no right to reckon myself one of so honourable a number) we have never won any battle except the one with the Biscayan, and even out of that your worship came with half an ear and half a helmet the less; and from that till now it has been all cudgellings and more cudgellings, cuffs and more cuffs, I getting the blanketing over and above, and falling in with enchanted persons on whom I cannot avenge myself so as to know what the delight, as your worship calls it, of conquering an enemy is like."

"That is what vexes me, and what ought to vex thee, Sancho," replied Don Quixote; "but henceforward I will endeavour to have at hand some sword made by such craft that no kind of enchantments can take effect upon him who carries it, and it is even possible that fortune may procure for me that which belonged to Amadis when he was called 'The Knight of the Burning Sword,' which was one of the best swords that ever knight in the world possessed, for, besides having the said virtue, it cut like a razor, and there was no armour, however strong and enchanted it might be, that could resist it."

"Such is my luck," said Sancho, "that even if that happened and your worship found some such sword, it would, like the balsam, turn out serviceable and good for dubbed knights only, and as for the squires, they might sup sorrow."

"Fear not that, Sancho," said Don Quixote: "Heaven will deal better by thee."

Thus talking, Don Quixote and his squire were going along, when, on the road they were following, Don Quixote perceived approaching them a large and thick cloud of dust, on seeing which he turned to Sancho and said:

"This is the day, Sancho, on which will be seen the boon my fortune is reserving for me; this, I say, is the day on which as much as on any other shall be displayed the might of my arm, and on which I shall do deeds that shall remain written in the book of fame for all ages to come. Seest thou that cloud of dust which rises yonder? Well, then, all that is churned up by a vast army composed of various and countless nations that comes marching there."

"According to that there must be two," said Sancho, "for on this opposite side also there rises just such another cloud of dust."

Don Quixote turned to look and found that it was true, and rejoicing exceedingly, he concluded that they were two armies about to engage and encounter in the midst of that broad plain; for at all times and seasons his fancy was full of the battles, enchantments, adventures, crazy feats, loves, and defiances that are recorded in the books of chivalry, and everything he said, thought, or did had reference to such things. Now the cloud of dust he had seen was raised by two great droves of sheep coming along the same road in opposite directions, which, because of the dust, did not become visible until they drew near, but Don Quixote asserted so positively that they were armies that Sancho was led to believe it and say, "Well, and what are we to do, senor?"

"What?" said Don Quixote: "give aid and assistance to the weak and those who need it; and thou must know, Sancho, that this which comes opposite to us is conducted and led by the mighty emperor Alifanfaron, lord of the great isle of Trapobana; this other that marches behind me is that of his enemy the king of the Garamantas, Pentapolin of the Bare Arm, for he always goes into battle with his right arm bare."

"But why are these two lords such enemies?"

"They are at enmity," replied Don Quixote, "because this Alifanfaron is a furious pagan and is in love with the daughter of Pentapolin, who is a very beautiful and moreover gracious lady, and a Christian, and her father is unwilling to bestow her upon the pagan king unless he first abandons the religion of his false prophet Mahomet, and adopts his own."

"By my beard," said Sancho, "but Pentapolin does quite right, and I will help him as much as I can."

"In that thou wilt do what is thy duty, Sancho," said Don Quixote; "for to engage in battles of this sort it is not requisite to be a dubbed knight."

"That I can well understand," answered Sancho; "but where shall we put this ass where we may be sure to find him after the fray is over? for I believe it has not been the custom so far to go into battle on a beast of this kind."

"That is true," said Don Quixote, "and what you had best do with him is to leave him to take his chance whether he be lost or not, for the horses we shall have when we come out victors will be so many that even Rocinante will run a risk of being changed for another. But attend to me and observe, for I wish to give thee some account of the chief knights who accompany these two armies; and that thou mayest the better see and mark, let us withdraw to that hillock which rises yonder, whence both armies may be seen."

They did so, and placed themselves on a rising ground from which the two droves that Don Quixote made armies of might have been plainly seen if the clouds of dust they raised had not obscured them and blinded the sight; nevertheless, seeing in his imagination what he did not see and what did not exist, he began thus in a loud voice:

"That knight whom thou seest yonder in yellow armour, who bears upon his shield a lion crowned crouching at the feet of a damsel, is the valiant Laurcalco, lord of the Silver Bridge; that one in armour with flowers of gold, who bears on his shield three crowns argent on an azure field, is the dreaded Micocolembo, grand duke of Quirocia; that other of gigantic frame, on his right hand, is the ever dauntless Brandabarbaran de Boliche, lord of the three Arabias, who for armour wears that serpent skin, and has for shield a gate which, according to tradition, is one of those of the temple that Samson brought to the ground when by his death he revenged himself upon his enemies. But turn thine eyes to the other side, and thou shalt see in front and in the van of this other army the ever victorious and never vanquished Timonel of Carcajona, prince of New Biscay, who comes in armour with arms quartered azure, vert, white, and yellow, and bears on his shield a cat or on a field tawny with a motto which says Miau, which is the beginning of the name of his lady, who according to report is the peerless Miaulina, daughter of the duke Alfeniquen of the Algarve; the other, who burdens and presses the loins of that powerful charger and bears arms white as snow and a shield blank and without any device, is a novice knight, a Frenchman by birth, Pierres Papin by name, lord of the baronies of Utrique; that other, who with iron-shod heels strikes the flanks of that nimble parti-coloured zebra, and for arms bears azure vair, is the mighty duke of Nerbia, Espartafilardo del Bosque, who bears for device on his shield an asparagus plant with a motto in Castilian that says, Rastrea mi suerte." And so he went on naming a number of knights of one squadron or the other out of his imagination, and to all he assigned off-hand their arms, colours, devices, and mottoes, carried away by the illusions of his unheard-of craze; and without a pause, he continued, "People of divers nations compose this squadron in front; here are those that drink of the sweet waters of the famous Xanthus, those that scour the woody Massilian plains, those that sift the pure fine gold of Arabia Felix, those that enjoy the famed cool banks of the crystal Thermodon, those that in many and various ways divert the streams of the golden Pactolus, the Numidians, faithless in their promises, the Persians renowned in archery, the Parthians and the Medes that fight as they fly, the Arabs that ever shift their dwellings, the Scythians as cruel as they are fair, the Ethiopians with pierced lips, and an infinity of other nations whose features I recognise and descry, though I cannot recall their names. In this other squadron there come those that drink of the crystal streams of the olive-bearing Betis, those that make smooth their countenances with the water of the ever rich and golden Tagus, those that rejoice in the fertilising flow of the divine Genil, those that roam the Tartesian plains abounding in pasture, those that take their pleasure in the Elysian meadows of Jerez, the rich Manchegans crowned with ruddy ears of corn, the wearers of iron, old relics of the Gothic race, those that bathe in the Pisuerga renowned for its gentle current, those that feed their herds along the spreading pastures of the winding Guadiana famed for its hidden course, those that tremble with the cold of the pineclad Pyrenees or the dazzling snows of the lofty Apennine; in a word, as many as all Europe includes and contains."

Good God! what a number of countries and nations he named! giving to each its proper attributes with marvellous readiness; brimful and saturated with what he had read in his lying books! Sancho Panza hung upon his words without speaking, and from time to time turned to try if he could see the knights and giants his master was describing, and as he could not make out one of them he said to him:

"Senor, devil take it if there's a sign of any man you talk of, knight or giant, in the whole thing; maybe it's all enchantment, like the phantoms last night."

"How canst thou say that!" answered Don Quixote; "dost thou not hear the neighing of the steeds, the braying of the trumpets, the roll of the drums?"

"I hear nothing but a great bleating of ewes and sheep," said Sancho; which was true, for by this time the two flocks had come close.

"The fear thou art in, Sancho," said Don Quixote, "prevents thee from seeing or hearing correctly, for one of the effects of fear is to derange the senses and make things appear different from what they are; if thou art in such fear, withdraw to one side and leave me to myself, for alone I suffice to bring victory to that side to which I shall give my aid;" and so saying he gave Rocinante the spur, and putting the lance in rest, shot down the slope like a thunderbolt.

Sancho shouted after him, crying, "Come back, Senor Don Quixote; I vow to God they are sheep and ewes you are charging! Come back! Unlucky the father that begot me! what madness is this! Look, there is no giant, nor knight, nor cats, nor arms, nor shields quartered or whole, nor vair azure or bedevilled. What are you about? Sinner that I am before God!" But not for all these entreaties did Don Quixote turn back; on the contrary he went on shouting out, "Ho, knights, ye who follow and fight under the banners of the valiant emperor Pentapolin of the Bare Arm, follow me all; ye shall see how easily I shall give him his revenge over his enemy Alifanfaron of the Trapobana."

So saying, he dashed into the midst of the squadron of ewes, and began spearing them with as much spirit and intrepidity as if he were transfixing mortal enemies in earnest. The shepherds and drovers accompanying the flock shouted to him to desist; seeing it was no use, they ungirt their slings and began to salute his ears with stones as big as one's fist. Don Quixote gave no heed to the stones, but, letting drive right and left kept saying:

"Where art thou, proud Alifanfaron? Come before me; I am a single knight who would fain prove thy prowess hand to hand, and make thee yield thy life a penalty for the wrong thou dost to the valiant Pentapolin Garamanta." Here came a sugar-plum from the brook that struck him on the side and buried a couple of ribs in his body. Feeling himself so smitten, he imagined himself slain or badly wounded for certain, and recollecting his liquor he drew out his flask, and putting it to his mouth began to pour the contents into his stomach; but ere he had succeeded in swallowing what seemed to him enough, there came another almond which struck him on the hand and on the flask so fairly that it smashed it to pieces, knocking three or four teeth and grinders out of his mouth in its course, and sorely crushing two fingers of his hand. Such was the force of the first blow and of the second, that the poor knight in spite of himself came down backwards off his horse. The shepherds came up, and felt sure they had killed him; so in all haste they collected their flock together, took up the dead beasts, of which there were more than seven, and made off without waiting to ascertain anything further.

All this time Sancho stood on the hill watching the crazy feats his master was performing, and tearing his beard and cursing the hour and the occasion when fortune had made him acquainted with him. Seeing him, then, brought to the ground, and that the shepherds had taken themselves off, he ran to him and found him in very bad case, though not unconscious; and said he:

"Did I not tell you to come back, Senor Don Quixote; and that what you were going to attack were not armies but droves of sheep?"

"That's how that thief of a sage, my enemy, can alter and falsify things," answered Don Quixote; "thou must know, Sancho, that it is a very easy matter for those of his sort to make us believe what they choose; and this malignant being who persecutes me, envious of the glory he knew I was to win in this battle, has turned the squadrons of the enemy into droves of sheep. At any rate, do this much, I beg of thee, Sancho, to undeceive thyself, and see that what I say is true; mount thy ass and follow them quietly, and thou shalt see that when they have gone some little distance from this they will return to their original shape and, ceasing to be sheep, become men in all respects as I described them to thee at first. But go not just yet, for I want thy help and assistance; come hither, and see how many of my teeth and grinders are missing, for I feel as if there was not one left in my mouth."

Sancho came so close that he almost put his eyes into his mouth; now just at that moment the balsam had acted on the stomach of Don Quixote, so, at the very instant when Sancho came to examine his mouth, he discharged all its contents with more force than a musket, and full into the beard of the compassionate squire.

"Holy Mary!" cried Sancho, "what is this that has happened me? Clearly this sinner is mortally wounded, as he vomits blood from the mouth;" but considering the matter a little more closely he perceived by the colour, taste, and smell, that it was not blood but the balsam from the flask which he had seen him drink; and he was taken with such a loathing that his stomach turned, and he vomited up his inside over his very master, and both were left in a precious state. Sancho ran to his ass to get something wherewith to clean himself, and relieve his master, out of his alforjas; but not finding them, he well-nigh took leave of his senses, and cursed himself anew, and in his heart resolved to quit his master and return home, even though he forfeited the wages of his service and all hopes of the promised island.

Don Quixote now rose, and putting his left hand to his mouth to keep his teeth from falling out altogether, with the other he laid hold of the bridle of Rocinante, who had never stirred from his master's side—so loyal and well-behaved was he—and betook himself to where the squire stood leaning over his ass with his hand to his cheek, like one in deep dejection. Seeing him in this mood, looking so sad, Don Quixote said to him:

"Bear in mind, Sancho, that one man is no more than another, unless he does more than another; all these tempests that fall upon us are signs that fair weather is coming shortly, and that things will go well with us, for it is impossible for good or evil to last for ever; and hence it follows that the evil having lasted long, the good must be now nigh at hand; so thou must not distress thyself at the misfortunes which happen to me, since thou hast no share in them."

"How have I not?" replied Sancho; "was he whom they blanketed yesterday perchance any other than my father's son? and the alforjas that are missing to-day with all my treasures, did they belong to any other but myself?"

"What! are the alforjas missing, Sancho?" said Don Quixote.

"Yes, they are missing," answered Sancho.

"In that case we have nothing to eat to-day," replied Don Quixote.

"It would be so," answered Sancho, "if there were none of the herbs your worship says you know in these meadows, those with which knights-errant as unlucky as your worship are wont to supply such-like shortcomings."

"For all that," answered Don Quixote, "I would rather have just now a quarter of bread, or a loaf and a couple of pilchards' heads, than all the herbs described by Dioscorides, even with Doctor Laguna's notes. Nevertheless, Sancho the Good, mount thy beast and come along with me, for God, who provides for all things, will not fail us (more especially when we are so active in his service as we are), since he fails not the midges of the air, nor the grubs of the earth, nor the tadpoles of the water, and is so merciful that he maketh his sun to rise on the good and on the evil, and sendeth rain on the unjust and on the just."

"Your worship would make a better preacher than knight-errant," said

Sancho.

"Knights-errant knew and ought to know everything, Sancho," said Don Quixote; "for there were knights-errant in former times as well qualified to deliver a sermon or discourse in the middle of an encampment, as if they had graduated in the University of Paris; whereby we may see that the lance has never blunted the pen, nor the pen the lance."

"Well, be it as your worship says," replied Sancho; "let us be off now and find some place of shelter for the night, and God grant it may be somewhere where there are no blankets, nor blanketeers, nor phantoms, nor enchanted Moors; for if there are, may the devil take the whole concern."

"Ask that of God, my son," said Don Quixote; "and do thou lead on where thou wilt, for this time I leave our lodging to thy choice; but reach me here thy hand, and feel with thy finger, and find out how many of my teeth and grinders are missing from this right side of the upper jaw, for it is there I feel the pain."

Sancho put in his fingers, and feeling about asked him, "How many grinders used your worship have on this side?"

"Four," replied Don Quixote, "besides the back-tooth, all whole and quite sound."

"Mind what you are saying, senor."

"I say four, if not five," answered Don Quixote, "for never in my life have I had tooth or grinder drawn, nor has any fallen out or been destroyed by any decay or rheum."

"Well, then," said Sancho, "in this lower side your worship has no more than two grinders and a half, and in the upper neither a half nor any at all, for it is all as smooth as the palm of my hand."

"Luckless that I am!" said Don Quixote, hearing the sad news his squire gave him; "I had rather they despoiled me of an arm, so it were not the sword-arm; for I tell thee, Sancho, a mouth without teeth is like a mill without a millstone, and a tooth is much more to be prized than a diamond; but we who profess the austere order of chivalry are liable to all this. Mount, friend, and lead the way, and I will follow thee at whatever pace thou wilt."

Sancho did as he bade him, and proceeded in the direction in which he thought he might find refuge without quitting the high road, which was there very much frequented. As they went along, then, at a slow pace—for the pain in Don Quixote's jaws kept him uneasy and ill-disposed for speed—Sancho thought it well to amuse and divert him by talk of some kind, and among the things he said to him was that which will be told in the following chapter.

CHAPTER XIX

OF THE SHREWD DISCOURSE WHICH SANCHO HELD WITH HIS MASTER, AND OF THE ADVENTURE THAT BEFELL HIM WITH A DEAD BODY, TOGETHER WITH OTHER NOTABLE OCCURRENCES

"It seems to me, senor, that all these mishaps that have befallen us of late have been without any doubt a punishment for the offence committed by your worship against the order of chivalry in not keeping the oath you made not to eat bread off a tablecloth or embrace the queen, and all the rest of it that your worship swore to observe until you had taken that helmet of Malandrino's, or whatever the Moor is called, for I do not very well remember."

"Thou art very right, Sancho," said Don Quixote, "but to tell the truth, it had escaped my memory; and likewise thou mayest rely upon it that the affair of the blanket happened to thee because of thy fault in not reminding me of it in time; but I will make amends, for there are ways of compounding for everything in the order of chivalry."

"Why! have I taken an oath of some sort, then?" said Sancho.

"It makes no matter that thou hast not taken an oath," said Don Quixote; "suffice it that I see thou art not quite clear of complicity; and whether or no, it will not be ill done to provide ourselves with a remedy."

"In that case," said Sancho, "mind that your worship does not forget this as you did the oath; perhaps the phantoms may take it into their heads to amuse themselves once more with me; or even with your worship if they see you so obstinate."

While engaged in this and other talk, night overtook them on the road before they had reached or discovered any place of shelter; and what made it still worse was that they were dying of hunger, for with the loss of the alforjas they had lost their entire larder and commissariat; and to complete the misfortune they met with an adventure which without any invention had really the appearance of one. It so happened that the night closed in somewhat darkly, but for all that they pushed on, Sancho feeling sure that as the road was the king's highway they might reasonably expect to find some inn within a league or two. Going along, then, in this way, the night dark, the squire hungry, the master sharp-set, they saw coming towards them on the road they were travelling a great number of lights which looked exactly like stars in motion. Sancho was taken aback at the sight of them, nor did Don Quixote altogether relish them: the one pulled up his ass by the halter, the other his hack by the bridle, and they stood still, watching anxiously to see what all this would turn out to be, and found that the lights were approaching them, and the nearer they came the greater they seemed, at which spectacle Sancho began to shake like a man dosed with mercury, and Don Quixote's hair stood on end; he, however, plucking up spirit a little, said:

"This, no doubt, Sancho, will be a most mighty and perilous adventure, in which it will be needful for me to put forth all my valour and resolution."

"Unlucky me!" answered Sancho; "if this adventure happens to be one of phantoms, as I am beginning to think it is, where shall I find the ribs to bear it?"

"Be they phantoms ever so much," said Don Quixote, "I will not permit them to touch a thread of thy garments; for if they played tricks with thee the time before, it was because I was unable to leap the walls of the yard; but now we are on a wide plain, where I shall be able to wield my sword as I please."

"And if they enchant and cripple you as they did the last time," said Sancho, "what difference will it make being on the open plain or not?"

"For all that," replied Don Quixote, "I entreat thee, Sancho, to keep a good heart, for experience will tell thee what mine is."

"I will, please God," answered Sancho, and the two retiring to one side of the road set themselves to observe closely what all these moving lights might be; and very soon afterwards they made out some twenty encamisados, all on horseback, with lighted torches in their hands, the awe-inspiring aspect of whom completely extinguished the courage of Sancho, who began to chatter with his teeth like one in the cold fit of an ague; and his heart sank and his teeth chattered still more when they perceived distinctly that behind them there came a litter covered over with black and followed by six more mounted figures in mourning down to the very feet of their mules—for they could perceive plainly they were not horses by the easy pace at which they went. And as the encamisados came along they muttered to themselves in a low plaintive tone. This strange spectacle at such an hour and in such a solitary place was quite enough to strike terror into Sancho's heart, and even into his master's; and (save in Don Quixote's case) did so, for all Sancho's resolution had now broken down. It was just the opposite with his master, whose imagination immediately conjured up all this to him vividly as one of the adventures of his books.

He took it into his head that the litter was a bier on which was borne some sorely wounded or slain knight, to avenge whom was a task reserved for him alone; and without any further reasoning he laid his lance in rest, fixed himself firmly in his saddle, and with gallant spirit and bearing took up his position in the middle of the road where the encamisados must of necessity pass; and as soon as he saw them near at hand he raised his voice and said:

"Halt, knights, or whosoever ye may be, and render me account of who ye are, whence ye come, where ye go, what it is ye carry upon that bier, for, to judge by appearances, either ye have done some wrong or some wrong has been done to you, and it is fitting and necessary that I should know, either that I may chastise you for the evil ye have done, or else that I may avenge you for the injury that has been inflicted upon you."

"We are in haste," answered one of the encamisados, "and the inn is far off, and we cannot stop to render you such an account as you demand;" and spurring his mule he moved on.

Don Quixote was mightily provoked by this answer, and seizing the mule by the bridle he said, "Halt, and be more mannerly, and render an account of what I have asked of you; else, take my defiance to combat, all of you."

The mule was shy, and was so frightened at her bridle being seized that rearing up she flung her rider to the ground over her haunches. An attendant who was on foot, seeing the encamisado fall, began to abuse Don Quixote, who now moved to anger, without any more ado, laying his lance in rest charged one of the men in mourning and brought him badly wounded to the ground, and as he wheeled round upon the others the agility with which he attacked and routed them was a sight to see, for it seemed just as if wings had that instant grown upon Rocinante, so lightly and proudly did he bear himself. The encamisados were all timid folk and unarmed, so they speedily made their escape from the fray and set off at a run across the plain with their lighted torches, looking exactly like maskers running on some gala or festival night. The mourners, too, enveloped and swathed in their skirts and gowns, were unable to bestir themselves, and so with entire safety to himself Don Quixote belaboured them all and drove them off against their will, for they all thought it was no man but a devil from hell come to carry away the dead body they had in the litter.

Sancho beheld all this in astonishment at the intrepidity of his lord, and said to himself, "Clearly this master of mine is as bold and valiant as he says he is."

A burning torch lay on the ground near the first man whom the mule had thrown, by the light of which Don Quixote perceived him, and coming up to him he presented the point of the lance to his face, calling on him to yield himself prisoner, or else he would kill him; to which the prostrate man replied, "I am prisoner enough as it is; I cannot stir, for one of my legs is broken: I entreat you, if you be a Christian gentleman, not to kill me, which will be committing grave sacrilege, for I am a licentiate and I hold first orders."

"Then what the devil brought you here, being a churchman?" said Don Quixote.

"What, senor?" said the other. "My bad luck."

"Then still worse awaits you," said Don Quixote, "if you do not satisfy me as to all I asked you at first."

"You shall be soon satisfied," said the licentiate; "you must know, then, that though just now I said I was a licentiate, I am only a bachelor, and my name is Alonzo Lopez; I am a native of Alcobendas, I come from the city of Baeza with eleven others, priests, the same who fled with the torches, and we are going to the city of Segovia accompanying a dead body which is in that litter, and is that of a gentleman who died in Baeza, where he was interred; and now, as I said, we are taking his bones to their burial-place, which is in Segovia, where he was born."

"And who killed him?" asked Don Quixote.

"God, by means of a malignant fever that took him," answered the bachelor.

"In that case," said Don Quixote, "the Lord has relieved me of the task of avenging his death had any other slain him; but, he who slew him having slain him, there is nothing for it but to be silent, and shrug one's shoulders; I should do the same were he to slay myself; and I would have your reverence know that I am a knight of La Mancha, Don Quixote by name, and it is my business and calling to roam the world righting wrongs and redressing injuries."

"I do not know how that about righting wrongs can be," said the bachelor, "for from straight you have made me crooked, leaving me with a broken leg that will never see itself straight again all the days of its life; and the injury you have redressed in my case has been to leave me injured in such a way that I shall remain injured for ever; and the height of misadventure it was to fall in with you who go in search of adventures."

"Things do not all happen in the same way," answered Don Quixote; "it all came, Sir Bachelor Alonzo Lopez, of your going, as you did, by night, dressed in those surplices, with lighted torches, praying, covered with mourning, so that naturally you looked like something evil and of the other world; and so I could not avoid doing my duty in attacking you, and I should have attacked you even had I known positively that you were the very devils of hell, for such I certainly believed and took you to be."

"As my fate has so willed it," said the bachelor, "I entreat you, sir knight-errant, whose errand has been such an evil one for me, to help me to get from under this mule that holds one of my legs caught between the stirrup and the saddle."

"I would have talked on till to-morrow," said Don Quixote; "how long were you going to wait before telling me of your distress?"

He at once called to Sancho, who, however, had no mind to come, as he was just then engaged in unloading a sumpter mule, well laden with provender, which these worthy gentlemen had brought with them. Sancho made a bag of his coat, and, getting together as much as he could, and as the bag would hold, he loaded his beast, and then hastened to obey his master's call, and helped him to remove the bachelor from under the mule; then putting him on her back he gave him the torch, and Don Quixote bade him follow the track of his companions, and beg pardon of them on his part for the wrong which he could not help doing them.

And said Sancho, "If by chance these gentlemen should want to know who was the hero that served them so, your worship may tell them that he is the famous Don Quixote of La Mancha, otherwise called the Knight of the Rueful Countenance."

The bachelor then took his departure.

I forgot to mention that before he did so he said to Don Quixote, "Remember that you stand excommunicated for having laid violent hands on a holy thing, juxta illud, si quis, suadente diabolo."

"I do not understand that Latin," answered Don Quixote, "but I know well I did not lay hands, only this pike; besides, I did not think I was committing an assault upon priests or things of the

Church, which, like a Catholic and faithful Christian as I am, I respect and revere, but upon phantoms and spectres of the other world; but even so, I remember how it fared with Cid Ruy Diaz when he broke the chair of the ambassador of that king before his Holiness the Pope, who excommunicated him for the same; and yet the good Roderick of Vivar bore himself that day like a very noble and valiant knight."

On hearing this the bachelor took his departure, as has been said, without making any reply; and Don Quixote asked Sancho what had induced him to call him the "Knight of the Rueful Countenance" more then than at any other time.

"I will tell you," answered Sancho; "it was because I have been looking at you for some time by the light of the torch held by that unfortunate, and verily your worship has got of late the most ill-favoured countenance I ever saw: it must be either owing to the fatigue of this combat, or else to the want of teeth and grinders."

"It is not that," replied Don Quixote, "but because the sage whose duty it will be to write the history of my achievements must have thought it proper that I should take some distinctive name as all knights of yore did; one being 'He of the Burning Sword,' another 'He of the Unicorn,' this one 'He of the Damsels,' that 'He of the Phoenix,' another 'The Knight of the Griffin,' and another 'He of the Death,' and by these names and designations they were known all the world round; and so I say that the sage aforesaid must have put it into your mouth and mind just now to call me 'The Knight of the Rueful Countenance,' as I intend to call myself from this day forward; and that the said name may fit me better, I mean, when the opportunity offers, to have a very rueful countenance painted on my shield."

"There is no occasion, senor, for wasting time or money on making that countenance," said Sancho; "for all that need be done is for your worship to show your own, face to face, to those who look at you, and without anything more, either image or shield, they will call you 'Him of the Rueful Countenance' and believe me I am telling you the truth, for I assure you, senor (and in good part be it said), hunger and the loss of your grinders have given you such an ill-favoured face that, as I say, the rueful picture may be very well spared."

Don Quixote laughed at Sancho's pleasantry; nevertheless he resolved to call himself by that name, and have his shield or buckler painted as he had devised.

Don Quixote would have looked to see whether the body in the litter were bones or not, but Sancho would not have it, saying:

"Senor, you have ended this perilous adventure more safely for yourself than any of those I have seen: perhaps these people, though beaten and routed, may bethink themselves that it is a single man that has beaten them, and feeling sore and ashamed of it may take heart and come in search of us and give us trouble enough. The ass is in proper trim, the mountains are near at hand, hunger presses, we have nothing more to do but make good our retreat, and, as the saying is, the dead to the grave and the living to the loaf."

And driving his ass before him he begged his master to follow, who, feeling that Sancho was right, did so without replying; and after proceeding some little distance between two hills they found themselves in a wide and retired valley, where they alighted, and Sancho unloaded his beast, and stretched upon the green grass, with hunger for sauce, they breakfasted, dined, lunched, and supped all at once, satisfying their appetites with more than one store of cold meat which the dead man's clerical gentlemen (who seldom put themselves on short allowance) had brought with them on their sumpter mule. But another piece of ill-luck befell them, which Sancho held the worst of all, and that was that they had no wine to drink, nor even water to moisten their lips; and as thirst tormented them, Sancho, observing that the meadow where they were was full of green and tender grass, said what will be told in the following chapter.

CHAPTER XX

OF THE UNEXAMPLED AND UNHEARD-OF ADVENTURE WHICH WAS ACHIEVED BY THE VALIANT DON QUIXOTE OF LA MANCHA WITH LESS PERIL THAN ANY EVER ACHIEVED BY ANY FAMOUS KNIGHT IN THE WORLD

"It cannot be, senor, but that this grass is a proof that there must be hard by some spring or brook to give it moisture, so it would be well to move a little farther on, that we may find some place where we may quench this terrible thirst that plagues us, which beyond a doubt is more distressing than hunger."

The advice seemed good to Don Quixote, and, he leading Rocinante by the bridle and Sancho the ass by the halter, after he had packed away upon him the remains of the supper, they advanced the meadow feeling their way, for the darkness of the night made it impossible to see anything; but they had not gone two hundred paces when a loud noise of water, as if falling from great rocks, struck their ears. The sound cheered them greatly; but halting to make out by listening from what quarter it came they heard unseasonably another noise which spoiled the satisfaction the sound of the water gave them, especially for Sancho, who was by nature timid and faint-hearted. They heard, I say, strokes falling with a measured beat, and a certain rattling of iron and chains that, together with the furious din of the water, would have struck terror into any heart but Don Quixote's. The night was, as has been said, dark, and they had happened to reach a spot in among some tall trees, whose leaves stirred by a gentle breeze made a low ominous sound; so that, what with the solitude, the place, the darkness, the noise of the water, and the rustling of the leaves, everything inspired awe and dread; more especially as they perceived that the strokes did not cease, nor the wind lull, nor morning approach; to all which might be added their ignorance as to where they were.

But Don Quixote, supported by his intrepid heart, leaped on Rocinante, and bracing his buckler on his arm, brought his pike to the slope, and said, "Friend Sancho, know that I by Heaven's will have been born in this our iron age to revive in it the age of gold, or the golden as it is called; I am he for whom perils, mighty achievements, and valiant deeds are reserved; I am, I say again, he who is to revive the Knights of the Round Table, the Twelve of France and the Nine Worthies; and he who is to consign to oblivion the Platirs, the Tablantes, the Olivantes and Tirantes, the Phoebuses and Belianises, with the whole herd of famous knights-errant of days gone by, performing in these in which I live such exploits, marvels, and feats of arms as shall obscure their brightest deeds. Thou dost mark well, faithful and trusty squire, the gloom of this night, its strange silence, the dull confused murmur of those trees, the awful sound of that water in quest of which we came, that seems as though it were precipitating and dashing itself down from the lofty mountains of the Moon, and that incessant hammering that wounds and pains our ears; which things all together and each of itself are enough to instil fear, dread, and dismay into the breast of Mars himself, much more into one not used to hazards and adventures of the kind. Well, then, all this that I put before thee is but an incentive and stimulant to my spirit, making my heart burst in my bosom through eagerness to engage in this adventure, arduous as it promises to be; therefore tighten Rocinante's girths a little, and God be with thee; wait for me here three days and no more, and if in that time I come not back, thou canst return to our village, and thence, to do me a favour and a service, thou wilt go to El Toboso, where thou shalt say to my incomparable lady Dulcinea that her captive knight hath died in attempting things that might make him worthy of being called hers."

When Sancho heard his master's words he began to weep in the most pathetic way, saying:

"Senor, I know not why your worship wants to attempt this so dreadful adventure; it is night now, no one sees us here, we can easily turn about and take ourselves out of danger, even if we don't drink for three days to come; and as there is no one to see us, all the less will there be anyone to set us down as cowards; besides, I have many a time heard the curate of our village, whom your worship knows well, preach that he who seeks danger perishes in it; so it is not right to tempt God by trying so tremendous a feat from which there can be no escape save by a miracle, and Heaven has performed enough of them for your worship in delivering you from being blanketed as I was, and bringing you out victorious and safe and sound from among all those enemies that were with the dead man; and if all this does not move or soften that hard heart, let this thought and reflection move it, that you will have hardly quitted this spot when from pure fear I shall yield my soul up to anyone that will take it. I left home and wife and children to come and serve your worship, trusting to do better and not worse; but as covetousness bursts the bag, it has rent my hopes asunder, for just as I had them highest about getting that wretched unlucky island your worship has so often promised me, I see that instead and in lieu of it you mean to desert me now in a place so far from human reach: for God's sake, master mine, deal not so unjustly by me, and if your worship will not entirely give up attempting this feat, at least put it off till morning, for by what the lore I learned when I was a shepherd tells me it cannot want three hours of dawn now, because the mouth of the Horn is overhead and makes midnight in the line of the left arm."

"How canst thou see, Sancho," said Don Quixote, "where it makes that line, or where this mouth or this occiput is that thou talkest of, when the night is so dark that there is not a star to be seen in the whole heaven?"

"That's true," said Sancho, "but fear has sharp eyes, and sees things underground, much more above in heavens; besides, there is good reason to show that it now wants but little of day."

"Let it want what it may," replied Don Quixote, "it shall not be said of me now or at any time that tears or entreaties turned me aside from doing what was in accordance with knightly usage; and so I beg of thee, Sancho, to hold thy peace, for God, who has put it into my heart to undertake now this so unexampled and terrible adventure, will take care to watch over my safety and console thy sorrow; what thou hast to do is to tighten Rocinante's girths well, and wait here, for I shall come back shortly, alive or dead."

Sancho perceiving it his master's final resolve, and how little his tears, counsels, and entreaties prevailed with him, determined to have recourse to his own ingenuity and compel him, if he could, to wait till daylight; and so, while tightening the girths of the horse, he quietly and without being felt, with his ass' halter tied both Rocinante's legs, so that when Don Quixote strove to go he was unable as the horse could only move by jumps. Seeing the success of his trick, Sancho Panza said:

"See there, senor! Heaven, moved by my tears and prayers, has so ordered it that Rocinante cannot stir; and if you will be obstinate, and spur and strike him, you will only provoke fortune, and kick, as they say, against the pricks."

Don Quixote at this grew desperate, but the more he drove his heels into the horse, the less he stirred him; and not having any suspicion of the tying, he was fain to resign himself and wait till daybreak or until Rocinante could move, firmly persuaded that all this came of something other than Sancho's ingenuity. So he said to him, "As it is so, Sancho, and as Rocinante cannot move, I am content to wait till dawn smiles upon us, even though I weep while it delays its coming."

"There is no need to weep," answered Sancho, "for I will amuse your worship by telling stories from this till daylight, unless indeed you like to dismount and lie down to sleep a little on the green grass after the fashion of knights-errant, so as to be fresher when day comes and the moment arrives for attempting this extraordinary adventure you are looking forward to."

"What art thou talking about dismounting or sleeping for?" said Don Quixote. "Am I, thinkest thou, one of those knights that take their rest in the presence of danger? Sleep thou who art born to sleep, or do as thou wilt, for I will act as I think most consistent with my character."

"Be not angry, master mine," replied Sancho, "I did not mean to say that;" and coming close to him he laid one hand on the pommel of the saddle and the other on the cantle so that he held his master's left thigh in his embrace, not daring to separate a finger's width from him; so much afraid was he of the strokes which still resounded with a regular beat. Don Quixote bade him tell some story to amuse him as he had proposed, to which Sancho replied that he would if his dread of what he heard would let him; "Still," said he, "I will strive to tell a story which, if I can manage to relate it, and nobody interferes with the telling, is the best of stories, and let your worship give me your attention, for here I begin. What was, was; and may the good that is to come be for all, and the evil for him who goes to look for it—your worship must know that the beginning the old folk used to put to their tales was not just as each one pleased; it was a maxim of Cato Zonzorino the Roman, that says 'the evil for him that goes to look for it,' and it comes as pat to the purpose now as ring to finger, to show that your worship should keep quiet and not go looking for evil in any quarter, and that we should go back by some other road, since nobody forces us to follow this in which so many terrors affright us."

"Go on with thy story, Sancho," said Don Quixote, "and leave the choice of our road to my care."

"I say then," continued Sancho, "that in a village of Estremadura there was a goat-shepherd—that is to say, one who tended goats—which shepherd or goatherd, as my story goes, was called Lope Ruiz, and this Lope Ruiz was in love with a shepherdess called Torralva, which shepherdess called Torralva was the daughter of a rich grazier, and this rich grazier-"

"If that is the way thou tellest thy tale, Sancho," said Don Quixote, "repeating twice all thou hast to say, thou wilt not have done these two days; go straight on with it, and tell it like a reasonable man, or else say nothing."

"Tales are always told in my country in the very way I am telling this," answered Sancho, "and I cannot tell it in any other, nor is it right of your worship to ask me to make new customs."

"Tell it as thou wilt," replied Don Quixote; "and as fate will have it that I cannot help listening to thee, go on."

"And so, lord of my soul," continued Sancho, as I have said, this shepherd was in love with Torralva the shepherdess, who was a wild buxom lass with something of the look of a man about her, for she had little moustaches; I fancy I see her now."

"Then you knew her?" said Don Quixote.

"I did not know her," said Sancho, "but he who told me the story said it was so true and certain that when I told it to another I might safely declare and swear I had seen it all myself. And so in course of time, the devil, who never sleeps and puts everything in confusion, contrived that the love the shepherd bore the shepherdess turned into hatred and ill-will, and the reason, according to evil tongues, was some little jealousy she caused him that crossed the line and trespassed on forbidden ground; and so much did the shepherd hate her from that time forward that, in order to escape from her, he determined to quit the country and go where he should never set eyes on her again. Torralva, when she found herself spurned by Lope, was immediately smitten with love for him, though she had never loved him before."

"That is the natural way of women," said Don Quixote, "to scorn the one that loves them, and love the one that hates them: go on, Sancho."

"It came to pass," said Sancho, "that the shepherd carried out his intention, and driving his goats before him took his way across the plains of Estremadura to pass over into the Kingdom of Portugal. Torralva, who knew of it, went after him, and on foot and barefoot followed him at a distance, with a pilgrim's staff in her hand and a scrip round her neck, in which she carried, it is said, a bit of looking-glass and a piece of a comb and some little pot or other of paint for her face; but let her carry what she did, I am not going to trouble myself to prove it; all I say is, that the shepherd, they say, came with his flock to cross over the river Guadiana, which was at that time swollen and almost overflowing its banks, and at the spot he came to there was neither ferry nor boat nor anyone to carry him or his flock to the other side, at which he was much vexed, for he perceived that Torralva was approaching and would give him great annoyance with her tears and entreaties; however, he went looking about so closely that he discovered a fisherman who had alongside of him a boat so small that it could only hold one person and one goat; but for all that he spoke to him and agreed with him to carry himself and his three hundred goats across. The fisherman got into the boat and carried one goat over; he came back and carried another over; he came back again, and again brought over another—let your worship keep count of the goats the fisherman is taking across, for if one escapes the memory there will be an end of the story, and it will be impossible to tell another word of it. To proceed, I must tell you the landing place on the other side was miry and slippery, and the fisherman lost a great deal of time in going and coming; still he returned for another goat, and another, and another."

"Take it for granted he brought them all across," said Don Quixote, "and don't keep going and coming in this way, or thou wilt not make an end of bringing them over this twelvemonth."

"How many have gone across so far?" said Sancho.

"How the devil do I know?" replied Don Quixote.

"There it is," said Sancho, "what I told you, that you must keep a good count; well then, by God, there is an end of the story, for there is no going any farther."

"How can that be?" said Don Quixote; "is it so essential to the story to know to a nicety the goats that have crossed over, that if there be a mistake of one in the reckoning, thou canst not go on with it?"

"No, senor, not a bit," replied Sancho; "for when I asked your worship to tell me how many goats had crossed, and you answered you did not know, at that very instant all I had to say passed away out of my memory, and, faith, there was much virtue in it, and entertainment."

"So, then," said Don Quixote, "the story has come to an end?"

"As much as my mother has," said Sancho.

"In truth," said Don Quixote, "thou hast told one of the rarest stories, tales, or histories, that anyone in the world could have imagined, and such a way of telling it and ending it was never seen nor will be in a lifetime; though I expected nothing else from thy excellent understanding. But I do not wonder, for perhaps those ceaseless strokes may have confused thy wits."

"All that may be," replied Sancho, "but I know that as to my story, all that can be said is that it ends there where the mistake in the count of the passage of the goats begins."

"Let it end where it will, well and good," said Don Quixote, "and let us see if Rocinante can go;" and again he spurred him, and again Rocinante made jumps and remained where he was, so well tied was he.

Just then, whether it was the cold of the morning that was now approaching, or that he had eaten something laxative at supper, or that it was only natural (as is most likely), Sancho felt a desire to do what no one could do for him; but so great was the fear that had penetrated his heart, he dared not separate himself from his master by as much as the black of his nail; to escape doing what he wanted was, however, also impossible; so what he did for peace's sake was to remove his right hand, which held the back of the saddle, and with it to untie gently and silently the running string which alone held up his breeches, so that on loosening it they at once fell down round his feet like fetters; he then raised his shirt as well as he could and bared his hind quarters, no slim ones. But, this accomplished, which he fancied was all he had to do to get out of this terrible strait and embarrassment, another still greater difficulty presented itself, for it seemed to him impossible to relieve himself without making some noise, and he ground his teeth and squeezed his shoulders together, holding his breath as much as he could; but in spite of his precautions he was unlucky enough after all to make a little noise, very different from that which was causing him so much fear.

Don Quixote, hearing it, said, "What noise is that, Sancho?"

"I don't know, senor," said he; "it must be something new, for adventures and misadventures never begin with a trifle." Once more he tried his luck, and succeeded so well, that without any further noise or disturbance he found himself relieved of the burden that had given him so much discomfort. But as Don Quixote's sense of smell was as acute as his hearing, and as Sancho was so closely linked with him that the fumes rose almost in a straight line, it could not be but that some should reach his nose, and as soon as they did he came to its relief by compressing it between his fingers, saying in a rather snuffing tone, "Sancho, it strikes me thou art in great fear."

"I am," answered Sancho; "but how does your worship perceive it now more than ever?"

"Because just now thou smellest stronger than ever, and not of ambergris," answered Don Quixote.

"Very likely," said Sancho, "but that's not my fault, but your worship's, for leading me about at unseasonable hours and at such unwonted paces."

"Then go back three or four, my friend," said Don Quixote, all the time with his fingers to his nose; "and for the future pay more attention to thy person and to what thou owest to mine; for it is my great familiarity with thee that has bred this contempt."

"I'll bet," replied Sancho, "that your worship thinks I have done something I ought not with my person."

"It makes it worse to stir it, friend Sancho," returned Don Quixote.

With this and other talk of the same sort master and man passed the night, till Sancho, perceiving that daybreak was coming on apace, very cautiously untied Rocinante and tied up his breeches. As soon as Rocinante found himself free, though by nature he was not at all mettlesome, he seemed to feel lively and began pawing—for as to capering, begging his pardon, he knew not what it meant. Don Quixote, then, observing that Rocinante could move, took it as a good sign and a signal that he should attempt the dread adventure. By this time day had fully broken and everything showed distinctly, and Don Quixote saw that he was among some tall trees, chestnuts, which cast a very deep shade; he perceived likewise that the sound of the strokes did not cease, but could not discover what caused it, and so without any further delay he let Rocinante feel the spur, and once more taking leave of Sancho, he told him to wait for him there three days at most, as he had said before, and if he should not have returned by that time, he might feel sure it had been God's will that he should end his days in that perilous adventure. He again repeated the message and commission with which he was to go on his behalf to his lady Dulcinea, and said he was not to be uneasy as to the payment of his services, for before leaving home he had made his will, in which he would find himself fully recompensed in the matter of wages in due proportion to the time he had served; but if God delivered him safe, sound, and unhurt out of that danger, he might look upon the promised island as much more than certain. Sancho began to weep afresh on again hearing the affecting words of his good master, and resolved to stay with him until the final issue and end of the business. From these tears and this honourable resolve of Sancho Panza's the author of this history infers that he must have been of good birth and at least an old Christian; and the feeling he displayed touched his but not so much as to make him show any weakness; on the contrary, hiding what he felt as well as he could, he began to move towards that quarter whence the sound of the water and of the strokes seemed to come.

Sancho followed him on foot, leading by the halter, as his custom was, his ass, his constant comrade in prosperity or adversity; and advancing some distance through the shady chestnut trees they came upon a little meadow at the foot of some high rocks, down which a mighty rush of water flung itself. At the foot of the rocks were some rudely constructed houses looking more like ruins than houses, from among which came, they perceived, the din and clatter of blows, which still continued without intermission. Rocinante took fright at the noise of the water and of the blows, but quieting him Don Quixote advanced step by step towards the houses, commending himself with all his heart to his lady, imploring her support in that dread pass and enterprise, and on the way commending himself to God, too, not to forget him. Sancho who never quitted his side, stretched his neck as far as he could and peered between the legs of Rocinante to see if he could now discover what it was that caused him such fear and apprehension. They went it might be a hundred paces farther, when on turning a corner the true cause, beyond the possibility of any mistake, of that dread-sounding and to them awe-inspiring noise that had kept them all the night in such fear and perplexity, appeared plain and obvious; and it was (if, reader, thou art not disgusted and disappointed) six fulling hammers which by their alternate strokes made all the din.

When Don Quixote perceived what it was, he was struck dumb and rigid from head to foot. Sancho glanced at him and saw him with his head bent down upon his breast in manifest mortification; and Don Quixote glanced at Sancho and saw him with his cheeks puffed out and his mouth full of laughter, and evidently ready to explode with it, and in spite of his vexation he could not help laughing at the sight of him; and when Sancho saw his master begin he let go so heartily that he had to hold his sides with both hands to keep himself from bursting with laughter. Four times he stopped, and as many times did his laughter break out afresh with the same violence as at first, whereat Don Quixote grew furious, above all when he heard him say mockingly, "Thou must know, friend Sancho, that of Heaven's will I was born in this our iron age to revive in it the golden or age of gold; I am he for whom are reserved perils, mighty achievements, valiant deeds;" and here he went on repeating the words that Don Quixote uttered the first time they heard the awful strokes.

Don Quixote, then, seeing that Sancho was turning him into ridicule, was so mortified and vexed that he lifted up his pike and smote him two such blows that if, instead of catching them on his shoulders, he had caught them on his head there would have been no wages to pay, unless indeed to his heirs. Sancho seeing that he was getting an awkward return in earnest for his jest, and fearing his master might carry it still further, said to him very humbly, "Calm yourself, sir, for by God I am only joking."

"Well, then, if you are joking I am not," replied Don Quixote. "Look here, my lively gentleman, if these, instead of being fulling hammers, had been some perilous adventure, have I not, think you, shown the courage required for the attempt and achievement? Am I, perchance, being, as I am, a gentleman, bound to know and distinguish sounds and tell whether they come from fulling mills or not; and that, when perhaps, as is the case, I have never in my life seen any as you have, low boor as you are, that have been born and bred among them? But turn me these six hammers into six giants, and bring them to beard me, one by one or all together, and if I do not knock them head over heels, then make what mockery you like of me."

"No more of that, senor," returned Sancho; "I own I went a little too far with the joke. But tell me, your worship, now that peace is made between us (and may God bring you out of all the adventures that may befall you as safe and sound as he has brought you out of this one), was it not a thing to laugh at, and is it not a good story, the great fear we were in?—at least that I was in; for as to your worship I see now that you neither know nor understand what either fear or dismay is."

"I do not deny," said Don Quixote, "that what happened to us may be worth laughing at, but it is not worth making a story about, for it is not everyone that is shrewd enough to hit the right point of a thing."

"At any rate," said Sancho, "your worship knew how to hit the right point with your pike, aiming at my head and hitting me on the shoulders, thanks be to God and my own smartness in dodging it. But let that pass; all will come out in the scouring; for I have heard say 'he loves thee well that makes thee weep;' and moreover that it is the way with great lords after any hard words they give a servant to give him a pair of breeches; though I do not know what they give after blows, unless it be that knights-errant after blows give islands, or kingdoms on the mainland."

"It may be on the dice," said Don Quixote, "that all thou sayest will come true; overlook the past, for thou art shrewd enough to know that our first movements are not in our own control; and one thing for the future bear in mind, that thou curb and restrain thy loquacity in my company; for in all the books of chivalry that I have read, and they are innumerable, I never met with a squire who talked so much to his lord as thou dost to thine; and in fact I feel it to be a great fault of thine and of mine: of thine, that thou hast so little respect for me; of mine, that I do not make myself more respected. There was Gandalin, the squire of Amadis of Gaul, that was Count of the Insula Firme, and we read of him that he always addressed his lord with his cap in his hand, his head bowed down and his body bent double, more turquesco. And then, what shall we say of Gasabal, the squire of Galaor, who was so silent that in order to indicate to us the greatness of his marvellous taciturnity his name is only once mentioned in the whole of that history, as long as it is truthful? From all I have said thou wilt gather, Sancho, that there must be a difference between master and man, between lord and lackey, between knight and squire: so that from this day forward in our intercourse we must observe more respect and take less liberties, for in whatever way I may be provoked with you it will be bad for the pitcher. The favours and benefits that I have promised you will come in due time, and if they do not your wages at least will not be lost, as I have already told you."

"All that your worship says is very well," said Sancho, "but I should like to know (in case the time of favours should not come, and it might be necessary to fall back upon wages) how much did the squire of a knight-errant get in those days, and did they agree by the month, or by the day like bricklayers?"

"I do not believe," replied Don Quixote, "that such squires were ever on wages, but were dependent on favour; and if I have now mentioned thine in the sealed will I have left at home, it was with a view to what may happen; for as yet I know not how chivalry will turn out in these wretched times of ours, and I do not wish my soul to suffer for trifles in the other world; for I would have thee know, Sancho, that in this there is no condition more hazardous than that of adventurers."

"That is true," said Sancho, "since the mere noise of the hammers of a fulling mill can disturb and disquiet the heart of such a valiant errant adventurer as your worship; but you may be sure I will not open my lips henceforward to make light of anything of your worship's, but only to honour you as my master and natural lord."

"By so doing," replied Don Quixote, "shalt thou live long on the face of the earth; for next to parents, masters are to be respected as though they were parents."

CHAPTER XXI

WHICH TREATS OF THE EXALTED ADVENTURE AND RICH PRIZE OF MAMBRINO'S HELMET, TOGETHER WITH OTHER THINGS THAT HAPPENED TO OUR INVINCIBLE KNIGHT

It now began to rain a little, and Sancho was for going into the fulling mills, but Don Quixote had taken such an abhorrence to them on account of the late joke that he would not enter them on any account; so turning aside to right they came upon another road, different from that which they had taken the night before. Shortly afterwards Don Quixote perceived a man on horseback who wore on his head something that shone like gold, and the moment he saw him he turned to Sancho and said:

"I think, Sancho, there is no proverb that is not true, all being maxims drawn from experience itself, the mother of all the sciences, especially that one that says, 'Where one door shuts, another opens.' I say so because if last night fortune shut the door of the adventure we were looking for against us, cheating us with the fulling mills, it now opens wide another one for another better and more certain adventure, and if I do not contrive to enter it, it will be my own fault, and I cannot lay it to my ignorance of fulling mills, or the darkness of the night. I say this because, if I mistake not, there comes towards us one who wears on his head the helmet of Mambrino, concerning which I took the oath thou rememberest."

"Mind what you say, your worship, and still more what you do," said Sancho, "for I don't want any more fulling mills to finish off fulling and knocking our senses out."

"The devil take thee, man," said Don Quixote; "what has a helmet to do with fulling mills?"

"I don't know," replied Sancho, "but, faith, if I might speak as I used, perhaps I could give such reasons that your worship would see you were mistaken in what you say."

"How can I be mistaken in what I say, unbelieving traitor?" returned Don Quixote; "tell me, seest thou not yonder knight coming towards us on a dappled grey steed, who has upon his head a helmet of gold?"

"What I see and make out," answered Sancho, "is only a man on a grey ass like my own, who has something that shines on his head."

"Well, that is the helmet of Mambrino," said Don Quixote; "stand to one side and leave me alone with him; thou shalt see how, without saying a word, to save time, I shall bring this adventure to an issue and possess myself of the helmet I have so longed for."

"I will take care to stand aside," said Sancho; "but God grant, I say once more, that it may be marjoram and not fulling mills."

"I have told thee, brother, on no account to mention those fulling mills to me again," said Don Quixote, "or I vow—and I say no more-I'll full the soul out of you."

Sancho held his peace in dread lest his master should carry out the vow he had hurled like a bowl at him.

The fact of the matter as regards the helmet, steed, and knight that Don Quixote saw, was this. In that neighbourhood there were two villages, one of them so small that it had neither apothecary's shop nor barber, which the other that was close to it had, so the barber of the larger served the smaller, and in it there was a sick man who required to be bled and another man who wanted to be shaved, and on this errand the barber was going, carrying with him a brass basin; but as luck would have it, as he was on the way it began to rain, and not to spoil his hat, which probably was a new one, he put the basin on his head, and being clean it glittered at half a league's distance. He rode upon a grey ass, as Sancho said, and this was what made it seem to Don Quixote to be a dapple-grey steed and a knight and a golden helmet; for everything he saw he made to fall in with his crazy chivalry and ill-errant notions; and when he saw the poor knight draw near, without entering into any parley with him, at Rocinante's top speed he bore down upon him with the pike pointed low, fully determined to run him through and through, and as he reached him, without checking the fury of his charge, he cried to him:

"Defend thyself, miserable being, or yield me of thine own accord that which is so reasonably my due."

The barber, who without any expectation or apprehension of it saw this apparition coming down upon him, had no other way of saving himself from the stroke of the lance but to let himself fall off his ass; and no sooner had he touched the ground than he sprang up more nimbly than a deer and sped away across the plain faster than the wind.

He left the basin on the ground, with which Don Quixote contented himself, saying that the pagan had shown his discretion and imitated the beaver, which finding itself pressed by the hunters bites and cuts off with its teeth that for which, by its natural instinct, it knows it is pursued.

He told Sancho to pick up the helmet, and he taking it in his hands said:

"By God the basin is a good one, and worth a real of eight if it is worth a maravedis," and handed it to his master, who immediately put it on his head, turning it round, now this way, now that, in search of fitment, and not finding it he said, "Clearly the pagan to whose measure this famous head-piece was first forged must have had a very large head; but the worst of it is half of it is wanting."

When Sancho heard him call the basin a headpiece he was unable to restrain his laughter, but remembering his master's wrath he checked himself in the midst of it.

"What art thou laughing at, Sancho?" said Don Quixote.

"I am laughing," said he, "to think of the great head the pagan must have had who owned this helmet, for it looks exactly like a regular barber's basin."

"Dost thou know what I suspect, Sancho?" said Don Quixote; "that this wonderful piece of this enchanted helmet must by some strange accident have come into the hands of some one who was unable to recognise or realise its value, and who, not knowing what he did, and seeing it to be of the purest gold, must have melted down one half for the sake of what it might be worth, and of the other made this which is like a barber's basin as thou sayest; but be it as it may, to me who recognise it, its transformation makes no difference, for I will set it to rights at the first village where there is a blacksmith, and in such style that that helmet the god of smithies forged for the god of battles shall not surpass it or even come up to it; and in the meantime I will wear it as well as I can, for something is better than nothing; all the more as it will be quite enough to protect me from any chance blow of a stone."

"That is," said Sancho, "if it is not shot with a sling as they were in the battle of the two armies, when they signed the cross on your worship's grinders and smashed the flask with that blessed draught that made me vomit my bowels up."

"It does not grieve me much to have lost it," said Don Quixote, "for thou knowest, Sancho, that I have the receipt in my memory."

"So have I," answered Sancho, "but if ever I make it, or try it again as long as I live, may this be my last hour; moreover, I have no intention of putting myself in the way of wanting it, for I mean, with all my five senses, to keep myself from being wounded or from wounding anyone: as to being blanketed again I say nothing, for it is hard to prevent mishaps of that sort, and if they come there is nothing for it but to squeeze our shoulders together, hold our breath, shut our eyes, and let ourselves go where luck and the blanket may send us."

"Thou art a bad Christian, Sancho," said Don Quixote on hearing this, "for once an injury has been done thee thou never forgettest it: but know that it is the part of noble and generous hearts not to attach importance to trifles. What lame leg hast thou got by it, what broken rib, what cracked head, that thou canst not forget that jest? For jest and sport it was, properly regarded, and had I not seen it in that light I would have returned and done more mischief in revenging thee than the Greeks did for the rape of Helen, who, if she were alive now, or if my Dulcinea had lived then, might depend upon it she would not be so famous for her beauty as she is;" and here he heaved a sigh and sent it aloft; and said Sancho, "Let it pass for a jest as it cannot be revenged in earnest, but I know what sort of jest and earnest it was, and I know it will never be rubbed out of my memory any more than off my shoulders. But putting that aside, will your worship tell me what are we to do with this dapple-grey steed that looks like a grey ass, which that Martino that your worship overthrew has left deserted here? for, from the way he took to his heels and bolted, he is not likely ever to come back for it; and by my beard but the grey is a good one."

"I have never been in the habit," said Don Quixote, "of taking spoil of those whom I vanquish, nor is it the practice of chivalry to take away their horses and leave them to go on foot, unless indeed it be that the victor have lost his own in the combat, in which case it is lawful to take that of the vanquished as a thing won in lawful war; therefore, Sancho, leave this horse, or ass, or whatever thou wilt have it to be; for when its owner sees us gone hence he will come back for it."

"God knows I should like to take it," returned Sancho, "or at least to change it for my own, which does not seem to me as good a one: verily the laws of chivalry are strict, since they cannot be stretched to let one ass be changed for another; I should like to know if I might at least change trappings."

"On that head I am not quite certain," answered Don Quixote, "and the matter being doubtful, pending better information, I say thou mayest change them, if so be thou hast urgent need of them."

"So urgent is it," answered Sancho, "that if they were for my own person I could not want them more;" and forthwith, fortified by this licence, he effected the mutatio capparum, rigging out his beast to the ninety-nines and making quite another thing of it. This done, they broke their fast on the remains of the spoils of war plundered from the sumpter mule, and drank of the brook that flowed from the fulling mills, without casting a look in that direction, in such loathing did they hold them for the alarm they had caused them; and, all anger and gloom removed, they mounted and, without taking any fixed road (not to fix upon any being the proper thing for true knights-errant), they set out, guided by Rocinante's will, which carried along with it that of his master, not to say that of the ass, which always followed him wherever he led, lovingly and sociably; nevertheless they returned to the high road, and pursued it at a venture without any other aim.

As they went along, then, in this way Sancho said to his master, "Senor, would your worship give me leave to speak a little to you? For since you laid that hard injunction of silence on me several things have gone to rot in my stomach, and I have now just one on the tip of my tongue that I don't want to be spoiled."

"Say, on, Sancho," said Don Quixote, "and be brief in thy discourse, for there is no pleasure in one that is long."

"Well then, senor," returned Sancho, "I say that for some days past I have been considering how little is got or gained by going in search of these adventures that your worship seeks in these wilds and cross-roads, where, even if the most perilous are victoriously achieved, there is no one to see or know of them, and so they must be left untold for ever, to the loss of your worship's object and the credit they deserve; therefore it seems to me it would be better (saving your worship's better judgment) if we were to go and serve some emperor or other great prince who may have some war on hand, in whose service your worship may prove the worth of your person, your great might, and greater understanding, on perceiving which the lord in whose service we may be will perforce have to reward us, each according to his merits; and there you will not be at a loss for some one to set down your achievements in writing so as to preserve their memory for ever. Of my own I say nothing, as they will not go beyond squirely limits, though I make bold to say that, if it be the practice in chivalry to write the achievements of squires, I think mine must not be left out."

"Thou speakest not amiss, Sancho," answered Don Quixote, "but before that point is reached it is requisite to roam the world, as it were on probation, seeking adventures, in order that, by achieving some, name and fame may be acquired, such that when he betakes himself to the court of some great monarch the knight may be already known by his deeds, and that the boys, the instant they see him enter the gate of the city, may all follow him and surround him, crying, 'This is the Knight of the Sun'-or the Serpent, or any other title under which he may have achieved great deeds. 'This,' they will say, 'is he who vanquished in single combat the gigantic Brocabruno of mighty strength; he who delivered the great Mameluke of Persia out of the long enchantment under which he had been for almost nine hundred years.' So from one to another they will go proclaiming his achievements; and presently at the tumult of the boys and the others the king of that kingdom will appear at the windows of his royal palace, and as soon as he beholds the knight, recognising him by his arms and the device on his shield, he will as a matter of course say, 'What ho! Forth all ye, the knights of my court, to receive the flower of chivalry who cometh hither!' At which command all will issue forth, and he himself, advancing half-way down the stairs, will embrace him closely, and salute him, kissing him on the cheek, and will then lead him to the queen's chamber, where the knight will find her with the princess her daughter, who will be one of the most beautiful and accomplished damsels that could with the utmost pains be discovered anywhere in the known world. Straightway it will come to pass that she will fix her eyes upon the knight and he his upon her, and each will seem to the other something more divine than human, and, without knowing how or why they will be taken and entangled in the inextricable toils of love, and sorely distressed in their hearts not to see any way of making their pains and sufferings known by speech. Thence they will lead him, no doubt, to some richly adorned chamber of the palace, where, having removed his armour, they will bring him a rich mantle of scarlet wherewith to robe himself, and if he looked noble in his armour he will look still more so in a doublet. When night comes he will sup with the king, queen, and princess; and all the time he will never take his eyes off her, stealing stealthy glances, unnoticed by those present, and she will do the same, and with equal cautiousness, being, as I have said, a damsel of great discretion. The tables being removed, suddenly through the door of the hall there will enter a hideous and diminutive dwarf followed by a fair dame, between two giants, who comes with a certain adventure, the work of an ancient sage; and he who shall achieve it shall be deemed the best knight in the world.

"The king will then command all those present to essay it, and none will bring it to an end and conclusion save the stranger knight, to the great enhancement of his fame, whereat the princess will be overjoyed and will esteem herself happy and fortunate in having fixed and placed her thoughts so high. And the best of it is that this king, or prince, or whatever he is, is engaged in a very bitter war with another as powerful as himself, and the stranger knight, after having been some days at his court, requests leave from him to go and serve him in the said war. The king will grant it very readily, and the knight will courteously kiss his hands for the favour done to him; and that night he will take leave of his lady the princess at the grating of the chamber where she sleeps, which looks upon a garden, and at which he has already many times conversed with her, the go-between and confidante in the matter being a damsel much trusted by the princess. He will sigh, she will swoon, the damsel will fetch water, much distressed because morning approaches, and for the honour of her lady he would not that they were discovered; at last the princess will come to herself and will present her white hands through the grating to the knight, who will kiss them a thousand and a thousand times, bathing them with his tears. It will be arranged between them how they are to inform each other of their good or evil fortunes, and the princess will entreat him to make his absence as short as possible, which he will promise to do with many oaths; once more he kisses her hands, and takes his leave in such grief that he is well-nigh ready to die. He betakes him thence to his chamber, flings himself on his bed, cannot sleep for sorrow at parting, rises early in the morning, goes to take leave of the king, queen, and princess, and, as he takes his leave of the pair, it is told him that the princess is indisposed and cannot receive a visit; the knight thinks it is from grief at his departure, his heart is pierced, and he is hardly able to keep from showing his pain. The confidante is present, observes all, goes to tell her mistress, who listens with tears and says that one of her greatest distresses is not knowing who this knight is, and whether he is of kingly lineage or not; the damsel assures her that so much courtesy, gentleness, and gallantry of bearing as her knight possesses could not exist in any save one who was royal and illustrious; her anxiety is thus relieved, and she strives to be of good cheer lest she should excite suspicion in her parents, and at the end of two days she appears in public. Meanwhile the knight has taken his departure; he fights in the war, conquers the king's enemy, wins many cities, triumphs in many battles, returns to the court, sees his lady where he was wont to see her, and it is agreed that he shall demand her in marriage of her parents as the reward of his services; the king is unwilling to give her, as he knows not who he is, but nevertheless, whether carried off or in whatever other way it may be, the princess comes to be his bride, and her father comes to regard it as very good fortune; for it so happens that this knight is proved to be the son of a valiant king of some kingdom, I know not what, for I fancy it is not likely to be on the map. The father dies, the princess inherits, and in two words the knight becomes king. And here comes in at once the bestowal of rewards upon his squire and all who have aided him in rising to so exalted a rank. He marries his squire to a damsel of the princess's, who will be, no doubt, the one who was confidante in their amour, and is daughter of a very great duke."

"That's what I want, and no mistake about it!" said Sancho. "That's what I'm waiting for; for all this, word for word, is in store for your worship under the title of the Knight of the Rueful Countenance."

"Thou needst not doubt it, Sancho," replied Don Quixote, "for in the same manner, and by the same steps as I have described here, knights-errant rise and have risen to be kings and emperors; all we want now is to find out what king, Christian or pagan, is at war and has a beautiful daughter; but there will be time enough to think of that, for, as I have told thee, fame must be won in other quarters before repairing to the court. There is another thing, too, that is wanting; for supposing we find a king who is at war and has a beautiful daughter, and that I have won incredible fame throughout the universe, I know not how it can be made out that I am of royal lineage, or even second cousin to an emperor; for the king will not be willing to give me his daughter in marriage unless he is first thoroughly satisfied on this point, however much my famous deeds may deserve it; so that by this deficiency I fear I shall lose what my arm has fairly earned. True it is I am a gentleman of known house, of estate and property, and entitled to the five hundred sueldos mulct; and it may be that the sage who shall write my history will so clear up my ancestry and pedigree that I may find myself fifth or sixth in descent from a king; for I would have thee know, Sancho, that there are two kinds of lineages in the world; some there be tracing and deriving their descent from kings and princes, whom time has reduced little by little until they end in a point like a pyramid upside down; and others who spring from the common herd and go on rising step by step until they come to be great lords; so that the difference is that the one were what they no longer are, and the others are what they formerly were not. And I may be of such that after investigation my origin may prove great and famous, with which the king, my father-in-law that is to be, ought to be satisfied; and should he not be, the princess will so love me that even though she well knew me to be the son of a water-carrier, she will take me for her lord and husband in spite of her father; if not, then it comes to seizing her and carrying her off where I please; for time or death will put an end to the wrath of her parents."

"It comes to this, too," said Sancho, "what some naughty people say, 'Never ask as a favour what thou canst take by force;' though it would fit better to say, 'A clear escape is better than good men's prayers.' I say so because if my lord the king, your worship's father-in-law, will not condescend to give you my lady the princess, there is nothing for it but, as your worship says, to seize her and transport her. But the mischief is that until peace is made and you come into the peaceful enjoyment of your kingdom, the poor squire is famishing as far as rewards go, unless it be that the confidante damsel that is to be his wife comes with the princess, and that with her he tides over his bad luck until Heaven otherwise orders things; for his master, I suppose, may as well give her to him at once for a lawful wife."

"Nobody can object to that," said Don Quixote.

"Then since that may be," said Sancho, "there is nothing for it but to commend ourselves to God, and let fortune take what course it will."

"God guide it according to my wishes and thy wants," said Don Quixote, "and mean be he who thinks himself mean."

"In God's name let him be so," said Sancho: "I am an old Christian, and to fit me for a count that's enough."

"And more than enough for thee," said Don Quixote; "and even wert thou not, it would make no difference, because I being the king can easily give thee nobility without purchase or service rendered by thee, for when I make thee a count, then thou art at once a gentleman; and they may say what they will, but by my faith they will have to call thee 'your lordship,' whether they like it or not."

"Not a doubt of it; and I'll know how to support the tittle," said Sancho.

"Title thou shouldst say, not tittle," said his master.

"So be it," answered Sancho. "I say I will know how to behave, for once in my life I was beadle of a brotherhood, and the beadle's gown sat so well on me that all said I looked as if I was to be steward of the same brotherhood. What will it be, then, when I put a duke's robe on my back, or dress myself in gold and pearls like a count? I believe they'll come a hundred leagues to see me."

"Thou wilt look well," said Don Quixote, "but thou must shave thy beard often, for thou hast it so thick and rough and unkempt, that if thou dost not shave it every second day at least, they will see what thou art at the distance of a musket shot."

"What more will it be," said Sancho, "than having a barber, and keeping him at wages in the house? and even if it be necessary, I will make him go behind me like a nobleman's equerry."

"Why, how dost thou know that noblemen have equerries behind them?" asked Don Quixote.

"I will tell you," answered Sancho. "Years ago I was for a month at the capital and there I saw taking the air a very small gentleman who they said was a very great man, and a man following him on horseback in every turn he took, just as if he was his tail. I asked why this man did not join the other man, instead of always going behind him; they answered me that he was his equerry, and that it was the custom with nobles to have such persons behind them, and ever since then I know it, for I have never forgotten it."

"Thou art right," said Don Quixote, "and in the same way thou mayest carry thy barber with thee, for customs did not come into use all together, nor were they all invented at once, and thou mayest be the first count to have a barber to follow him; and, indeed, shaving one's beard is a greater trust than saddling one's horse."

"Let the barber business be my look-out," said Sancho; "and your worship's be it to strive to become a king, and make me a count."

"So it shall be," answered Don Quixote, and raising his eyes he saw what will be told in the following chapter.

CHAPTER XXII

OF THE FREEDOM DON QUIXOTE CONFERRED ON SEVERAL UNFORTUNATES WHO AGAINST THEIR WILL WERE BEING CARRIED WHERE THEY HAD NO WISH TO GO

Cide Hamete Benengeli, the Arab and Manchegan author, relates in this most grave, high sounding, minute, delightful, and original history that after the discussion between the famous Don Quixote of La Mancha and his squire Sancho Panza which is set down at the end of chapter twenty-one, Don Quixote raised his eyes and saw coming along the road he was following some dozen men on foot strung together by the neck, like beads, on a great iron chain, and all with manacles on their hands. With them there came also two men on horseback and two on foot; those on horseback with wheel-lock muskets, those on foot with javelins and swords, and as soon as Sancho saw them he said:

"That is a chain of galley slaves, on the way to the galleys by force of the king's orders."

"How by force?" asked Don Quixote; "is it possible that the king uses force against anyone?"

"I do not say that," answered Sancho, "but that these are people condemned for their crimes to serve by force in the king's galleys."

"In fact," replied Don Quixote, "however it may be, these people are going where they are taking them by force, and not of their own will."

"Just so," said Sancho.

"Then if so," said Don Quixote, "here is a case for the exercise of my office, to put down force and to succour and help the wretched."

"Recollect, your worship," said Sancho, "Justice, which is the king himself, is not using force or doing wrong to such persons, but punishing them for their crimes."

The chain of galley slaves had by this time come up, and Don Quixote in very courteous language asked those who were in custody of it to be good enough to tell him the reason or reasons for which they were conducting these people in this manner. One of the guards on horseback answered that they were galley slaves belonging to his majesty, that they were going to the galleys, and that was all that was to be said and all he had any business to know.

"Nevertheless," replied Don Quixote, "I should like to know from each of them separately the reason of his misfortune;" to this he added more to the same effect to induce them to tell him what he wanted so civilly that the other mounted guard said to him:

"Though we have here the register and certificate of the sentence of every one of these wretches, this is no time to take them out or read them; come and ask themselves; they can tell if they choose, and they will, for these fellows take a pleasure in doing and talking about rascalities."

With this permission, which Don Quixote would have taken even had they not granted it, he approached the chain and asked the first for what offences he was now in such a sorry case.

He made answer that it was for being a lover.

"For that only?" replied Don Quixote; "why, if for being lovers they send people to the galleys I might have been rowing in them long ago."

"The love is not the sort your worship is thinking of," said the galley slave; "mine was that I loved a washerwoman's basket of clean linen so well, and held it so close in my embrace, that if the arm of the law had not forced it from me, I should never have let it go of my own will to this moment; I was caught in the act, there was no occasion for torture, the case was settled, they treated me to a hundred lashes on the back, and three years of gurapas besides, and that was the end of it."

"What are gurapas?" asked Don Quixote.

"Gurapas are galleys," answered the galley slave, who was a young man of about four-and-twenty, and said he was a native of Piedrahita.

Don Quixote asked the same question of the second, who made no reply, so downcast and melancholy was he; but the first answered for him, and said, "He, sir, goes as a canary, I mean as a musician and a singer."

"What!" said Don Quixote, "for being musicians and singers are people sent to the galleys too?"

"Yes, sir," answered the galley slave, "for there is nothing worse than singing under suffering."

"On the contrary, I have heard say," said Don Quixote, "that he who sings scares away his woes."

"Here it is the reverse," said the galley slave; "for he who sings once weeps all his life."

"I do not understand it," said Don Quixote; but one of the guards said to him, "Sir, to sing under suffering means with the non sancta fraternity to confess under torture; they put this sinner to the torture and he confessed his crime, which was being a cuatrero, that is a cattle-stealer, and on his confession they sentenced him to six years in the galleys, besides two hundred lashes that he has already had on the back; and he is always dejected and downcast because the other thieves that were left behind and that march here ill-treat, and snub, and jeer, and despise him for confessing and not having spirit enough to say nay; for, say they, 'nay' has no more letters in it than 'yea,' and a culprit is well off when life or death with him depends on his own tongue and not on that of witnesses or evidence; and to my thinking they are not very far out."

"And I think so too," answered Don Quixote; then passing on to the third he asked him what he had asked the others, and the man answered very readily and unconcernedly, "I am going for five years to their ladyships the gurapas for the want of ten ducats."

"I will give twenty with pleasure to get you out of that trouble," said Don Quixote.

"That," said the galley slave, "is like a man having money at sea when he is dying of hunger and has no way of buying what he wants; I say so because if at the right time I had had those twenty ducats that your worship now offers me, I would have greased the notary's pen and freshened up the attorney's wit with them, so that to-day I should be in the middle of the plaza of the Zocodover at Toledo, and not on this road coupled like a greyhound. But God is great; patience—there, that's enough of it."

Don Quixote passed on to the fourth, a man of venerable aspect with a white beard falling below his breast, who on hearing himself asked the reason of his being there began to weep without answering a word, but the fifth acted as his tongue and said, "This worthy man is going to the galleys for four years, after having gone the rounds in ceremony and on horseback."

"That means," said Sancho Panza, "as I take it, to have been exposed to shame in public."

"Just so," replied the galley slave, "and the offence for which they gave him that punishment was having been an ear-broker, nay body-broker; I mean, in short, that this gentleman goes as a pimp, and for having besides a certain touch of the sorcerer about him."

"If that touch had not been thrown in," said Don Quixote, "he would not deserve, for mere pimping, to row in the galleys, but rather to command and be admiral of them; for the office of pimp is no ordinary one, being the office of persons of discretion, one very necessary in a well-ordered state, and only to be exercised by persons of good birth; nay, there ought to be an inspector and overseer of them, as in other offices, and recognised number, as with the brokers on change; in this way many of the evils would be avoided which are caused by this office and calling being in the hands of stupid and ignorant people, such as women more or less silly, and pages and jesters of little standing and experience, who on the most urgent occasions, and when ingenuity of contrivance is needed, let the crumbs freeze on the way to their mouths, and know not which is their right hand. I should like to go farther, and give reasons to show that it is advisable to choose those who are to hold so necessary an office in the state, but this is not the fit place for it; some day I will expound the matter to some one able to see to and rectify it; all I say now is, that the additional fact of his being a sorcerer has removed the sorrow it gave me to see these white hairs and this venerable countenance in so painful a position on account of his being a pimp; though I know well there are no sorceries in the world that can move or compel the will as some simple folk fancy, for our will is free, nor is there herb or charm that can force it. All that certain silly women and quacks do is to turn men mad with potions and poisons, pretending that they have power to cause love, for, as I say, it is an impossibility to compel the will."

"It is true," said the good old man, "and indeed, sir, as far as the charge of sorcery goes I was not guilty; as to that of being a pimp I cannot deny it; but I never thought I was doing any harm by it, for my only object was that all the world should enjoy itself and live in peace and quiet, without quarrels or troubles; but my good intentions were unavailing to save me from going where I never expect to come back from, with this weight of years upon me and a urinary ailment that never gives me a moment's ease;" and again he fell to weeping as before, and such compassion did Sancho feel for him that he took out a real of four from his bosom and gave it to him in alms.

Don Quixote went on and asked another what his crime was, and the man answered with no less but rather much more sprightliness than the last one.

"I am here because I carried the joke too far with a couple of cousins of mine, and with a couple of other cousins who were none of mine; in short, I carried the joke so far with them all that it ended in such a complicated increase of kindred that no accountant could make it clear: it was all proved against me, I got no favour, I had no money, I was near having my neck stretched, they sentenced me to the galleys for six years, I accepted my fate, it is the punishment of my fault; I am a young man; let life only last, and with that all will come right. If you, sir, have anything wherewith to help the poor, God will repay it to you in heaven, and we on earth will take care in our petitions to him to pray for the life and health of your worship, that they may be as long and as good as your amiable appearance deserves."

This one was in the dress of a student, and one of the guards said he was a great talker and a very elegant Latin scholar.

Behind all these there came a man of thirty, a very personable fellow, except that when he looked, his eyes turned in a little one towards the other. He was bound differently from the rest, for he had to his leg a chain so long that it was wound all round his body, and two rings on his neck, one attached to the chain, the other to what they call a "keep-friend" or "friend's foot," from which hung two irons reaching to his waist with two manacles fixed to them in which his hands were secured by a big padlock, so that he could neither raise his hands to his mouth nor lower his head to his hands. Don Quixote asked why this man carried so many more chains than the others. The guard replied that it was because he alone had committed more crimes than all the rest put together, and was so daring and such a villain, that though they marched him in that fashion they did not feel sure of him, but were in dread of his making his escape.

"What crimes can he have committed," said Don Quixote, "if they have not deserved a heavier punishment than being sent to the galleys?"

"He goes for ten years," replied the guard, "which is the same thing as civil death, and all that need be said is that this good fellow is the famous Gines de Pasamonte, otherwise called Ginesillo de Parapilla."

"Gently, senor commissary," said the galley slave at this, "let us have no fixing of names or surnames; my name is Gines, not Ginesillo, and my family name is Pasamonte, not Parapilla as you say; let each one mind his own business, and he will be doing enough."

"Speak with less impertinence, master thief of extra measure," replied the commissary, "if you don't want me to make you hold your tongue in spite of your teeth."

"It is easy to see," returned the galley slave, "that man goes as God pleases, but some one shall know some day whether I am called Ginesillo de Parapilla or not."

"Don't they call you so, you liar?" said the guard.

"They do," returned Gines, "but I will make them give over calling me so, or I will be shaved, where, I only say behind my teeth. If you, sir, have anything to give us, give it to us at once, and God speed you, for you are becoming tiresome with all this inquisitiveness about the lives of others; if you want to know about mine, let me tell you I am Gines de Pasamonte, whose life is written by these fingers."

"He says true," said the commissary, "for he has himself written his story as grand as you please, and has left the book in the prison in pawn for two hundred reals."

"And I mean to take it out of pawn," said Gines, "though it were in for two hundred ducats."

"Is it so good?" said Don Quixote.

"So good is it," replied Gines, "that a fig for 'Lazarillo de Tormes,' and all of that kind that have been written, or shall be written compared with it: all I will say about it is that it deals with facts, and facts so neat and diverting that no lies could match them."

"And how is the book entitled?" asked Don Quixote.

"The 'Life of Gines de Pasamonte,'" replied the subject of it.

"And is it finished?" asked Don Quixote.

"How can it be finished," said the other, "when my life is not yet finished? All that is written is from my birth down to the point when they sent me to the galleys this last time."

"Then you have been there before?" said Don Quixote.

"In the service of God and the king I have been there for four years before now, and I know by this time what the biscuit and courbash are like," replied Gines; "and it is no great grievance to me to go back to them, for there I shall have time to finish my book; I have still many things left to say, and in the galleys of Spain there is more than enough leisure; though I do not want much for what I have to write, for I have it by heart."

"You seem a clever fellow," said Don Quixote.

"And an unfortunate one," replied Gines, "for misfortune always persecutes good wit."

"It persecutes rogues," said the commissary.

"I told you already to go gently, master commissary," said Pasamonte; "their lordships yonder never gave you that staff to ill-treat us wretches here, but to conduct and take us where his majesty orders you; if not, by the life of-never mind-; it may be that some day the stains made in the inn will come out in the scouring; let everyone hold his tongue and behave well and speak better; and now let us march on, for we have had quite enough of this entertainment."

The commissary lifted his staff to strike Pasamonte in return for his threats, but Don Quixote came between them, and begged him not to ill-use him, as it was not too much to allow one who had his hands tied to have his tongue a trifle free; and turning to the whole chain of them he said:

"From all you have told me, dear brethren, make out clearly that though they have punished you for your faults, the punishments you are about to endure do not give you much pleasure, and that you go to them very much against the grain and against your will, and that perhaps this one's want of courage under torture, that one's want of money, the other's want of advocacy, and lastly the perverted judgment of the judge may have been the cause of your ruin and of your failure to obtain the justice you had on your side. All which presents itself now to my mind, urging, persuading, and even compelling me to demonstrate in your case the purpose for which Heaven sent me into the world and caused me to make profession of the order of chivalry to which I belong, and the vow I took therein to give aid to those in need and under the oppression of the strong. But as I know that it is a mark of prudence not to do by foul means what may be done by fair, I will ask these gentlemen, the guards and commissary, to be so good as to release you and let you go in peace, as there will be no lack of others to serve the king under more favourable circumstances; for it seems to me a hard case to make slaves of those whom God and nature have made free. Moreover, sirs of the guard," added Don Quixote, "these poor fellows have done nothing to you; let each answer for his own sins yonder; there is a God in Heaven who will not forget to punish the wicked or reward the good; and it is not fitting that honest men should be the instruments of punishment to others, they being therein no way concerned. This request I make thus gently and quietly, that, if you comply with it, I may have reason for thanking you; and, if you will not voluntarily, this lance and sword together with the might of my arm shall compel you to comply with it by force."

"Nice nonsense!" said the commissary; "a fine piece of pleasantry he has come out with at last! He wants us to let the king's prisoners go, as if we had any authority to release them, or he to order us to do so! Go your way, sir, and good luck to you; put that basin straight that you've got on your head, and don't go looking for three feet on a cat."

"'Tis you that are the cat, rat, and rascal," replied Don Quixote, and acting on the word he fell upon him so suddenly that without giving him time to defend himself he brought him to the ground sorely wounded with a lance-thrust; and lucky it was for him that it was the one that had the musket. The other guards stood thunderstruck and amazed at this unexpected event, but recovering presence of mind, those on horseback seized their swords, and those on foot their javelins, and attacked Don Quixote, who was waiting for them with great calmness; and no doubt it would have gone badly with him if the galley slaves, seeing the chance before them of liberating themselves, had not effected it by contriving to break the chain on which they were strung. Such was the confusion, that the guards, now rushing at the galley slaves who were breaking loose, now to attack Don Quixote who was waiting for them, did nothing at all that was of any use. Sancho, on his part, gave a helping hand to release Gines de Pasamonte, who was the first to leap forth upon the plain free and unfettered, and who, attacking the prostrate commissary, took from him his sword and the musket, with which, aiming at one and levelling at another, he, without ever discharging it, drove every one of the guards off the field, for they took to flight, as well to escape Pasamonte's musket, as the showers of stones the now released galley slaves were raining upon them. Sancho was greatly grieved at the affair, because he anticipated that those who had fled would report the matter to the Holy Brotherhood, who at the summons of the alarm-bell would at once sally forth in quest of the offenders; and he said so to his master, and entreated him to leave the place at once, and go into hiding in the sierra that was close by.

"That is all very well," said Don Quixote, "but I know what must be done now;" and calling together all the galley slaves, who were now running riot, and had stripped the commissary to the skin, he collected them round him to hear what he had to say, and addressed them as follows: "To be grateful for benefits received is the part of persons of good birth, and one of the sins most offensive to God is ingratitude; I say so because, sirs, ye have already seen by manifest proof the benefit ye have received of me; in return for which I desire, and it is my good pleasure that, laden with that chain which I have taken off your necks, ye at once set out and proceed to the city of El Toboso, and there present yourselves before the lady Dulcinea del Toboso, and say to her that her knight, he of the Rueful Countenance, sends to commend himself to her; and that ye recount to her in full detail all the particulars of this notable adventure, up to the recovery of your longed-for liberty; and this done ye may go where ye will, and good fortune attend you."

Gines de Pasamonte made answer for all, saying, "That which you, sir, our deliverer, demand of us, is of all impossibilities the most impossible to comply with, because we cannot go together along the roads, but only singly and separate, and each one his own way, endeavouring to hide ourselves in the bowels of the earth to escape the Holy Brotherhood, which, no doubt, will come out in search of us. What your worship may do, and fairly do, is to change this service and tribute as regards the lady Dulcinea del Toboso for a certain quantity of ave-marias and credos which we will say for your worship's intention, and this is a condition that can be complied with by night as by day, running or resting, in peace or in war; but to imagine that we are going now to return to the flesh-pots of Egypt, I mean to take up our chain and set out for El Toboso, is to imagine that it is now night, though it is not yet ten in the morning, and to ask this of us is like asking pears of the elm tree."

"Then by all that's good," said Don Quixote (now stirred to wrath), "Don son of a bitch, Don Ginesillo de Paropillo, or whatever your name is, you will have to go yourself alone, with your tail between your legs and the whole chain on your back."

Pasamonte, who was anything but meek (being by this time thoroughly convinced that Don Quixote was not quite right in his head as he had committed such a vagary as to set them free), finding himself abused in this fashion, gave the wink to his companions, and falling back they began to shower stones on Don Quixote at such a rate that he was quite unable to protect himself with his buckler, and poor Rocinante no more heeded the spur than if he had been made of brass. Sancho planted himself behind his ass, and with him sheltered himself from the hailstorm that poured on both of them. Don Quixote was unable to shield himself so well but that more pebbles than I could count struck him full on the body with such force that they brought him to the ground; and the instant he fell the student pounced upon him, snatched the basin from his head, and with it struck three or four blows on his shoulders, and as many more on the ground, knocking it almost to pieces. They then stripped him of a jacket that he wore over his armour, and they would have stripped off his stockings if his greaves had not prevented them. From Sancho they took his coat, leaving him in his shirt-sleeves; and dividing among themselves the remaining spoils of the battle, they went each one his own way, more solicitous about keeping clear of the Holy Brotherhood they dreaded, than about burdening themselves with the chain, or going to present themselves before the lady Dulcinea del Toboso. The ass and Rocinante, Sancho and Don Quixote, were all that were left upon the spot; the ass with drooping head, serious, shaking his ears from time to time as if he thought the storm of stones that assailed them was not yet over; Rocinante stretched beside his master, for he too had been brought to the ground by a stone; Sancho stripped, and trembling with fear of the Holy Brotherhood; and Don Quixote fuming to find himself so served by the very persons for whom he had done so much.

CHAPTER XXIII

OF WHAT BEFELL DON QUIXOTE IN THE SIERRA MORENA, WHICH WAS ONE OF THE RAREST ADVENTURES RELATED IN THIS VERACIOUS HISTORY

Seeing himself served in this way, Don Quixote said to his squire, "I have always heard it said, Sancho, that to do good to boors is to throw water into the sea. If I had believed thy words, I should have avoided this trouble; but it is done now, it is only to have patience and take warning for the future."

"Your worship will take warning as much as I am a Turk," returned Sancho; "but, as you say this mischief might have been avoided if you had believed me, believe me now, and a still greater one will be avoided; for I tell you chivalry is of no account with the Holy Brotherhood, and they don't care two maravedis for all the knights-errant in the world; and I can tell you I fancy I hear their arrows whistling past my ears this minute."

"Thou art a coward by nature, Sancho," said Don Quixote, "but lest thou shouldst say I am obstinate, and that I never do as thou dost advise, this once I will take thy advice, and withdraw out of reach of that fury thou so dreadest; but it must be on one condition, that never, in life or in death, thou art to say to anyone that I retired or withdrew from this danger out of fear, but only in compliance with thy entreaties; for if thou sayest otherwise thou wilt lie therein, and from this time to that, and from that to this, I give thee lie, and say thou liest and wilt lie every time thou thinkest or sayest it; and answer me not again; for at the mere thought that I am withdrawing or retiring from any danger, above all from this, which does seem to carry some little shadow of fear with it, I am ready to take my stand here and await alone, not only that Holy Brotherhood you talk of and dread, but the brothers of the twelve tribes of Israel, and the Seven Maccabees, and Castor and Pollux, and all the brothers and brotherhoods in the world."

"Senor," replied Sancho, "to retire is not to flee, and there is no wisdom in waiting when danger outweighs hope, and it is the part of wise men to preserve themselves to-day for to-morrow, and not risk all in one day; and let me tell you, though I am a clown and a boor, I have got some notion of what they call safe conduct; so repent not of having taken my advice, but mount Rocinante if you can, and if not I will help you; and follow me, for my mother-wit tells me we have more need of legs than hands just now."

Don Quixote mounted without replying, and, Sancho leading the way on his ass, they entered the side of the Sierra Morena, which was close by, as it was Sancho's design to cross it entirely and come out again at El Viso or Almodovar del Campo, and hide for some days among its crags so as to escape the search of the Brotherhood should they come to look for them. He was encouraged in this by perceiving that the stock of provisions carried by the ass had come safe out of the fray with the galley slaves, a circumstance that he regarded as a miracle, seeing how they pillaged and ransacked.

That night they reached the very heart of the Sierra Morena, where it seemed prudent to Sancho to pass the night and even some days, at least as many as the stores he carried might last, and so they encamped between two rocks and among some cork trees; but fatal destiny, which, according to the opinion of those who have not the light of the true faith, directs, arranges, and settles everything in its own way, so ordered it that Gines de Pasamonte, the famous knave and thief who by the virtue and madness of Don Quixote had been released from the chain, driven by fear of the Holy Brotherhood, which he had good reason to dread, resolved to take hiding in the mountains; and his fate and fear led him to the same spot to which Don Quixote and Sancho Panza had been led by theirs, just in time to recognise them and leave them to fall asleep: and as the wicked are always ungrateful, and necessity leads to evildoing, and immediate advantage overcomes all considerations of the future, Gines, who was neither grateful nor well-principled, made up his mind to steal Sancho Panza's ass, not troubling himself about Rocinante, as being a prize that was no good either to pledge or sell. While Sancho slept he stole his ass, and before day dawned he was far out of reach.

Aurora made her appearance bringing gladness to the earth but sadness to Sancho Panza, for he found that his Dapple was missing, and seeing himself bereft of him he began the saddest and most doleful lament in the world, so loud that Don Quixote awoke at his exclamations and heard him saying, "O son of my bowels, born in my very house, my children's plaything, my wife's joy, the envy of my neighbours, relief of my burdens, and lastly, half supporter of myself, for with the six-and-twenty maravedis thou didst earn me daily I met half my charges."

Don Quixote, when he heard the lament and learned the cause, consoled Sancho with the best arguments he could, entreating him to be patient, and promising to give him a letter of exchange ordering three out of five ass-colts that he had at home to be given to him. Sancho took comfort at this, dried his tears, suppressed his sobs, and returned thanks for the kindness shown him by Don Quixote. He on his part was rejoiced to the heart on entering the mountains, as they seemed to him to be just the place for the adventures he was in quest of. They brought back to his memory the marvellous adventures that had befallen knights-errant in like solitudes and wilds, and he went along reflecting on these things, so absorbed and carried away by them that he had no thought for anything else.

Nor had Sancho any other care (now that he fancied he was travelling in a safe quarter) than to satisfy his appetite with such remains as were left of the clerical spoils, and so he marched behind his master laden with what Dapple used to carry, emptying the sack and packing his paunch, and so long as he could go that way, he would not have given a farthing to meet with another adventure.

While so engaged he raised his eyes and saw that his master had halted, and was trying with the point of his pike to lift some bulky object that lay upon the ground, on which he hastened to join him and help him if it were needful, and reached him just as with the point of the pike he was raising a saddle-pad with a valise attached to it, half or rather wholly rotten and torn; but so heavy were they that Sancho had to help to take them up, and his master directed him to see what the valise contained. Sancho did so with great alacrity, and though the valise was secured by a chain and padlock, from its torn and rotten condition he was able to see its contents, which were four shirts of fine holland, and other articles of linen no less curious than clean; and in a handkerchief he found a good lot of gold crowns, and as soon as he saw them he exclaimed:

"Blessed be all Heaven for sending us an adventure that is good for something!"

Searching further he found a little memorandum book richly bound; this Don Quixote asked of him, telling him to take the money and keep it for himself. Sancho kissed his hands for the favour, and cleared the valise of its linen, which he stowed away in the provision sack. Considering the whole matter, Don Quixote observed:

"It seems to me, Sancho—and it is impossible it can be otherwise-that some strayed traveller must have crossed this sierra and been attacked and slain by footpads, who brought him to this remote spot to bury him."

"That cannot be," answered Sancho, "because if they had been robbers they would not have left this money."

"Thou art right," said Don Quixote, "and I cannot guess or explain what this may mean; but stay; let us see if in this memorandum book there is anything written by which we may be able to trace out or discover what we want to know."

He opened it, and the first thing he found in it, written roughly but in a very good hand, was a sonnet, and reading it aloud that Sancho might hear it, he found that it ran as follows:

SONNET

>Or Love is lacking in intelligence,
>>Or to the height of cruelty attains,
>>Or else it is my doom to suffer pains
>
>Beyond the measure due to my offence.
>But if Love be a God, it follows thence
>>That he knows all, and certain it remains
>>No God loves cruelty; then who ordains
>
>This penance that enthrals while it torments?
>It were a falsehood, Chloe, thee to name;
>>Such evil with such goodness cannot live;
>
>And against Heaven I dare not charge the blame,
>>I only know it is my fate to die.
>>To him who knows not whence his malady
>
>A miracle alone a cure can give.

"There is nothing to be learned from that rhyme," said Sancho, "unless by that clue there's in it, one may draw out the ball of the whole matter."

"What clue is there?" said Don Quixote.

"I thought your worship spoke of a clue in it," said Sancho.

"I only said Chloe," replied Don Quixote; "and that no doubt, is the name of the lady of whom the author of the sonnet complains; and, faith, he must be a tolerable poet, or I know little of the craft."

"Then your worship understands rhyming too?"

"And better than thou thinkest," replied Don Quixote, "as thou shalt see when thou carriest a letter written in verse from beginning to end to my lady Dulcinea del Toboso, for I would have thee know, Sancho, that all or most of the knights-errant in days of yore were great troubadours and great musicians, for both of these accomplishments, or more properly speaking gifts, are the peculiar property of lovers-errant: true it is that the verses of the knights of old have more spirit than neatness in them."

"Read more, your worship," said Sancho, "and you will find something that will enlighten us."

Don Quixote turned the page and said, "This is prose and seems to be a letter."

"A correspondence letter, senor?"

"From the beginning it seems to be a love letter," replied Don Quixote.

"Then let your worship read it aloud," said Sancho, "for I am very fond of love matters."

"With all my heart," said Don Quixote, and reading it aloud as Sancho had requested him, he found it ran thus:

Thy false promise and my sure misfortune carry me to a place whence the news of my death will reach thy ears before the words of my complaint. Ungrateful one, thou hast rejected me for one more wealthy, but not more worthy; but if virtue were esteemed wealth I should neither envy the fortunes of others nor weep for misfortunes of my own. What thy beauty raised up thy deeds have laid low; by it I believed thee to be an angel, by them I know thou art a woman. Peace be with thee who hast sent war to me, and Heaven grant that the deceit of thy husband be ever hidden from thee, so that thou repent not of what thou hast done, and I reap not a revenge I would not have.

When he had finished the letter, Don Quixote said, "There is less to be gathered from this than from the verses, except that he who wrote it is some rejected lover;" and turning over nearly all the pages of the book he found more verses and letters, some of which he could read, while others he could not; but they were all made up of complaints, laments, misgivings, desires and aversions, favours and rejections, some rapturous, some doleful. While Don Quixote examined the book, Sancho examined the valise, not leaving a corner in the whole of it or in the pad that he did not search, peer into, and explore, or seam that he did not rip, or tuft of wool that he did not pick to pieces, lest anything should escape for want of care and pains; so keen was the covetousness excited in him by the discovery of the crowns, which amounted to near a hundred; and though he found no more booty, he held the blanket flights, balsam vomits, stake benedictions, carriers' fisticuffs, missing alforjas, stolen coat, and all the hunger, thirst, and weariness he had endured in the service of his good master, cheap at the price; as he considered himself more than fully indemnified for all by the payment he received in the gift of the treasure-trove.

The Knight of the Rueful Countenance was still very anxious to find out who the owner of the valise could be, conjecturing from the sonnet and letter, from the money in gold, and from the fineness of the shirts, that he must be some lover of distinction whom the scorn and cruelty of his lady had driven to some desperate course; but as in that uninhabited and rugged spot there was no one to be seen of whom he could inquire, he saw nothing else for it but to push on, taking whatever road Rocinante chose—which was where he could make his way—firmly persuaded that among these wilds he could not fail to meet some rare adventure. As he went along, then, occupied with these thoughts, he perceived on the summit of a height that rose before their eyes a man who went springing from rock to rock and from tussock to tussock with marvellous agility. As well as he could make out he was unclad, with a thick black beard, long tangled hair, and bare legs and feet, his thighs were covered by breeches apparently of tawny velvet but so ragged that they showed his skin in several places.

He was bareheaded, and notwithstanding the swiftness with which he passed as has been described, the Knight of the Rueful Countenance observed and noted all these trifles, and though he made the attempt, he was unable to follow him, for it was not granted to the feebleness of Rocinante to make way over such rough ground, he being, moreover, slow-paced and sluggish by nature. Don Quixote at once came to the conclusion that this was the owner of the saddle-pad and of the valise, and made up his mind to go in search of him, even though he should have to wander a year in those mountains before he found him, and so he directed Sancho to take a short cut over one side of the mountain, while he himself went by the other, and perhaps by this means they might light upon this man who had passed so quickly out of their sight.

"I could not do that," said Sancho, "for when I separate from your worship fear at once lays hold of me, and assails me with all sorts of panics and fancies; and let what I now say be a notice that from this time forth I am not going to stir a finger's width from your presence."

"It shall be so," said he of the Rueful Countenance, "and I am very glad that thou art willing to rely on my courage, which will never fail thee, even though the soul in thy body fail thee; so come on now behind me slowly as well as thou canst, and make lanterns of thine eyes; let us make the circuit of this ridge; perhaps we shall light upon this man that we saw, who no doubt is no other than the owner of what we found."

To which Sancho made answer, "Far better would it be not to look for him, for, if we find him, and he happens to be the owner of the money, it is plain I must restore it; it would be better, therefore, that without taking this needless trouble, I should keep possession of it until in some other less meddlesome and officious way the real owner may be discovered; and perhaps that will be when I shall have spent it, and then the king will hold me harmless."

"Thou art wrong there, Sancho," said Don Quixote, "for now that we have a suspicion who the owner is, and have him almost before us, we are bound to seek him and make restitution; and if we do not see him, the strong suspicion we have as to his being the owner makes us as guilty as if he were so; and so, friend Sancho, let not our search for him give thee any uneasiness, for if we find him it will relieve mine."

And so saying he gave Rocinante the spur, and Sancho followed him on foot and loaded, and after having partly made the circuit of the mountain they found lying in a ravine, dead and half devoured by dogs and pecked by jackdaws, a mule saddled and bridled, all which still further strengthened their suspicion that he who had fled was the owner of the mule and the saddle-pad.

As they stood looking at it they heard a whistle like that of a shepherd watching his flock, and suddenly on their left there appeared a great number of goats and behind them on the summit of the mountain the goatherd in charge of them, a man advanced in years. Don Quixote called aloud to him and begged him to come down to where they stood. He shouted in return, asking what had brought them to that spot, seldom or never trodden except by the feet of goats, or of the wolves and other wild beasts that roamed around. Sancho in return bade him come down, and they would explain all to him.

The goatherd descended, and reaching the place where Don Quixote stood, he said, "I will wager you are looking at that hack mule that lies dead in the hollow there, and, faith, it has been lying there now these six months; tell me, have you come upon its master about here?"

"We have come upon nobody," answered Don Quixote, "nor on anything except a saddle-pad and a little valise that we found not far from this."

"I found it too," said the goatherd, "but I would not lift it nor go near it for fear of some ill-luck or being charged with theft, for the devil is crafty, and things rise up under one's feet to make one fall without knowing why or wherefore."

"That's exactly what I say," said Sancho; "I found it too, and I would not go within a stone's throw of it; there I left it, and there it lies just as it was, for I don't want a dog with a bell."

"Tell me, good man," said Don Quixote, "do you know who is the owner of this property?"

"All I can tell you," said the goatherd, "is that about six months ago, more or less, there arrived at a shepherd's hut three leagues, perhaps, away from this, a youth of well-bred appearance and manners, mounted on that same mule which lies dead here, and with the same saddle-pad and valise which you say you found and did not touch. He asked us what part of this sierra was the most rugged and retired; we told him that it was where we now are; and so in truth it is, for if you push on half a league farther, perhaps you will not be able to find your way out; and I am wondering how you have managed to come here, for there is no road or path that leads to this spot. I say, then, that on hearing our answer the youth turned about and made for the place we pointed out to him, leaving us all charmed with his good looks, and wondering at his question and the haste with which we saw him depart in the direction of the sierra; and after that we saw him no more, until some days afterwards he crossed the path of one of our shepherds, and without saying a word to him, came up to him and gave him several cuffs and kicks, and then turned to the ass with our provisions and took all the bread and cheese it carried, and having done this made off back again into the sierra with extraordinary swiftness. When some of us goatherds learned this we went in search of him for about two days through the most remote portion of this sierra, at the end of which we found him lodged in the hollow of a large thick cork tree. He came out to meet us with great gentleness, with his dress now torn and his face so disfigured and burned by the sun, that we hardly recognised him but that his clothes, though torn, convinced us, from the recollection we had of them, that he was the person we were looking for. He saluted us courteously, and in a few well-spoken words he told us not to wonder at seeing him going about in this guise, as it was binding upon him in order that he might work out a penance which for his many sins had been imposed upon him. We asked him to tell us who he was, but we were never able to find out from him: we begged of him too, when he was in want of food, which he could not do without, to tell us where we should find him, as we would bring it to him with all good-will and readiness; or if this were not to his taste, at least to come and ask it of us and not take it by force from the shepherds. He thanked us for the offer, begged pardon for the late assault, and promised for the future to ask it in God's name without offering violence to anybody. As for fixed abode, he said he had no other than that which chance offered wherever night might overtake him; and his words ended in an outburst of weeping so bitter that we who listened to him must have been very stones had we not joined him in it, comparing what we saw of him the first time with what we saw now; for, as I said, he was a graceful and gracious youth, and in his courteous and polished language showed himself to be of good birth and courtly breeding, and rustics as we were that listened to him, even to our rusticity his gentle bearing sufficed to make it plain.

"But in the midst of his conversation he stopped and became silent, keeping his eyes fixed upon the ground for some time, during which we stood still waiting anxiously to see what would come of this abstraction; and with no little pity, for from his behaviour, now staring at the ground with fixed gaze and eyes wide open without moving an eyelid, again closing them, compressing his lips and raising his eyebrows, we could perceive plainly that a fit of madness of some kind had come upon him; and before long he showed that what we imagined was the truth, for he arose in a fury from the ground where he had thrown himself, and attacked the first he found near him with such rage and fierceness that if we had not dragged him off him, he would have beaten or bitten him to death, all the while exclaiming, 'Oh faithless Fernando, here, here shalt thou pay the penalty of the wrong thou hast done me; these hands shall tear out that heart of thine, abode and dwelling of all iniquity, but of deceit and fraud above all; and to these he added other words all in effect upbraiding this Fernando and charging him with treachery and faithlessness.

"We forced him to release his hold with no little difficulty, and without another word he left us, and rushing off plunged in among these brakes and brambles, so as to make it impossible for us to follow him; from this we suppose that madness comes upon him from time to time, and that some one called Fernando must have done him a wrong of a grievous nature such as the condition to which it had brought him seemed to show. All this has been since then confirmed on those occasions, and they have been many, on which he has crossed our path, at one time to beg the shepherds to give him some of the food they carry, at another to take it from them by force; for when there is a fit of madness upon him, even though the shepherds offer it freely, he will not accept it but snatches it from them by dint of blows; but when he is in his senses he begs it for the love of God, courteously and civilly, and receives it with many thanks and not a few tears. And to tell you the truth, sirs," continued the goatherd, "it was yesterday that we resolved, I and four of the lads, two of them our servants, and the other two friends of mine, to go in search of him until we find him, and when we do to take him, whether by force or of his own consent, to the town of Almodovar, which is eight leagues from this, and there strive to cure him (if indeed his malady admits of a cure), or learn when he is in his senses who he is, and if he has relatives to whom we may give notice of his misfortune. This, sirs, is all I can say in answer to what you have asked me; and be sure that the owner of the articles you found is he whom you saw pass by with such nimbleness and so naked."

For Don Quixote had already described how he had seen the man go bounding along the mountain side, and he was now filled with amazement at what he heard from the goatherd, and more eager than ever to discover who the unhappy madman was; and in his heart he resolved, as he had done before, to search for him all over the mountain, not leaving a corner or cave unexamined until he had found him. But chance arranged matters better than he expected or hoped, for at that very moment, in a gorge on the mountain that opened where they stood, the youth he wished to find made his appearance, coming along talking to himself in a way that would have been unintelligible near at hand, much more at a distance. His garb was what has been described, save that as he drew near, Don Quixote perceived that a tattered doublet which he wore was amber-tanned, from which he concluded that one who wore such garments could not be of very low rank.

Approaching them, the youth greeted them in a harsh and hoarse voice but with great courtesy. Don Quixote returned his salutation with equal politeness, and dismounting from Rocinante advanced with well-bred bearing and grace to embrace him, and held him for some time close in his arms as if he had known him for a long time. The other, whom we may call the Ragged One of the Sorry Countenance, as Don Quixote was of the Rueful, after submitting to the embrace pushed him back a little and, placing his hands on Don Quixote's shoulders, stood gazing at him as if seeking to see whether he knew him, not less amazed, perhaps, at the sight of the face, figure, and armour of Don Quixote than Don Quixote was at the sight of him. To be brief, the first to speak after embracing was the Ragged One, and he said what will be told farther on.

CHAPTER XXIV

IN WHICH IS CONTINUED THE ADVENTURE OF THE SIERRA MORENA

The history relates that it was with the greatest attention Don Quixote listened to the ragged knight of the Sierra, who began by saying:

"Of a surety, senor, whoever you are, for I know you not, I thank you for the proofs of kindness and courtesy you have shown me, and would I were in a condition to requite with something more than good-will that which you have displayed towards me in the cordial reception you have given me; but my fate does not afford me any other means of returning kindnesses done me save the hearty desire to repay them."

"Mine," replied Don Quixote, "is to be of service to you, so much so that I had resolved not to quit these mountains until I had found you, and learned of you whether there is any kind of relief to be found for that sorrow under which from the strangeness of your life you seem to labour; and to search for you with all possible diligence, if search had been necessary. And if your misfortune should prove to be one of those that refuse admission to any sort of consolation, it was my purpose to join you in lamenting and mourning over it, so far as I could; for it is still some comfort in misfortune to find one who can feel for it. And if my good intentions deserve to be acknowledged with any kind of courtesy, I entreat you, senor, by that which I perceive you possess in so high a degree, and likewise conjure you by whatever you love or have loved best in life, to tell me who you are and the cause that has brought you to live or die in these solitudes like a brute beast, dwelling among them in a manner so foreign to your condition as your garb and appearance show. And I swear," added Don Quixote, "by the order of knighthood which I have received, and by my vocation of knight-errant, if you gratify me in this, to serve you with all the zeal my calling demands of me, either in relieving your misfortune if it admits of relief, or in joining you in lamenting it as I promised to do."

The Knight of the Thicket, hearing him of the Rueful Countenance talk in this strain, did nothing but stare at him, and stare at him again, and again survey him from head to foot; and when he had thoroughly examined him, he said to him:

"If you have anything to give me to eat, for God's sake give it me, and after I have eaten I will do all you ask in acknowledgment of the goodwill you have displayed towards me."

Sancho from his sack, and the goatherd from his pouch, furnished the Ragged One with the means of appeasing his hunger, and what they gave him he ate like a half-witted being, so hastily that he took no time between mouthfuls, gorging rather than swallowing; and while he ate neither he nor they who observed him uttered a word. As soon as he had done he made signs to them to follow him, which they did, and he led them to a green plot which lay a little farther off round the corner of a rock. On reaching it he stretched himself upon the grass, and the others did the same, all keeping silence, until the Ragged One, settling himself in his place, said:

"If it is your wish, sirs, that I should disclose in a few words the surpassing extent of my misfortunes, you must promise not to break the thread of my sad story with any question or other interruption, for the instant you do so the tale I tell will come to an end."

These words of the Ragged One reminded Don Quixote of the tale his squire had told him, when he failed to keep count of the goats that had crossed the river and the story remained unfinished; but to return to the Ragged One, he went on to say:

"I give you this warning because I wish to pass briefly over the story of my misfortunes, for recalling them to memory only serves to add fresh ones, and the less you question me the sooner shall I make an end of the recital, though I shall not omit to relate anything of importance in order fully to satisfy your curiosity."

Don Quixote gave the promise for himself and the others, and with this assurance he began as follows:

"My name is Cardenio, my birthplace one of the best cities of this Andalusia, my family noble, my parents rich, my misfortune so great that my parents must have wept and my family grieved over it without being able by their wealth to lighten it; for the gifts of fortune can do little to relieve reverses sent by Heaven. In that same country there was a heaven in which love had placed all the glory I could desire; such was the beauty of Luscinda, a damsel as noble and as rich as I, but of happier fortunes, and of less firmness than was due to so worthy a passion as mine. This Luscinda I loved, worshipped, and adored from my earliest and tenderest years, and she loved me in all the innocence and sincerity of childhood. Our parents were aware of our feelings, and were not sorry to perceive them, for they saw clearly that as they ripened they must lead at last to a marriage between us, a thing that seemed almost prearranged by the equality of our families and wealth. We grew up, and with our growth grew the love between us, so that the father of Luscinda felt bound for propriety's sake to refuse me admission to his house, in this perhaps imitating the parents of that Thisbe so celebrated by the poets, and this refusal but added love to love and flame to flame; for though they enforced silence upon our tongues they could not impose it upon our pens, which can make known the heart's secrets to a loved one more freely than tongues; for many a time the presence of the object of love shakes the firmest will and strikes dumb the boldest tongue. Ah heavens! how many letters did I write her, and how many dainty modest replies did I receive! how many ditties and love-songs did I compose in which my heart declared and made known its feelings, described its ardent longings, revelled in its recollections and dallied with its desires! At length growing impatient and feeling my heart languishing with longing to see her, I resolved to put into execution and carry out what seemed to me the best mode of winning my desired and merited reward, to ask her of her father for my lawful wife, which I did. To this his answer was that he thanked me for the disposition I showed to do honour to him and to regard myself as honoured by the bestowal of his treasure; but that as my father was alive it was his by right to make this demand, for if it were not in accordance with his full will and pleasure, Luscinda was not to be taken or given by stealth. I thanked him for his kindness, reflecting that there was reason in what he said, and that my father would assent to it as soon as I should tell him, and with that view I went the very same instant to let him know what my desires were. When I entered the room where he was I found him with an open letter in his hand, which, before I could utter a word, he gave me, saying, 'By this letter thou wilt see, Cardenio, the disposition the Duke Ricardo has to serve thee.' This Duke Ricardo, as you, sirs, probably know already, is a grandee of Spain who has his seat in the best part of this Andalusia. I took and read the letter, which was couched in terms so flattering that even I myself felt it would be wrong in my father not to comply with the request the duke made in it, which was that he would send me immediately to him, as he wished me to become the companion, not servant, of his eldest son, and would take upon himself the charge of placing me in a position corresponding to the esteem in which he held me. On reading the letter my voice failed me, and still more when I heard my father say, 'Two days hence thou wilt depart, Cardenio, in accordance with the duke's wish, and give thanks to God who is opening a road to thee by which thou mayest attain what I know thou dost deserve; and to these words he added others of fatherly counsel. The time for my departure arrived; I spoke one night to

Luscinda, I told her all that had occurred, as I did also to her father, entreating him to allow some delay, and to defer the disposal of her hand until I should see what the Duke Ricardo sought of me: he gave me the promise, and she confirmed it with vows and swoonings unnumbered. Finally, I presented myself to the duke, and was received and treated by him so kindly that very soon envy began to do its work, the old servants growing envious of me, and regarding the duke's inclination to show me favour as an injury to themselves. But the one to whom my arrival gave the greatest pleasure was the duke's second son, Fernando by name, a gallant youth, of noble, generous, and amorous disposition, who very soon made so intimate a friend of me that it was remarked by everybody; for though the elder was attached to me, and showed me kindness, he did not carry his affectionate treatment to the same length as Don Fernando. It so happened, then, that as between friends no secret remains unshared, and as the favour I enjoyed with Don Fernando had grown into friendship, he made all his thoughts known to me, and in particular a love affair which troubled his mind a little. He was deeply in love with a peasant girl, a vassal of his father's, the daughter of wealthy parents, and herself so beautiful, modest, discreet, and virtuous, that no one who knew her was able to decide in which of these respects she was most highly gifted or most excelled. The attractions of the fair peasant raised the passion of Don Fernando to such a point that, in order to gain his object and overcome her virtuous resolutions, he determined to pledge his word to her to become her husband, for to attempt it in any other way was to attempt an impossibility. Bound to him as I was by friendship, I strove by the best arguments and the most forcible examples I could think of to restrain and dissuade him from such a course; but perceiving I produced no effect I resolved to make the Duke Ricardo, his father, acquainted with the matter; but Don Fernando, being sharp-witted and shrewd, foresaw and apprehended this, perceiving that by my duty as a good servant I was bound not to keep concealed a thing so much opposed to the honour of my lord the duke; and so, to mislead and deceive me, he told me he could find no better way of effacing from his mind the beauty that so enslaved him than by absenting himself for some months, and that he wished the absence to be effected by our going, both of us, to my father's house under the pretence, which he would make to the duke, of going to see and buy some fine horses that there were in my city, which produces the best in the world. When I heard him say so, even if his resolution had not been so good a one I should have hailed it as one of the happiest that could be imagined, prompted by my affection, seeing what a favourable chance and opportunity it offered me of returning to see my Luscinda. With this thought and wish I commended his idea and encouraged his design, advising him to put it into execution as quickly as possible, as, in truth, absence produced its effect in spite of the most deeply rooted feelings. But, as afterwards appeared, when he said this to me he had already enjoyed the peasant girl under the title of husband, and was waiting for an opportunity of making it known with safety to himself, being in dread of what his father the duke would do when he came to know of his folly. It happened, then, that as with young men love is for the most part nothing more than appetite, which, as its final object is enjoyment, comes to an end on obtaining it, and that which seemed to be love takes to flight, as it cannot pass the limit fixed by nature, which fixes no limit to true love—what I mean is that after Don Fernando had enjoyed this peasant girl his passion subsided and his eagerness cooled, and if at first he feigned a wish to absent himself in order to cure his love, he was now in reality anxious to go to avoid keeping his promise.

"The duke gave him permission, and ordered me to accompany him; we arrived at my city, and my father gave him the reception due to his rank; I saw Luscinda without delay, and, though it had not been dead or deadened, my love gathered fresh life. To my sorrow I told the story of it to Don Fernando, for I thought that in virtue of the great friendship he bore me I was bound to conceal nothing from him. I extolled her beauty, her gaiety, her wit, so warmly, that my praises excited in him a desire to see a damsel adorned by such attractions. To my misfortune I yielded to it, showing her to him one night by the light of a taper at a window where we used to talk to one another. As she appeared to him in her dressing-gown, she drove all the beauties he had seen until then out of his recollection; speech failed him, his head turned, he was spell-bound, and in the end love-smitten, as you will see in the course of the story of my misfortune; and to inflame still further his passion, which he hid from me and revealed to Heaven alone, it so happened that one day he found a note of hers entreating me to demand her of her father in marriage, so delicate, so modest, and so tender, that on reading it he told me that in Luscinda alone were combined all the charms of beauty and understanding that were distributed among all the other women in the world. It is true, and I own it now, that though I knew what good cause Don Fernando had to praise Luscinda, it gave me uneasiness to hear these praises from his mouth, and I began to fear, and with reason to feel distrust of him, for there was no moment when he was not ready to talk of Luscinda, and he would start the subject himself even though he dragged it in unseasonably, a circumstance that aroused in me a certain amount of jealousy; not that I feared any change in the constancy or faith of Luscinda; but still my fate led me to forebode what she assured me against. Don Fernando contrived always to read the letters I sent to Luscinda and her answers to me, under the pretence that he enjoyed the wit and sense of both. It so happened, then, that Luscinda having begged of me a book of chivalry to read, one that she was very fond of, Amadis of Gaul-"

Don Quixote no sooner heard a book of chivalry mentioned, than he said:

"Had your worship told me at the beginning of your story that the Lady Luscinda was fond of books of chivalry, no other laudation would have been requisite to impress upon me the superiority of her understanding, for it could not have been of the excellence you describe had a taste for such delightful reading been wanting; so, as far as I am concerned, you need waste no more words in describing her beauty, worth, and intelligence; for, on merely hearing what her taste was, I declare her to be the most beautiful and the most intelligent woman in the world; and I wish your worship had, along with Amadis of Gaul, sent her the worthy Don Rugel of Greece, for I know the Lady Luscinda would greatly relish Daraida and Garaya, and the shrewd sayings of the shepherd Darinel, and the admirable verses of his bucolics, sung and delivered by him with such sprightliness, wit, and ease; but a time may come when this omission can be remedied, and to rectify it nothing more is needed than for your worship to be so good as to come with me to my village, for there I can give you more than three hundred books which are the delight of my soul and the entertainment of my life;—though it occurs to me that I have not got one of them now, thanks to the spite of wicked and envious enchanters;—but pardon me for having broken the promise we made not to interrupt your discourse; for when I hear chivalry or knights-errant mentioned, I can no more help talking about them than the rays of the sun can help giving heat, or those of the moon moisture; pardon me, therefore, and proceed, for that is more to the purpose now."

While Don Quixote was saying this, Cardenio allowed his head to fall upon his breast, and seemed plunged in deep thought; and though twice Don Quixote bade him go on with his story, he neither looked up nor uttered a word in reply; but after some time he raised his head and said, "I cannot get rid of the idea, nor will anyone in the world remove it, or make me think otherwise—and he would be a blockhead who would hold or believe anything else than that that arrant knave Master Elisabad made free with Queen Madasima."

"That is not true, by all that's good," said Don Quixote in high wrath, turning upon him angrily, as his way was; "and it is a very great slander, or rather villainy. Queen Madasima was a very illustrious lady, and it is not to be supposed that so exalted a princess would have made free with a quack; and whoever maintains the contrary lies like a great scoundrel, and I will give him to know it, on foot or on horseback, armed or unarmed, by night or by day, or as he likes best."

Cardenio was looking at him steadily, and his mad fit having now come upon him, he had no disposition to go on with his story, nor would Don Quixote have listened to it, so much had what he had heard about Madasima disgusted him. Strange to say, he stood up for her as if she were in earnest his veritable born lady; to such a pass had his unholy books brought him. Cardenio, then, being, as I said, now mad, when he heard himself given the lie, and called a scoundrel and other insulting names, not relishing the jest, snatched up a stone that he found near him, and with it delivered such a blow on Don Quixote's breast that he laid him on his back. Sancho Panza, seeing his master treated in this fashion, attacked the madman with his closed fist; but the Ragged One received him in such a way that with a blow of his fist he stretched him at his feet, and then mounting upon him crushed his ribs to his own satisfaction; the goatherd, who came to the rescue, shared the same fate; and having beaten and pummelled them all he left them and quietly withdrew to his hiding-place on the mountain. Sancho rose, and with the rage he felt at finding himself so belaboured without deserving it, ran to take vengeance on the goatherd, accusing him of not giving them warning that this man was at times taken with a mad fit, for if they had known it they would have been on their guard to protect themselves. The goatherd replied that he had said so, and that if he had not heard him, that was no fault of his. Sancho retorted, and the goatherd rejoined, and the altercation ended in their seizing each other by the beard, and exchanging such fisticuffs that if Don Quixote had not made peace between them, they would have knocked one another to pieces.

"Leave me alone, Sir Knight of the Rueful Countenance," said Sancho, grappling with the goatherd, "for of this fellow, who is a clown like myself, and no dubbed knight, I can safely take satisfaction for the affront he has offered me, fighting with him hand to hand like an honest man."

"That is true," said Don Quixote, "but I know that he is not to blame for what has happened."

With this he pacified them, and again asked the goatherd if it would be possible to find Cardenio, as he felt the greatest anxiety to know the end of his story. The goatherd told him, as he had told him before, that there was no knowing of a certainty where his lair was; but that if he wandered about much in that neighbourhood he could not fail to fall in with him either in or out of his senses.

CHAPTER XXV

WHICH TREATS OF THE STRANGE THINGS THAT HAPPENED TO THE STOUT KNIGHT OF LA MANCHA IN THE SIERRA MORENA, AND OF HIS IMITATION OF THE PENANCE OF BELTENEBROS

Don Quixote took leave of the goatherd, and once more mounting Rocinante bade Sancho follow him, which he having no ass, did very discontentedly. They proceeded slowly, making their way into the most rugged part of the mountain, Sancho all the while dying to have a talk with his master, and longing for him to begin, so that there should be no breach of the injunction laid upon him; but unable to keep silence so long he said to him:

"Senor Don Quixote, give me your worship's blessing and dismissal, for I'd like to go home at once to my wife and children with whom I can at any rate talk and converse as much as I like; for to want me to go through these solitudes day and night and not speak to you when I have a mind is burying me alive. If luck would have it that animals spoke as they did in the days of Guisopete, it would not be so bad, because I could talk to Rocinante about whatever came into my head, and so put up with my ill-fortune; but it is a hard case, and not to be borne with patience, to go seeking adventures all one's life and get nothing but kicks and blanketings, brickbats and punches, and with all this to have to sew up one's mouth without daring to say what is in one's heart, just as if one were dumb."

"I understand thee, Sancho," replied Don Quixote; "thou art dying to have the interdict I placed upon thy tongue removed; consider it removed, and say what thou wilt while we are wandering in these mountains."

"So be it," said Sancho; "let me speak now, for God knows what will happen by-and-by; and to take advantage of the permit at once, I ask, what made your worship stand up so for that Queen Majimasa, or whatever her name is, or what did it matter whether that abbot was a friend of hers or not? for if your worship had let that pass—and you were not a judge in the matter—it is my belief the madman would have gone on with his story, and the blow of the stone, and the kicks, and more than half a dozen cuffs would have been escaped."

"In faith, Sancho," answered Don Quixote, "if thou knewest as I do what an honourable and illustrious lady Queen Madasima was,

I know thou wouldst say I had great patience that I did not break in pieces the mouth that uttered such blasphemies, for a very great blasphemy it is to say or imagine that a queen has made free with a surgeon. The truth of the story is that that Master Elisabad whom the madman mentioned was a man of great prudence and sound judgment, and served as governor and physician to the queen, but to suppose that she was his mistress is nonsense deserving very severe punishment; and as a proof that Cardenio did not know what he was saying, remember when he said it he was out of his wits."

"That is what I say," said Sancho; "there was no occasion for minding the words of a madman; for if good luck had not helped your worship, and he had sent that stone at your head instead of at your breast, a fine way we should have been in for standing up for my lady yonder, God confound her! And then, would not Cardenio have gone free as a madman?"

"Against men in their senses or against madmen," said Don Quixote, "every knight-errant is bound to stand up for the honour of women, whoever they may be, much more for queens of such high degree and dignity as Queen Madasima, for whom I have a particular regard on account of her amiable qualities; for, besides being extremely beautiful, she was very wise, and very patient under her misfortunes, of which she had many; and the counsel and society of the Master Elisabad were a great help and support to her in enduring her afflictions with wisdom and resignation; hence the ignorant and ill-disposed vulgar took occasion to say and think that she was his mistress; and they lie, I say it once more, and will lie two hundred times more, all who think and say so."

"I neither say nor think so," said Sancho; "let them look to it; with their bread let them eat it; they have rendered account to God whether they misbehaved or not; I come from my vineyard, I know nothing; I am not fond of prying into other men's lives; he who buys and lies feels it in his purse; moreover, naked was I born, naked I find myself, I neither lose nor gain; but if they did, what is that to me? many think there are flitches where there are no hooks; but who can put gates to the open plain? moreover they said of God-"

"God bless me," said Don Quixote, "what a set of absurdities thou art stringing together! What has what we are talking about got to do with the proverbs thou art threading one after the other? for God's sake hold thy tongue, Sancho, and henceforward keep to prodding thy ass and don't meddle in what does not concern thee; and understand with all thy five senses that everything I have done, am doing, or shall do, is well founded on reason and in conformity with the rules of chivalry, for I understand them better than all the world that profess them."

"Senor," replied Sancho, "is it a good rule of chivalry that we should go astray through these mountains without path or road, looking for a madman who when he is found will perhaps take a fancy to finish what he began, not his story, but your worship's head and my ribs, and end by breaking them altogether for us?"

"Peace, I say again, Sancho," said Don Quixote, "for let me tell thee it is not so much the desire of finding that madman that leads me into these regions as that which I have of performing among them an achievement wherewith I shall win eternal name and fame throughout the known world; and it shall be such that I shall thereby set the seal on all that can make a knight-errant perfect and famous."

"And is it very perilous, this achievement?"

"No," replied he of the Rueful Countenance; "though it may be in the dice that we may throw deuce-ace instead of sixes; but all will depend on thy diligence."

"On my diligence!" said Sancho.

"Yes," said Don Quixote, "for if thou dost return soon from the place where I mean to send thee, my penance will be soon over, and my glory will soon begin. But as it is not right to keep thee any longer in suspense, waiting to see what comes of my words, I would have thee know, Sancho, that the famous Amadis of Gaul was one of the most perfect knights-errant—I am wrong to say he was one; he stood alone, the first, the only one, the lord of all that were in the world in his time. A fig for Don Belianis, and for all who say he equalled him in any respect, for, my oath upon it, they are deceiving themselves! I say, too, that when a painter desires to become famous in his art he endeavours to copy the originals of the rarest painters that he knows; and the same rule holds good for all the most important crafts and callings that serve to adorn a state; thus must he who would be esteemed prudent and patient imitate Ulysses, in whose person and labours Homer presents to us a lively picture of prudence and patience; as Virgil, too, shows us in the person of AEneas the virtue of a pious son and the sagacity of a brave and skilful captain; not representing or describing them as they were, but as they ought to be, so as to leave the example of their virtues to posterity. In the same way Amadis was the polestar, day-star, sun of valiant and devoted knights, whom all we who fight under the banner of love and chivalry are bound to imitate. This, then, being so, I consider, friend Sancho, that the knight-errant who shall imitate him most closely will come nearest to reaching the perfection of chivalry. Now one of the instances in which this knight most conspicuously showed his prudence, worth, valour, endurance, fortitude, and love, was when he withdrew, rejected by the Lady Oriana, to do penance upon the Pena Pobre, changing his name into that of Beltenebros, a name assuredly significant and appropriate to the life which he had voluntarily adopted. So, as it is easier for me to imitate him in this than in cleaving giants asunder, cutting off serpents' heads, slaying dragons, routing armies, destroying fleets, and breaking enchantments, and as this place is so well suited for a similar purpose, I must not allow the opportunity to escape which now so conveniently offers me its forelock."

"What is it in reality," said Sancho, "that your worship means to do in such an out-of-the-way place as this?"

"Have I not told thee," answered Don Quixote, "that I mean to imitate Amadis here, playing the victim of despair, the madman, the maniac, so as at the same time to imitate the valiant Don Roland, when at the fountain he had evidence of the fair Angelica having disgraced herself with Medoro and through grief thereat went mad, and plucked up trees, troubled the waters of the clear springs, slew destroyed flocks, burned down huts, levelled houses, dragged mares after him, and perpetrated a hundred thousand other outrages worthy of everlasting renown and record? And though I have no intention of imitating Roland, or Orlando, or Rotolando (for he went by all these names), step by step in all the mad things he did, said, and thought, I will make a rough copy to the best of my power of all that seems to me most essential; but perhaps I shall content myself with the simple imitation of Amadis, who without giving way to any mischievous madness but merely to tears and sorrow, gained as much fame as the most famous."

"It seems to me," said Sancho, "that the knights who behaved in this way had provocation and cause for those follies and penances; but what cause has your worship for going mad? What lady has rejected you, or what evidence have you found to prove that the lady Dulcinea del Toboso has been trifling with Moor or Christian?"

"There is the point," replied Don Quixote, "and that is the beauty of this business of mine; no thanks to a knight-errant for going mad when he has cause; the thing is to turn crazy without any provocation, and let my lady know, if I do this in the dry, what I would do in the moist; moreover I have abundant cause in the long separation I have endured from my lady till death, Dulcinea del Toboso; for as thou didst hear that shepherd Ambrosio say the other day, in absence all ills are felt and feared; and so, friend Sancho, waste no time in advising me against so rare, so happy, and so unheard-of an imitation; mad I am, and mad I must be until thou returnest with the answer to a letter that I mean to send by thee to my lady Dulcinea; and if it be such as my constancy deserves, my insanity and penance will come to an end; and if it be to the opposite effect, I shall become mad in earnest, and, being so, I shall suffer no more; thus in whatever way she may answer I shall escape from the struggle and affliction in which thou wilt leave me, enjoying in my senses the boon thou bearest me, or as a madman not feeling the evil thou bringest me. But tell me, Sancho, hast thou got Mambrino's helmet safe? for I saw thee take it up from the ground when that ungrateful wretch tried to break it in pieces but could not, by which the fineness of its temper may be seen."

To which Sancho made answer, "By the living God, Sir Knight of the Rueful Countenance, I cannot endure or bear with patience some of the things that your worship says; and from them I begin to suspect that all you tell me about chivalry, and winning kingdoms and empires, and giving islands, and bestowing other rewards and dignities after the custom of knights-errant, must be all made up of wind and lies, and all pigments or figments, or whatever we may call them; for what would anyone think that heard your worship calling a barber's basin Mambrino's helmet without ever seeing the mistake all this time, but that one who says and maintains such things must have his brains addled? I have the basin in my sack all dinted, and I am taking it home to have it mended, to trim my beard in it, if, by God's grace, I am allowed to see my wife and children some day or other."

"Look here, Sancho," said Don Quixote, "by him thou didst swear by just now I swear thou hast the most limited understanding that any squire in the world has or ever had. Is it possible that all this time thou hast been going about with me thou hast never found out that all things belonging to knights-errant seem to be illusions and nonsense and ravings, and to go always by contraries? And not because it really is so, but because there is always a swarm of enchanters in attendance upon us that change and alter everything with us, and turn things as they please, and according as they are disposed to aid or destroy us; thus what seems to thee a barber's basin seems to me Mambrino's helmet, and to another it will seem something else; and rare foresight it was in the sage who is on my side to make what is really and truly Mambrine's helmet seem a basin to everybody, for, being held in such estimation as it is, all the world would pursue me to rob me of it; but when they see it is only a barber's basin they do not take the trouble to obtain it; as was plainly shown by him who tried to break it, and left it on the ground without taking it, for, by my faith, had he known it he would never have left it behind. Keep it safe, my friend, for just now I have no need of it; indeed, I shall have to take off all this armour and remain as naked as I was born, if I have a mind to follow Roland rather than Amadis in my penance."

Thus talking they reached the foot of a high mountain which stood like an isolated peak among the others that surrounded it. Past its base there flowed a gentle brook, all around it spread a meadow so green and luxuriant that it was a delight to the eyes to look upon it, and forest trees in abundance, and shrubs and flowers, added to the charms of the spot. Upon this place the Knight of the Rueful Countenance fixed his choice for the performance of his penance, and as he beheld it exclaimed in a loud voice as though he were out of his senses:

"This is the place, oh, ye heavens, that I select and choose for bewailing the misfortune in which ye yourselves have plunged me: this is the spot where the overflowings of mine eyes shall swell the waters of yon little brook, and my deep and endless sighs shall stir unceasingly the leaves of these mountain trees, in testimony and token of the pain my persecuted heart is suffering. Oh, ye rural deities, whoever ye be that haunt this lone spot, give ear to the complaint of a wretched lover whom long absence and brooding jealousy have driven to bewail his fate among these wilds and complain of the hard heart of that fair and ungrateful one, the end and limit of all human beauty! Oh, ye wood nymphs and dryads, that dwell in the thickets of the forest, so may the nimble wanton satyrs by whom ye are vainly wooed never disturb your sweet repose, help me to lament my hard fate or at least weary not at listening to it! Oh, Dulcinea del Toboso, day of my night, glory of my pain, guide of my path, star of my fortune, so may Heaven grant thee in full all thou seekest of it, bethink thee of the place and condition to which absence from thee has brought me, and make that return in kindness that is due to my fidelity! Oh, lonely trees, that from this day forward shall bear me company in my solitude, give me some sign by the gentle movement of your boughs that my presence is not distasteful to you! Oh, thou, my squire, pleasant companion in my prosperous and adverse fortunes, fix well in thy memory what thou shalt see me do here, so that thou mayest relate and report it to the sole cause of all," and so saying he dismounted from Rocinante, and in an instant relieved him of saddle and bridle, and giving him a slap on the croup, said, "He gives thee freedom who is bereft of it himself, oh steed as excellent in deed as thou art unfortunate in thy lot; begone where thou wilt, for thou bearest written on thy forehead that neither Astolfo's hippogriff, nor the famed Frontino that cost Bradamante so dear, could equal thee in speed."

Seeing this Sancho said, "Good luck to him who has saved us the trouble of stripping the pack-saddle off Dapple! By my faith he would not have gone without a slap on the croup and something said in his praise; though if he were here I would not let anyone strip him, for there would be no occasion, as he had nothing of the lover or victim of despair about him, inasmuch as his master, which I was while it was God's pleasure, was nothing of the sort; and indeed, Sir Knight of the Rueful Countenance, if my departure and your worship's madness are to come off in earnest, it will be as well to saddle Rocinante again in order that he may supply the want of Dapple, because it will save me time in going and returning: for if I go on foot I don't know when I shall get there or when I shall get back, as I am, in truth, a bad walker."

"I declare, Sancho," returned Don Quixote, "it shall be as thou wilt, for thy plan does not seem to me a bad one, and three days hence thou wilt depart, for I wish thee to observe in the meantime what I do and say for her sake, that thou mayest be able to tell it."

"But what more have I to see besides what I have seen?" said Sancho.

"Much thou knowest about it!" said Don Quixote. "I have now got to tear up my garments, to scatter about my armour, knock my head against these rocks, and more of the same sort of thing, which thou must witness."

"For the love of God," said Sancho, "be careful, your worship, how you give yourself those knocks on the head, for you may come across such a rock, and in such a way, that the very first may put an end to the whole contrivance of this penance; and I should think, if indeed knocks on the head seem necessary to you, and this business cannot be done without them, you might be content—as the whole thing is feigned, and counterfeit, and in joke—you might be content, I say, with giving them to yourself in the water, or against something soft, like cotton; and leave it all to me; for I'll tell my lady that your worship knocked your head against a point of rock harder than a diamond."

"I thank thee for thy good intentions, friend Sancho," answered Don Quixote, "but I would have thee know that all these things I am doing are not in joke, but very much in earnest, for anything else would be a transgression of the ordinances of chivalry, which forbid us to tell any lie whatever under the penalties due to apostasy; and to do one thing instead of another is just the same as lying; so my knocks on the head must be real, solid, and valid, without anything sophisticated or fanciful about them, and it will be needful to leave me some lint to dress my wounds, since fortune has compelled us to do without the balsam we lost."

"It was worse losing the ass," replied Sancho, "for with him lint and all were lost; but I beg of your worship not to remind me again of that accursed liquor, for my soul, not to say my stomach, turns at hearing the very name of it; and I beg of you, too, to reckon as past the three days you allowed me for seeing the mad things you do, for I take them as seen already and pronounced upon, and I will tell wonderful stories to my lady; so write the letter and send me off at once, for I long to return and take your worship out of this purgatory where I am leaving you."

"Purgatory dost thou call it, Sancho?" said Don Quixote, "rather call it hell, or even worse if there be anything worse."

"For one who is in hell," said Sancho, "nulla est retentio, as I have heard say."

"I do not understand what retentio means," said Don Quixote.

"Retentio," answered Sancho, "means that whoever is in hell never comes nor can come out of it, which will be the opposite case with your worship or my legs will be idle, that is if I have spurs to enliven Rocinante: let me once get to El Toboso and into the presence of my lady Dulcinea, and I will tell her such things of the follies and madnesses (for it is all one) that your worship has done and is still doing, that I will manage to make her softer than a glove though I find her harder than a cork tree; and with her sweet and honeyed answer I will come back through the air like a witch, and take your worship out of this purgatory that seems to be hell but is not, as there is hope of getting out of it; which, as I have said, those in hell have not, and I believe your worship will not say anything to the contrary."

"That is true," said he of the Rueful Countenance, "but how shall we manage to write the letter?"

"And the ass-colt order too," added Sancho.

"All shall be included," said Don Quixote; "and as there is no paper, it would be well done to write it on the leaves of trees, as the ancients did, or on tablets of wax; though that would be as hard to find just now as paper. But it has just occurred to me how it may be conveniently and even more than conveniently written, and that is in the note-book that belonged to Cardenio, and thou wilt take care to have it copied on paper, in a good hand, at the first village thou comest to where there is a schoolmaster, or if not, any sacristan will copy it; but see thou give it not to any notary to copy, for they write a law hand that Satan could not make out."

"But what is to be done about the signature?" said Sancho.

"The letters of Amadis were never signed," said Don Quixote.

"That is all very well," said Sancho, "but the order must needs be signed, and if it is copied they will say the signature is false, and I shall be left without ass-colts."

"The order shall go signed in the same book," said Don Quixote, "and on seeing it my niece will make no difficulty about obeying it; as to the loveletter thou canst put by way of signature, 'Yours till death, the Knight of the Rueful Countenance.' And it will be no great matter if it is in some other person's hand, for as well as I recollect Dulcinea can neither read nor write, nor in the whole course of her life has she seen handwriting or letter of mine, for my love and hers have been always platonic, not going beyond a modest look, and even that so seldom that I can safely swear I have not seen her four times in all these twelve years I have been loving her more than the light of these eyes that the earth will one day devour; and perhaps even of those four times she has not once perceived that I was looking at her: such is the retirement and seclusion in which her father Lorenzo Corchuelo and her mother Aldonza Nogales have brought her up."

"So, so!" said Sancho; "Lorenzo Corchuelo's daughter is the lady Dulcinea del Toboso, otherwise called Aldonza Lorenzo?"

"She it is," said Don Quixote, "and she it is that is worthy to be lady of the whole universe."

"I know her well," said Sancho, "and let me tell you she can fling a crowbar as well as the lustiest lad in all the town. Giver of all good! but she is a brave lass, and a right and stout one, and fit to be helpmate to any knight-errant that is or is to be, who may make her his lady: the whoreson wench, what sting she has and what a voice! I can tell you one day she posted herself on the top of the belfry of the village to call some labourers of theirs that were in a ploughed field of her father's, and though they were better than half a league off they heard her as well as if they were at the foot of the tower; and the best of her is that she is not a bit prudish, for she has plenty of affability, and jokes with everybody, and has a grin and a jest for everything. So, Sir Knight of the Rueful Countenance, I say you not only may and ought to do mad freaks for her sake, but you have a good right to give way to despair and hang yourself; and no one who knows of it but will say you did well, though the devil should take you; and I wish I were on my road already, simply to see her, for it is many a day since I saw her, and she must be altered by this time, for going about the fields always, and the sun and the air spoil women's looks greatly. But I must own the truth to your worship, Senor Don Quixote; until now I have been under a great mistake, for I believed truly and honestly that the lady Dulcinea must be some princess your worship was in love with, or some person great enough to deserve the rich presents you have sent her, such as the Biscayan and the galley slaves, and many more no doubt, for your worship must have won many victories in the time when I was not yet your squire. But all things considered, what good can it do the lady Aldonza Lorenzo, I mean the lady Dulcinea del Toboso, to have the vanquished your worship sends or will send coming to her and going down on their knees before her? Because may be when they came she'd be hackling flax or threshing on the threshing floor, and they'd be ashamed to see her, and she'd laugh, or resent the present."

"I have before now told thee many times, Sancho," said Don Quixote, "that thou art a mighty great chatterer, and that with a blunt wit thou art always striving at sharpness; but to show thee what a fool thou art and how rational I am, I would have thee listen to a short story. Thou must know that a certain widow, fair, young, independent, and rich, and above all free and easy, fell in love with a sturdy strapping young lay-brother; his superior came to know of it, and one day said to the worthy widow by way of brotherly remonstrance, 'I am surprised, senora, and not without good reason, that a woman of such high standing, so fair, and so rich as you are, should have fallen in love with such a mean, low, stupid fellow as So-and-so, when in this house there are so many masters, graduates, and divinity students from among whom you might choose as if they were a lot of pears, saying this one I'll take, that I won't take;' but she replied to him with great sprightliness and candour, 'My dear sir, you are very much mistaken, and your ideas are very old-fashioned, if you think that I have made a bad choice in So-and-so, fool as he seems; because for all I want with him he knows as much and more philosophy than Aristotle.' In the same way, Sancho, for all I want with Dulcinea del Toboso she is just as good as the most exalted princess on earth. It is not to be supposed that all those poets who sang the praises of ladies under the fancy names they give them, had any such mistresses. Thinkest thou that the Amarillises, the Phillises, the Sylvias, the Dianas, the Galateas, the Filidas, and all the rest of them, that the books, the ballads, the barber's shops, the theatres are full of, were really and truly ladies of flesh and blood, and mistresses of those that glorify and have glorified them? Nothing of the kind; they only invent them for the most part to furnish a subject for their verses, and that they may pass for lovers, or for men valiant enough to be so; and so it suffices me to think and believe that the good Aldonza Lorenzo is fair and virtuous; and as to her pedigree it is very little matter, for no one will examine into it for the purpose of conferring any order upon her, and I, for my part, reckon her the most exalted princess in the world. For thou shouldst know, Sancho, if thou dost not know, that two things alone beyond all others are incentives to love, and these are great beauty and a good name, and these two things are to be found in Dulcinea in the highest degree, for in beauty no one equals her and in good name few approach her; and to put the whole thing in a nutshell, I persuade myself that all I say is as I say, neither more nor less, and I picture her in my imagination as I would have her to be, as well in beauty as in condition; Helen approaches her not nor does Lucretia come up to her, nor any other of the famous women of times past, Greek, Barbarian, or Latin; and let each say what he will, for if in this I am taken to task by the ignorant, I shall not be censured by the critical."

"I say that your worship is entirely right," said Sancho, "and that I am an ass. But I know not how the name of ass came into my mouth, for a rope is not to be mentioned in the house of him who has been hanged; but now for the letter, and then, God be with you, I am off."

Don Quixote took out the note-book, and, retiring to one side, very deliberately began to write the letter, and when he had finished it he called to Sancho, saying he wished to read it to him, so that he might commit it to memory, in case of losing it on the road; for with evil fortune like his anything might be apprehended. To which Sancho replied, "Write it two or three times there in the book and give it to me, and I will carry it very carefully, because to expect me to keep it in my memory is all nonsense, for I have such a bad one that I often forget my own name; but for all that repeat it to me, as I shall like to hear it, for surely it will run as if it was in print."

"Listen," said Don Quixote, "this is what it says:

"DON QUIXOTE'S LETTER TO DULCINEA DEL TOBOSO

"Sovereign and exalted Lady,—The pierced by the point of absence, the wounded to the heart's core, sends thee, sweetest Dulcinea del Toboso, the health that he himself enjoys not. If thy beauty despises me, if thy worth is not for me, if thy scorn is my affliction, though I be sufficiently long-suffering, hardly shall I endure this anxiety, which, besides being oppressive, is protracted. My good squire Sancho will relate to thee in full, fair ingrate, dear enemy, the condition to which I am reduced on thy account: if it be thy pleasure to give me relief, I am thine; if not, do as may be pleasing to thee; for by ending my life I shall satisfy thy cruelty and my desire.

"Thine till death,

"The Knight of the Rueful Countenance."

"By the life of my father," said Sancho, when he heard the letter, "it is the loftiest thing I ever heard. Body of me! how your worship says everything as you like in it! And how well you fit in 'The Knight of the Rueful Countenance' into the signature. I declare your worship is indeed the very devil, and there is nothing you don't know."

"Everything is needed for the calling I follow," said Don Quixote.

"Now then," said Sancho, "let your worship put the order for the three ass-colts on the other side, and sign it very plainly, that they may recognise it at first sight."

"With all my heart," said Don Quixote, and as he had written it he read it to this effect:

"Mistress Niece,—By this first of ass-colts please pay to Sancho Panza, my squire, three of the five I left at home in your charge: said three ass-colts to be paid and delivered for the same number received here in hand, which upon this and upon his receipt shall be duly paid. Done in the heart of the Sierra Morena, the twenty-seventh of August of this present year."

"That will do," said Sancho; "now let your worship sign it."

"There is no need to sign it," said Don Quixote, "but merely to put my flourish, which is the same as a signature, and enough for three asses, or even three hundred."

"I can trust your worship," returned Sancho; "let me go and saddle Rocinante, and be ready to give me your blessing, for I mean to go at once without seeing the fooleries your worship is going to do; I'll say I saw you do so many that she will not want any more."

"At any rate, Sancho," said Don Quixote, "I should like—and there is reason for it—I should like thee, I say, to see me stripped to the skin and performing a dozen or two of insanities, which I can get done in less than half an hour; for having seen them with thine own eyes, thou canst then safely swear to the rest that thou wouldst add; and I promise thee thou wilt not tell of as many as I mean to perform."

"For the love of God, master mine," said Sancho, "let me not see your worship stripped, for it will sorely grieve me, and I shall not be able to keep from tears, and my head aches so with all I shed last night for Dapple, that I am not fit to begin any fresh weeping; but if it is your worship's pleasure that I should see some insanities, do them in your clothes, short ones, and such as come readiest to hand; for I myself want nothing of the sort, and, as I have said, it will be a saving of time for my return, which will be with the news your worship desires and deserves. If not, let the lady Dulcinea look to it; if she does not answer reasonably, I swear as solemnly as I can that I will fetch a fair answer out of her stomach with kicks and cuffs; for why should it be borne that a knight-errant as famous as your worship should go mad without rhyme or reason for a—? Her ladyship had best not drive me to say it, for by God I will speak out and let off everything cheap, even if it doesn't sell: I am pretty good at that! she little knows me; faith, if she knew me she'd be in awe of me."

"In faith, Sancho," said Don Quixote, "to all appearance thou art no sounder in thy wits than I."

"I am not so mad," answered Sancho, "but I am more peppery; but apart from all this, what has your worship to eat until I come back? Will you sally out on the road like Cardenio to force it from the shepherds?"

"Let not that anxiety trouble thee," replied Don Quixote, "for even if I had it I should not eat anything but the herbs and the fruits which this meadow and these trees may yield me; the beauty of this business of mine lies in not eating, and in performing other mortifications."

"Do you know what I am afraid of?" said Sancho upon this; "that I shall not be able to find my way back to this spot where I am leaving you, it is such an out-of-the-way place."

"Observe the landmarks well," said Don Quixote, "for I will try not to go far from this neighbourhood, and I will even take care to mount the highest of these rocks to see if I can discover thee returning; however, not to miss me and lose thyself, the best plan will be to cut some branches of the broom that is so abundant about here, and as thou goest to lay them at intervals until thou hast come out upon the plain; these will serve thee, after the fashion of the clue in the labyrinth of Theseus, as marks and signs for finding me on thy return."

"So I will," said Sancho Panza, and having cut some, he asked his master's blessing, and not without many tears on both sides, took his leave of him, and mounting Rocinante, of whom Don Quixote charged him earnestly to have as much care as of his own person, he set out for the plain, strewing at intervals the branches of broom as his master had recommended him; and so he went his way, though Don Quixote still entreated him to see him do were it only a couple of mad acts. He had not gone a hundred paces, however, when he returned and said:

"I must say, senor, your worship said quite right, that in order to be able to swear without a weight on my conscience that I had seen you do mad things, it would be well for me to see if it were only one; though in your worship's remaining here I have seen a very great one."

"Did I not tell thee so?" said Don Quixote. "Wait, Sancho, and I will do them in the saying of a credo," and pulling off his breeches in all haste he stripped himself to his skin and his shirt, and then, without more ado, he cut a couple of gambados in the air, and a couple of somersaults, heels over head, making such a display that, not to see it a second time, Sancho wheeled Rocinante round, and felt easy, and satisfied in his mind that he could swear he had left his master mad; and so we will leave him to follow his road until his return, which was a quick one.

CHAPTER XXVI

IN WHICH ARE CONTINUED THE REFINEMENTS WHEREWITH DON QUIXOTE PLAYED THE PART OF A LOVER IN THE SIERRA MORENA

Returning to the proceedings of him of the Rueful Countenance when he found himself alone, the history says that when Don Quixote had completed the performance of the somersaults or capers, naked from the waist down and clothed from the waist up, and saw that Sancho had gone off without waiting to see any more crazy feats, he climbed up to the top of a high rock, and there set himself to consider what he had several times before considered without ever coming to any conclusion on the point, namely whether it would be better and more to his purpose to imitate the outrageous madness of Roland, or the melancholy madness of Amadis; and communing with himself he said:

"What wonder is it if Roland was so good a knight and so valiant as everyone says he was, when, after all, he was enchanted, and nobody could kill him save by thrusting a corking pin into the sole of his foot, and he always wore shoes with seven iron soles? Though cunning devices did not avail him against Bernardo del Carpio, who knew all about them, and strangled him in his arms at Roncesvalles. But putting the question of his valour aside, let us come to his losing his wits, for certain it is that he did lose them in consequence of the proofs he discovered at the fountain, and the intelligence the shepherd gave him of Angelica having slept more than two siestas with Medoro, a little curly-headed Moor, and page to Agramante. If he was persuaded that this was true, and that his lady had wronged him, it is no wonder that he should have gone mad; but I, how am I to imitate him in his madness, unless I can imitate him in the cause of it? For my Dulcinea, I will venture to swear, never saw a Moor in her life, as he is, in his proper costume, and she is this day as the mother that bore her, and I should plainly be doing her a wrong if, fancying anything else, I were to go mad with the same kind of madness as Roland the Furious. On the other hand, I see that Amadis of Gaul, without losing his senses and without doing anything mad, acquired as a lover as much fame as the most famous; for, according to his history, on finding himself rejected by his lady Oriana, who had ordered him not to appear in her presence until it should be her pleasure, all he did was to retire to the Pena Pobre in company with a hermit, and there he took his fill of weeping until Heaven sent him relief in the midst of his great grief and need. And if this be true, as it is, why should I now take the trouble to strip stark naked, or do mischief to these trees which have done me no harm, or why am I to disturb the clear waters of these brooks which will give me to drink whenever I have a mind? Long live the memory of Amadis and let him be imitated so far as is possible by Don Quixote of La Mancha, of whom it will be said, as was said of the other, that if he did not achieve great things, he died in attempting them; and if I am not repulsed or rejected by my Dulcinea, it is enough for me, as I have said, to be absent from her. And so, now to business; come to my memory ye deeds of Amadis, and show me how I am to begin to imitate you. I know already that what he chiefly did was to pray and commend himself to God; but what am I to do for a rosary, for I have not got one?"

And then it occurred to him how he might make one, and that was by tearing a great strip off the tail of his shirt which hung down, and making eleven knots on it, one bigger than the rest, and this served him for a rosary all the time he was there, during which he repeated countless ave-marias. But what distressed him greatly was not having another hermit there to confess him and receive consolation from; and so he solaced himself with pacing up and down the little meadow, and writing and carving on the bark of the trees and on the fine sand a multitude of verses all in harmony with his sadness, and some in praise of Dulcinea; but, when he was found there afterwards, the only ones completely legible that could be discovered were those that follow here:

> Ye on the mountain side that grow,
>   Ye green things all, trees, shrubs, and bushes,
> Are ye aweary of the woe
>   That this poor aching bosom crushes?
> If it disturb you, and I owe
>   Some reparation, it may be a
> Defence for me to let you know
> Don Quixote's tears are on the flow,
>   And all for distant Dulcinea
>   Del Toboso.
>
> The lealest lover time can show,
>   Doomed for a lady-love to languish,
> Among these solitudes doth go,
>   A prey to every kind of anguish.

> Why Love should like a spiteful foe
> Thus use him, he hath no idea,
> But hogsheads full—this doth he know—
> Don Quixote's tears are on the flow,
> And all for distant Dulcinea
> Del Toboso.
>
> Adventure-seeking doth he go
> Up rugged heights, down rocky valleys,
> But hill or dale, or high or low,
> Mishap attendeth all his sallies:
> Love still pursues him to and fro,
> And plies his cruel scourge—ah me! a
> Relentless fate, an endless woe;
> Don Quixote's tears are on the flow,
> And all for distant Dulcinea
> Del Toboso.

The addition of "Del Toboso" to Dulcinea's name gave rise to no little laughter among those who found the above lines, for they suspected Don Quixote must have fancied that unless he added "del Toboso" when he introduced the name of Dulcinea the verse would be unintelligible; which was indeed the fact, as he himself afterwards admitted. He wrote many more, but, as has been said, these three verses were all that could be plainly and perfectly deciphered. In this way, and in sighing and calling on the fauns and satyrs of the woods and the nymphs of the streams, and Echo, moist and mournful, to answer, console, and hear him, as well as in looking for herbs to sustain him, he passed his time until Sancho's return; and had that been delayed three weeks, as it was three days, the Knight of the Rueful Countenance would have worn such an altered countenance that the mother that bore him would not have known him: and here it will be well to leave him, wrapped up in sighs and verses, to relate how Sancho Panza fared on his mission.

As for him, coming out upon the high road, he made for El Toboso, and the next day reached the inn where the mishap of the blanket had befallen him. As soon as he recognised it he felt as if he were once more living through the air, and he could not bring himself to enter it though it was an hour when he might well have done so, for it was dinner-time, and he longed to taste something hot as it had been all cold fare with him for many days past. This craving drove him to draw near to the inn, still undecided whether to go in or not, and as he was hesitating there came out two persons who at once recognised him, and said one to the other:

"Senor licentiate, is not he on the horse there Sancho Panza who, our adventurer's housekeeper told us, went off with her master as esquire?"

"So it is," said the licentiate, "and that is our friend Don Quixote's horse;" and if they knew him so well it was because they were the curate and the barber of his own village, the same who had carried out the scrutiny and sentence upon the books; and as soon as they recognised Sancho Panza and Rocinante, being anxious to hear of Don Quixote, they approached, and calling him by his name the curate said, "Friend Sancho Panza, where is your master?"

Sancho recognised them at once, and determined to keep secret the place and circumstances where and under which he had left his master, so he replied that his master was engaged in a certain quarter on a certain matter of great importance to him which he could not disclose for the eyes in his head.

"Nay, nay," said the barber, "if you don't tell us where he is, Sancho Panza, we will suspect as we suspect already, that you have murdered and robbed him, for here you are mounted on his horse; in fact, you must produce the master of the hack, or else take the consequences."

"There is no need of threats with me," said Sancho, "for I am not a man to rob or murder anybody; let his own fate, or God who made him, kill each one; my master is engaged very much to his taste doing penance in the midst of these mountains;" and then, offhand and without stopping, he told them how he had left him, what adventures had befallen him, and how he was carrying a letter to the lady Dulcinea del Toboso, the daughter of Lorenzo Corchuelo, with whom he was over head and ears in love. They were both amazed at what Sancho Panza told them; for though they were aware of Don Quixote's madness and the nature of it, each time they heard of it they were filled with fresh wonder. They then asked Sancho Panza to show them the letter he was carrying to the lady Dulcinea del Toboso. He said it was written in a notebook, and that his master's directions were that he should have it copied on paper at the first village he came to. On this the curate said if he showed it to him, he himself would make a fair copy of it. Sancho put his hand into his bosom in search of the note-book but could not find it, nor, if he had been searching until now, could he have found it, for Don Quixote had kept it, and had never given it to him, nor had he himself thought of asking for it. When Sancho discovered he could not find the book his face grew deadly pale, and in great haste he again felt his body all over, and seeing plainly it was not to be found, without more ado he seized his beard with both hands and plucked away half of it, and then, as quick as he could and without stopping, gave himself half a dozen cuffs on the face and nose till they were bathed in blood.

Seeing this, the curate and the barber asked him what had happened him that he gave himself such rough treatment.

"What should happen me?" replied Sancho, "but to have lost from one hand to the other, in a moment, three ass-colts, each of them like a castle?"

"How is that?" said the barber.

"I have lost the note-book," said Sancho, "that contained the letter to Dulcinea, and an order signed by my master in which he directed his niece to give me three ass-colts out of four or five he had at home;" and he then told them about the loss of Dapple.

The curate consoled him, telling him that when his master was found he would get him to renew the order, and make a fresh draft on paper, as was usual and customary; for those made in notebooks were never accepted or honoured.

Sancho comforted himself with this, and said if that were so the loss of Dulcinea's letter did not trouble him much, for he had it almost by heart, and it could be taken down from him wherever and whenever they liked.

"Repeat it then, Sancho," said the barber, "and we will write it down afterwards."

Sancho Panza stopped to scratch his head to bring back the letter to his memory, and balanced himself now on one foot, now the other, one moment staring at the ground, the next at the sky, and after having half gnawed off the end of a finger and kept them in suspense waiting for him to begin, he said, after a long pause, "By God, senor licentiate, devil a thing can I recollect of the letter; but it said at the beginning, 'Exalted and scrubbing Lady.'"

"It cannot have said 'scrubbing,'" said the barber, "but 'superhuman' or 'sovereign.'"

"That is it," said Sancho; "then, as well as I remember, it went on, 'The wounded, and wanting of sleep, and the pierced, kisses your worship's hands, ungrateful and very unrecognised fair one; and it said something or other about health and sickness that he was sending her; and from that it went tailing off until it ended with 'Yours till death, the Knight of the Rueful Countenance.'"

It gave them no little amusement, both of them, to see what a good memory Sancho had, and they complimented him greatly upon it, and begged him to repeat the letter a couple of times more, so that they too might get it by heart to write it out by-and-by. Sancho repeated it three times, and as he did, uttered three thousand more absurdities; then he told them more about his master but he never said a word about the blanketing that had befallen himself in that inn, into which he refused to enter. He told them, moreover, how his lord, if he brought him a favourable answer from the lady Dulcinea del Toboso, was to put himself in the way of endeavouring to become an emperor, or at least a monarch; for it had been so settled between them, and with his personal worth and the might of his arm it was an easy matter to come to be one: and how on becoming one his lord was to make a marriage for him (for he would be a widower by that time, as a matter of course) and was to give him as a wife one of the damsels of the empress, the heiress of some rich and grand state on the mainland, having nothing to do with islands of any sort, for he did not care for them now. All this Sancho delivered with so much composure—wiping his nose from time to time—and with so little common-sense that his two hearers were again filled with wonder at the force of Don Quixote's madness that could run away with this poor man's reason. They did not care to take the trouble of disabusing him of his error, as they considered that since it did not in any way hurt his conscience it would be better to leave him in it, and they would have all the more amusement in listening to his simplicities; and so they bade him pray to God for his lord's health, as it was a very likely and a very feasible thing for him in course of time to come to be an emperor, as he said, or at least an archbishop or some other dignitary of equal rank.

To which Sancho made answer, "If fortune, sirs, should bring things about in such a way that my master should have a mind, instead of being an emperor, to be an archbishop, I should like to know what archbishops-errant commonly give their squires?"

"They commonly give them," said the curate, some simple benefice or cure, or some place as sacristan which brings them a good fixed income, not counting the altar fees, which may be reckoned at as much more."

"But for that," said Sancho, "the squire must be unmarried, and must know, at any rate, how to help at mass, and if that be so, woe is me, for I am married already and I don't know the first letter of the A B C. What will become of me if my master takes a fancy to be an archbishop and not an emperor, as is usual and customary with knights-errant?"

"Be not uneasy, friend Sancho," said the barber, "for we will entreat your master, and advise him, even urging it upon him as a case of conscience, to become an emperor and not an archbishop, because it will be easier for him as he is more valiant than lettered."

"So I have thought," said Sancho; "though I can tell you he is fit for anything: what I mean to do for my part is to pray to our Lord to place him where it may be best for him, and where he may be able to bestow most favours upon me."

"You speak like a man of sense," said the curate, "and you will be acting like a good Christian; but what must now be done is to take steps to coax your master out of that useless penance you say he is performing; and we had best turn into this inn to consider what plan to adopt, and also to dine, for it is now time."

Sancho said they might go in, but that he would wait there outside, and that he would tell them afterwards the reason why he was unwilling, and why it did not suit him to enter it; but he begged them to bring him out something to eat, and to let it be hot, and also to bring barley for Rocinante. They left him and went in, and presently the barber brought him out something to eat. By-and-by, after they had between them carefully thought over what they should do to carry out their object, the curate hit upon an idea very well adapted to humour Don Quixote, and effect their purpose; and his notion, which he explained to the barber, was that he himself should assume the disguise of a wandering damsel, while the other should try as best he could to pass for a squire, and that they should thus proceed to where Don Quixote was, and he, pretending to be an aggrieved and distressed damsel, should ask a favour of him, which as a valiant knight-errant he could not refuse to grant; and the favour he meant to ask him was that he should accompany her whither she would conduct him, in order to redress a wrong which a wicked knight had done her, while at the same time she should entreat him not to require her to remove her mask, nor ask her any question touching her circumstances until he had righted her with the wicked knight. And he had no doubt that Don Quixote would comply with any request made in these terms, and that in this way they might remove him and take him to his own village, where they would endeavour to find out if his extraordinary madness admitted of any kind of remedy.

CHAPTER XXVII

OF HOW THE CURATE AND THE BARBER PROCEEDED WITH THEIR SCHEME; TOGETHER WITH OTHER MATTERS WORTHY OF RECORD IN THIS GREAT HISTORY

The curate's plan did not seem a bad one to the barber, but on the contrary so good that they immediately set about putting it in execution. They begged a petticoat and hood of the landlady, leaving her in pledge a new cassock of the curate's; and the barber made a beard out of a grey-brown or red ox-tail in which the landlord used to stick his comb. The landlady asked them what they wanted these things for, and the curate told her in a few words about the madness of Don Quixote, and how this disguise was intended to get him away from the mountain where he then was. The landlord and landlady immediately came to the conclusion that the madman was their guest, the balsam man and master of the blanketed squire, and they told the curate all that had passed between him and them, not omitting what Sancho had been so silent about. Finally the landlady dressed up the curate in a style that left nothing to be desired; she put on him a cloth petticoat with black velvet stripes a palm broad, all slashed, and a bodice of green velvet set off by a binding of white satin, which as well as the petticoat must have been made in the time of king Wamba. The curate would not let them hood him, but put on his head a little quilted linen cap which he used for a night-cap, and bound his forehead with a strip of black silk, while with another he made a mask with which he concealed his beard and face very well. He then put on his hat, which was broad enough to serve him for an umbrella, and enveloping himself in his cloak seated himself woman-fashion on his mule, while the barber mounted his with a beard down to the waist of mingled red and white, for it was, as has been said, the tail of a clay-red ox.

They took leave of all, and of the good Maritornes, who, sinner as she was, promised to pray a rosary of prayers that God might grant them success in such an arduous and Christian undertaking as that they had in hand. But hardly had he sallied forth from the inn when it struck the curate that he was doing wrong in rigging himself out in that fashion, as it was an indecorous thing for a priest to dress himself that way even though much might depend upon it; and saying so to the barber he begged him to change dresses, as it was fitter he should be the distressed damsel, while he himself would play the squire's part, which would be less derogatory to his dignity; otherwise he was resolved to have nothing more to do with the matter, and let the devil take Don Quixote. Just at this moment Sancho came up, and on seeing the pair in such a costume he was unable to restrain his laughter; the barber, however, agreed to do as the curate wished, and, altering their plan, the curate went on to instruct him how to play his part and what to say to Don Quixote to induce and compel him to come with them and give up his fancy for the place he had chosen for his idle penance. The barber told him he could manage it properly without any instruction, and as he did not care to dress himself up until they were near where Don Quixote was, he folded up the garments, and the curate adjusted his beard, and they set out under the guidance of Sancho Panza, who went along telling them of the encounter with the madman they met in the Sierra, saying nothing, however, about the finding of the valise and its contents; for with all his simplicity the lad was a trifle covetous.

The next day they reached the place where Sancho had laid the broom-branches as marks to direct him to where he had left his master, and recognising it he told them that here was the entrance, and that they would do well to dress themselves, if that was required to deliver his master; for they had already told him that going in this guise and dressing in this way were of the highest importance in order to rescue his master from the pernicious life he had adopted; and they charged him strictly not to tell his master who they were, or that he knew them, and should he ask, as ask he would, if he had given the letter to Dulcinea, to say that he had, and that, as she did not know how to read, she had given an answer by word of mouth, saying that she commanded him, on pain of her displeasure, to come and see her at once; and it was a very important matter for himself, because in this way and with what they meant to say to him they felt sure of bringing him back to a better mode of life and inducing him to take immediate steps to become an emperor or monarch, for there was no fear of his becoming an archbishop. All this Sancho listened to and fixed it well in his memory, and thanked them heartily for intending to recommend his master to be an emperor instead of an archbishop, for he felt sure that in the way of bestowing rewards on their squires emperors could do more than archbishops-errant. He said, too, that it would be as well for him to go on before them to find him, and give him his lady's answer; for that perhaps might be enough to bring him away from the place without putting them to all this trouble. They approved of what Sancho proposed, and resolved to wait for him until he brought back word of having found his master.

Sancho pushed on into the glens of the Sierra, leaving them in one through which there flowed a little gentle rivulet, and where the rocks and trees afforded a cool and grateful shade. It was an August day with all the heat of one, and the heat in those parts is intense, and the hour was three in the afternoon, all which made the spot the more inviting and tempted them to wait there for Sancho's return, which they did. They were reposing, then, in the shade, when a voice unaccompanied by the notes of any instrument, but sweet and pleasing in its tone, reached their ears, at which they were not a little astonished, as the place did not seem to them likely quarters for one who sang so well; for though it is often said that shepherds of rare voice are to be found in the woods and fields, this is rather a flight of the poet's fancy than the truth. And still more surprised were they when they perceived that what they heard sung were the verses not of rustic shepherds, but of the polished wits of the city; and so it proved, for the verses they heard were these:

>What makes my quest of happiness seem vain?
>>Disdain.
>
>What bids me to abandon hope of ease?
>>Jealousies.
>
>What holds my heart in anguish of suspense?
>>Absence.
>
>If that be so, then for my grief
>Where shall I turn to seek relief,
>When hope on every side lies slain
>By Absence, Jealousies, Disdain?
>
>What the prime cause of all my woe doth prove?
>>Love.
>
>What at my glory ever looks askance?
>>Chance.
>
>Whence is permission to afflict me given?
>>Heaven.
>
>If that be so, I but await
>The stroke of a resistless fate,
>Since, working for my woe, these three,
>Love, Chance and Heaven, in league I see.
>
>What must I do to find a remedy?
>>Die.
>
>What is the lure for love when coy and strange?
>>Change.

What, if all fail, will cure the heart of sadness?
Madness.
If that be so, it is but folly
To seek a cure for melancholy:
Ask where it lies; the answer saith
In Change, in Madness, or in Death.

The hour, the summer season, the solitary place, the voice and skill of the singer, all contributed to the wonder and delight of the two listeners, who remained still waiting to hear something more; finding, however, that the silence continued some little time, they resolved to go in search of the musician who sang with so fine a voice; but just as they were about to do so they were checked by the same voice, which once more fell upon their ears, singing this

SONNET

When heavenward, holy Friendship, thou didst go
   Soaring to seek thy home beyond the sky,
   And take thy seat among the saints on high,
It was thy will to leave on earth below
Thy semblance, and upon it to bestow
   Thy veil, wherewith at times hypocrisy,
   Parading in thy shape, deceives the eye,
And makes its vileness bright as virtue show.
Friendship, return to us, or force the cheat
   That wears it now, thy livery to restore,
   By aid whereof sincerity is slain.
If thou wilt not unmask thy counterfeit,
   This earth will be the prey of strife once more,
   As when primaeval discord held its reign.

The song ended with a deep sigh, and again the listeners remained waiting attentively for the singer to resume; but perceiving that the music had now turned to sobs and heart-rending moans they determined to find out who the unhappy being could be whose voice was as rare as his sighs were piteous, and they had not proceeded far when on turning the corner of a rock they discovered a man of the same aspect and appearance as Sancho had described to them when he told them the story of Cardenio. He, showing no astonishment when he saw them, stood still with his head bent down upon his breast like one in deep thought, without raising his eyes to look at them after the first glance when they suddenly came upon him. The curate, who was aware of his misfortune and recognised him by the description, being a man of good address, approached him and in a few sensible words entreated and urged him to quit a life of such misery, lest he should end it there, which would be the greatest of all misfortunes. Cardenio was then in his right mind, free from any attack of that madness which so frequently carried him away, and seeing them dressed in a fashion so unusual among the frequenters of those wilds, could not help showing some surprise, especially when he heard them speak of his case as if it were a well-known matter (for the curate's words gave him to understand as much) so he replied to them thus:

"I see plainly, sirs, whoever you may be, that Heaven, whose care it is to succour the good, and even the wicked very often, here, in this remote spot, cut off from human intercourse, sends me, though I deserve it not, those who seek to draw me away from this to some better retreat, showing me by many and forcible arguments how unreasonably I act in leading the life I do; but as they know, that if I escape from this evil I shall fall into another still greater, perhaps they will set me down as a weak-minded man, or, what is worse, one devoid of reason; nor would it be any wonder, for I myself can perceive that the effect of the recollection of my misfortunes is so great and works so powerfully to my ruin, that in spite of myself I become at times like a stone, without feeling or consciousness; and I come to feel the truth of it when they tell me and show me proofs of the things I have done when the terrible fit overmasters me; and all I can do is bewail my lot in vain, and idly curse my destiny, and plead for my madness by telling how it was caused, to any that care to hear it; for no reasonable beings on learning the cause will wonder at the effects; and if they cannot help me at least they will not blame me, and the repugnance they feel at my wild ways will turn into pity for my woes. If it be, sirs, that you are here with the same design as others have come wah, before you proceed with your wise arguments, I entreat you to hear the story of my countless misfortunes, for perhaps when you have heard it you will spare yourselves the trouble you would take in offering consolation to grief that is beyond the reach of it."

As they, both of them, desired nothing more than to hear from his own lips the cause of his suffering, they entreated him to tell it, promising not to do anything for his relief or comfort that he did not wish; and thereupon the unhappy gentleman began his sad story in nearly the same words and manner in which he had related it to Don Quixote and the goatherd a few days before, when, through Master Elisabad, and Don Quixote's scrupulous observance of what was due to chivalry, the tale was left unfinished, as this history has already recorded; but now fortunately the mad fit kept off, allowed him to tell it to the end; and so, coming to the incident of the note which Don

Fernando had found in the volume of "Amadis of Gaul," Cardenio said that he remembered it perfectly and that it was in these words:

"Luscinda to Cardenio.

"Every day I discover merits in you that oblige and compel me to hold you in higher estimation; so if you desire to relieve me of this obligation without cost to my honour, you may easily do so. I have a father who knows you and loves me dearly, who without putting any constraint on my inclination will grant what will be reasonable for you to have, if it be that you value me as you say and as I believe you do."

"By this letter I was induced, as I told you, to demand Luscinda for my wife, and it was through it that Luscinda came to be regarded by Don Fernando as one of the most discreet and prudent women of the day, and this letter it was that suggested his design of ruining me before mine could be carried into effect. I told Don Fernando that all Luscinda's father was waiting for was that mine should ask her of him, which I did not dare to suggest to him, fearing that he would not consent to do so; not because he did not know perfectly well the rank, goodness, virtue, and beauty of Luscinda, and that she had qualities that would do honour to any family in Spain, but because I was aware that he did not wish me to marry so soon, before seeing what the Duke Ricardo would do for me. In short, I told him I did not venture to mention it to my father, as well on account of that difficulty, as of many others that discouraged me though I knew not well what they were, only that it seemed to me that what I desired was never to come to pass. To all this Don Fernando answered that he would take it upon himself to speak to my father, and persuade him to speak to Luscinda's father. O, ambitious Marius! O, cruel Catiline! O, wicked Sylla! O, perfidious Ganelon! O, treacherous Vellido! O, vindictive Julian! O, covetous Judas! Traitor, cruel, vindictive, and perfidious, wherein had this poor wretch failed in his fidelity, who with such frankness showed thee the secrets and the joys of his heart? What offence did I commit? What words did I utter, or what counsels did I give that had not the furtherance of thy honour and welfare for their aim? But, woe is me, wherefore do I complain? for sure it is that when misfortunes spring from the stars, descending from on high they fall upon us with such fury and violence that no power on earth can check their course nor human device stay their coming. Who could have thought that Don Fernando, a highborn gentleman, intelligent, bound to me by gratitude for my services, one that could win the object of his love wherever he might set his affections, could have become so obdurate, as they say, as to rob me of my one ewe lamb that was not even yet in my possession? But laying aside these useless and unavailing reflections, let us take up the broken thread of my unhappy story.

"To proceed, then: Don Fernando finding my presence an obstacle to the execution of his treacherous and wicked design, resolved to send me to his elder brother under the pretext of asking money from him to pay for six horses which, purposely, and with the sole object of sending me away that he might the better carry out his infernal scheme, he had purchased the very day he offered to speak to my father, and the price of which he now desired me to fetch. Could I have anticipated this treachery? Could I by any chance have suspected it? Nay; so far from that, I offered with the greatest pleasure to go at once, in my satisfaction at the good bargain that had been made. That night I spoke with Luscinda, and told her what had been agreed upon with Don Fernando, and how I had strong hopes of our fair and reasonable wishes being realised. She, as unsuspicious as I was of the treachery of Don Fernando, bade me try to return speedily, as she believed the fulfilment of our desires would be delayed only so long as my father put off speaking to hers. I know not why it was that on saying this to me her eyes filled with tears, and there came a lump in her throat that prevented her from uttering a word of many more that it seemed to me she was striving to say to me. I was astonished at this unusual turn, which I never before observed in her. for we always conversed, whenever good fortune and my ingenuity gave us the chance, with the greatest gaiety and cheerfulness, mingling tears, sighs, jealousies, doubts, or fears with our words; it was all on my part a eulogy of my good fortune that Heaven should have given her to me for my mistress; I glorified her beauty, I extolled her worth and her understanding; and she paid me back by praising in me what in her love for me she thought worthy of praise; and besides we had a hundred thousand trifles and doings of our neighbours and acquaintances to talk about, and the utmost extent of my boldness was to take, almost by force, one of her fair white hands and carry it to my lips, as well as the closeness of the low grating that separated us allowed me. But the night before the unhappy day of my departure she wept, she moaned, she sighed, and she withdrew leaving me filled with perplexity and amazement, overwhelmed at the sight of such strange and affecting signs of grief and sorrow in Luscinda; but not to dash my hopes I ascribed it all to the depth of her love for me and the pain that separation gives those who love tenderly. At last I took my departure, sad and dejected, my heart filled with fancies and suspicions, but not knowing well what it was I suspected or fancied; plain omens pointing to the sad event and misfortune that was awaiting me.

"I reached the place whither I had been sent, gave the letter to Don Fernando's brother, and was kindly received but not promptly dismissed, for he desired me to wait, very much against my will, eight days in some place where the duke his father was not likely to see me, as his brother wrote that the money was to be sent without his knowledge; all of which was a scheme of the treacherous Don Fernando, for his brother had no want of money to enable him to despatch me at once.

"The command was one that exposed me to the temptation of disobeying it, as it seemed to me impossible to endure life for so many days separated from Luscinda, especially after leaving her in the sorrowful mood I have described to you; nevertheless as a dutiful servant I obeyed, though I felt it would be at the cost of my well-being. But four days later there came a man in quest of me with a letter which he gave me, and which by the address I perceived to be from Luscinda, as the writing was hers. I opened it with fear and trepidation, persuaded that it must be something serious that had impelled her to write to me when at a distance, as she seldom did so when I was near. Before reading it I asked the man who it was that had given it to him, and how long he had been upon the road; he told me that as he happened to be passing through one of the streets of the city at the hour of noon, a very beautiful lady called to him from a window, and with tears in her eyes said to him hurriedly, 'Brother, if you are, as you seem to be, a Christian, for the love of God I entreat you to have this letter despatched without a moment's delay to the place and person named in the address, all which is well known, and by this you will render a great service to our Lord; and that you may be at no inconvenience in doing so take what is in this handkerchief;' and said he, 'with this she threw me a handkerchief out of the window in which were tied up a hundred reals and this gold ring which I bring here together with the letter I have given you. And then without waiting for any answer she left the window, though not before she saw me take the letter and the handkerchief, and I had by signs let her know that I would do as she bade me; and so, seeing myself so well paid for the trouble I would have in bringing it to you, and knowing by the address that it was to you it was sent (for, senor, I know you very well), and also unable to resist that beautiful lady's tears, I resolved to trust no one else, but to come myself and give it to you, and in sixteen hours from the time when it was given me I have made the journey, which, as you know, is eighteen leagues.'

"All the while the good-natured improvised courier was telling me this, I hung upon his words, my legs trembling under me so that I could scarcely stand. However, I opened the letter and read these words:

"'The promise Don Fernando gave you to urge your father to speak to mine, he has fulfilled much more to his own satisfaction than to your advantage. I have to tell you, senor, that he has demanded me for a wife, and my father, led away by what he considers Don Fernando's superiority over you, has favoured his suit so cordially, that in two days hence the betrothal is to take place with such secrecy and so privately that the only witnesses are to be the Heavens above and a few of the household. Picture to yourself the state I am in; judge if it be urgent for you to come; the issue of the affair will show you whether I love you or not. God grant this may come to your hand before mine shall be forced to link itself with his who keeps so ill the faith that he has pledged.'

"Such, in brief, were the words of the letter, words that made me set out at once without waiting any longer for reply or money; for I now saw clearly that it was not the purchase of horses but of his own pleasure that had made Don Fernando send me to his brother. The exasperation I felt against Don Fernando, joined with the fear of losing the prize I had won by so many years of love and devotion, lent me wings; so that almost flying I reached home the same day, by the hour which served for speaking with Luscinda. I arrived unobserved, and left the mule on which I had come at the house of the worthy man who had brought me the letter, and fortune was pleased to be for once so kind that I found Luscinda at the grating that was the witness of our loves. She recognised me at once, and I her, but not as she ought to have recognised me, or I her. But who is there in the world that can boast of having fathomed or understood the wavering mind and unstable nature of a woman? Of a truth no one. To proceed: as soon as Luscinda saw me she said, 'Cardenio, I am in my bridal dress, and the treacherous Don Fernando and my covetous father are waiting for me in the hall with the other witnesses, who shall be the witnesses of my death before they witness my betrothal. Be not distressed, my friend, but contrive to be present at this sacrifice, and if that cannot be prevented by my words, I have a dagger concealed which will prevent more deliberate violence, putting an end to my life and giving thee a first proof of the love I have borne and bear thee.' I replied to her distractedly and hastily, in fear lest I should not have time to reply, 'May thy words be verified by thy deeds, lady; and if thou hast a dagger to save thy honour, I have a sword to defend thee or kill myself if fortune be against us.'

"I think she could not have heard all these words, for I perceived that they called her away in haste, as the bridegroom was waiting. Now the night of my sorrow set in, the sun of my happiness went down, I felt my eyes bereft of sight, my mind of reason. I could not enter the house, nor was I capable of any movement; but reflecting how important it was that I should be present at what might take place on the occasion, I nerved myself as best I could and went in, for I well knew all the entrances and outlets; and besides, with the confusion that in secret pervaded the house no one took notice of me, so, without being seen, I found an opportunity of placing myself in the recess formed by a window of the hall itself, and concealed by the ends and borders of two tapestries, from between which I could, without being seen, see all that took place in the room. Who could describe the agitation of heart I suffered as I stood there—the thoughts that came to me—the reflections that passed through my mind? They were such as cannot be, nor were it well they should be, told. Suffice it to say that the bridegroom entered the hall in his usual dress, without ornament of any kind; as groomsman he had with him a cousin of Luscinda's and except the servants of the house there was no one else in the chamber. Soon afterwards Luscinda came out from an antechamber, attended by her mother and two of her damsels, arrayed and adorned as became her rank and beauty, and in full festival and ceremonial attire. My anxiety and distraction did not allow me to observe or notice particularly what she wore; I could only perceive the colours, which were crimson and white, and the glitter of the gems and jewels on her head dress and apparel, surpassed by the rare beauty of her lovely auburn hair that vying with the precious stones and the light of the four torches that stood in the hall shone with a brighter gleam than all. Oh memory, mortal foe of my peace! why bring before me now the incomparable beauty of that adored enemy of mine? Were it not better, cruel memory, to remind me and recall what she then did, that stirred by a wrong so glaring I may seek, if not vengeance now, at least to rid myself of life? Be not weary, sirs, of listening to these digressions; my sorrow is not one of those that can or should be told tersely and briefly, for to me each incident seems to call for many words."

To this the curate replied that not only were they not weary of listening to him, but that the details he mentioned interested them greatly, being of a kind by no means to be omitted and deserving of the same attention as the main story.

"To proceed, then," continued Cardenio: "all being assembled in the hall, the priest of the parish came in and as he took the pair by the hand to perform the requisite ceremony, at the words, 'Will you, Senora Luscinda, take Senor Don Fernando, here present, for your lawful husband, as the holy Mother Church ordains?' I thrust my head and neck out from between the tapestries, and with eager ears and throbbing heart set myself to listen to Luscinda's answer, awaiting in her reply the sentence of death or the grant of life. Oh, that I had but dared at that moment to rush forward crying aloud, 'Luscinda, Luscinda! have a care what thou dost; remember what thou owest me; bethink thee thou art mine and canst not be another's; reflect that thy utterance of "Yes" and the end of my life will come at the same instant. O, treacherous Don Fernando! robber of my glory, death of my life! What seekest thou? Remember that thou canst not as a Christian attain the object of thy wishes, for Luscinda is my bride, and I am her husband!' Fool that I am! now that I am far away, and out of danger, I say I should have done what I did not do: now that I have allowed my precious treasure to be robbed from me, I curse the robber, on whom I might have taken vengeance had I as much heart for it as I have for bewailing my fate; in short, as I was then a coward and a fool, little wonder is it if I am now dying shame-stricken, remorseful, and mad.

"The priest stood waiting for the answer of Luscinda, who for a long time withheld it; and just as I thought she was taking out the dagger to save her honour, or struggling for words to make some declaration of the truth on my behalf, I heard her say in a faint and feeble voice, 'I will:' Don Fernando said the same, and giving her the ring they stood linked by a knot that could never be loosed. The bridegroom then approached to embrace his bride; and she, pressing her hand upon her heart, fell fainting in her mother's arms. It only remains now for me to tell you the state I was in when in that consent that I heard I saw all my hopes mocked, the words and promises of Luscinda proved falsehoods, and the recovery of the prize I had that instant lost rendered impossible for ever. I stood stupefied, wholly abandoned, it seemed, by Heaven, declared the enemy of the earth that bore me, the air refusing me breath for my sighs, the water moisture for my tears; it was only the fire that gathered strength so that my whole frame glowed with rage and jealousy. They were all thrown into confusion by Luscinda's fainting, and as her mother was unlacing her to give her air a sealed paper was discovered in her bosom which Don Fernando seized at once and began to read by the light of one of the torches. As soon as he had read it he seated himself in a chair, leaning his cheek on his hand in the attitude of one deep in thought, without taking any part in the efforts that were being made to recover his bride from her fainting fit.

"Seeing all the household in confusion, I ventured to come out regardless whether I were seen or not, and determined, if I were, to do some frenzied deed that would prove to all the world the righteous indignation of my breast in the punishment of the treacherous Don Fernando, and even in that of the fickle fainting traitress. But my fate, doubtless reserving me for greater sorrows, if such there be, so ordered it that just then I had enough and to spare of that reason which has since been wanting to me; and so, without seeking to take vengeance on my greatest enemies (which might have been easily taken, as all thought of me was so far from their minds), I resolved to take it upon myself, and on myself to inflict the pain they deserved, perhaps with even greater severity than I should have dealt out to them had I then slain them; for sudden pain is soon over, but that which is protracted by tortures is ever slaying without ending life. In a word, I quitted the house and reached that of the man with whom I had left my mule; I made him saddle it for me, mounted without bidding him farewell, and rode out of the city, like another Lot, not daring to turn my head to look back upon it; and when I found myself alone in the open country, screened by the darkness of the night, and tempted by the stillness to give vent to my grief without apprehension or fear of being heard or seen, then I broke silence and lifted up my voice in maledictions upon Luscinda and Don Fernando, as if I could thus avenge the wrong they had done me. I called her cruel, ungrateful, false, thankless, but above all covetous, since the wealth of my enemy had blinded the eyes of her affection, and turned it from me to transfer it to one to whom fortune had been more generous and liberal. And yet, in the midst of this outburst of execration and upbraiding, I found excuses for her, saying it was no wonder that a young girl in the seclusion of her parents' house, trained and schooled to obey them always, should have been ready to yield to their wishes when they offered her for a husband a gentleman of such distinction, wealth, and noble birth, that if she had refused to accept him she would have been thought out of her senses, or to have set her affection elsewhere, a suspicion injurious to her fair name and fame. But then again, I said, had she declared I was her husband, they would have seen that in choosing me she had not chosen so ill but that they might excuse her, for before Don Fernando had made his offer, they themselves could not have desired, if their desires had been ruled by reason, a more eligible husband for their daughter than I was; and she, before taking the last fatal step of giving her hand, might easily have said that I had already given her mine, for I should have come forward to support any assertion of hers to that effect. In short, I came to the conclusion that feeble love, little reflection, great ambition, and a craving for rank, had made her forget the words with which she had deceived me, encouraged and supported by my firm hopes and honourable passion.

"Thus soliloquising and agitated, I journeyed onward for the remainder of the night, and by daybreak I reached one of the passes of these mountains, among which I wandered for three days more without taking any path or road, until I came to some meadows lying on I know not which side of the mountains, and there I inquired of some herdsmen in what direction the most rugged part of the range lay. They told me that it was in this quarter, and I at once directed my course hither, intending to end my life here; but as I was making my way among these crags, my mule dropped dead through fatigue and hunger, or, as I think more likely, in order to have done with such a worthless burden as it bore in me. I was left on foot, worn out, famishing, without anyone to help me or any thought of seeking help: and so thus I lay stretched on the ground, how long I know not, after which I rose up free from hunger, and found beside me some goatherds, who no doubt were the persons who had relieved me in my need, for they told me how they had found me, and how I had been uttering ravings that showed plainly I had lost my reason; and since then I am conscious that I am not always in full possession of it, but at times so deranged and crazed that I do a thousand mad things, tearing my clothes, crying aloud in these solitudes, cursing my fate, and idly calling on the dear name of her who is my enemy, and only seeking to end my life in lamentation; and when I recover my senses I find myself so exhausted and weary that I can scarcely move. Most commonly my dwelling is the hollow of a cork tree large enough to shelter this miserable body; the herdsmen and goatherds who frequent these mountains, moved by compassion, furnish me with food, leaving it by the wayside or on the rocks, where they think I may perhaps pass and find it; and so, even though I may be then out of my senses, the wants of nature teach me what is required to sustain me, and make me crave it and eager to take it. At other times, so they tell me when they find me in a rational mood, I sally out upon the road, and though they would gladly give it me, I snatch food by force from the shepherds bringing it from the village to their huts. Thus do pass the wretched life that remains to me, until it be Heaven's will to bring it to a close, or so to order my memory that I no longer recollect the beauty and treachery of Luscinda, or the wrong done me by Don Fernando; for if it will do this without depriving me of life, I will turn my thoughts into some better channel; if not, I can only implore it to have full mercy on my soul, for in myself I feel no power or strength to release my body from this strait in which I have of my own accord chosen to place it.

"Such, sirs, is the dismal story of my misfortune: say if it be one that can be told with less emotion than you have seen in me; and do not trouble yourselves with urging or pressing upon me what reason suggests as likely to serve for my relief, for it will avail me as much as the medicine prescribed by a wise physician avails the sick man who will not take it. I have no wish for health without Luscinda; and since it is her pleasure to be another's, when she is or should be mine, let it be mine to be a prey to misery when I might have enjoyed happiness. She by her fickleness strove to make my ruin irretrievable; I will strive to gratify her wishes by seeking destruction; and it will show generations to come that I alone was deprived of that of which all others in misfortune have a superabundance, for to them the impossibility of being consoled is itself a consolation, while to me it is the cause of greater sorrows and sufferings, for I think that even in death there will not be an end of them."

Here Cardenio brought to a close his long discourse and story, as full of misfortune as it was of love; but just as the curate was going to address some words of comfort to him, he was stopped by a voice that reached his ear, saying in melancholy tones what will be told in the Fourth Part of this narrative; for at this point the sage and sagacious historian, Cide Hamete Benengeli, brought the Third to a conclusion.

CHAPTER XXVIII

WHICH TREATS OF THE STRANGE AND DELIGHTFUL ADVENTURE THAT BEFELL THE CURATE AND THE BARBER IN THE SAME SIERRA

Happy and fortunate were the times when that most daring knight Don Quixote of La Mancha was sent into the world; for by reason of his having formed a resolution so honourable as that of seeking to revive and restore to the world the long-lost and almost defunct order of knight-errantry, we now enjoy in this age of ours, so poor in light entertainment, not only the charm of his veracious history, but also of the tales and episodes contained in it which are, in a measure, no less pleasing, ingenious, and truthful, than the history itself; which, resuming its thread, carded, spun, and wound, relates that just as the curate was going to offer consolation to Cardenio, he was interrupted by a voice that fell upon his ear saying in plaintive tones:

"O God! is it possible I have found a place that may serve as a secret grave for the weary load of this body that I support so unwillingly? If the solitude these mountains promise deceives me not, it is so; ah! woe is me! how much more grateful to my mind will be the society of these rocks and brakes that permit me to complain of my misfortune to Heaven, than that of any human being, for there is none on earth to look to for counsel in doubt, comfort in sorrow, or relief in distress!"

All this was heard distinctly by the curate and those with him, and as it seemed to them to be uttered close by, as indeed it was, they got up to look for the speaker, and before they had gone twenty paces they discovered behind a rock, seated at the foot of an ash tree, a youth in the dress of a peasant, whose face they were unable at the moment to see as he was leaning forward, bathing his feet in the brook that flowed past. They approached so silently that he did not perceive them, being fully occupied in bathing his feet, which were so fair that they looked like two pieces of shining crystal brought forth among the other stones of the brook. The whiteness and beauty of these feet struck them with surprise, for they did not seem to have been made to crush clods or to follow the plough and the oxen as their owner's dress suggested; and so, finding they had not been noticed, the curate, who was in front, made a sign to the other two to conceal themselves behind some fragments of rock that lay there; which they did, observing closely what the youth was about. He had on a loose double-skirted dark brown jacket bound tight to his body with a white cloth; he wore besides breeches and gaiters of brown cloth, and on his head a brown montera; and he had the gaiters turned up as far as the middle of the leg, which verily seemed to be of pure alabaster.

As soon as he had done bathing his beautiful feet, he wiped them with a towel he took from under the montera, on taking off which he raised his face, and those who were watching him had an opportunity of seeing a beauty so exquisite that Cardenio said to the curate in a whisper:

"As this is not Luscinda, it is no human creature but a divine being."

The youth then took off the montera, and shaking his head from side to side there broke loose and spread out a mass of hair that the beams of the sun might have envied; by this they knew that what had seemed a peasant was a lovely woman, nay the most beautiful the eyes of two of them had ever beheld, or even Cardenio's if they had not seen and known Luscinda, for he afterwards declared that only the beauty of Luscinda could compare with this. The long auburn tresses not only covered her shoulders, but such was their length and abundance, concealed her all round beneath their masses, so that except the feet nothing of her form was visible. She now used her hands as a comb, and if her feet had seemed like bits of crystal in the water, her hands looked like pieces of driven snow among her locks; all which increased not only the admiration of the three beholders, but their anxiety to learn who she was. With this object they resolved to show themselves, and at the stir they made in getting upon their feet the fair damsel raised her head, and parting her hair from before her eyes with both hands, she looked to see who had made the noise, and the instant she perceived them she started to her feet, and without waiting to put on her shoes or gather up her hair, hastily snatched up a bundle as though of clothes that she had beside her, and, scared and alarmed, endeavoured to take flight; but before she had gone six paces she fell to the ground, her delicate feet being unable to bear the roughness of the stones; seeing which, the three hastened towards her, and the curate addressing her first said:

"Stay, senora, whoever you may be, for those whom you see here only desire to be of service to you; you have no need to attempt a flight so heedless, for neither can your feet bear it, nor we allow it."

Taken by surprise and bewildered, she made no reply to these words. They, however, came towards her, and the curate taking her hand went on to say:

"What your dress would hide, senora, is made known to us by your hair; a clear proof that it can be no trifling cause that has disguised your beauty in a garb so unworthy of it, and sent it into solitudes like these where we have had the good fortune to find you, if not to relieve your distress, at least to offer you comfort; for no distress, so long as life lasts, can be so oppressive or reach such a height as to make the sufferer refuse to listen to comfort offered with good intention. And so, senora, or senor, or whatever you prefer to be, dismiss the fears that our appearance has caused you and make us acquainted with your good or evil fortunes, for from all of us together, or from each one of us, you will receive sympathy in your trouble."

While the curate was speaking, the disguised damsel stood as if spell-bound, looking at them without opening her lips or uttering a word, just like a village rustic to whom something strange that he has never seen before has been suddenly shown; but on the curate addressing some further words to the same effect to her, sighing deeply she broke silence and said:

"Since the solitude of these mountains has been unable to conceal me, and the escape of my dishevelled tresses will not allow my tongue to deal in falsehoods, it would be idle for me now to make any further pretence of what, if you were to believe me, you would believe more out of courtesy than for any other reason. This being so, I say I thank you, sirs, for the offer you have made me, which places me under the obligation of complying with the request you have made of me; though I fear the account I shall give you of my misfortunes will excite in you as much concern as compassion, for you will be unable to suggest anything to remedy them or any consolation to alleviate them. However, that my honour may not be left a matter of doubt in your minds, now that you have discovered me to be a woman, and see that I am young, alone, and in this dress, things that taken together or separately would be enough to destroy any good name, I feel bound to tell what I would willingly keep secret if I could."

All this she who was now seen to be a lovely woman delivered without any hesitation, with so much ease and in so sweet a voice that they were not less charmed by her intelligence than by her beauty, and as they again repeated their offers and entreaties to her to fulfil her promise, she without further pressing, first modestly covering her feet and gathering up her hair, seated herself on a stone with the three placed around her, and, after an effort to restrain some tears that came to her eyes, in a clear and steady voice began her story thus:

"In this Andalusia there is a town from which a duke takes a title which makes him one of those that are called Grandees of Spain.

This nobleman has two sons, the elder heir to his dignity and apparently to his good qualities; the younger heir to I know not what, unless it be the treachery of Vellido and the falsehood of Ganelon. My parents are this lord's vassals, lowly in origin, but so wealthy that if birth had conferred as much on them as fortune, they would have had nothing left to desire, nor should I have had reason to fear trouble like that in which I find myself now; for it may be that my ill fortune came of theirs in not having been nobly born. It is true they are not so low that they have any reason to be ashamed of their condition, but neither are they so high as to remove from my mind the impression that my mishap comes of their humble birth. They are, in short, peasants, plain homely people, without any taint of disreputable blood, and, as the saying is, old rusty Christians, but so rich that by their wealth and free-handed way of life they are coming by degrees to be considered gentlefolk by birth, and even by position; though the wealth and nobility they thought most of was having me for their daughter; and as they have no other child to make their heir, and are affectionate parents, I was one of the most indulged daughters that ever parents indulged.

"I was the mirror in which they beheld themselves, the staff of their old age, and the object in which, with submission to Heaven, all their wishes centred, and mine were in accordance with theirs, for I knew their worth; and as I was mistress of their hearts, so was I also of their possessions. Through me they engaged or dismissed their servants; through my hands passed the accounts and returns of what was sown and reaped; the oil-mills, the wine-presses, the count of the flocks and herds, the beehives, all in short that a rich farmer like my father has or can have, I had under my care, and I acted as steward and mistress with an assiduity on my part and satisfaction on theirs that I cannot well describe to you. The leisure hours left to me after I had given the requisite orders to the head-shepherds, overseers, and other labourers, I passed in such employments as are not only allowable but necessary for young girls, those that the needle, embroidery cushion, and spinning wheel usually afford, and if to refresh my mind I quitted them for a while, I found recreation in reading some devotional book or playing the harp, for experience taught me that music soothes the troubled mind and relieves weariness of spirit. Such was the life I led in my parents' house and if I have depicted it thus minutely, it is not out of ostentation, or to let you know that I am rich, but that you may see how, without any fault of mine, I have fallen from the happy condition I have described, to the misery I am in at present. The truth is, that while I was leading this busy life, in a retirement that might compare with that of a monastery, and unseen as I thought by any except the servants of the house (for when I went to Mass it was so early in the morning, and I was so closely attended by my mother and the women of the household, and so thickly veiled and so shy, that my eyes scarcely saw more ground than I trod on), in spite of all this, the eyes of love, or idleness, more properly speaking, that the lynx's cannot rival, discovered me, with the help of the assiduity of Don Fernando; for that is the name of the younger son of the duke I told of."

The moment the speaker mentioned the name of Don Fernando, Cardenio changed colour and broke into a sweat, with such signs of emotion that the curate and the barber, who observed it, feared that one of the mad fits which they heard attacked him sometimes was coming upon him; but Cardenio showed no further agitation and remained quiet, regarding the peasant girl with fixed attention, for he began to suspect who she was. She, however, without noticing the excitement of Cardenio, continuing her story, went on to say:

"And they had hardly discovered me, when, as he owned afterwards, he was smitten with a violent love for me, as the manner in which it displayed itself plainly showed. But to shorten the long recital of my woes, I will pass over in silence all the artifices employed by Don Fernando for declaring his passion for me. He bribed all the household, he gave and offered gifts and presents to my parents; every day was like a holiday or a merry-making in our street; by night no one could sleep for the music; the love letters that used to come to my hand, no one knew how, were innumerable, full of tender pleadings and pledges, containing more promises and oaths than there were letters in them; all which not only did not soften me, but hardened my heart against him, as if he had been my mortal enemy, and as if everything he did to make me yield were done with the opposite intention. Not that the high-bred bearing of Don Fernando was disagreeable to me, or that I found his importunities wearisome; for it gave me a certain sort of satisfaction to find myself so sought and prized by a gentleman of such distinction, and I was not displeased at seeing my praises in his letters (for however ugly we women may be, it seems to me it always pleases us to hear ourselves called beautiful) but that my own sense of right was opposed to all this, as well as the repeated advice of my parents, who now very plainly perceived Don Fernando's purpose, for he cared very little if all the world knew it. They told me they trusted and confided their honour and good name to my virtue and rectitude alone, and bade me consider the disparity between Don Fernando and myself, from which I might conclude that his intentions, whatever he might say to the contrary, had for their aim his own pleasure rather than my advantage; and if I were at all desirous of opposing an obstacle to his unreasonable suit, they were ready, they said, to marry me at once to anyone I preferred, either among the leading people of our own town, or of any of those in the neighbourhood; for with their wealth and my good name, a match might be looked for in any quarter. This offer, and their sound advice strengthened my resolution, and I never gave Don Fernando a word in reply that could hold out to him any hope of success, however remote.

"All this caution of mine, which he must have taken for coyness, had apparently the effect of increasing his wanton appetite—for that is the name I give to his passion for me; had it been what he declared it to be, you would not know of it now, because there would have been no occasion to tell you of it. At length he learned that my parents were contemplating marriage for me in order to put an end to his hopes of obtaining possession of me, or at least to secure additional protectors to watch over me, and this intelligence or suspicion made him act as you shall hear. One night, as I was in my chamber with no other companion than a damsel who waited on me, with the doors carefully locked lest my honour should be imperilled through any carelessness, I know not nor can conceive how it happened, but, with all this seclusion and these precautions, and in the solitude and silence of my retirement, I found him standing before me, a vision that so astounded me that it deprived my eyes of sight, and my tongue of speech. I had no power to utter a cry, nor, I think, did he give me time to utter one, as he immediately approached me, and taking me in his arms (for, overwhelmed as I was, I was powerless, I say, to help myself), he began to make such professions to me that I know not how falsehood could have had the power of dressing them up to seem so like truth; and the traitor contrived that his tears should vouch for his words, and his sighs for his sincerity.

"I, a poor young creature alone, ill versed among my people in cases such as this, began, I know not how, to think all these lying protestations true, though without being moved by his sighs and tears to anything more than pure compassion; and so, as the first feeling of bewilderment passed away, and I began in some degree to recover myself, I said to him with more courage than I thought I could have possessed, 'If, as I am now in your arms, senor, I were in the claws of a fierce lion, and my deliverance could be procured by doing or saying anything to the prejudice of my honour, it would no more be in my power to do it or say it, than it would be possible that what was should not have been; so then, if you hold my body clasped in your arms, I hold my soul secured by virtuous intentions, very different from yours, as you will see if you attempt to carry them into effect by force. I am your vassal, but I am not your slave; your nobility neither has nor should have any right to dishonour or degrade my humble birth; and low-born peasant as I am, I have my self-respect as much as you, a lord and gentleman: with me your violence will be to no purpose, your wealth will have no weight, your words will have no power to deceive me, nor your sighs or tears to soften me: were I to see any of the things I speak of in him whom my parents gave me as a husband, his will should be mine, and mine should be bounded by his; and my honour being preserved even though my inclinations were not would willingly yield him what you, senor, would now obtain by force; and this I say lest you should suppose that any but my lawful husband shall ever win anything of me.' 'If that,' said this disloyal gentleman, 'be the only scruple you feel, fairest Dorothea' (for that is the name of this unhappy being), 'see here I give you my hand to be yours, and let Heaven, from which nothing is hid, and this image of Our Lady you have here, be witnesses of this pledge.'"

When Cardenio heard her say she was called Dorothea, he showed fresh agitation and felt convinced of the truth of his former suspicion, but he was unwilling to interrupt the story, and wished to hear the end of what he already all but knew, so he merely said:

"What! is Dorothea your name, senora? I have heard of another of the same name who can perhaps match your misfortunes. But proceed; by-and-by I may tell you something that will astonish you as much as it will excite your compassion."

Dorothea was struck by Cardenio's words as well as by his strange and miserable attire, and begged him if he knew anything concerning her to tell it to her at once, for if fortune had left her any blessing it was courage to bear whatever calamity might fall upon her, as she felt sure that none could reach her capable of increasing in any degree what she endured already.

"I would not let the occasion pass, senora," replied Cardenio, "of telling you what I think, if what I suspect were the truth, but so far there has been no opportunity, nor is it of any importance to you to know it."

"Be it as it may," replied Dorothea, "what happened in my story was that Don Fernando, taking an image that stood in the chamber, placed it as a witness of our betrothal, and with the most binding words and extravagant oaths gave me his promise to become my husband; though before he had made an end of pledging himself I bade him consider well what he was doing, and think of the anger his father would feel at seeing him married to a peasant girl and one of his vassals; I told him not to let my beauty, such as it was, blind him, for that was not enough to furnish an excuse for his transgression; and if in the love he bore me he wished to do me any kindness, it would be to leave my lot to follow its course at the level my condition required; for marriages so unequal never brought happiness, nor did they continue long to afford the enjoyment they began with.

"All this that I have now repeated I said to him, and much more which I cannot recollect; but it had no effect in inducing him to forego his purpose; he who has no intention of paying does not trouble himself about difficulties when he is striking the bargain. At the same time I argued the matter briefly in my own mind, saying to myself, 'I shall not be the first who has risen through marriage from a lowly to a lofty station, nor will Don Fernando be the first whom beauty or, as is more likely, a blind attachment, has led to mate himself below his rank. Then, since I am introducing no new usage or practice, I may as well avail myself of the honour that chance offers me, for even though his inclination for me should not outlast the attainment of his wishes, I shall be, after all, his wife before God. And if I strive to repel him by scorn, I can see that, fair means failing, he is in a mood to use force, and I shall be left dishonoured and without any means of proving my innocence to those who cannot know how innocently I have come to be in this position; for what arguments would persuade my parents that this gentleman entered my chamber without my consent?'

"All these questions and answers passed through my mind in a moment; but the oaths of Don Fernando, the witnesses he appealed to, the tears he shed, and lastly the charms of his person and his high-bred grace, which, accompanied by such signs of genuine love, might well have conquered a heart even more free and coy than mine—these were the things that more than all began to influence me and lead me unawares to my ruin. I called my waiting-maid to me, that there might be a witness on earth besides those in Heaven, and again Don Fernando renewed and repeated his oaths, invoked as witnesses fresh saints in addition to the former ones, called down upon himself a thousand curses hereafter should he fail to keep his promise, shed more tears, redoubled his sighs and pressed me closer in his arms, from which he had never allowed me to escape; and so I was left by my maid, and ceased to be one, and he became a traitor and a perjured man.

"The day which followed the night of my misfortune did not come so quickly, I imagine, as Don Fernando wished, for when desire has attained its object, the greatest pleasure is to fly from the scene of pleasure. I say so because Don Fernando made all haste to leave me, and by the adroitness of my maid, who was indeed the one who had admitted him, gained the street before daybreak; but on taking leave of me he told me, though not with as much earnestness and fervour as when he came, that I might rest assured of his faith and of the sanctity and sincerity of his oaths; and to confirm his words he drew a rich ring off his finger and placed it upon mine. He then took his departure and I was left, I know not whether sorrowful or happy; all I can say is, I was left agitated and troubled in mind and almost bewildered by what had taken place, and I had not the spirit, or else it did not occur to me, to chide my maid for the treachery she had been guilty of in concealing Don Fernando in my chamber; for as yet I was unable to make up my mind whether what had befallen me was for good or evil. I told Don Fernando at parting, that as I was now his, he might see me on other nights in the same way, until it should be his pleasure to let the matter become known; but, except the following night, he came no more, nor for more than a month could I catch a glimpse of him in the street or in church, while I wearied myself with watching for one; although I knew he was in the town, and almost every day went out hunting, a pastime he was very fond of. I remember well how sad and dreary those days and hours were to me; I remember well how I began to doubt as they went by, and even to lose confidence in the faith of Don Fernando; and I remember, too, how my maid heard those words in reproof of her audacity that she had not heard before, and how I was forced to put a constraint on my tears and on the expression of my countenance, not to give my parents cause to ask me why I was so melancholy, and drive me to invent falsehoods in reply. But all this was suddenly brought to an end, for the time came when all such considerations were disregarded, and there was no further question of honour, when my patience gave way and the secret of my heart became known abroad. The reason was, that a few days later it was reported in the town that Don Fernando had been married in a neighbouring city to a maiden of rare beauty, the daughter of parents of distinguished position, though not so rich that her portion would entitle her to look for so brilliant a match; it was said, too, that her name was Luscinda, and that at the betrothal some strange things had happened."

Cardenio heard the name of Luscinda, but he only shrugged his shoulders, bit his lips, bent his brows, and before long two streams of tears escaped from his eyes. Dorothea, however, did not interrupt her story, but went on in these words:

"This sad intelligence reached my ears, and, instead of being struck with a chill, with such wrath and fury did my heart burn that I scarcely restrained myself from rushing out into the streets, crying aloud and proclaiming openly the perfidy and treachery of which I was the victim; but this transport of rage was for the time checked by a resolution I formed, to be carried out the same night, and that was to assume this dress, which I got from a servant of my father's, one of the zagals, as they are called in farmhouses, to whom I confided the whole of my misfortune, and whom I entreated to accompany me to the city where I heard my enemy was. He, though he remonstrated with me for my boldness, and condemned my resolution, when he saw me bent upon my purpose, offered to bear me company, as he said, to the end of the world. I at once packed up in a linen pillow-case a woman's dress, and some jewels and money to provide for emergencies, and in the silence of the night, without letting my treacherous maid know, I sallied forth from the house, accompanied by my servant and abundant anxieties, and on foot set out for the city, but borne as it were on wings by my eagerness to reach it, if not to prevent what I presumed to be already done, at least to call upon Don Fernando to tell me with what conscience he had done it. I reached my destination in two days and a half, and on entering the city inquired for the house of Luscinda's parents. The first person I asked gave me more in reply than I sought to know; he showed me the house, and told me all that had occurred at the betrothal of the daughter of the family, an affair of such notoriety in the city that it was the talk of every knot of idlers in the street. He said that on the night of Don Fernando's betrothal with Luscinda, as soon as she had consented to be his bride by saying 'Yes,' she was taken with a sudden fainting fit, and that on the bridegroom approaching to unlace the bosom of her dress to give her air, he found a paper in her own handwriting, in which she said and declared that she could not be Don Fernando's bride, because she was already Cardenio's, who, according to the man's account, was a gentleman of distinction of the same city; and that if she had accepted Don Fernando, it was only in obedience to her parents. In short, he said, the words of the paper made it clear she meant to kill herself on the completion of the betrothal, and gave her reasons for putting an end to herself all which was confirmed, it was said, by a dagger they found somewhere in her clothes. On seeing this, Don Fernando, persuaded that Luscinda had befooled, slighted, and trifled with him, assailed her before she had recovered from her swoon, and tried to stab her with the dagger that had been found, and would have succeeded had not her parents and those who were present prevented him. It was said, moreover, that Don Fernando went away at once, and that Luscinda did not recover from her prostration until the next day, when she told her parents how she was really the bride of that Cardenio I have mentioned. I learned besides that Cardenio, according to report, had been present at the betrothal; and that upon seeing her betrothed contrary to his expectation, he had quitted the city in despair, leaving behind him a letter declaring the wrong Luscinda had done him, and his intention of going where no one should ever see him again. All this was a matter of notoriety in the city, and everyone spoke of it; especially when it became known that Luscinda was missing from her father's house and from the city, for she was not to be found anywhere, to the distraction of her parents, who knew not what steps to take to recover her. What I learned revived my hopes, and I was better pleased not to have found Don Fernando than to find him married, for it seemed to me that the door was not yet entirely shut upon relief in my case, and I thought that perhaps Heaven had put this impediment in the way of the second marriage, to lead him to recognise his obligations under the former one, and reflect that as a Christian he was bound to consider his soul above all human objects. All this passed through my mind, and I strove to comfort myself without comfort, indulging in faint and distant hopes of cherishing that life that I now abhor.

"But while I was in the city, uncertain what to do, as I could not find Don Fernando, I heard notice given by the public crier offering a great reward to anyone who should find me, and giving the particulars of my age and of the very dress I wore; and I heard it said that the lad who came with me had taken me away from my father's house; a thing that cut me to the heart, showing how low my good name had fallen, since it was not enough that I should lose it by my flight, but they must add with whom I had fled, and that one so much beneath me and so unworthy of my consideration. The instant I heard the notice I quitted the city with my servant, who now began to show signs of wavering in his fidelity to me, and the same night, for fear of discovery, we entered the most thickly wooded part of these mountains. But, as is commonly said, one evil calls up another and the end of one misfortune is apt to be the beginning of one still greater, and so it proved in my case; for my worthy servant, until then so faithful and trusty when he found me in this lonely spot, moved more by his own villainy than by my beauty, sought to take advantage of the opportunity which these solitudes seemed to present him, and with little shame and less fear of God and respect for me, began to make overtures to me; and finding that I replied to the effrontery of his proposals with justly severe language, he laid aside the entreaties which he had employed at first, and began to use violence.

"But just Heaven, that seldom fails to watch over and aid good intentions, so aided mine that with my slight strength and with little exertion I pushed him over a precipice, where I left him, whether dead or alive I know not; and then, with greater speed than seemed possible in my terror and fatigue, I made my way into the mountains, without any other thought or purpose save that of hiding myself among them, and escaping my father and those despatched in search of me by his orders. It is now I know not how many months since with this object I came here, where I met a herdsman who engaged me as his servant at a place in the heart of this Sierra, and all this time I have been serving him as herd, striving to keep always afield to hide these locks which have now unexpectedly betrayed me. But all my care and pains were unavailing, for my master made the discovery that I was not a man, and harboured the same base designs as my servant; and as fortune does not always supply a remedy in cases of difficulty, and I had no precipice or ravine at hand down which to fling the master and cure his passion, as I had in the servant's case, I thought it a lesser evil to leave him and again conceal myself among these crags, than make trial of my strength and argument with him. So, as I say, once more I went into hiding to seek for some place where I might with sighs and tears implore Heaven to have pity on my misery, and grant me help and strength to escape from it, or let me die among the solitudes, leaving no trace of an unhappy being who, by no fault of hers, has furnished matter for talk and scandal at home and abroad."

CHAPTER XXIX

WHICH TREATS OF THE DROLL DEVICE AND METHOD ADOPTED TO EXTRICATE OUR LOVE-STRICKEN KNIGHT FROM THE SEVERE PENANCE HE HAD IMPOSED UPON HIMSELF

"Such, sirs, is the true story of my sad adventures; judge for yourselves now whether the sighs and lamentations you heard, and the tears that flowed from my eyes, had not sufficient cause even if I had indulged in them more freely; and if you consider the nature of my misfortune you will see that consolation is idle, as there is no possible remedy for it. All I ask of you is, what you may easily and reasonably do, to show me where I may pass my life unharassed by the fear and dread of discovery by those who are in search of me; for though the great love my parents bear me makes me feel sure of being kindly received by them, so great is my feeling of shame at the mere thought that I cannot present myself before them as they expect, that I had rather banish myself from their sight for ever than look them in the face with the reflection that they beheld mine stripped of that purity they had a right to expect in me."

With these words she became silent, and the colour that overspread her face showed plainly the pain and shame she was suffering at heart. In theirs the listeners felt as much pity as wonder at her misfortunes; but as the curate was just about to offer her some consolation and advice Cardenio forestalled him, saying, "So then, senora, you are the fair Dorothea, the only daughter of the rich Clenardo?" Dorothea was astonished at hearing her father's name, and at the miserable appearance of him who mentioned it, for it has been already said how wretchedly clad Cardenio was; so she said to him:

"And who may you be, brother, who seem to know my father's name so well? For so far, if I remember rightly, I have not mentioned it in the whole story of my misfortunes."

"I am that unhappy being, senora," replied Cardenio, "whom, as you have said, Luscinda declared to be her husband; I am the unfortunate Cardenio, whom the wrong-doing of him who has brought you to your present condition has reduced to the state you see me in, bare, ragged, bereft of all human comfort, and what is worse, of reason, for I only possess it when Heaven is pleased for some short space to restore it to me. I, Dorothea, am he who witnessed the wrong done by Don Fernando, and waited to hear the 'Yes' uttered by which Luscinda owned herself his betrothed: I am he who had not courage enough to see how her fainting fit ended, or what came of the paper that was found in her bosom, because my heart had not the fortitude to endure so many strokes of ill-fortune at once; and so losing patience I quitted the house, and leaving a letter with my host, which I entreated him to place in Luscinda's hands, I betook myself to these solitudes, resolved to end here the life I hated as if it were my mortal enemy. But fate would not rid me of it, contenting itself with robbing me of my reason, perhaps to preserve me for the good fortune I have had in meeting you; for if that which you have just told us be true, as I believe it to be, it may be that Heaven has yet in store for both of us a happier termination to our misfortunes than we look for; because seeing that Luscinda cannot marry Don Fernando, being mine, as she has herself so openly declared, and that Don Fernando cannot marry her as he is yours, we may reasonably hope that Heaven will restore to us what is ours, as it is still in existence and not yet alienated or destroyed. And as we have this consolation springing from no very visionary hope or wild fancy, I entreat you, senora, to form new resolutions in your better mind, as I mean to do in mine, preparing yourself to look forward to happier fortunes; for I swear to you by the faith of a gentleman and a Christian not to desert you until I see you in possession of Don Fernando, and if I cannot by words induce him to recognise his obligation to you, in that case to avail myself of the right which my rank as a gentleman gives me, and with just cause challenge him on account of the injury he has done you, not regarding my own wrongs, which I shall leave to Heaven to avenge, while I on earth devote myself to yours."

Cardenio's words completed the astonishment of Dorothea, and not knowing how to return thanks for such an offer, she attempted to kiss his feet; but Cardenio would not permit it, and the licentiate replied for both, commended the sound reasoning of Cardenio, and lastly, begged, advised, and urged them to come with him to his village, where they might furnish themselves with what they needed, and take measures to discover Don Fernando, or restore Dorothea to her parents, or do what seemed to them most advisable. Cardenio and Dorothea thanked him, and accepted the kind offer he made them; and the barber, who had been listening to all attentively and in silence, on his part some kindly words also, and with no less good-will than the curate offered his services in any way that might be of use to them. He also explained to them in a few words the object that had brought them there, and the strange nature of Don Quixote's madness, and how they were waiting for his squire, who had gone in search of him. Like the recollection of a dream, the quarrel he had had with Don Quixote came back to Cardenio's memory, and he described it to the others; but he was unable to say what the dispute was about.

At this moment they heard a shout, and recognised it as coming from Sancho Panza, who, not finding them where he had left them, was calling aloud to them. They went to meet him, and in answer to their inquiries about Don Quixote, he told them how he had found him stripped to his shirt, lank, yellow, half dead with hunger, and sighing for his lady Dulcinea; and although he had told him that she commanded him to quit that place and come to El Toboso, where she was expecting him, he had answered that he was determined not to appear in the presence of her beauty until he had done deeds to make him worthy of her favour; and if this went on, Sancho said, he ran the risk of not becoming an emperor as in duty bound, or even an archbishop, which was the least he could be; for which reason they ought to consider what was to be done to get him away from there. The licentiate in reply told him not to be uneasy, for they would fetch him away in spite of himself. He then told Cardenio and Dorothea what they had proposed to do to cure Don Quixote, or at any rate take him home; upon which Dorothea said that she could play the distressed damsel better than the barber; especially as she had there the dress in which to do it to the life, and that they might trust to her acting the part in every particular requisite for carrying out their scheme, for she had read a great many books of chivalry, and knew exactly the style in which afflicted damsels begged boons of knights-errant.

"In that case," said the curate, "there is nothing more required than to set about it at once, for beyond a doubt fortune is declaring itself in our favour, since it has so unexpectedly begun to open a door for your relief, and smoothed the way for us to our object."

Dorothea then took out of her pillow-case a complete petticoat of some rich stuff, and a green mantle of some other fine material, and a necklace and other ornaments out of a little box, and with these in an instant she so arrayed herself that she looked like a great and rich lady. All this, and more, she said, she had taken from home in case of need, but that until then she had had no occasion to make use of it. They were all highly delighted with her grace, air, and beauty, and declared Don Fernando to be a man of very little taste when he rejected such charms. But the one who admired her most was Sancho Panza, for it seemed to him (what indeed was true) that in all the days of his life he had never seen such a lovely creature; and he asked the curate with great eagerness who this beautiful lady was, and what she wanted in these out-of-the-way quarters.

"This fair lady, brother Sancho," replied the curate, "is no less a personage than the heiress in the direct male line of the great kingdom of Micomicon, who has come in search of your master to beg a boon of him, which is that he redress a wrong or injury that a wicked giant has done her; and from the fame as a good knight which your master has acquired far and wide, this princess has come from Guinea to seek him."

"A lucky seeking and a lucky finding!" said Sancho Panza at this; "especially if my master has the good fortune to redress that injury, and right that wrong, and kill that son of a bitch of a giant your worship speaks of; as kill him he will if he meets him, unless, indeed, he happens to be a phantom; for my master has no power at all against phantoms. But one thing among others I would beg of you, senor licentiate, which is, that, to prevent my master taking a fancy to be an archbishop, for that is what I'm afraid of, your worship would recommend him to marry this princess at once; for in this way he will be disabled from taking archbishop's orders, and will easily come into his empire, and I to the end of my desires; I have been thinking over the matter carefully, and by what I can make out I find it will not do for me that my master should become an archbishop, because I am no good for the Church, as I am married; and for me now, having as I have a wife and children, to set about obtaining dispensations to enable me to hold a place of profit under the Church, would be endless work; so that, senor, it all turns on my master marrying this lady at once—for as yet I do not know her grace, and so I cannot call her by her name."

"She is called the Princess Micomicona," said the curate; "for as her kingdom is Micomicon, it is clear that must be her name."

"There's no doubt of that," replied Sancho, "for I have known many to take their name and title from the place where they were born and call themselves Pedro of Alcala, Juan of Ubeda, and Diego of Valladolid; and it may be that over there in Guinea queens have the same way of taking the names of their kingdoms."

"So it may," said the curate; "and as for your master's marrying, I will do all in my power towards it:" with which Sancho was as much pleased as the curate was amazed at his simplicity and at seeing what a hold the absurdities of his master had taken of his fancy, for he had evidently persuaded himself that he was going to be an emperor.

By this time Dorothea had seated herself upon the curate's mule, and the barber had fitted the ox-tail beard to his face, and they now told Sancho to conduct them to where Don Quixote was, warning him not to say that he knew either the licentiate or the barber, as his master's becoming an emperor entirely depended on his not recognising them; neither the curate nor Cardenio, however, thought fit to go with them; Cardenio lest he should remind Don Quixote of the quarrel he had with him, and the curate as there was no necessity for his presence just yet, so they allowed the others to go on before them, while they themselves followed slowly on foot. The curate did not forget to instruct Dorothea how to act, but she said they might make their minds easy, as everything would be done exactly as the books of chivalry required and described.

They had gone about three-quarters of a league when they discovered Don Quixote in a wilderness of rocks, by this time clothed, but without his armour; and as soon as Dorothea saw him and was told by Sancho that that was Don Quixote, she whipped her palfrey, the well-bearded barber following her, and on coming up to him her squire sprang from his mule and came forward to receive her in his arms, and she dismounting with great ease of manner advanced to kneel before the feet of Don Quixote; and though he strove to raise her up, she without rising addressed him in this fashion:

"From this spot I will not rise, valiant and doughty knight, until your goodness and courtesy grant me a boon, which will redound to the honour and renown of your person and render a service to the most disconsolate and afflicted damsel the sun has seen; and if the might of your strong arm corresponds to the repute of your immortal fame, you are bound to aid the helpless being who, led by the savour of your renowned name, hath come from far distant lands to seek your aid in her misfortunes."

"I will not answer a word, beauteous lady," replied Don Quixote, "nor will I listen to anything further concerning you, until you rise from the earth."

"I will not rise, senor," answered the afflicted damsel, "unless of your courtesy the boon I ask is first granted me."

"I grant and accord it," said Don Quixote, "provided without detriment or prejudice to my king, my country, or her who holds the key of my heart and freedom, it may be complied with."

"It will not be to the detriment or prejudice of any of them, my worthy lord," said the afflicted damsel; and here Sancho Panza drew close to his master's ear and said to him very softly, "Your worship may very safely grant the boon she asks; it's nothing at all; only to kill a big giant; and she who asks it is the exalted Princess Micomicona, queen of the great kingdom of Micomicon of Ethiopia."

"Let her be who she may," replied Don Quixote, "I will do what is my bounden duty, and what my conscience bids me, in conformity with what I have professed;" and turning to the damsel he said, "Let your great beauty rise, for I grant the boon which you would ask of me."

"Then what I ask," said the damsel, "is that your magnanimous person accompany me at once whither I will conduct you, and that you promise not to engage in any other adventure or quest until you have avenged me of a traitor who against all human and divine law, has usurped my kingdom."

"I repeat that I grant it," replied Don Quixote; "and so, lady, you may from this day forth lay aside the melancholy that distresses you, and let your failing hopes gather new life and strength, for with the help of God and of my arm you will soon see yourself restored to your kingdom, and seated upon the throne of your ancient and mighty realm, notwithstanding and despite of the felons who would gainsay it; and now hands to the work, for in delay there is apt to be danger."

The distressed damsel strove with much pertinacity to kiss his hands; but Don Quixote, who was in all things a polished and courteous knight, would by no means allow it, but made her rise and embraced her with great courtesy and politeness, and ordered Sancho to look to Rocinante's girths, and to arm him without a moment's delay. Sancho took down the armour, which was hung up on a tree like a trophy, and having seen to the girths armed his master in a trice, who as soon as he found himself in his armour exclaimed:

"Let us be gone in the name of God to bring aid to this great lady."

The barber was all this time on his knees at great pains to hide his laughter and not let his beard fall, for had it fallen maybe their fine scheme would have come to nothing; but now seeing the boon granted, and the promptitude with which Don Quixote prepared to set out in compliance with it, he rose and took his lady's hand, and between them they placed her upon the mule. Don Quixote then mounted Rocinante, and the barber settled himself on his beast, Sancho being left to go on foot, which made him feel anew the loss of his Dapple, finding the want of him now. But he bore all with cheerfulness, being persuaded that his master had now fairly started and was just on the point of becoming an emperor; for he felt no doubt at all that he would marry this princess, and be king of Micomicon at least. The only thing that troubled him was the reflection that this kingdom was in the land of the blacks, and that the people they would give him for vassals would be all black; but for this he soon found a remedy in his fancy, and said he to himself, "What is it to me if my vassals are blacks? What more have I to do than make a cargo of them and carry them to Spain, where I can sell them and get ready money for them, and with it buy some title or some office in which to live at ease all the days of my life? Not unless you go to sleep and haven't the wit or skill to turn things to account and sell three, six, or ten thousand vassals while you would be talking about it! By God I will stir them up, big and little, or as best I can, and let them be ever so black I'll turn them into white or yellow. Come, come, what a fool I am!" And so he jogged on, so occupied with his thoughts and easy in his mind that he forgot all about the hardship of travelling on foot.

Cardenio and the curate were watching all this from among some bushes, not knowing how to join company with the others; but the curate, who was very fertile in devices, soon hit upon a way of effecting their purpose, and with a pair of scissors he had in a case he quickly cut off Cardenio's beard, and putting on him a grey jerkin of his own he gave him a black cloak, leaving himself in his breeches and doublet, while Cardenio's appearance was so different from what it had been that he would not have known himself had he seen himself in a mirror. Having effected this, although the others had gone on ahead while they were disguising themselves, they easily came out on the high road before them, for the brambles and awkward places they encountered did not allow those on horseback to go as fast as those on foot. They then posted themselves on the level ground at the outlet of the Sierra, and as soon as Don Quixote and his companions emerged from it the curate began to examine him very deliberately, as though he were striving to recognise him, and after having stared at him for some time he hastened towards him with open arms exclaiming, "A happy meeting with the mirror of chivalry, my worthy compatriot Don Quixote of La Mancha, the flower and cream of high breeding, the protection and relief of the distressed, the quintessence of knights-errant!" And so saying he clasped in his arms the knee of Don Quixote's left leg. He, astonished at the stranger's words and behaviour, looked at him attentively, and at length recognised him, very much surprised to see him there, and made great efforts to dismount. This, however, the curate would not allow, on which Don Quixote said, "Permit me, senor licentiate, for it is not fitting that I should be on horseback and so reverend a person as your worship on foot."

"On no account will I allow it," said the curate; "your mightiness must remain on horseback, for it is on horseback you achieve the greatest deeds and adventures that have been beheld in our age; as for me, an unworthy priest, it will serve me well enough to mount on the haunches of one of the mules of these gentlefolk who accompany your worship, if they have no objection, and I will fancy I am mounted on the steed Pegasus, or on the zebra or charger that bore the famous Moor, Muzaraque, who to this day lies enchanted in the great hill of Zulema, a little distance from the great Complutum."

"Nor even that will I consent to, senor licentiate," answered Don Quixote, "and I know it will be the good pleasure of my lady the princess, out of love for me, to order her squire to give up the saddle of his mule to your worship, and he can sit behind if the beast will bear it."

"It will, I am sure," said the princess, "and I am sure, too, that I need not order my squire, for he is too courteous and considerate to allow a Churchman to go on foot when he might be mounted."

"That he is," said the barber, and at once alighting, he offered his saddle to the curate, who accepted it without much entreaty; but unfortunately as the barber was mounting behind, the mule, being as it happened a hired one, which is the same thing as saying ill-conditioned, lifted its hind hoofs and let fly a couple of kicks in the air, which would have made Master Nicholas wish his expedition in quest of Don Quixote at the devil had they caught him on the breast or head. As it was, they so took him by surprise that he came to the ground, giving so little heed to his beard that it fell off, and all he could do when he found himself without it was to cover his face hastily with both his hands and moan that his teeth were knocked out. Don Quixote when he saw all that bundle of beard detached, without jaws or blood, from the face of the fallen squire, exclaimed:

"By the living God, but this is a great miracle! it has knocked off and plucked away the beard from his face as if it had been shaved off designedly."

The curate, seeing the danger of discovery that threatened his scheme, at once pounced upon the beard and hastened with it to where Master Nicholas lay, still uttering moans, and drawing his head to his breast had it on in an instant, muttering over him some words which he said were a certain special charm for sticking on beards, as they would see; and as soon as he had it fixed he left him, and the squire appeared well bearded and whole as before, whereat Don Quixote was beyond measure astonished, and begged the curate to teach him that charm when he had an opportunity, as he was persuaded its virtue must extend beyond the sticking on of beards, for it was clear that where the beard had been stripped off the flesh must have remained torn and lacerated, and when it could heal all that it must be good for more than beards.

"And so it is," said the curate, and he promised to teach it to him on the first opportunity. They then agreed that for the present the curate should mount, and that the three should ride by turns until they reached the inn, which might be about six leagues from where they were.

Three then being mounted, that is to say, Don Quixote, the princess, and the curate, and three on foot, Cardenio, the barber, and Sancho Panza, Don Quixote said to the damsel:

"Let your highness, lady, lead on whithersoever is most pleasing to you;" but before she could answer the licentiate said:

"Towards what kingdom would your ladyship direct our course? Is it perchance towards that of Micomicon? It must be, or else I know little about kingdoms."

She, being ready on all points, understood that she was to answer "Yes," so she said "Yes, senor, my way lies towards that kingdom."

"In that case," said the curate, "we must pass right through my village, and there your worship will take the road to Cartagena, where you will be able to embark, fortune favouring; and if the wind be fair and the sea smooth and tranquil, in somewhat less than nine years you may come in sight of the great lake Meona, I mean Meotides, which is little more than a hundred days' journey this side of your highness's kingdom."

"Your worship is mistaken, senor," said she; "for it is not two years since I set out from it, and though I never had good weather, nevertheless I am here to behold what I so longed for, and that is my lord Don Quixote of La Mancha, whose fame came to my ears as soon as I set foot in Spain and impelled me to go in search of him, to commend myself to his courtesy, and entrust the justice of my cause to the might of his invincible arm."

"Enough; no more praise," said Don Quixote at this, "for I hate all flattery; and though this may not be so, still language of the kind is offensive to my chaste ears. I will only say, senora, that whether it has might or not, that which it may or may not have shall be devoted to your service even to death; and now, leaving this to its proper season, I would ask the senor licentiate to tell me what it is that has brought him into these parts, alone, unattended, and so lightly clad that I am filled with amazement."

"I will answer that briefly," replied the curate; "you must know then, Senor Don Quixote, that Master Nicholas, our friend and barber, and I were going to Seville to receive some money that a relative of mine who went to the Indies many years ago had sent me, and not such a small sum but that it was over sixty thousand pieces of eight, full weight, which is something; and passing by this place yesterday we were attacked by four footpads, who stripped us even to our beards, and them they stripped off so that the barber found it necessary to put on a false one, and even this young man here"-pointing to Cardenio—"they completely transformed. But the best of it is, the story goes in the neighbourhood that those who attacked us belong to a number of galley slaves who, they say, were set free almost on the very same spot by a man of such valour that, in spite of the commissary and of the guards, he released the whole of them; and beyond all doubt he must have been out of his senses, or he must be as great a scoundrel as they, or some man without heart or conscience to let the wolf loose among the sheep, the fox among the hens, the fly among the honey. He has defrauded justice, and opposed his king and lawful master, for he opposed his just commands; he has, I say, robbed the galleys of their feet, stirred up the Holy Brotherhood which for many years past has been quiet, and, lastly, has done a deed by which his soul may be lost without any gain to his body." Sancho had told the curate and the barber of the adventure of the galley slaves, which, so much to his glory, his master had achieved, and hence the curate in alluding to it made the most of it to see what would be said or done by Don Quixote; who changed colour at every word, not daring to say that it was he who had been the liberator of those worthy people. "These, then," said the curate, "were they who robbed us; and God in his mercy pardon him who would not let them go to the punishment they deserved."

CHAPTER XXX

WHICH TREATS OF ADDRESS DISPLAYED BY THE FAIR DOROTHEA, WITH OTHER MATTERS PLEASANT AND AMUSING

The curate had hardly ceased speaking, when Sancho said, "In faith, then, senor licentiate, he who did that deed was my master; and it was not for want of my telling him beforehand and warning him to mind what he was about, and that it was a sin to set them at liberty, as they were all on the march there because they were special scoundrels."

"Blockhead!" said Don Quixote at this, "it is no business or concern of knights-errant to inquire whether any persons in affliction, in chains, or oppressed that they may meet on the high roads go that way and suffer as they do because of their faults or because of their misfortunes. It only concerns them to aid them as persons in need of help, having regard to their sufferings and not to their rascalities. I encountered a chaplet or string of miserable and unfortunate people, and did for them what my sense of duty demands of me, and as for the rest be that as it may; and whoever takes objection to it, saving the sacred dignity of the senor licentiate and his honoured person, I say he knows little about chivalry and lies like a whoreson villain, and this I will give him to know to the fullest extent with my sword;" and so saying he settled himself in his stirrups and pressed down his morion; for the barber's basin, which according to him was Mambrino's helmet, he carried hanging at the saddle-bow until he could repair the damage done to it by the galley slaves.

Dorothea, who was shrewd and sprightly, and by this time thoroughly understood Don Quixote's crazy turn, and that all except Sancho Panza were making game of him, not to be behind the rest said to him, on observing his irritation, "Sir Knight, remember the boon you have promised me, and that in accordance with it you must not engage in any other adventure, be it ever so pressing; calm yourself, for if the licentiate had known that the galley slaves had been set free by that unconquered arm he would have stopped his mouth thrice over, or even bitten his tongue three times before he would have said a word that tended towards disrespect of your worship."

"That I swear heartily," said the curate, "and I would have even plucked off a moustache."

"I will hold my peace, senora," said Don Quixote, "and I will curb the natural anger that had arisen in my breast, and will proceed in peace and quietness until I have fulfilled my promise; but in return for this consideration I entreat you to tell me, if you have no objection to do so, what is the nature of your trouble, and how many, who, and what are the persons of whom I am to require due satisfaction, and on whom I am to take vengeance on your behalf?"

"That I will do with all my heart," replied Dorothea, "if it will not be wearisome to you to hear of miseries and misfortunes."

"It will not be wearisome, senora," said Don Quixote; to which Dorothea replied, "Well, if that be so, give me your attention." As soon as she said this, Cardenio and the barber drew close to her side, eager to hear what sort of story the quick-witted Dorothea would invent for herself; and Sancho did the same, for he was as much taken in by her as his master; and she having settled herself comfortably in the saddle, and with the help of coughing and other preliminaries taken time to think, began with great sprightliness of manner in this fashion.

"First of all, I would have you know, sirs, that my name is-" and here she stopped for a moment, for she forgot the name the curate had given her; but he came to her relief, seeing what her difficulty was, and said, "It is no wonder, senora, that your highness should be confused and embarrassed in telling the tale of your misfortunes; for such afflictions often have the effect of depriving the sufferers of memory, so that they do not even remember their own names, as is the case now with your ladyship, who has forgotten that she is called the Princess Micomicona, lawful heiress of the great kingdom of Micomicon; and with this cue your highness may now recall to your sorrowful recollection all you may wish to tell us."

"That is the truth," said the damsel; "but I think from this on I shall have no need of any prompting, and I shall bring my true story safe into port, and here it is. The king my father, who was called Tinacrio the Sapient, was very learned in what they call magic arts, and became aware by his craft that my mother, who was called Queen Jaramilla, was to die before he did, and that soon after he too was to depart this life, and I was to be left an orphan without father or mother. But all this, he declared, did not so much grieve or distress him as his certain knowledge that a prodigious giant, the lord of a great island close to our kingdom, Pandafilando of the Scowl by name—for it is averred that, though his eyes are properly placed and straight, he always looks askew as if he squinted, and this he does out of malignity, to strike fear and terror into those he looks at—that he knew, I say, that this giant on becoming aware of my orphan condition would overrun my kingdom with a mighty force and strip me of all, not leaving me even a small village to shelter me; but that I could avoid all this ruin and misfortune if I were willing to marry him; however, as far as he could see, he never expected that I would consent to a marriage so unequal; and he said no more than the truth in this, for it has never entered my mind to marry that giant, or any other, let him be ever so great or enormous. My father said, too, that when he was dead, and I saw Pandafilando about to invade my kingdom, I was not to wait and attempt to defend myself, for that would be destructive to me, but that I should leave the kingdom entirely open to him if I wished to avoid the death and total destruction of my good and loyal vassals, for there would be no possibility of defending myself against the giant's devilish power; and that I should at once with some of my followers set out for Spain, where I should obtain relief in my distress on finding a certain knight-errant whose fame by that time would extend over the whole kingdom, and who would be called, if I remember rightly, Don Azote or Don Gigote."

"'Don Quixote,' he must have said, senora," observed Sancho at this, "otherwise called the Knight of the Rueful Countenance."

"That is it," said Dorothea; "he said, moreover, that he would be tall of stature and lank featured; and that on his right side under the left shoulder, or thereabouts, he would have a grey mole with hairs like bristles."

On hearing this, Don Quixote said to his squire, "Here, Sancho my son, bear a hand and help me to strip, for I want to see if I am the knight that sage king foretold."

"What does your worship want to strip for?" said Dorothea.

"To see if I have that mole your father spoke of," answered Don Quixote.

"There is no occasion to strip," said Sancho; "for I know your worship has just such a mole on the middle of your backbone, which is the mark of a strong man."

"That is enough," said Dorothea, "for with friends we must not look too closely into trifles; and whether it be on the shoulder or on the backbone matters little; it is enough if there is a mole, be it where it may, for it is all the same flesh; no doubt my good father hit the truth in every particular, and I have made a lucky hit in commending myself to Don Quixote; for he is the one my father spoke of, as the features of his countenance correspond with those assigned to this knight by that wide fame he has acquired not only in Spain but in all La Mancha; for I had scarcely landed at Osuna when I heard such accounts of his achievements, that at once my heart told me he was the very one I had come in search of."

"But how did you land at Osuna, senora," asked Don Quixote, "when it is not a seaport?"

But before Dorothea could reply the curate anticipated her, saying, "The princess meant to say that after she had landed at Malaga the first place where she heard of your worship was Osuna."

"That is what I meant to say," said Dorothea.

"And that would be only natural," said the curate. "Will your majesty please proceed?"

"There is no more to add," said Dorothea, "save that in finding Don Quixote I have had such good fortune, that I already reckon and regard myself queen and mistress of my entire dominions, since of his courtesy and magnanimity he has granted me the boon of accompanying me whithersoever I may conduct him, which will be only to bring him face to face with Pandafilando of the Scowl, that he may slay him and restore to me what has been unjustly usurped by him: for all this must come to pass satisfactorily since my good father Tinacrio the Sapient foretold it, who likewise left it declared in writing in Chaldee or Greek characters (for I cannot read them), that if this predicted knight, after having cut the giant's throat, should be disposed to marry me I was to offer myself at once without demur as his lawful wife, and yield him possession of my kingdom together with my person."

"What thinkest thou now, friend Sancho?" said Don Quixote at this. "Hearest thou that? Did I not tell thee so? See how we have already got a kingdom to govern and a queen to marry!"

"On my oath it is so," said Sancho; "and foul fortune to him who won't marry after slitting Senor Pandahilado's windpipe! And then, how ill-favoured the queen is! I wish the fleas in my bed were that sort!"

And so saying he cut a couple of capers in the air with every sign of extreme satisfaction, and then ran to seize the bridle of Dorothea's mule, and checking it fell on his knees before her, begging her to give him her hand to kiss in token of his acknowledgment of her as his queen and mistress. Which of the bystanders could have helped laughing to see the madness of the master and the simplicity of the servant? Dorothea therefore gave her hand, and promised to make him a great lord in her kingdom, when Heaven should be so good as to permit her to recover and enjoy it, for which Sancho returned thanks in words that set them all laughing again.

"This, sirs," continued Dorothea, "is my story; it only remains to tell you that of all the attendants I took with me from my kingdom I have none left except this well-bearded squire, for all were drowned in a great tempest we encountered when in sight of port; and he and I came to land on a couple of planks as if by a miracle; and indeed the whole course of my life is a miracle and a mystery as you may have observed; and if I have been over minute in any respect or not as precise as I ought, let it be accounted for by what the licentiate said at the beginning of my tale, that constant and excessive troubles deprive the sufferers of their memory."

"They shall not deprive me of mine, exalted and worthy princess," said Don Quixote, "however great and unexampled those which I shall endure in your service may be; and here I confirm anew the boon I have promised you, and I swear to go with you to the end of the world until I find myself in the presence of your fierce enemy, whose haughty head I trust by the aid of my arm to cut off with the edge of this—I will not say good sword, thanks to Gines de Pasamonte who carried away mine"—(this he said between his teeth, and then continued), "and when it has been cut off and you have been put in peaceful possession of your realm it shall be left to your own decision to dispose of your person as may be most pleasing to you; for so long as my memory is occupied, my will enslaved, and my understanding enthralled by her-I say no more—it is impossible for me for a moment to contemplate marriage, even with a Phoenix."

The last words of his master about not wanting to marry were so disagreeable to Sancho that raising his voice he exclaimed with great irritation:

"By my oath, Senor Don Quixote, you are not in your right senses; for how can your worship possibly object to marrying such an exalted princess as this? Do you think Fortune will offer you behind every stone such a piece of luck as is offered you now? Is my lady Dulcinea fairer, perchance? Not she; nor half as fair; and I will even go so far as to say she does not come up to the shoe of this one here. A poor chance I have of getting that county I am waiting for if your worship goes looking for dainties in the bottom of the sea. In the devil's name, marry, marry, and take this kingdom that comes to hand without any trouble, and when you are king make me a marquis or governor of a province, and for the rest let the devil take it all."

Don Quixote, when he heard such blasphemies uttered against his lady Dulcinea, could not endure it, and lifting his pike, without saying anything to Sancho or uttering a word, he gave him two such thwacks that he brought him to the ground; and had it not been that Dorothea cried out to him to spare him he would have no doubt taken his life on the spot.

"Do you think," he said to him after a pause, "you scurvy clown, that you are to be always interfering with me, and that you are to be always offending and I always pardoning? Don't fancy it, impious scoundrel, for that beyond a doubt thou art, since thou hast set thy tongue going against the peerless Dulcinea. Know you not, lout, vagabond, beggar, that were it not for the might that she infuses into my arm I should not have strength enough to kill a flea? Say, scoffer with a viper's tongue, what think you has won this kingdom and cut off this giant's head and made you a marquis (for all this I count as already accomplished and decided), but the might of Dulcinea, employing my arm as the instrument of her achievements? She fights in me and conquers in me, and I live and breathe in her, and owe my life and being to her. O whoreson scoundrel, how ungrateful you are, you see yourself raised from the dust of the earth to be a titled lord, and the return you make for so great a benefit is to speak evil of her who has conferred it upon you!"

Sancho was not so stunned but that he heard all his master said, and rising with some degree of nimbleness he ran to place himself behind Dorothea's palfrey, and from that position he said to his master:

"Tell me, senor; if your worship is resolved not to marry this great princess, it is plain the kingdom will not be yours; and not being so, how can you bestow favours upon me? That is what I complain of. Let your worship at any rate marry this queen, now that we have got her here as if showered down from heaven, and afterwards you may go back to my lady Dulcinea; for there must have been kings in the world who kept mistresses. As to beauty, I have nothing to do with it; and if the truth is to be told, I like them both; though I have never seen the lady Dulcinea."

"How! never seen her, blasphemous traitor!" exclaimed Don Quixote; "hast thou not just now brought me a message from her?"

"I mean," said Sancho, "that I did not see her so much at my leisure that I could take particular notice of her beauty, or of her charms piecemeal; but taken in the lump I like her."

"Now I forgive thee," said Don Quixote; "and do thou forgive me the injury I have done thee; for our first impulses are not in our control."

"That I see," replied Sancho, "and with me the wish to speak is always the first impulse, and I cannot help saying, once at any rate, what I have on the tip of my tongue."

"For all that, Sancho," said Don Quixote, "take heed of what thou sayest, for the pitcher goes so often to the well—I need say no more to thee."

"Well, well," said Sancho, "God is in heaven, and sees all tricks, and will judge who does most harm, I in not speaking right, or your worship in not doing it."

"That is enough," said Dorothea; "run, Sancho, and kiss your lord's hand and beg his pardon, and henceforward be more circumspect with your praise and abuse; and say nothing in disparagement of that lady Toboso, of whom I know nothing save that I am her servant; and put your trust in God, for you will not fail to obtain some dignity so as to live like a prince."

Sancho advanced hanging his head and begged his master's hand, which Don Quixote with dignity presented to him, giving him his blessing as soon as he had kissed it; he then bade him go on ahead a little, as he had questions to ask him and matters of great importance to discuss with him. Sancho obeyed, and when the two had gone some distance in advance Don Quixote said to him, "Since thy return I have had no opportunity or time to ask thee many particulars touching thy mission and the answer thou hast brought back, and now that chance has granted us the time and opportunity, deny me not the happiness thou canst give me by such good news."

"Let your worship ask what you will," answered Sancho, "for I shall find a way out of all as as I found a way in; but I implore you, senor, not not to be so revengeful in future."

"Why dost thou say that, Sancho?" said Don Quixote.

"I say it," he returned, "because those blows just now were more because of the quarrel the devil stirred up between us both the other night, than for what I said against my lady Dulcinea, whom I love and reverence as I would a relic—though there is nothing of that about her—merely as something belonging to your worship."

"Say no more on that subject for thy life, Sancho," said Don Quixote, "for it is displeasing to me; I have already pardoned thee for that, and thou knowest the common saying, 'for a fresh sin a fresh penance.'"

While this was going on they saw coming along the road they were following a man mounted on an ass, who when he came close seemed to be a gipsy; but Sancho Panza, whose eyes and heart were there wherever he saw asses, no sooner beheld the man than he knew him to be Gines de Pasamonte; and by the thread of the gipsy he got at the ball, his ass, for it was, in fact, Dapple that carried Pasamonte, who to escape recognition and to sell the ass had disguised himself as a gipsy, being able to speak the gipsy language, and many more, as well as if they were his own. Sancho saw him and recognised him, and the instant he did so he shouted to him, "Ginesillo, you thief, give up my treasure, release my life, embarrass thyself not with my repose, quit my ass, leave my delight, be off, rip, get thee gone, thief, and give up what is not thine."

There was no necessity for so many words or objurgations, for at the first one Gines jumped down, and at a like racing speed made off and got clear of them all. Sancho hastened to his Dapple, and embracing him he said, "How hast thou fared, my blessing, Dapple of my eyes, my comrade?" all the while kissing him and caressing him as if he were a human being. The ass held his peace, and let himself be kissed and caressed by Sancho without answering a single word. They all came up and congratulated him on having found Dapple, Don Quixote especially, who told him that notwithstanding this he would not cancel the order for the three ass-colts, for which Sancho thanked him.

While the two had been going along conversing in this fashion, the curate observed to Dorothea that she had shown great cleverness, as well in the story itself as in its conciseness, and the resemblance it bore to those of the books of chivalry. She said that she had many times amused herself reading them; but that she did not know the situation of the provinces or seaports, and so she had said at haphazard that she had landed at Osuna.

"So I saw," said the curate, "and for that reason I made haste to say what I did, by which it was all set right. But is it not a strange thing to see how readily this unhappy gentleman believes all these figments and lies, simply because they are in the style and manner of the absurdities of his books?"

"So it is," said Cardenio; "and so uncommon and unexampled, that were one to attempt to invent and concoct it in fiction, I doubt if there be any wit keen enough to imagine it."

"But another strange thing about it," said the curate, "is that, apart from the silly things which this worthy gentleman says in connection with his craze, when other subjects are dealt with, he can discuss them in a perfectly rational manner, showing that his mind is quite clear and composed; so that, provided his chivalry is not touched upon, no one would take him to be anything but a man of thoroughly sound understanding."

While they were holding this conversation Don Quixote continued his with Sancho, saying:

"Friend Panza, let us forgive and forget as to our quarrels, and tell me now, dismissing anger and irritation, where, how, and when didst thou find Dulcinea? What was she doing? What didst thou say to her? What did she answer? How did she look when she was reading my letter? Who copied it out for thee? and everything in the matter that seems to thee worth knowing, asking, and learning; neither adding nor falsifying to give me pleasure, nor yet curtailing lest you should deprive me of it."

"Senor," replied Sancho, "if the truth is to be told, nobody copied out the letter for me, for I carried no letter at all."

"It is as thou sayest," said Don Quixote, "for the note-book in which I wrote it I found in my own possession two days after thy departure, which gave me very great vexation, as I knew not what thou wouldst do on finding thyself without any letter; and I made sure thou wouldst return from the place where thou didst first miss it."

"So I should have done," said Sancho, "if I had not got it by heart when your worship read it to me, so that I repeated it to a sacristan, who copied it out for me from hearing it, so exactly that he said in all the days of his life, though he had read many a letter of excommunication, he had never seen or read so pretty a letter as that."

"And hast thou got it still in thy memory, Sancho?" said Don Quixote.

"No, senor," replied Sancho, "for as soon as I had repeated it, seeing there was no further use for it, I set about forgetting it; and if I recollect any of it, it is that about 'Scrubbing,' I mean to say 'Sovereign Lady,' and the end 'Yours till death, the Knight of the Rueful Countenance;' and between these two I put into it more than three hundred 'my souls' and 'my life's' and 'my eyes.'"

CHAPTER XXXI

OF THE DELECTABLE DISCUSSION BETWEEN DON QUIXOTE AND SANCHO PANZA, HIS SQUIRE, TOGETHER WITH OTHER INCIDENTS

"All that is not unsatisfactory to me," said Don Quixote. "Go on; thou didst reach her; and what was that queen of beauty doing? Surely thou didst find her stringing pearls, or embroidering some device in gold thread for this her enslaved knight."

"I did not," said Sancho, "but I found her winnowing two bushels of wheat in the yard of her house."

"Then depend upon it," said Don Quixote, "the grains of that wheat were pearls when touched by her hands; and didst thou look, friend? was it white wheat or brown?"

"It was neither, but red," said Sancho.

"Then I promise thee," said Don Quixote, "that, winnowed by her hands, beyond a doubt the bread it made was of the whitest; but go on; when thou gavest her my letter, did she kiss it? Did she place it on her head? Did she perform any ceremony befitting it, or what did she do?"

"When I went to give it to her," replied Sancho, "she was hard at it swaying from side to side with a lot of wheat she had in the sieve, and she said to me, 'Lay the letter, friend, on the top of that sack, for I cannot read it until I have done sifting all this.'"

"Discreet lady!" said Don Quixote; "that was in order to read it at her leisure and enjoy it; proceed, Sancho; while she was engaged in her occupation what converse did she hold with thee? What did she ask about me, and what answer didst thou give? Make haste; tell me all, and let not an atom be left behind in the ink-bottle."

"She asked me nothing," said Sancho; "but I told her how your worship was left doing penance in her service, naked from the waist up, in among these mountains like a savage, sleeping on the ground, not eating bread off a tablecloth nor combing your beard, weeping and cursing your fortune."

"In saying I cursed my fortune thou saidst wrong," said Don Quixote; "for rather do I bless it and shall bless it all the days of my life for having made me worthy of aspiring to love so lofty a lady as Dulcinea del Toboso."

"And so lofty she is," said Sancho, "that she overtops me by more than a hand's-breadth."

"What! Sancho," said Don Quixote, "didst thou measure with her?"

"I measured in this way," said Sancho; "going to help her to put a sack of wheat on the back of an ass, we came so close together that I could see she stood more than a good palm over me."

"Well!" said Don Quixote, "and doth she not of a truth accompany and adorn this greatness with a thousand million charms of mind! But one thing thou wilt not deny, Sancho; when thou camest close to her didst thou not perceive a Sabaean odour, an aromatic fragrance, a, I know not what, delicious, that I cannot find a name for; I mean a redolence, an exhalation, as if thou wert in the shop of some dainty glover?"

"All I can say is," said Sancho, "that I did perceive a little odour, something goaty; it must have been that she was all in a sweat with hard work."

"It could not be that," said Don Quixote, "but thou must have been suffering from cold in the head, or must have smelt thyself; for I know well what would be the scent of that rose among thorns, that lily of the field, that dissolved amber."

"Maybe so," replied Sancho; "there often comes from myself that same odour which then seemed to me to come from her grace the lady Dulcinea; but that's no wonder, for one devil is like another."

"Well then," continued Don Quixote, "now she has done sifting the corn and sent it to the mill; what did she do when she read the letter?"

"As for the letter," said Sancho, "she did not read it, for she said she could neither read nor write; instead of that she tore it up into small pieces, saying that she did not want to let anyone read it lest her secrets should become known in the village, and that what I had told her by word of mouth about the love your worship bore her, and the extraordinary penance you were doing for her sake, was enough; and, to make an end of it, she told me to tell your worship that she kissed your hands, and that she had a greater desire to see you than to write to you; and that therefore she entreated and commanded you, on sight of this present, to come out of these thickets, and to have done with carrying on absurdities, and to set out at once for El Toboso, unless something else of greater importance should happen, for she had a great desire to see your worship. She laughed greatly when I told her how your worship was called The Knight of the Rueful Countenance; I asked her if that Biscayan the other day had been there; and she told me he had, and that he was an honest fellow; I asked her too about the galley slaves, but she said she had not seen any as yet."

"So far all goes well," said Don Quixote; "but tell me what jewel was it that she gave thee on taking thy leave, in return for thy tidings of me? For it is a usual and ancient custom with knights and ladies errant to give the squires, damsels, or dwarfs who bring tidings of their ladies to the knights, or of their knights to the ladies, some rich jewel as a guerdon for good news,' and acknowledgment of the message."

"That is very likely," said Sancho, "and a good custom it was, to my mind; but that must have been in days gone by, for now it would seem to be the custom only to give a piece of bread and cheese; because that was what my lady Dulcinea gave me over the top of the yard-wall when I took leave of her; and more by token it was sheep's-milk cheese."

"She is generous in the extreme," said Don Quixote, "and if she did not give thee a jewel of gold, no doubt it must have been because she had not one to hand there to give thee; but sleeves are good after Easter; I shall see her and all shall be made right. But knowest thou what amazes me, Sancho? It seems to me thou must have gone and come through the air, for thou hast taken but little more than three days to go to El Toboso and return, though it is more than thirty leagues from here to there. From which I am inclined to think that the sage magician who is my friend, and watches over my interests (for of necessity there is and must be one, or else I should not be a right knight-errant), that this same, I say, must have helped thee to travel without thy knowledge; for some of these sages will catch up a knight-errant sleeping in his bed, and without his knowing how or in what way it happened, he wakes up the next day more than a thousand leagues away from the place where he went to sleep. And if it were not for this, knights-errant would not be able to give aid to one another in peril, as they do at every turn. For a knight, maybe, is fighting in the mountains of Armenia with some dragon, or fierce serpent, or another knight, and gets the worst of the battle, and is at the point of death; but when he least looks for it, there appears over against him on a cloud, or chariot of fire, another knight, a friend of his, who just before had been in England, and who takes his part, and delivers him from death; and at night he finds himself in his own quarters supping very much to his satisfaction; and yet from one place to the other will have been two or three thousand leagues. And all this is done by the craft and skill of the sage enchanters who take care of those valiant knights; so that, friend Sancho, I find no difficulty in believing that thou mayest have gone from this place to El Toboso and returned in such a short time, since, as I have said, some friendly sage must have carried thee through the air without thee perceiving it."

"That must have been it," said Sancho, "for indeed Rocinante went like a gipsy's ass with quicksilver in his ears."

"Quicksilver!" said Don Quixote, "aye and what is more, a legion of devils, folk that can travel and make others travel without being weary, exactly as the whim seizes them. But putting this aside, what thinkest thou I ought to do about my lady's command to go and see her? For though I feel that I am bound to obey her mandate, I feel too that I am debarred by the boon I have accorded to the princess that accompanies us, and the law of chivalry compels me to have regard for my word in preference to my inclination; on the one hand the desire to see my lady pursues and harasses me, on the other my solemn promise and the glory I shall win in this enterprise urge and call me; but what I think I shall do is to travel with all speed and reach quickly the place where this giant is, and on my arrival I shall cut off his head, and establish the princess peacefully in her realm, and forthwith I shall return to behold the light that lightens my senses, to whom I shall make such excuses that she will be led to approve of my delay, for she will see that it entirely tends to increase her glory and fame; for all that I have won, am winning, or shall win by arms in this life, comes to me of the favour she extends to me, and because I am hers."

"Ah! what a sad state your worship's brains are in!" said Sancho. "Tell me, senor, do you mean to travel all that way for nothing, and to let slip and lose so rich and great a match as this where they give as a portion a kingdom that in sober truth I have heard say is more than twenty thousand leagues round about, and abounds with all things necessary to support human life, and is bigger than Portugal and Castile put together? Peace, for the love of God! Blush for what you have said, and take my advice, and forgive me, and marry at once in the first village where there is a curate; if not, here is our licentiate who will do the business beautifully; remember, I am old enough to give advice, and this I am giving comes pat to the purpose; for a sparrow in the hand is better than a vulture on the wing, and he who has the good to his hand and chooses the bad, that the good he complains of may not come to him."

"Look here, Sancho," said Don Quixote. "If thou art advising me to marry, in order that immediately on slaying the giant I may become king, and be able to confer favours on thee, and give thee what I have promised, let me tell thee I shall be able very easily to satisfy thy desires without marrying; for before going into battle I will make it a stipulation that, if I come out of it victorious, even I do not marry, they shall give me a portion of the kingdom, that I may bestow it upon whomsoever I choose, and when they give it to me upon whom wouldst thou have me bestow it but upon thee?"

"That is plain speaking," said Sancho; "but let your worship take care to choose it on the seacoast, so that if I don't like the life, I may be able to ship off my black vassals and deal with them as I have said; don't mind going to see my lady Dulcinea now, but go and kill this giant and let us finish off this business; for by God it strikes me it will be one of great honour and great profit."

"I hold thou art in the right of it, Sancho," said Don Quixote, "and I will take thy advice as to accompanying the princess before going to see Dulcinea; but I counsel thee not to say anything to any one, or to those who are with us, about what we have considered and discussed, for as Dulcinea is so decorous that she does not wish her thoughts to be known it is not right that I or anyone for me should disclose them."

"Well then, if that be so," said Sancho, "how is it that your worship makes all those you overcome by your arm go to present themselves before my lady Dulcinea, this being the same thing as signing your name to it that you love her and are her lover? And as those who go must perforce kneel before her and say they come from your worship to submit themselves to her, how can the thoughts of both of you be hid?"

"O, how silly and simple thou art!" said Don Quixote; "seest thou not, Sancho, that this tends to her greater exaltation? For thou must know that according to our way of thinking in chivalry, it is a high honour to a lady to have many knights-errant in her service, whose thoughts never go beyond serving her for her own sake, and who look for no other reward for their great and true devotion than that she should be willing to accept them as her knights."

"It is with that kind of love," said Sancho, "I have heard preachers say we ought to love our Lord, for himself alone, without being moved by the hope of glory or the fear of punishment; though for my part, I would rather love and serve him for what he could do."

"The devil take thee for a clown!" said Don Quixote, "and what shrewd things thou sayest at times! One would think thou hadst studied."

"In faith, then, I cannot even read."

Master Nicholas here called out to them to wait a while, as they wanted to halt and drink at a little spring there was there. Don Quixote drew up, not a little to the satisfaction of Sancho, for he was by this time weary of telling so many lies, and in dread of his master catching him tripping, for though he knew that Dulcinea was a peasant girl of El Toboso, he had never seen her in all his life. Cardenio had now put on the clothes which Dorothea was wearing when they found her, and though they were not very good, they were far better than those he put off. They dismounted together by the side of the spring, and with what the curate had provided himself with at the inn they appeased, though not very well, the keen appetite they all of them brought with them.

While they were so employed there happened to come by a youth passing on his way, who stopping to examine the party at the spring, the next moment ran to Don Quixote and clasping him round the legs, began to weep freely, saying, "O, senor, do you not know me? Look at me well; I am that lad Andres that your worship released from the oak-tree where I was tied."

Don Quixote recognised him, and taking his hand he turned to those present and said: "That your worships may see how important it is to have knights-errant to redress the wrongs and injuries done by tyrannical and wicked men in this world, I may tell you that some days ago passing through a wood, I heard cries and piteous complaints as of a person in pain and distress; I immediately hastened, impelled by my bounden duty, to the quarter whence the plaintive accents seemed to me to proceed, and I found tied to an oak this lad who now stands before you, which in my heart I rejoice at, for his testimony will not permit me to depart from the truth in any particular. He was, I say, tied to an oak, naked from the waist up, and a clown, whom I afterwards found to be his master, was scarifying him by lashes with the reins of his mare. As soon as I saw him I asked the reason of so cruel a flagellation. The boor replied that he was flogging him because he was his servant and because of carelessness that proceeded rather from dishonesty than stupidity; on which this boy said, 'Senor, he flogs me only because I ask for my wages.' The master made I know not what speeches and explanations, which, though I listened to them, I did not accept. In short, I compelled the clown to unbind him, and to swear he would take him with him, and pay him real by real, and perfumed into the bargain. Is not all this true, Andres my son? Didst thou not mark with what authority I commanded him, and with what humility he promised to do all I enjoined, specified, and required of him? Answer without hesitation; tell these gentlemen what took place, that they may see that it is as great an advantage as I say to have knights-errant abroad."

"All that your worship has said is quite true," answered the lad; "but the end of the business turned out just the opposite of what your worship supposes."

"How! the opposite?" said Don Quixote; "did not the clown pay thee then?"

"Not only did he not pay me," replied the lad, "but as soon as your worship had passed out of the wood and we were alone, he tied me up again to the same oak and gave me a fresh flogging, that left me like a flayed Saint Bartholomew; and every stroke he gave me he followed up with some jest or gibe about having made a fool of your worship, and but for the pain I was suffering I should have laughed at the things he said. In short he left me in such a condition that I have been until now in a hospital getting cured of the injuries which that rascally clown inflicted on me then; for all which your worship is to blame; for if you had gone your own way and not come where there was no call for you, nor meddled in other people's affairs, my master would have been content with giving me one or two dozen lashes, and would have then loosed me and paid me what he owed me; but when your worship abused him so out of measure, and gave him so many hard words, his anger was kindled; and as he could not revenge himself on you, as soon as he saw you had left him the storm burst upon me in such a way, that I feel as if I should never be a man again."

"The mischief," said Don Quixote, "lay in my going away; for I should not have gone until I had seen thee paid; because I ought to have known well by long experience that there is no clown who will keep his word if he finds it will not suit him to keep it; but thou rememberest, Andres, that I swore if he did not pay thee I would go and seek him, and find him though he were to hide himself in the whale's belly."

"That is true," said Andres; "but it was of no use."

"Thou shalt see now whether it is of use or not," said Don Quixote; and so saying, he got up hastily and bade Sancho bridle Rocinante, who was browsing while they were eating. Dorothea asked him what he meant to do. He replied that he meant to go in search of this clown and chastise him for such iniquitous conduct, and see Andres paid to the last maravedi, despite and in the teeth of all the clowns in the world. To which she replied that he must remember that in accordance with his promise he could not engage in any enterprise until he had concluded hers; and that as he knew this better than anyone, he should restrain his ardour until his return from her kingdom.

"That is true," said Don Quixote, "and Andres must have patience until my return as you say, senora; but I once more swear and promise not to stop until I have seen him avenged and paid."

"I have no faith in those oaths," said Andres; "I would rather have now something to help me to get to Seville than all the revenges in the world; if you have here anything to eat that I can take with me, give it me, and God be with your worship and all knights-errant; and may their errands turn out as well for themselves as they have for me."

Sancho took out from his store a piece of bread and another of cheese, and giving them to the lad he said, "Here, take this, brother Andres, for we have all of us a share in your misfortune."

"Why, what share have you got?"

"This share of bread and cheese I am giving you," answered Sancho; "and God knows whether I shall feel the want of it myself or not; for I would have you know, friend, that we squires to knights-errant have to bear a great deal of hunger and hard fortune, and even other things more easily felt than told."

Andres seized his bread and cheese, and seeing that nobody gave him anything more, bent his head, and took hold of the road, as the saying is. However, before leaving he said, "For the love of God, sir knight-errant, if you ever meet me again, though you may see them cutting me to pieces, give me no aid or succour, but leave me to my misfortune, which will not be so great but that a greater will come to me by being helped by your worship, on whom and all the knights-errant that have ever been born God send his curse."

Don Quixote was getting up to chastise him, but he took to his heels at such a pace that no one attempted to follow him; and mightily chapfallen was Don Quixote at Andres' story, and the others had to take great care to restrain their laughter so as not to put him entirely out of countenance.

CHAPTER XXXII

WHICH TREATS OF WHAT BEFELL DON QUIXOTE'S PARTY AT THE INN

Their dainty repast being finished, they saddled at once, and without any adventure worth mentioning they reached next day the inn, the object of Sancho Panza's fear and dread; but though he would have rather not entered it, there was no help for it. The landlady, the landlord, their daughter, and Maritornes, when they saw Don Quixote and Sancho coming, went out to welcome them with signs of hearty satisfaction, which Don Quixote received with dignity and gravity, and bade them make up a better bed for him than the last time: to which the landlady replied that if he paid better than he did the last time she would give him one fit for a prince. Don Quixote said he would, so they made up a tolerable one for him in the same garret as before; and he lay down at once, being sorely shaken and in want of sleep.

No sooner was the door shut upon him than the landlady made at the barber, and seizing him by the beard, said:

"By my faith you are not going to make a beard of my tail any longer; you must give me back tail, for it is a shame the way that thing of my husband's goes tossing about on the floor; I mean the comb that I used to stick in my good tail."

But for all she tugged at it the barber would not give it up until the licentiate told him to let her have it, as there was now no further occasion for that stratagem, because he might declare himself and appear in his own character, and tell Don Quixote that he had fled to this inn when those thieves the galley slaves robbed him; and should he ask for the princess's squire, they could tell him that she had sent him on before her to give notice to the people of her kingdom that she was coming, and bringing with her the deliverer of them all. On this the barber cheerfully restored the tail to the landlady, and at the same time they returned all the accessories they had borrowed to effect Don Quixote's deliverance. All the people of the inn were struck with astonishment at the beauty of Dorothea, and even at the comely figure of the shepherd Cardenio. The curate made them get ready such fare as there was in the inn, and the landlord, in hope of better payment, served them up a tolerably good dinner. All this time Don Quixote was asleep, and they thought it best not to waken him, as sleeping would now do him more good than eating.

While at dinner, the company consisting of the landlord, his wife, their daughter, Maritornes, and all the travellers, they discussed the strange craze of Don Quixote and the manner in which he had been found; and the landlady told them what had taken place between him and the carrier; and then, looking round to see if Sancho was there, when she saw he was not, she gave them the whole story of his blanketing, which they received with no little amusement. But on the curate observing that it was the books of chivalry which Don Quixote had read that had turned his brain, the landlord said:

"I cannot understand how that can be, for in truth to my mind there is no better reading in the world, and I have here two or three of them, with other writings that are the very life, not only of myself but of plenty more; for when it is harvest-time, the reapers flock here on holidays, and there is always one among them who can read and who takes up one of these books, and we gather round him, thirty or more of us, and stay listening to him with a delight that makes our grey hairs grow young again. At least I can say for myself that when I hear of what furious and terrible blows the knights deliver, I am seized with the longing to do the same, and I would like to be hearing about them night and day."

"And I just as much," said the landlady, "because I never have a quiet moment in my house except when you are listening to some one reading; for then you are so taken up that for the time being you forget to scold."

"That is true," said Maritornes; "and, faith, I relish hearing these things greatly too, for they are very pretty; especially when they describe some lady or another in the arms of her knight under the orange trees, and the duenna who is keeping watch for them half dead with envy and fright; all this I say is as good as honey."

"And you, what do you think, young lady?" said the curate turning to the landlord's daughter.

"I don't know indeed, senor," said she; "I listen too, and to tell the truth, though I do not understand it, I like hearing it; but it is not the blows that my father likes that I like, but the laments the knights utter when they are separated from their ladies; and indeed they sometimes make me weep with the pity I feel for them."

"Then you would console them if it was for you they wept, young lady?" said Dorothea.

"I don't know what I should do," said the girl; "I only know that there are some of those ladies so cruel that they call their knights tigers and lions and a thousand other foul names: and Jesus! I don't know what sort of folk they can be, so unfeeling and heartless, that rather than bestow a glance upon a worthy man they leave him to die or go mad. I don't know what is the good of such prudery; if it is for honour's sake, why not marry them? That's all they want."

"Hush, child," said the landlady; "it seems to me thou knowest a great deal about these things, and it is not fit for girls to know or talk so much."

"As the gentleman asked me, I could not help answering him," said the girl.

"Well then," said the curate, "bring me these books, senor landlord, for I should like to see them."

"With all my heart," said he, and going into his own room he brought out an old valise secured with a little chain, on opening which the curate found in it three large books and some manuscripts written in a very good hand. The first that he opened he found to be "Don Cirongilio of Thrace," and the second "Don Felixmarte of Hircania," and the other the "History of the Great Captain Gonzalo Hernandez de Cordova, with the Life of Diego Garcia de Paredes."

When the curate read the two first titles he looked over at the barber and said, "We want my friend's housekeeper and niece here now."

"Nay," said the barber, "I can do just as well to carry them to the yard or to the hearth, and there is a very good fire there."

"What! your worship would burn my books!" said the landlord.

"Only these two," said the curate, "Don Cirongilio, and Felixmarte."

"Are my books, then, heretics or phlegmaties that you want to burn them?" said the landlord.

"Schismatics you mean, friend," said the barber, "not phlegmatics."

"That's it," said the landlord; "but if you want to burn any, let it be that about the Great Captain and that Diego Garcia; for I would rather have a child of mine burnt than either of the others."

"Brother," said the curate, "those two books are made up of lies, and are full of folly and nonsense; but this of the Great Captain is a true history, and contains the deeds of Gonzalo Hernandez of Cordova, who by his many and great achievements earned the title all over the world of the Great Captain, a famous and illustrious name, and deserved by him alone; and this Diego Garcia de Paredes was a distinguished knight of the city of Trujillo in Estremadura, a most gallant soldier, and of such bodily strength that with one finger he stopped a mill-wheel in full motion; and posted with a two-handed sword at the foot of a bridge he kept the whole of an immense army from passing over it, and achieved such other exploits that if, instead of his relating them himself with the modesty of a knight and of one writing his own history, some free and unbiassed writer had recorded them, they would have thrown into the shade all the deeds of the Hectors, Achilleses, and Rolands."

"Tell that to my father," said the landlord. "There's a thing to be astonished at! Stopping a mill-wheel! By God your worship should read what I have read of Felixmarte of Hircania, how with one single backstroke he cleft five giants asunder through the middle as if they had been made of bean-pods like the little friars the children make; and another time he attacked a very great and powerful army, in which there were more than a million six hundred thousand soldiers, all armed from head to foot, and he routed them all as if they had been flocks of sheep.

"And then, what do you say to the good Cirongilio of Thrace, that was so stout and bold; as may be seen in the book, where it is related that as he was sailing along a river there came up out of the midst of the water against him a fiery serpent, and he, as soon as he saw it, flung himself upon it and got astride of its scaly shoulders, and squeezed its throat with both hands with such force that the serpent, finding he was throttling it, had nothing for it but to let itself sink to the bottom of the river, carrying with it the knight who would not let go his hold; and when they got down there he found himself among palaces and gardens so pretty that it was a wonder to see; and then the serpent changed itself into an old ancient man, who told him such things as were never heard. Hold your peace, senor; for if you were to hear this you would go mad with delight. A couple of figs for your Great Captain and your Diego Garcia!"

Hearing this Dorothea said in a whisper to Cardenio, "Our landlord is almost fit to play a second part to Don Quixote."

"I think so," said Cardenio, "for, as he shows, he accepts it as a certainty that everything those books relate took place exactly as it is written down; and the barefooted friars themselves would not persuade him to the contrary."

"But consider, brother," said the curate once more, "there never was any Felixmarte of Hircania in the world, nor any Cirongilio of

Thrace, or any of the other knights of the same sort, that the books of chivalry talk of; the whole thing is the fabrication and invention of idle wits, devised by them for the purpose you describe of beguiling the time, as your reapers do when they read; for I swear to you in all seriousness there never were any such knights in the world, and no such exploits or nonsense ever happened anywhere."

"Try that bone on another dog," said the landlord; "as if I did not know how many make five, and where my shoe pinches me; don't think to feed me with pap, for by God I am no fool. It is a good joke for your worship to try and persuade me that everything these good books say is nonsense and lies, and they printed by the license of the Lords of the Royal Council, as if they were people who would allow such a lot of lies to be printed all together, and so many battles and enchantments that they take away one's senses."

"I have told you, friend," said the curate, "that this is done to divert our idle thoughts; and as in well-ordered states games of chess, fives, and billiards are allowed for the diversion of those who do not care, or are not obliged, or are unable to work, so books of this kind are allowed to be printed, on the supposition that, what indeed is the truth, there can be nobody so ignorant as to take any of them for true stories; and if it were permitted me now, and the present company desired it, I could say something about the qualities books of chivalry should possess to be good ones, that would be to the advantage and even to the taste of some; but I hope the time will come when I can communicate my ideas to some one who may be able to mend matters; and in the meantime, senor landlord, believe what I have said, and take your books, and make up your mind about their truth or falsehood, and much good may they do you; and God grant you may not fall lame of the same foot your guest Don Quixote halts on."

"No fear of that," returned the landlord; "I shall not be so mad as to make a knight-errant of myself; for I see well enough that things are not now as they used to be in those days, when they say those famous knights roamed about the world."

Sancho had made his appearance in the middle of this conversation, and he was very much troubled and cast down by what he heard said about knights-errant being now no longer in vogue, and all books of chivalry being folly and lies; and he resolved in his heart to wait and see what came of this journey of his master's, and if it did not turn out as happily as his master expected, he determined to leave him and go back to his wife and children and his ordinary labour.

The landlord was carrying away the valise and the books, but the curate said to him, "Wait; I want to see what those papers are that are written in such a good hand." The landlord taking them out handed them to him to read, and he perceived they were a work of about eight sheets of manuscript, with, in large letters at the beginning, the title of "Novel of the Ill-advised Curiosity." The curate read three or four lines to himself, and said, "I must say the title of this novel does not seem to me a bad one, and I feel an inclination to read it all." To which the landlord replied, "Then your reverence will do well to read it, for I can tell you that some guests who have read it here have been much pleased with it, and have begged it of me very earnestly; but I would not give it, meaning to return it to the person who forgot the valise, books, and papers here, for maybe he will return here some time or other; and though I know I shall miss the books, faith I mean to return them; for though I am an innkeeper, still I am a Christian."

"You are very right, friend," said the curate; "but for all that, if the novel pleases me you must let me copy it."

"With all my heart," replied the host.

While they were talking Cardenio had taken up the novel and begun to read it, and forming the same opinion of it as the curate, he begged him to read it so that they might all hear it.

"I would read it," said the curate, "if the time would not be better spent in sleeping."

"It will be rest enough for me," said Dorothea, "to while away the time by listening to some tale, for my spirits are not yet tranquil enough to let me sleep when it would be seasonable."

"Well then, in that case," said the curate, "I will read it, if it were only out of curiosity; perhaps it may contain something pleasant."

Master Nicholas added his entreaties to the same effect, and Sancho too; seeing which, and considering that he would give pleasure to all, and receive it himself, the curate said, "Well then, attend to me everyone, for the novel begins thus."

CHAPTER XXXIII

IN WHICH IS RELATED THE NOVEL OF "THE ILL-ADVISED CURIOSITY"

In Florence, a rich and famous city of Italy in the province called Tuscany, there lived two gentlemen of wealth and quality, Anselmo and Lothario, such great friends that by way of distinction they were called by all that knew them "The Two Friends." They were unmarried, young, of the same age and of the same tastes, which was enough to account for the reciprocal friendship between them. Anselmo, it is true, was somewhat more inclined to seek pleasure in love than Lothario, for whom the pleasures of the chase had more attraction; but on occasion Anselmo would forego his own tastes to yield to those of Lothario, and Lothario would surrender his to fall in with those of Anselmo, and in this way their inclinations kept pace one with the other with a concord so perfect that the best regulated clock could not surpass it.

Anselmo was deep in love with a high-born and beautiful maiden of the same city, the daughter of parents so estimable, and so estimable herself, that he resolved, with the approval of his friend Lothario, without whom he did nothing, to ask her of them in marriage, and did so, Lothario being the bearer of the demand, and conducting the negotiation so much to the satisfaction of his friend that in a short time he was in possession of the object of his desires, and Camilla so happy in having won Anselmo for her husband, that she gave thanks unceasingly to heaven and to Lothario, by whose means such good fortune had fallen to her. The first few days, those of a wedding being usually days of merry-making, Lothario frequented his friend Anselmo's house as he had been wont, striving to do honour to him and to the occasion, and to gratify him in every way he could; but when the wedding days were over and the succession of visits and congratulations had slackened, he began purposely to leave off going to the house of Anselmo, for it seemed to him, as it naturally would to all men of sense, that friends' houses ought not to be visited after marriage with the same frequency as in their masters' bachelor days: because, though true and genuine friendship cannot and should not be in any way suspicious, still a married man's honour is a thing of such delicacy that it is held liable to injury from brothers, much more from friends. Anselmo remarked the cessation of Lothario's visits, and complained of it to him, saying that if he had known that marriage was to keep him from enjoying his society as he used, he would have never married; and that, if by the thorough harmony that subsisted between them while he was a bachelor they had earned such a sweet name as that of "The Two Friends," he should not allow a title so rare and so delightful to be lost through a needless anxiety to act circumspectly; and so he entreated him, if such a phrase was allowable between them, to be once more master of his house and to come in and go out as formerly, assuring him that his wife Camilla had no other desire or inclination than that which he would wish her to have, and that knowing how sincerely they loved one another she was grieved to see such coldness in him.

To all this and much more that Anselmo said to Lothario to persuade him to come to his house as he had been in the habit of doing, Lothario replied with so much prudence, sense, and judgment, that Anselmo was satisfied of his friend's good intentions, and it was agreed that on two days in the week, and on holidays, Lothario should come to dine with him; but though this arrangement was made between them Lothario resolved to observe it no further than he considered to be in accordance with the honour of his friend, whose good name was more to him than his own. He said, and justly, that a married man upon whom heaven had bestowed a beautiful wife should consider as carefully what friends he brought to his house as what female friends his wife associated with, for what cannot be done or arranged in the market-place, in church, at public festivals or at stations (opportunities that husbands cannot always deny their wives), may be easily managed in the house of the female friend or relative in whom most confidence is reposed. Lothario said, too, that every married man should have some friend who would point out to him any negligence he might be guilty of in his conduct, for it will sometimes happen that owing to the deep affection the husband bears his wife either he does not caution her, or, not to vex her, refrains from telling her to do or not to do certain things, doing or avoiding which may be a matter of honour or reproach to him; and errors of this kind he could easily correct if warned by a friend. But where is such a friend to be found as Lothario would have, so judicious, so loyal, and so true?

Of a truth I know not; Lothario alone was such a one, for with the utmost care and vigilance he watched over the honour of his friend, and strove to diminish, cut down, and reduce the number of days for going to his house according to their agreement, lest the visits of a young man, wealthy, high-born, and with the attractions he was conscious of possessing, at the house of a woman so beautiful as Camilla, should be regarded with suspicion by the inquisitive and malicious eyes of the idle public. For though his integrity and reputation might bridle slanderous tongues, still he was unwilling to hazard either his own good name or that of his friend; and for this reason most of the days agreed upon he devoted to some other business which he pretended was unavoidable; so that a great portion of the day was taken up with complaints on one side and excuses on the other. It happened, however, that on one occasion when the two were strolling together outside the city, Anselmo addressed the following words to Lothario.

"Thou mayest suppose, Lothario my friend, that I am unable to give sufficient thanks for the favours God has rendered me in making me the son of such parents as mine were, and bestowing upon me with no niggard hand what are called the gifts of nature as well as those of fortune, and above all for what he has done in giving me thee for a friend and Camilla for a wife—two treasures that I value, if not as highly as I ought, at least as highly as I am able. And yet, with all these good things, which are commonly all that men need to enable them to live happily, I am the most discontented and dissatisfied man in the whole world; for, I know not how long since, I have been harassed and oppressed by a desire so strange and so unusual, that I wonder at myself and blame and chide myself when I am alone, and strive to stifle it and hide it from my own thoughts, and with no better success than if I were endeavouring deliberately to publish it to all the world; and as, in short, it must come out, I would confide it to thy safe keeping, feeling sure that by this means, and by thy readiness as a true friend to afford me relief, I shall soon find myself freed from the distress it causes me, and that thy care will give me happiness in the same degree as my own folly has caused me misery."

The words of Anselmo struck Lothario with astonishment, unable as he was to conjecture the purport of such a lengthy preamble; and though be strove to imagine what desire it could be that so troubled his friend, his conjectures were all far from the truth, and to relieve the anxiety which this perplexity was causing him, he told him he was doing a flagrant injustice to their great friendship in seeking circuitous methods of confiding to him his most hidden thoughts, for he well knew he might reckon upon his counsel in diverting them, or his help in carrying them into effect.

"That is the truth," replied Anselmo, "and relying upon that I will tell thee, friend Lothario, that the desire which harasses me is that of knowing whether my wife Camilla is as good and as perfect as I think her to be; and I cannot satisfy myself of the truth on this point except by testing her in such a way that the trial may prove the purity of her virtue as the fire proves that of gold; because I am persuaded, my friend, that a woman is virtuous only in proportion as she is or is not tempted; and that she alone is strong who does not yield to the promises, gifts, tears, and importunities of earnest lovers; for what thanks does a woman deserve for being good if no one urges her to be bad, and what wonder is it that she is reserved and circumspect to whom no opportunity is given of going wrong and who knows she has a husband that will take her life the first time he detects her in an impropriety? I do not therefore hold her who is virtuous through fear or want of opportunity in the same estimation as her who comes out of temptation and trial with a crown of victory; and so, for these reasons and many others that I could give thee to justify and support the opinion I hold, I am desirous that my wife Camilla should pass this crisis, and be refined and tested by the fire of finding herself wooed and by one worthy to set his affections upon her; and if she comes out, as I know she will, victorious from this struggle, I shall look upon my good fortune as unequalled, I shall be able to say that the cup of my desire is full, and that the virtuous woman of whom the sage says 'Who shall find her?' has fallen to my lot. And if the result be the contrary of what I expect, in the satisfaction of knowing that I have been right in my opinion, I shall bear without complaint the pain which my so dearly bought experience will naturally cause me. And, as nothing of all thou wilt urge in opposition to my wish will avail to keep me from carrying it into effect, it is my desire, friend Lothario, that thou shouldst consent to become the instrument for effecting this purpose that I am bent upon, for I will afford thee opportunities to that end, and nothing shall be wanting that I may think necessary for the pursuit of a virtuous, honourable, modest and high-minded woman. And among other reasons, I am induced to entrust this arduous task to thee by the consideration that if Camilla be conquered by thee the conquest will not be pushed to extremes, but only far enough to account that accomplished which from a sense of honour will be left undone; thus I shall not be wronged in anything more than intention, and my wrong will remain buried in the integrity of thy silence, which I know well will be as lasting as that of death in what concerns me. If, therefore, thou wouldst have me enjoy what can be called life, thou wilt at once engage in this love struggle, not lukewarmly nor slothfully, but with the energy and zeal that my desire demands, and with the loyalty our friendship assures me of."

Such were the words Anselmo addressed to Lothario, who listened to them with such attention that, except to say what has been already mentioned, he did not open his lips until the other had finished. Then perceiving that he had no more to say, after regarding him for awhile, as one would regard something never before seen that excited wonder and amazement, he said to him, "I cannot persuade myself, Anselmo my friend, that what thou hast said to me is not in jest; if I thought that thou wert speaking seriously I would not have allowed thee to go so far; so as to put a stop to thy long harangue by not listening to thee I verily suspect that either thou dost not know me, or I do not know thee; but no, I know well thou art Anselmo, and thou knowest that I am Lothario; the misfortune is, it seems to me, that thou art not the Anselmo thou wert, and must have thought that I am not the Lothario I should be; for the things that thou hast said to me are not those of that Anselmo who was my friend, nor are those that thou demandest of me what should be asked of the Lothario thou knowest. True friends will prove their friends and make use of them, as a poet has said, usque ad aras; whereby he meant that they will not make use of their friendship in things that are contrary to God's will. If this, then, was a heathen's feeling about friendship, how much more should it be a Christian's, who knows that the divine must not be forfeited for the sake of any human friendship? And if a friend should go so far as to put aside his duty to Heaven to fulfil his duty to his friend, it should not be in matters that are trifling or of little moment, but in such as affect the friend's life and honour. Now tell me, Anselmo, in which of these two art thou imperilled, that I should hazard myself to gratify thee, and do a thing so detestable as that thou seekest of me? Neither forsooth; on the contrary, thou dost ask of me, so far as I understand, to strive and labour to rob thee of honour and life, and to rob myself of them at the same time; for if I take away thy honour it is plain I take away thy life, as a man without honour is worse than dead; and being the instrument, as thou wilt have it so, of so much wrong to thee, shall not I, too, be left without honour, and consequently without life? Listen to me, Anselmo my friend, and be not impatient to answer me until I have said what occurs to me touching the object of thy desire, for there will be time enough left for thee to reply and for me to hear."

"Be it so," said Anselmo, "say what thou wilt."

Lothario then went on to say, "It seems to me, Anselmo, that thine is just now the temper of mind which is always that of the Moors, who can never be brought to see the error of their creed by quotations from the Holy Scriptures, or by reasons which depend upon the examination of the understanding or are founded upon the articles of faith, but must have examples that are palpable, easy, intelligible, capable of proof, not admitting of doubt, with mathematical demonstrations that cannot be denied, like, 'If equals be taken from equals, the remainders are equal:' and if they do not understand this in words, and indeed they do not, it has to be shown to them with the hands, and put before their eyes, and even with all this no one succeeds in convincing them of the truth of our holy religion. This same mode of proceeding I shall have to adopt with thee, for the desire which has sprung up in thee is so absurd and remote from everything that has a semblance of reason, that I feel it would be a waste of time to employ it in reasoning with thy simplicity, for at present I will call it by no other name; and I am even tempted to leave thee in thy folly as a punishment for thy pernicious desire; but the friendship I bear thee, which will not allow me to desert thee in such manifest danger of destruction, keeps me from dealing so harshly by thee. And that thou mayest clearly see this, say, Anselmo, hast thou not told me that I must force my suit upon a modest woman, decoy one that is virtuous, make overtures to one that is pure-minded, pay court to one that is prudent? Yes, thou hast told me so. Then, if thou knowest that thou hast a wife, modest, virtuous, pure-minded and prudent, what is it that thou seekest? And if thou believest that she will come forth victorious from all my attacks—as doubtless she would—what higher titles than those she possesses now dost thou think thou canst upon her then, or in what will she be better then than she is now? Either thou dost not hold her to be what thou sayest, or thou knowest not what thou dost demand. If thou dost not hold her to be what thou why dost thou seek to prove her instead of treating her as guilty in the way that may seem best to thee? but if she be as virtuous as thou believest, it is an uncalled-for proceeding to make trial of truth itself, for, after trial, it will but be in the same estimation as before. Thus, then, it is conclusive that to attempt things from which harm rather than advantage may come to us is the part of unreasoning and reckless minds, more especially when they are things which we are not forced or compelled to attempt, and which show from afar that it is plainly madness to attempt them.

"Difficulties are attempted either for the sake of God or for the sake of the world, or for both; those undertaken for God's sake are those which the saints undertake when they attempt to live the lives of angels in human bodies; those undertaken for the sake of the world are those of the men who traverse such a vast expanse of water, such a variety of climates, so many strange countries, to acquire what are called the blessings of fortune; and those undertaken for the sake of God and the world together are those of brave soldiers, who no sooner do they see in the enemy's wall a breach as wide as a cannon ball could make, than, casting aside all fear, without hesitating, or heeding the manifest peril that threatens them, borne onward by the desire of defending their faith, their country, and their king, they fling themselves dauntlessly into the midst of the thousand opposing deaths that await them. Such are the things that men are wont to attempt, and there is honour, glory, gain, in attempting them, however full of difficulty and peril they may be; but that which thou sayest it is thy wish to attempt and carry out will not win thee the glory of God nor the blessings of fortune nor fame among men; for even if the issue be as thou wouldst have it, thou wilt be no happier, richer, or more honoured than thou art this moment; and if it be otherwise thou wilt be reduced to misery greater than can be imagined, for then it will avail thee nothing to reflect that no one is aware of the misfortune that has befallen thee; it will suffice to torture and crush thee that thou knowest it thyself. And in confirmation of the truth of what I say, let me repeat to thee a stanza made by the famous poet Luigi Tansillo at the end of the first part of his 'Tears of Saint Peter,' which says thus:

The anguish and the shame but greater grew In Peter's heart as morning slowly came; No eye was there to see him, well he knew, Yet he himself was to himself a shame; Exposed to all men's gaze, or screened from view, A noble heart will feel the pang the same; A prey to shame the sinning soul will be, Though none but heaven and earth its shame can see.

Thus by keeping it secret thou wilt not escape thy sorrow, but rather thou wilt shed tears unceasingly, if not tears of the eyes, tears of blood from the heart, like those shed by that simple doctor our poet tells us of, that tried the test of the cup, which the wise Rinaldo, better advised, refused to do; for though this may be a poetic fiction it contains a moral lesson worthy of attention and study and imitation. Moreover by what I am about to say to thee thou wilt be led to see the great error thou wouldst commit.

"Tell me, Anselmo, if Heaven or good fortune had made thee master and lawful owner of a diamond of the finest quality, with the excellence and purity of which all the lapidaries that had seen it had been satisfied, saying with one voice and common consent that in purity, quality, and fineness, it was all that a stone of the kind could possibly be, thou thyself too being of the same belief, as knowing nothing to the contrary, would it be reasonable in thee to desire to take that diamond and place it between an anvil and a hammer, and by mere force of blows and strength of arm try if it were as hard and as fine as they said? And if thou didst, and if the stone should resist so silly a test, that would add nothing to its value or reputation; and if it were broken, as it might be, would not all be lost? Undoubtedly it would, leaving its owner to be rated as a fool in the opinion of all. Consider, then, Anselmo my friend, that Camilla is a diamond of the finest quality as well in thy estimation as in that of others, and that it is contrary to reason to expose her to the risk of being broken; for if she remains intact she cannot rise to a higher value than she now possesses; and if she give way and be unable to resist, bethink thee now how thou wilt be deprived of her, and with what good reason thou wilt complain of thyself for having been the cause of her ruin and thine own. Remember there is no jewel in the world so precious as a chaste and virtuous woman, and that the whole honour of women consists in reputation; and since thy wife's is of that high excellence that thou knowest, wherefore shouldst thou seek to call that truth in question? Remember, my friend, that woman is an imperfect animal, and that impediments are not to be placed in her way to make her trip and fall, but that they should be removed, and her path left clear of all obstacles, so that without hindrance she may run her course freely to attain the desired perfection, which consists in being virtuous. Naturalists tell us that the ermine is a little animal which has a fur of purest white, and that when the hunters wish to take it, they make use of this artifice. Having ascertained the places which it frequents and passes, they stop the way to them with mud, and then rousing it, drive it towards the spot, and as soon as the ermine comes to the mud it halts, and allows itself to be taken captive rather than pass through the mire, and spoil and sully its whiteness, which it values more than life and liberty. The virtuous and chaste woman is an ermine, and whiter and purer than snow is the virtue of modesty; and he who wishes her not to lose it, but to keep and preserve it, must adopt a course different from that employed with the ermine; he must not put before her the mire of the gifts and attentions of persevering lovers, because perhaps—and even without a perhaps—she may not have sufficient virtue and natural strength in herself to pass through and tread under foot these impediments; they must be removed, and the brightness of virtue and the beauty of a fair fame must be put before her. A virtuous woman, too, is like a mirror, of clear shining crystal, liable to be tarnished and dimmed by every breath that touches it. She must be treated as relics are; adored, not touched. She must be protected and prized as one protects and prizes a fair garden full of roses and flowers, the owner of which allows no one to trespass or pluck a blossom; enough for others that from afar and through the iron grating they may enjoy its fragrance and its beauty. Finally let me repeat to thee some verses that come to my mind; I heard them in a modern comedy, and it seems to me they bear upon the point we are discussing. A prudent old man was giving advice to another, the father of a young girl, to lock her up, watch over her and keep her in seclusion, and among other arguments he used these:

> Woman is a thing of glass;
> But her brittleness 'tis best
> Not too curiously to test:
> Who knows what may come to pass?
>
> Breaking is an easy matter,
> And it's folly to expose
> What you cannot mend to blows;
> What you can't make whole to shatter.
>
> This, then, all may hold as true,
> And the reason's plain to see;
> For if Danaes there be,
> There are golden showers too.

"All that I have said to thee so far, Anselmo, has had reference to what concerns thee; now it is right that I should say something of what regards myself; and if I be prolix, pardon me, for the labyrinth into which thou hast entered and from which thou wouldst have me extricate thee makes it necessary.

"Thou dost reckon me thy friend, and thou wouldst rob me of honour, a thing wholly inconsistent with friendship; and not only dost thou aim at this, but thou wouldst have me rob thee of it also. That thou wouldst rob me of it is clear, for when Camilla sees that I pay court to her as thou requirest, she will certainly regard me as a man without honour or right feeling, since I attempt and do a thing so much opposed to what I owe to my own position and thy friendship. That thou wouldst have me rob thee of it is beyond a doubt, for Camilla, seeing that I press my suit upon her, will suppose that I have perceived in her something light that has encouraged me to make known to her my base desire; and if she holds herself dishonoured, her dishonour touches thee as belonging to her; and hence arises what so commonly takes place, that the husband of the adulterous woman, though he may not be aware of or have given any cause for his wife's failure in her duty, or (being careless or negligent) have had it in his power to prevent his dishonour, nevertheless is stigmatised by a vile and reproachful name, and in a manner regarded with eyes of contempt instead of pity by all who know of his wife's guilt, though they see that he is unfortunate not by his own fault, but by the lust of a vicious consort. But I will tell thee why with good reason dishonour attaches to the husband of the unchaste wife, though he know not that she is so, nor be to blame, nor have done anything, or given any provocation to make her so; and be not weary with listening to me, for it will be for thy good.

"When God created our first parent in the earthly paradise, the Holy Scripture says that he infused sleep into Adam and while he slept took a rib from his left side of which he formed our mother Eve, and when Adam awoke and beheld her he said, 'This is flesh of my flesh, and bone of my bone.' And God said 'For this shall a man leave his father and his mother, and they shall be two in one flesh; and then was instituted the divine sacrament of marriage, with such ties that death alone can loose them. And such is the force and virtue of this miraculous sacrament that it makes two different persons one and the same flesh; and even more than this when the virtuous are married; for though they have two souls they have but one will. And hence it follows that as the flesh of the wife is one and the same with that of her husband the stains that may come upon it, or the injuries it incurs fall upon the husband's flesh, though he, as has been said, may have given no cause for them; for as the pain of the foot or any member of the body is felt by the whole body, because all is one flesh, as the head feels the hurt to the ankle without having caused it, so the husband, being one with her, shares the dishonour of the wife; and as all worldly honour or dishonour comes of flesh and blood, and the erring wife's is of that kind, the husband must needs bear his part of it and be held dishonoured without knowing it. See, then, Anselmo, the peril thou art encountering in seeking to disturb the peace of thy virtuous consort; see for what an empty and ill-advised curiosity thou wouldst rouse up passions that now repose in quiet in the breast of thy chaste wife; reflect that what thou art staking all to win is little, and what thou wilt lose so much that I leave it undescribed, not having the words to express it. But if all I have said be not enough to turn thee from thy vile purpose, thou must seek some other instrument for thy dishonour and misfortune; for such I will not consent to be, though I lose thy friendship, the greatest loss that I can conceive."

Having said this, the wise and virtuous Lothario was silent, and Anselmo, troubled in mind and deep in thought, was unable for a while to utter a word in reply; but at length he said, "I have listened, Lothario my friend, attentively, as thou hast seen, to what thou hast chosen to say to me, and in thy arguments, examples, and comparisons I have seen that high intelligence thou dost possess, and the perfection of true friendship thou hast reached; and likewise I see and confess that if I am not guided by thy opinion, but follow my own, I am flying from the good and pursuing the evil. This being so, thou must remember that I am now labouring under that infirmity which women sometimes suffer from, when the craving seizes them to eat clay, plaster, charcoal, and things even worse, disgusting to look at, much more to eat; so that it will be necessary to have recourse to some artifice to cure me; and this can be easily effected if only thou wilt make a beginning, even though it be in a lukewarm and make-believe fashion, to pay court to Camilla, who will not be so yielding that her virtue will give way at the first attack: with this mere attempt I shall rest satisfied, and thou wilt have done what our friendship binds thee to do, not only in giving me life, but in persuading me not to discard my honour. And this thou art bound to do for one reason alone, that, being, as I am, resolved to apply this test, it is not for thee to permit me to reveal my weakness to another, and so imperil that honour thou art striving to keep me from losing; and if thine may not stand as high as it ought in the estimation of Camilla while thou art paying court to her, that is of little or no importance, because ere long, on finding in her that constancy which we expect, thou canst tell her the plain truth as regards our stratagem, and so regain thy place in her esteem; and as thou art venturing so little, and by the venture canst afford me so much satisfaction, refuse not to undertake it, even if further difficulties present themselves to thee; for, as I have said, if thou wilt only make a beginning I will acknowledge the issue decided."

Lothario seeing the fixed determination of Anselmo, and not knowing what further examples to offer or arguments to urge in order to dissuade him from it, and perceiving that he threatened to confide his pernicious scheme to some one else, to avoid a greater evil resolved to gratify him and do what he asked, intending to manage the business so as to satisfy Anselmo without corrupting the mind of Camilla; so in reply he told him not to communicate his purpose to any other, for he would undertake the task himself, and would begin it as soon as he pleased. Anselmo embraced him warmly and affectionately, and thanked him for his offer as if he had bestowed some great favour upon him; and it was agreed between them to set about it the next day, Anselmo affording opportunity and time to Lothario to converse alone with Camilla, and furnishing him with money and jewels to offer and present to her. He suggested, too, that he should treat her to music, and write verses in her praise, and if he was unwilling to take the trouble of composing them, he offered to do it himself. Lothario agreed to all with an intention very different from what Anselmo supposed, and with this understanding they returned to Anselmo's house, where they found Camilla awaiting her husband anxiously and uneasily, for he was later than usual in returning that day. Lothario repaired to his own house, and Anselmo remained in his, as well satisfied as Lothario was troubled in mind; for he could see no satisfactory way out of this ill-advised business. That night, however, he thought of a plan by which he might deceive Anselmo without any injury to Camilla. The next day he went to dine with his friend, and was welcomed by Camilla, who received and treated him with great cordiality, knowing the affection her husband felt for him. When dinner was over and the cloth removed, Anselmo told Lothario to stay there with Camilla while he attended to some pressing business, as he would return in an hour and a half. Camilla begged him not to go, and Lothario offered to accompany him, but nothing could persuade Anselmo, who on the contrary pressed Lothario to remain waiting for him as he had a matter of great importance to discuss with him. At the same time he bade Camilla not to leave Lothario alone until he came back. In short he contrived to put so good a face on the reason, or the folly, of his absence that no one could have suspected it was a pretence.

Anselmo took his departure, and Camilla and Lothario were left alone at the table, for the rest of the household had gone to dinner. Lothario saw himself in the lists according to his friend's wish, and facing an enemy that could by her beauty alone vanquish a squadron of armed knights; judge whether he had good reason to fear; but what he did was to lean his elbow on the arm of the chair, and his cheek upon his hand, and, asking Camilla's pardon for his ill manners, he said he wished to take a little sleep until Anselmo returned. Camilla in reply said he could repose more at his ease in the reception-room than in his chair, and begged of him to go in and sleep there; but Lothario declined, and there he remained asleep until the return of Anselmo, who finding Camilla in her own room, and Lothario asleep, imagined that he had stayed away so long as to have afforded them time enough for conversation and even for sleep, and was all impatience until Lothario should wake up, that he might go out with him and question him as to his success. Everything fell out as he wished; Lothario awoke, and the two at once left the house, and Anselmo asked what he was anxious to know, and Lothario in answer told him that he had not thought it advisable to declare himself entirely the first time, and therefore had only extolled the charms of Camilla, telling her that all the city spoke of nothing else but her beauty and wit, for this seemed to him an excellent way of beginning to gain her good-will and render her disposed to listen to him with pleasure the next time, thus availing himself of the device the devil has recourse to when he would deceive one who is on the watch; for he being the angel of darkness transforms himself into an angel of light, and, under cover of a fair seeming, discloses himself at length, and effects his purpose if at the beginning his wiles are not discovered. All this gave great satisfaction to Anselmo, and he said he would afford the same opportunity every day, but without leaving the house, for he would find things to do at home so that Camilla should not detect the plot.

Thus, then, several days went by, and Lothario, without uttering a word to Camilla, reported to Anselmo that he had talked with her and that he had never been able to draw from her the slightest indication of consent to anything dishonourable, nor even a sign or shadow of hope; on the contrary, he said she would inform her husband of it.

"So far well," said Anselmo; "Camilla has thus far resisted words; we must now see how she will resist deeds. I will give you to-morrow two thousand crowns in gold for you to offer or even present, and as many more to buy jewels to lure her, for women are fond of being becomingly attired and going gaily dressed, and all the more so if they are beautiful, however chaste they may be; and if she resists this temptation, I will rest satisfied and will give you no more trouble."

Lothario replied that now he had begun he would carry on the undertaking to the end, though he perceived he was to come out of it wearied and vanquished. The next day he received the four thousand crowns, and with them four thousand perplexities, for he knew not what to say by way of a new falsehood; but in the end he made up his mind to tell him that Camilla stood as firm against gifts and promises as against words, and that there was no use in taking any further trouble, for the time was all spent to no purpose.

But chance, directing things in a different manner, so ordered it that Anselmo, having left Lothario and Camilla alone as on other occasions, shut himself into a chamber and posted himself to watch and listen through the keyhole to what passed between them, and perceived that for more than half an hour Lothario did not utter a word to Camilla, nor would utter a word though he were to be there for an age; and he came to the conclusion that what his friend had told him about the replies of Camilla was all invention and falsehood, and to ascertain if it were so, he came out, and calling

Lothario aside asked him what news he had and in what humour Camilla was. Lothario replied that he was not disposed to go on with the business, for she had answered him so angrily and harshly that he had no heart to say anything more to her.

"Ah, Lothario, Lothario," said Anselmo, "how ill dost thou meet thy obligations to me, and the great confidence I repose in thee! I have been just now watching through this keyhole, and I have seen that thou has not said a word to Camilla, whence I conclude that on the former occasions thou hast not spoken to her either, and if this be so, as no doubt it is, why dost thou deceive me, or wherefore seekest thou by craft to deprive me of the means I might find of attaining my desire?"

Anselmo said no more, but he had said enough to cover Lothario with shame and confusion, and he, feeling as it were his honour touched by having been detected in a lie, swore to Anselmo that he would from that moment devote himself to satisfying him without any deception, as he would see if he had the curiosity to watch; though he need not take the trouble, for the pains he would take to satisfy him would remove all suspicions from his mind. Anselmo believed him, and to afford him an opportunity more free and less liable to surprise, he resolved to absent himself from his house for eight days, betaking himself to that of a friend of his who lived in a village not far from the city; and, the better to account for his departure to Camilla, he so arranged it that the friend should send him a very pressing invitation.

Unhappy, shortsighted Anselmo, what art thou doing, what art thou plotting, what art thou devising? Bethink thee thou art working against thyself, plotting thine own dishonour, devising thine own ruin. Thy wife Camilla is virtuous, thou dost possess her in peace and quietness, no one assails thy happiness, her thoughts wander not beyond the walls of thy house, thou art her heaven on earth, the object of her wishes, the fulfilment of her desires, the measure wherewith she measures her will, making it conform in all things to thine and Heaven's. If, then, the mine of her honour, beauty, virtue, and modesty yields thee without labour all the wealth it contains and thou canst wish for, why wilt thou dig the earth in search of fresh veins, of new unknown treasure, risking the collapse of all, since it but rests on the feeble props of her weak nature? Bethink thee that from him who seeks impossibilities that which is possible may with justice be withheld, as was better expressed by a poet who said:

'Tis mine to seek for life in death,
Health in disease seek I,
I seek in prison freedom's breath,
In traitors loyalty.
So Fate that ever scorns to grant
Or grace or boon to me,
Since what can never be I want,
Denies me what might be.

The next day Anselmo took his departure for the village, leaving instructions with Camilla that during his absence Lothario would come to look after his house and to dine with her, and that she was to treat him as she would himself. Camilla was distressed, as a discreet and right-minded woman would be, at the orders her husband left her, and bade him remember that it was not becoming that anyone should occupy his seat at the table during his absence, and if he acted thus from not feeling confidence that she would be able to manage his house, let him try her this time, and he would find by experience that she was equal to greater responsibilities. Anselmo replied that it was his pleasure to have it so, and that she had only to submit and obey. Camilla said she would do so, though against her will.

Anselmo went, and the next day Lothario came to his house, where he was received by Camilla with a friendly and modest welcome; but she never suffered Lothario to see her alone, for she was always attended by her men and women servants, especially by a handmaid of hers, Leonela by name, to whom she was much attached (for they had been brought up together from childhood in her father's house), and whom she had kept with her after her marriage with Anselmo. The first three days Lothario did not speak to her, though he might have done so when they removed the cloth and the servants retired to dine hastily; for such were Camilla's orders; nay more, Leonela had directions to dine earlier than Camilla and never to leave her side. She, however, having her thoughts fixed upon other things more to her taste, and wanting that time and opportunity for her own pleasures, did not always obey her mistress's commands, but on the contrary left them alone, as if they had ordered her to do so; but the modest bearing of Camilla, the calmness of her countenance, the composure of her aspect were enough to bridle the tongue of Lothario. But the influence which the many virtues of Camilla exerted in imposing silence on Lothario's tongue proved mischievous for both of them, for if his tongue was silent his thoughts were busy, and could dwell at leisure upon the perfections of Camilla's goodness and beauty one by one, charms enough to warm with love a marble statue, not to say a heart of flesh. Lothario gazed upon her when he might have been speaking to her, and thought how worthy of being loved she was; and thus reflection began little by little to assail his allegiance to Anselmo, and a thousand times he thought of withdrawing from the city and going where Anselmo should never see him nor he see Camilla. But already the delight he found in gazing on her interposed and held him fast. He put a constraint upon himself, and struggled to repel and repress the pleasure he found in contemplating Camilla; when alone he blamed himself for his weakness, called himself a bad friend, nay a bad Christian; then he argued the matter and compared himself with Anselmo; always coming to the conclusion that the folly and rashness of Anselmo had been worse than his faithlessness, and that if he could excuse his intentions as easily before God as with man, he had no reason to fear any punishment for his offence.

In short the beauty and goodness of Camilla, joined with the opportunity which the blind husband had placed in his hands, overthrew the loyalty of Lothario; and giving heed to nothing save the object towards which his inclinations led him, after Anselmo had been three days absent, during which he had been carrying on a continual struggle with his passion, he began to make love to Camilla with so much vehemence and warmth of language that she was overwhelmed with amazement, and could only rise from her place and retire to her room without answering him a word. But the hope which always springs up with love was not weakened in Lothario by this repelling demeanour; on the contrary his passion for Camilla increased, and she discovering in him what she had never expected, knew not what to do; and considering it neither safe nor right to give him the chance or opportunity of speaking to her again, she resolved to send, as she did that very night, one of her servants with a letter to Anselmo, in which she addressed the following words to him..

CHAPTER XXXIV

IN WHICH IS CONTINUED THE NOVEL OF "THE ILL-ADVISED CURIOSITY"

"It is commonly said that an army looks ill without its general and a castle without its castellan, and I say that a young married woman looks still worse without her husband unless there are very good reasons for it. I find myself so ill at ease without you, and so incapable of enduring this separation, that unless you return quickly I shall have to go for relief to my parents' house, even if I leave yours without a protector; for the one you left me, if indeed he deserved that title, has, I think, more regard to his own pleasure than to what concerns you: as you are possessed of discernment I need say no more to you, nor indeed is it fitting I should say more."

Anselmo received this letter, and from it he gathered that Lothario had already begun his task and that Camilla must have replied to him as he would have wished; and delighted beyond measure at such intelligence he sent word to her not to leave his house on any account, as he would very shortly return. Camilla was astonished at Anselmo's reply, which placed her in greater perplexity than before, for she neither dared to remain in her own house, nor yet to go to her parents'; for in remaining her virtue was imperilled, and in going she was opposing her husband's commands. Finally she decided upon what was the worse course for her, to remain, resolving not to fly from the presence of Lothario, that she might not give food for gossip to her servants; and she now began to regret having written as she had to her husband, fearing he might imagine that Lothario had perceived in her some lightness which had impelled him to lay aside the respect he owed her; but confident of her rectitude she put her trust in God and in her own virtuous intentions, with which she hoped to resist in silence all the solicitations of Lothario, without saying anything to her husband so as not to involve him in any quarrel or trouble; and she even began to consider how to excuse Lothario to Anselmo when he should ask her what it was that induced her to write that letter. With these resolutions, more honourable than judicious or effectual, she remained the next day listening to Lothario, who pressed his suit so strenuously that Camilla's firmness began to waver, and her virtue had enough to do to come to the rescue of her eyes and keep them from showing signs of a certain tender compassion which the tears and appeals of Lothario had awakened in her bosom. Lothario observed all this, and it inflamed him all the more. In short he felt that while Anselmo's absence afforded time and opportunity he must press the siege of the fortress, and so he assailed her self-esteem with praises of her beauty, for there is nothing that more quickly reduces and levels the castle towers of fair women's vanity than vanity itself upon the tongue of flattery. In fact with the utmost assiduity he undermined the rock of her purity with such engines that had Camilla been of brass she must have fallen. He wept, he entreated, he promised, he flattered, he importuned, he pretended with so much feeling and apparent sincerity, that he overthrew the virtuous resolves of Camilla and won the triumph he least expected and most longed for. Camilla yielded, Camilla fell; but what wonder if the friendship of Lothario could not stand firm? A clear proof to us that the passion of love is to be conquered only by flying from it, and that no one should engage in a struggle with an enemy so mighty; for divine strength is needed to overcome his human power. Leonela alone knew of her mistress's weakness, for the two false friends and new lovers were unable to conceal it. Lothario did not care to tell Camilla the object Anselmo had in view, nor that he had afforded him the opportunity of attaining such a result, lest she should undervalue his love and think that it was by chance and without intending it and not of his own accord that he had made love to her.

 A few days later Anselmo returned to his house and did not perceive what it had lost, that which he so lightly treated and so highly prized. He went at once to see Lothario, and found him at home; they embraced each other, and Anselmo asked for the tidings of his life or his death.

 "The tidings I have to give thee, Anselmo my friend," said Lothario, "are that thou dost possess a wife that is worthy to be the pattern and crown of all good wives. The words that I have addressed to her were borne away on the wind, my promises have been despised, my presents have been refused, such feigned tears as I shed have been turned into open ridicule. In short, as Camilla is the essence of all beauty, so is she the treasure-house where purity dwells, and gentleness and modesty abide with all the virtues that can confer praise, honour, and happiness upon a woman. Take back thy money, my friend; here it is, and I have had no need to touch it, for the chastity of Camilla yields not to things so base as gifts or promises. Be content, Anselmo, and refrain from making further proof; and as thou hast passed dryshod through the sea of those doubts and suspicions that are and may be entertained of women, seek not to plunge again into the deep ocean of new embarrassments, or with another pilot make trial of the goodness and strength of the bark that Heaven has granted thee for thy passage across the sea of this world; but reckon thyself now safe in port, moor thyself with the anchor of sound reflection, and rest in peace until thou art called upon to pay that debt which no nobility on earth can escape paying."

Anselmo was completely satisfied by the words of Lothario, and believed them as fully as if they had been spoken by an oracle; nevertheless he begged of him not to relinquish the undertaking, were it but for the sake of curiosity and amusement; though thenceforward he need not make use of the same earnest endeavours as before; all he wished him to do was to write some verses to her, praising her under the name of Chloris, for he himself would give her to understand that he was in love with a lady to whom he had given that name to enable him to sing her praises with the decorum due to her modesty; and if Lothario were unwilling to take the trouble of writing the verses he would compose them himself.

"That will not be necessary," said Lothario, "for the muses are not such enemies of mine but that they visit me now and then in the course of the year. Do thou tell Camilla what thou hast proposed about a pretended amour of mine; as for the verses will make them, and if not as good as the subject deserves, they shall be at least the best I can produce." An agreement to this effect was made between the friends, the ill-advised one and the treacherous, and Anselmo returning to his house asked Camilla the question she already wondered he had not asked before—what it was that had caused her to write the letter she had sent him. Camilla replied that it had seemed to her that Lothario looked at her somewhat more freely than when he had been at home; but that now she was undeceived and believed it to have been only her own imagination, for Lothario now avoided seeing her, or being alone with her. Anselmo told her she might be quite easy on the score of that suspicion, for he knew that Lothario was in love with a damsel of rank in the city whom he celebrated under the name of Chloris, and that even if he were not, his fidelity and their great friendship left no room for fear. Had not Camilla, however, been informed beforehand by Lothario that this love for Chloris was a pretence, and that he himself had told Anselmo of it in order to be able sometimes to give utterance to the praises of Camilla herself, no doubt she would have fallen into the despairing toils of jealousy; but being forewarned she received the startling news without uneasiness.

The next day as the three were at table Anselmo asked Lothario to recite something of what he had composed for his mistress Chloris; for as Camilla did not know her, he might safely say what he liked.

"Even did she know her," returned Lothario, "I would hide nothing, for when a lover praises his lady's beauty, and charges her with cruelty, he casts no imputation upon her fair name; at any rate, all I can say is that yesterday I made a sonnet on the ingratitude of this Chloris, which goes thus:

SONNET

> At midnight, in the silence, when the eyes
> Of happier mortals balmy slumbers close,
> The weary tale of my unnumbered woes
> To Chloris and to Heaven is wont to rise.
> And when the light of day returning dyes
> The portals of the east with tints of rose,
> With undiminished force my sorrow flows
> In broken accents and in burning sighs.
> And when the sun ascends his star-girt throne,
> And on the earth pours down his midday beams,
> Noon but renews my wailing and my tears;
> And with the night again goes up my moan.
> Yet ever in my agony it seems
> To me that neither Heaven nor Chloris hears."

The sonnet pleased Camilla, and still more Anselmo, for he praised it and said the lady was excessively cruel who made no return for sincerity so manifest. On which Camilla said, "Then all that love-smitten poets say is true?"

"As poets they do not tell the truth," replied Lothario; "but as lovers they are not more defective in expression than they are truthful."

"There is no doubt of that," observed Anselmo, anxious to support and uphold Lothario's ideas with Camilla, who was as regardless of his design as she was deep in love with Lothario; and so taking delight in anything that was his, and knowing that his thoughts and writings had her for their object, and that she herself was the real Chloris, she asked him to repeat some other sonnet or verses if he recollected any.

"I do," replied Lothario, "but I do not think it as good as the first one, or, more correctly speaking, less bad; but you can easily judge, for it is this.

SONNET

>I know that I am doomed; death is to me
>>As certain as that thou, ungrateful fair,
>>Dead at thy feet shouldst see me lying, ere
>My heart repented of its love for thee.
>If buried in oblivion I should be,
>>Bereft of life, fame, favour, even there
>>It would be found that I thy image bear
>Deep graven in my breast for all to see.
>This like some holy relic do I prize
>>To save me from the fate my truth entails,
>>Truth that to thy hard heart its vigour owes.
>Alas for him that under lowering skies,
>>In peril o'er a trackless ocean sails,
>>Where neither friendly port nor pole-star shows."

Anselmo praised this second sonnet too, as he had praised the first; and so he went on adding link after link to the chain with which he was binding himself and making his dishonour secure; for when Lothario was doing most to dishonour him he told him he was most honoured; and thus each step that Camilla descended towards the depths of her abasement, she mounted, in his opinion, towards the summit of virtue and fair fame.

It so happened that finding herself on one occasion alone with her maid, Camilla said to her, "I am ashamed to think, my dear Leonela, how lightly I have valued myself that I did not compel Lothario to purchase by at least some expenditure of time that full possession of me that I so quickly yielded him of my own free will. I fear that he will think ill of my pliancy or lightness, not considering the irresistible influence he brought to bear upon me."

"Let not that trouble you, my lady," said Leonela, "for it does not take away the value of the thing given or make it the less precious to give it quickly if it be really valuable and worthy of being prized; nay, they are wont to say that he who gives quickly gives twice."

"They say also," said Camilla, "that what costs little is valued less."

"That saying does not hold good in your case," replied Leonela, "for love, as I have heard say, sometimes flies and sometimes walks; with this one it runs, with that it moves slowly; some it cools, others it burns; some it wounds, others it slays; it begins the course of its desires, and at the same moment completes and ends it; in the morning it will lay siege to a fortress and by night will have taken it, for there is no power that can resist it; so what are you in dread of, what do you fear, when the same must have befallen Lothario, love having chosen the absence of my lord as the instrument for subduing you? and it was absolutely necessary to complete then what love had resolved upon, without affording the time to let Anselmo return and by his presence compel the work to be left unfinished; for love has no better agent for carrying out his designs than opportunity; and of opportunity he avails himself in all his feats, especially at the outset. All this I know well myself, more by experience than by hearsay, and some day, senora, I will enlighten you on the subject, for I am of your flesh and blood too. Moreover, lady Camilla, you did not surrender yourself or yield so quickly but that first you saw Lothario's whole soul in his eyes, in his sighs, in his words, his promises and his gifts, and by it and his good qualities perceived how worthy he was of your love. This, then, being the case, let not these scrupulous and prudish ideas trouble your imagination, but be assured that Lothario prizes you as you do him, and rest content and satisfied that as you are caught in the noose of love it is one of worth and merit that has taken you, and one that has not only the four S's that they say true lovers ought to have, but a complete alphabet; only listen to me and you will see how I can repeat it by rote. He is to my eyes and thinking, Amiable, Brave, Courteous, Distinguished, Elegant, Fond, Gay, Honourable, Illustrious, Loyal, Manly, Noble, Open, Polite, Quickwitted, Rich, and the S's according to the saying, and then Tender, Veracious: X does not suit him, for it is a rough letter; Y has been given already; and Z Zealous for your honour."

Camilla laughed at her maid's alphabet, and perceived her to be more experienced in love affairs than she said, which she admitted, confessing to Camilla that she had love passages with a young man of good birth of the same city. Camilla was uneasy at this, dreading lest it might prove the means of endangering her honour, and asked whether her intrigue had gone beyond words, and she with little shame and much effrontery said it had; for certain it is that ladies' imprudences make servants shameless, who, when they see their mistresses make a false step, think nothing of going astray themselves, or of its being known. All that Camilla could do was to entreat Leonela to say nothing about her doings to him whom she called her lover, and to conduct her own affairs secretly lest they should come to the knowledge of Anselmo or of Lothario. Leonela said she would, but kept her word in such a way that she confirmed Camilla's apprehension of losing her reputation through her means; for this abandoned and bold Leonela, as soon as she perceived that her mistress's demeanour was not what it was wont to be, had the audacity to introduce her lover into the house, confident that even if her mistress saw him she would not dare to expose him; for the sins of mistresses entail this mischief among others; they make themselves the slaves of their own servants, and are obliged to hide their laxities and depravities; as was the case with Camilla, who though she perceived, not once but many times, that Leonela was with her lover in some room of the house, not only did not dare to chide her, but afforded her opportunities for concealing him and removed all difficulties, lest he should be seen by her husband. She was unable, however, to prevent him from being seen on one occasion, as he sallied forth at daybreak, by Lothario, who, not knowing who he was, at first took him for a spectre; but, as soon as he saw him hasten away, muffling his face with his cloak and concealing himself carefully and cautiously, he rejected this foolish idea, and adopted another, which would have been the ruin of all had not Camilla found a remedy. It did not occur to Lothario that this man he had seen issuing at such an untimely hour from Anselmo's house could have entered it on Leonela's account, nor did he even remember there was such a person as Leonela; all he thought was that as Camilla had been light and yielding with him, so she had been with another; for this further penalty the erring woman's sin brings with it, that her honour is distrusted even by him to whose overtures and persuasions she has yielded; and he believes her to have surrendered more easily to others, and gives implicit credence to every suspicion that comes into his mind. All Lothario's good sense seems to have failed him at this juncture; all his prudent maxims escaped his memory; for without once reflecting rationally, and without more ado, in his impatience and in the blindness of the jealous rage that gnawed his heart, and dying to revenge himself upon Camilla, who had done him no wrong, before Anselmo had risen he hastened to him and said to him, "Know, Anselmo, that for several days past I have been struggling with myself, striving to withhold from thee what it is no longer possible or right that I should conceal from thee. Know that Camilla's fortress has surrendered and is ready to submit to my will; and if I have been slow to reveal this fact to thee, it was in order to see if it were some light caprice of hers, or if she sought to try me and ascertain if the love I began to make to her with thy permission was made with a serious intention. I thought, too, that she, if she were what she ought to be, and what we both believed her, would have ere this given thee information of my addresses; but seeing that she delays, I believe the truth of the promise she has given me that the next time thou art absent from the house she will grant me an interview in the closet where thy jewels are kept (and it was true that Camilla used to meet him there); but I do not wish thee to rush precipitately to take vengeance, for the sin is as yet only committed in intention, and Camilla's may change perhaps between this and the appointed time, and repentance spring up in its place. As hitherto thou hast always followed my advice wholly or in part, follow and observe this that I will give thee now, so that, without mistake, and with mature deliberation, thou mayest satisfy thyself as to what may seem the best course; pretend to absent thyself for two or three days as thou hast been wont to do on other occasions, and contrive to hide thyself in the closet; for the tapestries and other things there afford great facilities for thy concealment, and then thou wilt see with thine own eyes and I with mine what Camilla's purpose may be. And if it be a guilty one, which may be feared rather than expected, with silence, prudence, and discretion thou canst thyself become the instrument of punishment for the wrong done thee."

Anselmo was amazed, overwhelmed, and astounded at the words of Lothario, which came upon him at a time when he least expected to hear them, for he now looked upon Camilla as having triumphed over the pretended attacks of Lothario, and was beginning to enjoy the glory of her victory. He remained silent for a considerable time, looking on the ground with fixed gaze, and at length said, "Thou hast behaved, Lothario, as I expected of thy friendship: I will follow thy advice in everything; do as thou wilt, and keep this secret as thou seest it should be kept in circumstances so unlooked for."

Lothario gave him his word, but after leaving him he repented altogether of what he had said to him, perceiving how foolishly he had acted, as he might have revenged himself upon Camilla in some less cruel and degrading way. He cursed his want of sense, condemned his hasty resolution, and knew not what course to take to undo the mischief or find some ready escape from it. At last he decided upon revealing all to Camilla, and, as there was no want of opportunity for doing so, he found her alone the same day; but she, as soon as she had the chance of speaking to him, said, "Lothario my friend, I must tell thee I have a sorrow in my heart which fills it so that it seems ready to burst; and it will be a wonder if it does not; for the audacity of Leonela has now reached such a pitch that every night she conceals a gallant of hers in this house and remains with him till morning, at the expense of my reputation; inasmuch as it is open to anyone to question it who may see him quitting my house at such unseasonable hours; but what distresses me is that I cannot punish or chide her, for her privity to our intrigue bridles my mouth and keeps me silent about hers, while I am dreading that some catastrophe will come of it."

As Camilla said this Lothario at first imagined it was some device to delude him into the idea that the man he had seen going out was Leonela's lover and not hers; but when he saw how she wept and suffered, and begged him to help her, he became convinced of the truth, and the conviction completed his confusion and remorse; however, he told Camilla not to distress herself, as he would take measures to put a stop to the insolence of Leonela. At the same time he told her what, driven by the fierce rage of jealousy, he had said to Anselmo, and how he had arranged to hide himself in the closet that he might there see plainly how little she preserved her fidelity to him; and he entreated her pardon for this madness, and her advice as to how to repair it, and escape safely from the intricate labyrinth in which his imprudence had involved him. Camilla was struck with alarm at hearing what Lothario said, and with much anger, and great good sense, she reproved him and rebuked his base design and the foolish and mischievous resolution he had made; but as woman has by nature a nimbler wit than man for good and for evil, though it is apt to fail when she sets herself deliberately to reason, Camilla on the spur of the moment thought of a way to remedy what was to all appearance irremediable, and told Lothario to contrive that the next day Anselmo should conceal himself in the place he mentioned, for she hoped from his concealment to obtain the means of their enjoying themselves for the future without any apprehension; and without revealing her purpose to him entirely she charged him to be careful, as soon as Anselmo was concealed, to come to her when Leonela should call him, and to all she said to him to answer as he would have answered had he not known that Anselmo was listening. Lothario pressed her to explain her intention fully, so that he might with more certainty and precaution take care to do what he saw to be needful.

"I tell you," said Camilla, "there is nothing to take care of except to answer me what I shall ask you;" for she did not wish to explain to him beforehand what she meant to do, fearing lest he should be unwilling to follow out an idea which seemed to her such a good one, and should try or devise some other less practicable plan.

Lothario then retired, and the next day Anselmo, under pretence of going to his friend's country house, took his departure, and then returned to conceal himself, which he was able to do easily, as Camilla and Leonela took care to give him the opportunity; and so he placed himself in hiding in the state of agitation that it may be imagined he would feel who expected to see the vitals of his honour laid bare before his eyes, and found himself on the point of losing the supreme blessing he thought he possessed in his beloved Camilla. Having made sure of Anselmo's being in his hiding-place, Camilla and Leonela entered the closet, and the instant she set foot within it Camilla said, with a deep sigh, "Ah! dear Leonela, would it not be better, before I do what I am unwilling you should know lest you should seek to prevent it, that you should take Anselmo's dagger that I have asked of you and with it pierce this vile heart of mine? But no; there is no reason why I should suffer the punishment of another's fault. I will first know what it is that the bold licentious eyes of Lothario have seen in me that could have encouraged him to reveal to me a design so base as that which he has disclosed regardless of his friend and of my honour. Go to the window, Leonela, and call him, for no doubt he is in the street waiting to carry out his vile project; but mine, cruel it may be, but honourable, shall be carried out first."

"Ah, senora," said the crafty Leonela, who knew her part, "what is it you want to do with this dagger? Can it be that you mean to take your own life, or Lothario's? for whichever you mean to do, it will lead to the loss of your reputation and good name. It is better to dissemble your wrong and not give this wicked man the chance of entering the house now and finding us alone; consider, senora, we are weak women and he is a man, and determined, and as he comes with such a base purpose, blind and urged by passion, perhaps before you can put yours into execution he may do what will be worse for you than taking your life. Ill betide my master, Anselmo, for giving such authority in his house to this shameless fellow! And supposing you kill him, senora, as I suspect you mean to do, what shall we do with him when he is dead?"

"What, my friend?" replied Camilla, "we shall leave him for Anselmo to bury him; for in reason it will be to him a light labour to hide his own infamy under ground. Summon him, make haste, for all the time I delay in taking vengeance for my wrong seems to me an offence against the loyalty I owe my husband."

Anselmo was listening to all this, and every word that Camilla uttered made him change his mind; but when he heard that it was resolved to kill Lothario his first impulse was to come out and show himself to avert such a disaster; but in his anxiety to see the issue of a resolution so bold and virtuous he restrained himself, intending to come forth in time to prevent the deed. At this moment Camilla, throwing herself upon a bed that was close by, swooned away, and Leonela began to weep bitterly, exclaiming, "Woe is me! that I should be fated to have dying here in my arms the flower of virtue upon earth, the crown of true wives, the pattern of chastity!"

with more to the same effect, so that anyone who heard her would have taken her for the most tender-hearted and faithful handmaid in the world, and her mistress for another persecuted Penelope.

Camilla was not long in recovering from her fainting fit and on coming to herself she said, "Why do you not go, Leonela, to call hither that friend, the falsest to his friend the sun ever shone upon or night concealed? Away, run, haste, speed! lest the fire of my wrath burn itself out with delay, and the righteous vengeance that I hope for melt away in menaces and maledictions."

"I am just going to call him, senora," said Leonela; "but you must first give me that dagger, lest while I am gone you should by means of it give cause to all who love you to weep all their lives."

"Go in peace, dear Leonela, I will not do so," said Camilla, "for rash and foolish as I may be, to your mind, in defending my honour, I am not going to be so much so as that Lucretia who they say killed herself without having done anything wrong, and without having first killed him on whom the guilt of her misfortune lay. I shall die, if I am to die; but it must be after full vengeance upon him who has brought me here to weep over audacity that no fault of mine gave birth to."

Leonela required much pressing before she would go to summon Lothario, but at last she went, and while awaiting her return Camilla continued, as if speaking to herself, "Good God! would it not have been more prudent to have repulsed Lothario, as I have done many a time before, than to allow him, as I am now doing, to think me unchaste and vile, even for the short time I must wait until I undeceive him? No doubt it would have been better; but I should not be avenged, nor the honour of my husband vindicated, should he find so clear and easy an escape from the strait into which his depravity has led him. Let the traitor pay with his life for the temerity of his wanton wishes, and let the world know (if haply it shall ever come to know) that Camilla not only preserved her allegiance to her husband, but avenged him of the man who dared to wrong him. Still, I think it might be better to disclose this to Anselmo. But then I have called his attention to it in the letter I wrote to him in the country, and, if he did nothing to prevent the mischief I there pointed out to him, I suppose it was that from pure goodness of heart and trustfulness he would not and could not believe that any thought against his honour could harbour in the breast of so stanch a friend; nor indeed did I myself believe it for many days, nor should I have ever believed it if his insolence had not gone so far as to make it manifest by open presents, lavish promises, and ceaseless tears. But why do I argue thus? Does a bold determination stand in need of arguments? Surely not. Then traitors avaunt! Vengeance to my aid! Let the false one come, approach, advance, die, yield up his life, and then befall what may. Pure I came to him whom Heaven bestowed upon me, pure I shall leave him; and at the worst bathed in my own chaste blood and in the foul blood of the falsest friend that friendship ever saw in the world;" and as she uttered these words she paced the room holding the unsheathed dagger, with such irregular and disordered steps, and such gestures that one would have supposed her to have lost her senses, and taken her for some violent desperado instead of a delicate woman.

Anselmo, hidden behind some tapestries where he had concealed himself, beheld and was amazed at all, and already felt that what he had seen and heard was a sufficient answer to even greater suspicions; and he would have been now well pleased if the proof afforded by Lothario's coming were dispensed with, as he feared some sudden mishap; but as he was on the point of showing himself and coming forth to embrace and undeceive his wife he paused as he saw Leonela returning, leading Lothario. Camilla when she saw him, drawing a long line in front of her on the floor with the dagger, said to him, "Lothario, pay attention to what I say to thee: if by any chance thou darest to cross this line thou seest, or even approach it, the instant I see thee attempt it that same instant will I pierce my bosom with this dagger that I hold in my hand; and before thou answerest me a word desire thee to listen to a few from me, and afterwards thou shalt reply as may please thee. First, I desire thee to tell me, Lothario, if thou knowest my husband Anselmo, and in what light thou regardest him; and secondly I desire to know if thou knowest me too. Answer me this, without embarrassment or reflecting deeply what thou wilt answer, for they are no riddles I put to thee."

Lothario was not so dull but that from the first moment when Camilla directed him to make Anselmo hide himself he understood what she intended to do, and therefore he fell in with her idea so readily and promptly that between them they made the imposture look more true than truth; so he answered her thus: "I did not think, fair Camilla, that thou wert calling me to ask questions so remote from the object with which I come; but if it is to defer the promised reward thou art doing so, thou mightst have put it off still longer, for the longing for happiness gives the more distress the nearer comes the hope of gaining it; but lest thou shouldst say that I do not answer thy questions, I say that I know thy husband Anselmo, and that we have known each other from our earliest years; I will not speak of what thou too knowest, of our friendship, that I may not compel myself to testify against the wrong that love, the mighty excuse for greater errors, makes me inflict upon him. Thee I know and hold in the same estimation as he does, for were it not so I had not for a lesser prize acted in opposition to what I owe to my station and the holy laws of true friendship, now broken and violated by me through that powerful enemy, love."

"If thou dost confess that," returned Camilla, "mortal enemy of all that rightly deserves to be loved, with what face dost thou dare to come before one whom thou knowest to be the mirror wherein he is reflected on whom thou shouldst look to see how unworthily thou him? But, woe is me, I now comprehend what has made thee give so little heed to what thou owest to thyself; it must have been some freedom of mine, for I will not call it immodesty, as it did not proceed from any deliberate intention, but from some heedlessness such as women are guilty of through inadvertence when they think they have no occasion for reserve. But tell me, traitor, when did I by word or sign give a reply to thy prayers that could awaken in thee a shadow of hope of attaining thy base wishes? When were not thy professions of love sternly and scornfully rejected and rebuked? When were thy frequent pledges and still more frequent gifts believed or accepted? But as I am persuaded that no one can long persevere in the attempt to win love unsustained by some hope, I am willing to attribute to myself the blame of thy assurance, for no doubt some thoughtlessness of mine has all this time fostered thy hopes; and therefore will I punish myself and inflict upon myself the penalty thy guilt deserves. And that thou mayest see that being so relentless to myself I cannot possibly be otherwise to thee, I have summoned thee to be a witness of the sacrifice I mean to offer to the injured honour of my honoured husband, wronged by thee with all the assiduity thou wert capable of, and by me too through want of caution in avoiding every occasion, if I have given any, of encouraging and sanctioning thy base designs. Once more I say the suspicion in my mind that some imprudence of mine has engendered these lawless thoughts in thee, is what causes me most distress and what I desire most to punish with my own hands, for were any other instrument of punishment employed my error might become perhaps more widely known; but before I do so, in my death I mean to inflict death, and take with me one that will fully satisfy my longing for the revenge I hope for and have; for I shall see, wheresoever it may be that I go, the penalty awarded by inflexible, unswerving justice on him who has placed me in a position so desperate."

As she uttered these words, with incredible energy and swiftness she flew upon Lothario with the naked dagger, so manifestly bent on burying it in his breast that he was almost uncertain whether these demonstrations were real or feigned, for he was obliged to have recourse to all his skill and strength to prevent her from striking him; and with such reality did she act this strange farce and mystification that, to give it a colour of truth, she determined to stain it with her own blood; for perceiving, or pretending, that she could not wound Lothario, she said, "Fate, it seems, will not grant my just desire complete satisfaction, but it will not be able to keep me from satisfying it partially at least;" and making an effort to free the hand with the dagger which Lothario held in his grasp, she released it, and directing the point to a place where it could not inflict a deep wound, she plunged it into her left side high up close to the shoulder, and then allowed herself to fall to the ground as if in a faint.

Leonela and Lothario stood amazed and astounded at the catastrophe, and seeing Camilla stretched on the ground and bathed in her blood they were still uncertain as to the true nature of the act. Lothario, terrified and breathless, ran in haste to pluck out the dagger; but when he saw how slight the wound was he was relieved of his fears and once more admired the subtlety, coolness, and ready wit of the fair Camilla; and the better to support the part he had to play he began to utter profuse and doleful lamentations over her body as if she were dead, invoking maledictions not only on himself but also on him who had been the means of placing him in such a position: and knowing that his friend Anselmo heard him he spoke in such a way as to make a listener feel much more pity for him than for Camilla, even though he supposed her dead. Leonela took her up in her arms and laid her on the bed, entreating Lothario to go in quest of some one to attend to her wound in secret, and at the same time asking his advice and opinion as to what they should say to Anselmo about his lady's wound if he should chance to return before it was healed. He replied they might say what they liked, for he was not in a state to give advice that would be of any use; all he could tell her was to try and stanch the blood, as he was going where he should never more be seen; and with every appearance of deep grief and sorrow he left the house; but when he found himself alone, and where there was nobody to see him, he crossed himself unceasingly, lost in wonder at the adroitness of Camilla and the consistent acting of Leonela. He reflected how convinced Anselmo would be that he had a second Portia for a wife, and he looked forward anxiously to meeting him in order to rejoice together over falsehood and truth the most craftily veiled that could be imagined.

Leonela, as he told her, stanched her lady's blood, which was no more than sufficed to support her deception; and washing the wound with a little wine she bound it up to the best of her skill, talking all the time she was tending her in a strain that, even if nothing else had been said before, would have been enough to assure Anselmo that he had in Camilla a model of purity. To Leonela's words Camilla added her own, calling herself cowardly and wanting in spirit, since she had not enough at the time she had most need of it to rid herself of the life she so much loathed. She asked her attendant's advice as to whether or not she ought to inform her beloved husband of all that had happened, but the other bade her say nothing about it, as she would lay upon him the obligation of taking vengeance on Lothario, which he could not do but at great risk to himself; and it was the duty of a true wife not to give her husband provocation to quarrel, but, on the contrary, to remove it as far as possible from him.

Camilla replied that she believed she was right and that she would follow her advice, but at any rate it would be well to consider how she was to explain the wound to Anselmo, for he could not help seeing it; to which Leonela answered that she did not know how to tell a lie even in jest.

"How then can I know, my dear?" said Camilla, "for I should not dare to forge or keep up a falsehood if my life depended on it. If we can think of no escape from this difficulty, it will be better to tell him the plain truth than that he should find us out in an untrue story."

"Be not uneasy, senora," said Leonela; "between this and to-morrow I will think of what we must say to him, and perhaps the wound being where it is it can be hidden from his sight, and Heaven will be pleased to aid us in a purpose so good and honourable. Compose yourself, senora, and endeavour to calm your excitement lest my lord find you agitated; and leave the rest to my care and God's, who always supports good intentions."

Anselmo had with the deepest attention listened to and seen played out the tragedy of the death of his honour, which the performers acted with such wonderfully effective truth that it seemed as if they had become the realities of the parts they played. He longed for night and an opportunity of escaping from the house to go and see his good friend Lothario, and with him give vent to his joy over the precious pearl he had gained in having established his wife's purity. Both mistress and maid took care to give him time and opportunity to get away, and taking advantage of it he made his escape, and at once went in quest of Lothario, and it would be impossible to describe how he embraced him when he found him, and the things he said to him in the joy of his heart, and the praises he bestowed upon Camilla; all which Lothario listened to without being able to show any pleasure, for he could not forget how deceived his friend was, and how dishonourably he had wronged him; and though Anselmo could see that Lothario was not glad, still he imagined it was only because he had left Camilla wounded and had been himself the cause of it; and so among other things he told him not to be distressed about Camilla's accident, for, as they had agreed to hide it from him, the wound was evidently trifling; and that being so, he had no cause for fear, but should henceforward be of good cheer and rejoice with him, seeing that by his means and adroitness he found himself raised to the greatest height of happiness that he could have ventured to hope for, and desired no better pastime than making verses in praise of Camilla that would preserve her name for all time to come. Lothario commended his purpose, and promised on his own part to aid him in raising a monument so glorious.

And so Anselmo was left the most charmingly hoodwinked man there could be in the world. He himself, persuaded he was conducting the instrument of his glory, led home by the hand of him who had been the utter destruction of his good name; whom Camilla received with averted countenance, though with smiles in her heart. The deception was carried on for some time, until at the end of a few months Fortune turned her wheel and the guilt which had been until then so skilfully concealed was published abroad, and Anselmo paid with his life the penalty of his ill-advised curiosity.

CHAPTER XXXV

WHICH TREATS OF THE HEROIC AND PRODIGIOUS BATTLE DON QUIXOTE HAD WITH CERTAIN SKINS OF RED WINE, AND BRINGS THE NOVEL OF "THE ILL-ADVISED CURIOSITY" TO A CLOSE

There remained but little more of the novel to be read, when Sancho Panza burst forth in wild excitement from the garret where Don Quixote was lying, shouting, "Run, sirs! quick; and help my master, who is in the thick of the toughest and stiffest battle I ever laid eyes on. By the living God he has given the giant, the enemy of my lady the Princess Micomicona, such a slash that he has sliced his head clean off as if it were a turnip."

"What are you talking about, brother?" said the curate, pausing as he was about to read the remainder of the novel. "Are you in your senses, Sancho? How the devil can it be as you say, when the giant is two thousand leagues away?"

Here they heard a loud noise in the chamber, and Don Quixote shouting out, "Stand, thief, brigand, villain; now I have got thee, and thy scimitar shall not avail thee!" And then it seemed as though he were slashing vigorously at the wall.

"Don't stop to listen," said Sancho, "but go in and part them or help my master: though there is no need of that now, for no doubt the giant is dead by this time and giving account to God of his past wicked life; for I saw the blood flowing on the ground, and the head cut off and fallen on one side, and it is as big as a large wine-skin."

"May I die," said the landlord at this, "if Don Quixote or Don Devil has not been slashing some of the skins of red wine that stand full at his bed's head, and the spilt wine must be what this good fellow takes for blood;" and so saying he went into the room and the rest after him, and there they found Don Quixote in the strangest costume in the world. He was in his shirt, which was not long enough in front to cover his thighs completely and was six fingers shorter behind; his legs were very long and lean, covered with hair, and anything but clean; on his head he had a little greasy red cap that belonged to the host, round his left arm he had rolled the blanket of the bed, to which Sancho, for reasons best known to himself, owed a grudge, and in his right hand he held his unsheathed sword, with which he was slashing about on all sides, uttering exclamations as if he were actually fighting some giant: and the best of it was his eyes were not open, for he was fast asleep, and dreaming that he was doing battle with the giant. For his imagination was so wrought upon by the adventure he was going to accomplish, that it made him dream he had already reached the kingdom of Micomicon, and was engaged in combat with his enemy; and believing he was laying on the giant, he had given so many sword cuts to the skins that the whole room was full of wine. On seeing this the landlord was so enraged that he fell on Don Quixote, and with his clenched fist began to pummel him in such a way, that if Cardenio and the curate had not dragged him off, he would have brought the war of the giant to an end. But in spite of all the poor gentleman never woke until the barber brought a great pot of cold water from the well and flung it with one dash all over his body, on which Don Quixote woke up, but not so completely as to understand what was the matter. Dorothea, seeing how short and slight his attire was, would not go in to witness the battle between her champion and her opponent. As for Sancho, he went searching all over the floor for the head of the giant, and not finding it he said, "I see now that it's all enchantment in this house; for the last time, on this very spot where I am now, I got ever so many thumps without knowing who gave them to me, or being able to see anybody; and now this head is not to be seen anywhere about, though I saw it cut off with my own eyes and the blood running from the body as if from a fountain."

"What blood and fountains are you talking about, enemy of God and his saints?" said the landlord. "Don't you see, you thief, that the blood and the fountain are only these skins here that have been stabbed and the red wine swimming all over the room?—and I wish I saw the soul of him that stabbed them swimming in hell."

"I know nothing about that," said Sancho; "all I know is it will be my bad luck that through not finding this head my county will melt away like salt in water;"—for Sancho awake was worse than his master asleep, so much had his master's promises addled his wits.

The landlord was beside himself at the coolness of the squire and the mischievous doings of the master, and swore it should not be like the last time when they went without paying; and that their privileges of chivalry should not hold good this time to let one or other of them off without paying, even to the cost of the plugs that would have to be put to the damaged wine-skins. The curate was holding Don Quixote's hands, who, fancying he had now ended the adventure and was in the presence of the Princess Micomicona, knelt before the curate and said, "Exalted and beauteous lady, your highness may live from this day forth fearless of any harm this base being could do you; and I too from this day forth am released from the promise I gave you, since by the help of God on high and by the favour of her by whom I live and breathe, I have fulfilled it so successfully."

"Did not I say so?" said Sancho on hearing this. "You see I wasn't drunk; there you see my master has already salted the giant; there's no doubt about the bulls; my county is all right!"

Who could have helped laughing at the absurdities of the pair, master and man? And laugh they did, all except the landlord, who cursed himself; but at length the barber, Cardenio, and the curate contrived with no small trouble to get Don Quixote on the bed, and he fell asleep with every appearance of excessive weariness. They left him to sleep, and came out to the gate of the inn to console Sancho Panza on not having found the head of the giant; but much more work had they to appease the landlord, who was furious at the sudden death of his wine-skins; and said the landlady half scolding, half crying, "At an evil moment and in an unlucky hour he came into my house, this knight-errant—would that I had never set eyes on him, for dear he has cost me; the last time he went off with the overnight score against him for supper, bed, straw, and barley, for himself and his squire and a hack and an ass, saying he was a knight adventurer—God send unlucky adventures to him and all the adventurers in the world—and therefore not bound to pay anything, for it was so settled by the knight-errantry tariff: and then, all because of him, came the other gentleman and carried off my tail, and gives it back more than two cuartillos the worse, all stripped of its hair, so that it is no use for my husband's purpose; and then, for a finishing touch to all, to burst my wine-skins and spill my wine! I wish I saw his own blood spilt! But let him not deceive himself, for, by the bones of my father and the shade of my mother, they shall pay me down every quarts; or my name is not what it is, and I am not my father's daughter." All this and more to the same effect the landlady delivered with great irritation, and her good maid Maritornes backed her up, while the daughter held her peace and smiled from time to time. The curate smoothed matters by promising to make good all losses to the best of his power, not only as regarded the wine-skins but also the wine, and above all the depreciation of the tail which they set such store by. Dorothea comforted Sancho, telling him that she pledged herself, as soon as it should appear certain that his master had decapitated the giant, and she found herself peacefully established in her kingdom, to bestow upon him the best county there was in it. With this Sancho consoled himself, and assured the princess she might rely upon it that he had seen the head of the giant, and more by token it had a beard that reached to the girdle, and that if it was not to be seen now it was because everything that happened in that house went by enchantment, as he himself had proved the last time he had lodged there. Dorothea said she fully believed it, and that he need not be uneasy, for all would go well and turn out as he wished. All therefore being appeased, the curate was anxious to go on with the novel, as he saw there was but little more left to read. Dorothea and the others begged him to finish it, and he, as he was willing to please them, and enjoyed reading it himself, continued the tale in these words:

The result was, that from the confidence Anselmo felt in Camilla's virtue, he lived happy and free from anxiety, and Camilla purposely looked coldly on Lothario, that Anselmo might suppose her feelings towards him to be the opposite of what they were; and the better to support the position, Lothario begged to be excused from coming to the house, as the displeasure with which Camilla regarded his presence was plain to be seen. But the befooled Anselmo said he would on no account allow such a thing, and so in a thousand ways he became the author of his own dishonour, while he believed he was insuring his happiness. Meanwhile the satisfaction with which Leonela saw herself empowered to carry on her amour reached such a height that, regardless of everything else, she followed her inclinations unrestrainedly, feeling confident that her mistress would screen her, and even show her how to manage it safely. At last one night Anselmo heard footsteps in Leonela's room, and on trying to enter to see who it was, he found that the door was held against him, which made him all the more determined to open it; and exerting his strength he forced it open, and entered the room in time to see a man leaping through the window into the street. He ran quickly to seize him or discover who he was, but he was unable to effect either purpose, for Leonela flung her arms round him crying, "Be calm, senor; do not give way to passion or follow him who has escaped from this; he belongs to me, and in fact he is my husband."

Anselmo would not believe it, but blind with rage drew a dagger and threatened to stab Leonela, bidding her tell the truth or he would kill her. She, in her fear, not knowing what she was saying, exclaimed, "Do not kill me, senor, for I can tell you things more important than any you can imagine."

"Tell me then at once or thou diest," said Anselmo.

"It would be impossible for me now," said Leonela, "I am so agitated: leave me till to-morrow, and then you shall hear from me what will fill you with astonishment; but rest assured that he who leaped through the window is a young man of this city, who has given me his promise to become my husband."

Anselmo was appeased with this, and was content to wait the time she asked of him, for he never expected to hear anything against Camilla, so satisfied and sure of her virtue was he; and so he quitted the room, and left Leonela locked in, telling her she should not come out until she had told him all she had to make known to him. He went at once to see Camilla, and tell her, as he did, all that had passed between him and her handmaid, and the promise she had given him to inform him matters of serious importance.

There is no need of saying whether Camilla was agitated or not, for so great was her fear and dismay, that, making sure, as she had good reason to do, that Leonela would tell Anselmo all she knew of her faithlessness, she had not the courage to wait and see if her suspicions were confirmed; and that same night, as soon as she thought that Anselmo was asleep, she packed up the most valuable jewels she had and some money, and without being observed by anybody escaped from the house and betook herself to Lothario's, to whom she related what had occurred, imploring him to convey her to some place of safety or fly with her where they might be safe from Anselmo. The state of perplexity to which Camilla reduced Lothario was such that he was unable to utter a word in reply, still less to decide upon what he should do. At length he resolved to conduct her to a convent of which a sister of his was prioress; Camilla agreed to this, and with the speed which the circumstances demanded, Lothario took her to the convent and left her there, and then himself quitted the city without letting anyone know of his departure.

As soon as daylight came Anselmo, without missing Camilla from his side, rose eager to learn what Leonela had to tell him, and hastened to the room where he had locked her in. He opened the door, entered, but found no Leonela; all he found was some sheets knotted to the window, a plain proof that she had let herself down from it and escaped. He returned, uneasy, to tell Camilla, but not finding her in bed or anywhere in the house he was lost in amazement. He asked the servants of the house about her, but none of them could give him any explanation. As he was going in search of Camilla it happened by chance that he observed her boxes were lying open, and that the greater part of her jewels were gone; and now he became fully aware of his disgrace, and that Leonela was not the cause of his misfortune; and, just as he was, without delaying to dress himself completely, he repaired, sad at heart and dejected, to his friend Lothario to make known his sorrow to him; but when he failed to find him and the servants reported that he had been absent from his house all night and had taken with him all the money he had, he felt as though he were losing his senses; and to make all complete on returning to his own house he found it deserted and empty, not one of all his servants, male or female, remaining in it. He knew not what to think, or say, or do, and his reason seemed to be deserting him little by little. He reviewed his position, and saw himself in a moment left without wife, friend, or servants, abandoned, he felt, by the heaven above him, and more than all robbed of his honour, for in Camilla's disappearance he saw his own ruin. After long reflection he resolved at last to go to his friend's village, where he had been staying when he afforded opportunities for the contrivance of this complication of misfortune. He locked the doors of his house, mounted his horse, and with a broken spirit set out on his journey; but he had hardly gone half-way when, harassed by his reflections, he had to dismount and tie his horse to a tree, at the foot of which he threw himself, giving vent to piteous heartrending sighs; and there he remained till nearly nightfall, when he observed a man approaching on horseback from the city, of whom, after saluting him, he asked what was the news in Florence.

The citizen replied, "The strangest that have been heard for many a day; for it is reported abroad that Lothario, the great friend of the wealthy Anselmo, who lived at San Giovanni, carried off last night Camilla, the wife of Anselmo, who also has disappeared. All this has been told by a maid-servant of Camilla's, whom the governor found last night lowering herself by a sheet from the windows of Anselmo's house. I know not indeed, precisely, how the affair came to pass; all I know is that the whole city is wondering at the occurrence, for no one could have expected a thing of the kind, seeing the great and intimate friendship that existed between them, so great, they say, that they were called 'The Two Friends.'"

"Is it known at all," said Anselmo, "what road Lothario and Camilla took?"

"Not in the least," said the citizen, "though the governor has been very active in searching for them."

"God speed you, senor," said Anselmo.

"God be with you," said the citizen and went his way.

This disastrous intelligence almost robbed Anselmo not only of his senses but of his life. He got up as well as he was able and reached the house of his friend, who as yet knew nothing of his misfortune, but seeing him come pale, worn, and haggard, perceived that he was suffering some heavy affliction. Anselmo at once begged to be allowed to retire to rest, and to be given writing materials. His wish was complied with and he was left lying down and alone, for he desired this, and even that the door should be locked. Finding himself alone he so took to heart the thought of his misfortune that by the signs of death he felt within him he knew well his life was drawing to a close, and therefore he resolved to leave behind him a declaration of the cause of his strange end. He began to write, but before he had put down all he meant to say, his breath failed him and he yielded up his life, a victim to the suffering which his ill-advised curiosity had entailed upon him. The master of the house observing that it was now late and that Anselmo did not call, determined to go in and ascertain if his indisposition was increasing, and found him lying on his face, his body partly in the bed, partly on the writing-table, on which he lay with the written paper open and the pen still in his hand. Having first called to him without receiving any answer, his host approached him, and taking him by the hand, found that it was cold, and saw that he was dead. Greatly surprised and distressed he summoned the household to witness the sad fate which had befallen Anselmo; and then he read the paper, the handwriting of which he recognised as his, and which contained these words:

"A foolish and ill-advised desire has robbed me of life. If the news of my death should reach the ears of Camilla, let her know that I forgive her, for she was not bound to perform miracles, nor ought I to have required her to perform them; and since I have been the author of my own dishonour, there is no reason why-"

So far Anselmo had written, and thus it was plain that at this point, before he could finish what he had to say, his life came to an end. The next day his friend sent intelligence of his death to his relatives, who had already ascertained his misfortune, as well as the convent where Camilla lay almost on the point of accompanying her husband on that inevitable journey, not on account of the tidings of his death, but because of those she received of her lover's departure. Although she saw herself a widow, it is said she refused either to quit the convent or take the veil, until, not long afterwards, intelligence reached her that Lothario had been killed in a battle in which M. de Lautrec had been recently engaged with the Great Captain Gonzalo Fernandez de Cordova in the kingdom of Naples, whither her too late repentant lover had repaired. On learning this Camilla took the veil, and shortly afterwards died, worn out by grief and melancholy. This was the end of all three, an end that came of a thoughtless beginning.

"I like this novel," said the curate; "but I cannot persuade myself of its truth; and if it has been invented, the author's invention is faulty, for it is impossible to imagine any husband so foolish as to try such a costly experiment as Anselmo's. If it had been represented as occurring between a gallant and his mistress it might pass; but between husband and wife there is something of an impossibility about it. As to the way in which the story is told, however, I have no fault to find."

CHAPTER XXXVI

WHICH TREATS OF MORE CURIOUS INCIDENTS THAT OCCURRED AT THE INN

Just at that instant the landlord, who was standing at the gate of the inn, exclaimed, "Here comes a fine troop of guests; if they stop here we may say gaudeamus."

"What are they?" said Cardenio.

"Four men," said the landlord, "riding a la jineta, with lances and bucklers, and all with black veils, and with them there is a woman in white on a side-saddle, whose face is also veiled, and two attendants on foot."

"Are they very near?" said the curate.

"So near," answered the landlord, "that here they come."

Hearing this Dorothea covered her face, and Cardenio retreated into Don Quixote's room, and they hardly had time to do so before the whole party the host had described entered the inn, and the four that were on horseback, who were of highbred appearance and bearing, dismounted, and came forward to take down the woman who rode on the side-saddle, and one of them taking her in his arms placed her in a chair that stood at the entrance of the room where Cardenio had hidden himself. All this time neither she nor they had removed their veils or spoken a word, only on sitting down on the chair the woman gave a deep sigh and let her arms fall like one that was ill and weak. The attendants on foot then led the horses away to the stable. Observing this the curate, curious to know who these people in such a dress and preserving such silence were, went to where the servants were standing and put the question to one of them, who answered him.

"Faith, sir, I cannot tell you who they are, I only know they seem to be people of distinction, particularly he who advanced to take the lady you saw in his arms; and I say so because all the rest show him respect, and nothing is done except what he directs and orders."

"And the lady, who is she?" asked the curate.

"That I cannot tell you either," said the servant, "for I have not seen her face all the way: I have indeed heard her sigh many times and utter such groans that she seems to be giving up the ghost every time; but it is no wonder if we do not know more than we have told you, as my comrade and I have only been in their company two days, for having met us on the road they begged and persuaded us to accompany them to Andalusia, promising to pay us well."

"And have you heard any of them called by his name?" asked the curate.

"No, indeed," replied the servant; "they all preserve a marvellous silence on the road, for not a sound is to be heard among them except the poor lady's sighs and sobs, which make us pity her; and we feel sure that wherever it is she is going, it is against her will, and as far as one can judge from her dress she is a nun or, what is more likely, about to become one; and perhaps it is because taking the vows is not of her own free will, that she is so unhappy as she seems to be."

"That may well be," said the curate, and leaving them he returned to where Dorothea was, who, hearing the veiled lady sigh, moved by natural compassion drew near to her and said, "What are you suffering from, senora? If it be anything that women are accustomed and know how to relieve, I offer you my services with all my heart."

To this the unhappy lady made no reply; and though Dorothea repeated her offers more earnestly she still kept silence, until the gentleman with the veil, who, the servant said, was obeyed by the rest, approached and said to Dorothea, "Do not give yourself the trouble, senora, of making any offers to that woman, for it is her way to give no thanks for anything that is done for her; and do not try to make her answer unless you want to hear some lie from her lips."

"I have never told a lie," was the immediate reply of her who had been silent until now; "on the contrary, it is because I am so truthful and so ignorant of lying devices that I am now in this miserable condition; and this I call you yourself to witness, for it is my unstained truth that has made you false and a liar."

Cardenio heard these words clearly and distinctly, being quite close to the speaker, for there was only the door of Don Quixote's room between them, and the instant he did so, uttering a loud exclamation he cried, "Good God! what is this I hear? What voice is this that has reached my ears?" Startled at the voice the lady turned her head; and not seeing the speaker she stood up and attempted to enter the room; observing which the gentleman held her back, preventing her from moving a step. In her agitation and sudden movement the silk with which she had covered her face fell off and disclosed a countenance of incomparable and marvellous beauty, but pale and terrified; for she kept turning her eyes, everywhere she could direct her gaze, with an eagerness that made her look as if she had lost her senses, and so marked that it excited the pity of Dorothea and all who beheld her, though they knew not what caused it. The gentleman grasped her firmly by the shoulders, and being so fully occupied with holding her back, he was unable to put a hand to his veil which was falling off, as it did at length entirely, and Dorothea, who was holding the lady in her arms, raising her eyes saw that he who likewise held her was her husband, Don Fernando. The instant she recognised him, with a prolonged plaintive cry drawn from the depths of her heart, she fell backwards fainting, and but for the barber being close by to catch her in his arms, she would have fallen completely to the ground. The curate at once hastened to uncover her face and throw water on it, and as he did so Don Fernando, for he it was who held the other in his arms, recognised her and stood as if death-stricken by the sight; not, however, relaxing his grasp of Luscinda, for it was she that was struggling to release herself from his hold, having recognised Cardenio by his voice, as he had recognised her. Cardenio also heard Dorothea's cry as she fell fainting, and imagining that it came from his Luscinda burst forth in terror from the room, and the first thing he saw was Don Fernando with Luscinda in his arms. Don Fernando, too, knew Cardenio at once; and all three, Luscinda, Cardenio, and Dorothea, stood in silent amazement scarcely knowing what had happened to them.

They gazed at one another without speaking, Dorothea at Don Fernando, Don Fernando at Cardenio, Cardenio at Luscinda, and Luscinda at Cardenio. The first to break silence was Luscinda, who thus addressed Don Fernando: "Leave me, Senor Don Fernando, for the sake of what you owe to yourself; if no other reason will induce you, leave me to cling to the wall of which I am the ivy, to the support from which neither your importunities, nor your threats, nor your promises, nor your gifts have been able to detach me. See how Heaven, by ways strange and hidden from our sight, has brought me face to face with my true husband; and well you know by dear-bought experience that death alone will be able to efface him from my memory. May this plain declaration, then, lead you, as you can do nothing else, to turn your love into rage, your affection into resentment, and so to take my life; for if I yield it up in the presence of my beloved husband I count it well bestowed; it may be by my death he will be convinced that I kept my faith to him to the last moment of life."

Meanwhile Dorothea had come to herself, and had heard Luscinda's words, by means of which she divined who she was; but seeing that Don Fernando did not yet release her or reply to her, summoning up her resolution as well as she could she rose and knelt at his feet, and with a flood of bright and touching tears addressed him thus:

"If, my lord, the beams of that sun that thou holdest eclipsed in thine arms did not dazzle and rob thine eyes of sight thou wouldst have seen by this time that she who kneels at thy feet is, so long as thou wilt have it so, the unhappy and unfortunate Dorothea. I am that lowly peasant girl whom thou in thy goodness or for thy pleasure wouldst raise high enough to call herself thine; I am she who in the seclusion of innocence led a contented life until at the voice of thy importunity, and thy true and tender passion, as it seemed, she opened the gates of her modesty and surrendered to thee the keys of her liberty; a gift received by thee but thanklessly, as is clearly shown by my forced retreat to the place where thou dost find me, and by thy appearance under the circumstances in which I see thee. Nevertheless, I would not have thee suppose that I have come here driven by my shame; it is only grief and sorrow at seeing myself forgotten by thee that have led me. It was thy will to make me thine, and thou didst so follow thy will, that now, even though thou repentest, thou canst not help being mine. Bethink thee, my lord, the unsurpassable affection I bear thee may compensate for the beauty and noble birth for which thou wouldst desert me. Thou canst not be the fair Luscinda's because thou art mine, nor can she be thine because she is Cardenio's; and it will be easier, remember, to bend thy will to love one who adores thee, than to lead one to love thee who abhors thee now. Thou didst address thyself to my simplicity, thou didst lay siege to my virtue, thou wert not ignorant of my station, well dost thou know how I yielded wholly to thy will; there is no ground or reason for thee to plead deception, and if it be so, as it is, and if thou art a Christian as thou art a gentleman, why dost thou by such subterfuges put off making me as happy at last as thou didst at first? And if thou wilt not have me for what I am, thy true and lawful wife, at least take and accept me as thy slave, for so long as I am thine I will count myself happy and fortunate. Do not by deserting me let my shame become the talk of the gossips in the streets; make not the old age of my parents miserable; for the loyal services they as faithful vassals have ever rendered thine are not deserving of such a return; and if thou thinkest it will debase thy blood to mingle it with mine, reflect that there is little or no nobility in the world that has not travelled the same road, and that in illustrious lineages it is not the woman's blood that is of account; and, moreover, that true nobility consists in virtue, and if thou art wanting in that, refusing me what in justice thou owest me, then even I have higher claims to nobility than thine. To make an end, senor, these are my last words to thee: whether thou wilt, or wilt not, I am thy wife; witness thy words, which must not and ought not to be false, if thou dost pride thyself on that for want of which thou scornest me; witness the pledge which thou didst give me, and witness Heaven, which thou thyself didst call to witness the promise thou hadst made me; and if all this fail, thy own conscience will not fail to lift up its silent voice in the midst of all thy gaiety, and vindicate the truth of what I say and mar thy highest pleasure and enjoyment."

All this and more the injured Dorothea delivered with such earnest feeling and such tears that all present, even those who came with Don Fernando, were constrained to join her in them. Don Fernando listened to her without replying, until, ceasing to speak, she gave way to such sobs and sighs that it must have been a heart of brass that was not softened by the sight of so great sorrow. Luscinda stood regarding her with no less compassion for her sufferings than admiration for her intelligence and beauty, and would have gone to her to say some words of comfort to her, but was prevented by Don Fernando's grasp which held her fast. He, overwhelmed with confusion and astonishment, after regarding Dorothea for some moments with a fixed gaze, opened his arms, and, releasing Luscinda, exclaimed:

"Thou hast conquered, fair Dorothea, thou hast conquered, for it is impossible to have the heart to deny the united force of so many truths."

Luscinda in her feebleness was on the point of falling to the ground when Don Fernando released her, but Cardenio, who stood near, having retreated behind Don Fernando to escape recognition, casting fear aside and regardless of what might happen, ran forward to support her, and said as he clasped her in his arms, "If Heaven in its compassion is willing to let thee rest at last, mistress of my heart, true, constant, and fair, nowhere canst thou rest more safely than in these arms that now receive thee, and received thee before when fortune permitted me to call thee mine."

At these words Luscinda looked up at Cardenio, at first beginning to recognise him by his voice and then satisfying herself by her eyes that it was he, and hardly knowing what she did, and heedless of all considerations of decorum, she flung her arms around his neck and pressing her face close to his, said, "Yes, my dear lord, you are the true master of this your slave, even though adverse fate interpose again, and fresh dangers threaten this life that hangs on yours."

A strange sight was this for Don Fernando and those that stood around, filled with surprise at an incident so unlooked for. Dorothea fancied that Don Fernando changed colour and looked as though he meant to take vengeance on Cardenio, for she observed him put his hand to his sword; and the instant the idea struck her, with wonderful quickness she clasped him round the knees, and kissing them and holding him so as to prevent his moving, she said, while her tears continued to flow, "What is it thou wouldst do, my only refuge, in this unforeseen event? Thou hast thy wife at thy feet, and she whom thou wouldst have for thy wife is in the arms of her husband: reflect whether it will be right for thee, whether it will be possible for thee to undo what Heaven has done, or whether it will be becoming in thee to seek to raise her to be thy mate who in spite of every obstacle, and strong in her truth and constancy, is before thine eyes, bathing with the tears of love the face and bosom of her lawful husband. For God's sake I entreat of thee, for thine own I implore thee, let not this open manifestation rouse thy anger; but rather so calm it as to allow these two lovers to live in peace and quiet without any interference from thee so long as Heaven permits them; and in so doing thou wilt prove the generosity of thy lofty noble spirit, and the world shall see that with thee reason has more influence than passion."

All the time Dorothea was speaking, Cardenio, though he held Luscinda in his arms, never took his eyes off Don Fernando, determined, if he saw him make any hostile movement, to try and defend himself and resist as best he could all who might assail him, though it should cost him his life. But now Don Fernando's friends, as well as the curate and the barber, who had been present all the while, not forgetting the worthy Sancho Panza, ran forward and gathered round Don Fernando, entreating him to have regard for the tears of Dorothea, and not suffer her reasonable hopes to be disappointed, since, as they firmly believed, what she said was but the truth; and bidding him observe that it was not, as it might seem, by accident, but by a special disposition of Providence that they had all met in a place where no one could have expected a meeting. And the curate bade him remember that only death could part Luscinda from Cardenio; that even if some sword were to separate them they would think their death most happy; and that in a case that admitted of no remedy his wisest course was, by conquering and putting a constraint upon himself, to show a generous mind, and of his own accord suffer these two to enjoy the happiness Heaven had granted them. He bade him, too, turn his eyes upon the beauty of Dorothea and he would see that few if any could equal much less excel her; while to that beauty should be added her modesty and the surpassing love she bore him. But besides all this, he reminded him that if he prided himself on being a gentleman and a Christian, he could not do otherwise than keep his plighted word; and that in doing so he would obey God and meet the approval of all sensible people, who know and recognised it to be the privilege of beauty, even in one of humble birth, provided virtue accompany it, to be able to raise itself to the level of any rank, without any slur upon him who places it upon an equality with himself; and furthermore that when the potent sway of passion asserts itself, so long as there be no mixture of sin in it, he is not to be blamed who gives way to it.

To be brief, they added to these such other forcible arguments that Don Fernando's manly heart, being after all nourished by noble blood, was touched, and yielded to the truth which, even had he wished it, he could not gainsay; and he showed his submission, and acceptance of the good advice that had been offered to him, by stooping down and embracing Dorothea, saying to her, "Rise, dear lady, it is not right that what I hold in my heart should be kneeling at my feet; and if until now I have shown no sign of what I own, it may have been by Heaven's decree in order that, seeing the constancy with which you love me, I may learn to value you as you deserve. What I entreat of you is that you reproach me not with my transgression and grievous wrong-doing; for the same cause and force that drove me to make you mine impelled me to struggle against being yours; and to prove this, turn and look at the eyes of the now happy Luscinda, and you will see in them an excuse for all my errors: and as she has found and gained the object of her desires, and I have found in you what satisfies all my wishes, may she live in peace and contentment as many happy years with her Cardenio, as on my knees I pray Heaven to allow me to live with my Dorothea;" and with these words he once more embraced her and pressed his face to hers with so much tenderness that he had to take great heed to keep his tears from completing the proof of his love and repentance in the sight of all. Not so Luscinda, and Cardenio, and almost all the others, for they shed so many tears, some in their own happiness, some at that of the others, that one would have supposed a heavy calamity had fallen upon them all. Even Sancho Panza was weeping; though afterwards he said he only wept because he saw that Dorothea was not as he fancied the queen Micomicona, of whom he expected such great favours. Their wonder as well as their weeping lasted some time, and then Cardenio and Luscinda went and fell on their knees before Don Fernando, returning him thanks for the favour he had rendered them in language so grateful that he knew not how to answer them, and raising them up embraced them with every mark of affection and courtesy.

He then asked Dorothea how she had managed to reach a place so far removed from her own home, and she in a few fitting words told all that she had previously related to Cardenio, with which Don Fernando and his companions were so delighted that they wished the story had been longer; so charmingly did Dorothea describe her misadventures. When she had finished Don Fernando recounted what had befallen him in the city after he had found in Luscinda's bosom the paper in which she declared that she was Cardenio's wife, and never could be his. He said he meant to kill her, and would have done so had he not been prevented by her parents, and that he quitted the house full of rage and shame, and resolved to avenge himself when a more convenient opportunity should offer. The next day he learned that Luscinda had disappeared from her father's house, and that no one could tell whither she had gone. Finally, at the end of some months he ascertained that she was in a convent and meant to remain there all the rest of her life, if she were not to share it with Cardenio; and as soon as he had learned this, taking these three gentlemen as his companions, he arrived at the place where she was, but avoided speaking to her, fearing that if it were known he was there stricter precautions would be taken in the convent; and watching a time when the porter's lodge was open he left two to guard the gate, and he and the other entered the convent in quest of Luscinda, whom they found in the cloisters in conversation with one of the nuns, and carrying her off without giving her time to resist, they reached a place with her where they provided themselves with what they required for taking her away; all which they were able to do in complete safety, as the convent was in the country at a considerable distance from the city. He added that when Luscinda found herself in his power she lost all consciousness, and after returning to herself did nothing but weep and sigh without speaking a word; and thus in silence and tears they reached that inn, which for him was reaching heaven where all the mischances of earth are over and at an end.

CHAPTER XXXVII

IN WHICH IS CONTINUED THE STORY OF THE FAMOUS PRINCESS MICOMICONA, WITH OTHER DROLL ADVENTURES

To all this Sancho listened with no little sorrow at heart to see how his hopes of dignity were fading away and vanishing in smoke, and how the fair Princess Micomicona had turned into Dorothea, and the giant into Don Fernando, while his master was sleeping tranquilly, totally unconscious of all that had come to pass. Dorothea was unable to persuade herself that her present happiness was not all a dream; Cardenio was in a similar state of mind, and Luscinda's thoughts ran in the same direction. Don Fernando gave thanks to Heaven for the favour shown to him and for having been rescued from the intricate labyrinth in which he had been brought so near the destruction of his good name and of his soul; and in short everybody in the inn was full of contentment and satisfaction at the happy issue of such a complicated and hopeless business. The curate as a sensible man made sound reflections upon the whole affair, and congratulated each upon his good fortune; but the one that was in the highest spirits and good humour was the landlady, because of the promise Cardenio and the curate had given her to pay for all the losses and damage she had sustained through Don Quixote's means. Sancho, as has been already said, was the only one who was distressed, unhappy, and dejected; and so with a long face he went in to his master, who had just awoke, and said to him:

"Sir Rueful Countenance, your worship may as well sleep on as much as you like, without troubling yourself about killing any giant or restoring her kingdom to the princess; for that is all over and settled now."

"I should think it was," replied Don Quixote, "for I have had the most prodigious and stupendous battle with the giant that I ever remember having had all the days of my life; and with one back-stroke-swish!—I brought his head tumbling to the ground, and so much blood gushed forth from him that it ran in rivulets over the earth like water."

"Like red wine, your worship had better say," replied Sancho; "for I would have you know, if you don't know it, that the dead giant is a hacked wine-skin, and the blood four-and-twenty gallons of red wine that it had in its belly, and the cut-off head is the bitch that bore me; and the devil take it all."

"What art thou talking about, fool?" said Don Quixote; "art thou in thy senses?"

"Let your worship get up," said Sancho, "and you will see the nice business you have made of it, and what we have to pay; and you will see the queen turned into a private lady called Dorothea, and other things that will astonish you, if you understand them."

"I shall not be surprised at anything of the kind," returned Don Quixote; "for if thou dost remember the last time we were here I told thee that everything that happened here was a matter of enchantment, and it would be no wonder if it were the same now."

"I could believe all that," replied Sancho, "if my blanketing was the same sort of thing also; only it wasn't, but real and genuine; for I saw the landlord, Who is here to-day, holding one end of the blanket and jerking me up to the skies very neatly and smartly, and with as much laughter as strength; and when it comes to be a case of knowing people, I hold for my part, simple and sinner as I am, that there is no enchantment about it at all, but a great deal of bruising and bad luck."

"Well, well, God will give a remedy," said Don Quixote; "hand me my clothes and let me go out, for I want to see these transformations and things thou speakest of."

Sancho fetched him his clothes; and while he was dressing, the curate gave Don Fernando and the others present an account of Don Quixote's madness and of the stratagem they had made use of to withdraw him from that Pena Pobre where he fancied himself stationed because of his lady's scorn. He described to them also nearly all the adventures that Sancho had mentioned, at which they marvelled and laughed not a little, thinking it, as all did, the strangest form of madness a crazy intellect could be capable of. But now, the curate said, that the lady Dorothea's good fortune prevented her from proceeding with their purpose, it would be necessary to devise or discover some other way of getting him home.

Cardenio proposed to carry out the scheme they had begun, and suggested that Luscinda would act and support Dorothea's part sufficiently well.

"No," said Don Fernando, "that must not be, for I want Dorothea to follow out this idea of hers; and if the worthy gentleman's village is not very far off, I shall be happy if I can do anything for his relief."

"It is not more than two days' journey from this," said the curate.

"Even if it were more," said Don Fernando, "I would gladly travel so far for the sake of doing so good a work.

"At this moment Don Quixote came out in full panoply, with Mambrino's helmet, all dinted as it was, on his head, his buckler on his arm, and leaning on his staff or pike. The strange figure he presented filled Don Fernando and the rest with amazement as they contemplated his lean yellow face half a league long, his armour of all sorts, and the solemnity of his deportment. They stood silent waiting to see what he would say, and he, fixing his eyes on the air Dorothea, addressed her with great gravity and composure:

"I am informed, fair lady, by my squire here that your greatness has been annihilated and your being abolished, since, from a queen and lady of high degree as you used to be, you have been turned into a private maiden. If this has been done by the command of the magician king your father, through fear that I should not afford you the aid you need and are entitled to, I may tell you he did not know and does not know half the mass, and was little versed in the annals of chivalry; for, if he had read and gone through them as attentively and deliberately as I have, he would have found at every turn that knights of less renown than mine have accomplished things more difficult: it is no great matter to kill a whelp of a giant, however arrogant he may be; for it is not many hours since I myself was engaged with one, and-I will not speak of it, that they may not say I am lying; time, however, that reveals all, will tell the tale when we least expect it."

"You were engaged with a couple of wine-skins, and not a giant," said the landlord at this; but Don Fernando told him to hold his tongue and on no account interrupt Don Quixote, who continued, "I say in conclusion, high and disinherited lady, that if your father has brought about this metamorphosis in your person for the reason I have mentioned, you ought not to attach any importance to it; for there is no peril on earth through which my sword will not force a way, and with it, before many days are over, I will bring your enemy's head to the ground and place on yours the crown of your kingdom."

Don Quixote said no more, and waited for the reply of the princess, who aware of Don Fernando's determination to carry on the deception until Don Quixote had been conveyed to his home, with great ease of manner and gravity made answer, "Whoever told you, valiant Knight of the Rueful Countenance, that I had undergone any change or transformation did not tell you the truth, for I am the same as I was yesterday. It is true that certain strokes of good fortune, that have given me more than I could have hoped for, have made some alteration in me; but I have not therefore ceased to be what I was before, or to entertain the same desire I have had all through of availing myself of the might of your valiant and invincible arm. And so, senor, let your goodness reinstate the father that begot me in your good opinion, and be assured that he was a wise and prudent man, since by his craft he found out such a sure and easy way of remedying my misfortune; for I believe, senor, that had it not been for you I should never have lit upon the good fortune I now possess; and in this I am saying what is perfectly true; as most of these gentlemen who are present can fully testify. All that remains is to set out on our journey to-morrow, for to-day we could not make much way; and for the rest of the happy result I am looking forward to, I trust to God and the valour of your heart."

So said the sprightly Dorothea, and on hearing her Don Quixote turned to Sancho, and said to him, with an angry air, "I declare now, little Sancho, thou art the greatest little villain in Spain. Say, thief and vagabond, hast thou not just now told me that this princess had been turned into a maiden called Dorothea, and that the head which I am persuaded I cut off from a giant was the bitch that bore thee, and other nonsense that put me in the greatest perplexity I have ever been in all my life? I vow" (and here he looked to heaven and ground his teeth) "I have a mind to play the mischief with thee, in a way that will teach sense for the future to all lying squires of knights-errant in the world."

"Let your worship be calm, senor," returned Sancho, "for it may well be that I have been mistaken as to the change of the lady princess Micomicona; but as to the giant's head, or at least as to the piercing of the wine-skins, and the blood being red wine, I make no mistake, as sure as there is a God; because the wounded skins are there at the head of your worship's bed, and the wine has made a lake of the room; if not you will see when the eggs come to be fried; I mean when his worship the landlord calls for all the damages: for the rest, I am heartily glad that her ladyship the queen is as she was, for it concerns me as much as anyone."

"I tell thee again, Sancho, thou art a fool," said Don Quixote; "forgive me, and that will do."

"That will do," said Don Fernando; "let us say no more about it; and as her ladyship the princess proposes to set out to-morrow because it is too late to-day, so be it, and we will pass the night in pleasant conversation, and to-morrow we will all accompany Senor Don Quixote; for we wish to witness the valiant and unparalleled achievements he is about to perform in the course of this mighty enterprise which he has undertaken."

"It is I who shall wait upon and accompany you," said Don Quixote; "and I am much gratified by the favour that is bestowed upon me, and the good opinion entertained of me, which I shall strive to justify or it shall cost me my life, or even more, if it can possibly cost me more."

Many were the compliments and expressions of politeness that passed between Don Quixote and Don Fernando; but they were brought to an end by a traveller who at this moment entered the inn, and who seemed from his attire to be a Christian lately come from the country of the Moors, for he was dressed in a short-skirted coat of blue cloth with half-sleeves and without a collar; his breeches were also of blue cloth, and his cap of the same colour, and he wore yellow buskins and had a Moorish cutlass slung from a baldric across his breast. Behind him, mounted upon an ass, there came a woman dressed in Moorish fashion, with her face veiled and a scarf on her head, and wearing a little brocaded cap, and a mantle that covered her from her shoulders to her feet. The man was of a robust and well-proportioned frame, in age a little over forty, rather swarthy in complexion, with long moustaches and a full beard, and, in short, his appearance was such that if he had been well dressed he would have been taken for a person of quality and good birth. On entering he asked for a room, and when they told him there was none in the inn he seemed distressed, and approaching her who by her dress seemed to be a Moor he her down from saddle in his arms. Luscinda, Dorothea, the landlady, her daughter and Maritornes, attracted by the strange, and to them entirely new costume, gathered round her; and Dorothea, who was always kindly, courteous, and quick-witted, perceiving that both she and the man who had brought her were annoyed at not finding a room, said to her, "Do not be put out, senora, by the discomfort and want of luxuries here, for it is the way of roadside inns to be without them; still, if you will be pleased to share our lodging with us (pointing to Luscinda) perhaps you will have found worse accommodation in the course of your journey."

To this the veiled lady made no reply; all she did was to rise from her seat, crossing her hands upon her bosom, bowing her head and bending her body as a sign that she returned thanks. From her silence they concluded that she must be a Moor and unable to speak a Christian tongue.

At this moment the captive came up, having been until now otherwise engaged, and seeing that they all stood round his companion and that she made no reply to what they addressed to her, he said, "Ladies, this damsel hardly understands my language and can speak none but that of her own country, for which reason she does not and cannot answer what has been asked of her."

"Nothing has been asked of her," returned Luscinda; "she has only been offered our company for this evening and a share of the quarters we occupy, where she shall be made as comfortable as the circumstances allow, with the good-will we are bound to show all strangers that stand in need of it, especially if it be a woman to whom the service is rendered."

"On her part and my own, senora," replied the captive, "I kiss your hands, and I esteem highly, as I ought, the favour you have offered, which, on such an occasion and coming from persons of your appearance, is, it is plain to see, a very great one."

"Tell me, senor," said Dorothea, "is this lady a Christian or a Moor? for her dress and her silence lead us to imagine that she is what we could wish she was not."

"In dress and outwardly," said he, "she is a Moor, but at heart she is a thoroughly good Christian, for she has the greatest desire to become one."

"Then she has not been baptised?" returned Luscinda.

"There has been no opportunity for that," replied the captive, "since she left Algiers, her native country and home; and up to the present she has not found herself in any such imminent danger of death as to make it necessary to baptise her before she has been instructed in all the ceremonies our holy mother Church ordains; but, please God, ere long she shall be baptised with the solemnity befitting her which is higher than her dress or mine indicates."

By these words he excited a desire in all who heard him, to know who the Moorish lady and the captive were, but no one liked to ask just then, seeing that it was a fitter moment for helping them to rest themselves than for questioning them about their lives. Dorothea took the Moorish lady by the hand and leading her to a seat beside herself, requested her to remove her veil. She looked at the captive as if to ask him what they meant and what she was to do. He said to her in Arabic that they asked her to take off her veil, and thereupon she removed it and disclosed a countenance so lovely, that to Dorothea she seemed more beautiful than Luscinda, and to

Luscinda more beautiful than Dorothea, and all the bystanders felt that if any beauty could compare with theirs it was the Moorish lady's, and there were even those who were inclined to give it somewhat the preference. And as it is the privilege and charm of beauty to win the heart and secure good-will, all forthwith became eager to show kindness and attention to the lovely Moor.

Don Fernando asked the captive what her name was, and he replied that it was Lela Zoraida; but the instant she heard him, she guessed what the Christian had asked, and said hastily, with some displeasure and energy, "No, not Zoraida; Maria, Maria!" giving them to understand that she was called "Maria" and not "Zoraida." These words, and the touching earnestness with which she uttered them, drew more than one tear from some of the listeners, particularly the women, who are by nature tender-hearted and compassionate. Luscinda embraced her affectionately, saying, "Yes, yes, Maria, Maria," to which the Moor replied, "Yes, yes, Maria; Zoraida macange," which means "not Zoraida."

Night was now approaching, and by the orders of those who accompanied Don Fernando the landlord had taken care and pains to prepare for them the best supper that was in his power. The hour therefore having arrived they all took their seats at a long table like a refectory one, for round or square table there was none in the inn, and the seat of honour at the head of it, though he was for refusing it, they assigned to Don Quixote, who desired the lady Micomicona to place herself by his side, as he was her protector. Luscinda and Zoraida took their places next her, opposite to them were Don Fernando and Cardenio, and next the captive and the other gentlemen, and by the side of the ladies, the curate and the barber. And so they supped in high enjoyment, which was increased when they observed Don Quixote leave off eating, and, moved by an impulse like that which made him deliver himself at such length when he supped with the goatherds, begin to address them:

"Verily, gentlemen, if we reflect upon it, great and marvellous are the things they see, who make profession of the order of knight-errantry. Say, what being is there in this world, who entering the gate of this castle at this moment, and seeing us as we are here, would suppose or imagine us to be what we are? Who would say that this lady who is beside me was the great queen that we all know her to be, or that I am that Knight of the Rueful Countenance, trumpeted far and wide by the mouth of Fame? Now, there can be no doubt that this art and calling surpasses all those that mankind has invented, and is the more deserving of being held in honour in proportion as it is the more exposed to peril. Away with those who assert that letters have the preeminence over arms; I will tell them, whosoever they may be, that they know not what they say. For the reason which such persons commonly assign, and upon which they chiefly rest, is, that the labours of the mind are greater than those of the body, and that arms give employment to the body alone; as if the calling were a porter's trade, for which nothing more is required than sturdy strength; or as if, in what we who profess them call arms, there were not included acts of vigour for the execution of which high intelligence is requisite; or as if the soul of the warrior, when he has an army, or the defence of a city under his care, did not exert itself as much by mind as by body. Nay; see whether by bodily strength it be possible to learn or divine the intentions of the enemy, his plans, stratagems, or obstacles, or to ward off impending mischief; for all these are the work of the mind, and in them the body has no share whatever. Since, therefore, arms have need of the mind, as much as letters, let us see now which of the two minds, that of the man of letters or that of the warrior, has most to do; and this will be seen by the end and goal that each seeks to attain; for that purpose is the more estimable which has for its aim the nobler object. The end and goal of letters—I am not speaking now of divine letters, the aim of which is to raise and direct the soul to Heaven; for with an end so infinite no other can be compared—I speak of human letters, the end of which is to establish distributive justice, give to every man that which is his, and see and take care that good laws are observed: an end undoubtedly noble, lofty, and deserving of high praise, but not such as should be given to that sought by arms, which have for their end and object peace, the greatest boon that men can desire in this life. The first good news the world and mankind received was that which the angels announced on the night that was our day, when they sang in the air, 'Glory to God in the highest, and peace on earth to men of good-will;' and the salutation which the great Master of heaven and earth taught his disciples and chosen followers when they entered any house, was to say, 'Peace be on this house;' and many other times he said to them, 'My peace I give unto you, my peace I leave you, peace be with you;' a jewel and a precious gift given and left by such a hand: a jewel without which there can be no happiness either on earth or in heaven. This peace is the true end of war; and war is only another name for arms. This, then, being admitted, that the end of war is peace, and that so far it has the advantage of the end of letters, let us turn to the bodily labours of the man of letters, and those of him who follows the profession of arms, and see which are the greater."

   Don Quixote delivered his discourse in such a manner and in such correct language, that for the time being he made it impossible for any of his hearers to consider him a madman; on the contrary, as they were mostly gentlemen, to whom arms are an appurtenance by birth, they listened to him with great pleasure as he continued: "Here, then, I say is what the student has to undergo; first of all poverty: not that all are poor, but to put the case as strongly as possible: and when I have said that he endures poverty, I think nothing more need be said about his hard fortune, for he who is poor has no share of the good things of life. This poverty he suffers from in various ways, hunger, or cold, or nakedness, or all together; but for all that it is not so extreme but that he gets something to eat, though it may be at somewhat unseasonable hours and from the leavings of the rich; for the greatest misery of the student is what they themselves call 'going out for soup,' and there is always some neighbour's brazier or hearth for them, which, if it does not warm, at least tempers the cold to them, and lastly, they sleep comfortably at night under a roof. I will not go into other particulars, as for example want of shirts, and no superabundance of shoes, thin and threadbare garments, and gorging themselves to surfeit in their voracity when good luck has treated them to a banquet of some sort. By this road that I have described, rough and hard, stumbling here, falling there, getting up again to fall again, they reach the rank they desire, and that once attained, we have seen many who have passed these Syrtes and Scyllas and Charybdises, as if borne flying on the wings of favouring fortune; we have seen them, I say, ruling and governing the world from a chair, their hunger turned into satiety, their cold into comfort, their nakedness into fine raiment, their sleep on a mat into repose in holland and damask, the justly earned reward of their virtue; but, contrasted and compared with what the warrior undergoes, all they have undergone falls far short of it, as I am now about to show."

CHAPTER XXXVIII

WHICH TREATS OF THE CURIOUS DISCOURSE DON QUIXOTE DELIVERED ON ARMS AND LETTERS

Continuing his discourse Don Quixote said: "As we began in the student's case with poverty and its accompaniments, let us see now if the soldier is richer, and we shall find that in poverty itself there is no one poorer; for he is dependent on his miserable pay, which comes late or never, or else on what he can plunder, seriously imperilling his life and conscience; and sometimes his nakedness will be so great that a slashed doublet serves him for uniform and shirt, and in the depth of winter he has to defend himself against the inclemency of the weather in the open field with nothing better than the breath of his mouth, which I need not say, coming from an empty place, must come out cold, contrary to the laws of nature. To be sure he looks forward to the approach of night to make up for all these discomforts on the bed that awaits him, which, unless by some fault of his, never sins by being over narrow, for he can easily measure out on the ground as he likes, and roll himself about in it to his heart's content without any fear of the sheets slipping away from him. Then, after all this, suppose the day and hour for taking his degree in his calling to have come; suppose the day of battle to have arrived, when they invest him with the doctor's cap made of lint, to mend some bullet-hole, perhaps, that has gone through his temples, or left him with a crippled arm or leg. Or if this does not happen, and merciful Heaven watches over him and keeps him safe and sound, it may be he will be in the same poverty he was in before, and he must go through more engagements and more battles, and come victorious out of all before he betters himself; but miracles of that sort are seldom seen. For tell me, sirs, if you have ever reflected upon it, by how much do those who have gained by war fall short of the number of those who have perished in it? No doubt you will reply that there can be no comparison, that the dead cannot be numbered, while the living who have been rewarded may be summed up with three figures. All which is the reverse in the case of men of letters; for by skirts, to say nothing of sleeves, they all find means of support; so that though the soldier has more to endure, his reward is much less. But against all this it may be urged that it is easier to reward two thousand soldiers, for the former may be remunerated by giving them places, which must perforce be conferred upon men of their calling, while the latter can only be recompensed out of the very property of the master they serve; but this impossibility only strengthens my argument.

"Putting this, however, aside, for it is a puzzling question for which it is difficult to find a solution, let us return to the superiority of arms over letters, a matter still undecided, so many are the arguments put forward on each side; for besides those I have mentioned, letters say that without them arms cannot maintain themselves, for war, too, has its laws and is governed by them, and laws belong to the domain of letters and men of letters. To this arms make answer that without them laws cannot be maintained, for by arms states are defended, kingdoms preserved, cities protected, roads made safe, seas cleared of pirates; and, in short, if it were not for them, states, kingdoms, monarchies, cities, ways by sea and land would be exposed to the violence and confusion which war brings with it, so long as it lasts and is free to make use of its privileges and powers. And then it is plain that whatever costs most is valued and deserves to be valued most. To attain to eminence in letters costs a man time, watching, hunger, nakedness, headaches, indigestions, and other things of the sort, some of which I have already referred to. But for a man to come in the ordinary course of things to be a good soldier costs him all the student suffers, and in an incomparably higher degree, for at every step he runs the risk of losing his life. For what dread of want or poverty that can reach or harass the student can compare with what the soldier feels, who finds himself beleaguered in some stronghold mounting guard in some ravelin or cavalier, knows that the enemy is pushing a mine towards the post where he is stationed, and cannot under any circumstances retire or fly from the imminent danger that threatens him? All he can do is to inform his captain of what is going on so that he may try to remedy it by a counter-mine, and then stand his ground in fear and expectation of the moment when he will fly up to the clouds without wings and descend into the deep against his will. And if this seems a trifling risk, let us see whether it is equalled or surpassed by the encounter of two galleys stem to stem, in the midst of the open sea, locked and entangled one with the other, when the soldier has no more standing room than two feet of the plank of the spur; and yet, though he sees before him threatening him as many ministers of death as there are cannon of the foe pointed at him, not a lance length from his body, and sees too that with the first heedless step he will go down to visit the profundities of Neptune's bosom, still with dauntless heart, urged on by honour that nerves him, he makes himself a target for all that musketry, and struggles to cross that narrow path to the enemy's ship. And what is still more marvellous, no sooner has one gone down into the depths he will never rise from till the end of the world, than another takes his place; and if he too falls into the sea that waits for him like an enemy, another and another will succeed him without a moment's pause between their deaths: courage and daring the greatest that all the chances of war can show. Happy the blest ages that knew not the dread fury of those devilish engines of artillery, whose inventor I am persuaded is in hell receiving the reward of his diabolical invention, by which he made it easy for a base and cowardly arm to take the life of a gallant gentleman; and that, when he knows not how or whence, in the height of the ardour and enthusiasm that fire and animate brave hearts, there should come some random bullet, discharged perhaps by one who fled in terror at the flash when he fired off his accursed machine, which in an instant puts an end to the projects and cuts off the life of one who deserved to live for ages to come. And thus when I reflect on this, I am almost tempted to say that in my heart I repent of having adopted this profession of knight-errant in so detestable an age as we live in now; for though no peril can make me fear, still it gives me some uneasiness to think that powder and lead may rob me of the opportunity of making myself famous and renowned throughout the known earth by the might of my arm and the edge of my sword. But Heaven's will be done; if I succeed in my attempt I shall be all the more honoured, as I have faced greater dangers than the knights-errant of yore exposed themselves to."

All this lengthy discourse Don Quixote delivered while the others supped, forgetting to raise a morsel to his lips, though Sancho more than once told him to eat his supper, as he would have time enough afterwards to say all he wanted. It excited fresh pity in those who had heard him to see a man of apparently sound sense, and with rational views on every subject he discussed, so hopelessly wanting in all, when his wretched unlucky chivalry was in question. The curate told him he was quite right in all he had said in favour of arms, and that he himself, though a man of letters and a graduate, was of the same opinion.

They finished their supper, the cloth was removed, and while the hostess, her daughter, and Maritornes were getting Don Quixote of La Mancha's garret ready, in which it was arranged that the women were to be quartered by themselves for the night, Don Fernando begged the captive to tell them the story of his life, for it could not fail to be strange and interesting, to judge by the hints he had let fall on his arrival in company with Zoraida. To this the captive replied that he would very willingly yield to his request, only he feared his tale would not give them as much pleasure as he wished; nevertheless, not to be wanting in compliance, he would tell it. The curate and the others thanked him and added their entreaties, and he finding himself so pressed said there was no occasion ask, where a command had such weight, and added, "If your worships will give me your attention you will hear a true story which, perhaps, fictitious ones constructed with ingenious and studied art cannot come up to." These words made them settle themselves in their places and preserve a deep silence, and he seeing them waiting on his words in mute expectation, began thus in a pleasant quiet voice.

CHAPTER XXXIX

WHEREIN THE CAPTIVE RELATES HIS LIFE AND ADVENTURES

My family had its origin in a village in the mountains of Leon, and nature had been kinder and more generous to it than fortune; though in the general poverty of those communities my father passed for being even a rich man; and he would have been so in reality had he been as clever in preserving his property as he was in spending it. This tendency of his to be liberal and profuse he had acquired from having been a soldier in his youth, for the soldier's life is a school in which the niggard becomes free-handed and the free-handed prodigal; and if any soldiers are to be found who are misers, they are monsters of rare occurrence. My father went beyond liberality and bordered on prodigality, a disposition by no means advantageous to a married man who has children to succeed to his name and position. My father had three, all sons, and all of sufficient age to make choice of a profession. Finding, then, that he was unable to resist his propensity, he resolved to divest himself of the instrument and cause of his prodigality and lavishness, to divest himself of wealth, without which Alexander himself would have seemed parsimonious; and so calling us all three aside one day into a room, he addressed us in words somewhat to the following effect:

"My sons, to assure you that I love you, no more need be known or said than that you are my sons; and to encourage a suspicion that I do not love you, no more is needed than the knowledge that I have no self-control as far as preservation of your patrimony is concerned; therefore, that you may for the future feel sure that I love you like a father, and have no wish to ruin you like a stepfather, I propose to do with you what I have for some time back meditated, and after mature deliberation decided upon. You are now of an age to choose your line of life or at least make choice of a calling that will bring you honour and profit when you are older; and what I have resolved to do is to divide my property into four parts; three I will give to you, to each his portion without making any difference, and the other I will retain to live upon and support myself for whatever remainder of life Heaven may be pleased to grant me. But I wish each of you on taking possession of the share that falls to him to follow one of the paths I shall indicate. In this Spain of ours there is a proverb, to my mind very true—as they all are, being short aphorisms drawn from long practical experience—and the one I refer to says, 'The church, or the sea, or the king's house;' as much as to say, in plainer language, whoever wants to flourish and become rich, let him follow the church, or go to sea, adopting commerce as his calling, or go into the king's service in his household, for they say, 'Better a king's crumb than a lord's favour.' I say so because it is my will and pleasure that one of you should follow letters, another trade, and the third serve the king in the wars, for it is a difficult matter to gain admission to his service in his household, and if war does not bring much wealth it confers great distinction and fame. Eight days hence I will give you your full shares in money, without defrauding you of a farthing, as you will see in the end. Now tell me if you are willing to follow out my idea and advice as I have laid it before you."

Having called upon me as the eldest to answer, I, after urging him not to strip himself of his property but to spend it all as he pleased, for we were young men able to gain our living, consented to comply with his wishes, and said that mine were to follow the profession of arms and thereby serve God and my king. My second brother having made the same proposal, decided upon going to the Indies, embarking the portion that fell to him in trade. The youngest, and in my opinion the wisest, said he would rather follow the church, or go to complete his studies at Salamanca. As soon as we had come to an understanding, and made choice of our professions, my father embraced us all, and in the short time he mentioned carried into effect all he had promised; and when he had given to each his share, which as well as I remember was three thousand ducats apiece in cash (for an uncle of ours bought the estate and paid for it down, not to let it go out of the family), we all three on the same day took leave of our good father; and at the same time, as it seemed to me inhuman to leave my father with such scanty means in his old age, I induced him to take two of my three thousand ducats, as the remainder would be enough to provide me with all a soldier needed. My two brothers, moved by my example, gave him each a thousand ducats, so that there was left for my father four thousand ducats in money, besides three thousand, the value of the portion that fell to him which he preferred to retain in land instead of selling it. Finally, as I said, we took leave of him, and of our uncle whom I have mentioned, not without sorrow and tears on both sides, they charging us to let them know whenever an opportunity offered how we fared, whether well or ill. We promised to do so, and when he had embraced us and given us his blessing, one set out for Salamanca, the other for Seville, and I for

Alicante, where I had heard there was a Genoese vessel taking in a cargo of wool for Genoa.

It is now some twenty-two years since I left my father's house, and all that time, though I have written several letters, I have had no news whatever of him or of my brothers; my own adventures during that period I will now relate briefly. I embarked at Alicante, reached Genoa after a prosperous voyage, and proceeded thence to Milan, where I provided myself with arms and a few soldier's accoutrements; thence it was my intention to go and take service in Piedmont, but as I was already on the road to Alessandria della Paglia, I learned that the great Duke of Alva was on his way to Flanders. I changed my plans, joined him, served under him in the campaigns he made, was present at the deaths of the Counts Egmont and Horn, and was promoted to be ensign under a famous captain of Guadalajara, Diego de Urbina by name. Some time after my arrival in Flanders news came of the league that his Holiness Pope Pius V of happy memory, had made with Venice and Spain against the common enemy, the Turk, who had just then with his fleet taken the famous island of Cyprus, which belonged to the Venetians, a loss deplorable and disastrous. It was known as a fact that the Most Serene Don John of Austria, natural brother of our good king Don Philip, was coming as commander-in-chief of the allied forces, and rumours were abroad of the vast warlike preparations which were being made, all which stirred my heart and filled me with a longing to take part in the campaign which was expected; and though I had reason to believe, and almost certain promises, that on the first opportunity that presented itself I should be promoted to be captain, I preferred to leave all and betake myself, as I did, to Italy; and it was my good fortune that Don John had just arrived at Genoa, and was going on to Naples to join the Venetian fleet, as he afterwards did at Messina. I may say, in short, that I took part in that glorious expedition, promoted by this time to be a captain of infantry, to which honourable charge my good luck rather than my merits raised me; and that day—so fortunate for Christendom, because then all the nations of the earth were disabused of the error under which they lay in imagining the Turks to be invincible on sea-on that day, I say, on which the Ottoman pride and arrogance were broken, among all that were there made happy (for the Christians who died that day were happier than those who remained alive and victorious) I alone was miserable; for, instead of some naval crown that I might have expected had it been in Roman times, on the night that followed that famous day I found myself with fetters on my feet and manacles on my hands.

It happened in this way: El Uchali, the king of Algiers, a daring and successful corsair, having attacked and taken the leading Maltese galley (only three knights being left alive in it, and they badly wounded), the chief galley of John Andrea, on board of which I and my company were placed, came to its relief, and doing as was bound to do in such a case, I leaped on board the enemy's galley, which, sheering off from that which had attacked it, prevented my men from following me, and so I found myself alone in the midst of my enemies, who were in such numbers that I was unable to resist; in short I was taken, covered with wounds; El Uchali, as you know, sirs, made his escape with his entire squadron, and I was left a prisoner in his power, the only sad being among so many filled with joy, and the only captive among so many free; for there were fifteen thousand Christians, all at the oar in the Turkish fleet, that regained their longed-for liberty that day.

They carried me to Constantinople, where the Grand Turk, Selim, made my master general at sea for having done his duty in the battle and carried off as evidence of his bravery the standard of the Order of Malta. The following year, which was the year seventy-two, I found myself at Navarino rowing in the leading galley with the three lanterns. There I saw and observed how the opportunity of capturing the whole Turkish fleet in harbour was lost; for all the marines and janizzaries that belonged to it made sure that they were about to be attacked inside the very harbour, and had their kits and pasamaques, or shoes, ready to flee at once on shore without waiting to be assailed, in so great fear did they stand of our fleet. But Heaven ordered it otherwise, not for any fault or neglect of the general who commanded on our side, but for the sins of Christendom, and because it was God's will and pleasure that we should always have instruments of punishment to chastise us. As it was, El Uchali took refuge at Modon, which is an island near Navarino, and landing forces fortified the mouth of the harbour and waited quietly until Don John retired. On this expedition was taken the galley called the Prize, whose captain was a son of the famous corsair Barbarossa. It was taken by the chief Neapolitan galley called the She-wolf, commanded by that thunderbolt of war, that father of his men, that successful and unconquered captain Don Alvaro de Bazan, Marquis of Santa Cruz; and I cannot help telling you what took place at the capture of the Prize.

The son of Barbarossa was so cruel, and treated his slaves so badly, that, when those who were at the oars saw that the She-wolf galley was bearing down upon them and gaining upon them, they all at once dropped their oars and seized their captain who stood on the stage at the end of the gangway shouting to them to row lustily; and passing him on from bench to bench, from the poop to the prow, they so bit him that before he had got much past the mast his soul had already got to hell; so great, as I said, was the cruelty with which he treated them, and the hatred with which they hated him.

We returned to Constantinople, and the following year, seventy-three, it became known that Don John had seized Tunis and taken the kingdom from the Turks, and placed Muley Hamet in possession, putting an end to the hopes which Muley Hamida, the cruelest and bravest Moor in the world, entertained of returning to reign there. The Grand Turk took the loss greatly to heart, and with the cunning which all his race possess, he made peace with the Venetians (who were much more eager for it than he was), and the following year, seventy-four, he attacked the Goletta and the fort which Don John had left half built near Tunis. While all these events were occurring, I was labouring at the oar without any hope of freedom; at least I had no hope of obtaining it by ransom, for I was firmly resolved not to write to my father telling him of my misfortunes. At length the Goletta fell, and the fort fell, before which places there were seventy-five thousand regular Turkish soldiers, and more than four hundred thousand Moors and Arabs from all parts of Africa, and in the train of all this great host such munitions and engines of war, and so many pioneers that with their hands they might have covered the Goletta and the fort with handfuls of earth. The first to fall was the Goletta, until then reckoned impregnable, and it fell, not by any fault of its defenders, who did all that they could and should have done, but because experiment proved how easily entrenchments could be made in the desert sand there; for water used to be found at two palms depth, while the Turks found none at two yards; and so by means of a quantity of sand-bags they raised their works so high that they commanded the walls of the fort, sweeping them as if from a cavalier, so that no one was able to make a stand or maintain the defence.

It was a common opinion that our men should not have shut themselves up in the Goletta, but should have waited in the open at the landing-place; but those who say so talk at random and with little knowledge of such matters; for if in the Goletta and in the fort there were barely seven thousand soldiers, how could such a small number, however resolute, sally out and hold their own against numbers like those of the enemy? And how is it possible to help losing a stronghold that is not relieved, above all when surrounded by a host of determined enemies in their own country? But many thought, and I thought so too, that it was special favour and mercy which Heaven showed to Spain in permitting the destruction of that source and hiding place of mischief, that devourer, sponge, and moth of countless money, fruitlessly wasted there to no other purpose save preserving the memory of its capture by the invincible Charles V; as if to make that eternal, as it is and will be, these stones were needed to support it. The fort also fell; but the Turks had to win it inch by inch, for the soldiers who defended it fought so gallantly and stoutly that the number of the enemy killed in twenty-two general assaults exceeded twenty-five thousand. Of three hundred that remained alive not one was taken unwounded, a clear and manifest proof of their gallantry and resolution, and how sturdily they had defended themselves and held their post. A small fort or tower which was in the middle of the lagoon under the command of Don Juan Zanoguera, a Valencian gentleman and a famous soldier, capitulated upon terms. They took prisoner Don Pedro Puertocarrero, commandant of the Goletta, who had done all in his power to defend his fortress, and took the loss of it so much to heart that he died of grief on the way to Constantinople, where they were carrying him a prisoner. They also took the commandant of the fort, Gabrio Cerbellon by name, a Milanese gentleman, a great engineer and a very brave soldier. In these two fortresses perished many persons of note, among whom was Pagano Doria, knight of the Order of St. John, a man of generous disposition, as was shown by his extreme liberality to his brother, the famous John Andrea Doria; and what made his death the more sad was that he was slain by some Arabs to whom, seeing that the fort was now lost, he entrusted himself, and who offered to conduct him in the disguise of a Moor to Tabarca, a small fort or station on the coast held by the Genoese employed in the coral fishery. These Arabs cut off his head and carried it to the commander of the Turkish fleet, who proved on them the truth of our Castilian proverb, that "though the treason may please, the traitor is hated;" for they say he ordered those who brought him the present to be hanged for not having brought him alive.

 Among the Christians who were taken in the fort was one named Don Pedro de Aguilar, a native of some place, I know not what, in Andalusia, who had been ensign in the fort, a soldier of great repute and rare intelligence, who had in particular a special gift for what they call poetry. I say so because his fate brought him to my galley and to my bench, and made him a slave to the same master; and before we left the port this gentleman composed two sonnets by way of epitaphs, one on the Goletta and the other on the fort; indeed, I may as well repeat them, for I have them by heart, and I think they will be liked rather than disliked.

The instant the captive mentioned the name of Don Pedro de Aguilar, Don Fernando looked at his companions and they all three smiled; and when he came to speak of the sonnets one of them said, "Before your worship proceeds any further I entreat you to tell me what became of that Don Pedro de Aguilar you have spoken of."

"All I know is," replied the captive, "that after having been in Constantinople two years, he escaped in the disguise of an Arnaut, in company with a Greek spy; but whether he regained his liberty or not I cannot tell, though I fancy he did, because a year afterwards I saw the Greek at Constantinople, though I was unable to ask him what the result of the journey was."

"Well then, you are right," returned the gentleman, "for that Don Pedro is my brother, and he is now in our village in good health, rich, married, and with three children."

"Thanks be to God for all the mercies he has shown him," said the captive; "for to my mind there is no happiness on earth to compare with recovering lost liberty."

"And what is more," said the gentleman, "I know the sonnets my brother made."

"Then let your worship repeat them," said the captive, "for you will recite them better than I can."

"With all my heart," said the gentleman; "that on the Goletta runs thus."

CHAPTER XL

IN WHICH THE STORY OF THE CAPTIVE IS CONTINUED

SONNET

"Blest souls, that, from this mortal husk set free,
   In guerdon of brave deeds beatified,
   Above this lowly orb of ours abide
Made heirs of heaven and immortality,
With noble rage and ardour glowing ye
   Your strength, while strength was yours, in battle plied,
   And with your own blood and the foeman's dyed
The sandy soil and the encircling sea.
It was the ebbing life-blood first that failed
The weary arms; the stout hearts never quailed.
   Though vanquished, yet ye earned the victor's crown:
Though mourned, yet still triumphant was your fall
For there ye won, between the sword and wall,
   In Heaven glory and on earth renown."

"That is it exactly, according to my recollection," said the captive.

"Well then, that on the fort," said the gentleman, "if my memory serves me, goes thus:

SONNET

"Up from this wasted soil, this shattered shell,
   Whose walls and towers here in ruin lie,
   Three thousand soldier souls took wing on high,
In the bright mansions of the blest to dwell.
The onslaught of the foeman to repel
   By might of arm all vainly did they try,
   And when at length 'twas left them but to die,
Wearied and few the last defenders fell.
And this same arid soil hath ever been
A haunt of countless mournful memories,
   As well in our day as in days of yore.
But never yet to Heaven it sent, I ween,
From its hard bosom purer souls than these,
   Or braver bodies on its surface bore."

The sonnets were not disliked, and the captive was rejoiced at the tidings they gave him of his comrade, and continuing his tale, he went on to say:

The Goletta and the fort being thus in their hands, the Turks gave orders to dismantle the Goletta—for the fort was reduced to such a state that there was nothing left to level—and to do the work more quickly and easily they mined it in three places; but nowhere were they able to blow up the part which seemed to be the least strong, that is to say, the old walls, while all that remained standing of the new fortifications that the Fratin had made came to the ground with the greatest ease. Finally the fleet returned victorious and triumphant to Constantinople, and a few months later died my master, El Uchali, otherwise Uchali Fartax, which means in Turkish "the scabby renegade;" for that he was; it is the practice with the Turks to name people from some defect or virtue they may possess; the reason being that there are among them only four surnames belonging to families tracing their descent from the Ottoman house, and the others, as I have said, take their names and surnames either from bodily blemishes or moral qualities. This "scabby one" rowed at the oar as a slave of the Grand Signor's for fourteen years, and when over thirty-four years of age, in resentment at having been struck by a Turk while at the oar, turned renegade and renounced his faith in order to be able to revenge himself; and such was his valour that, without owing his advancement to the base ways and means by which most favourites of the Grand Signor rise to power, he came to be king of Algiers, and afterwards general-on-sea, which is the third place of trust in the realm. He was a Calabrian by birth, and a worthy man morally, and he treated his slaves with great humanity. He had three thousand of them, and after his death they were divided, as he directed by his will, between the Grand Signor (who is heir of all who die and shares with the children of the deceased) and his renegades. I fell to the lot of a Venetian renegade who, when a cabin boy on board a ship, had been taken by Uchali and was so much beloved by him that he became one of his most favoured youths. He came to be the most cruel renegade I ever saw: his name was Hassan Aga, and he grew very rich and became king of Algiers. With him I went there from Constantinople, rather glad to be so near Spain, not that I intended to write to anyone about my unhappy lot, but to try if fortune would be kinder to me in Algiers than in Constantinople, where I had attempted in a thousand ways to escape without ever finding a favourable time or chance; but in Algiers I resolved to seek for other means of effecting the purpose I cherished so dearly; for the hope of obtaining my liberty never deserted me; and when in my plots and schemes and attempts the result did not answer my expectations, without giving way to despair I immediately began to look out for or conjure up some new hope to support me, however faint or feeble it might be.

In this way I lived on immured in a building or prison called by the Turks a bano in which they confine the Christian captives, as well those that are the king's as those belonging to private individuals, and also what they call those of the Almacen, which is as much as to say the slaves of the municipality, who serve the city in the public works and other employments; but captives of this kind recover their liberty with great difficulty, for, as they are public property and have no particular master, there is no one with whom to treat for their ransom, even though they may have the means. To these banos, as I have said, some private individuals of the town are in the habit of bringing their captives, especially when they are to be ransomed; because there they can keep them in safety and comfort until their ransom arrives. The king's captives also, that are on ransom, do not go out to work with the rest of the crew, unless when their ransom is delayed; for then, to make them write for it more pressingly, they compel them to work and go for wood, which is no light labour.

I, however, was one of those on ransom, for when it was discovered that I was a captain, although I declared my scanty means and want of fortune, nothing could dissuade them from including me among the gentlemen and those waiting to be ransomed. They put a chain on me, more as a mark of this than to keep me safe, and so I passed my life in that bano with several other gentlemen and persons of quality marked out as held to ransom; but though at times, or rather almost always, we suffered from hunger and scanty clothing, nothing distressed us so much as hearing and seeing at every turn the unexampled and unheard-of cruelties my master inflicted upon the Christians. Every day he hanged a man, impaled one, cut off the ears of another; and all with so little provocation, or so entirely without any, that the Turks acknowledged he did it merely for the sake of doing it, and because he was by nature murderously disposed towards the whole human race. The only one that fared at all well with him was a Spanish soldier, something de Saavedra by name, to whom he never gave a blow himself, or ordered a blow to be given, or addressed a hard word, although he had done things that will dwell in the memory of the people there for many a year, and all to recover his liberty; and for the least of the many things he did we all dreaded that he would be impaled, and he himself was in fear of it more than once; and only that time does not allow, I could tell you now something of what that soldier did, that would interest and astonish you much more than the narration of my own tale.

To go on with my story; the courtyard of our prison was overlooked by the windows of the house belonging to a wealthy Moor of high position; and these, as is usual in Moorish houses, were rather loopholes than windows, and besides were covered with thick and close lattice-work. It so happened, then, that as I was one day on the terrace of our prison with three other comrades, trying, to pass away the time, how far we could leap with our chains, we being alone, for all the other Christians had gone out to work, I chanced to raise my eyes, and from one of these little closed windows I saw a reed appear with a cloth attached to the end of it, and it kept waving to and fro, and moving as if making signs to us to come and take it. We watched it, and one of those who were with me went and stood under the reed to see whether they would let it drop, or what they would do, but as he did so the reed was raised and moved from side to side, as if they meant to say "no" by a shake of the head. The Christian came back, and it was again lowered, making the same movements as before. Another of my comrades went, and with him the same happened as with the first, and then the third went forward, but with the same result as the first and second. Seeing this I did not like not to try my luck, and as soon as I came under the reed it was dropped and fell inside the bano at my feet. I hastened to untie the cloth, in which I perceived a knot, and in this were ten cianis, which are coins of base gold, current among the Moors, and each worth ten reals of our money.

It is needless to say I rejoiced over this godsend, and my joy was not less than my wonder as I strove to imagine how this good fortune could have come to us, but to me specially; for the evident unwillingness to drop the reed for any but me showed that it was for me the favour was intended. I took my welcome money, broke the reed, and returned to the terrace, and looking up at the window, I saw a very white hand put out that opened and shut very quickly. From this we gathered or fancied that it must be some woman living in that house that had done us this kindness, and to show that we were grateful for it, we made salaams after the fashion of the Moors, bowing the head, bending the body, and crossing the arms on the breast. Shortly afterwards at the same window a small cross made of reeds was put out and immediately withdrawn. This sign led us to believe that some Christian woman was a captive in the house, and that it was she who had been so good to us; but the whiteness of the hand and the bracelets we had perceived made us dismiss that idea, though we thought it might be one of the Christian renegades whom their masters very often take as lawful wives, and gladly, for they prefer them to the women of their own nation. In all our conjectures we were wide of the truth; so from that time forward our sole occupation was watching and gazing at the window where the cross had appeared to us, as if it were our pole-star; but at least fifteen days passed without our seeing either it or the hand, or any other sign and though meanwhile we endeavoured with the utmost pains to ascertain who it was that lived in the house, and whether there were any Christian renegade in it, nobody could ever tell us anything more than that he who lived there was a rich Moor of high position, Hadji Morato by name, formerly alcaide of La Pata, an office of high dignity among them. But when we least thought it was going to rain any more cianis from that quarter, we saw the reed suddenly appear with another cloth tied in a larger knot attached to it, and this at a time when, as on the former occasion, the bano was deserted and unoccupied.

We made trial as before, each of the same three going forward before I did; but the reed was delivered to none but me, and on my approach it was let drop. I untied the knot and I found forty Spanish gold crowns with a paper written in Arabic, and at the end of the writing there was a large cross drawn. I kissed the cross, took the crowns and returned to the terrace, and we all made our salaams; again the hand appeared, I made signs that I would read the paper, and then the window was closed. We were all puzzled, though filled with joy at what had taken place; and as none of us understood Arabic, great was our curiosity to know what the paper contained, and still greater the difficulty of finding some one to read it. At last I resolved to confide in a renegade, a native of Murcia, who professed a very great friendship for me, and had given pledges that bound him to keep any secret I might entrust to him; for it is the custom with some renegades, when they intend to return to Christian territory, to carry about them certificates from captives of mark testifying, in whatever form they can, that such and such a renegade is a worthy man who has always shown kindness to Christians, and is anxious to escape on the first opportunity that may present itself. Some obtain these testimonials with good intentions, others put them to a cunning use; for when they go to pillage on Christian territory, if they chance to be cast away, or taken prisoners, they produce their certificates and say that from these papers may be seen the object they came for, which was to remain on Christian ground, and that it was to this end they joined the Turks in their foray. In this way they escape the consequences of the first outburst and make their peace with the Church before it does them any harm, and then when they have the chance they return to Barbary to become what they were before. Others, however, there are who procure these papers and make use of them honestly, and remain on Christian soil. This friend of mine, then, was one of these renegades that I have described; he had certificates from all our comrades, in which we testified in his favour as strongly as we could; and if the Moors had found the papers they would have burned him alive.

I knew that he understood Arabic very well, and could not only speak but also write it; but before I disclosed the whole matter to him, I asked him to read for me this paper which I had found by accident in a hole in my cell. He opened it and remained some time examining it and muttering to himself as he translated it. I asked him if he understood it, and he told me he did perfectly well, and that if I wished him to tell me its meaning word for word, I must give him pen and ink that he might do it more satisfactorily. We at once gave him what he required, and he set about translating it bit by bit, and when he had done he said:

"All that is here in Spanish is what the Moorish paper contains, and you must bear in mind that when it says 'Lela Marien' it means 'Our Lady the Virgin Mary.'"

We read the paper and it ran thus:

"When I was a child my father had a slave who taught me to pray the Christian prayer in my own language, and told me many things about Lela Marien. The Christian died, and I know that she did not go to the fire, but to Allah, because since then I have seen her twice, and she told me to go to the land of the Christians to see Lela Marien, who had great love for me. I know not how to go. I have seen many Christians, but except thyself none has seemed to me to be a gentleman. I am young and beautiful, and have plenty of money to take with me. See if thou canst contrive how we may go, and if thou wilt thou shalt be my husband there, and if thou wilt not it will not distress me, for Lela Marien will find me some one to marry me. I myself have written this: have a care to whom thou givest it to read: trust no Moor, for they are all perfidious. I am greatly troubled on this account, for I would not have thee confide in anyone, because if my father knew it he would at once fling me down a well and cover me with stones. I will put a thread to the reed; tie the answer to it, and if thou hast no one to write for thee in Arabic, tell it to me by signs, for Lela Marien will make me understand thee. She and Allah and this cross, which I often kiss as the captive bade me, protect thee."

Judge, sirs, whether we had reason for surprise and joy at the words of this paper; and both one and the other were so great, that the renegade perceived that the paper had not been found by chance, but had been in reality addressed to some one of us, and he begged us, if what he suspected were the truth, to trust him and tell him all, for he would risk his life for our freedom; and so saying he took out from his breast a metal crucifix, and with many tears swore by the God the image represented, in whom, sinful and wicked as he was, he truly and faithfully believed, to be loyal to us and keep secret whatever we chose to reveal to him; for he thought and almost foresaw that by means of her who had written that paper, he and all of us would obtain our liberty, and he himself obtain the object he so much desired, his restoration to the bosom of the Holy Mother Church, from which by his own sin and ignorance he was now severed like a corrupt limb. The renegade said this with so many tears and such signs of repentance, that with one consent we all agreed to tell him the whole truth of the matter, and so we gave him a full account of all, without hiding anything from him. We pointed out to him the window at which the reed appeared, and he by that means took note of the house, and resolved to ascertain with particular care who lived in it. We agreed also that it would be advisable to answer the Moorish lady's letter, and the renegade without a moment's delay took down the words I dictated to him, which were exactly what I shall tell you, for nothing of importance that took place in this affair has escaped my memory, or ever will while life lasts. This, then, was the answer returned to the Moorish lady:

"The true Allah protect thee, Lady, and that blessed Marien who is the true mother of God, and who has put it into thy heart to go to the land of the Christians, because she loves thee. Entreat her that she be pleased to show thee how thou canst execute the command she gives thee, for she will, such is her goodness. On my own part, and on that of all these Christians who are with me, I promise to do all that we can for thee, even to death. Fail not to write to me and inform me what thou dost mean to do, and I will always answer thee; for the great Allah has given us a Christian captive who can speak and write thy language well, as thou mayest see by this paper; without fear, therefore, thou canst inform us of all thou wouldst. As to what thou sayest, that if thou dost reach the land of the Christians thou wilt be my wife, I give thee my promise upon it as a good Christian; and know that the Christians keep their promises better than the Moors. Allah and Marien his mother watch over thee, my Lady."

The paper being written and folded I waited two days until the bano was empty as before, and immediately repaired to the usual walk on the terrace to see if there were any sign of the reed, which was not long in making its appearance. As soon as I saw it, although I could not distinguish who put it out, I showed the paper as a sign to attach the thread, but it was already fixed to the reed, and to it I tied the paper; and shortly afterwards our star once more made its appearance with the white flag of peace, the little bundle. It was dropped, and I picked it up, and found in the cloth, in gold and silver coins of all sorts, more than fifty crowns, which fifty times more strengthened our joy and doubled our hope of gaining our liberty. That very night our renegade returned and said he had learned that the Moor we had been told of lived in that house, that his name was Hadji Morato, that he was enormously rich, that he had one only daughter the heiress of all his wealth, and that it was the general opinion throughout the city that she was the most beautiful woman in Barbary, and that several of the viceroys who came there had sought her for a wife, but that she had been always unwilling to marry; and he had learned, moreover, that she had a Christian slave who was now dead; all which agreed with the contents of the paper. We immediately took counsel with the renegade as to what means would have to be adopted in order to carry off the Moorish lady and bring us all to Christian territory; and in the end it was agreed that for the present we should wait for a second communication from Zoraida (for that was the name of her who now desires to be called Maria), because we saw clearly that she and no one else could find a way out of all these difficulties. When we had decided upon this the renegade told us not to be uneasy, for he would lose his life or restore us to liberty. For four days the bano was filled with people, for which reason the reed delayed its appearance for four days, but at the end of that time, when the bano was, as it generally was, empty, it appeared with the cloth so bulky that it promised a happy birth. Reed and cloth came down to me, and I found another paper and a hundred crowns in gold, without any other coin. The renegade was present, and in our cell we gave him the paper to read, which was to this effect:

"I cannot think of a plan, senor, for our going to Spain, nor has Lela Marien shown me one, though I have asked her. All that can be done is for me to give you plenty of money in gold from this window. With it ransom yourself and your friends, and let one of you go to the land of the Christians, and there buy a vessel and come back for the others; and he will find me in my father's garden, which is at the Babazon gate near the seashore, where I shall be all this summer with my father and my servants. You can carry me away from there by night without any danger, and bring me to the vessel. And remember thou art to be my husband, else I will pray to Marien to punish thee. If thou canst not trust anyone to go for the vessel, ransom thyself and do thou go, for I know thou wilt return more surely than any other, as thou art a gentleman and a Christian. Endeavour to make thyself acquainted with the garden; and when I see thee walking yonder I shall know that the bano is empty and I will give thee abundance of money. Allah protect thee, senor."

These were the words and contents of the second paper, and on hearing them, each declared himself willing to be the ransomed one, and promised to go and return with scrupulous good faith; and I too made the same offer; but to all this the renegade objected, saying that he would not on any account consent to one being set free before all went together, as experience had taught him how ill those who have been set free keep promises which they made in captivity; for captives of distinction frequently had recourse to this plan, paying the ransom of one who was to go to Valencia or Majorca with money to enable him to arm a bark and return for the others who had ransomed him, but who never came back; for recovered liberty and the dread of losing it again efface from the memory all the obligations in the world. And to prove the truth of what he said, he told us briefly what had happened to a certain Christian gentleman almost at that very time, the strangest case that had ever occurred even there, where astonishing and marvellous things are happening every instant. In short, he ended by saying that what could and ought to be done was to give the money intended for the ransom of one of us Christians to him, so that he might with it buy a vessel there in Algiers under the pretence of becoming a merchant and trader at Tetuan and along the coast; and when master of the vessel, it would be easy for him to hit on some way of getting us all out of the bano and putting us on board; especially if the Moorish lady gave, as she said, money enough to ransom all, because once free it would be the easiest thing in the world for us to embark even in open day; but the greatest difficulty was that the Moors do not allow any renegade to buy or own any craft, unless it be a large vessel for going on roving expeditions, because they are afraid that anyone who buys a small vessel, especially if he be a Spaniard, only wants it for the purpose of escaping to Christian territory. This however he could get over by arranging with a Tagarin Moor to go shares with him in the purchase of the vessel, and in the profit on the cargo; and under cover of this he could become master of the vessel, in which case he looked upon all the rest as accomplished. But though to me and my comrades it had seemed a better plan to send to Majorca for the vessel, as the Moorish lady suggested, we did not dare to oppose him, fearing that if we did not do as he said he would denounce us, and place us in danger of losing all our lives if he were to disclose our dealings with Zoraida, for whose life we would have all given our own. We therefore resolved to put ourselves in the hands of God and in the renegade's; and at the same time an answer was given to Zoraida, telling her that we would do all she recommended, for she had given as good advice as if Lela Marien had delivered it, and that it depended on her alone whether we were to defer the business or put it in execution at once. I renewed my promise to be her husband; and thus the next day that the bano chanced to be empty she at different times gave us by means of the reed and cloth two thousand gold crowns and a paper in which she said that the next Juma, that is to say Friday, she was going to her father's garden, but that before she went she would give us more money; and if it were not enough we were to let her know, as she would give us as much as we asked, for her father had so much he would not miss it, and besides she kept all the keys.

We at once gave the renegade five hundred crowns to buy the vessel, and with eight hundred I ransomed myself, giving the money to a Valencian merchant who happened to be in Algiers at the time, and who had me released on his word, pledging it that on the arrival of the first ship from Valencia he would pay my ransom; for if he had given the money at once it would have made the king suspect that my ransom money had been for a long time in Algiers, and that the merchant had for his own advantage kept it secret. In fact my master was so difficult to deal with that I dared not on any account pay down the money at once. The Thursday before the Friday on which the fair Zoraida was to go to the garden she gave us a thousand crowns more, and warned us of her departure, begging me, if I were ransomed, to find out her father's garden at once, and by all means to seek an opportunity of going there to see her. I answered in a few words that I would do so, and that she must remember to commend us to Lela Marien with all the prayers the captive had taught her. This having been done, steps were taken to ransom our three comrades, so as to enable them to quit the bano, and lest, seeing me ransomed and themselves not, though the money was forthcoming, they should make a disturbance about it and the devil should prompt them to do something that might injure Zoraida; for though their position might be sufficient to relieve me from this apprehension, nevertheless I was unwilling to run any risk in the matter; and so I had them ransomed in the same way as I was, handing over all the money to the merchant so that he might with safety and confidence give security; without, however, confiding our arrangement and secret to him, which might have been dangerous.

CHAPTER XLI

IN WHICH THE CAPTIVE STILL CONTINUES HIS ADVENTURES

Before fifteen days were over our renegade had already purchased an excellent vessel with room for more than thirty persons; and to make the transaction safe and lend a colour to it, he thought it well to make, as he did, a voyage to a place called Shershel, twenty leagues from Algiers on the Oran side, where there is an extensive trade in dried figs. Two or three times he made this voyage in company with the Tagarin already mentioned. The Moors of Aragon are called Tagarins in Barbary, and those of Granada Mudejars; but in the Kingdom of Fez they call the Mudejars Elches, and they are the people the king chiefly employs in war. To proceed: every time he passed with his vessel he anchored in a cove that was not two crossbow shots from the garden where Zoraida was waiting; and there the renegade, together with the two Moorish lads that rowed, used purposely to station himself, either going through his prayers, or else practising as a part what he meant to perform in earnest. And thus he would go to Zoraida's garden and ask for fruit, which her father gave him, not knowing him; but though, as he afterwards told me, he sought to speak to Zoraida, and tell her who he was, and that by my orders he was to take her to the land of the Christians, so that she might feel satisfied and easy, he had never been able to do so; for the Moorish women do not allow themselves to be seen by any Moor or Turk, unless their husband or father bid them: with Christian captives they permit freedom of intercourse and communication, even more than might be considered proper. But for my part I should have been sorry if he had spoken to her, for perhaps it might have alarmed her to find her affairs talked of by renegades. But God, who ordered it otherwise, afforded no opportunity for our renegade's well-meant purpose; and he, seeing how safely he could go to Shershel and return, and anchor when and how and where he liked, and that the Tagarin his partner had no will but his, and that, now I was ransomed, all we wanted was to find some Christians to row, told me to look out for any I should be willing to take with me, over and above those who had been ransomed, and to engage them for the next Friday, which he fixed upon for our departure. On this I spoke to twelve Spaniards, all stout rowers, and such as could most easily leave the city; but it was no easy matter to find so many just then, because there were twenty ships out on a cruise and they had taken all the rowers with them; and these would not have been found were it not that their master remained at home that summer without going to sea in order to finish a galliot that he had upon the stocks. To these men I said nothing more than that the next Friday in the evening they were to come out stealthily one by one and hang about Hadji Morato's garden, waiting for me there until I came. These directions I gave each one separately, with orders that if they saw any other Christians there they were not to say anything to them except that I had directed them to wait at that spot.

This preliminary having been settled, another still more necessary step had to be taken, which was to let Zoraida know how matters stood that she might be prepared and forewarned, so as not to be taken by surprise if we were suddenly to seize upon her before she thought the Christians' vessel could have returned. I determined, therefore, to go to the garden and try if I could speak to her; and the day before my departure I went there under the pretence of gathering herbs. The first person I met was her father, who addressed me in the language that all over Barbary and even in Constantinople is the medium between captives and Moors, and is neither Morisco nor Castilian, nor of any other nation, but a mixture of all languages, by means of which we can all understand one another. In this sort of language, I say, he asked me what I wanted in his garden, and to whom I belonged. I replied that I was a slave of the Arnaut Mami (for I knew as a certainty that he was a very great friend of his), and that I wanted some herbs to make a salad. He asked me then whether I were on ransom or not, and what my master demanded for me. While these questions and answers were proceeding, the fair Zoraida, who had already perceived me some time before, came out of the house in the garden, and as Moorish women are by no means particular about letting themselves be seen by Christians, or, as I have said before, at all coy, she had no hesitation in coming to where her father stood with me; moreover her father, seeing her approaching slowly, called to her to come. It would be beyond my power now to describe to you the great beauty, the high-bred air, the brilliant attire of my beloved Zoraida as she presented herself before my eyes. I will content myself with saying that more pearls hung from her fair neck, her ears, and her hair than she had hairs on her head. On her ankles, which as is customary were bare, she had carcajes (for so bracelets or anklets are called in Morisco) of the purest gold, set with so many diamonds that she told me afterwards her father valued them at ten thousand doubloons, and those she had on her wrists were worth as much more. The pearls were in profusion and very fine, for the highest display and adornment of the Moorish women is decking themselves with rich pearls and seed-pearls; and of these there are therefore more among the Moors than among any other people. Zoraida's father had to the reputation of possessing a great number, and the purest in all Algiers, and of possessing also more than two hundred thousand Spanish crowns; and she, who is now mistress of me only, was mistress of all this. Whether thus adorned she would have been beautiful or not, and what she must have been in her prosperity, may be imagined from the beauty remaining to her after so many hardships; for, as everyone knows, the beauty of some women has its times and its seasons, and is increased or diminished by chance causes; and naturally the emotions of the mind will heighten or impair it, though indeed more frequently they totally destroy it. In a word she presented herself before me that day attired with the utmost splendour, and supremely beautiful; at any rate, she seemed to me the most beautiful object I had ever seen; and when, besides, I thought of all I owed to her I felt as though I had before me some heavenly being come to earth to bring me relief and happiness.

As she approached her father told her in his own language that I was a captive belonging to his friend the Arnaut Mami, and that I had come for salad.

She took up the conversation, and in that mixture of tongues I have spoken of she asked me if I was a gentleman, and why I was not ransomed.

I answered that I was already ransomed, and that by the price it might be seen what value my master set on me, as I had given one thousand five hundred zoltanis for me; to which she replied, "Hadst thou been my father's, I can tell thee, I would not have let him part with thee for twice as much, for you Christians always tell lies about yourselves and make yourselves out poor to cheat the Moors."

"That may be, lady," said I; "but indeed I dealt truthfully with my master, as I do and mean to do with everybody in the world."

"And when dost thou go?" said Zoraida.

"To-morrow, I think," said I, "for there is a vessel here from France which sails to-morrow, and I think I shall go in her."

"Would it not be better," said Zoraida, "to wait for the arrival of ships from Spain and go with them and not with the French who are not your friends?"

"No," said I; "though if there were intelligence that a vessel were now coming from Spain it is true I might, perhaps, wait for it; however, it is more likely I shall depart to-morrow, for the longing I feel to return to my country and to those I love is so great that it will not allow me to wait for another opportunity, however more convenient, if it be delayed."

"No doubt thou art married in thine own country," said Zoraida, "and for that reason thou art anxious to go and see thy wife."

"I am not married," I replied, "but I have given my promise to marry on my arrival there."

"And is the lady beautiful to whom thou hast given it?" said Zoraida.

"So beautiful," said I, "that, to describe her worthily and tell thee the truth, she is very like thee."

At this her father laughed very heartily and said, "By Allah, Christian, she must be very beautiful if she is like my daughter, who is the most beautiful woman in all this kingdom: only look at her well and thou wilt see I am telling the truth."

Zoraida's father as the better linguist helped to interpret most of these words and phrases, for though she spoke the bastard language, that, as I have said, is employed there, she expressed her meaning more by signs than by words.

While we were still engaged in this conversation, a Moor came running up, exclaiming that four Turks had leaped over the fence or wall of the garden, and were gathering the fruit though it was not yet ripe. The old man was alarmed and Zoraida too, for the Moors commonly, and, so to speak, instinctively have a dread of the Turks, but particularly of the soldiers, who are so insolent and domineering to the Moors who are under their power that they treat them worse than if they were their slaves. Her father said to Zoraida, "Daughter, retire into the house and shut thyself in while I go and speak to these dogs; and thou, Christian, pick thy herbs, and go in peace, and Allah bring thee safe to thy own country."

I bowed, and he went away to look for the Turks, leaving me alone with Zoraida, who made as if she were about to retire as her father bade her; but the moment he was concealed by the trees of the garden, turning to me with her eyes full of tears she said, "Tameji, cristiano, tameji?" that is to say, "Art thou going, Christian, art thou going?"

I made answer, "Yes, lady, but not without thee, come what may: be on the watch for me on the next Juma, and be not alarmed when thou seest us; for most surely we shall go to the land of the Christians."

This I said in such a way that she understood perfectly all that passed between us, and throwing her arm round my neck she began with feeble steps to move towards the house; but as fate would have it (and it might have been very unfortunate if Heaven had not otherwise ordered it), just as we were moving on in the manner and position I have described, with her arm round my neck, her father, as he returned after having sent away the Turks, saw how we were walking and we perceived that he saw us; but Zoraida, ready and quickwitted, took care not to remove her arm from my neck, but on the contrary drew closer to me and laid her head on my breast, bending her knees a little and showing all the signs and tokens of fainting, while I at the same time made it seem as though I were supporting her against my will. Her father came running up to where we were, and seeing his daughter in this state asked what was the matter with her; she, however, giving no answer, he said, "No doubt she has fainted in alarm at the entrance of those dogs," and taking her from mine he drew her to his own breast, while she sighing, her eyes still wet with tears, said again, "Ameji, cristiano, ameji"—"Go, Christian, go." To this her father replied, "There is no need, daughter, for the Christian to go, for he has done thee no harm, and the Turks have now gone; feel no alarm, there is nothing to hurt thee, for as I say, the Turks at my request have gone back the way they came."

"It was they who terrified her, as thou hast said, senor," said I to her father; "but since she tells me to go, I have no wish to displease her: peace be with thee, and with thy leave I will come back to this garden for herbs if need be, for my master says there are nowhere better herbs for salad then here."

"Come back for any thou hast need of," replied Hadji Morato; "for my daughter does not speak thus because she is displeased with thee or any Christian: she only meant that the Turks should go, not thou; or that it was time for thee to look for thy herbs."

With this I at once took my leave of both; and she, looking as though her heart were breaking, retired with her father. While pretending to look for herbs I made the round of the garden at my ease, and studied carefully all the approaches and outlets, and the fastenings of the house and everything that could be taken advantage of to make our task easy.

Having done so I went and gave an account of all that had taken place to the renegade and my comrades, and looked forward with impatience to the hour when, all fear at an end, I should find myself in possession of the prize which fortune held out to me in the fair and lovely Zoraida. The time passed at length, and the appointed day we so longed for arrived; and, all following out the arrangement and plan which, after careful consideration and many a long discussion, we had decided upon, we succeeded as fully as we could have wished; for on the Friday following the day upon which I spoke to Zoraida in the garden, the renegade anchored his vessel at nightfall almost opposite the spot where she was. The Christians who were to row were ready and in hiding in different places round about, all waiting for me, anxious and elated, and eager to attack the vessel they had before their eyes; for they did not know the renegade's plan, but expected that they were to gain their liberty by force of arms and by killing the Moors who were on board the vessel. As soon, then, as I and my comrades made our appearance, all those that were in hiding seeing us came and joined us. It was now the time when the city gates are shut, and there was no one to be seen in all the space outside. When we were collected together we debated whether it would be better first to go for Zoraida, or to make prisoners of the Moorish rowers who rowed in the vessel; but while we were still uncertain our renegade came up asking us what kept us, as it was now the time, and all the Moors were off their guard and most of them asleep. We told him why we hesitated, but he said it was of more importance first to secure the vessel, which could be done with the greatest ease and without any danger, and then we could go for Zoraida. We all approved of what he said, and so without further delay, guided by him we made for the vessel, and he leaping on board first, drew his cutlass and said in Morisco, "Let no one stir from this if he does not want it to cost him his life." By this almost all the Christians were on board, and the Moors, who were fainthearted, hearing their captain speak in this way, were cowed, and without any one of them taking to his arms (and indeed they had few or hardly any) they submitted without saying a word to be bound by the Christians, who quickly secured them, threatening them that if they raised any kind of outcry they would be all put to the sword. This having been accomplished, and half of our party being left to keep guard over them, the rest of us, again taking the renegade as our guide, hastened towards Hadji Morato's garden, and as good luck would have it, on trying the gate it opened as easily as if it had not been locked; and so, quite quietly and in silence, we reached the house without being perceived by anybody. The lovely Zoraida was watching for us at a window, and as soon as she perceived that there were people there, she asked in a low voice if we were "Nizarani," as much as to say or ask if we were Christians. I answered that we were, and begged her to come down. As soon as she recognised me she did not delay an instant, but without answering a word came down immediately, opened the door and presented herself before us all, so beautiful and so richly attired that I cannot attempt to describe her. The moment I saw her I took her hand and kissed it, and the renegade and my two comrades did the same; and the rest, who knew nothing of the circumstances, did as they saw us do, for it only seemed as if we were returning thanks to her, and recognising her as the giver of our liberty. The renegade asked her in the Morisco language if her father was in the house. She replied that he was and that he was asleep.

"Then it will be necessary to waken him and take him with us," said the renegade, "and everything of value in this fair mansion."

"Nay," said she, "my father must not on any account be touched, and there is nothing in the house except what I shall take, and that will be quite enough to enrich and satisfy all of you; wait a little and you shall see," and so saying she went in, telling us she would return immediately and bidding us keep quiet making any noise.

I asked the renegade what had passed between them, and when he told me, I declared that nothing should be done except in accordance with the wishes of Zoraida, who now came back with a little trunk so full of gold crowns that she could scarcely carry it. Unfortunately her father awoke while this was going on, and hearing a noise in the garden, came to the window, and at once perceiving that all those who were there were Christians, raising a prodigiously loud outcry, he began to call out in Arabic, "Christians, Christians! thieves, thieves!" by which cries we were all thrown into the greatest fear and embarrassment; but the renegade seeing the danger we were in and how important it was for him to effect his purpose before we were heard, mounted with the utmost quickness to where Hadji Morato was, and with him went some of our party; I, however, did not dare to leave Zoraida, who had fallen almost fainting in my arms. To be brief, those who had gone upstairs acted so promptly that in an instant they came down, carrying Hadji Morato with his hands bound and a napkin tied over his mouth, which prevented him from uttering a word, warning him at the same time that to attempt to speak would cost him his life. When his daughter caught sight of him she covered her eyes so as not to see him, and her father was horror-stricken, not knowing how willingly she had placed herself in our hands. But it was now most essential for us to be on the move, and carefully and quickly we regained the vessel, where those who had remained on board were waiting for us in apprehension of some mishap having befallen us. It was barely two hours after night set in when we were all on board the vessel, where the cords were removed from the hands of Zoraida's father, and the napkin from his mouth; but the renegade once more told him not to utter a word, or they would take his life. He, when he saw his daughter there, began to sigh piteously, and still more when he perceived that I held her closely embraced and that she lay quiet without resisting or complaining, or showing any reluctance; nevertheless he remained silent lest they should carry into effect the repeated threats the renegade had addressed to him.

Finding herself now on board, and that we were about to give way with the oars, Zoraida, seeing her father there, and the other Moors bound, bade the renegade ask me to do her the favour of releasing the Moors and setting her father at liberty, for she would rather drown herself in the sea than suffer a father that had loved her so dearly to be carried away captive before her eyes and on her account. The renegade repeated this to me, and I replied that I was very willing to do so; but he replied that it was not advisable, because if they were left there they would at once raise the country and stir up the city, and lead to the despatch of swift cruisers in pursuit, and our being taken, by sea or land, without any possibility of escape; and that all that could be done was to set them free on the first Christian ground we reached. On this point we all agreed; and Zoraida, to whom it was explained, together with the reasons that prevented us from doing at once what she desired, was satisfied likewise; and then in glad silence and with cheerful alacrity each of our stout rowers took his oar, and commending ourselves to God with all our hearts, we began to shape our course for the island of Majorca, the nearest Christian land. Owing, however, to the Tramontana rising a little, and the sea growing somewhat rough, it was impossible for us to keep a straight course for Majorca, and we were compelled to coast in the direction of Oran, not without great uneasiness on our part lest we should be observed from the town of Shershel, which lies on that coast, not more than sixty miles from Algiers. Moreover we were afraid of meeting on that course one of the galliots that usually come with goods from Tetuan; although each of us for himself and all of us together felt confident that, if we were to meet a merchant galliot, so that it were not a cruiser, not only should we not be lost, but that we should take a vessel in which we could more safely accomplish our voyage. As we pursued our course Zoraida kept her head between my hands so as not to see her father, and I felt that she was praying to Lela Marien to help us.

We might have made about thirty miles when daybreak found us some three musket-shots off the land, which seemed to us deserted, and without anyone to see us. For all that, however, by hard rowing we put out a little to sea, for it was now somewhat calmer, and having gained about two leagues the word was given to row by batches, while we ate something, for the vessel was well provided; but the rowers said it was not a time to take any rest; let food be served out to those who were not rowing, but they would not leave their oars on any account. This was done, but now a stiff breeze began to blow, which obliged us to leave off rowing and make sail at once and steer for Oran, as it was impossible to make any other course. All this was done very promptly, and under sail we ran more than eight miles an hour without any fear, except that of coming across some vessel out on a roving expedition. We gave the Moorish rowers some food, and the renegade comforted them by telling them that they were not held as captives, as we should set them free on the first opportunity.

The same was said to Zoraida's father, who replied, "Anything else, Christian, I might hope for or think likely from your generosity and good behaviour, but do not think me so simple as to imagine you will give me my liberty; for you would have never exposed yourselves to the danger of depriving me of it only to restore it to me so generously, especially as you know who I am and the sum you may expect to receive on restoring it; and if you will only name that, I here offer you all you require for myself and for my unhappy daughter there; or else for her alone, for she is the greatest and most precious part of my soul."

As he said this he began to weep so bitterly that he filled us all with compassion and forced Zoraida to look at him, and when she saw him weeping she was so moved that she rose from my feet and ran to throw her arms round him, and pressing her face to his, they both gave way to such an outburst of tears that several of us were constrained to keep them company.

But when her father saw her in full dress and with all her jewels about her, he said to her in his own language, "What means this, my daughter? Last night, before this terrible misfortune in which we are plunged befell us, I saw thee in thy everyday and indoor garments; and now, without having had time to attire thyself, and without my bringing thee any joyful tidings to furnish an occasion for adorning and bedecking thyself, I see thee arrayed in the finest attire it would be in my power to give thee when fortune was most kind to us. Answer me this; for it causes me greater anxiety and surprise than even this misfortune itself."

The renegade interpreted to us what the Moor said to his daughter; she, however, returned him no answer. But when he observed in one corner of the vessel the little trunk in which she used to keep her jewels, which he well knew he had left in Algiers and had not brought to the garden, he was still more amazed, and asked her how that trunk had come into our hands, and what there was in it. To which the renegade, without waiting for Zoraida to reply, made answer, "Do not trouble thyself by asking thy daughter Zoraida so many questions, senor, for the one answer I will give thee will serve for all; I would have thee know that she is a Christian, and that it is she who has been the file for our chains and our deliverer from captivity. She is here of her own free will, as glad, I imagine, to find herself in this position as he who escapes from darkness into the light, from death to life, and from suffering to glory."

"Daughter, is this true, what he says?" cried the Moor.

"It is," replied Zoraida.

"That thou art in truth a Christian," said the old man, "and that thou hast given thy father into the power of his enemies?"

To which Zoraida made answer, "A Christian I am, but it is not I who have placed thee in this position, for it never was my wish to leave thee or do thee harm, but only to do good to myself."

"And what good hast thou done thyself, daughter?" said he.

"Ask thou that," said she, "of Lela Marien, for she can tell thee better than I."

The Moor had hardly heard these words when with marvellous quickness he flung himself headforemost into the sea, where no doubt he would have been drowned had not the long and full dress he wore held him up for a little on the surface of the water. Zoraida cried aloud to us to save him, and we all hastened to help, and seizing him by his robe we drew him in half drowned and insensible, at which Zoraida was in such distress that she wept over him as piteously and bitterly as though he were already dead. We turned him upon his face and he voided a great quantity of water, and at the end of two hours came to himself. Meanwhile, the wind having changed we were compelled to head for the land, and ply our oars to avoid being driven on shore; but it was our good fortune to reach a creek that lies on one side of a small promontory or cape, called by the Moors that of the "Cava rumia," which in our language means "the wicked Christian woman;" for it is a tradition among them that La Cava, through whom Spain was lost, lies buried at that spot; "cava" in their language meaning "wicked woman," and "rumia" "Christian;" moreover, they count it unlucky to anchor there when necessity compels them, and they never do so otherwise. For us, however, it was not the resting-place of the wicked woman but a haven of safety for our relief, so much had the sea now got up. We posted a look-out on shore, and never let the oars out of our hands, and ate of the stores the renegade had laid in, imploring God and Our Lady with all our hearts to help and protect us, that we might give a happy ending to a beginning so prosperous. At the entreaty of Zoraida orders were given to set on shore her father and the other Moors who were still bound, for she could not endure, nor could her tender heart bear to see her father in bonds and her fellow-countrymen prisoners before her eyes. We promised her to do this at the moment of departure, for as it was uninhabited we ran no risk in releasing them at that place.

Our prayers were not so far in vain as to be unheard by Heaven, for after a while the wind changed in our favour, and made the sea calm, inviting us once more to resume our voyage with a good heart. Seeing this we unbound the Moors, and one by one put them on shore, at which they were filled with amazement; but when we came to land Zoraida's father, who had now completely recovered his senses, he said:

"Why is it, think ye, Christians, that this wicked woman is rejoiced at your giving me my liberty? Think ye it is because of the affection she bears me? Nay verily, it is only because of the hindrance my presence offers to the execution of her base designs. And think not that it is her belief that yours is better than ours that has led her to change her religion; it is only because she knows that immodesty is more freely practised in your country than in ours." Then turning to Zoraida, while I and another of the Christians held him fast by both arms, lest he should do some mad act, he said to her, "Infamous girl, misguided maiden, whither in thy blindness and madness art thou going in the hands of these dogs, our natural enemies? Cursed be the hour when I begot thee! Cursed the luxury and indulgence in which I reared thee!"

But seeing that he was not likely soon to cease I made haste to put him on shore, and thence he continued his maledictions and lamentations aloud; calling on Mohammed to pray to Allah to destroy us, to confound us, to make an end of us; and when, in consequence of having made sail, we could no longer hear what he said we could see what he did; how he plucked out his beard and tore his hair and lay writhing on the ground. But once he raised his voice to such a pitch that we were able to hear what he said. "Come back, dear daughter, come back to shore; I forgive thee all;

let those men have the money, for it is theirs now, and come back to comfort thy sorrowing father, who will yield up his life on this barren strand if thou dost leave him."

All this Zoraida heard, and heard with sorrow and tears, and all she could say in answer was, "Allah grant that Lela Marien, who has made me become a Christian, give thee comfort in thy sorrow, my father. Allah knows that I could not do otherwise than I have done, and that these Christians owe nothing to my will; for even had I wished not to accompany them, but remain at home, it would have been impossible for me, so eagerly did my soul urge me on to the accomplishment of this purpose, which I feel to be as righteous as to thee, dear father, it seems wicked."

But neither could her father hear her nor we see him when she said this; and so, while I consoled Zoraida, we turned our attention to our voyage, in which a breeze from the right point so favoured us that we made sure of finding ourselves off the coast of Spain on the morrow by daybreak. But, as good seldom or never comes pure and unmixed, without being attended or followed by some disturbing evil that gives a shock to it, our fortune, or perhaps the curses which the Moor had hurled at his daughter (for whatever kind of father they may come from these are always to be dreaded), brought it about that when we were now in mid-sea, and the night about three hours spent, as we were running with all sail set and oars lashed, for the favouring breeze saved us the trouble of using them, we saw by the light of the moon, which shone brilliantly, a square-rigged vessel in full sail close to us, luffing up and standing across our course, and so close that we had to strike sail to avoid running foul of her, while they too put the helm hard up to let us pass. They came to the side of the ship to ask who we were, whither we were bound, and whence we came, but as they asked this in French our renegade said, "Let no one answer, for no doubt these are French corsairs who plunder all comers."

Acting on this warning no one answered a word, but after we had gone a little ahead, and the vessel was now lying to leeward, suddenly they fired two guns, and apparently both loaded with chain-shot, for with one they cut our mast in half and brought down both it and the sail into the sea, and the other, discharged at the same moment, sent a ball into our vessel amidships, staving her in completely, but without doing any further damage. We, however, finding ourselves sinking began to shout for help and call upon those in the ship to pick us up as we were beginning to fill. They then lay to, and lowering a skiff or boat, as many as a dozen Frenchmen, well armed with match-locks, and their matches burning, got into it and came alongside; and seeing how few we were, and that our vessel was going down, they took us in, telling us that this had come to us through our incivility in not giving them an answer. Our renegade took the trunk containing Zoraida's wealth and dropped it into the sea without anyone perceiving what he did. In short we went on board with the Frenchmen, who, after having ascertained all they wanted to know about us, rifled us of everything we had, as if they had been our bitterest enemies, and from Zoraida they took even the anklets she wore on her feet; but the distress they caused her did not distress me so much as the fear I was in that from robbing her of her rich and precious jewels they would proceed to rob her of the most precious jewel that she valued more than all. The desires, however, of those people do not go beyond money, but of that their covetousness is insatiable, and on this occasion it was carried to such a pitch that they would have taken even the clothes we wore as captives if they had been worth anything to them. It was the advice of some of them to throw us all into the sea wrapped up in a sail; for their purpose was to trade at some of the ports of Spain, giving themselves out as Bretons, and if they brought us alive they would be punished as soon as the robbery was discovered; but the captain (who was the one who had plundered my beloved Zoraida) said he was satisfied with the prize he had got, and that he would not touch at any Spanish port, but pass the Straits of Gibraltar by night, or as best he could, and make for La Rochelle, from which he had sailed. So they agreed by common consent to give us the skiff belonging to their ship and all we required for the short voyage that remained to us, and this they did the next day on coming in sight of the Spanish coast, with which, and the joy we felt, all our sufferings and miseries were as completely forgotten as if they had never been endured by us, such is the delight of recovering lost liberty.

It may have been about mid-day when they placed us in the boat, giving us two kegs of water and some biscuit; and the captain, moved by I know not what compassion, as the lovely Zoraida was about to embark, gave her some forty gold crowns, and would not permit his men to take from her those same garments which she has on now. We got into the boat, returning them thanks for their kindness to us, and showing ourselves grateful rather than indignant. They stood out to sea, steering for the straits; we, without looking to any compass save the land we had before us, set ourselves to row with such energy that by sunset we were so near that we might easily, we thought, land before the night was far advanced. But as the moon did not show that night, and the sky was clouded, and as we knew not whereabouts we were, it did not seem to us a prudent thing to make for the shore, as several of us advised, saying we ought to run ourselves ashore even if it were on rocks and far from any habitation, for in this way we should be relieved from the apprehensions we naturally felt of the prowling vessels of the Tetuan corsairs, who leave Barbary at nightfall and are on the Spanish coast by daybreak, where they commonly take some prize, and then go home to sleep in their own houses. But of the conflicting counsels the one which was adopted was that we should approach gradually, and land where we could if the sea were calm enough to permit us. This was done, and a little before midnight we drew near to the foot of a huge and lofty mountain, not so close to the sea but that it left a narrow space on which to land conveniently. We ran our boat up on the sand, and all sprang out and kissed the ground, and with tears of joyful satisfaction returned thanks to God our Lord for all his incomparable goodness to us on our voyage. We took out of the boat the provisions it contained, and drew it up on the shore, and then climbed a long way up the mountain, for even there we could not feel easy in our hearts, or persuade ourselves that it was Christian soil that was now under our feet.

The dawn came, more slowly, I think, than we could have wished; we completed the ascent in order to see if from the summit any habitation or any shepherds' huts could be discovered, but strain our eyes as we might, neither dwelling, nor human being, nor path nor road could we perceive. However, we determined to push on farther, as it could not but be that ere long we must see some one who could tell us where we were. But what distressed me most was to see Zoraida going on foot over that rough ground; for though I once carried her on my shoulders, she was more wearied by my weariness than rested by the rest; and so she would never again allow me to undergo the exertion, and went on very patiently and cheerfully, while I led her by the hand. We had gone rather less than a quarter of a league when the sound of a little bell fell on our ears, a clear proof that there were flocks hard by, and looking about carefully to see if any were within view, we observed a young shepherd tranquilly and unsuspiciously trimming a stick with his knife at the foot of a cork tree. We called to him, and he, raising his head, sprang nimbly to his feet, for, as we afterwards learned, the first who presented themselves to his sight were the renegade and Zoraida, and seeing them in Moorish dress he imagined that all the Moors of Barbary were upon him; and plunging with marvellous swiftness into the thicket in front of him, he began to raise a prodigious outcry, exclaiming, "The Moors—the Moors have landed! To arms, to arms!" We were all thrown into perplexity by these cries, not knowing what to do; but reflecting that the shouts of the shepherd would raise the country and that the mounted coast-guard would come at once to see what was the matter, we agreed that the renegade must strip off his Turkish garments and put on a captive's jacket or coat which one of our party gave him at once, though he himself was reduced to his shirt; and so commending ourselves to God, we followed the same road which we saw the shepherd take, expecting every moment that the coast-guard would be down upon us. Nor did our expectation deceive us, for two hours had not passed when, coming out of the brushwood into the open ground, we perceived some fifty mounted men swiftly approaching us at a hand-gallop. As soon as we saw them we stood still, waiting for them; but as they came close and, instead of the Moors they were in quest of, saw a set of poor Christians, they were taken aback, and one of them asked if it could be we who were the cause of the shepherd having raised the call to arms. I said "Yes," and as I was about to explain to him what had occurred, and whence we came and who we were, one of the Christians of our party recognised the horseman who had put the question to us, and before I could say anything more he exclaimed:

"Thanks be to God, sirs, for bringing us to such good quarters; for, if I do not deceive myself, the ground we stand on is that of Velez Malaga unless, indeed, all my years of captivity have made me unable to recollect that you, senor, who ask who we are, are Pedro de Bustamante, my uncle."

The Christian captive had hardly uttered these words, when the horseman threw himself off his horse, and ran to embrace the young man, crying:

"Nephew of my soul and life! I recognise thee now; and long have I mourned thee as dead, I, and my sister, thy mother, and all thy kin that are still alive, and whom God has been pleased to preserve that they may enjoy the happiness of seeing thee. We knew long since that thou wert in Algiers, and from the appearance of thy garments and those of all this company, I conclude that ye have had a miraculous restoration to liberty."

"It is true," replied the young man, "and by-and-by we will tell you all."

As soon as the horsemen understood that we were Christian captives, they dismounted from their horses, and each offered his to carry us to the city of Velez Malaga, which was a league and a half distant. Some of them went to bring the boat to the city, we having told them where we had left it; others took us up behind them, and Zoraida was placed on the horse of the young man's uncle. The whole town came out to meet us, for they had by this time heard of our arrival from one who had gone on in advance. They were not astonished to see liberated captives or captive Moors, for people on that coast are well used to see both one and the other; but they were astonished at the beauty of Zoraida, which was just then heightened, as well by the exertion of travelling as by joy at finding herself on Christian soil, and relieved of all fear of being lost; for this had brought such a glow upon her face, that unless my affection for her were deceiving me, I would venture to say that there was not a more beautiful creature in the world—at least, that I had ever seen. We went straight to the church to return thanks to God for the mercies we had received, and when Zoraida entered it she said there were faces there like Lela Marien's. We told her they were her images; and as well as he could the renegade explained to her what they meant, that she might adore them as if each of them were the very same Lela Marien that had spoken to her; and she, having great intelligence and a quick and clear instinct, understood at once all he said to her about them. Thence they took us away and distributed us all in different houses in the town; but as for the renegade, Zoraida, and myself, the Christian who came with us brought us to the house of his parents, who had a fair share of the gifts of fortune, and treated us with as much kindness as they did their own son.

We remained six days in Velez, at the end of which the renegade, having informed himself of all that was requisite for him to do, set out for the city of Granada to restore himself to the sacred bosom of the Church through the medium of the Holy Inquisition. The other released captives took their departures, each the way that seemed best to him, and Zoraida and I were left alone, with nothing more than the crowns which the courtesy of the Frenchman had bestowed upon Zoraida, out of which I bought the beast on which she rides; and, I for the present attending her as her father and squire and not as her husband, we are now going to ascertain if my father is living, or if any of my brothers has had better fortune than mine has been; though, as Heaven has made me the companion of Zoraida, I think no other lot could be assigned to me, however happy, that I would rather have. The patience with which she endures the hardships that poverty brings with it, and the eagerness she shows to become a Christian, are such that they fill me with admiration, and bind me to serve her all my life; though the happiness I feel in seeing myself hers, and her mine, is disturbed and marred by not knowing whether I shall find any corner to shelter her in my own country, or whether time and death may not have made such changes in the fortunes and lives of my father and brothers, that I shall hardly find anyone who knows me, if they are not alive.

I have no more of my story to tell you, gentlemen; whether it be an interesting or a curious one let your better judgments decide; all I can say is I would gladly have told it to you more briefly; although my fear of wearying you has made me leave out more than one circumstance.

CHAPTER XLII

WHICH TREATS OF WHAT FURTHER TOOK PLACE IN THE INN, AND OF SEVERAL OTHER THINGS WORTH KNOWING

With these words the captive held his peace, and Don Fernando said to him, "In truth, captain, the manner in which you have related this remarkable adventure has been such as befitted the novelty and strangeness of the matter. The whole story is curious and uncommon, and abounds with incidents that fill the hearers with wonder and astonishment; and so great is the pleasure we have found in listening to it that we should be glad if it were to begin again, even though to-morrow were to find us still occupied with the same tale." And while he said this Cardenio and the rest of them offered to be of service to him in any way that lay in their power, and in words and language so kindly and sincere that the captain was much gratified by their good-will. In particular Don Fernando offered, if he would go back with him, to get his brother the marquis to become godfather at the baptism of Zoraida, and on his own part to provide him with the means of making his appearance in his own country with the credit and comfort he was entitled to. For all this the captive returned thanks very courteously, although he would not accept any of their generous offers.

By this time night closed in, and as it did, there came up to the inn a coach attended by some men on horseback, who demanded accommodation; to which the landlady replied that there was not a hand's breadth of the whole inn unoccupied.

"Still, for all that," said one of those who had entered on horseback, "room must be found for his lordship the Judge here."

At this name the landlady was taken aback, and said, "Senor, the fact is I have no beds; but if his lordship the Judge carries one with him, as no doubt he does, let him come in and welcome; for my husband and I will give up our room to accommodate his worship."

"Very good, so be it," said the squire; but in the meantime a man had got out of the coach whose dress indicated at a glance the office and post he held, for the long robe with ruffled sleeves that he wore showed that he was, as his servant said, a Judge of appeal. He led by the hand a young girl in a travelling dress, apparently about sixteen years of age, and of such a high-bred air, so beautiful and so graceful, that all were filled with admiration when she made her appearance, and but for having seen Dorothea, Luscinda, and Zoraida, who were there in the inn, they would have fancied that a beauty like that of this maiden's would have been hard to find. Don Quixote was present at the entrance of the Judge with the young lady, and as soon as he saw him he said, "Your worship may with confidence enter and take your ease in this castle; for though the accommodation be scanty and poor, there are no quarters so cramped or inconvenient that they cannot make room for arms and letters; above all if arms and letters have beauty for a guide and leader, as letters represented by your worship have in this fair maiden, to whom not only ought castles to throw themselves open and yield themselves up, but rocks should rend themselves asunder and mountains divide and bow themselves down to give her a reception. Enter, your worship, I say, into this paradise, for here you will find stars and suns to accompany the heaven your worship brings with you, here you will find arms in their supreme excellence, and beauty in its highest perfection."

The Judge was struck with amazement at the language of Don Quixote, whom he scrutinized very carefully, no less astonished by his figure than by his talk; and before he could find words to answer him he had a fresh surprise, when he saw opposite to him Luscinda, Dorothea, and Zoraida, who, having heard of the new guests and of the beauty of the young lady, had come to see her and welcome her; Don Fernando, Cardenio, and the curate, however, greeted him in a more intelligible and polished style. In short, the Judge made his entrance in a state of bewilderment, as well with what he saw as what he heard, and the fair ladies of the inn gave the fair damsel a cordial welcome. On the whole he could perceive that all who were there were people of quality; but with the figure, countenance, and bearing of Don Quixote he was at his wits' end; and all civilities having been exchanged, and the accommodation of the inn inquired into, it was settled, as it had been before settled, that all the women should retire to the garret that has been already mentioned, and that the men should remain outside as if to guard them; the Judge, therefore, was very well pleased to allow his daughter, for such the damsel was, to go with the ladies, which she did very willingly; and with part of the host's narrow bed and half of what the Judge had brought with him, they made a more comfortable arrangement for the night than they had expected.

The captive, whose heart had leaped within him the instant he saw the Judge, telling him somehow that this was his brother, asked one of the servants who accompanied him what his name was, and whether he knew from what part of the country he came. The servant replied that he was called the Licentiate Juan Perez de Viedma, and that he had heard it said he came from a village in the mountains of Leon. From this statement, and what he himself had seen, he felt convinced that this was his brother who had adopted letters by his father's advice; and excited and rejoiced, he called Don Fernando and Cardenio and the curate aside, and told them how the matter stood, assuring them that the judge was his brother. The servant had further informed him that he was now going to the Indies with the appointment of Judge of the Supreme Court of Mexico; and he had learned, likewise, that the young lady was his daughter, whose mother had died in giving birth to her, and that he was very rich in consequence of the dowry left to him with the daughter. He asked their advice as to what means he should adopt to make himself known, or to ascertain beforehand whether, when he had made himself known, his brother, seeing him so poor, would be ashamed of him, or would receive him with a warm heart.

"Leave it to me to find out that," said the curate; "though there is no reason for supposing, senor captain, that you will not be kindly received, because the worth and wisdom that your brother's bearing shows him to possess do not make it likely that he will prove haughty or insensible, or that he will not know how to estimate the accidents of fortune at their proper value."

"Still," said the captain, "I would not make myself known abruptly, but in some indirect way."

"I have told you already," said the curate, "that I will manage it in a way to satisfy us all."

By this time supper was ready, and they all took their seats at the table, except the captive, and the ladies, who supped by themselves in their own room. In the middle of supper the curate said:

"I had a comrade of your worship's name, Senor Judge, in Constantinople, where I was a captive for several years, and that same comrade was one of the stoutest soldiers and captains in the whole Spanish infantry; but he had as large a share of misfortune as he had of gallantry and courage."

"And how was the captain called, senor?" asked the Judge.

"He was called Ruy Perez de Viedma," replied the curate, "and he was born in a village in the mountains of Leon; and he mentioned a circumstance connected with his father and his brothers which, had it not been told me by so truthful a man as he was, I should have set down as one of those fables the old women tell over the fire in winter; for he said his father had divided his property among his three sons and had addressed words of advice to them sounder than any of Cato's. But I can say this much, that the choice he made of going to the wars was attended with such success, that by his gallant conduct and courage, and without any help save his own merit, he rose in a few years to be captain of infantry, and to see himself on the high-road and in position to be given the command of a corps before long; but Fortune was against him, for where he might have expected her favour he lost it, and with it his liberty, on that glorious day when so many recovered theirs, at the battle of Lepanto. I lost mine at the Goletta, and after a variety of adventures we found ourselves comrades at Constantinople. Thence he went to Algiers, where he met with one of the most extraordinary adventures that ever befell anyone in the world."

Here the curate went on to relate briefly his brother's adventure with Zoraida; to all which the Judge gave such an attentive hearing that he never before had been so much of a hearer. The curate, however, only went so far as to describe how the Frenchmen plundered those who were in the boat, and the poverty and distress in which his comrade and the fair Moor were left, of whom he said he had not been able to learn what became of them, or whether they had reached Spain, or been carried to France by the Frenchmen.

The captain, standing a little to one side, was listening to all the curate said, and watching every movement of his brother, who, as soon as he perceived the curate had made an end of his story, gave a deep sigh and said with his eyes full of tears, "Oh, senor, if you only knew what news you have given me and how it comes home to me, making me show how I feel it with these tears that spring from my eyes in spite of all my worldly wisdom and self-restraint! That brave captain that you speak of is my eldest brother, who, being of a bolder and loftier mind than my other brother or myself, chose the honourable and worthy calling of arms, which was one of the three careers our father proposed to us, as your comrade mentioned in that fable you thought he was telling you. I followed that of letters, in which God and my own exertions have raised me to the position in which you see me. My second brother is in Peru, so wealthy that with what he has sent to my father and to me he has fully repaid the portion he took with him, and has even furnished my father's hands with the means of gratifying his natural generosity, while I too have been enabled to pursue my studies in a more becoming and creditable fashion, and so to attain my present standing. My father is still alive, though dying with anxiety to hear of his eldest son, and he prays God unceasingly that death may not close his eyes until he has looked upon those of his son; but with regard to him what surprises me is, that having so much common sense as he had, he should have neglected to give any intelligence about himself, either in his troubles and sufferings, or in his prosperity, for if his father or any of us had known of his condition he need not have waited for that miracle of the reed to obtain his ransom; but what now disquiets me is the uncertainty whether those Frenchmen may have restored him to liberty, or murdered him to hide the robbery. All this will make me continue my journey, not with the satisfaction in which I began it, but in the deepest melancholy and sadness. Oh dear brother! that I only knew where thou art now, and I would hasten to seek thee out and deliver thee from thy sufferings, though it were to cost me suffering myself! Oh that I could bring news to our old father that thou art alive, even wert thou the deepest dungeon of Barbary; for his wealth and my brother's and mine would rescue thee thence! Oh beautiful and generous Zoraida, that I could repay thy good goodness to a brother! That I could be present at the new birth of thy soul, and at thy bridal that would give us all such happiness!"

All this and more the Judge uttered with such deep emotion at the news he had received of his brother that all who heard him shared in it, showing their sympathy with his sorrow. The curate, seeing, then, how well he had succeeded in carrying out his purpose and the captain's wishes, had no desire to keep them unhappy any longer, so he rose from the table and going into the room where Zoraida was he took her by the hand, Luscinda, Dorothea, and the Judge's daughter following her. The captain was waiting to see what the curate would do, when the latter, taking him with the other hand, advanced with both of them to where the Judge and the other gentlemen were and said, "Let your tears cease to flow, Senor Judge, and the wish of your heart be gratified as fully as you could desire, for you have before you your worthy brother and your good sister-in-law. He whom you see here is the Captain Viedma, and this is the fair Moor who has been so good to him. The Frenchmen I told you of have reduced them to the state of poverty you see that you may show the generosity of your kind heart."

The captain ran to embrace his brother, who placed both hands on his breast so as to have a good look at him, holding him a little way off but as soon as he had fully recognised him he clasped him in his arms so closely, shedding such tears of heartfelt joy, that most of those present could not but join in them. The words the brothers exchanged, the emotion they showed can scarcely be imagined, I fancy, much less put down in writing. They told each other in a few words the events of their lives; they showed the true affection of brothers in all its strength; then the judge embraced Zoraida, putting all he possessed at her disposal; then he made his daughter embrace her, and the fair Christian and the lovely Moor drew fresh tears from every eye. And there was Don Quixote observing all these strange proceedings attentively without uttering a word, and attributing the whole to chimeras of knight-errantry. Then they agreed that the captain and Zoraida should return with his brother to Seville, and send news to his father of his having been delivered and found, so as to enable him to come and be present at the marriage and baptism of Zoraida, for it was impossible for the Judge to put off his journey, as he was informed that in a month from that time the fleet was to sail from Seville for New Spain, and to miss the passage would have been a great inconvenience to him. In short, everybody was well pleased and glad at the captive's good fortune; and as now almost two-thirds of the night were past, they resolved to retire to rest for the remainder of it. Don Quixote offered to mount guard over the castle lest they should be attacked by some giant or other malevolent scoundrel, covetous of the great treasure of beauty the castle contained. Those who understood him returned him thanks for this service, and they gave the Judge an account of his extraordinary humour, with which he was not a little amused. Sancho Panza alone was fuming at the lateness of the hour for retiring to rest; and he of all was the one that made himself most comfortable, as he stretched himself on the trappings of his ass, which, as will be told farther on, cost him so dear.

The ladies, then, having retired to their chamber, and the others having disposed themselves with as little discomfort as they could, Don Quixote sallied out of the inn to act as sentinel of the castle as he had promised. It happened, however, that a little before the approach of dawn a voice so musical and sweet reached the ears of the ladies that it forced them all to listen attentively, but especially Dorothea, who had been awake, and by whose side Dona Clara de Viedma, for so the Judge's daughter was called, lay sleeping. No one could imagine who it was that sang so sweetly, and the voice was unaccompanied by any instrument. At one moment it seemed to them as if the singer were in the courtyard, at another in the stable; and as they were all attention, wondering, Cardenio came to the door and said, "Listen, whoever is not asleep, and you will hear a muleteer's voice that enchants as it chants."

"We are listening to it already, senor," said Dorothea; on which Cardenio went away; and Dorothea, giving all her attention to it, made out the words of the song to be these:

CHAPTER XLIII

WHEREIN IS RELATED THE PLEASANT STORY OF THE MULETEER, TOGETHER WITH OTHER STRANGE THINGS THAT CAME TO PASS IN THE INN

> Ah me, Love's mariner am I
>   On Love's deep ocean sailing;
> I know not where the haven lies,
>   I dare not hope to gain it.
>
> One solitary distant star
>   Is all I have to guide me,
> A brighter orb than those of old
>   That Palinurus lighted.
>
> And vaguely drifting am I borne,
>   I know not where it leads me;
> I fix my gaze on it alone,
>   Of all beside it heedless.
>
> But over-cautious prudery,
>   And coyness cold and cruel,
> When most I need it, these, like clouds,
>   Its longed-for light refuse me.
>
> Bright star, goal of my yearning eyes
>   As thou above me beamest,
> When thou shalt hide thee from my sight
>   I'll know that death is near me.

The singer had got so far when it struck Dorothea that it was not fair to let Clara miss hearing such a sweet voice, so, shaking her from side to side, she woke her, saying:

"Forgive me, child, for waking thee, but I do so that thou mayest have the pleasure of hearing the best voice thou hast ever heard, perhaps, in all thy life."

Clara awoke quite drowsy, and not understanding at the moment what Dorothea said, asked her what it was; she repeated what she had said, and Clara became attentive at once; but she had hardly heard two lines, as the singer continued, when a strange trembling seized her, as if she were suffering from a severe attack of quartan ague, and throwing her arms round Dorothea she said:

"Ah, dear lady of my soul and life! why did you wake me? The greatest kindness fortune could do me now would be to close my eyes and ears so as neither to see or hear that unhappy musician."

"What art thou talking about, child?" said Dorothea. "Why, they say this singer is a muleteer!"

"Nay, he is the lord of many places," replied Clara, "and that one in my heart which he holds so firmly shall never be taken from him, unless he be willing to surrender it."

Dorothea was amazed at the ardent language of the girl, for it seemed to be far beyond such experience of life as her tender years gave any promise of, so she said to her:

"You speak in such a way that I cannot understand you, Senora Clara; explain yourself more clearly, and tell me what is this you are saying about hearts and places and this musician whose voice has so moved you? But do not tell me anything now; I do not want to lose the pleasure I get from listening to the singer by giving my attention to your transports, for I perceive he is beginning to sing a new strain and a new air."

"Let him, in Heaven's name," returned Clara; and not to hear him she stopped both ears with her hands, at which Dorothea was again surprised; but turning her attention to the song she found that it ran in this fashion:

> Sweet Hope, my stay,
> That onward to the goal of thy intent
> Dost make thy way,
> Heedless of hindrance or impediment,
> Have thou no fear
> If at each step thou findest death is near.
>
> No victory,
> No joy of triumph doth the faint heart know;
> Unblest is he
> That a bold front to Fortune dares not show,
> But soul and sense
> In bondage yieldeth up to indolence.
>
> If Love his wares
> Do dearly sell, his right must be contest;
> What gold compares
> With that whereon his stamp he hath imprest?

>   And all men know
>   What costeth little that we rate but low.
>
>   Love resolute
>   Knows not the word "impossibility;"
>   And though my suit
>   Beset by endless obstacles I see,
>   Yet no despair
>   Shall hold me bound to earth while heaven is there.

Here the voice ceased and Clara's sobs began afresh, all which excited Dorothea's curiosity to know what could be the cause of singing so sweet and weeping so bitter, so she again asked her what it was she was going to say before. On this Clara, afraid that Luscinda might overhear her, winding her arms tightly round Dorothea put her mouth so close to her ear that she could speak without fear of being heard by anyone else, and said:

"This singer, dear senora, is the son of a gentleman of Aragon, lord of two villages, who lives opposite my father's house at Madrid; and though my father had curtains to the windows of his house in winter, and lattice-work in summer, in some way—I know not how—this gentleman, who was pursuing his studies, saw me, whether in church or elsewhere, I cannot tell, and, in fact, fell in love with me, and gave me to know it from the windows of his house, with so many signs and tears that I was forced to believe him, and even to love him, without knowing what it was he wanted of me. One of the signs he used to make me was to link one hand in the other, to show me he wished to marry me; and though I should have been glad if that could be, being alone and motherless I knew not whom to open my mind to, and so I left it as it was, showing him no favour, except when my father, and his too, were from home, to raise the curtain or the lattice a little and let him see me plainly, at which he would show such delight that he seemed as if he were going mad. Meanwhile the time for my father's departure arrived, which he became aware of, but not from me, for I had never been able to tell him of it. He fell sick, of grief I believe, and so the day we were going away I could not see him to take farewell of him, were it only with the eyes. But after we had been two days on the road, on entering the posada of a village a day's journey from this, I saw him at the inn door in the dress of a muleteer, and so well disguised, that if I did not carry his image graven on my heart it would have been impossible for me to recognise him. But I knew him, and I was surprised, and glad; he watched me, unsuspected by my father, from whom he always hides himself when he crosses my path on the road, or in the posadas where we halt; and, as I know what he is, and reflect that for love of me he makes this journey on foot in all this hardship, I am ready to die of sorrow; and where he sets foot there I set my eyes. I know not with what object he has come; or how he could have got away from his father, who loves him beyond measure, having no other heir, and because he deserves it, as you will perceive when you see him. And moreover, I can tell you, all that he sings is out of his own head; for I have heard them say he is a great scholar and poet; and what is more, every time I see him or hear him sing I tremble all over, and am terrified lest my father should recognise him and come to know of our loves. I have never spoken a word to him in my life; and for all that I love him so that I could not live without him. This, dear senora, is all I have to tell you about the musician whose voice has delighted you so much; and from it alone you might easily perceive he is no muleteer, but a lord of hearts and towns, as I told you already."

"Say no more, Dona Clara," said Dorothea at this, at the same time kissing her a thousand times over, "say no more, I tell you, but wait till day comes; when I trust in God to arrange this affair of yours so that it may have the happy ending such an innocent beginning deserves."

"Ah, senora," said Dona Clara, "what end can be hoped for when his father is of such lofty position, and so wealthy, that he would think I was not fit to be even a servant to his son, much less wife? And as to marrying without the knowledge of my father, I would not do it for all the world. I would not ask anything more than that this youth should go back and leave me; perhaps with not seeing him, and the long distance we shall have to travel, the pain I suffer now may become easier; though I daresay the remedy I propose will do me very little good. I don't know how the devil this has come about, or how this love I have for him got in; I such a young girl, and he such a mere boy; for I verily believe we are both of an age, and I am not sixteen yet; for I will be sixteen Michaelmas Day, next, my father says."

Dorothea could not help laughing to hear how like a child Dona Clara spoke. "Let us go to sleep now, senora," said she, "for the little of the night that I fancy is left to us: God will soon send us daylight, and we will set all to rights, or it will go hard with me."

With this they fell asleep, and deep silence reigned all through the inn. The only persons not asleep were the landlady's daughter and her servant Maritornes, who, knowing the weak point of

Don Quixote's humour, and that he was outside the inn mounting guard in armour and on horseback, resolved, the pair of them, to play some trick upon him, or at any rate to amuse themselves for a while by listening to his nonsense. As it so happened there was not a window in the whole inn that looked outwards except a hole in the wall of a straw-loft through which they used to throw out the straw. At this hole the two demi-damsels posted themselves, and observed Don Quixote on his horse, leaning on his pike and from time to time sending forth such deep and doleful sighs, that he seemed to pluck up his soul by the roots with each of them; and they could hear him, too, saying in a soft, tender, loving tone, "Oh my lady Dulcinea del Toboso, perfection of all beauty, summit and crown of discretion, treasure house of grace, depository of virtue, and finally, ideal of all that is good, honourable, and delectable in this world! What is thy grace doing now? Art thou, perchance, mindful of thy enslaved knight who of his own free will hath exposed himself to so great perils, and all to serve thee? Give me tidings of her, oh luminary of the three faces! Perhaps at this moment, envious of hers, thou art regarding her, either as she paces to and fro some gallery of her sumptuous palaces, or leans over some balcony, meditating how, whilst preserving her purity and greatness, she may mitigate the tortures this wretched heart of mine endures for her sake, what glory should recompense my sufferings, what repose my toil, and lastly what death my life, and what reward my services? And thou, oh sun, that art now doubtless harnessing thy steeds in haste to rise betimes and come forth to see my lady; when thou seest her I entreat of thee to salute her on my behalf: but have a care, when thou shalt see her and salute her, that thou kiss not her face; for I shall be more jealous of thee than thou wert of that light-footed ingrate that made thee sweat and run so on the plains of Thessaly, or on the banks of the Peneus (for I do not exactly recollect where it was thou didst run on that occasion) in thy jealousy and love."

Don Quixote had got so far in his pathetic speech when the landlady's daughter began to signal to him, saying, "Senor, come over here, please."

At these signals and voice Don Quixote turned his head and saw by the light of the moon, which then was in its full splendour, that some one was calling to him from the hole in the wall, which seemed to him to be a window, and what is more, with a gilt grating, as rich castles, such as he believed the inn to be, ought to have; and it immediately suggested itself to his imagination that, as on the former occasion, the fair damsel, the daughter of the lady of the castle, overcome by love for him, was once more endeavouring to win his affections; and with this idea, not to show himself discourteous, or ungrateful, he turned Rocinante's head and approached the hole, and as he perceived the two wenches he said:

"I pity you, beauteous lady, that you should have directed your thoughts of love to a quarter from whence it is impossible that such a return can be made to you as is due to your great merit and gentle birth, for which you must not blame this unhappy knight-errant whom love renders incapable of submission to any other than her whom, the first moment his eyes beheld her, he made absolute mistress of his soul. Forgive me, noble lady, and retire to your apartment, and do not, by any further declaration of your passion, compel me to show myself more ungrateful; and if, of the love you bear me, you should find that there is anything else in my power wherein I can gratify you, provided it be not love itself, demand it of me; for I swear to you by that sweet absent enemy of mine to grant it this instant, though it be that you require of me a lock of Medusa's hair, which was all snakes, or even the very beams of the sun shut up in a vial."

"My mistress wants nothing of that sort, sir knight," said Maritornes at this.

"What then, discreet dame, is it that your mistress wants?" replied Don Quixote.

"Only one of your fair hands," said Maritornes, "to enable her to vent over it the great passion which has brought her to this loophole, so much to the risk of her honour; for if the lord her father had heard her, the least slice he would cut off her would be her ear."

"I should like to see that tried," said Don Quixote; "but he had better beware of that, if he does not want to meet the most disastrous end that ever father in the world met for having laid hands on the tender limbs of a love-stricken daughter."

Maritornes felt sure that Don Quixote would present the hand she had asked, and making up her mind what to do, she got down from the hole and went into the stable, where she took the halter of Sancho Panza's ass, and in all haste returned to the hole, just as Don Quixote had planted himself standing on Rocinante's saddle in order to reach the grated window where he supposed the lovelorn damsel to be; and giving her his hand, he said, "Lady, take this hand, or rather this scourge of the evil-doers of the earth; take, I say, this hand which no other hand of woman has ever touched, not even hers who has complete possession of my entire body. I present it to you, not that you may kiss it, but that you may observe the contexture of the sinews, the close network of the muscles, the breadth and capacity of the veins, whence you may infer what must be the strength of the arm that has such a hand."

"That we shall see presently," said Maritornes, and making a running knot on the halter, she passed it over his wrist and coming down from the hole tied the other end very firmly to the bolt of the door of the straw-loft.

Don Quixote, feeling the roughness of the rope on his wrist, exclaimed, "Your grace seems to be grating rather than caressing my hand; treat it not so harshly, for it is not to blame for the offence my resolution has given you, nor is it just to wreak all your vengeance on so small a part; remember that one who loves so well should not revenge herself so cruelly."

But there was nobody now to listen to these words of Don Quixote's, for as soon as Maritornes had tied him she and the other made off, ready to die with laughing, leaving him fastened in such a way that it was impossible for him to release himself.

He was, as has been said, standing on Rocinante, with his arm passed through the hole and his wrist tied to the bolt of the door, and in mighty fear and dread of being left hanging by the arm if Rocinante were to stir one side or the other; so he did not dare to make the least movement, although from the patience and imperturbable disposition of Rocinante, he had good reason to expect that he would stand without budging for a whole century. Finding himself fast, then, and that the ladies had retired, he began to fancy that all this was done by enchantment, as on the former occasion when in that same castle that enchanted Moor of a carrier had belaboured him; and he cursed in his heart his own want of sense and judgment in venturing to enter the castle again, after having come off so badly the first time; it being a settled point with knights-errant that when they have tried an adventure, and have not succeeded in it, it is a sign that it is not reserved for them but for others, and that therefore they need not try it again. Nevertheless he pulled his arm to see if he could release himself, but it had been made so fast that all his efforts were in vain. It is true he pulled it gently lest Rocinante should move, but try as he might to seat himself in the saddle, he had nothing for it but to stand upright or pull his hand off. Then it was he wished for the sword of Amadis, against which no enchantment whatever had any power; then he cursed his ill fortune; then he magnified the loss the world would sustain by his absence while he remained there enchanted, for that he believed he was beyond all doubt; then he once more took to thinking of his beloved Dulcinea del Toboso; then he called to his worthy squire Sancho Panza, who, buried in sleep and stretched upon the pack-saddle of his ass, was oblivious, at that moment, of the mother that bore him; then he called upon the sages Lirgandeo and Alquife to come to his aid; then he invoked his good friend Urganda to succour him; and then, at last, morning found him in such a state of desperation and perplexity that he was bellowing like a bull, for he had no hope that day would bring any relief to his suffering, which he believed would last for ever, inasmuch as he was enchanted; and of this he was convinced by seeing that Rocinante never stirred, much or little, and he felt persuaded that he and his horse were to remain in this state, without eating or drinking or sleeping, until the malign influence of the stars was overpast, or until some other more sage enchanter should disenchant him.

But he was very much deceived in this conclusion, for daylight had hardly begun to appear when there came up to the inn four men on horseback, well equipped and accoutred, with firelocks across their saddle-bows. They called out and knocked loudly at the gate of the inn, which was still shut; on seeing which, Don Quixote, even there where he was, did not forget to act as sentinel, and said in a loud and imperious tone, "Knights, or squires, or whatever ye be, ye have no right to knock at the gates of this castle; for it is plain enough that they who are within are either asleep, or else are not in the habit of throwing open the fortress until the sun's rays are spread over the whole surface of the earth. Withdraw to a distance, and wait till it is broad daylight, and then we shall see whether it will be proper or not to open to you."

"What the devil fortress or castle is this," said one, "to make us stand on such ceremony? If you are the innkeeper bid them open to us; we are travellers who only want to feed our horses and go on, for we are in haste."

"Do you think, gentlemen, that I look like an innkeeper?" said Don Quixote.

"I don't know what you look like," replied the other; "but I know that you are talking nonsense when you call this inn a castle."

"A castle it is," returned Don Quixote, "nay, more, one of the best in this whole province, and it has within it people who have had the sceptre in the hand and the crown on the head."

"It would be better if it were the other way," said the traveller, "the sceptre on the head and the crown in the hand; but if so, may be there is within some company of players, with whom it is a common thing to have those crowns and sceptres you speak of; for in such a small inn as this, and where such silence is kept, I do not believe any people entitled to crowns and sceptres can have taken up their quarters."

"You know but little of the world," returned Don Quixote, "since you are ignorant of what commonly occurs in knight-errantry."

But the comrades of the spokesman, growing weary of the dialogue with Don Quixote, renewed their knocks with great vehemence, so much so that the host, and not only he but everybody in the inn, awoke, and he got up to ask who knocked. It happened at this moment that one of the horses of the four who were seeking admittance went to smell Rocinante, who melancholy, dejected, and with drooping ears stood motionless, supporting his sorely stretched master; and as he was, after all, flesh, though he looked as if he were made of wood, he could not help giving way and in return smelling the one who had come to offer him attentions. But he had hardly moved at all when Don Quixote lost his footing; and slipping off the saddle, he would have come to the ground, but for being suspended by the arm, which caused him such agony that he believed either his wrist would be cut through or his arm torn off; and he hung so near the ground that he could just touch it with his feet, which was all the worse for him; for, finding how little was wanted to enable him to plant his feet firmly, he struggled and stretched himself as much as he could to gain a footing; just like those undergoing the torture of the strappado, when they are fixed at "touch and no touch," who aggravate their own sufferings by their violent efforts to stretch themselves, deceived by the hope which makes them fancy that with a very little more they will reach the ground.

CHAPTER XLIV

IN WHICH ARE CONTINUED THE UNHEARD OF ADVENTURES OF THE INN

So loud, in fact, were the shouts of Don Quixote, that the landlord opening the gate of the inn in all haste, came out in dismay, and ran to see who was uttering such cries, and those who were outside joined him. Maritornes, who had been by this time roused up by the same outcry, suspecting what it was, ran to the loft and, without anyone seeing her, untied the halter by which Don Quixote was suspended, and down he came to the ground in the sight of the landlord and the travellers, who approaching asked him what was the matter with him that he shouted so. He without replying a word took the rope off his wrist, and rising to his feet leaped upon Rocinante, braced his buckler on his arm, put his lance in rest, and making a considerable circuit of the plain came back at a half-gallop exclaiming:

"Whoever shall say that I have been enchanted with just cause, provided my lady the Princess Micomicona grants me permission to do so, I give him the lie, challenge him and defy him to single combat."

The newly arrived travellers were amazed at the words of Don Quixote; but the landlord removed their surprise by telling them who he was, and not to mind him as he was out of his senses. They then asked the landlord if by any chance a youth of about fifteen years of age had come to that inn, one dressed like a muleteer, and of such and such an appearance, describing that of Dona Clara's lover. The landlord replied that there were so many people in the inn he had not noticed the person they were inquiring for; but one of them observing the coach in which the Judge had come, said, "He is here no doubt, for this is the coach he is following: let one of us stay at the gate, and the rest go in to look for him; or indeed it would be as well if one of us went round the inn, lest he should escape over the wall of the yard." "So be it," said another; and while two of them went in, one remained at the gate and the other made the circuit of the inn; observing all which, the landlord was unable to conjecture for what reason they were taking all these precautions, though he understood they were looking for the youth whose description they had given him.

It was by this time broad daylight; and for that reason, as well as in consequence of the noise Don Quixote had made, everybody was awake and up, but particularly Dona Clara and Dorothea; for they had been able to sleep but badly that night, the one from agitation at having her lover so near her, the other from curiosity to see him. Don Quixote, when he saw that not one of the four travellers took any notice of him or replied to his challenge, was furious and ready to die with indignation and wrath; and if he could have found in the ordinances of chivalry that it was lawful for a knight-errant to undertake or engage in another enterprise, when he had plighted his word and faith not to involve himself in any until he had made an end of the one to which he was pledged, he would have attacked the whole of them, and would have made them return an answer in spite of themselves. But considering that it would not become him, nor be right, to begin any new emprise until he had established Micomicona in her kingdom, he was constrained to hold his peace and wait quietly to see what would be the upshot of the proceedings of those same travellers; one of whom found the youth they were seeking lying asleep by the side of a muleteer, without a thought of anyone coming in search of him, much less finding him.

The man laid hold of him by the arm, saying, "It becomes you well indeed, Senor Don Luis, to be in the dress you wear, and well the bed in which I find you agrees with the luxury in which your mother reared you."

The youth rubbed his sleepy eyes and stared for a while at him who held him, but presently recognised him as one of his father's servants, at which he was so taken aback that for some time he could not find or utter a word; while the servant went on to say, "There is nothing for it now, Senor Don Luis, but to submit quietly and return home, unless it is your wish that my lord, your father, should take his departure for the other world, for nothing else can be the consequence of the grief he is in at your absence."

"But how did my father know that I had gone this road and in this dress?" said Don Luis.

"It was a student to whom you confided your intentions," answered the servant, "that disclosed them, touched with pity at the distress he saw your father suffer on missing you; he therefore despatched four of his servants in quest of you, and here we all are at your service, better pleased than you can imagine that we shall return so soon and be able to restore you to those eyes that so yearn for you."

"That shall be as I please, or as heaven orders," returned Don Luis.

"What can you please or heaven order," said the other, "except to agree to go back? Anything else is impossible."

All this conversation between the two was overheard by the muleteer at whose side Don Luis lay, and rising, he went to report what had taken place to Don Fernando, Cardenio, and the others, who had by this time dressed themselves; and told them how the man had addressed the youth as "Don," and what words had passed, and how he wanted him to return to his father, which the youth was unwilling to do. With this, and what they already knew of the rare voice that heaven had bestowed upon him, they all felt very anxious to know more particularly who he was, and even to help him if it was attempted to employ force against him; so they hastened to where he was still talking and arguing with his servant. Dorothea at this instant came out of her room, followed by Dona Clara all in a tremor; and calling Cardenio aside, she told him in a few words the story of the musician and Dona Clara, and he at the same time told her what had happened, how his father's servants had come in search of him; but in telling her so, he did not speak low enough but that Dona Clara heard what he said, at which she was so much agitated that had not Dorothea hastened to support her she would have fallen to the ground. Cardenio then bade Dorothea return to her room, as he would endeavour to make the whole matter right, and they did as he desired. All the four who had come in quest of Don Luis had now come into the inn and surrounded him, urging him to return and console his father at once and without a moment's delay. He replied that he could not do so on any account until he had concluded some business in which his life, honour, and heart were at stake. The servants pressed him, saying that most certainly they would not return without him, and that they would take him away whether he liked it or not.

"You shall not do that," replied Don Luis, "unless you take me dead; though however you take me, it will be without life."

By this time most of those in the inn had been attracted by the dispute, but particularly Cardenio, Don Fernando, his companions, the Judge, the curate, the barber, and Don Quixote; for he now considered there was no necessity for mounting guard over the castle any longer. Cardenio being already acquainted with the young man's story, asked the men who wanted to take him away, what object they had in seeking to carry off this youth against his will.

"Our object," said one of the four, "is to save the life of his father, who is in danger of losing it through this gentleman's disappearance."

Upon this Don Luis exclaimed, "There is no need to make my affairs public here; I am free, and I will return if I please; and if not, none of you shall compel me."

"Reason will compel your worship," said the man, "and if it has no power over you, it has power over us, to make us do what we came for, and what it is our duty to do."

"Let us hear what the whole affair is about," said the Judge at this; but the man, who knew him as a neighbour of theirs, replied, "Do you not know this gentleman, Senor Judge? He is the son of your neighbour, who has run away from his father's house in a dress so unbecoming his rank, as your worship may perceive."

The judge on this looked at him more carefully and recognised him, and embracing him said, "What folly is this, Senor Don Luis, or what can have been the cause that could have induced you to come here in this way, and in this dress, which so ill becomes your condition?"

Tears came into the eyes of the young man, and he was unable to utter a word in reply to the Judge, who told the four servants not to be uneasy, for all would be satisfactorily settled; and then taking Don Luis by the hand, he drew him aside and asked the reason of his having come there.

But while he was questioning him they heard a loud outcry at the gate of the inn, the cause of which was that two of the guests who had passed the night there, seeing everybody busy about finding out what it was the four men wanted, had conceived the idea of going off without paying what they owed; but the landlord, who minded his own affairs more than other people's, caught them going out of the gate and demanded his reckoning, abusing them for their dishonesty with such language that he drove them to reply with their fists, and so they began to lay on him in such a style that the poor man was forced to cry out, and call for help. The landlady and her daughter could see no one more free to give aid than Don Quixote, and to him the daughter said, "Sir knight, by the virtue God has given you, help my poor father, for two wicked men are beating him to a mummy."

To which Don Quixote very deliberately and phlegmatically replied, "Fair damsel, at the present moment your request is inopportune, for I am debarred from involving myself in any adventure until I have brought to a happy conclusion one to which my word has pledged me; but that which I can do for you is what I will now mention: run and tell your father to stand his ground as well as he can in this battle, and on no account to allow himself to be vanquished, while I go and request permission of the Princess Micomicona to enable me to succour him in his distress; and if she grants it, rest assured I will relieve him from it."

"Sinner that I am," exclaimed Maritornes, who stood by; "before you have got your permission my master will be in the other world."

"Give me leave, senora, to obtain the permission I speak of," returned Don Quixote; "and if I get it, it will matter very little if he is in the other world; for I will rescue him thence in spite of all the same world can do; or at any rate I will give you such a revenge over those who shall have sent him there that you will be more than moderately satisfied;" and without saying anything more he went and knelt before Dorothea, requesting her Highness in knightly and errant phrase to be pleased to grant him permission to aid and succour the castellan of that castle, who now stood in grievous jeopardy. The princess granted it graciously, and he at once, bracing his buckler on his arm and drawing his sword, hastened to the inn-gate, where the two guests were still handling the landlord roughly; but as soon as he reached the spot he stopped short and stood still, though Maritornes and the landlady asked him why he hesitated to help their master and husband.

"I hesitate," said Don Quixote, "because it is not lawful for me to draw sword against persons of squirely condition; but call my squire Sancho to me; for this defence and vengeance are his affair and business."

Thus matters stood at the inn-gate, where there was a very lively exchange of fisticuffs and punches, to the sore damage of the landlord and to the wrath of Maritornes, the landlady, and her daughter, who were furious when they saw the pusillanimity of Don Quixote, and the hard treatment their master, husband and father was undergoing. But let us leave him there; for he will surely find some one to help him, and if not, let him suffer and hold his tongue who attempts more than his strength allows him to do; and let us go back fifty paces to see what Don Luis said in reply to the Judge whom we left questioning him privately as to his reasons for coming on foot and so meanly dressed.

To which the youth, pressing his hand in a way that showed his heart was troubled by some great sorrow, and shedding a flood of tears, made answer:

"Senor, I have no more to tell you than that from the moment when, through heaven's will and our being near neighbours, I first saw Dona Clara, your daughter and my lady, from that instant I made her the mistress of my will, and if yours, my true lord and father, offers no impediment, this very day she shall become my wife. For her I left my father's house, and for her I assumed this disguise, to follow her whithersoever she may go, as the arrow seeks its mark or the sailor the pole-star. She knows nothing more of my passion than what she may have learned from having sometimes seen from a distance that my eyes were filled with tears. You know already, senor, the wealth and noble birth of my parents, and that I am their sole heir; if this be a sufficient inducement for you to venture to make me completely happy, accept me at once as your son; for if my father, influenced by other objects of his own, should disapprove of this happiness I have sought for myself, time has more power to alter and change things, than human will."

With this the love-smitten youth was silent, while the Judge, after hearing him, was astonished, perplexed, and surprised, as well at the manner and intelligence with which Don Luis had confessed the secret of his heart, as at the position in which he found himself, not knowing what course to take in a matter so sudden and unexpected. All the answer, therefore, he gave him was to bid him to make his mind easy for the present, and arrange with his servants not to take him back that day, so that there might be time to consider what was best for all parties. Don Luis kissed his hands by force, nay, bathed them with his tears, in a way that would have touched a heart of marble, not to say that of the Judge, who, as a shrewd man, had already perceived how advantageous the marriage would be to his daughter; though, were it possible, he would have preferred that it should be brought about with the consent of the father of Don Luis, who he knew looked for a title for his son.

The guests had by this time made peace with the landlord, for, by persuasion and Don Quixote's fair words more than by threats, they had paid him what he demanded, and the servants of Don Luis were waiting for the end of the conversation with the Judge and their master's decision, when the devil, who never sleeps, contrived that the barber, from whom Don Quixote had taken Mambrino's helmet, and Sancho Panza the trappings of his ass in exchange for those of his own, should at this instant enter the inn; which said barber, as he led his ass to the stable, observed Sancho Panza engaged in repairing something or other belonging to the pack-saddle; and the moment he saw it he knew it, and made bold to attack Sancho, exclaiming, "Ho, sir thief, I have caught you! hand over my basin and my pack-saddle, and all my trappings that you robbed me of."

Sancho, finding himself so unexpectedly assailed, and hearing the abuse poured upon him, seized the pack-saddle with one hand, and with the other gave the barber a cuff that bathed his teeth in blood. The barber, however, was not so ready to relinquish the prize he had made in the pack-saddle; on the contrary, he raised such an outcry that everyone in the inn came running to know what the noise and quarrel meant. "Here, in the name of the king and justice!" he cried, "this thief and highwayman wants to kill me for trying to recover my property."

"You lie," said Sancho, "I am no highwayman; it was in fair war my master Don Quixote won these spoils."

Don Quixote was standing by at the time, highly pleased to see his squire's stoutness, both offensive and defensive, and from that time forth he reckoned him a man of mettle, and in his heart resolved to dub him a knight on the first opportunity that presented itself, feeling sure that the order of chivalry would be fittingly bestowed upon him.

In the course of the altercation, among other things the barber said, "Gentlemen, this pack-saddle is mine as surely as I owe God a death, and I know it as well as if I had given birth to it, and here is my ass in the stable who will not let me lie; only try it, and if it does not fit him like a glove, call me a rascal; and what is more, the same day I was robbed of this, they robbed me likewise of a new brass basin, never yet handselled, that would fetch a crown any day."

At this Don Quixote could not keep himself from answering; and interposing between the two, and separating them, he placed the pack-saddle on the ground, to lie there in sight until the truth was established, and said, "Your worships may perceive clearly and plainly the error under which this worthy squire lies when he calls a basin which was, is, and shall be the helmet of Mambrino which I won from him in fair war, and made myself master of by legitimate and lawful possession. With the pack-saddle I do not concern myself; but I may tell you on that head that my squire Sancho asked my permission to strip off the caparison of this vanquished poltroon's steed, and with it adorn his own; I allowed him, and he took it; and as to its having been changed from a caparison into a pack-saddle, I can give no explanation except the usual one, that such transformations will take place in adventures of chivalry. To confirm all which, run, Sancho my son, and fetch hither the helmet which this good fellow calls a basin."

"Egad, master," said Sancho, "if we have no other proof of our case than what your worship puts forward, Mambrino's helmet is just as much a basin as this good fellow's caparison is a pack-saddle."

"Do as I bid thee," said Don Quixote; "it cannot be that everything in this castle goes by enchantment."

Sancho hastened to where the basin was, and brought it back with him, and when Don Quixote saw it, he took hold of it and said:

"Your worships may see with what a face this squire can assert that this is a basin and not the helmet I told you of; and I swear by the order of chivalry I profess, that this helmet is the identical one I took from him, without anything added to or taken from it."

"There is no doubt of that," said Sancho, "for from the time my master won it until now he has only fought one battle in it, when he let loose those unlucky men in chains; and if had not been for this basin-helmet he would not have come off over well that time, for there was plenty of stone-throwing in that affair."

CHAPTER XLV

IN WHICH THE DOUBTFUL QUESTION OF MAMBRINO'S HELMET AND THE PACK-SADDLE IS FINALLY SETTLED, WITH OTHER ADVENTURES THAT OCCURRED IN TRUTH AND EARNEST

"What do you think now, gentlemen," said the barber, "of what these gentles say, when they want to make out that this is a helmet?"

"And whoever says the contrary," said Don Quixote, "I will let him know he lies if he is a knight, and if he is a squire that he lies again a thousand times."

Our own barber, who was present at all this, and understood Don Quixote's humour so thoroughly, took it into his head to back up his delusion and carry on the joke for the general amusement; so addressing the other barber he said:

"Senor barber, or whatever you are, you must know that I belong to your profession too, and have had a licence to practise for more than twenty years, and I know the implements of the barber craft, every one of them, perfectly well; and I was likewise a soldier for some time in the days of my youth, and I know also what a helmet is, and a morion, and a headpiece with a visor, and other things pertaining to soldiering, I meant to say to soldiers' arms; and I say-saving better opinions and always with submission to sounder judgments—that this piece we have now before us, which this worthy gentleman has in his hands, not only is no barber's basin, but is as far from being one as white is from black, and truth from falsehood; I say, moreover, that this, although it is a helmet, is not a complete helmet."

"Certainly not," said Don Quixote, "for half of it is wanting, that is to say the beaver."

"It is quite true," said the curate, who saw the object of his friend the barber; and Cardenio, Don Fernando and his companions agreed with him, and even the Judge, if his thoughts had not been so full of Don Luis's affair, would have helped to carry on the joke; but he was so taken up with the serious matters he had on his mind that he paid little or no attention to these facetious proceedings.

"God bless me!" exclaimed their butt the barber at this; "is it possible that such an honourable company can say that this is not a basin but a helmet? Why, this is a thing that would astonish a whole university, however wise it might be! That will do; if this basin is a helmet, why, then the pack-saddle must be a horse's caparison, as this gentleman has said."

"To me it looks like a pack-saddle," said Don Quixote; "but I have already said that with that question I do not concern myself."

"As to whether it be pack-saddle or caparison," said the curate, "it is only for Senor Don Quixote to say; for in these matters of chivalry all these gentlemen and I bow to his authority."

"By God, gentlemen," said Don Quixote, "so many strange things have happened to me in this castle on the two occasions on which I have sojourned in it, that I will not venture to assert anything positively in reply to any question touching anything it contains; for it is my belief that everything that goes on within it goes by enchantment. The first time, an enchanted Moor that there is in it gave me sore trouble, nor did Sancho fare well among certain followers of his; and last night I was kept hanging by this arm for nearly two hours, without knowing how or why I came by such a mishap. So that now, for me to come forward to give an opinion in such a puzzling matter, would be to risk a rash decision. As regards the assertion that this is a basin and not a helmet I have already given an answer; but as to the question whether this is a pack-saddle or a caparison I will not venture to give a positive opinion, but will leave it to your worships' better judgment. Perhaps as you are not dubbed knights like myself, the enchantments of this place have nothing to do with you, and your faculties are unfettered, and you can see things in this castle as they really and truly are, and not as they appear to me."

"There can be no question," said Don Fernando on this, "but that Senor Don Quixote has spoken very wisely, and that with us rests the decision of this matter; and that we may have surer ground to go on, I will take the votes of the gentlemen in secret, and declare the result clearly and fully."

To those who were in the secret of Don Quixote's humour all this afforded great amusement; but to those who knew nothing about it, it seemed the greatest nonsense in the world, in particular to the four servants of Don Luis, as well as to Don Luis himself, and to three other travellers who had by chance come to the inn, and had the appearance of officers of the Holy Brotherhood, as indeed they were; but the one who above all was at his wits' end, was the barber whose basin, there before his very eyes, had been turned into Mambrino's helmet, and whose pack-saddle he had no doubt whatever was about to become a rich caparison for a horse.

All laughed to see Don Fernando going from one to another collecting the votes, and whispering to them to give him their private opinion whether the treasure over which there had been so much fighting was a pack-saddle or a caparison; but after he had taken the votes of those who knew Don Quixote, he said aloud, "The fact is, my good fellow, that I am tired collecting such a number of opinions, for I find that there is not one of whom I ask what I desire to know, who does not tell me that it is absurd to say that this is the pack-saddle of an ass, and not the caparison of a horse, nay, of a thoroughbred horse; so you must submit, for, in spite of you and your ass, this is a caparison and no pack-saddle, and you have stated and proved your case very badly."

"May I never share heaven," said the poor barber, "if your worships are not all mistaken; and may my soul appear before God as that appears to me a pack-saddle and not a caparison; but, 'laws go,'-I say no more; and indeed I am not drunk, for I am fasting, except it be from sin."

The simple talk of the barber did not afford less amusement than the absurdities of Don Quixote, who now observed:

"There is no more to be done now than for each to take what belongs to him, and to whom God has given it, may St. Peter add his blessing."

But said one of the four servants, "Unless, indeed, this is a deliberate joke, I cannot bring myself to believe that men so intelligent as those present are, or seem to be, can venture to declare and assert that this is not a basin, and that not a pack-saddle; but as I perceive that they do assert and declare it, I can only come to the conclusion that there is some mystery in this persistence in what is so opposed to the evidence of experience and truth itself; for I swear by"—and here he rapped out a round oath-"all the people in the world will not make me believe that this is not a barber's basin and that a jackass's pack-saddle."

"It might easily be a she-ass's," observed the curate.

"It is all the same," said the servant; "that is not the point; but whether it is or is not a pack-saddle, as your worships say."

On hearing this one of the newly arrived officers of the Brotherhood, who had been listening to the dispute and controversy, unable to restrain his anger and impatience, exclaimed, "It is a pack-saddle as sure as my father is my father, and whoever has said or will say anything else must be drunk."

"You lie like a rascally clown," returned Don Quixote; and lifting his pike, which he had never let out of his hand, he delivered such a blow at his head that, had not the officer dodged it, it would have stretched him at full length. The pike was shivered in pieces against the ground, and the rest of the officers, seeing their comrade assaulted, raised a shout, calling for help for the Holy Brotherhood. The landlord, who was of the fraternity, ran at once to fetch his staff of office and his sword, and ranged himself on the side of his comrades; the servants of Don Luis clustered round him, lest he should escape from them in the confusion; the barber, seeing the house turned upside down, once more laid hold of his pack-saddle and Sancho did the same; Don Quixote drew his sword and charged the officers; Don Luis cried out to his servants to leave him alone and go and help Don Quixote, and Cardenio and Don Fernando, who were supporting him; the curate was shouting at the top of his voice, the landlady was screaming, her daughter was wailing, Maritornes was weeping, Dorothea was aghast, Luscinda terror-stricken, and Dona Clara in a faint. The barber cudgelled Sancho, and Sancho pommelled the barber; Don Luis gave one of his servants, who ventured to catch him by the arm to keep him from escaping, a cuff that bathed his teeth in blood; the Judge took his part; Don Fernando had got one of the officers down and was belabouring him heartily; the landlord raised his voice again calling for help for the Holy Brotherhood; so that the whole inn was nothing but cries, shouts, shrieks, confusion, terror, dismay, mishaps, sword-cuts, fisticuffs, cudgellings, kicks, and bloodshed; and in the midst of all this chaos, complication, and general entanglement, Don Quixote took it into his head that he had been plunged into the thick of the discord of Agramante's camp; and, in a voice that shook the inn like thunder, he cried out:

"Hold all, let all sheathe their swords, let all be calm and attend to me as they value their lives!"

All paused at his mighty voice, and he went on to say, "Did I not tell you, sirs, that this castle was enchanted, and that a legion or so of devils dwelt in it? In proof whereof I call upon you to behold with your own eyes how the discord of Agramante's camp has come hither, and been transferred into the midst of us. See how they fight, there for the sword, here for the horse, on that side for the eagle, on this for the helmet; we are all fighting, and all at cross purposes. Come then, you, Senor Judge, and you, senor curate; let the one represent King Agramante and the other King Sobrino, and make peace among us; for by God Almighty it is a sorry business that so many persons of quality as we are should slay one another for such trifling cause." The officers, who did not understand Don Quixote's mode of speaking, and found themselves roughly handled by Don Fernando, Cardenio, and their companions, were not to be appeased; the barber was, however, for both his beard and his pack-saddle were the worse for the struggle; Sancho like a good servant obeyed the slightest word of his master; while the four servants of Don Luis kept quiet when they saw how little they gained by not being so. The landlord alone insisted upon it that they must punish the insolence of this madman, who at every turn raised a disturbance in the inn; but at length the uproar was stilled for the present; the pack-saddle remained a caparison till the day of judgment, and the basin a helmet and the inn a castle in Don Quixote's imagination.

All having been now pacified and made friends by the persuasion of the Judge and the curate, the servants of Don Luis began again to urge him to return with them at once; and while he was discussing the matter with them, the Judge took counsel with Don Fernando, Cardenio, and the curate as to what he ought to do in the case, telling them how it stood, and what Don Luis had said to him. It was agreed at length that Don Fernando should tell the servants of Don Luis who he was, and that it was his desire that Don Luis should accompany him to Andalusia, where he would receive from the marquis his brother the welcome his quality entitled him to; for, otherwise, it was easy to see from the determination of Don Luis that he would not return to his father at present, though they tore him to pieces. On learning the rank of Don Fernando and the resolution of Don Luis the four then settled it between themselves that three of them should return to tell his father how matters stood, and that the other should remain to wait upon Don Luis, and not leave him until they came back for him, or his father's orders were known. Thus by the authority of Agramante and the wisdom of King Sobrino all this complication of disputes was arranged; but the enemy of concord and hater of peace, feeling himself slighted and made a fool of, and seeing how little he had gained after having involved them all in such an elaborate entanglement, resolved to try his hand once more by stirring up fresh quarrels and disturbances.

It came about in this wise: the officers were pacified on learning the rank of those with whom they had been engaged, and withdrew from the contest, considering that whatever the result might be they were likely to get the worst of the battle; but one of them, the one who had been thrashed and kicked by Don Fernando, recollected that among some warrants he carried for the arrest of certain delinquents, he had one against Don Quixote, whom the

Holy Brotherhood had ordered to be arrested for setting the galley slaves free, as Sancho had, with very good reason, apprehended. Suspecting how it was, then, he wished to satisfy himself as to whether Don Quixote's features corresponded; and taking a parchment out of his bosom he lit upon what he was in search of, and setting himself to read it deliberately, for he was not a quick reader, as he made out each word he fixed his eyes on Don Quixote, and went on comparing the description in the warrant with his face, and discovered that beyond all doubt he was the person described in it. As soon as he had satisfied himself, folding up the parchment, he took the warrant in his left hand and with his right seized Don Quixote by the collar so tightly that he did not allow him to breathe, and shouted aloud, "Help for the Holy Brotherhood! and that you may see I demand it in earnest, read this warrant which says this highwayman is to be arrested."

The curate took the warrant and saw that what the officer said was true, and that it agreed with Don Quixote's appearance, who, on his part, when he found himself roughly handled by this rascally clown, worked up to the highest pitch of wrath, and all his joints cracking with rage, with both hands seized the officer by the throat with all his might, so that had he not been helped by his comrades he would have yielded up his life ere Don Quixote released his hold. The landlord, who had perforce to support his brother officers, ran at once to aid them. The landlady, when she saw her husband engaged in a fresh quarrel, lifted up her voice afresh, and its note was immediately caught up by Maritornes and her daughter, calling upon heaven and all present for help; and Sancho, seeing what was going on, exclaimed, "By the Lord, it is quite true what my master says about the enchantments of this castle, for it is impossible to live an hour in peace in it!"

Don Fernando parted the officer and Don Quixote, and to their mutual contentment made them relax the grip by which they held, the one the coat collar, the other the throat of his adversary; for all this, however, the officers did not cease to demand their prisoner and call on them to help, and deliver him over bound into their power, as was required for the service of the King and of the Holy Brotherhood, on whose behalf they again demanded aid and assistance to effect the capture of this robber and footpad of the highways.

Don Quixote smiled when he heard these words, and said very calmly, "Come now, base, ill-born brood; call ye it highway robbery to give freedom to those in bondage, to release the captives, to succour the miserable, to raise up the fallen, to relieve the needy?

Infamous beings, who by your vile grovelling intellects deserve that heaven should not make known to you the virtue that lies in knight-errantry, or show you the sin and ignorance in which ye lie when ye refuse to respect the shadow, not to say the presence, of any knight-errant! Come now; band, not of officers, but of thieves; footpads with the licence of the Holy Brotherhood; tell me who was the ignoramus who signed a warrant of arrest against such a knight as I am? Who was he that did not know that knights-errant are independent of all jurisdictions, that their law is their sword, their charter their prowess, and their edicts their will? Who, I say again, was the fool that knows not that there are no letters patent of nobility that confer such privileges or exemptions as a knight-errant acquires the day he is dubbed a knight, and devotes himself to the arduous calling of chivalry? What knight-errant ever paid poll-tax, duty, queen's pin-money, king's dues, toll or ferry? What tailor ever took payment of him for making his clothes? What castellan that received him in his castle ever made him pay his shot? What king did not seat him at his table? What damsel was not enamoured of him and did not yield herself up wholly to his will and pleasure? And, lastly, what knight-errant has there been, is there, or will there ever be in the world, not bold enough to give, single-handed, four hundred cudgellings to four hundred officers of the Holy Brotherhood if they come in his way?"

CHAPTER XLVI

OF THE END OF THE NOTABLE ADVENTURE OF THE OFFICERS OF THE HOLY BROTHERHOOD; AND OF THE GREAT FEROCITY OF OUR WORTHY KNIGHT, DON QUIXOTE

While Don Quixote was talking in this strain, the curate was endeavouring to persuade the officers that he was out of his senses, as they might perceive by his deeds and his words, and that they need not press the matter any further, for even if they arrested him and carried him off, they would have to release him by-and-by as a madman; to which the holder of the warrant replied that he had nothing to do with inquiring into Don Quixote's madness, but only to execute his superior's orders, and that once taken they might let him go three hundred times if they liked.

"For all that," said the curate, "you must not take him away this time, nor will he, it is my opinion, let himself be taken away."

In short, the curate used such arguments, and Don Quixote did such mad things, that the officers would have been more mad than he was if they had not perceived his want of wits, and so they thought it best to allow themselves to be pacified, and even to act as peacemakers between the barber and Sancho Panza, who still continued their altercation with much bitterness. In the end they, as officers of justice, settled the question by arbitration in such a manner that both sides were, if not perfectly contented, at least to some extent satisfied; for they changed the pack-saddles, but not the girths or head-stalls; and as to Mambrino's helmet, the curate, under the rose and without Don Quixote's knowing it, paid eight reals for the basin, and the barber executed a full receipt and engagement to make no further demand then or thenceforth for evermore, amen. These two disputes, which were the most important and gravest, being settled, it only remained for the servants of Don Luis to consent that three of them should return while one was left to accompany him whither Don Fernando desired to take him; and good luck and better fortune, having already begun to solve difficulties and remove obstructions in favour of the lovers and warriors of the inn, were pleased to persevere and bring everything to a happy issue; for the servants agreed to do as Don Luis wished; which gave Dona Clara such happiness that no one could have looked into her face just then without seeing the joy of her heart. Zoraida, though she did not fully comprehend all she saw, was grave or gay without knowing why, as she watched and studied the various countenances, but particularly her Spaniard's, whom she followed with her eyes and clung to with her soul. The gift and compensation which the curate gave the barber had not escaped the landlord's notice, and he demanded Don Quixote's reckoning, together with the amount of the damage to his wine-skins, and the loss of his wine, swearing that neither Rocinante nor Sancho's ass should leave the inn until he had been paid to the very last farthing. The curate settled all amicably, and Don Fernando paid; though the Judge had also very readily offered to pay the score; and all became so peaceful and quiet that the inn no longer reminded one of the discord of Agramante's camp, as Don Quixote said, but of the peace and tranquillity of the days of Octavianus: for all which it was the universal opinion that their thanks were due to the great zeal and eloquence of the curate, and to the unexampled generosity of Don Fernando.

Finding himself now clear and quit of all quarrels, his squire's as well as his own, Don Quixote considered that it would be advisable to continue the journey he had begun, and bring to a close that great adventure for which he had been called and chosen; and with this high resolve he went and knelt before Dorothea, who, however, would not allow him to utter a word until he had risen; so to obey her he rose, and said, "It is a common proverb, fair lady, that 'diligence is the mother of good fortune,' and experience has often shown in important affairs that the earnestness of the negotiator brings the doubtful case to a successful termination; but in nothing does this truth show itself more plainly than in war, where quickness and activity forestall the devices of the enemy, and win the victory before the foe has time to defend himself. All this I say, exalted and esteemed lady, because it seems to me that for us to remain any longer in this castle now is useless, and may be injurious to us in a way that we shall find out some day; for who knows but that your enemy the giant may have learned by means of secret and diligent spies that I am going to destroy him, and if the opportunity be given him he may seize it to fortify himself in some impregnable castle or stronghold, against which all my efforts and the might of my indefatigable arm may avail but little? Therefore, lady, let us, as I say, forestall his schemes by our activity, and let us depart at once in quest of fair fortune; for your highness is only kept from enjoying it as fully as you could desire by my delay in encountering your adversary."

Don Quixote held his peace and said no more, calmly awaiting the reply of the beauteous princess, who, with commanding dignity and in a style adapted to Don Quixote's own, replied to him in these words, "I give you thanks, sir knight, for the eagerness you, like a good knight to whom it is a natural obligation to succour the orphan and the needy, display to afford me aid in my sore trouble; and heaven grant that your wishes and mine may be realised, so that you may see that there are women in this world capable of gratitude; as to my departure, let it be forthwith, for I have no will but yours; dispose of me entirely in accordance with your good pleasure; for she who has once entrusted to you the defence of her person, and placed in your hands the recovery of her dominions, must not think of offering opposition to that which your wisdom may ordain."

"On, then, in God's name," said Don Quixote; "for, when a lady humbles herself to me, I will not lose the opportunity of raising her up and placing her on the throne of her ancestors. Let us depart at once, for the common saying that in delay there is danger, lends spurs to my eagerness to take the road; and as neither heaven has created nor hell seen any that can daunt or intimidate me, saddle Rocinante, Sancho, and get ready thy ass and the queen's palfrey, and let us take leave of the castellan and these gentlemen, and go hence this very instant."

Sancho, who was standing by all the time, said, shaking his head, "Ah! master, master, there is more mischief in the village than one hears of, begging all good bodies' pardon."

"What mischief can there be in any village, or in all the cities of the world, you booby, that can hurt my reputation?" said Don Quixote.

"If your worship is angry," replied Sancho, "I will hold my tongue and leave unsaid what as a good squire I am bound to say, and what a good servant should tell his master."

"Say what thou wilt," returned Don Quixote, "provided thy words be not meant to work upon my fears; for thou, if thou fearest, art behaving like thyself; but I like myself, in not fearing."

"It is nothing of the sort, as I am a sinner before God," said Sancho, "but that I take it to be sure and certain that this lady, who calls herself queen of the great kingdom of Micomicon, is no more so than my mother; for, if she was what she says, she would not go rubbing noses with one that is here every instant and behind every door."

Dorothea turned red at Sancho's words, for the truth was that her husband Don Fernando had now and then, when the others were not looking, gathered from her lips some of the reward his love had earned, and Sancho seeing this had considered that such freedom was more like a courtesan than a queen of a great kingdom; she, however, being unable or not caring to answer him, allowed him to proceed, and he continued, "This I say, senor, because, if after we have travelled roads and highways, and passed bad nights and worse days, one who is now enjoying himself in this inn is to reap the fruit of our labours, there is no need for me to be in a hurry to saddle Rocinante, put the pad on the ass, or get ready the palfrey; for it will be better for us to stay quiet, and let every jade mind her spinning, and let us go to dinner."

Good God, what was the indignation of Don Quixote when he heard the audacious words of his squire! So great was it, that in a voice inarticulate with rage, with a stammering tongue, and eyes that flashed living fire, he exclaimed, "Rascally clown, boorish, insolent, and ignorant, ill-spoken, foul-mouthed, impudent back-biter and slanderer! Hast thou dared to utter such words in my presence and in that of these illustrious ladies? Hast thou dared to harbour such gross and shameless thoughts in thy muddled imagination? Begone from my presence, thou born monster, storehouse of lies, hoard of untruths, garner of knaveries, inventor of scandals, publisher of absurdities, enemy of the respect due to royal personages! Begone, show thyself no more before me under pain of my wrath;" and so saying he knitted his brows, puffed out his cheeks, gazed around him, and stamped on the ground violently with his right foot, showing in every way the rage that was pent up in his heart; and at his words and furious gestures Sancho was so scared and terrified that he would have been glad if the earth had opened that instant and swallowed him, and his only thought was to turn round and make his escape from the angry presence of his master.

But the ready-witted Dorothea, who by this time so well understood Don Quixote's humour, said, to mollify his wrath, "Be not irritated at the absurdities your good squire has uttered, Sir Knight of the Rueful Countenance, for perhaps he did not utter them without cause, and from his good sense and Christian conscience it is not likely that he would bear false witness against anyone. We may therefore believe, without any hesitation, that since, as you say, sir knight, everything in this castle goes and is brought about by means of enchantment, Sancho, I say, may possibly have seen, through this diabolical medium, what he says he saw so much to the detriment of my modesty."

"I swear by God Omnipotent," exclaimed Don Quixote at this, "your highness has hit the point; and that some vile illusion must have come before this sinner of a Sancho, that made him see what it would have been impossible to see by any other means than enchantments; for I know well enough, from the poor fellow's goodness and harmlessness, that he is incapable of bearing false witness against anybody."

"True, no doubt," said Don Fernando, "for which reason, Senor Don Quixote, you ought to forgive him and restore him to the bosom of your favour, sicut erat in principio, before illusions of this sort had taken away his senses."

Don Quixote said he was ready to pardon him, and the curate went for Sancho, who came in very humbly, and falling on his knees begged for the hand of his master, who having presented it to him and allowed him to kiss it, gave him his blessing and said, "Now, Sancho my son, thou wilt be convinced of the truth of what I have many a time told thee, that everything in this castle is done by means of enchantment."

"So it is, I believe," said Sancho, "except the affair of the blanket, which came to pass in reality by ordinary means."

"Believe it not," said Don Quixote, "for had it been so, I would have avenged thee that instant, or even now; but neither then nor now could I, nor have I seen anyone upon whom to avenge thy wrong."

They were all eager to know what the affair of the blanket was, and the landlord gave them a minute account of Sancho's flights, at which they laughed not a little, and at which Sancho would have been no less out of countenance had not his master once more assured him it was all enchantment. For all that his simplicity never reached so high a pitch that he could persuade himself it was not the plain and simple truth, without any deception whatever about it, that he had been blanketed by beings of flesh and blood, and not by visionary and imaginary phantoms, as his master believed and protested.

The illustrious company had now been two days in the inn; and as it seemed to them time to depart, they devised a plan so that, without giving Dorothea and Don Fernando the trouble of going back with Don Quixote to his village under pretence of restoring Queen Micomicona, the curate and the barber might carry him away with them as they proposed, and the curate be able to take his madness in hand at home; and in pursuance of their plan they arranged with the owner of an oxcart who happened to be passing that way to carry him after this fashion. They constructed a kind of cage with wooden bars, large enough to hold Don Quixote comfortably; and then Don Fernando and his companions, the servants of Don Luis, and the officers of the Brotherhood, together with the landlord, by the directions and advice of the curate, covered their faces and disguised themselves, some in one way, some in another, so as to appear to Don Quixote quite different from the persons he had seen in the castle. This done, in profound silence they entered the room where he was asleep, taking his rest after the past frays, and advancing to where he was sleeping tranquilly, not dreaming of anything of the kind happening, they seized him firmly and bound him fast hand and foot, so that, when he awoke startled, he was unable to move, and could only marvel and wonder at the strange figures he saw before him; upon which he at once gave way to the idea which his crazed fancy invariably conjured up before him, and took it into his head that all these shapes were phantoms of the enchanted castle, and that he himself was unquestionably enchanted as he could neither move nor help himself; precisely what the curate, the concoctor of the scheme, expected would happen. Of all that were there Sancho was the only one who was at once in his senses and in his own proper character, and he, though he was within very little of sharing his master's infirmity, did not fail to perceive who all these disguised figures were; but he did not dare to open his lips until he saw what came of this assault and capture of his master; nor did the latter utter a word, waiting to the upshot of his mishap; which was that bringing in the cage, they shut him up in it and nailed the bars so firmly that they could not be easily burst open.

They then took him on their shoulders, and as they passed out of the room an awful voice—as much so as the barber, not he of the pack-saddle but the other, was able to make it—was heard to say, "O Knight of the Rueful Countenance, let not this captivity in which thou art placed afflict thee, for this must needs be, for the more speedy accomplishment of the adventure in which thy great heart has engaged thee; the which shall be accomplished when the raging Manchegan lion and the white Tobosan dove shall be linked together, having first humbled their haughty necks to the gentle yoke of matrimony. And from this marvellous union shall come forth to the light of the world brave whelps that shall rival the ravening claws of their valiant father; and this shall come to pass ere the pursuer of the flying nymph shall in his swift natural course have twice visited the starry signs. And thou, O most noble and obedient squire that ever bore sword at side, beard on face, or nose to smell with, be not dismayed or grieved to see the flower of knight-errantry carried away thus before thy very eyes; for soon, if it so please the Framer of the universe, thou shalt see thyself exalted to such a height that thou shalt not know thyself, and the promises which thy good master has made thee shall not prove false; and I assure thee, on the authority of the sage Mentironiana, that thy wages shall be paid thee, as thou shalt see in due season. Follow then the footsteps of the valiant enchanted knight, for it is expedient that thou shouldst go to the destination assigned to both of you; and as it is not permitted to me to say more, God be with thee; for I return to that place I wot of;" and as he brought the prophecy to a close he raised his voice to a high pitch, and then lowered it to such a soft tone, that even those who knew it was all a joke were almost inclined to take what they heard seriously.

Don Quixote was comforted by the prophecy he heard, for he at once comprehended its meaning perfectly, and perceived it was promised to him that he should see himself united in holy and lawful matrimony with his beloved Dulcinea del Toboso, from whose blessed womb should proceed the whelps, his sons, to the eternal glory of La Mancha; and being thoroughly and firmly persuaded of this, he lifted up his voice, and with a deep sigh exclaimed, "Oh thou, whoever thou art, who hast foretold me so much good, I implore of thee that on my part thou entreat that sage enchanter who takes charge of my interests, that he leave me not to perish in this captivity in which they are now carrying me away, ere I see fulfilled promises so joyful and incomparable as those which have been now made me; for, let this but come to pass, and I shall glory in the pains of my prison, find comfort in these chains wherewith they bind me, and regard this bed whereon they stretch me, not as a hard battle-field, but as a soft and happy nuptial couch; and touching the consolation of Sancho Panza, my squire, I rely upon his goodness and rectitude that he will not desert me in good or evil fortune; for if, by his ill luck or mine, it may not happen to be in my power to give him the island I have promised, or any equivalent for it, at least his wages shall not be lost; for in my will, which is already made, I have declared the sum that shall be paid to him, measured, not by his many faithful services, but by the means at my disposal."

Sancho bowed his head very respectfully and kissed both his hands, for, being tied together, he could not kiss one; and then the apparitions lifted the cage upon their shoulders and fixed it upon the ox-cart.

CHAPTER XLVII

OF THE STRANGE MANNER IN WHICH DON QUIXOTE OF LA MANCHA WAS CARRIED AWAY ENCHANTED, TOGETHER WITH OTHER REMARKABLE INCIDENTS

When Don Quixote saw himself caged and hoisted on the cart in this way, he said, "Many grave histories of knights-errant have I read; but never yet have I read, seen, or heard of their carrying off enchanted knights-errant in this fashion, or at the slow pace that these lazy, sluggish animals promise; for they always take them away through the air with marvellous swiftness, enveloped in a dark thick cloud, or on a chariot of fire, or it may be on some hippogriff or other beast of the kind; but to carry me off like this on an ox-cart! By God, it puzzles me! But perhaps the chivalry and enchantments of our day take a different course from that of those in days gone by; and it may be, too, that as I am a new knight in the world, and the first to revive the already forgotten calling of knight-adventurers, they may have newly invented other kinds of enchantments and other modes of carrying off the enchanted. What thinkest thou of the matter, Sancho my son?"

"I don't know what to think," answered Sancho, "not being as well read as your worship in errant writings; but for all that I venture to say and swear that these apparitions that are about us are not quite catholic."

"Catholic!" said Don Quixote. "Father of me! how can they be Catholic when they are all devils that have taken fantastic shapes to come and do this, and bring me to this condition? And if thou wouldst prove it, touch them, and feel them, and thou wilt find they have only bodies of air, and no consistency except in appearance."

"By God, master," returned Sancho, "I have touched them already; and that devil, that goes about there so busily, has firm flesh, and another property very different from what I have heard say devils have, for by all accounts they all smell of brimstone and other bad smells; but this one smells of amber half a league off." Sancho was here speaking of Don Fernando, who, like a gentleman of his rank, was very likely perfumed as Sancho said.

"Marvel not at that, Sancho my friend," said Don Quixote; "for let me tell thee devils are crafty; and even if they do carry odours about with them, they themselves have no smell, because they are spirits; or, if they have any smell, they cannot smell of anything sweet, but of something foul and fetid; and the reason is that as they carry hell with them wherever they go, and can get no ease whatever from their torments, and as a sweet smell is a thing that gives pleasure and enjoyment, it is impossible that they can smell sweet; if, then, this devil thou speakest of seems to thee to smell of amber, either thou art deceiving thyself, or he wants to deceive thee by making thee fancy he is not a devil."

Such was the conversation that passed between master and man; and Don Fernando and Cardenio, apprehensive of Sancho's making a complete discovery of their scheme, towards which he had already gone some way, resolved to hasten their departure, and calling the landlord aside, they directed him to saddle Rocinante and put the pack-saddle on Sancho's ass, which he did with great alacrity. In the meantime the curate had made an arrangement with the officers that they should bear them company as far as his village, he paying them so much a day. Cardenio hung the buckler on one side of the bow of Rocinante's saddle and the basin on the other, and by signs commanded Sancho to mount his ass and take Rocinante's bridle, and at each side of the cart he placed two officers with their muskets; but before the cart was put in motion, out came the landlady and her daughter and Maritornes to bid Don Quixote farewell, pretending to weep with grief at his misfortune; and to them Don Quixote said:

"Weep not, good ladies, for all these mishaps are the lot of those who follow the profession I profess; and if these reverses did not befall me I should not esteem myself a famous knight-errant; for such things never happen to knights of little renown and fame, because nobody in the world thinks about them; to valiant knights they do, for these are envied for their virtue and valour by many princes and other knights who compass the destruction of the worthy by base means. Nevertheless, virtue is of herself so mighty, that, in spite of all the magic that Zoroaster its first inventor knew, she will come victorious out of every trial, and shed her light upon the earth as the sun does upon the heavens. Forgive me, fair ladies, if, through inadvertence, I have in aught offended you; for intentionally and wittingly I have never done so to any; and pray to God that he deliver me from this captivity to which some malevolent enchanter has consigned me; and should I find myself released therefrom, the favours that ye have bestowed upon me in this castle shall be held in memory by me, that I may acknowledge, recognise, and requite them as they deserve."

While this was passing between the ladies of the castle and Don Quixote, the curate and the barber bade farewell to Don Fernando and his companions, to the captain, his brother, and the ladies, now all made happy, and in particular to Dorothea and Luscinda. They all embraced one another, and promised to let each other know how things went with them, and Don Fernando directed the curate where to write to him, to tell him what became of Don Quixote, assuring him that there was nothing that could give him more pleasure than to hear of it, and that he too, on his part, would send him word of everything he thought he would like to know, about his marriage, Zoraida's baptism, Don Luis's affair, and Luscinda's return to her home. The curate promised to comply with his request carefully, and they embraced once more, and renewed their promises.

The landlord approached the curate and handed him some papers, saying he had discovered them in the lining of the valise in which the novel of "The Ill-advised Curiosity" had been found, and that he might take them all away with him as their owner had not since returned; for, as he could not read, he did not want them himself. The curate thanked him, and opening them he saw at the beginning of the manuscript the words, "Novel of Rinconete and Cortadillo," by which he perceived that it was a novel, and as that of "The Ill-advised Curiosity" had been good he concluded this would be so too, as they were both probably by the same author; so he kept it, intending to read it when he had an opportunity. He then mounted and his friend the barber did the same, both masked, so as not to be recognised by Don Quixote, and set out following in the rear of the cart. The order of march was this: first went the cart with the owner leading it; at each side of it marched the officers of the Brotherhood, as has been said, with their muskets; then followed Sancho Panza on his ass, leading Rocinante by the bridle; and behind all came the curate and the barber on their mighty mules, with faces covered, as aforesaid, and a grave and serious air, measuring their pace to suit the slow steps of the oxen. Don Quixote was seated in the cage, with his hands tied and his feet stretched out, leaning against the bars as silent and as patient as if he were a stone statue and not a man of flesh. Thus slowly and silently they made, it might be, two leagues, until they reached a valley which the carter thought a convenient place for resting and feeding his oxen, and he said so to the curate, but the barber was of opinion that they ought to push on a little farther, as at the other side of a hill which appeared close by he knew there was a valley that had more grass and much better than the one where they proposed to halt; and his advice was taken and they continued their journey.

Just at that moment the curate, looking back, saw coming on behind them six or seven mounted men, well found and equipped, who soon overtook them, for they were travelling, not at the sluggish, deliberate pace of oxen, but like men who rode canons' mules, and in haste to take their noontide rest as soon as possible at the inn which was in sight not a league off. The quick travellers came up with the slow, and courteous salutations were exchanged; and one of the new comers, who was, in fact, a canon of Toledo and master of the others who accompanied him, observing the regular order of the procession, the cart, the officers, Sancho, Rocinante, the curate and the barber, and above all Don Quixote caged and confined, could not help asking what was the meaning of carrying the man in that fashion; though, from the badges of the officers, he already concluded that he must be some desperate highwayman or other malefactor whose punishment fell within the jurisdiction of the Holy Brotherhood. One of the officers to whom he had put the question, replied, "Let the gentleman himself tell you the meaning of his going this way, senor, for we do not know."

Don Quixote overheard the conversation and said, "Haply, gentlemen, you are versed and learned in matters of errant chivalry? Because if you are I will tell you my misfortunes; if not, there is no good in my giving myself the trouble of relating them;" but here the curate and the barber, seeing that the travellers were engaged in conversation with Don Quixote, came forward, in order to answer in such a way as to save their stratagem from being discovered.

The canon, replying to Don Quixote, said, "In truth, brother, I know more about books of chivalry than I do about Villalpando's elements of logic; so if that be all, you may safely tell me what you please."

"In God's name, then, senor," replied Don Quixote; "if that be so, I would have you know that I am held enchanted in this cage by the envy and fraud of wicked enchanters; for virtue is more persecuted by the wicked than loved by the good. I am a knight-errant, and not one of those whose names Fame has never thought of immortalising in her record, but of those who, in defiance and in spite of envy itself, and all the magicians that Persia, or Brahmans that India, or Gymnosophists that Ethiopia ever produced, will place their names in the temple of immortality, to serve as examples and patterns for ages to come, whereby knights-errant may see the footsteps in which they must tread if they would attain the summit and crowning point of honour in arms."

"What Senor Don Quixote of La Mancha says," observed the curate, "is the truth; for he goes enchanted in this cart, not from any fault or sins of his, but because of the malevolence of those to whom virtue is odious and valour hateful. This, senor, is the Knight of the Rueful Countenance, if you have ever heard him named, whose valiant achievements and mighty deeds shall be written on lasting brass and imperishable marble, notwithstanding all the efforts of envy to obscure them and malice to hide them."

When the canon heard both the prisoner and the man who was at liberty talk in such a strain he was ready to cross himself in his astonishment, and could not make out what had befallen him; and all his attendants were in the same state of amazement.

At this point Sancho Panza, who had drawn near to hear the conversation, said, in order to make everything plain, "Well, sirs, you may like or dislike what I am going to say, but the fact of the matter is, my master, Don Quixote, is just as much enchanted as my mother. He is in his full senses, he eats and he drinks, and he has his calls like other men and as he had yesterday, before they caged him. And if that's the case, what do they mean by wanting me to believe that he is enchanted? For I have heard many a one say that enchanted people neither eat, nor sleep, nor talk; and my master, if you don't stop him, will talk more than thirty lawyers." Then turning to the curate he exclaimed, "Ah, senor curate, senor curate! do you think I don't know you? Do you think I don't guess and see the drift of these new enchantments? Well then, I can tell you I know you, for all your face is covered, and I can tell you I am up to you, however you may hide your tricks. After all, where envy reigns virtue cannot live, and where there is niggardliness there can be no liberality. Ill betide the devil! if it had not been for your worship my master would be married to the Princess Micomicona this minute, and I should be a count at least; for no less was to be expected, as well from the goodness of my master, him of the Rueful Countenance, as from the greatness of my services. But I see now how true it is what they say in these parts, that the wheel of fortune turns faster than a mill-wheel, and that those who were up yesterday are down to-day. I am sorry for my wife and children, for when they might fairly and reasonably expect to see their father return to them a governor or viceroy of some island or kingdom, they will see him come back a horse-boy. I have said all this, senor curate, only to urge your paternity to lay to your conscience your ill-treatment of my master; and have a care that God does not call you to account in another life for making a prisoner of him in this way, and charge against you all the succours and good deeds that my lord Don Quixote leaves undone while he is shut up.

"Trim those lamps there!" exclaimed the barber at this; "so you are of the same fraternity as your master, too, Sancho? By God,

I begin to see that you will have to keep him company in the cage, and be enchanted like him for having caught some of his humour and chivalry. It was an evil hour when you let yourself be got with child by his promises, and that island you long so much for found its way into your head."

"I am not with child by anyone," returned Sancho, "nor am I a man to let myself be got with child, if it was by the King himself. Though I am poor I am an old Christian, and I owe nothing to nobody, and if I long for an island, other people long for worse. Each of us is the son of his own works; and being a man I may come to be pope, not to say governor of an island, especially as my master may win so many that he will not know whom to give them to. Mind how you talk, master barber; for shaving is not everything, and there is some difference between Peter and Peter. I say this because we all know one another, and it will not do to throw false dice with me; and as to the enchantment of my master, God knows the truth; leave it as it is; it only makes it worse to stir it."

The barber did not care to answer Sancho lest by his plain speaking he should disclose what the curate and he himself were trying so hard to conceal; and under the same apprehension the curate had asked the canon to ride on a little in advance, so that he might tell him the mystery of this man in the cage, and other things that would amuse him. The canon agreed, and going on ahead with his servants, listened with attention to the account of the character, life, madness, and ways of Don Quixote, given him by the curate, who described to him briefly the beginning and origin of his craze, and told him the whole story of his adventures up to his being confined in the cage, together with the plan they had of taking him home to try if by any means they could discover a cure for his madness. The canon and his servants were surprised anew when they heard Don Quixote's strange story, and when it was finished he said, "To tell the truth, senor curate, I for my part consider what they call books of chivalry to be mischievous to the State; and though, led by idle and false taste, I have read the beginnings of almost all that have been printed, I never could manage to read any one of them from beginning to end; for it seems to me they are all more or less the same thing; and one has nothing more in it than another; this no more than that. And in my opinion this sort of writing and composition is of the same species as the fables they call the Milesian, nonsensical tales that aim solely at giving amusement and not instruction, exactly the opposite of the apologue fables which amuse and instruct at the same time.

And though it may be the chief object of such books to amuse, I do not know how they can succeed, when they are so full of such monstrous nonsense. For the enjoyment the mind feels must come from the beauty and harmony which it perceives or contemplates in the things that the eye or the imagination brings before it; and nothing that has any ugliness or disproportion about it can give any pleasure. What beauty, then, or what proportion of the parts to the whole, or of the whole to the parts, can there be in a book or fable where a lad of sixteen cuts down a giant as tall as a tower and makes two halves of him as if he was an almond cake? And when they want to give us a picture of a battle, after having told us that there are a million of combatants on the side of the enemy, let the hero of the book be opposed to them, and we have perforce to believe, whether we like it or not, that the said knight wins the victory by the single might of his strong arm. And then, what shall we say of the facility with which a born queen or empress will give herself over into the arms of some unknown wandering knight? What mind, that is not wholly barbarous and uncultured, can find pleasure in reading of how a great tower full of knights sails away across the sea like a ship with a fair wind, and will be to-night in Lombardy and to-morrow morning in the land of Prester John of the Indies, or some other that Ptolemy never described nor Marco Polo saw? And if, in answer to this, I am told that the authors of books of the kind write them as fiction, and therefore are not bound to regard niceties of truth, I would reply that fiction is all the better the more it looks like truth, and gives the more pleasure the more probability and possibility there is about it. Plots in fiction should be wedded to the understanding of the reader, and be constructed in such a way that, reconciling impossibilities, smoothing over difficulties, keeping the mind on the alert, they may surprise, interest, divert, and entertain, so that wonder and delight joined may keep pace one with the other; all which he will fail to effect who shuns verisimilitude and truth to nature, wherein lies the perfection of writing. I have never yet seen any book of chivalry that puts together a connected plot complete in all its numbers, so that the middle agrees with the beginning, and the end with the beginning and middle; on the contrary, they construct them with such a multitude of members that it seems as though they meant to produce a chimera or monster rather than a well-proportioned figure. And besides all this they are harsh in their style, incredible in their achievements, licentious in their amours, uncouth in their courtly speeches, prolix in their battles, silly in their arguments, absurd in their travels, and, in short, wanting in everything like intelligent art; for which reason they deserve to be banished from the Christian commonwealth as a worthless breed."

The curate listened to him attentively and felt that he was a man of sound understanding, and that there was good reason in what he said; so he told him that, being of the same opinion himself, and bearing a grudge to books of chivalry, he had burned all Don Quixote's, which were many; and gave him an account of the scrutiny he had made of them, and of those he had condemned to the flames and those he had spared, with which the canon was not a little amused, adding that though he had said so much in condemnation of these books, still he found one good thing in them, and that was the opportunity they afforded to a gifted intellect for displaying itself; for they presented a wide and spacious field over which the pen might range freely, describing shipwrecks, tempests, combats, battles, portraying a valiant captain with all the qualifications requisite to make one, showing him sagacious in foreseeing the wiles of the enemy, eloquent in speech to encourage or restrain his soldiers, ripe in counsel, rapid in resolve, as bold in biding his time as in pressing the attack; now picturing some sad tragic incident, now some joyful and unexpected event; here a beauteous lady, virtuous, wise, and modest; there a Christian knight, brave and gentle; here a lawless, barbarous braggart; there a courteous prince, gallant and gracious; setting forth the devotion and loyalty of vassals, the greatness and generosity of nobles. "Or again," said he, "the author may show himself to be an astronomer, or a skilled cosmographer, or musician, or one versed in affairs of state, and sometimes he will have a chance of coming forward as a magician if he likes. He can set forth the craftiness of Ulysses, the piety of AEneas, the valour of Achilles, the misfortunes of Hector, the treachery of Sinon, the friendship of Euryalus, the generosity of Alexander, the boldness of Caesar, the clemency and truth of Trajan, the fidelity of Zopyrus, the wisdom of Cato, and in short all the faculties that serve to make an illustrious man perfect, now uniting them in one individual, again distributing them among many; and if this be done with charm of style and ingenious invention, aiming at the truth as much as possible, he will assuredly weave a web of bright and varied threads that, when finished, will display such perfection and beauty that it will attain the worthiest object any writing can seek, which, as I said before, is to give instruction and pleasure combined; for the unrestricted range of these books enables the author to show his powers, epic, lyric, tragic, or comic, and all the moods the sweet and winning arts of poesy and oratory are capable of; for the epic may be written in prose just as well as in verse."

CHAPTER XLVIII

IN WHICH THE CANON PURSUES THE SUBJECT OF THE BOOKS OF CHIVALRY, WITH OTHER MATTERS WORTHY OF HIS WIT

"It is as you say, senor canon," said the curate; "and for that reason those who have hitherto written books of the sort deserve all the more censure for writing without paying any attention to good taste or the rules of art, by which they might guide themselves and become as famous in prose as the two princes of Greek and Latin poetry are in verse."

"I myself, at any rate," said the canon, "was once tempted to write a book of chivalry in which all the points I have mentioned were to be observed; and if I must own the truth I have more than a hundred sheets written; and to try if it came up to my own opinion of it, I showed them to persons who were fond of this kind of reading, to learned and intelligent men as well as to ignorant people who cared for nothing but the pleasure of listening to nonsense, and from all I obtained flattering approval; nevertheless I proceeded no farther with it, as well because it seemed to me an occupation inconsistent with my profession, as because I perceived that the fools are more numerous than the wise; and, though it is better to be praised by the wise few than applauded by the foolish many, I have no mind to submit myself to the stupid judgment of the silly public, to whom the reading of such books falls for the most part.

"But what most of all made me hold my hand and even abandon all idea of finishing it was an argument I put to myself taken from the plays that are acted now-a-days, which was in this wise: if those that are now in vogue, as well those that are pure invention as those founded on history, are, all or most of them, downright nonsense and things that have neither head nor tail, and yet the public listens to them with delight, and regards and cries them up as perfection when they are so far from it; and if the authors who write them, and the players who act them, say that this is what they must be, for the public wants this and will have nothing else; and that those that go by rule and work out a plot according to the laws of art will only find some half-dozen intelligent people to understand them, while all the rest remain blind to the merit of their composition; and that for themselves it is better to get bread from the many than praise from the few; then my book will fare the same way, after I have burnt off my eyebrows in trying to observe the principles I have spoken of, and I shall be 'the tailor of the corner.' And though I have sometimes endeavoured to convince actors that they are mistaken in this notion they have adopted, and that they would attract more people, and get more credit, by producing plays in accordance with the rules of art, than by absurd ones, they are so thoroughly wedded to their own opinion that no argument or evidence can wean them from it.

"I remember saying one day to one of these obstinate fellows, 'Tell me, do you not recollect that a few years ago, there were three tragedies acted in Spain, written by a famous poet of these kingdoms, which were such that they filled all who heard them with admiration, delight, and interest, the ignorant as well as the wise, the masses as well as the higher orders, and brought in more money to the performers, these three alone, than thirty of the best that have been since produced?'

"'No doubt,' replied the actor in question, 'you mean the "Isabella," the

"Phyllis," and the "Alexandra."'

"'Those are the ones I mean,' said I; 'and see if they did not observe the principles of art, and if, by observing them, they failed to show their superiority and please all the world; so that the fault does not lie with the public that insists upon nonsense, but with those who don't know how to produce something else. "The Ingratitude Revenged" was not nonsense, nor was there any in "The Numantia," nor any to be found in "The Merchant Lover," nor yet in "The Friendly Fair Foe," nor in some others that have been written by certain gifted poets, to their own fame and renown, and to the profit of those that brought them out;' some further remarks I added to these, with which, I think, I left him rather dumbfoundered, but not so satisfied or convinced that I could disabuse him of his error."

"You have touched upon a subject, senor canon," observed the curate here, "that has awakened an old enmity I have against the plays in vogue at the present day, quite as strong as that which I bear to the books of chivalry; for while the drama, according to Tully, should be the mirror of human life, the model of manners, and the image of the truth, those which are presented now-a-days are mirrors of nonsense, models of folly, and images of lewdness. For what greater nonsense can there be in connection with what we are now discussing than for an infant to appear in swaddling clothes in the first scene of the first act, and in the second a grown-up bearded man? Or what greater absurdity can there be than putting before us an old man as a swashbuckler, a young man as a poltroon, a lackey using fine language, a page giving sage advice, a king plying as a porter, a princess who is a kitchen-maid? And then what shall I say of their attention to the time in which the action they represent may or can take place, save that I have seen a play where the first act began in Europe, the second in Asia, the third finished in Africa, and no doubt, had it been in four acts, the fourth would have ended in America, and so it would have been laid in all four quarters of the globe? And if truth to life is the main thing the drama should keep in view, how is it possible for any average understanding to be satisfied when the action is supposed to pass in the time of King Pepin or Charlemagne, and the principal personage in it they represent to be the Emperor Heraclius who entered Jerusalem with the cross and won the Holy Sepulchre, like Godfrey of Bouillon, there being years innumerable between the one and the other? or, if the play is based on fiction and historical facts are introduced, or bits of what occurred to different people and at different times mixed up with it, all, not only without any semblance of probability, but with obvious errors that from every point of view are inexcusable? And the worst of it is, there are ignorant people who say that this is perfection, and that anything beyond this is affected refinement. And then if we turn to sacred dramas—what miracles they invent in them! What apocryphal, ill-devised incidents, attributing to one saint the miracles of another! And even in secular plays they venture to introduce miracles without any reason or object except that they think some such miracle, or transformation as they call it, will come in well to astonish stupid people and draw them to the play. All this tends to the prejudice of the truth and the corruption of history, nay more, to the reproach of the wits of Spain; for foreigners who scrupulously observe the laws of the drama look upon us as barbarous and ignorant, when they see the absurdity and nonsense of the plays we produce. Nor will it be a sufficient excuse to say that the chief object well-ordered governments have in view when they permit plays to be performed in public is to entertain the people with some harmless amusement occasionally, and keep it from those evil humours which idleness is apt to engender; and that, as this may be attained by any sort of play, good or bad, there is no need to lay down laws, or bind those who write or act them to make them as they ought to be made, since, as I say, the object sought for may be secured by any sort. To this I would reply that the same end would be, beyond all comparison, better attained by means of good plays than by those that are not so; for after listening to an artistic and properly constructed play, the hearer will come away enlivened by the jests, instructed by the serious parts, full of admiration at the incidents, his wits sharpened by the arguments, warned by the tricks, all the wiser for the examples, inflamed against vice, and in love with virtue; for in all these ways a good play will stimulate the mind of the hearer be he ever so boorish or dull; and of all impossibilities the greatest is that a play endowed with all these qualities will not entertain, satisfy, and please much more than one wanting in them, like the greater number of those which are commonly acted now-a-days. Nor are the poets who write them to be blamed for this; for some there are among them who are perfectly well aware of their faults, and know what they ought to do; but as plays have become a salable commodity, they say, and with truth, that the actors will not buy them unless they are after this fashion; and so the poet tries to adapt himself to the requirements of the actor who is to pay him for his work. And that this is the truth may be seen by the countless plays that a most fertile wit of these kingdoms has written, with so much brilliancy, so much grace and gaiety, such polished versification, such choice language, such profound reflections, and in a word, so rich in eloquence and elevation of style, that he has filled the world with his fame; and yet, in consequence of his desire to suit the taste of the actors, they have not all, as some of them have, come as near perfection as they ought. Others write plays with such heedlessness that, after they have been acted, the actors have to fly and abscond, afraid of being punished, as they often have been, for having acted something offensive to some king or other, or insulting to some noble family. All which evils, and many more that I say nothing of, would be removed if there were some intelligent and sensible person at the capital to examine all plays before they were acted, not only those produced in the capital itself, but all that were intended to be acted in Spain; without whose approval, seal, and signature, no local magistracy should allow any play to be acted. In that case actors would take care to send their plays to the capital, and could act them in safety, and those who write them would be more careful and take more pains with their work, standing in awe of having to submit it to the strict examination of one who understood the matter; and so good plays would be produced and the objects they aim at happily attained; as well the amusement of the people, as the credit of the wits of Spain, the interest and safety of the actors, and the saving of trouble in inflicting punishment on them. And if the same or some other person were authorised to examine the newly written books of chivalry, no doubt some would appear with all the perfections you have described, enriching our language with the gracious and precious treasure of eloquence, and driving the old books into obscurity before the light of the new ones that would come out for the harmless entertainment, not merely of the idle but of the very busiest; for the bow cannot be always bent, nor can weak human nature exist without some lawful amusement."

The canon and the curate had proceeded thus far with their conversation, when the barber, coming forward, joined them, and said to the curate, "This is the spot, senor licentiate, that I said was a good one for fresh and plentiful pasture for the oxen, while we take our noontide rest."

"And so it seems," returned the curate, and he told the canon what he proposed to do, on which he too made up his mind to halt with them, attracted by the aspect of the fair valley that lay before their eyes; and to enjoy it as well as the conversation of the curate, to whom he had begun to take a fancy, and also to learn more particulars about the doings of Don Quixote, he desired some of his servants to go on to the inn, which was not far distant, and fetch from it what eatables there might be for the whole party, as he meant to rest for the afternoon where he was; to which one of his servants replied that the sumpter mule, which by this time ought to have reached the inn, carried provisions enough to make it unnecessary to get anything from the inn except barley.

"In that case," said the canon, "take all the beasts there, and bring the sumpter mule back."

While this was going on, Sancho, perceiving that he could speak to his master without having the curate and the barber, of whom he had his suspicions, present all the time, approached the cage in which Don Quixote was placed, and said, "Senor, to ease my conscience I want to tell you the state of the case as to your enchantment, and that is that these two here, with their faces covered, are the curate of our village and the barber; and I suspect they have hit upon this plan of carrying you off in this fashion, out of pure envy because your worship surpasses them in doing famous deeds; and if this be the truth it follows that you are not enchanted, but hoodwinked and made a fool of. And to prove this I want to ask you one thing; and if you answer me as I believe you will answer, you will be able to lay your finger on the trick, and you will see that you are not enchanted but gone wrong in your wits."

"Ask what thou wilt, Sancho my son," returned Don Quixote, "for I will satisfy thee and answer all thou requirest. As to what thou sayest, that these who accompany us yonder are the curate and the barber, our neighbours and acquaintances, it is very possible that they may seem to be those same persons; but that they are so in reality and in fact, believe it not on any account; what thou art to believe and think is that, if they look like them, as thou sayest, it must be that those who have enchanted me have taken this shape and likeness; for it is easy for enchanters to take any form they please, and they may have taken those of our friends in order to make thee think as thou dost, and lead thee into a labyrinth of fancies from which thou wilt find no escape though thou hadst the cord of Theseus; and they may also have done it to make me uncertain in my mind, and unable to conjecture whence this evil comes to me; for if on the one hand thou dost tell me that the barber and curate of our village are here in company with us, and on the other I find myself shut up in a cage, and know in my heart that no power on earth that was not supernatural would have been able to shut me in, what wouldst thou have me say or think, but that my enchantment is of a sort that transcends all I have ever read of in all the histories that deal with knights-errant that have been enchanted? So thou mayest set thy mind at rest as to the idea that they are what thou sayest, for they are as much so as I am a Turk. But touching thy desire to ask me something, say on, and I will answer thee, though thou shouldst ask questions from this till to-morrow morning."

"May Our Lady be good to me!" said Sancho, lifting up his voice; "and is it possible that your worship is so thick of skull and so short of brains that you cannot see that what I say is the simple truth, and that malice has more to do with your imprisonment and misfortune than enchantment? But as it is so, I will prove plainly to you that you are not enchanted. Now tell me, so may God deliver you from this affliction, and so may you find yourself when you least expect it in the arms of my lady Dulcinea-"

"Leave off conjuring me," said Don Quixote, "and ask what thou wouldst know; I have already told thee I will answer with all possible precision."

"That is what I want," said Sancho; "and what I would know, and have you tell me, without adding or leaving out anything, but telling the whole truth as one expects it to be told, and as it is told, by all who profess arms, as your worship professes them, under the title of knights-errant-"

"I tell thee I will not lie in any particular," said Don Quixote; "finish thy question; for in truth thou weariest me with all these asseverations, requirements, and precautions, Sancho."

"Well, I rely on the goodness and truth of my master," said Sancho; "and so, because it bears upon what we are talking about, I would ask, speaking with all reverence, whether since your worship has been shut up and, as you think, enchanted in this cage, you have felt any desire or inclination to go anywhere, as the saying is?"

"I do not understand 'going anywhere,'" said Don Quixote; "explain thyself more clearly, Sancho, if thou wouldst have me give an answer to the point."

"Is it possible," said Sancho, "that your worship does not understand 'going anywhere'? Why, the schoolboys know that from the time they were babes. Well then, you must know I mean have you had any desire to do what cannot be avoided?"

"Ah! now I understand thee, Sancho," said Don Quixote; "yes, often, and even this minute; get me out of this strait, or all will not go right."

CHAPTER XLIX

WHICH TREATS OF THE SHREWD CONVERSATION WHICH SANCHO PANZA HELD WITH HIS MASTER DON QUIXOTE

"Aha, I have caught you," said Sancho; "this is what in my heart and soul I was longing to know. Come now, senor, can you deny what is commonly said around us, when a person is out of humour, 'I don't know what ails so-and-so, that he neither eats, nor drinks, nor sleeps, nor gives a proper answer to any question; one would think he was enchanted'? From which it is to be gathered that those who do not eat, or drink, or sleep, or do any of the natural acts I am speaking of-that such persons are enchanted; but not those that have the desire your worship has, and drink when drink is given them, and eat when there is anything to eat, and answer every question that is asked them."

"What thou sayest is true, Sancho," replied Don Quixote; "but I have already told thee there are many sorts of enchantments, and it may be that in the course of time they have been changed one for another, and that now it may be the way with enchanted people to do all that I do, though they did not do so before; so it is vain to argue or draw inferences against the usage of the time. I know and feel that I am enchanted, and that is enough to ease my conscience; for it would weigh heavily on it if I thought that I was not enchanted, and that in a faint-hearted and cowardly way I allowed myself to lie in this cage, defrauding multitudes of the succour I might afford to those in need and distress, who at this very moment may be in sore want of my aid and protection."

"Still for all that," replied Sancho, "I say that, for your greater and fuller satisfaction, it would be well if your worship were to try to get out of this prison (and I promise to do all in my power to help, and even to take you out of it), and see if you could once more mount your good Rocinante, who seems to be enchanted too, he is so melancholy and dejected; and then we might try our chance in looking for adventures again; and if we have no luck there will be time enough to go back to the cage; in which, on the faith of a good and loyal squire, I promise to shut myself up along with your worship, if so be you are so unfortunate, or I so stupid, as not to be able to carry out my plan."

"I am content to do as thou sayest, brother Sancho," said Don Quixote, "and when thou seest an opportunity for effecting my release I will obey thee absolutely; but thou wilt see, Sancho, how mistaken thou art in thy conception of my misfortune."

The knight-errant and the ill-errant squire kept up their conversation till they reached the place where the curate, the canon, and the barber, who had already dismounted, were waiting for them. The carter at once unyoked the oxen and left them to roam at large about the pleasant green spot, the freshness of which seemed to invite, not enchanted people like Don Quixote, but wide-awake, sensible folk like his squire, who begged the curate to allow his master to leave the cage for a little; for if they did not let him out, the prison might not be as clean as the propriety of such a gentleman as his master required. The curate understood him, and said he would very gladly comply with his request, only that he feared his master, finding himself at liberty, would take to his old courses and make off where nobody could ever find him again.

"I will answer for his not running away," said Sancho.

"And I also," said the canon, "especially if he gives me his word as a knight not to leave us without our consent."

Don Quixote, who was listening to all this, said, "I give it;-moreover one who is enchanted as I am cannot do as he likes with himself; for he who had enchanted him could prevent his moving from one place for three ages, and if he attempted to escape would bring him back flying."—And that being so, they might as well release him, particularly as it would be to the advantage of all; for, if they did not let him out, he protested he would be unable to avoid offending their nostrils unless they kept their distance.

The canon took his hand, tied together as they both were, and on his word and promise they unbound him, and rejoiced beyond measure he was to find himself out of the cage. The first thing he did was to stretch himself all over, and then he went to where Rocinante was standing and giving him a couple of slaps on the haunches said, "I still trust in God and in his blessed mother, O flower and mirror of steeds, that we shall soon see ourselves, both of us, as we wish to be, thou with thy master on thy back, and I mounted upon thee, following the calling for which God sent me into the world." And so saying, accompanied by Sancho, he withdrew to a retired spot, from which he came back much relieved and more eager than ever to put his squire's scheme into execution.

The canon gazed at him, wondering at the extraordinary nature of his madness, and that in all his remarks and replies he should show such excellent sense, and only lose his stirrups, as has been already said, when the subject of chivalry was broached. And so, moved by compassion, he said to him, as they all sat on the green grass awaiting the arrival of the provisions:

"Is it possible, gentle sir, that the nauseous and idle reading of books of chivalry can have had such an effect on your worship as to upset your reason so that you fancy yourself enchanted, and the like, all as far from the truth as falsehood itself is? How can there be any human understanding that can persuade itself there ever was all that infinity of Amadises in the world, or all that multitude of famous knights, all those emperors of Trebizond, all those Felixmartes of Hircania, all those palfreys, and damsels-errant, and serpents, and monsters, and giants, and marvellous adventures, and enchantments of every kind, and battles, and prodigious encounters, splendid costumes, love-sick princesses, squires made counts, droll dwarfs, love letters, billings and cooings, swashbuckler women, and, in a word, all that nonsense the books of chivalry contain? For myself, I can only say that when I read them, so long as I do not stop to think that they are all lies and frivolity, they give me a certain amount of pleasure; but when I come to consider what they are, I fling the very best of them at the wall, and would fling it into the fire if there were one at hand, as richly deserving such punishment as cheats and impostors out of the range of ordinary toleration, and as founders of new sects and modes of life, and teachers that lead the ignorant public to believe and accept as truth all the folly they contain. And such is their audacity, they even dare to unsettle the wits of gentlemen of birth and intelligence, as is shown plainly by the way they have served your worship, when they have brought you to such a pass that you have to be shut up in a cage and carried on an ox-cart as one would carry a lion or a tiger from place to place to make money by showing it. Come, Senor Don Quixote, have some compassion for yourself, return to the bosom of common sense, and make use of the liberal share of it that heaven has been pleased to bestow upon you, employing your abundant gifts of mind in some other reading that may serve to benefit your conscience and add to your honour. And if, still led away by your natural bent, you desire to read books of achievements and of chivalry, read the Book of Judges in the Holy Scriptures, for there you will find grand reality, and deeds as true as they are heroic. Lusitania had a Viriatus, Rome a Caesar, Carthage a Hannibal, Greece an Alexander, Castile a Count Fernan Gonzalez, Valencia a Cid, Andalusia a Gonzalo Fernandez, Estremadura a Diego Garcia de Paredes, Jerez a Garci Perez de Vargas, Toledo a Garcilaso, Seville a Don Manuel de Leon, to read of whose valiant deeds will entertain and instruct the loftiest minds and fill them with delight and wonder. Here, Senor Don Quixote, will be reading worthy of your sound understanding; from which you will rise learned in history, in love with virtue, strengthened in goodness, improved in manners, brave without rashness, prudent without cowardice; and all to the honour of God, your own advantage and the glory of La Mancha, whence, I am informed, your worship derives your birth."

Don Quixote listened with the greatest attention to the canon's words, and when he found he had finished, after regarding him for some time, he replied to him:

"It appears to me, gentle sir, that your worship's discourse is intended to persuade me that there never were any knights-errant in the world, and that all the books of chivalry are false, lying, mischievous and useless to the State, and that I have done wrong in reading them, and worse in believing them, and still worse in imitating them, when I undertook to follow the arduous calling of knight-errantry which they set forth; for you deny that there ever were Amadises of Gaul or of Greece, or any other of the knights of whom the books are full."

"It is all exactly as you state it," said the canon; to which Don Quixote returned, "You also went on to say that books of this kind had done me much harm, inasmuch as they had upset my senses, and shut me up in a cage, and that it would be better for me to reform and change my studies, and read other truer books which would afford more pleasure and instruction."

"Just so," said the canon.

"Well then," returned Don Quixote, "to my mind it is you who are the one that is out of his wits and enchanted, as you have ventured to utter such blasphemies against a thing so universally acknowledged and accepted as true that whoever denies it, as you do, deserves the same punishment which you say you inflict on the books that irritate you when you read them. For to try to persuade anybody that Amadis, and all the other knights-adventurers with whom the books are filled, never existed, would be like trying to persuade him that the sun does not yield light, or ice cold, or earth nourishment. What wit in the world can persuade another that the story of the Princess Floripes and Guy of Burgundy is not true, or that of Fierabras and the bridge of Mantible, which happened in the time of Charlemagne? For by all that is good it is as true as that it is daylight now; and if it be a lie, it must be a lie too that there was a Hector, or Achilles, or Trojan war, or Twelve Peers of France, or Arthur of England, who still lives changed into a raven, and is unceasingly looked for in his kingdom. One might just as well try to make out that the history of Guarino Mezquino, or of the quest of the Holy Grail, is false, or that the loves of Tristram and the Queen Yseult are apocryphal, as well as those of Guinevere and Lancelot, when there are persons who can almost remember having seen the Dame Quintanona, who was the best cupbearer in Great Britain. And so true is this, that I recollect a grandmother of mine on the father's side, whenever she saw any dame in a venerable hood, used to say to me, 'Grandson, that one is like Dame Quintanona,' from which I conclude that she must have known her, or at least had managed to see some portrait of her. Then who can deny that the story of Pierres and the fair Magalona is true, when even to this day may be seen in the king's armoury the pin with which the valiant Pierres guided the wooden horse he rode through the air, and it is a trifle bigger than the pole of a cart? And alongside of the pin is Babieca's saddle, and at Roncesvalles there is Roland's horn, as large as a large beam; whence we may infer that there were Twelve Peers, and a Pierres, and a Cid, and other knights like them, of the sort people commonly call adventurers. Or perhaps I shall be told, too, that there was no such knight-errant as the valiant Lusitanian Juan de Merlo, who went to Burgundy and in the city of Arras fought with the famous lord of Charny, Mosen Pierres by name, and afterwards in the city of Basle with Mosen Enrique de Remesten, coming out of both encounters covered with fame and honour; or adventures and challenges achieved and delivered, also in Burgundy, by the valiant Spaniards Pedro Barba and Gutierre Quixada (of whose family I come in the direct male line), when they vanquished the sons of the Count of San Polo. I shall be told, too, that Don Fernando de Guevara did not go in quest of adventures to Germany, where he engaged in combat with Micer George, a knight of the house of the Duke of Austria. I shall be told that the jousts of Suero de Quinones, him of the 'Paso,' and the emprise of Mosen Luis de Falces against the Castilian knight, Don Gonzalo de Guzman, were mere mockeries; as well as many other achievements of Christian knights of these and foreign realms, which are so authentic and true, that, I repeat, he who denies them must be totally wanting in reason and good sense."

The canon was amazed to hear the medley of truth and fiction Don Quixote uttered, and to see how well acquainted he was with everything relating or belonging to the achievements of his knight-errantry; so he said in reply:

"I cannot deny, Senor Don Quixote, that there is some truth in what you say, especially as regards the Spanish knights-errant; and

I am willing to grant too that the Twelve Peers of France existed, but I am not disposed to believe that they did all the things that the Archbishop Turpin relates of them. For the truth of the matter is they were knights chosen by the kings of France, and called 'Peers' because they were all equal in worth, rank and prowess (at least if they were not they ought to have been), and it was a kind of religious order like those of Santiago and Calatrava in the present day, in which it is assumed that those who take it are valiant knights of distinction and good birth; and just as we say now a Knight of St. John, or of Alcantara, they used to say then a Knight of the Twelve Peers, because twelve equals were chosen for that military order. That there was a Cid, as well as a Bernardo del Carpio, there can be no doubt; but that they did the deeds people say they did, I hold to be very doubtful. In that other matter of the pin of Count Pierres that you speak of, and say is near Babieca's saddle in the Armoury, I confess my sin; for I am either so stupid or so short-sighted, that, though I have seen the saddle, I have never been able to see the pin, in spite of it being as big as your worship says it is."

"For all that it is there, without any manner of doubt," said Don Quixote; "and more by token they say it is inclosed in a sheath of cowhide to keep it from rusting."

"All that may be," replied the canon; "but, by the orders I have received, I do not remember seeing it. However, granting it is there, that is no reason why I am bound to believe the stories of all those Amadises and of all that multitude of knights they tell us about, nor is it reasonable that a man like your worship, so worthy, and with so many good qualities, and endowed with such a good understanding, should allow himself to be persuaded that such wild crazy things as are written in those absurd books of chivalry are really true."

CHAPTER L

OF THE SHREWD CONTROVERSY WHICH DON QUIXOTE AND THE CANON HELD, TOGETHER WITH OTHER INCIDENTS

"A good joke, that!" returned Don Quixote. "Books that have been printed with the king's licence, and with the approbation of those to whom they have been submitted, and read with universal delight, and extolled by great and small, rich and poor, learned and ignorant, gentle and simple, in a word by people of every sort, of whatever rank or condition they may be—that these should be lies! And above all when they carry such an appearance of truth with them; for they tell us the father, mother, country, kindred, age, place, and the achievements, step by step, and day by day, performed by such a knight or knights! Hush, sir; utter not such blasphemy; trust me I am advising you now to act as a sensible man should; only read them, and you will see the pleasure you will derive from them. For, come, tell me, can there be anything more delightful than to see, as it were, here now displayed before us a vast lake of bubbling pitch with a host of snakes and serpents and lizards, and ferocious and terrible creatures of all sorts swimming about in it, while from the middle of the lake there comes a plaintive voice saying: 'Knight, whosoever thou art who beholdest this dread lake, if thou wouldst win the prize that lies hidden beneath these dusky waves, prove the valour of thy stout heart and cast thyself into the midst of its dark burning waters, else thou shalt not be worthy to see the mighty wonders contained in the seven castles of the seven Fays that lie beneath this black expanse;' and then the knight, almost ere the awful voice has ceased, without stopping to consider, without pausing to reflect upon the danger to which he is exposing himself, without even relieving himself of the weight of his massive armour, commending himself to God and to his lady, plunges into the midst of the boiling lake, and when he little looks for it, or knows what his fate is to be, he finds himself among flowery meadows, with which the Elysian fields are not to be compared.

"The sky seems more transparent there, and the sun shines with a strange brilliancy, and a delightful grove of green leafy trees presents itself to the eyes and charms the sight with its verdure, while the ear is soothed by the sweet untutored melody of the countless birds of gay plumage that flit to and fro among the interlacing branches. Here he sees a brook whose limpid waters, like liquid crystal, ripple over fine sands and white pebbles that look like sifted gold and purest pearls. There he perceives a cunningly wrought fountain of many-coloured jasper and polished marble; here another of rustic fashion where the little mussel-shells and the spiral white and yellow mansions of the snail disposed in studious disorder, mingled with fragments of glittering crystal and mock emeralds, make up a work of varied aspect, where art, imitating nature, seems to have outdone it.

"Suddenly there is presented to his sight a strong castle or gorgeous palace with walls of massy gold, turrets of diamond and gates of jacinth; in short, so marvellous is its structure that though the materials of which it is built are nothing less than diamonds, carbuncles, rubies, pearls, gold, and emeralds, the workmanship is still more rare. And after having seen all this, what can be more charming than to see how a bevy of damsels comes forth from the gate of the castle in gay and gorgeous attire, such that, were I to set myself now to depict it as the histories describe it to us, I should never have done; and then how she who seems to be the first among them all takes the bold knight who plunged into the boiling lake by the hand, and without addressing a word to him leads him into the rich palace or castle, and strips him as naked as when his mother bore him, and bathes him in lukewarm water, and anoints him all over with sweet-smelling unguents, and clothes him in a shirt of the softest sendal, all scented and perfumed, while another damsel comes and throws over his shoulders a mantle which is said to be worth at the very least a city, and even more? How charming it is, then, when they tell us how, after all this, they lead him to another chamber where he finds the tables set out in such style that he is filled with amazement and wonder; to see how they pour out water for his hands distilled from amber and sweet-scented flowers; how they seat him on an ivory chair; to see how the damsels wait on him all in profound silence; how they bring him such a variety of dainties so temptingly prepared that the appetite is at a loss which to select; to hear the music that resounds while he is at table, by whom or whence produced he knows not. And then when the repast is over and the tables removed, for the knight to recline in the chair, picking his teeth perhaps as usual, and a damsel, much lovelier than any of the others, to enter unexpectedly by the chamber door, and herself by his side, and begin to tell him what the castle is, and how she is held enchanted there, and other things that amaze the knight and astonish the readers who are perusing his history.

"But I will not expatiate any further upon this, as it may be gathered from it that whatever part of whatever history of a knight-errant one reads, it will fill the reader, whoever he be, with delight and wonder; and take my advice, sir, and, as I said before, read these books and you will see how they will banish any melancholy you may feel and raise your spirits should they be depressed. For myself I can say that since I have been a knight-errant I have become valiant, polite, generous, well-bred, magnanimous, courteous, dauntless, gentle, patient, and have learned to bear hardships, imprisonments, and enchantments; and though it be such a short time since I have seen myself shut up in a cage like a madman, I hope by the might of my arm, if heaven aid me and fortune thwart me not, to see myself king of some kingdom where I may be able to show the gratitude and generosity that dwell in my heart; for by my faith, senor, the poor man is incapacitated from showing the virtue of generosity to anyone, though he may possess it in the highest degree; and gratitude that consists of disposition only is a dead thing, just as faith without works is dead. For this reason I should be glad were fortune soon to offer me some opportunity of making myself an emperor, so as to show my heart in doing good to my friends, particularly to this poor Sancho Panza, my squire, who is the best fellow in the world; and I would gladly give him a county I have promised him this ever so long, only that I am afraid he has not the capacity to govern his realm."

Sancho partly heard these last words of his master, and said to him, "Strive hard you, Senor Don Quixote, to give me that county so often promised by you and so long looked for by me, for I promise you there will be no want of capacity in me to govern it; and even if there is, I have heard say there are men in the world who farm seigniories, paying so much a year, and they themselves taking charge of the government, while the lord, with his legs stretched out, enjoys the revenue they pay him, without troubling himself about anything else. That's what I'll do, and not stand haggling over trifles, but wash my hands at once of the whole business, and enjoy my rents like a duke, and let things go their own way."

"That, brother Sancho," said the canon, "only holds good as far as the enjoyment of the revenue goes; but the lord of the seigniory must attend to the administration of justice, and here capacity and sound judgment come in, and above all a firm determination to find out the truth; for if this be wanting in the beginning, the middle and the end will always go wrong; and God as commonly aids the honest intentions of the simple as he frustrates the evil designs of the crafty."

"I don't understand those philosophies," returned Sancho Panza; "all I know is I would I had the county as soon as I shall know how to govern it; for I have as much soul as another, and as much body as anyone, and I shall be as much king of my realm as any other of his; and being so I should do as I liked, and doing as I liked I should please myself, and pleasing myself I should be content, and when one is content he has nothing more to desire, and when one has nothing more to desire there is an end of it; so let the county come, and God be with you, and let us see one another, as one blind man said to the other."

"That is not bad philosophy thou art talking, Sancho," said the canon; "but for all that there is a good deal to be said on this matter of counties."

To which Don Quixote returned, "I know not what more there is to be said; I only guide myself by the example set me by the great Amadis of Gaul, when he made his squire count of the Insula Firme; and so, without any scruples of conscience, I can make a count of Sancho Panza, for he is one of the best squires that ever knight-errant had."

The canon was astonished at the methodical nonsense (if nonsense be capable of method) that Don Quixote uttered, at the way in which he had described the adventure of the knight of the lake, at the impression that the deliberate lies of the books he read had made upon him, and lastly he marvelled at the simplicity of Sancho, who desired so eagerly to obtain the county his master had promised him.

By this time the canon's servants, who had gone to the inn to fetch the sumpter mule, had returned, and making a carpet and the green grass of the meadow serve as a table, they seated themselves in the shade of some trees and made their repast there, that the carter might not be deprived of the advantage of the spot, as has been already said. As they were eating they suddenly heard a loud noise and the sound of a bell that seemed to come from among some brambles and thick bushes that were close by, and the same instant they observed a beautiful goat, spotted all over black, white, and brown, spring out of the thicket with a goatherd after it, calling to it and uttering the usual cries to make it stop or turn back to the fold. The fugitive goat, scared and frightened, ran towards the company as if seeking their protection and then stood still, and the goatherd coming up seized it by the horns and began to talk to it as if it were possessed of reason and understanding: "Ah wanderer, wanderer, Spotty, Spotty; how have you gone limping all this time? What wolves have frightened you, my daughter? Won't you tell me what is the matter, my beauty? But what else can it be except that you are a she, and cannot keep quiet? A plague on your humours and the humours of those you take after! Come back, come back, my darling; and if you will not be so happy, at any rate you will be safe in the fold or with your companions; for if you who ought to keep and lead them, go wandering astray, what will become of them?"

The goatherd's talk amused all who heard it, but especially the canon, who said to him, "As you live, brother, take it easy, and be not in such a hurry to drive this goat back to the fold; for, being a female, as you say, she will follow her natural instinct in spite of all you can do to prevent it. Take this morsel and drink a sup, and that will soothe your irritation, and in the meantime the goat will rest herself," and so saying, he handed him the loins of a cold rabbit on a fork.

The goatherd took it with thanks, and drank and calmed himself, and then said, "I should be sorry if your worships were to take me for a simpleton for having spoken so seriously as I did to this animal; but the truth is there is a certain mystery in the words I used. I am a clown, but not so much of one but that I know how to behave to men and to beasts."

"That I can well believe," said the curate, "for I know already by experience that the woods breed men of learning, and shepherds' harbour philosophers."

"At all events, senor," returned the goatherd, "they shelter men of experience; and that you may see the truth of this and grasp it, though I may seem to put myself forward without being asked, I will, if it will not tire you, gentlemen, and you will give me your attention for a little, tell you a true story which will confirm this gentleman's word (and he pointed to the curate) as well as my own."

To this Don Quixote replied, "Seeing that this affair has a certain colour of chivalry about it, I for my part, brother, will hear you most gladly, and so will all these gentlemen, from the high intelligence they possess and their love of curious novelties that interest, charm, and entertain the mind, as I feel quite sure your story will do. So begin, friend, for we are all prepared to listen."

"I draw my stakes," said Sancho, "and will retreat with this pasty to the brook there, where I mean to victual myself for three days; for I have heard my lord, Don Quixote, say that a knight-errant's squire should eat until he can hold no more, whenever he has the chance, because it often happens them to get by accident into a wood so thick that they cannot find a way out of it for six days; and if the man is not well filled or his alforjas well stored, there he may stay, as very often he does, turned into a dried mummy."

"Thou art in the right of it, Sancho," said Don Quixote; "go where thou wilt and eat all thou canst, for I have had enough, and only want to give my mind its refreshment, as I shall by listening to this good fellow's story."

"It is what we shall all do," said the canon; and then begged the goatherd to begin the promised tale.

The goatherd gave the goat which he held by the horns a couple of slaps on the back, saying, "Lie down here beside me, Spotty, for we have time enough to return to our fold." The goat seemed to understand him, for as her master seated himself, she stretched herself quietly beside him and looked up in his face to show him she was all attention to what he was going to say, and then in these words he began his story.

CHAPTER LI

WHICH DEALS WITH WHAT THE GOATHERD TOLD THOSE WHO WERE CARRYING OFF DON QUIXOTE

Three leagues from this valley there is a village which, though small, is one of the richest in all this neighbourhood, and in it there lived a farmer, a very worthy man, and so much respected that, although to be so is the natural consequence of being rich, he was even more respected for his virtue than for the wealth he had acquired. But what made him still more fortunate, as he said himself, was having a daughter of such exceeding beauty, rare intelligence, gracefulness, and virtue, that everyone who knew her and beheld her marvelled at the extraordinary gifts with which heaven and nature had endowed her. As a child she was beautiful, she continued to grow in beauty, and at the age of sixteen she was most lovely. The fame of her beauty began to spread abroad through all the villages around—but why do I say the villages around, merely, when it spread to distant cities, and even made its way into the halls of royalty and reached the ears of people of every class, who came from all sides to see her as if to see something rare and curious, or some wonder-working image?

Her father watched over her and she watched over herself; for there are no locks, or guards, or bolts that can protect a young girl better than her own modesty. The wealth of the father and the beauty of the daughter led many neighbours as well as strangers to seek her for a wife; but he, as one might well be who had the disposal of so rich a jewel, was perplexed and unable to make up his mind to which of her countless suitors he should entrust her. I was one among the many who felt a desire so natural, and, as her father knew who I was, and I was of the same town, of pure blood, in the bloom of life, and very rich in possessions, I had great hopes of success. There was another of the same place and qualifications who also sought her, and this made her father's choice hang in the balance, for he felt that on either of us his daughter would be well bestowed; so to escape from this state of perplexity he resolved to refer the matter to Leandra (for that is the name of the rich damsel who has reduced me to misery), reflecting that as we were both equal it would be best to leave it to his dear daughter to choose according to her inclination—a course that is worthy of imitation by all fathers who wish to settle their children in life. I do not mean that they ought to leave them to make a choice of what is contemptible and bad, but that they should place before them what is good and then allow them to make a good choice as they please. I do not know which Leandra chose; I only know her father put us both off with the tender age of his daughter and vague words that neither bound him nor dismissed us. My rival is called Anselmo and I myself Eugenio—that you may know the names of the personages that figure in this tragedy, the end of which is still in suspense, though it is plain to see it must be disastrous.

About this time there arrived in our town one Vicente de la Roca, the son of a poor peasant of the same town, the said Vicente having returned from service as a soldier in Italy and divers other parts. A captain who chanced to pass that way with his company had carried him off from our village when he was a boy of about twelve years, and now twelve years later the young man came back in a soldier's uniform, arrayed in a thousand colours, and all over glass trinkets and fine steel chains. To-day he would appear in one gay dress, to-morrow in another; but all flimsy and gaudy, of little substance and less worth. The peasant folk, who are naturally malicious, and when they have nothing to do can be malice itself, remarked all this, and took note of his finery and jewellery, piece by piece, and discovered that he had three suits of different colours, with garters and stockings to match; but he made so many arrangements and combinations out of them, that if they had not counted them, anyone would have sworn that he had made a display of more than ten suits of clothes and twenty plumes. Do not look upon all this that I am telling you about the clothes as uncalled for or spun out, for they have a great deal to do with the story. He used to seat himself on a bench under the great poplar in our plaza, and there he would keep us all hanging open-mouthed on the stories he told us of his exploits. There was no country on the face of the globe he had not seen, nor battle he had not been engaged in; he had killed more Moors than there are in Morocco and Tunis, and fought more single combats, according to his own account, than Garcilaso, Diego Garcia de Paredes and a thousand others he named, and out of all he had come victorious without losing a drop of blood. On the other hand he showed marks of wounds, which, though they could not be made out, he said were gunshot wounds received in divers encounters and actions. Lastly, with monstrous impudence he used to say "you" to his equals and even those who knew what he was, and declare that his arm was his father and his deeds his pedigree, and that being a soldier he was as good as the king himself. And to add to these swaggering ways he was a trifle of a musician, and played the guitar with such a flourish that some said he made it speak; nor did his accomplishments end here, for he was something of a poet too, and on every trifle that happened in the town he made a ballad a league long.

This soldier, then, that I have described, this Vicente de la Roca, this bravo, gallant, musician, poet, was often seen and watched by Leandra from a window of her house which looked out on the plaza. The glitter of his showy attire took her fancy, his ballads bewitched her (for he gave away twenty copies of every one he made), the tales of his exploits which he told about himself came to her ears; and in short, as the devil no doubt had arranged it, she fell in love with him before the presumption of making love to her had suggested itself to him; and as in love-affairs none are more easily brought to an issue than those which have the inclination of the lady for an ally, Leandra and Vicente came to an understanding without any difficulty; and before any of her numerous suitors had any suspicion of her design, she had already carried it into effect, having left the house of her dearly beloved father (for mother she had none), and disappeared from the village with the soldier, who came more triumphantly out of this enterprise than out of any of the large number he laid claim to. All the village and all who heard of it were amazed at the affair; I was aghast, Anselmo thunderstruck, her father full of grief, her relations indignant, the authorities all in a ferment, the officers of the Brotherhood in arms. They scoured the roads, they searched the woods and all quarters, and at the end of three days they found the flighty Leandra in a mountain cave, stript to her shift, and robbed of all the money and precious jewels she had carried away from home with her.

They brought her back to her unhappy father, and questioned her as to her misfortune, and she confessed without pressure that Vicente de la Roca had deceived her, and under promise of marrying her had induced her to leave her father's house, as he meant to take her to the richest and most delightful city in the whole world, which was Naples; and that she, ill-advised and deluded, had believed him, and robbed her father, and handed over all to him the night she disappeared; and that he had carried her away to a rugged mountain and shut her up in the cave where they had found her. She said, moreover, that the soldier, without robbing her of her honour, had taken from her everything she had, and made off, leaving her in the cave, a thing that still further surprised everybody. It was not easy for us to credit the young man's continence, but she asserted it with such earnestness that it helped to console her distressed father, who thought nothing of what had been taken since the jewel that once lost can never be recovered had been left to his daughter. The same day that Leandra made her appearance her father removed her from our sight and took her away to shut her up in a convent in a town near this, in the hope that time may wear away some of the disgrace she has incurred. Leandra's youth furnished an excuse for her fault, at least with those to whom it was of no consequence whether she was good or bad; but those who knew her shrewdness and intelligence did not attribute her misdemeanour to ignorance but to wantonness and the natural disposition of women, which is for the most part flighty and ill-regulated.

Leandra withdrawn from sight, Anselmo's eyes grew blind, or at any rate found nothing to look at that gave them any pleasure, and mine were in darkness without a ray of light to direct them to anything enjoyable while Leandra was away. Our melancholy grew greater, our patience grew less; we cursed the soldier's finery and railed at the carelessness of Leandra's father. At last Anselmo and I agreed to leave the village and come to this valley; and, he feeding a great flock of sheep of his own, and I a large herd of goats of mine, we pass our life among the trees, giving vent to our sorrows, together singing the fair Leandra's praises, or upbraiding her, or else sighing alone, and to heaven pouring forth our complaints in solitude. Following our example, many more of Leandra's lovers have come to these rude mountains and adopted our mode of life, and they are so numerous that one would fancy the place had been turned into the pastoral Arcadia, so full is it of shepherds and sheep-folds; nor is there a spot in it where the name of the fair Leandra is not heard. Here one curses her and calls her capricious, fickle, and immodest, there another condemns her as frail and frivolous; this pardons and absolves her, that spurns and reviles her; one extols her beauty, another assails her character, and in short all abuse her, and all adore her, and to such a pitch has this general infatuation gone that there are some who complain of her scorn without ever having exchanged a word with her, and even some that bewail and mourn the raging fever of jealousy, for which she never gave anyone cause, for, as I have already said, her misconduct was known before her passion. There is no nook among the rocks, no brookside, no shade beneath the trees that is not haunted by some shepherd telling his woes to the breezes; wherever there is an echo it repeats the name of Leandra; the mountains ring with "Leandra," "Leandra" murmur the brooks, and Leandra keeps us all bewildered and bewitched, hoping without hope and fearing without knowing what we fear. Of all this silly set the one that shows the least and also the most sense is my rival Anselmo, for having so many other things to complain of, he only complains of separation, and to the accompaniment of a rebeck, which he plays admirably, he sings his complaints in verses that show his ingenuity. I follow another, easier, and to my mind wiser course, and that is to rail at the frivolity of women, at their inconstancy, their double dealing, their broken promises, their unkept pledges, and in short the want of reflection they show in fixing their affections and inclinations. This, sirs, was the reason of words and expressions I made use of to this goat when I came up just now; for as she is a female I have a contempt for her, though she is the best in all my fold. This is the story I promised to tell you, and if I have been tedious in telling it, I will not be slow to serve you; my hut is close by, and I have fresh milk and dainty cheese there, as well as a variety of toothsome fruit, no less pleasing to the eye than to the palate.

CHAPTER LII

OF THE QUARREL THAT DON QUIXOTE HAD WITH THE GOATHERD, TOGETHER WITH THE RARE ADVENTURE OF THE PENITENTS, WHICH WITH AN EXPENDITURE OF SWEAT HE BROUGHT TO A HAPPY CONCLUSION

The goatherd's tale gave great satisfaction to all the hearers, and the canon especially enjoyed it, for he had remarked with particular attention the manner in which it had been told, which was as unlike the manner of a clownish goatherd as it was like that of a polished city wit; and he observed that the curate had been quite right in saying that the woods bred men of learning. They all offered their services to Eugenio but he who showed himself most liberal in this way was Don Quixote, who said to him, "Most assuredly, brother goatherd, if I found myself in a position to attempt any adventure, I would, this very instant, set out on your behalf, and would rescue Leandra from that convent (where no doubt she is kept against her will), in spite of the abbess and all who might try to prevent me, and would place her in your hands to deal with her according to your will and pleasure, observing, however, the laws of chivalry which lay down that no violence of any kind is to be offered to any damsel. But I trust in God our Lord that the might of one malignant enchanter may not prove so great but that the power of another better disposed may prove superior to it, and then I promise you my support and assistance, as I am bound to do by my profession, which is none other than to give aid to the weak and needy."

The goatherd eyed him, and noticing Don Quixote's sorry appearance and looks, he was filled with wonder, and asked the barber, who was next him, "Senor, who is this man who makes such a figure and talks in such a strain?"

"Who should it be," said the barber, "but the famous Don Quixote of La Mancha, the undoer of injustice, the righter of wrongs, the protector of damsels, the terror of giants, and the winner of battles?"

"That," said the goatherd, "sounds like what one reads in the books of the knights-errant, who did all that you say this man does; though it is my belief that either you are joking, or else this gentleman has empty lodgings in his head."

"You are a great scoundrel," said Don Quixote, "and it is you who are empty and a fool. I am fuller than ever was the whoreson bitch that bore you;" and passing from words to deeds, he caught up a loaf that was near him and sent it full in the goatherd's face, with such force that he flattened his nose; but the goatherd, who did not understand jokes, and found himself roughly handled in such good earnest, paying no respect to carpet, tablecloth, or diners, sprang upon Don Quixote, and seizing him by the throat with both hands would no doubt have throttled him, had not Sancho Panza that instant come to the rescue, and grasping him by the shoulders flung him down on the table, smashing plates, breaking glasses, and upsetting and scattering everything on it. Don Quixote, finding himself free, strove to get on top of the goatherd, who, with his face covered with blood, and soundly kicked by Sancho, was on all fours feeling about for one of the table-knives to take a bloody revenge with. The canon and the curate, however, prevented him, but the barber so contrived it that he got Don Quixote under him, and rained down upon him such a shower of fisticuffs that the poor knight's face streamed with blood as freely as his own. The canon and the curate were bursting with laughter, the officers were capering with delight, and both the one and the other hissed them on as they do dogs that are worrying one another in a fight. Sancho alone was frantic, for he could not free himself from the grasp of one of the canon's servants, who kept him from going to his master's assistance.

At last, while they were all, with the exception of the two bruisers who were mauling each other, in high glee and enjoyment, they heard a trumpet sound a note so doleful that it made them all look in the direction whence the sound seemed to come. But the one that was most excited by hearing it was Don Quixote, who though sorely against his will he was under the goatherd, and something more than pretty well pummelled, said to him, "Brother devil (for it is impossible but that thou must be one since thou hast had might and strength enough to overcome mine), I ask thee to agree to a truce for but one hour for the solemn note of yonder trumpet that falls on our ears seems to me to summon me to some new adventure." The goatherd, who was by this time tired of pummelling and being pummelled, released him at once, and Don Quixote rising to his feet and turning his eyes to the quarter where the sound had been heard, suddenly saw coming down the slope of a hill several men clad in white like penitents.

The fact was that the clouds had that year withheld their moisture from the earth, and in all the villages of the district they were organising processions, rogations, and penances, imploring God to open the hands of his mercy and send the rain; and to this end the people of a village that was hard by were going in procession to a holy hermitage there was on one side of that valley. Don Quixote when he saw the strange garb of the penitents, without reflecting how often he had seen it before, took it into his head that this was a case of adventure, and that it fell to him alone as a knight-errant to engage in it; and he was all the more confirmed in this notion, by the idea that an image draped in black they had with them was some illustrious lady that these villains and discourteous thieves were carrying off by force. As soon as this occurred to him he ran with all speed to Rocinante who was grazing at large, and taking the bridle and the buckler from the saddle-bow, he had him bridled in an instant, and calling to Sancho for his sword he mounted Rocinante, braced his buckler on his arm, and in a loud voice exclaimed to those who stood by, "Now, noble company, ye shall see how important it is that there should be knights in the world professing the order of knight-errantry; now, I say, ye shall see, by the deliverance of that worthy lady who is borne captive there, whether knights-errant deserve to be held in estimation," and so saying he brought his legs to bear on Rocinante—for he had no spurs—and at a full canter (for in all this veracious history we never read of Rocinante fairly galloping) set off to encounter the penitents, though the curate, the canon, and the barber ran to prevent him. But it was out of their power, nor did he even stop for the shouts of Sancho calling after him, "Where are you going, Senor Don Quixote? What devils have possessed you to set you on against our Catholic faith? Plague take me! mind, that is a procession of penitents, and the lady they are carrying on that stand there is the blessed image of the immaculate Virgin. Take care what you are doing, senor, for this time it may be safely said you don't know what you are about." Sancho laboured in vain, for his master was so bent on coming to quarters with these sheeted figures and releasing the lady in black that he did not hear a word; and even had he heard, he would not have turned back if the king had ordered him. He came up with the procession and reined in Rocinante, who was already anxious enough to slacken speed a little, and in a hoarse, excited voice he exclaimed, "You who hide your faces, perhaps because you are not good subjects, pay attention and listen to what I am about to say to you." The first to halt were those who were carrying the image, and one of the four ecclesiastics who were chanting the Litany, struck by the strange figure of Don Quixote, the leanness of Rocinante, and the other ludicrous peculiarities he observed, said in reply to him, "Brother, if you have anything to say to us say it quickly, for these brethren are whipping themselves, and we cannot stop, nor is it reasonable we should stop to hear anything, unless indeed it is short enough to be said in two words."

"I will say it in one," replied Don Quixote, "and it is this; that at once, this very instant, ye release that fair lady whose tears and sad aspect show plainly that ye are carrying her off against her will, and that ye have committed some scandalous outrage against her; and I, who was born into the world to redress all such like wrongs, will not permit you to advance another step until you have restored to her the liberty she pines for and deserves."

From these words all the hearers concluded that he must be a madman, and began to laugh heartily, and their laughter acted like gunpowder on Don Quixote's fury, for drawing his sword without another word he made a rush at the stand. One of those who supported it, leaving the burden to his comrades, advanced to meet him, flourishing a forked stick that he had for propping up the stand when resting, and with this he caught a mighty cut Don Quixote made at him that severed it in two; but with the portion that remained in his hand he dealt such a thwack on the shoulder of Don Quixote's sword arm (which the buckler could not protect against the clownish assault) that poor Don Quixote came to the ground in a sad plight.

Sancho Panza, who was coming on close behind puffing and blowing, seeing him fall, cried out to his assailant not to strike him again, for he was a poor enchanted knight, who had never harmed anyone all the days of his life; but what checked the clown was, not Sancho's shouting, but seeing that Don Quixote did not stir hand or foot; and so, fancying he had killed him, he hastily hitched up his tunic under his girdle and took to his heels across the country like a deer.

By this time all Don Quixote's companions had come up to where he lay; but the processionists seeing them come running, and with them the officers of the Brotherhood with their crossbows, apprehended mischief, and clustering round the image, raised their hoods, and grasped their scourges, as the priests did their tapers, and awaited the attack, resolved to defend themselves and even to take the offensive against their assailants if they could. Fortune, however, arranged the matter better than they expected, for all Sancho did was to fling himself on his master's body, raising over him the most doleful and laughable lamentation that ever was heard, for he believed he was dead. The curate was known to another curate who walked in the procession, and their recognition of one another set at rest the apprehensions of both parties; the first then told the other in two words who Don Quixote was, and he and the whole troop of penitents went to see if the poor gentleman was dead, and heard Sancho Panza saying, with tears in his eyes, "Oh flower of chivalry, that with one blow of a stick hast ended the course of thy well-spent life! Oh pride of thy race, honour and glory of all La Mancha, nay, of all the world, that for want of thee will be full of evil-doers, no longer in fear of punishment for their misdeeds! Oh thou, generous above all the Alexanders, since for only eight months of service thou hast given me the best island the sea girds or surrounds! Humble with the proud, haughty with the humble, encounterer of dangers, endurer of outrages, enamoured without reason, imitator of the good, scourge of the wicked, enemy of the mean, in short, knight-errant, which is all that can be said!"

At the cries and moans of Sancho, Don Quixote came to himself, and the first word he said was, "He who lives separated from you, sweetest Dulcinea, has greater miseries to endure than these. Aid me, friend Sancho, to mount the enchanted cart, for I am not in a condition to press the saddle of Rocinante, as this shoulder is all knocked to pieces."

"That I will do with all my heart, senor," said Sancho; "and let us return to our village with these gentlemen, who seek your good, and there we will prepare for making another sally, which may turn out more profitable and creditable to us."

"Thou art right, Sancho," returned Don Quixote; "It will be wise to let the malign influence of the stars which now prevails pass off."

The canon, the curate, and the barber told him he would act very wisely in doing as he said; and so, highly amused at Sancho Panza's simplicities, they placed Don Quixote in the cart as before. The procession once more formed itself in order and proceeded on its road; the goatherd took his leave of the party; the officers of the Brotherhood declined to go any farther, and the curate paid them what was due to them; the canon begged the curate to let him know how Don Quixote did, whether he was cured of his madness or still suffered from it, and then begged leave to continue his journey; in short, they all separated and went their ways, leaving to themselves the curate and the barber, Don Quixote, Sancho Panza, and the good Rocinante, who regarded everything with as great resignation as his master. The carter yoked his oxen and made Don Quixote comfortable on a truss of hay, and at his usual deliberate pace took the road the curate directed, and at the end of six days they reached Don Quixote's village, and entered it about the middle of the day, which it so happened was a Sunday, and the people were all in the plaza, through which Don Quixote's cart passed. They all flocked to see what was in the cart, and when they recognised their townsman they were filled with amazement, and a boy ran off to bring the news to his housekeeper and his niece that their master and uncle had come back all lean and yellow and stretched on a truss of hay on an ox-cart. It was piteous to hear the cries the two good ladies raised, how they beat their breasts and poured out fresh maledictions on those accursed books of chivalry; all which was renewed when they saw Don Quixote coming in at the gate.

At the news of Don Quixote's arrival Sancho Panza's wife came running, for she by this time knew that her husband had gone away with him as his squire, and on seeing Sancho, the first thing she asked him was if the ass was well. Sancho replied that he was, better than his master was.

"Thanks be to God," said she, "for being so good to me; but now tell me, my friend, what have you made by your squirings? What gown have you brought me back? What shoes for your children?"

"I bring nothing of that sort, wife," said Sancho; "though I bring other things of more consequence and value."

"I am very glad of that," returned his wife; "show me these things of more value and consequence, my friend; for I want to see them to cheer my heart that has been so sad and heavy all these ages that you have been away."

"I will show them to you at home, wife," said Sancho; "be content for the present; for if it please God that we should again go on our travels in search of adventures, you will soon see me a count, or governor of an island, and that not one of those everyday ones, but the best that is to be had."

"Heaven grant it, husband," said she, "for indeed we have need of it. But tell me, what's this about islands, for I don't understand it?"

"Honey is not for the mouth of the ass," returned Sancho; "all in good time thou shalt see, wife—nay, thou wilt be surprised to hear thyself called 'your ladyship' by all thy vassals."

"What are you talking about, Sancho, with your ladyships, islands, and vassals?" returned Teresa Panza—for so Sancho's wife was called, though they were not relations, for in La Mancha it is customary for wives to take their husbands' surnames.

"Don't be in such a hurry to know all this, Teresa," said Sancho; "it is enough that I am telling you the truth, so shut your mouth. But I may tell you this much by the way, that there is nothing in the world more delightful than to be a person of consideration, squire to a knight-errant, and a seeker of adventures. To be sure most of those one finds do not end as pleasantly as one could wish, for out of a hundred, ninety-nine will turn out cross and contrary. I know it by experience, for out of some I came blanketed, and out of others belaboured. Still, for all that, it is a fine thing to be on the look-out for what may happen, crossing mountains, searching woods, climbing rocks, visiting castles, putting up at inns, all at free quarters, and devil take the maravedi to pay."

While this conversation passed between Sancho Panza and his wife, Don Quixote's housekeeper and niece took him in and undressed him and laid him in his old bed. He eyed them askance, and could not make out where he was. The curate charged his niece to be very careful to make her uncle comfortable and to keep a watch over him lest he should make his escape from them again, telling her what they had been obliged to do to bring him home. On this the pair once more lifted up their voices and renewed their maledictions upon the books of chivalry, and implored heaven to plunge the authors of such lies and nonsense into the midst of the bottomless pit. They were, in short, kept in anxiety and dread lest their uncle and master should give them the slip the moment he found himself somewhat better, and as they feared so it fell out.

But the author of this history, though he has devoted research and industry to the discovery of the deeds achieved by Don Quixote in his third sally, has been unable to obtain any information respecting them, at any rate derived from authentic documents; tradition has merely preserved in the memory of La Mancha the fact that Don Quixote, the third time he sallied forth from his home, betook himself to Saragossa, where he was present at some famous jousts which came off in that city, and that he had adventures there worthy of his valour and high intelligence. Of his end and death he could learn no particulars, nor would he have ascertained it or known of it, if good fortune had not produced an old physician for him who had in his possession a leaden box, which, according to his account, had been discovered among the crumbling foundations of an ancient hermitage that was being rebuilt; in which box were found certain parchment manuscripts in Gothic character, but in Castilian verse, containing many of his achievements, and setting forth the beauty of Dulcinea, the form of Rocinante, the fidelity of Sancho Panza, and the burial of Don Quixote himself, together with sundry epitaphs and eulogies on his life and character; but all that could be read and deciphered were those which the trustworthy author of this new and unparalleled history here presents. And the said author asks of those that shall read it nothing in return for the vast toil which it has cost him in examining and searching the Manchegan archives in order to bring it to light, save that they give him the same credit that people of sense give to the books of chivalry that pervade the world and are so popular; for with this he will consider himself amply paid and fully satisfied, and will be encouraged to seek out and produce other histories, if not as truthful, at least equal in invention and not less entertaining. The first words written on the parchment found in the leaden box were these:

THE ACADEMICIANS OF ARGAMASILLA, A VILLAGE OF LA MANCHA, ON THE LIFE AND DEATH OF DON QUIXOTE OF LA MANCHA, HOC SCRIPSERUNT MONICONGO, ACADEMICIAN OF ARGAMASILLA

ON THE TOMB OF DON QUIXOTE EPITAPH

> The scatterbrain that gave La Mancha more
>   Rich spoils than Jason's; who a point so keen
>   Had to his wit, and happier far had been
> If his wit's weathercock a blunter bore;
> The arm renowned far as Gaeta's shore,
>   Cathay, and all the lands that lie between;
>   The muse discreet and terrible in mien
> As ever wrote on brass in days of yore;
> He who surpassed the Amadises all,
>   And who as naught the Galaors accounted,
>   Supported by his love and gallantry:
> Who made the Belianises sing small,
>   And sought renown on Rocinante mounted;
>   Here, underneath this cold stone, doth he lie.

PANIAGUADO, ACADEMICIAN OF ARGAMASILLA, IN LAUDEM DULCINEAE DEL TOBOSO

SONNET

> She, whose full features may be here descried,
>   High-bosomed, with a bearing of disdain,
>   Is Dulcinea, she for whom in vain
> The great Don Quixote of La Mancha sighed.
> For her, Toboso's queen, from side to side
>   He traversed the grim sierra, the champaign
>   Of Aranjuez, and Montiel's famous plain:

On Rocinante oft a weary ride.
Malignant planets, cruel destiny,
Pursued them both, the fair Manchegan dame,
And the unconquered star of chivalry.
Nor youth nor beauty saved her from the claim
Of death; he paid love's bitter penalty,
And left the marble to preserve his name.

CAPRICHOSO, A MOST ACUTE ACADEMICIAN OF ARGAMASILLA, IN PRAISE OF ROCINANTE, STEED OF DON QUIXOTE OF LA MANCHA

SONNET

On that proud throne of diamantine sheen,
Which the blood-reeking feet of Mars degrade,
The mad Manchegan's banner now hath been
By him in all its bravery displayed.
There hath he hung his arms and trenchant blade
Wherewith, achieving deeds till now unseen,
He slays, lays low, cleaves, hews; but art hath made
A novel style for our new paladin.
If Amadis be the proud boast of Gaul,
If by his progeny the fame of Greece
Through all the regions of the earth be spread,
Great Quixote crowned in grim Bellona's hall
To-day exalts La Mancha over these,
And above Greece or Gaul she holds her head.
Nor ends his glory here, for his good steed
Doth Brillador and Bayard far exceed;
As mettled steeds compared with Rocinante,
The reputation they have won is scanty.

BURLADOR, ACADEMICIAN OF ARGAMASILLA, ON SANCHO PANZA

SONNET

The worthy Sancho Panza here you see;
A great soul once was in that body small,
Nor was there squire upon this earthly ball
So plain and simple, or of guile so free.
Within an ace of being Count was he,
And would have been but for the spite and gall
Of this vile age, mean and illiberal,
That cannot even let a donkey be.

>For mounted on an ass (excuse the word),
>By Rocinante's side this gentle squire
>Was wont his wandering master to attend.
>Delusive hopes that lure the common herd
>With promises of ease, the heart's desire,
>In shadows, dreams, and smoke ye always end.

CACHIDIABLO, ACADEMICIAN OF ARGAMASILLA, ON THE TOMB OF DON QUIXOTE EPITAPH

>The knight lies here below,
>Ill-errant and bruised sore,
>Whom Rocinante bore
>In his wanderings to and fro.
>By the side of the knight is laid
>Stolid man Sancho too,
>Than whom a squire more true
>Was not in the esquire trade.

TIQUITOC, ACADEMICIAN OF ARGAMASILLA, ON THE TOMB OF DULCINEA DEL TOBOSO

>EPITAPH
>Here Dulcinea lies.
>Plump was she and robust:
>Now she is ashes and dust:
>The end of all flesh that dies.
>A lady of high degree,
>With the port of a lofty dame,
>And the great Don Quixote's flame,
>And the pride of her village was she.

These were all the verses that could be deciphered; the rest, the writing being worm-eaten, were handed over to one of the Academicians to make out their meaning conjecturally. We have been informed that at the cost of many sleepless nights and much toil he has succeeded, and that he means to publish them in hopes of Don Quixote's third sally.

"Forse altro cantera con miglior plectro."

Made in United States
Orlando, FL
29 May 2025